D1544411

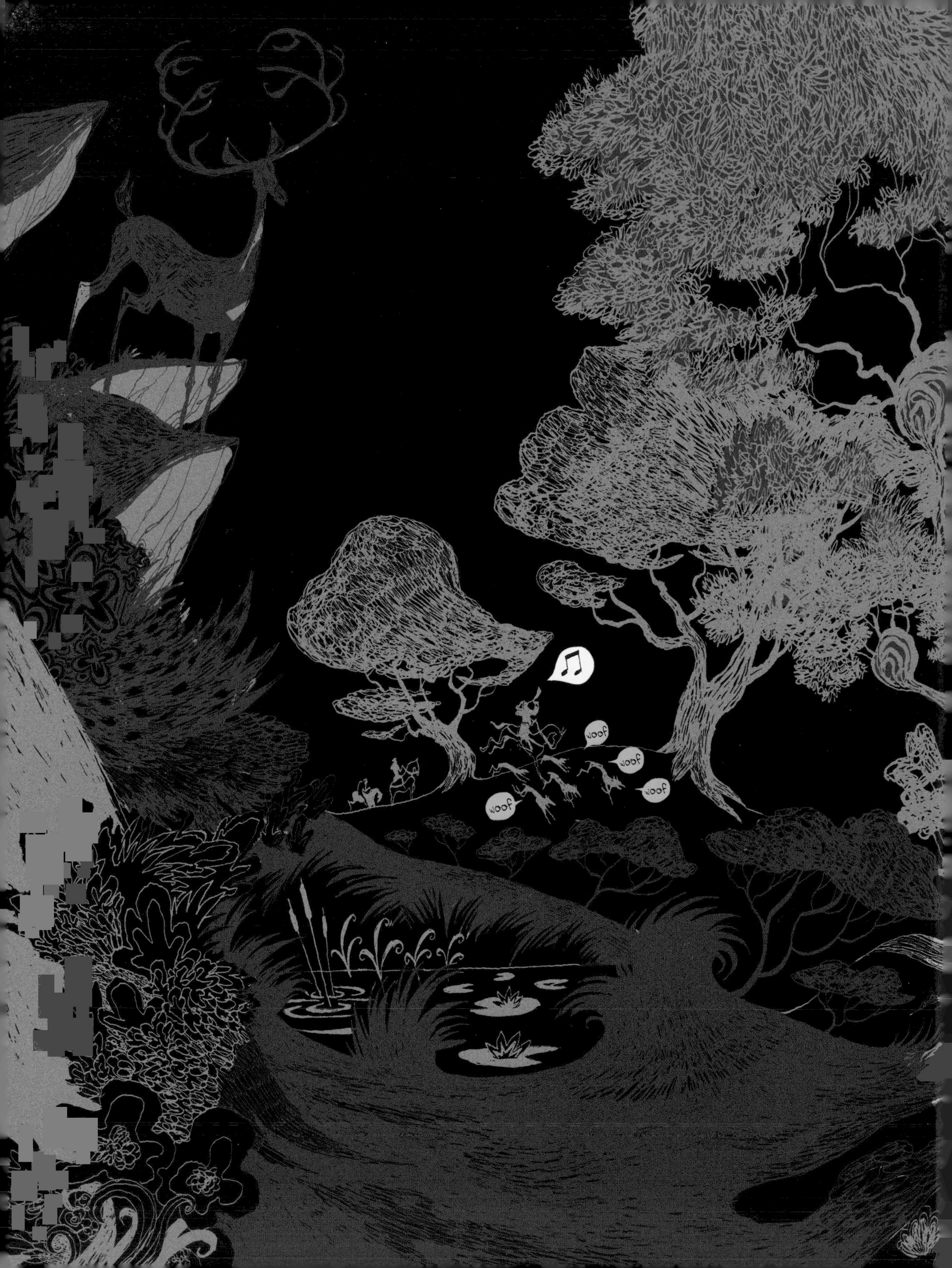
woof
woof
woof
woof

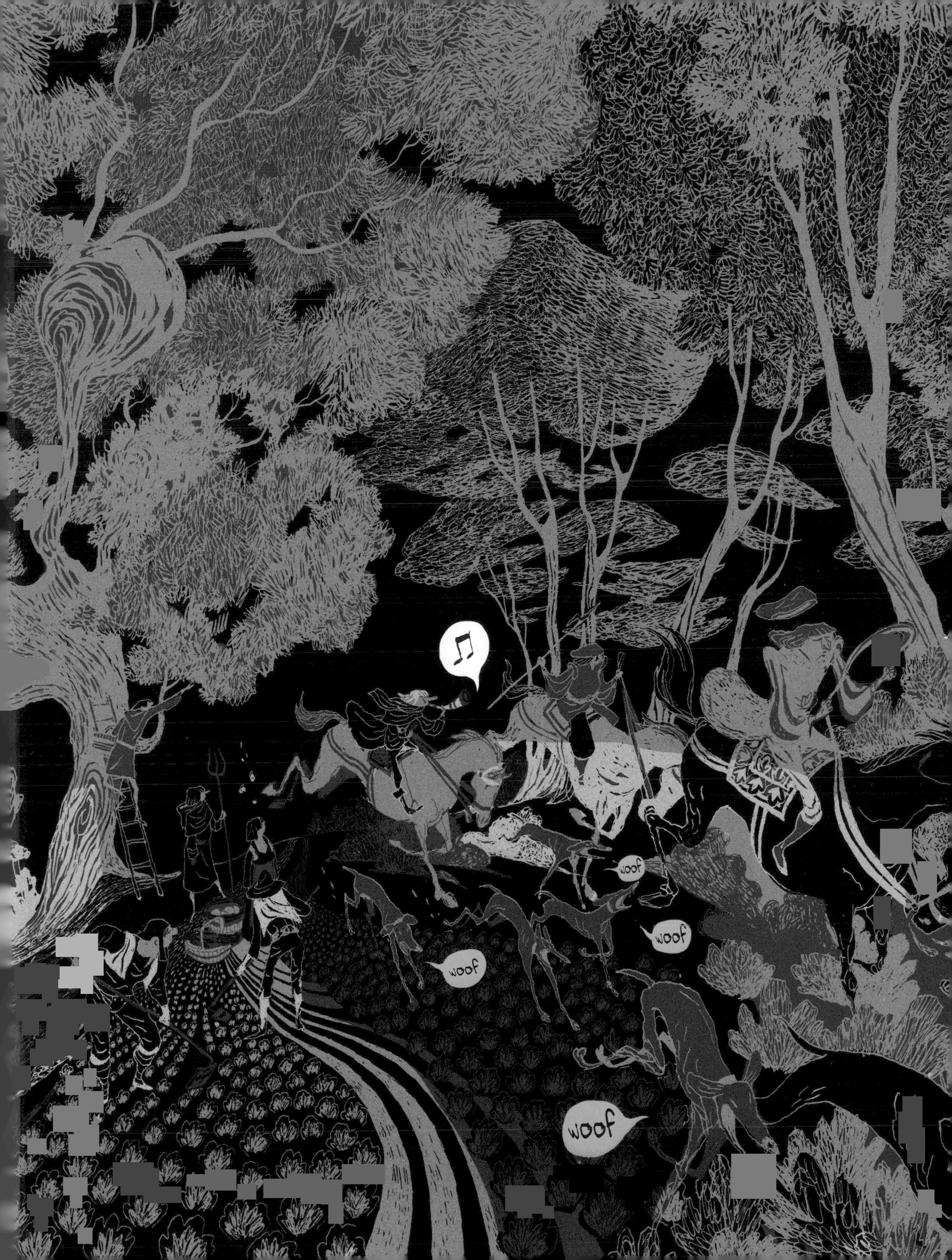
woof
woof
woof
woof

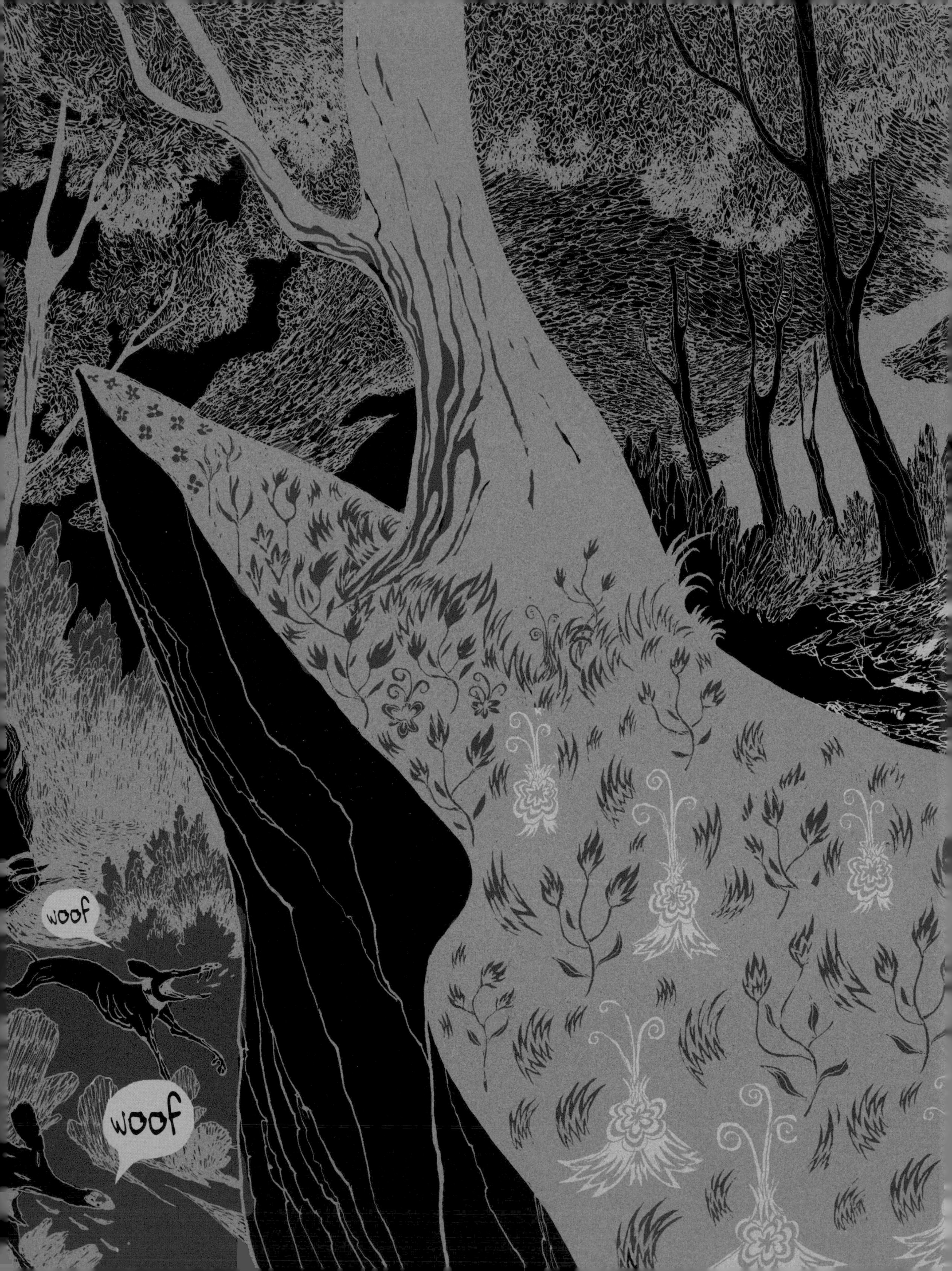
woof
woof

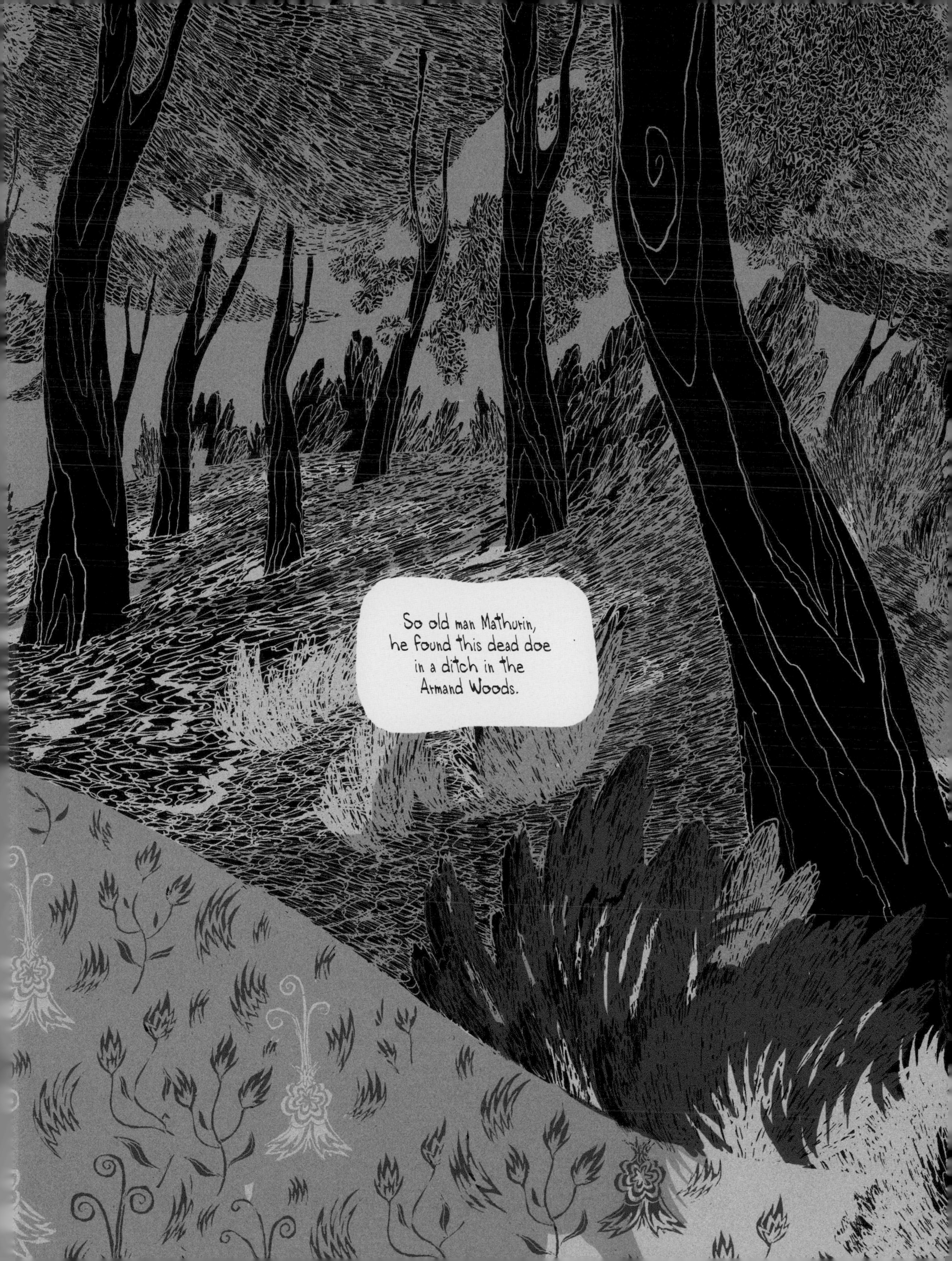
So old man Mathurin, he found this dead doe in a ditch in the Armand Woods.

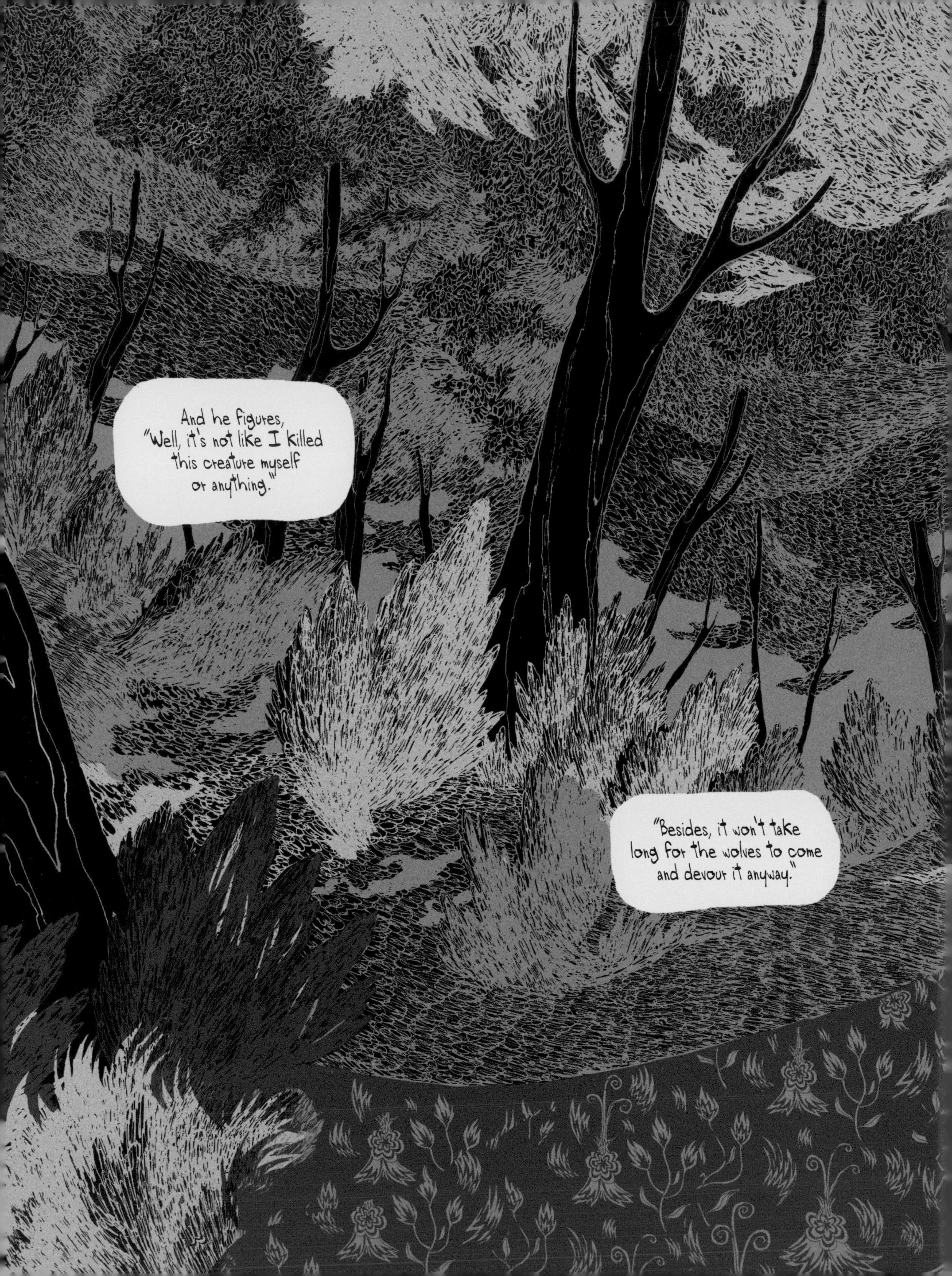
And he figures, "Well, it's not like I killed this creature myself or anything."
"Besides, it won't take long for the wolves to come and devour it anyway."

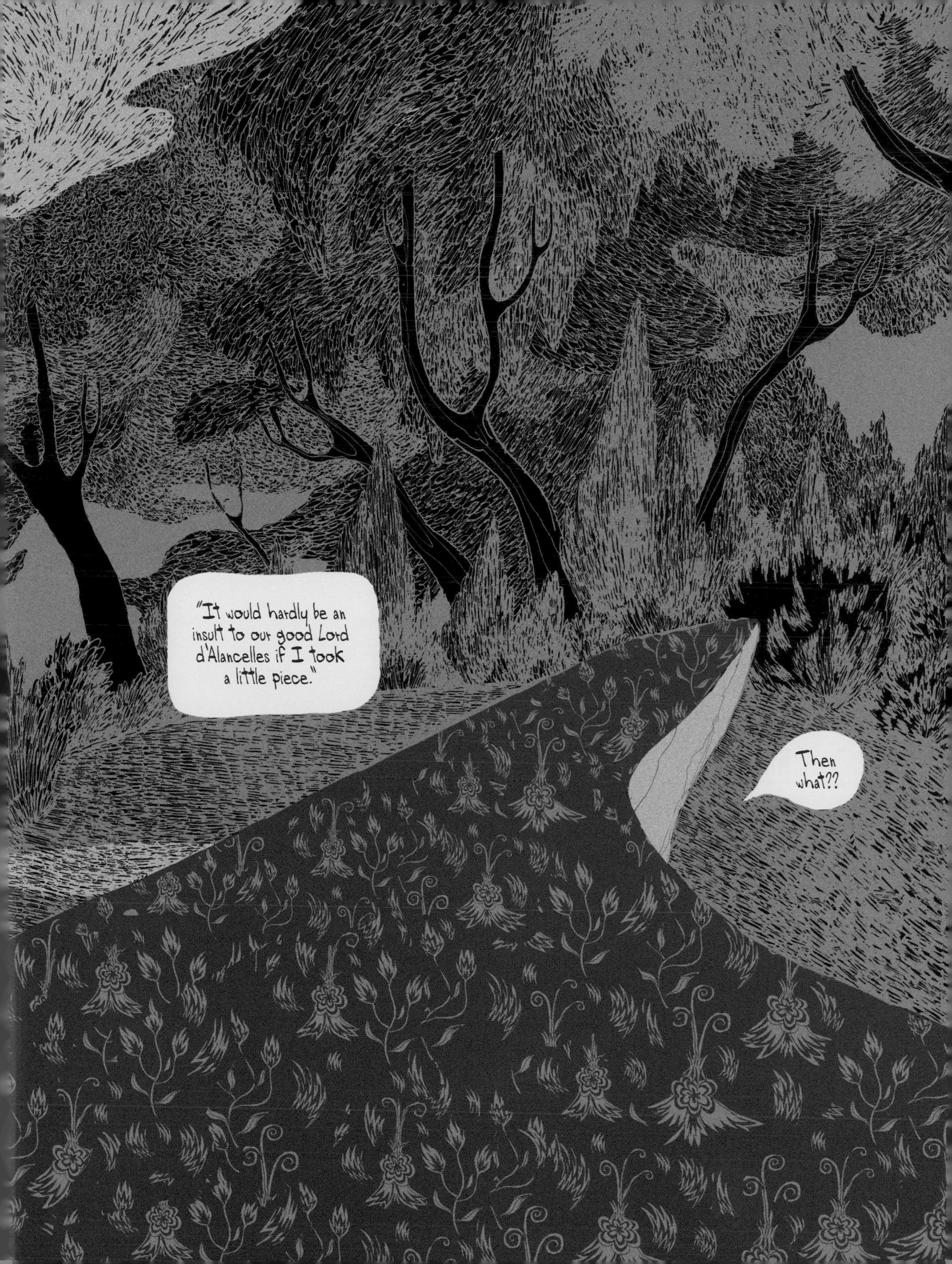
"It would hardly be an insult to our good Lord d'Alancelles if I took a little piece."
Then what??

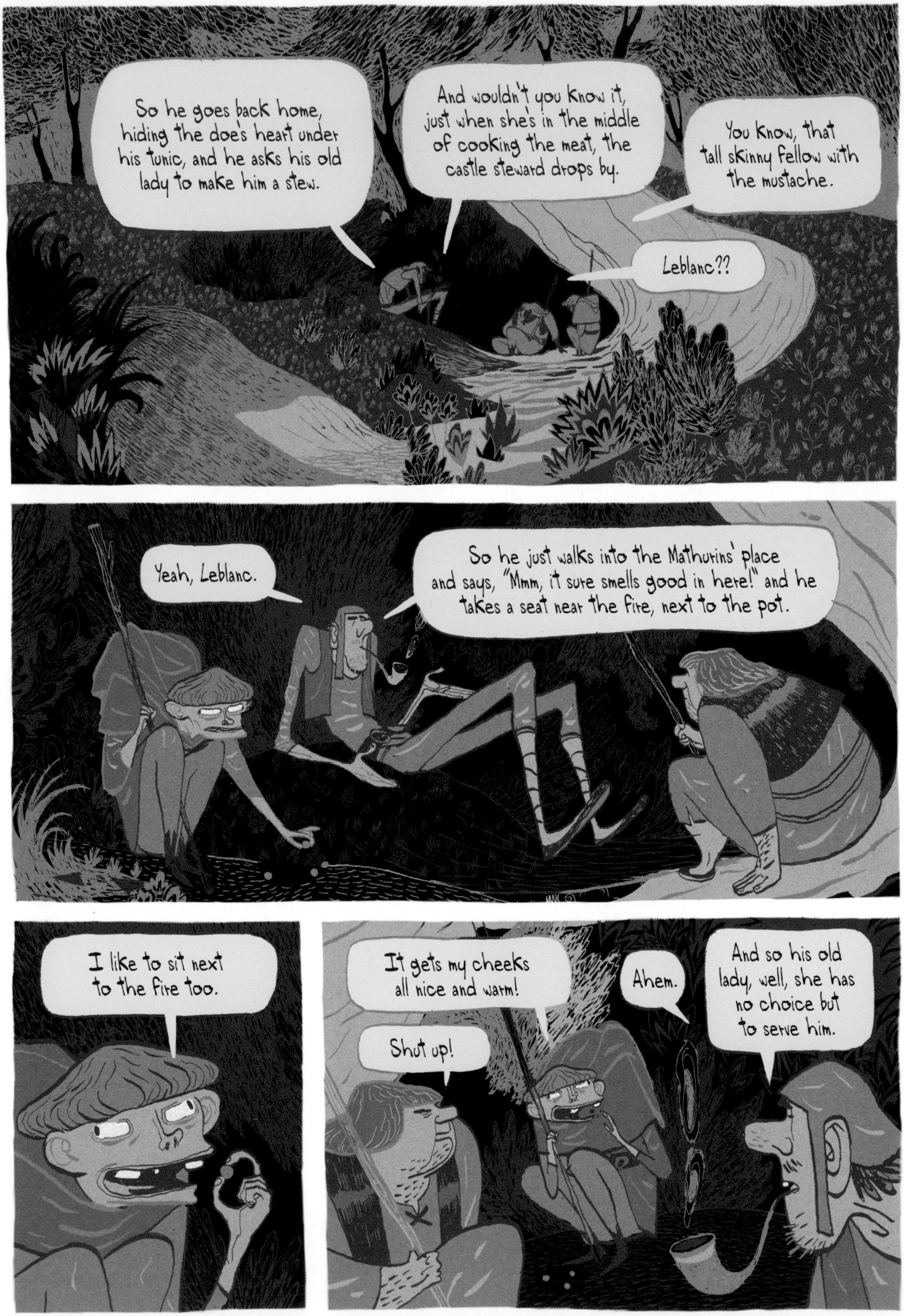
So he goes back home, hiding the doe's heart under his tunic, and he asks his old lady to make him a stew.
And wouldn't you know it, just when she's in the middle of cooking the meat, the castle steward drops by.
You know, that tall skinny fellow with the mustache.
Leblanc??
Yeah, Leblanc.
So he just walks into the Mathurins' place and says, "Mmm, it sure smells good in here!" and he takes a seat near the fire, next to the pot.
I like to sit next to the fire too.
It gets my cheeks all nice and warm!
Shut up!
Ahem.
And so his old lady, well, she has no choice but to serve him.

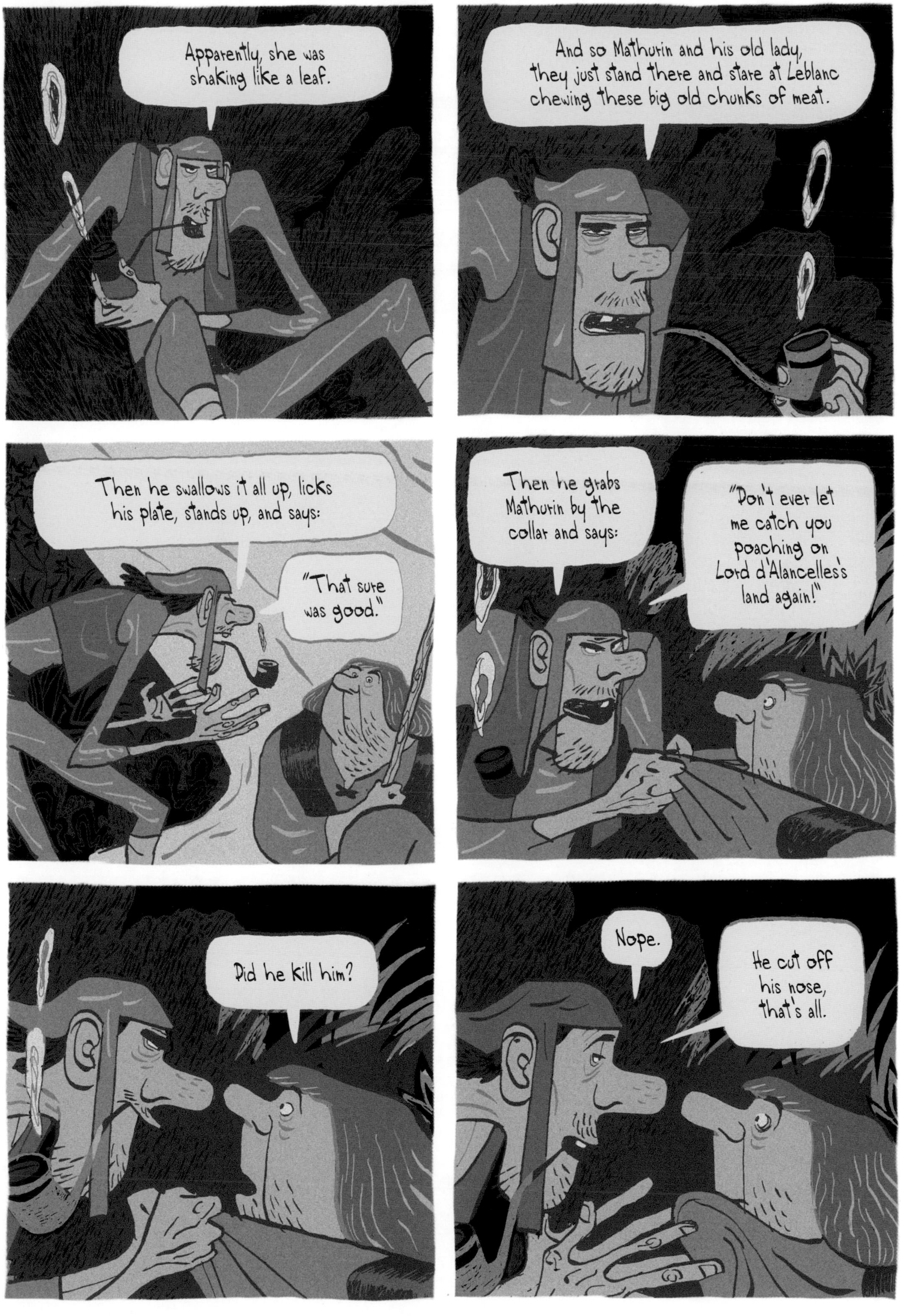
Apparently, she was shaking like a leaf.
And so Mathurin and his old lady, they just stand there and stare at Leblanc chewing these big old chunks of meat.
Then he swallows it all up, licks his plate, stands up, and says:
"That sure was good."
Then he grabs Mathurin by the collar and says:
"Don't ever let me catch you poaching on Lord d'Alancelles's land again!"
Did he kill him?
Nope.
He cut off his nose, that's all.

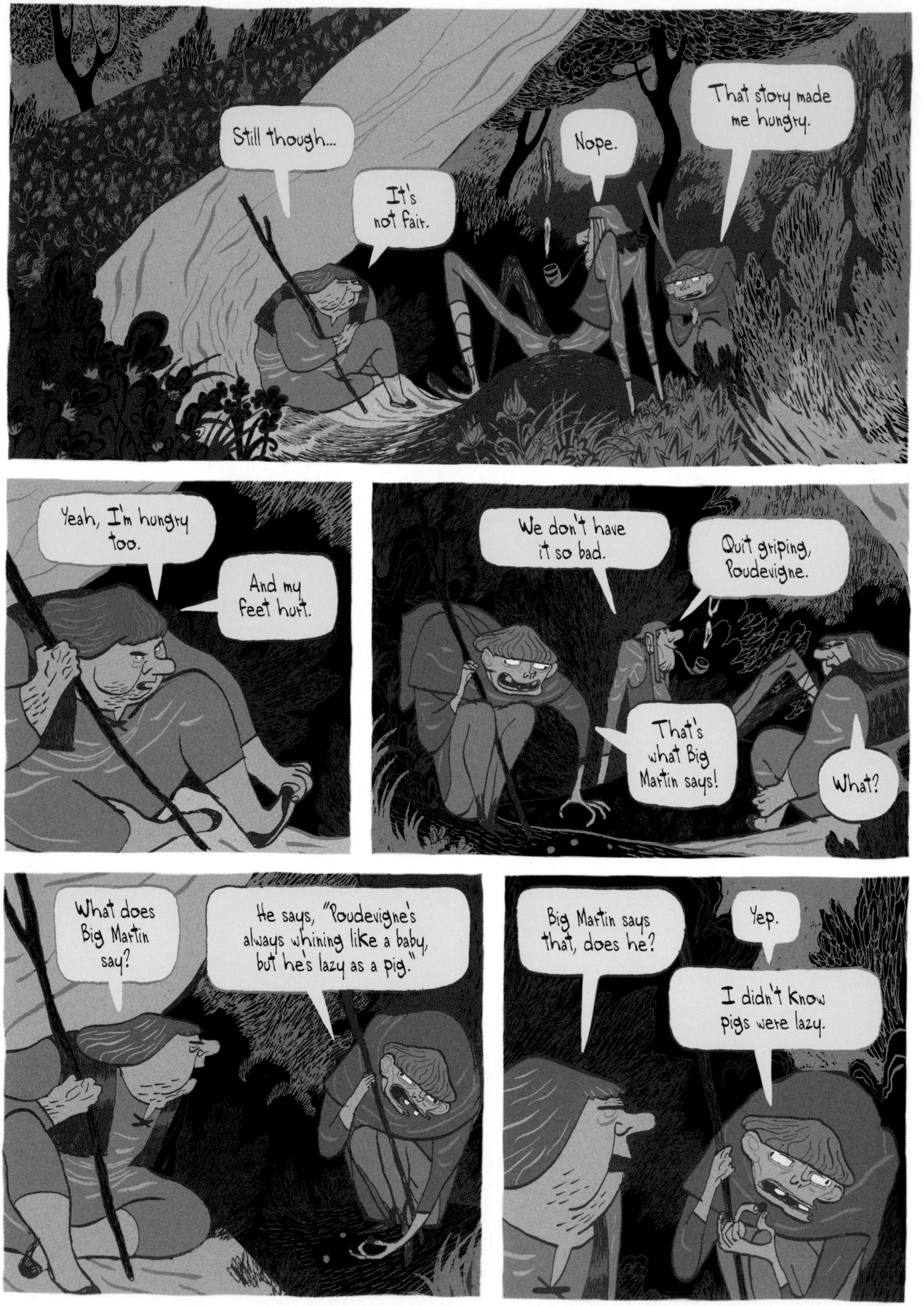
Still though...
It's not fair.
Nope.
That story made me hungry.
Yeah, I'm hungry too.
And my feet hurt.
We don't have it so bad.
Quit griping, Poudevigne.
That's what Big Martin says!
What?
What does Big Martin say?
He says, "Poudevigne's always whining like a baby, but he's lazy as a pig."
Big Martin says that, does he?
Yep.
I didn't know pigs were lazy.

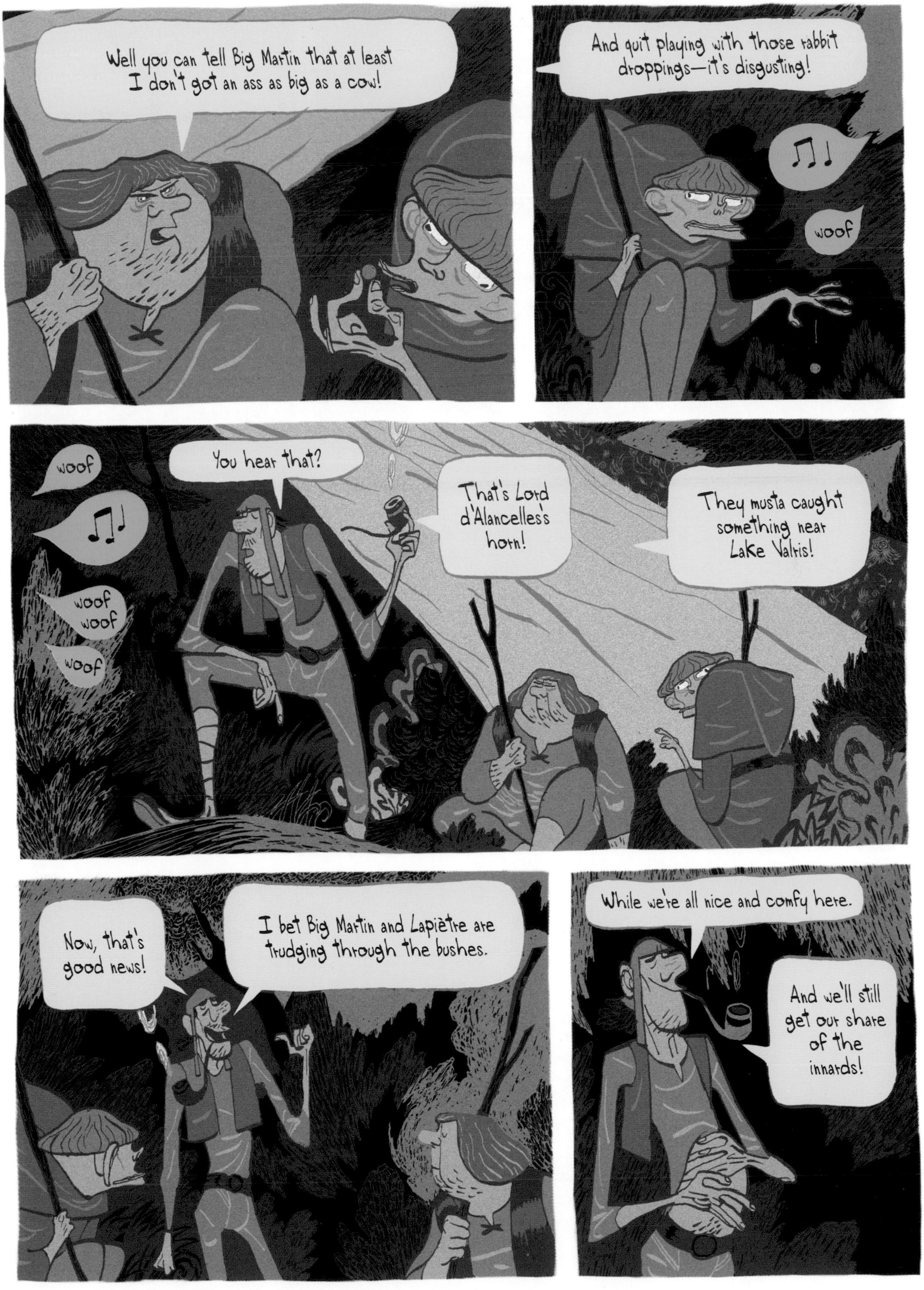
Well you can tell Big Martin that at least I don't got an ass as big as a cow!
And quit playing with those rabbit droppings—it's disgusting!
♫♩
woof
woof
♫♩
You hear that?
That's Lord d'Alancelles's horn!
They musta caught something near Lake Valtris!
woof woof
woof
Now, that's good news!
I bet Big Martin and Lapiètre are trudging through the bushes.
While we're all nice and comfy here.
And we'll still get our share of the innards!

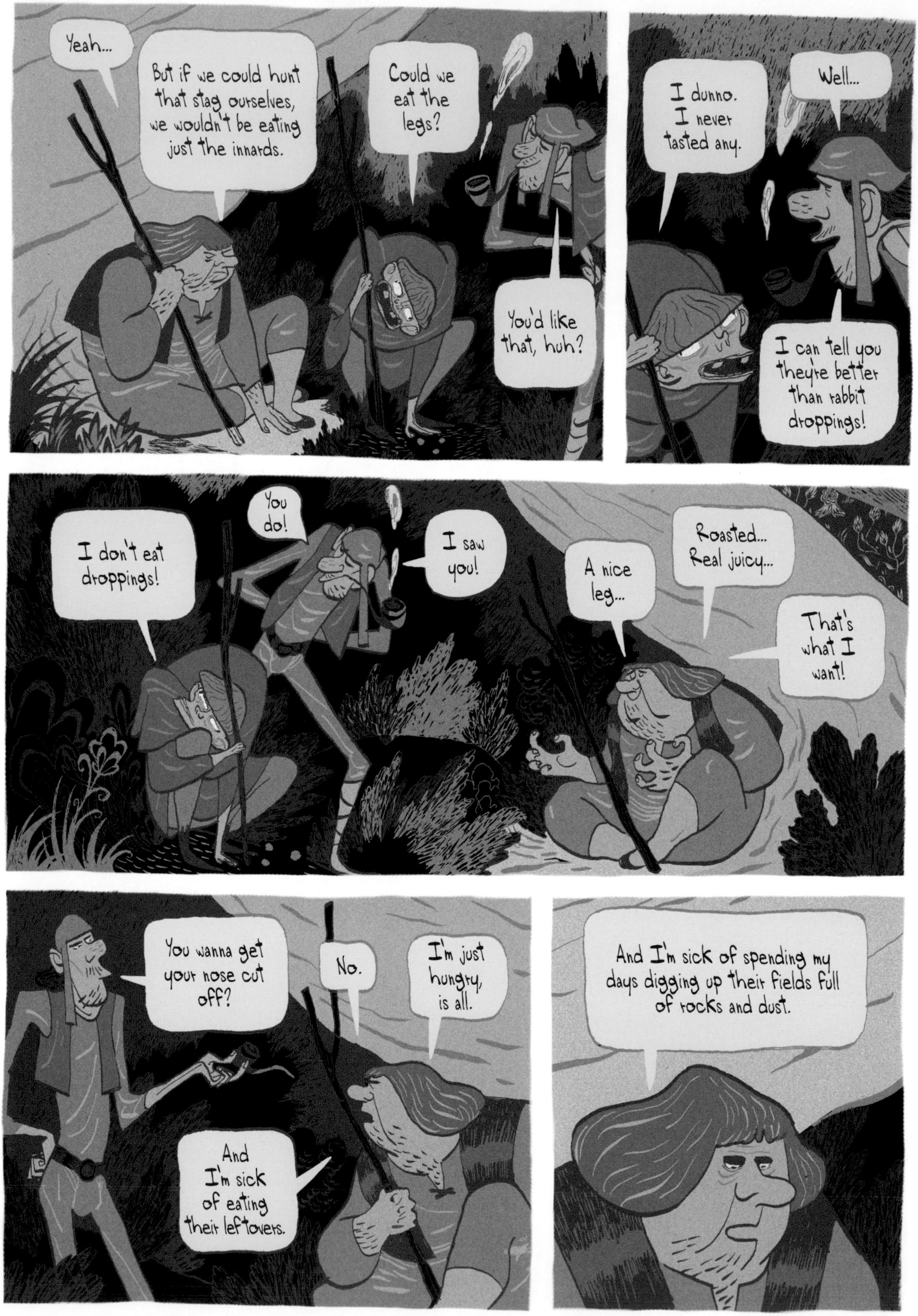
Yeah...
But if we could hunt that stag ourselves, we wouldn't be eating just the innards.
Could we eat the legs?
You'd like that, huh?
I dunno. I never tasted any.
Well...
I can tell you they're better than rabbit droppings!
I don't eat droppings!
You do!
I saw you!
A nice leg...
Roasted... Real juicy...
That's what I want!
You wanna get your nose cut off?
No.
I'm just hungry, is all.
And I'm sick of eating their leftovers.
And I'm sick of spending my days digging up their fields full of rocks and dust.

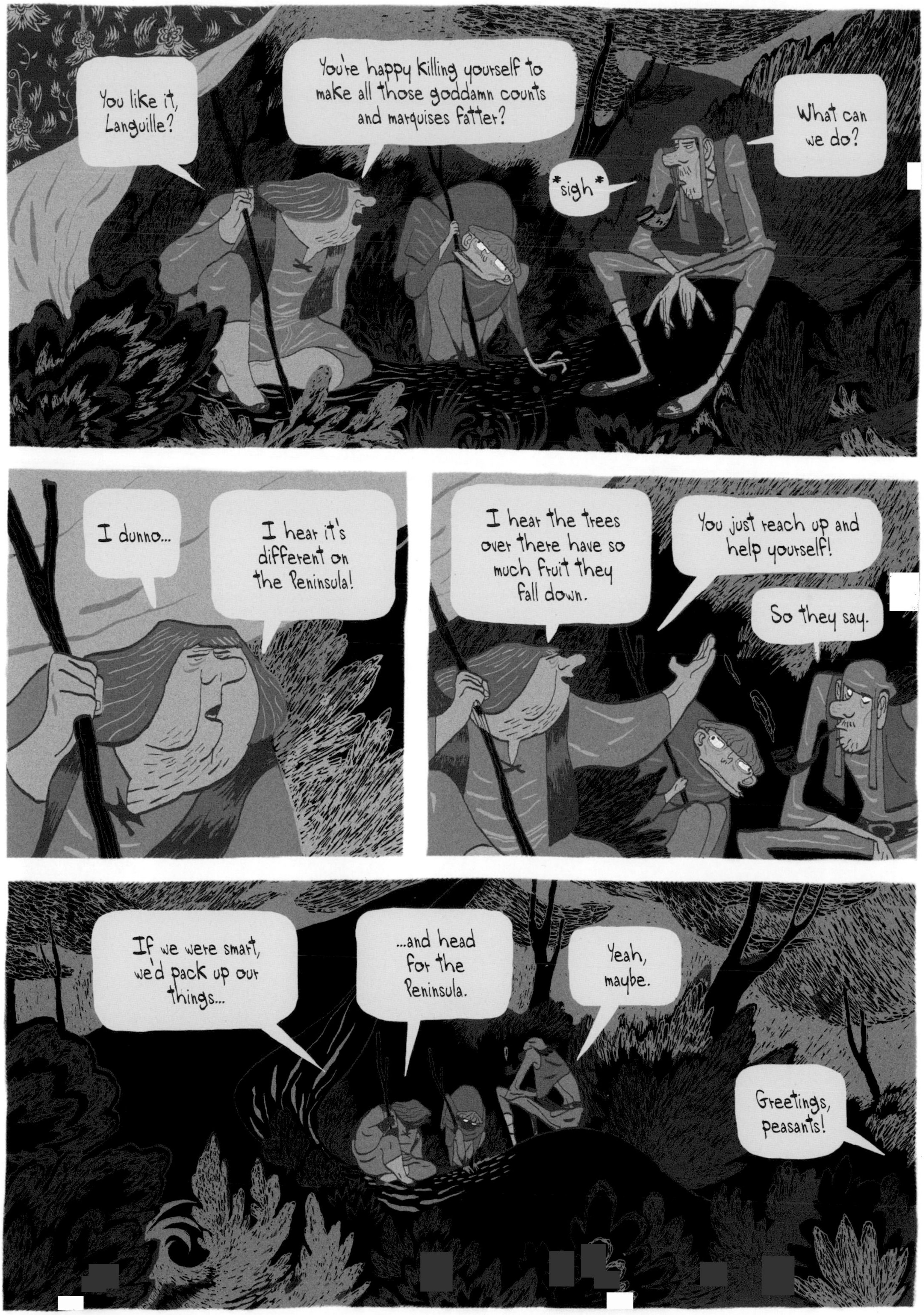

You like it, Languille?
You're happy killing yourself to make all those goddamn counts and marquises fatter?
sigh
What can we do?
I dunno...
I hear it's different on the Peninsula!
I hear the trees over there have so much fruit they fall down.
You just reach up and help yourself!
So they say.
If we were smart, we'd pack up our things...
...and head for the Peninsula.
Yeah, maybe.
Greetings, peasants!

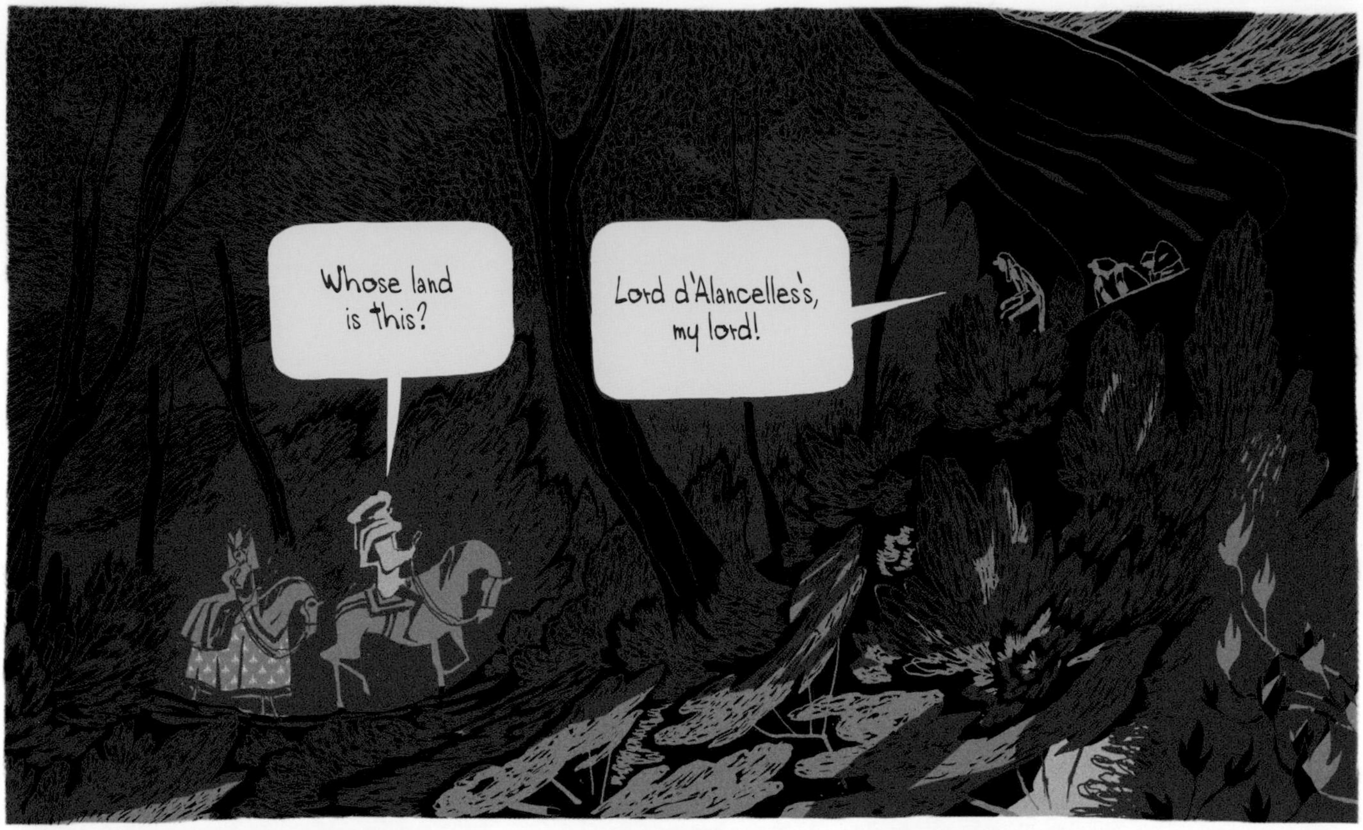
Whose land is this?
Lord d'Alancelles's, my lord!

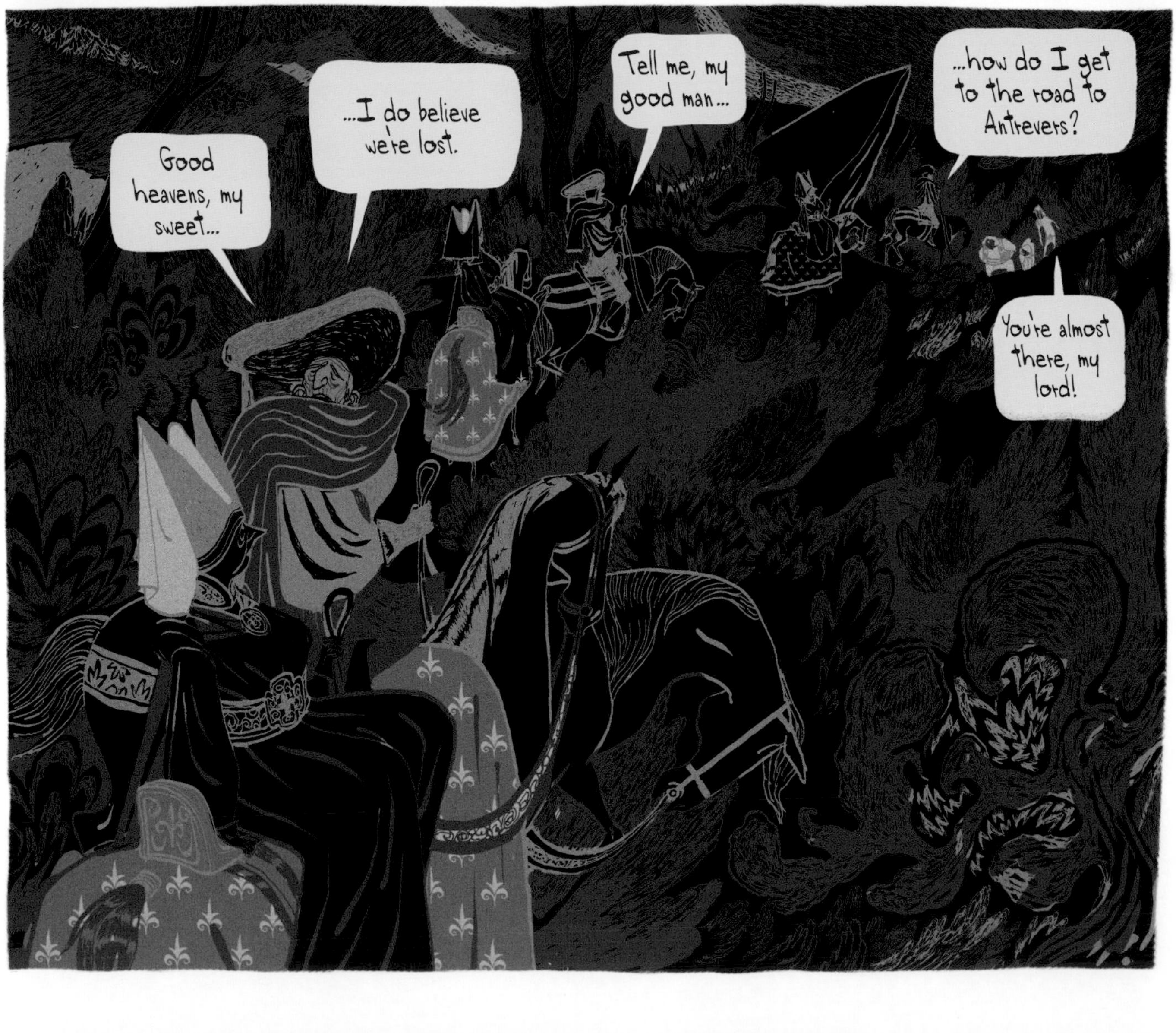
Good heavens, my sweet...
...I do believe we're lost.
Tell me, my good man...
...how do I get to the road to Antrevers?
You're almost there, my lord!

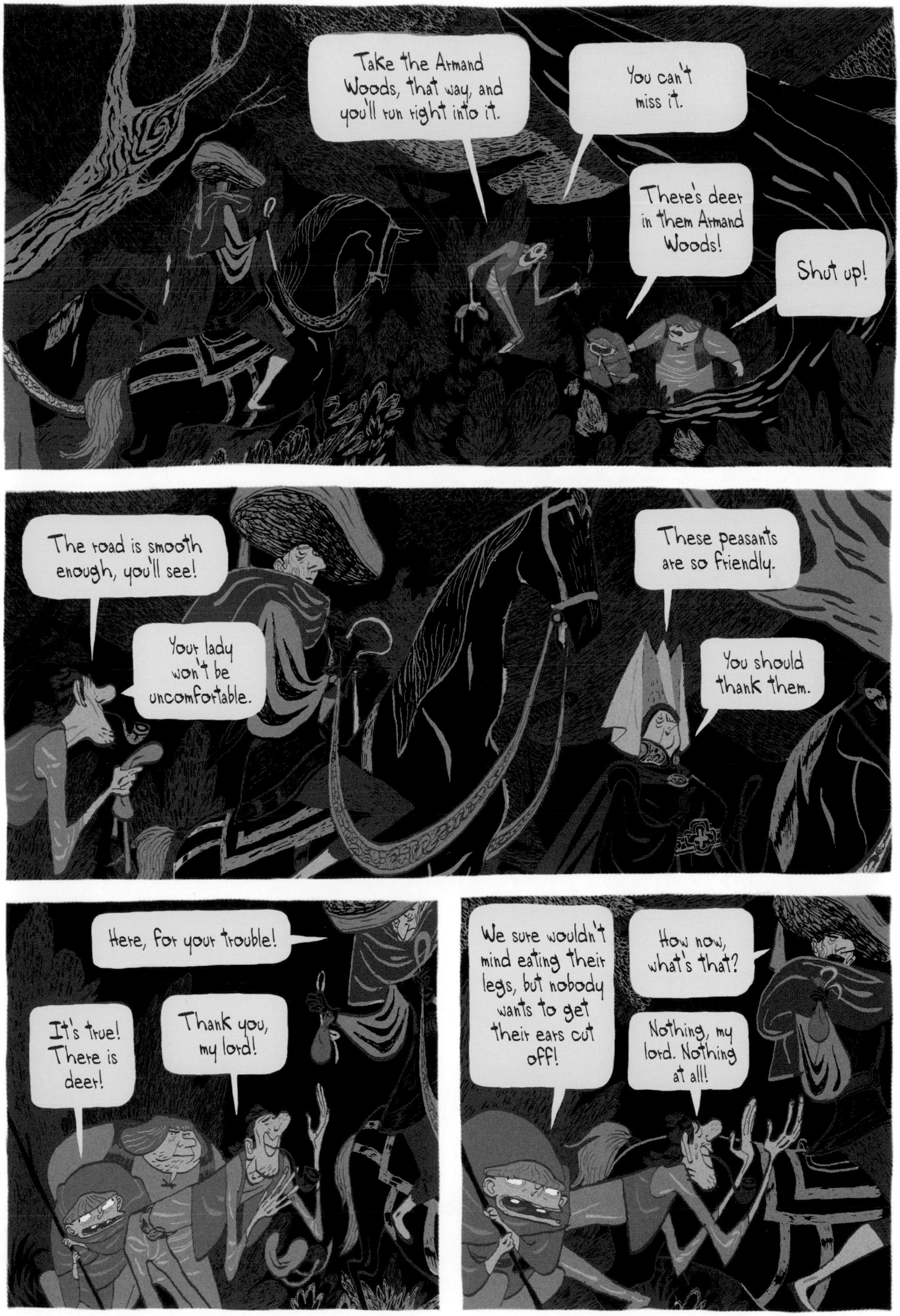
Take the Armand Woods, that way, and you'll run right into it.
You can't miss it.
There's deer in them Armand Woods!
Shut up!
The road is smooth enough, you'll see!
Your lady won't be uncomfortable.
These peasants are so friendly.
You should thank them.
Here, for your trouble!
It's true! There is deer!
Thank you, my lord!
We sure wouldn't mind eating their legs, but nobody wants to get their ears cut off!
How now, what's that?
Nothing, my lord. Nothing at all!

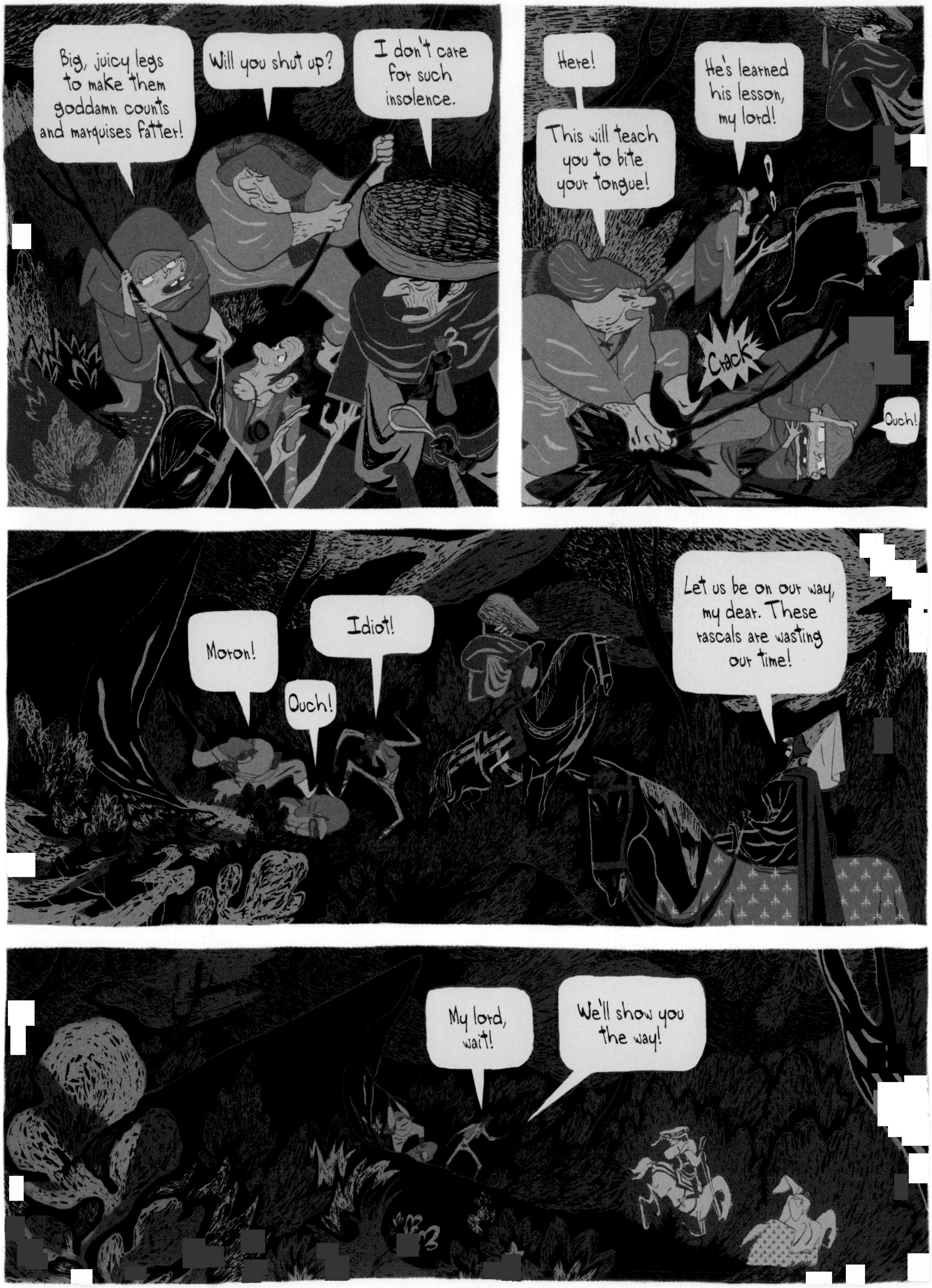
Big, juicy legs to make them goddamn counts and marquises fatter!
Will you shut up?
I don't care for such insolence.
Here!
This will teach you to bite your tongue!
He's learned his lesson, my lord!
Crack
Ouch!
Moron!
Idiot!
Ouch!
Let us be on our way, my dear. These rascals are wasting our time!
My lord, wait!
We'll show you the way!

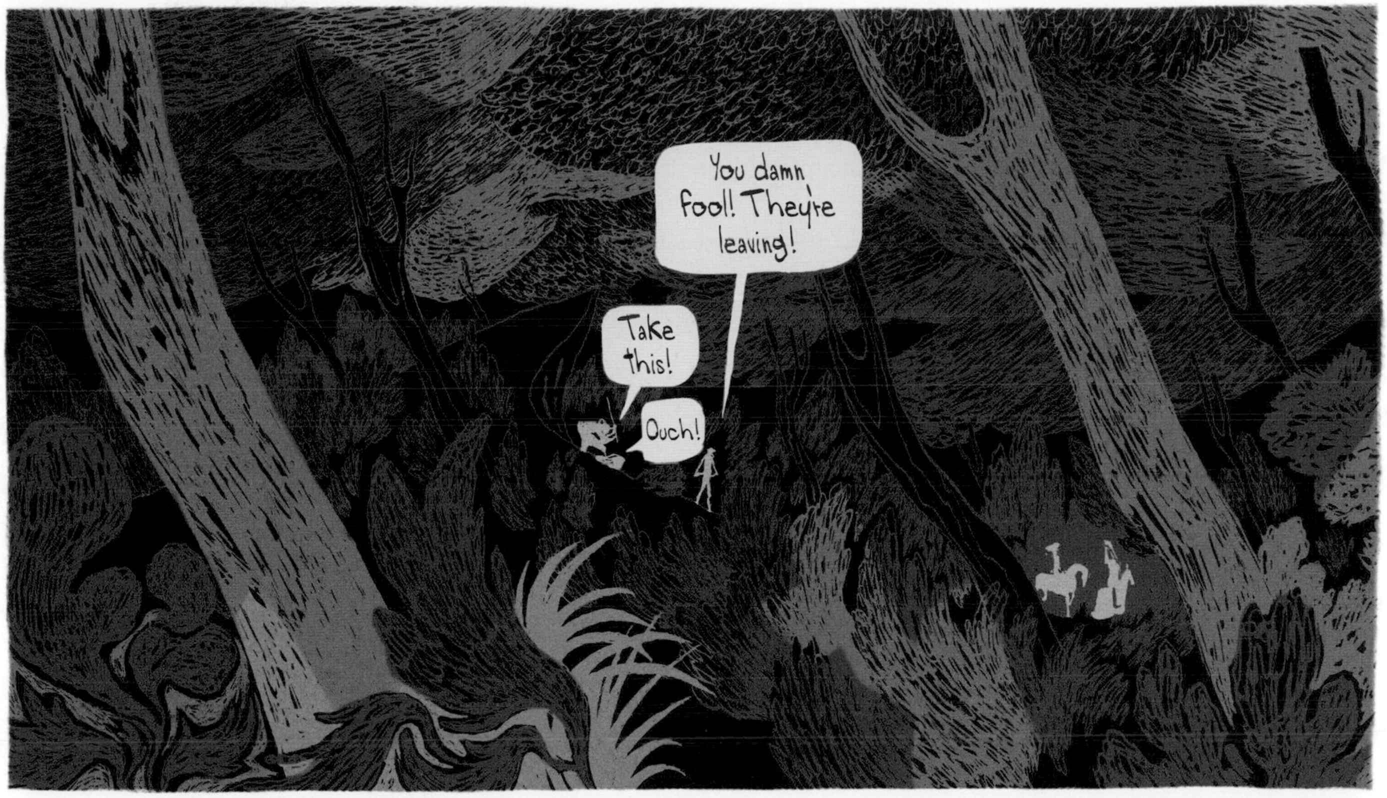
Take this!
Ouch!
You damn fool! They're leaving!

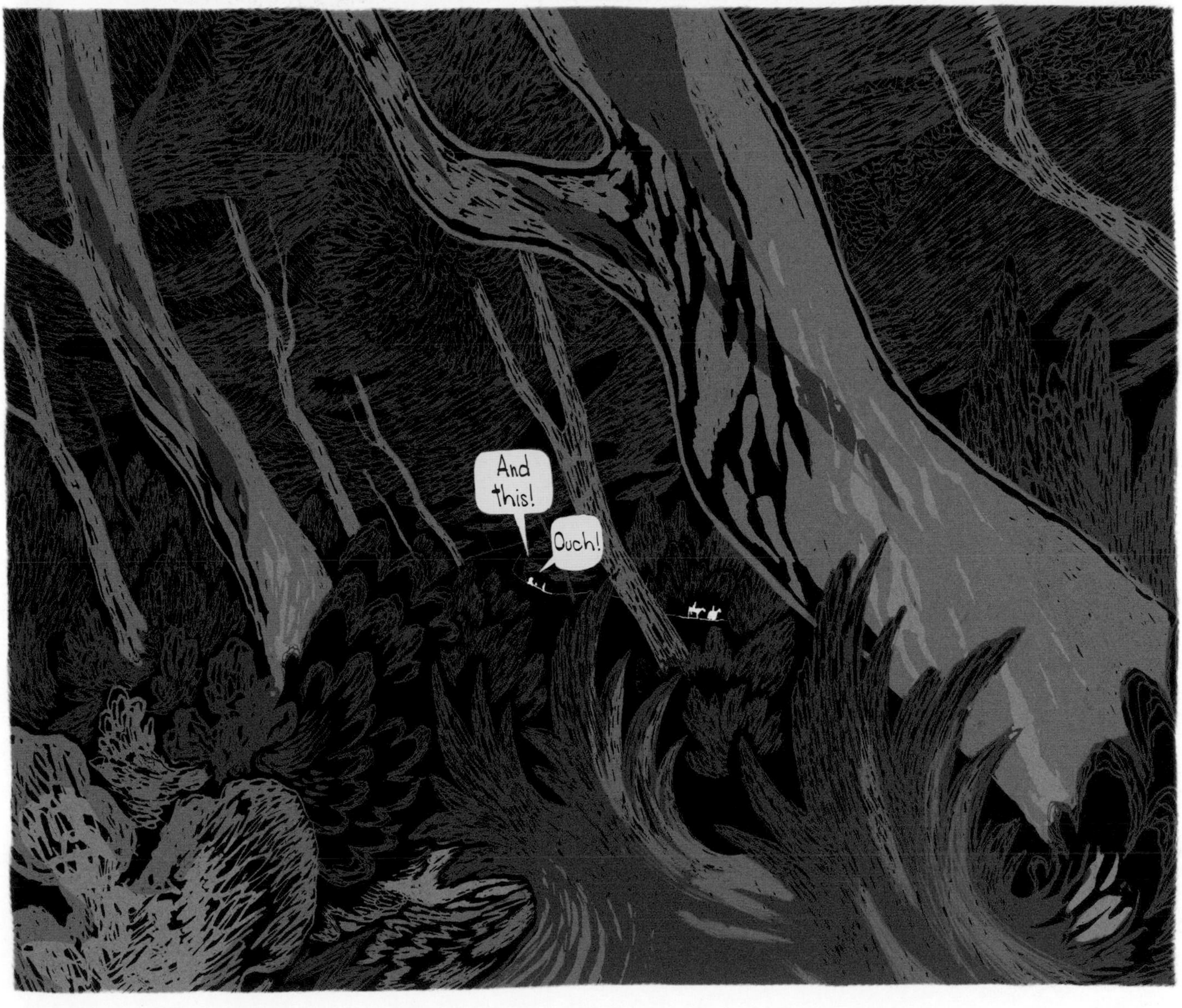
And this!
Ouch!

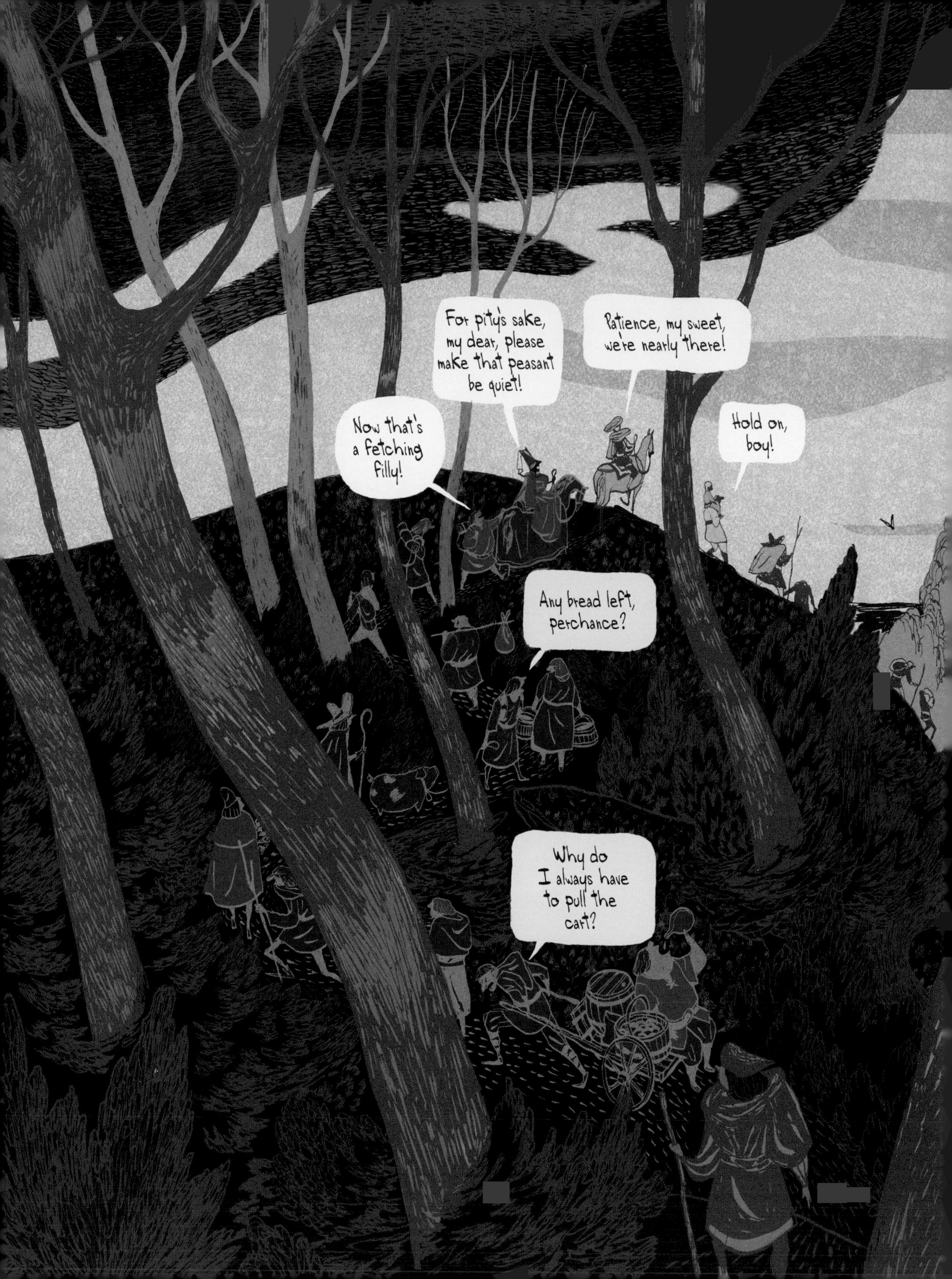
For pity's sake, my dear, please make that peasant be quiet!
Patience, my sweet, we're nearly there!
Now that's a fetching filly!
Hold on, boy!
Any bread left, perchance?
Why do I always have to pull the cart?

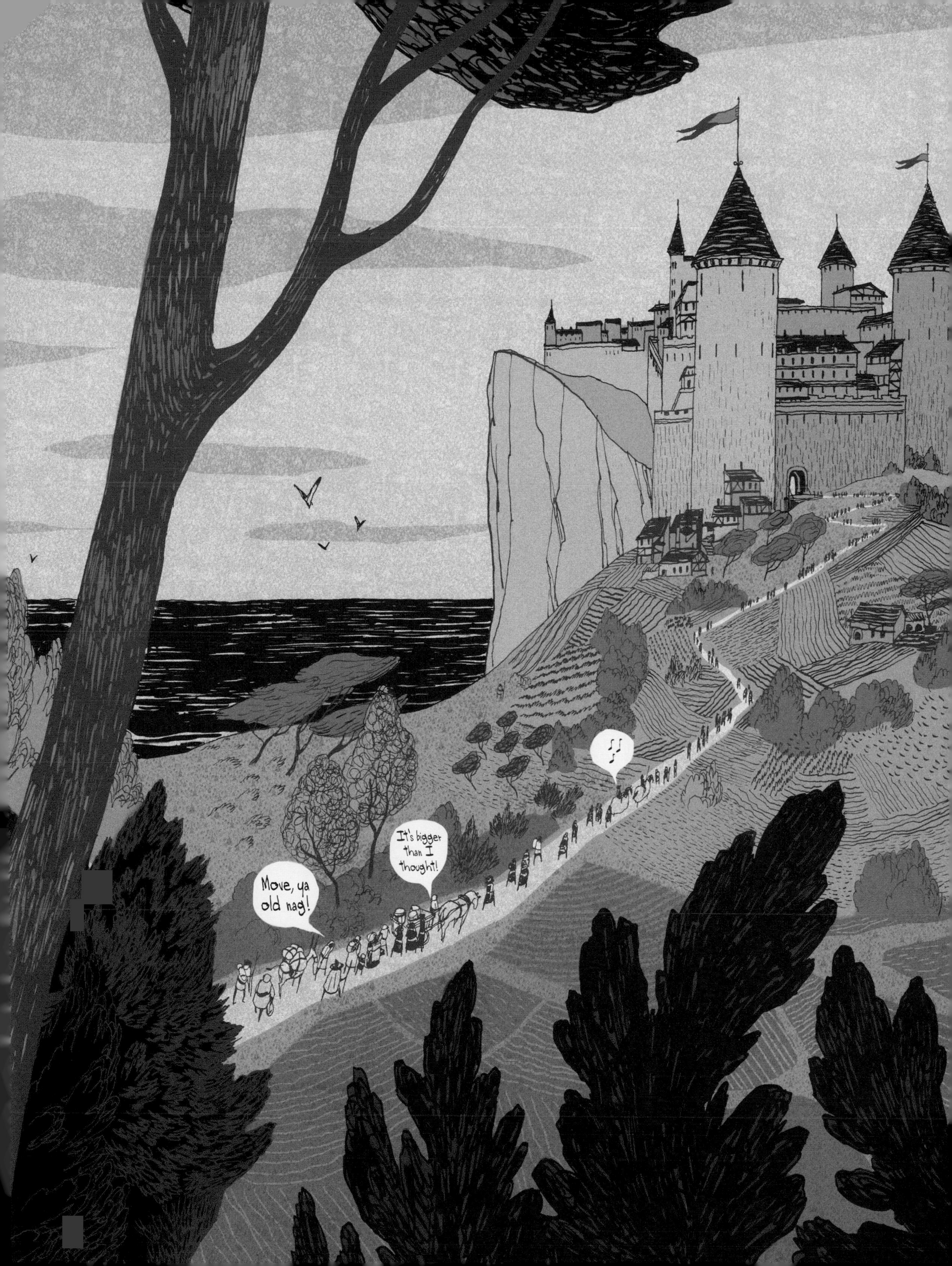
Move, ya old nag!
It's bigger than I thought!

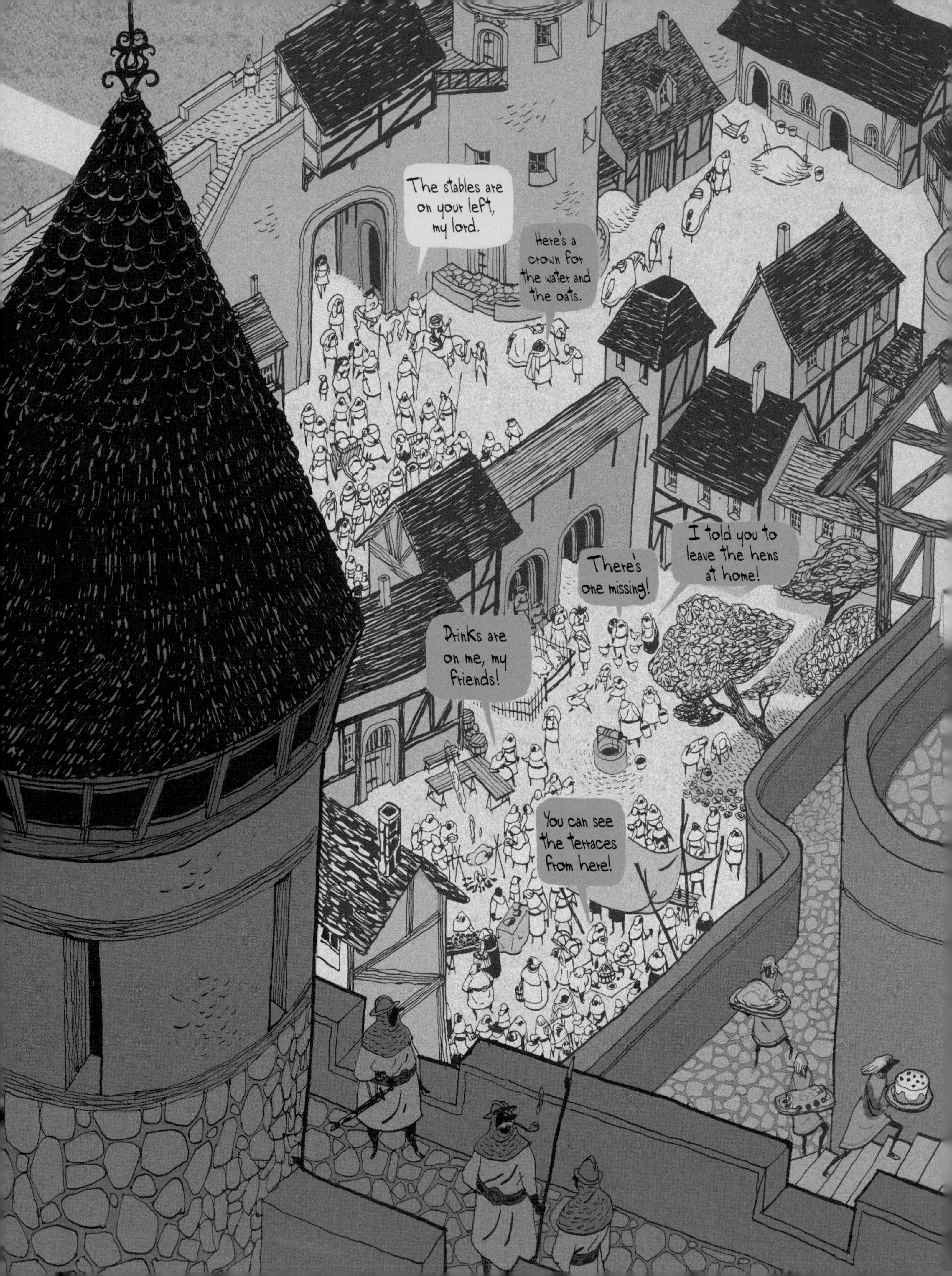
The stables are on your left, my lord.
Here's a crown for the water and the oats.
There's one missing!
I told you to leave the hens at home!
Drinks are on me, my friends!
You can see the terraces from here!

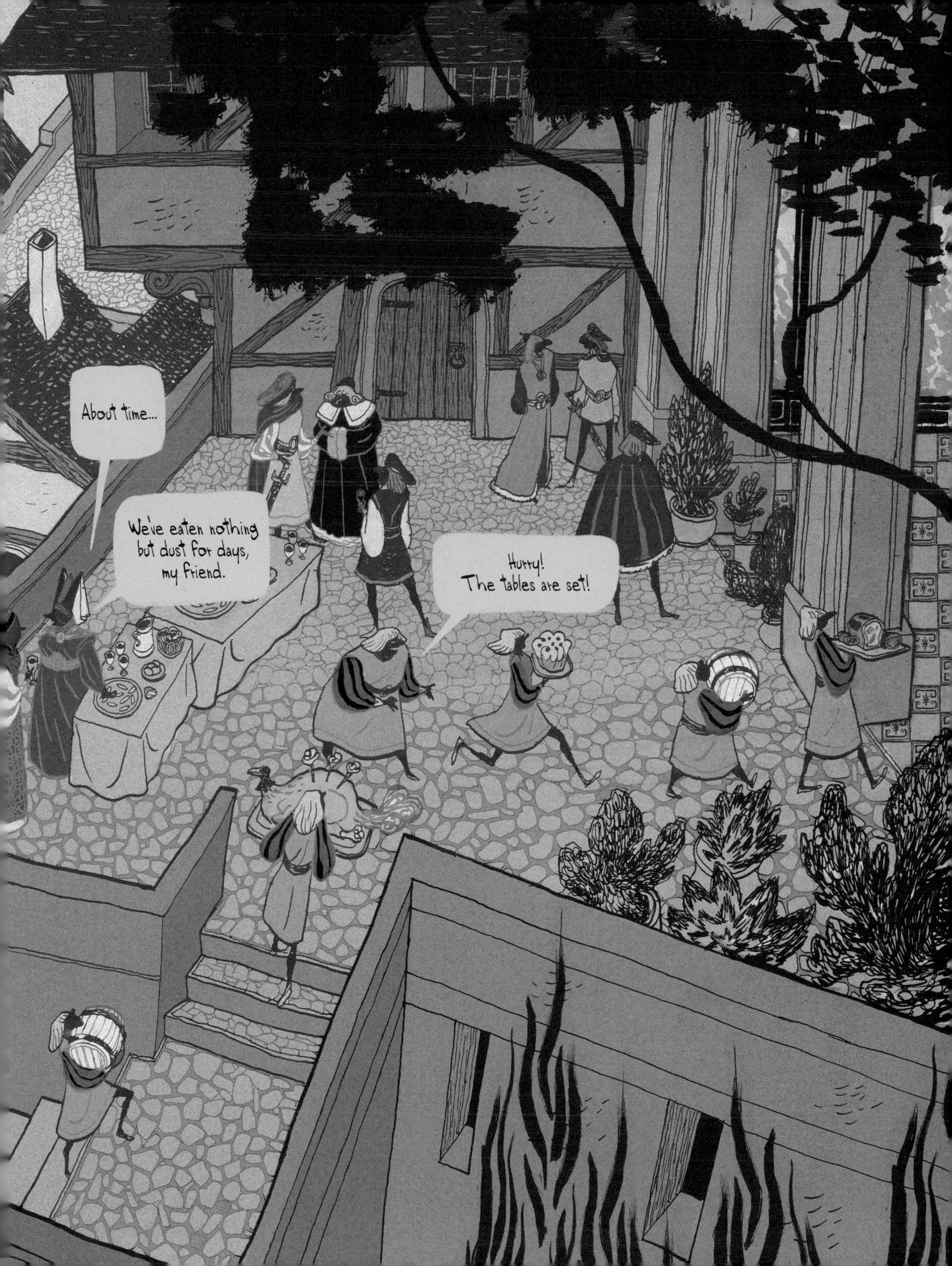
About time...
We've eaten nothing but dust for days, my friend.
Hurry! The tables are set!

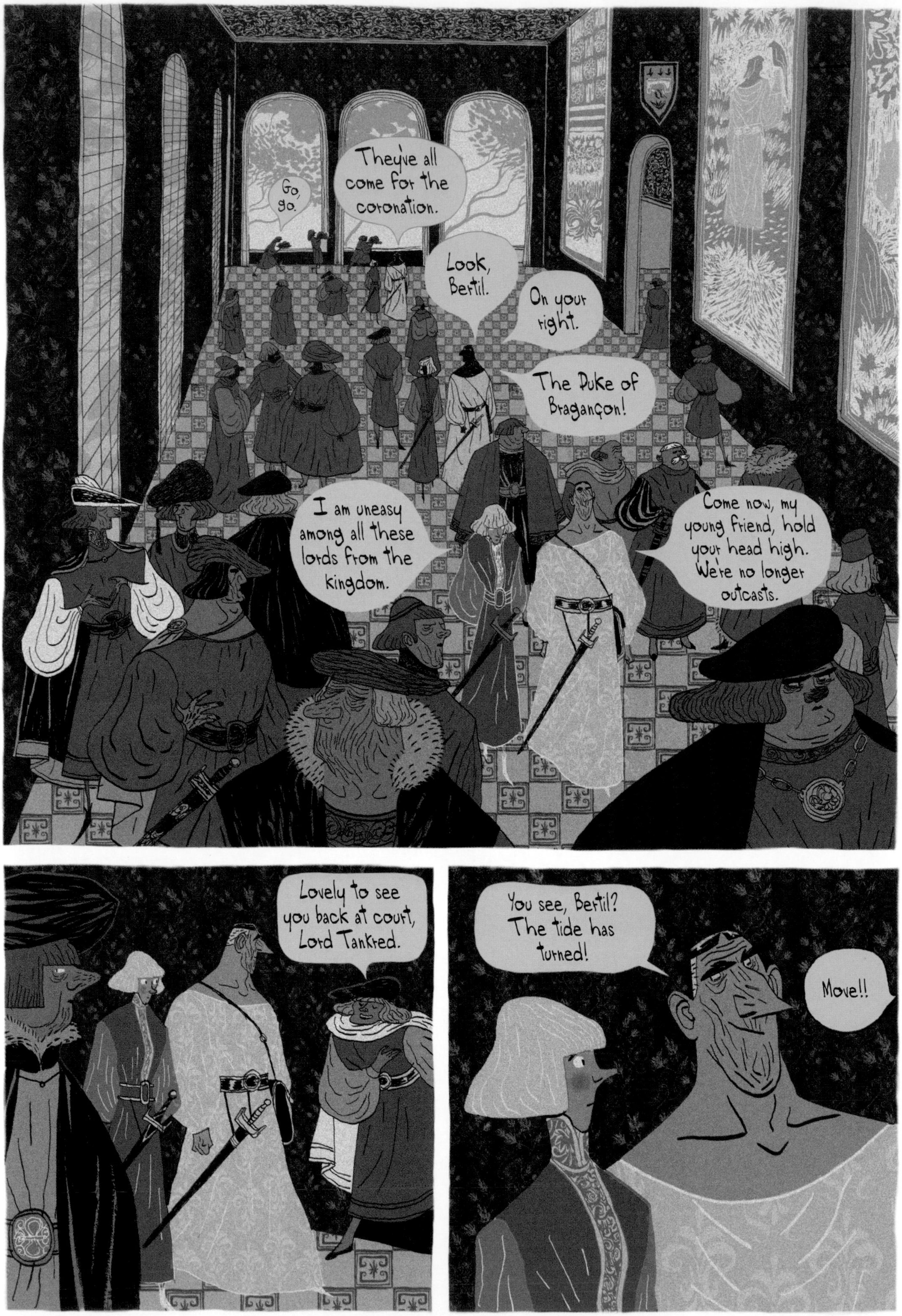

Go, go.
They've all come for the coronation.
Look, Bertil.
On your right.
The Duke of Bragançon!
I am uneasy among all these lords from the kingdom.
Come now, my young friend, hold your head high. We're no longer outcasts.
Lovely to see you back at court, Lord Tankred.
You see, Bertil? The tide has turned!
Move!!

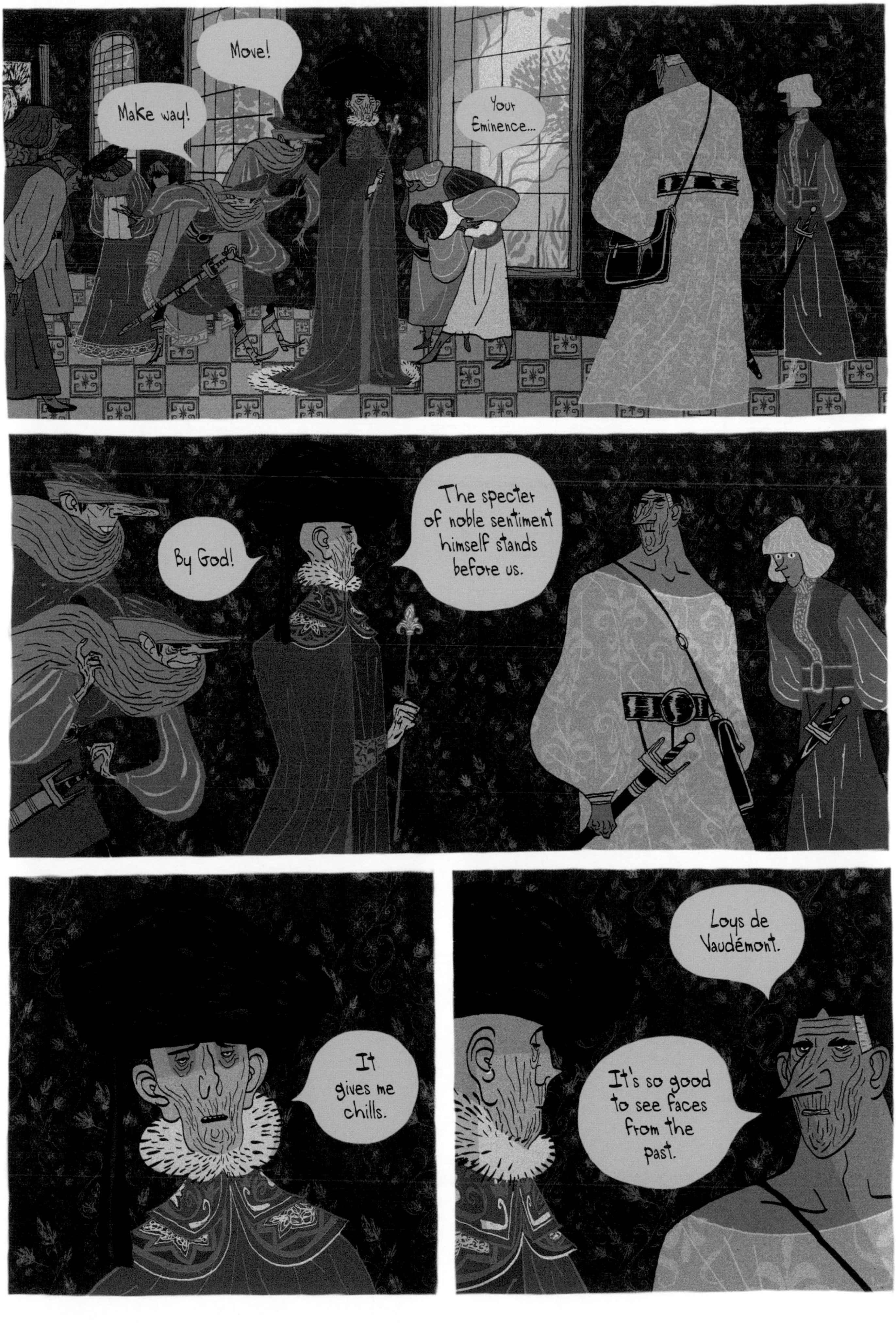
Make way!
Move!
Your Eminence...
By God!
The specter of noble sentiment himself stands before us.
It gives me chills.
Loys de Vaudémont.
It's so good to see faces from the past.

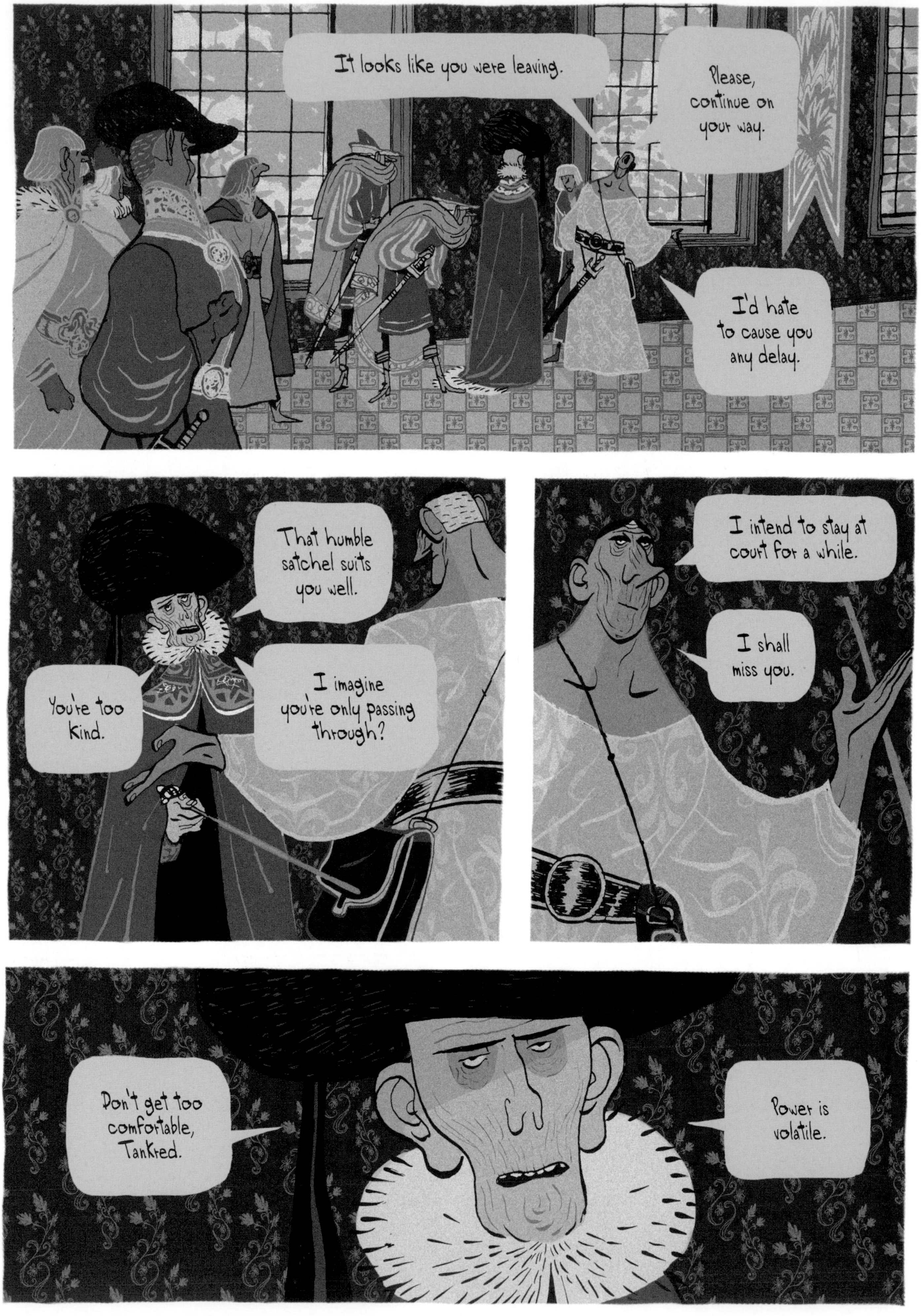
It looks like you were leaving.
Please, continue on your way.
I'd hate to cause you any delay.
That humble satchel suits you well.
I imagine you're only passing through?
You're too kind.
I intend to stay at court for a while.
I shall miss you.
Don't get too comfortable, Tankred.
Power is volatile.

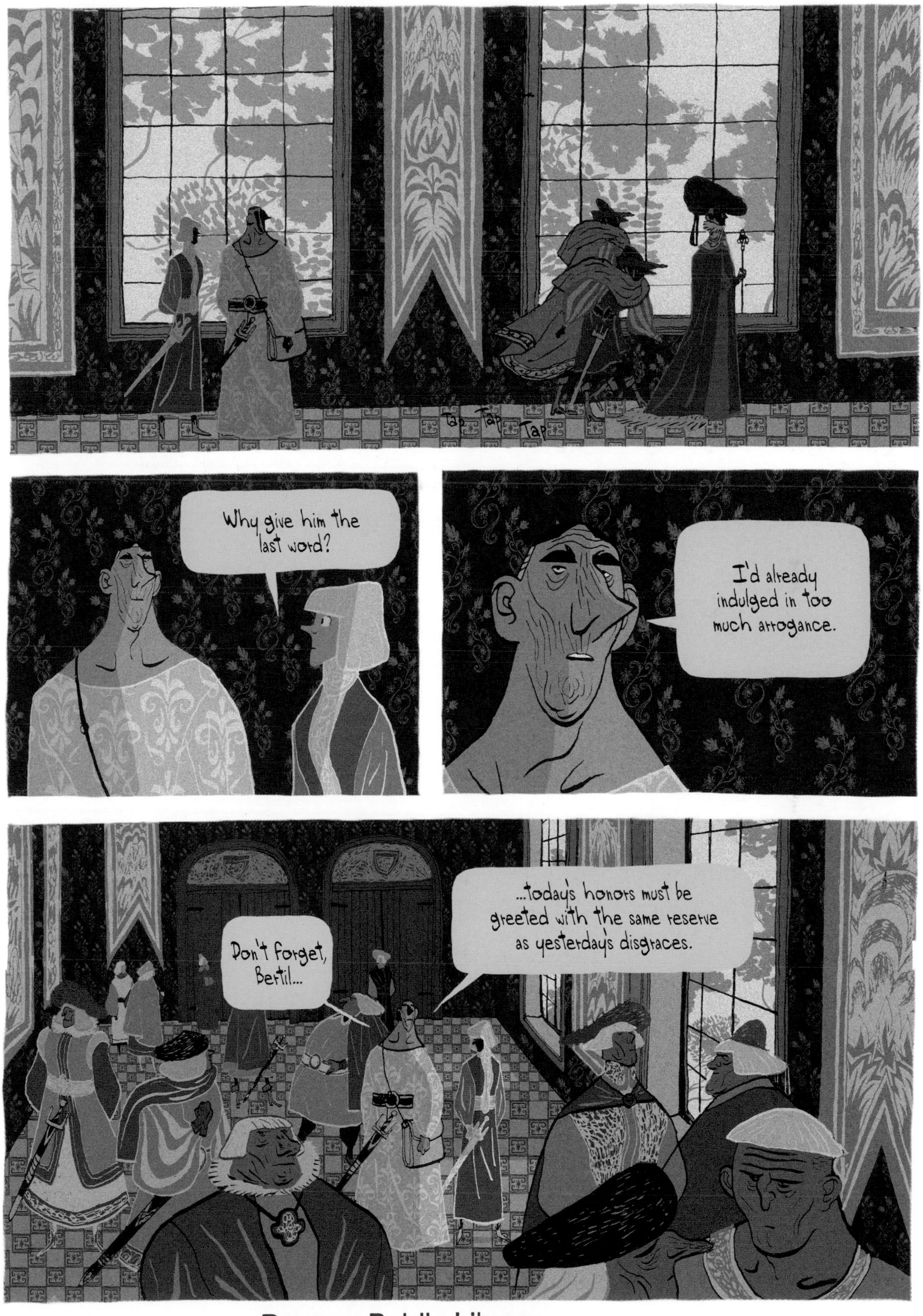
Tap Tap Tap
Why give him the last word?
I'd already indulged in too much arrogance.
Don't forget, Bertil...
...today's honors must be greeted with the same reserve as yesterday's disgraces.

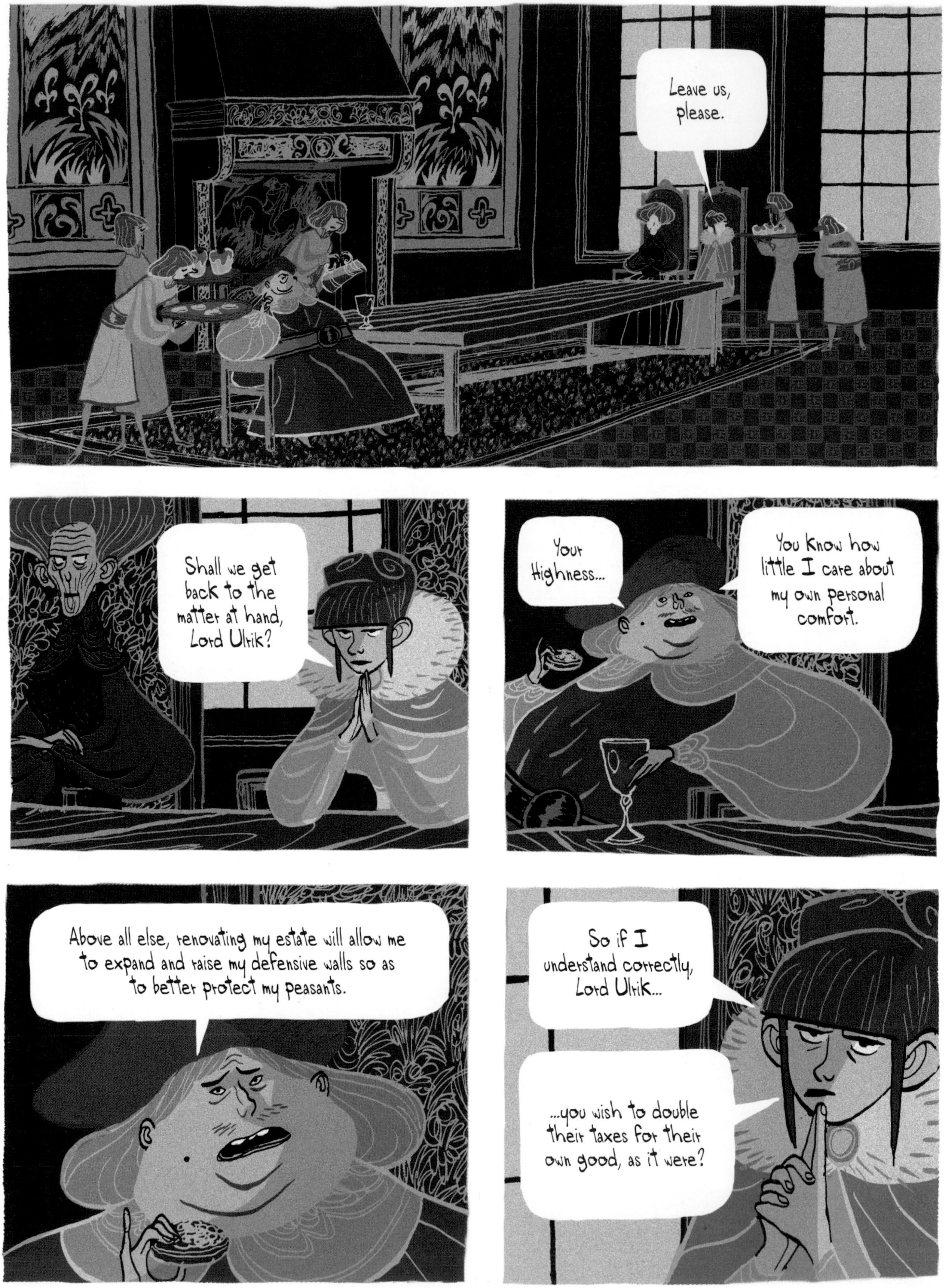
Leave us, please.
Shall we get back to the matter at hand, Lord Ulrik?
Your Highness...
You know how little I care about my own personal comfort.
Above all else, renovating my estate will allow me to expand and raise my defensive walls so as to better protect my peasants.
So if I understand correctly, Lord Ulrik...
...you wish to double their taxes for their own good, as it were?

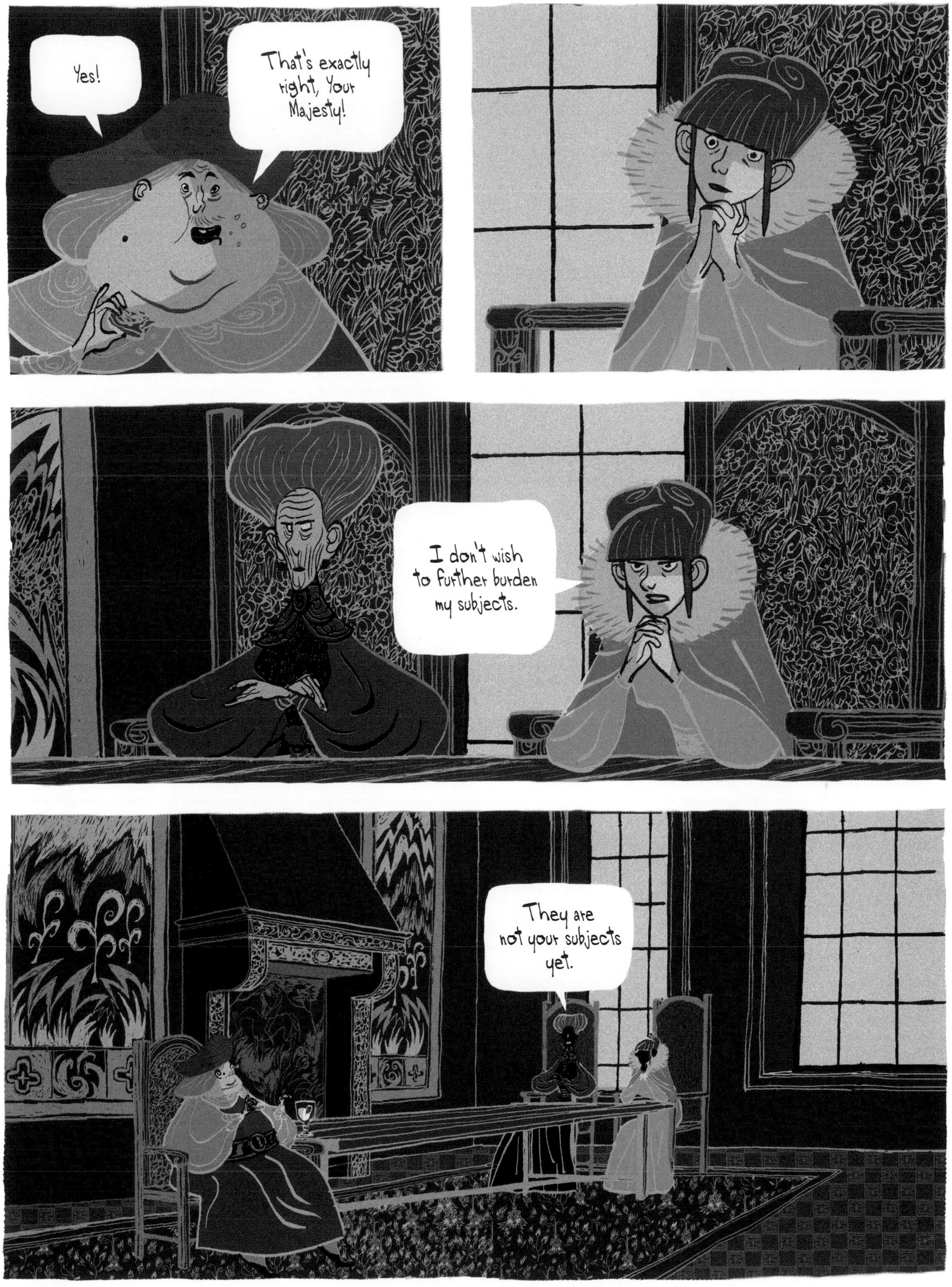
Yes!
That's exactly right, Your Majesty!
I don't wish to further burden my subjects.
They are not your subjects yet.

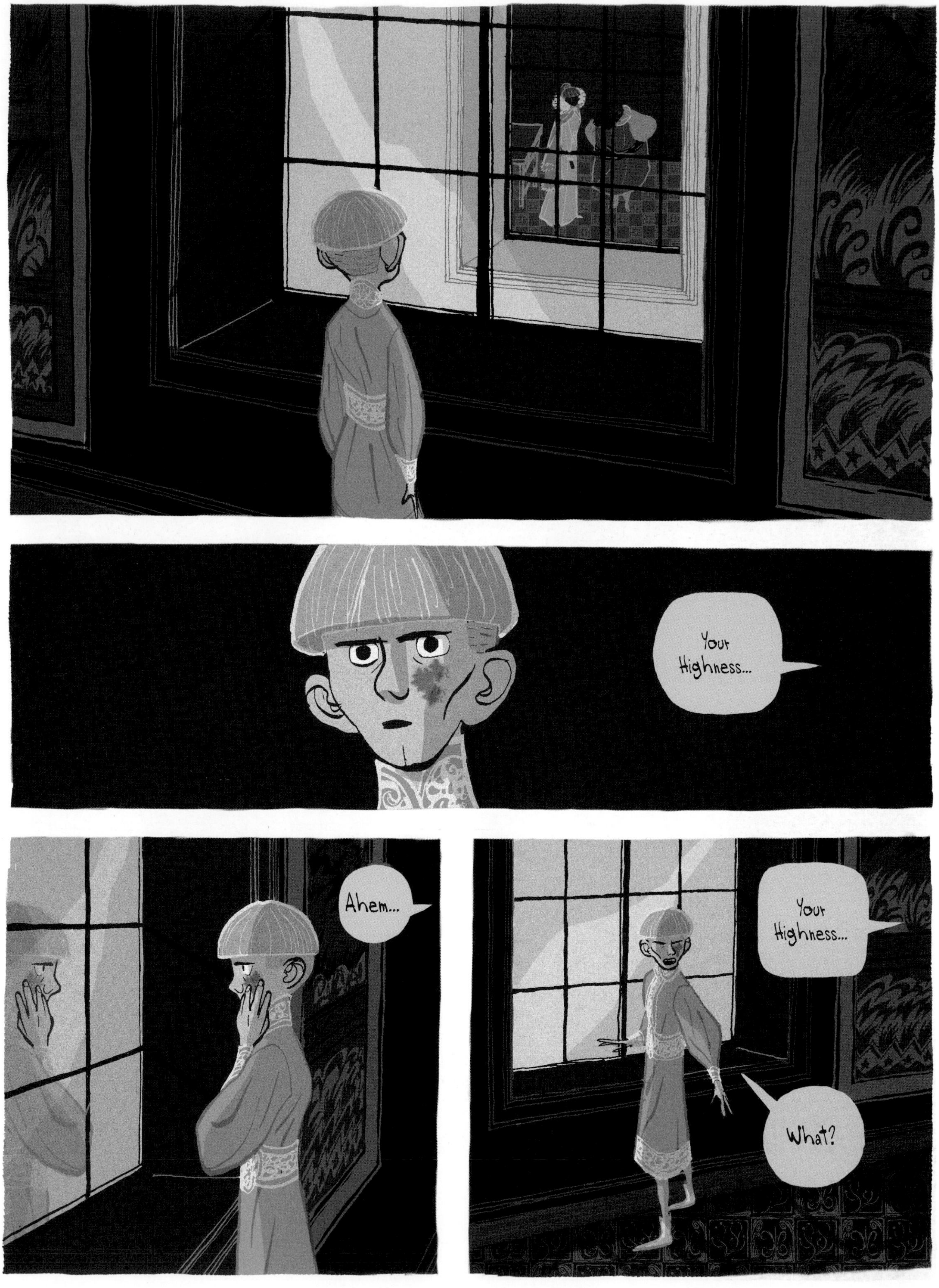
Your Highness...
Ahem...
Your Highness...
What?

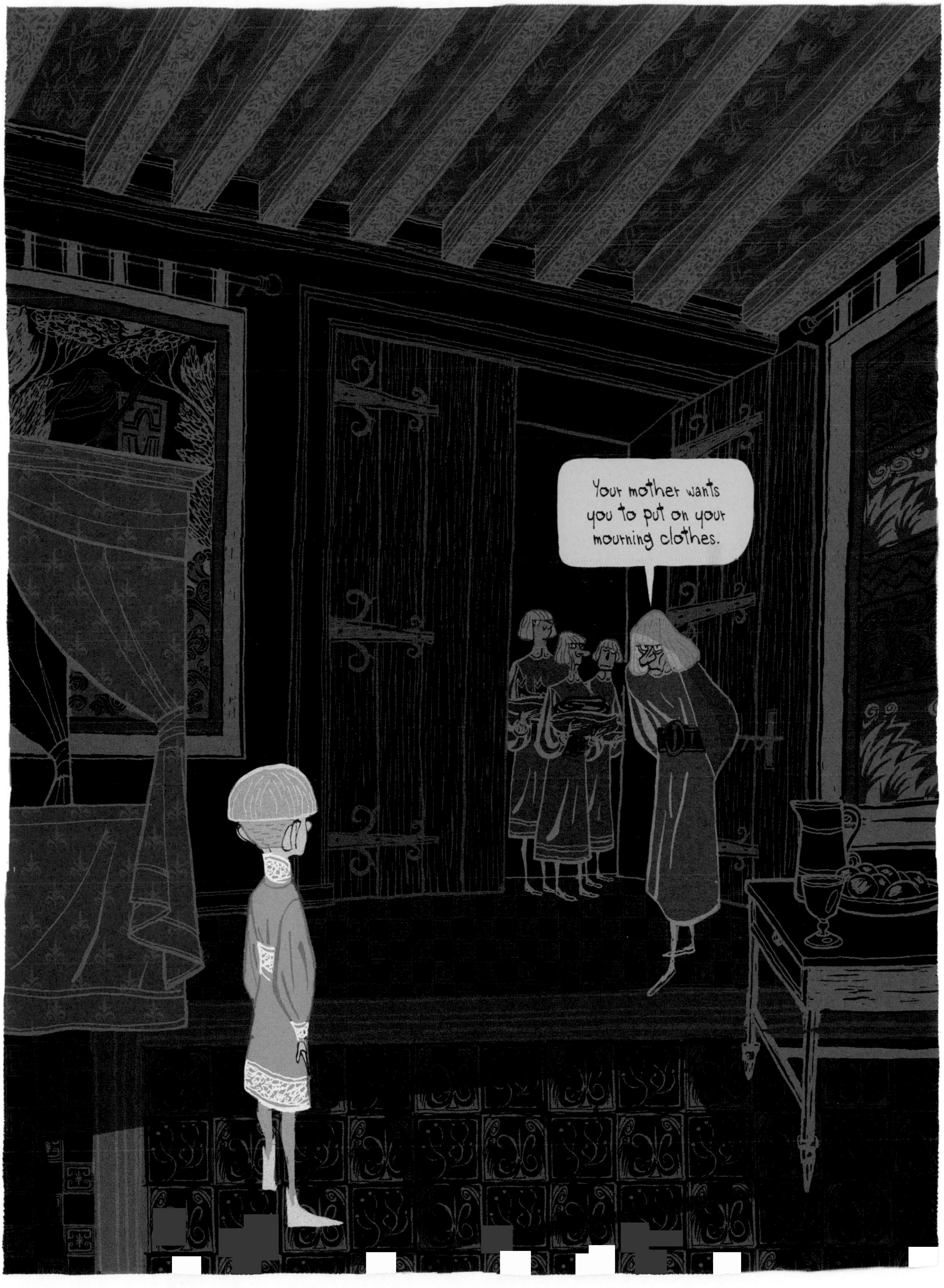
Your mother wants you to put on your mourning clothes.

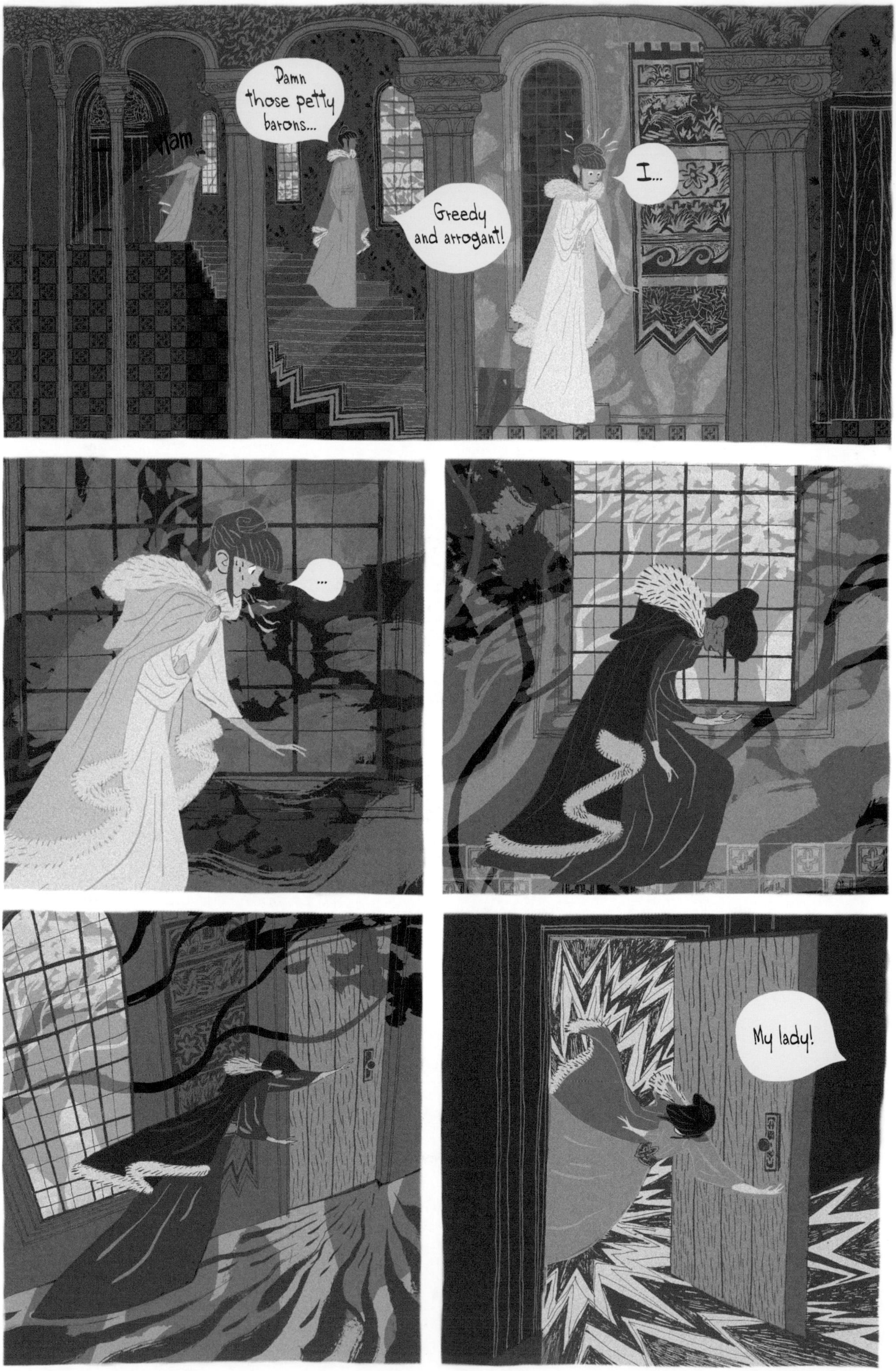
Slam
Damn those petty barons...
Greedy and arrogant!
I...
...
My lady!

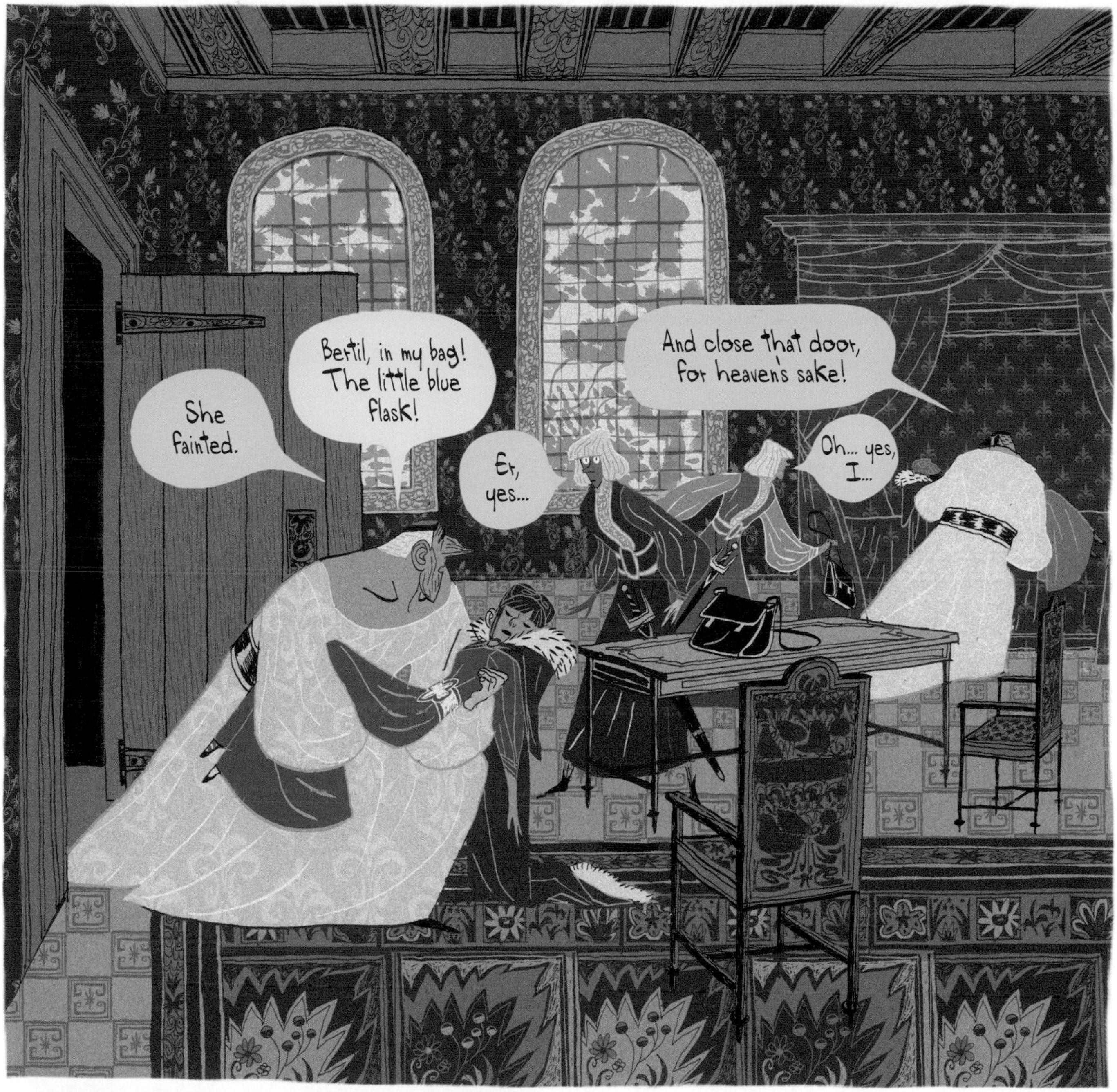
She fainted.
Bertil, in my bag! The little blue flask!
Er, yes...
And close that door, for heaven's sake!
Oh... yes, I...

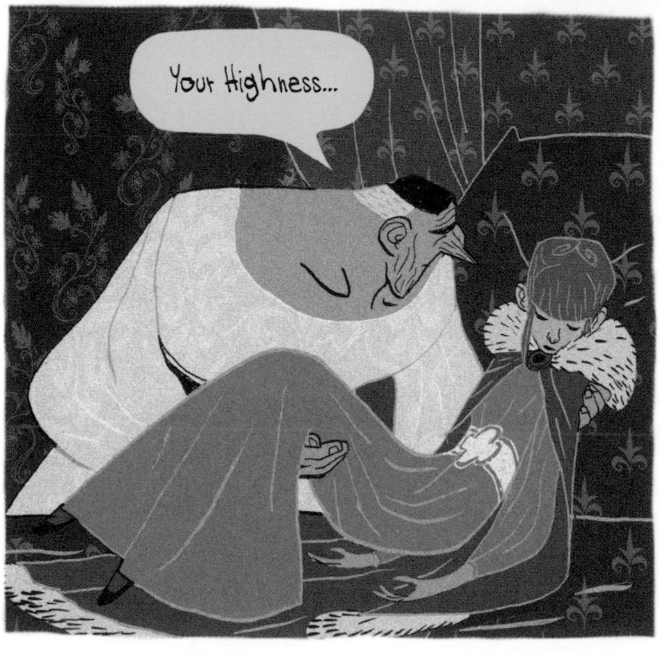
Your Highness...

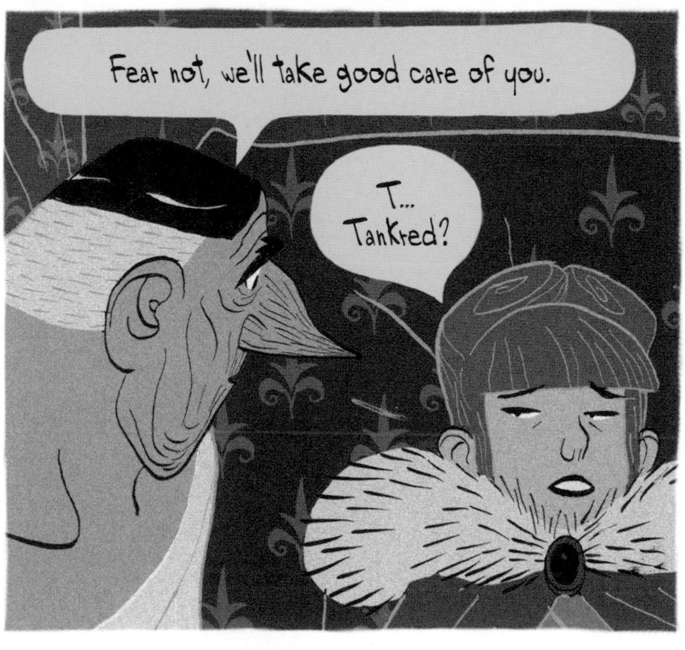
Fear not, we'll take good care of you.
T... Tankred?

Here.
A few drops of this should help.
Kof Kof Kof
How do you feel?
Better.
You are always there right when I need you.
I came as soon as I could.
The sudden death of His Majesty, your father, came as a big shock.
For me as well.
Ahem...
Perhaps a few more drops of—
Mercy, Tankred! Your remedy is worse than my condition!

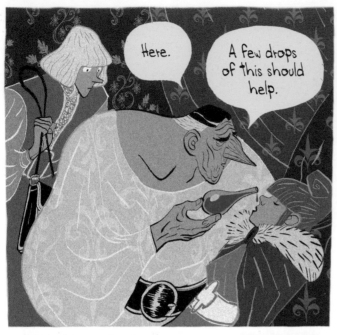

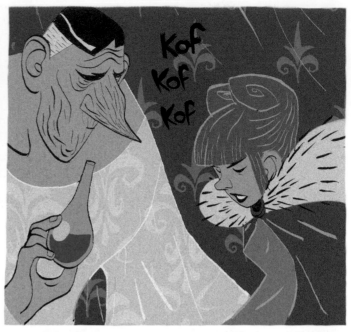

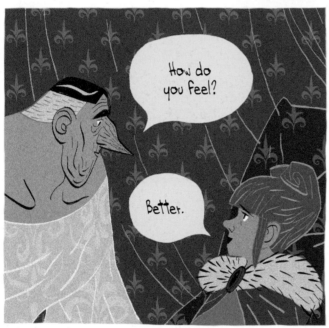

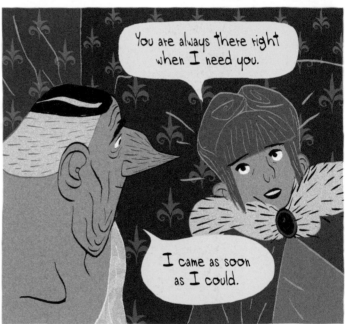

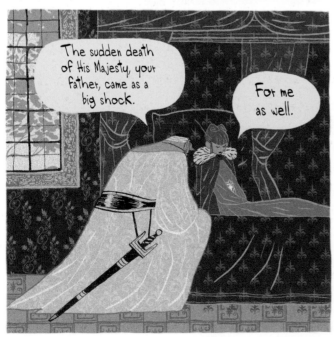

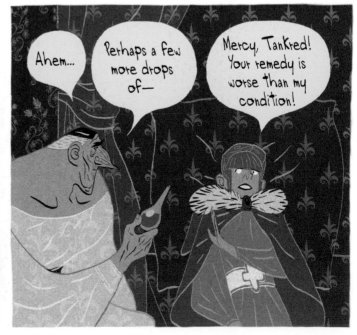

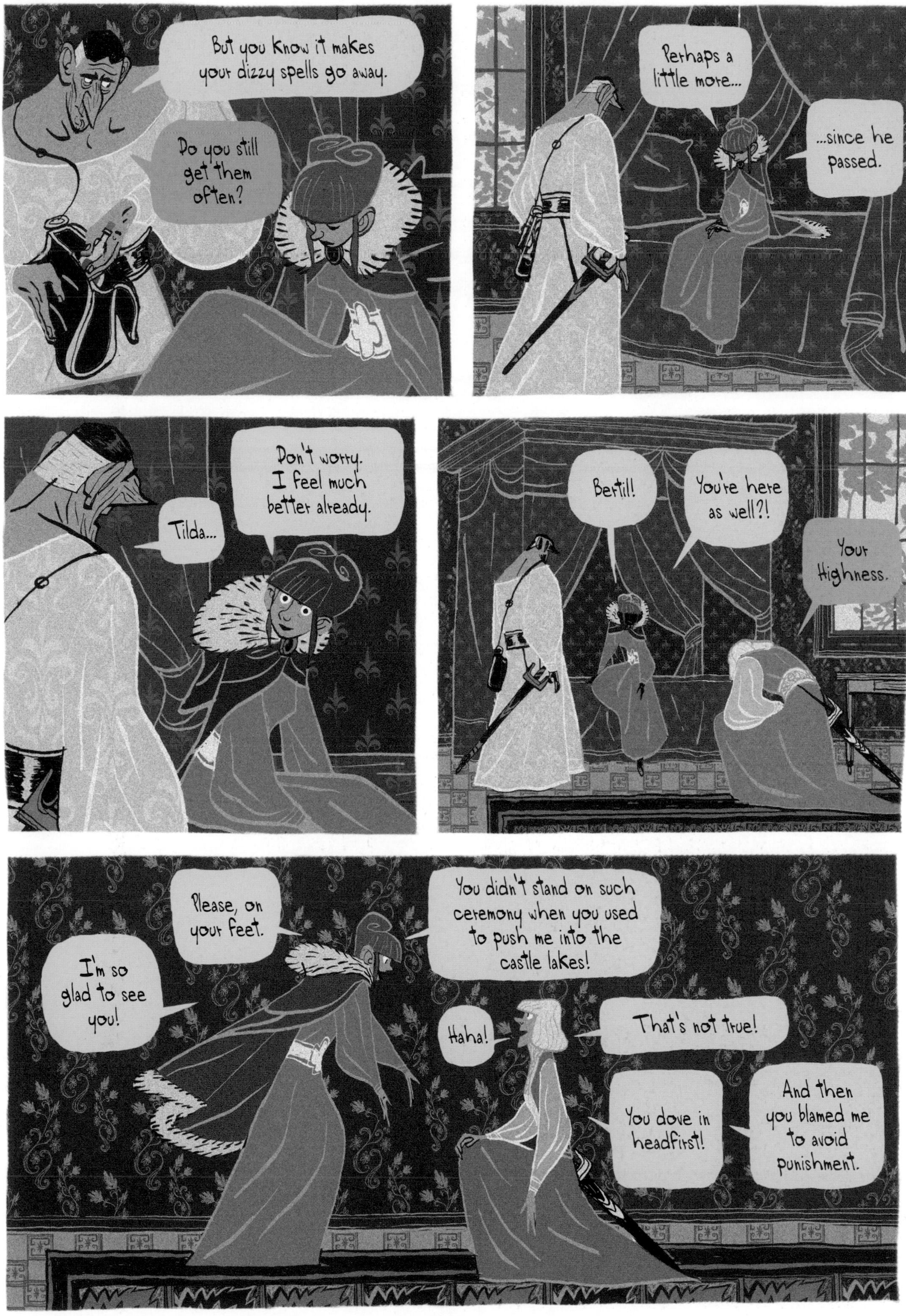

But you know it makes your dizzy spells go away.
Do you still get them often?
Perhaps a little more...
...since he passed.
Tilda...
Don't worry. I feel much better already.
Bertil!
You're here as well?!
Your Highness.
I'm so glad to see you!
Please, on your feet.
You didn't stand on such ceremony when you used to push me into the castle lakes!
Haha!
That's not true!
You dove in headfirst!
And then you blamed me to avoid punishment.

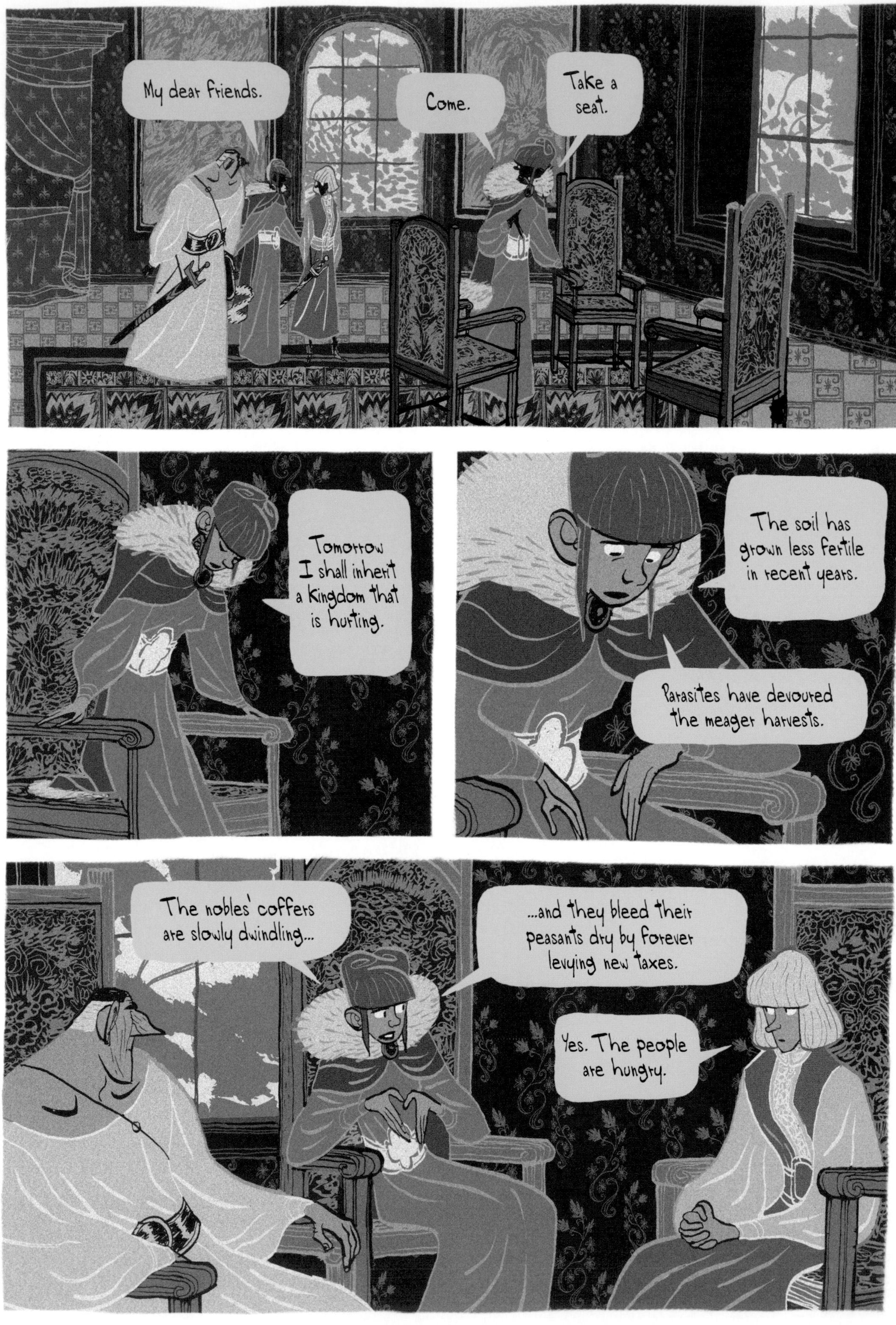
My dear friends.
Come.
Take a seat.
Tomorrow I shall inherit a Kingdom that is hurting.
The soil has grown less fertile in recent years.
Parasites have devoured the meager harvests.
The nobles' coffers are slowly dwindling...
...and they bleed their peasants dry by forever levying new taxes.
Yes. The people are hungry.

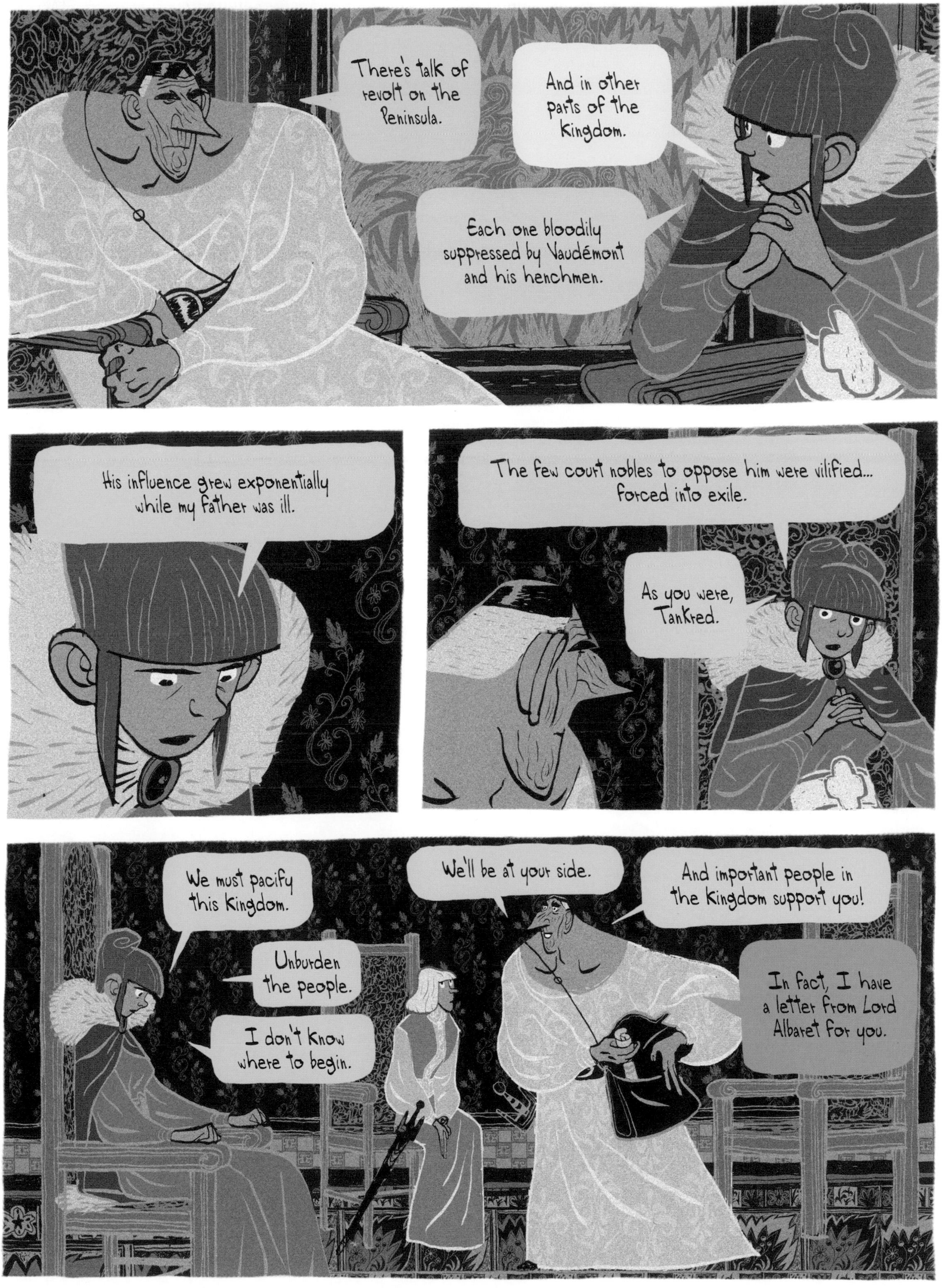
There's talk of revolt on the Peninsula.
And in other parts of the Kingdom.
Each one bloodily suppressed by Vaudémont and his henchmen.
His influence grew exponentially while my father was ill.
The few court nobles to oppose him were vilified... forced into exile.
As you were, Tankred.
We must pacify this kingdom.
Unburden the people.
I don't know where to begin.
We'll be at your side.
And important people in the kingdom support you!
In fact, I have a letter from Lord Albaret for you.

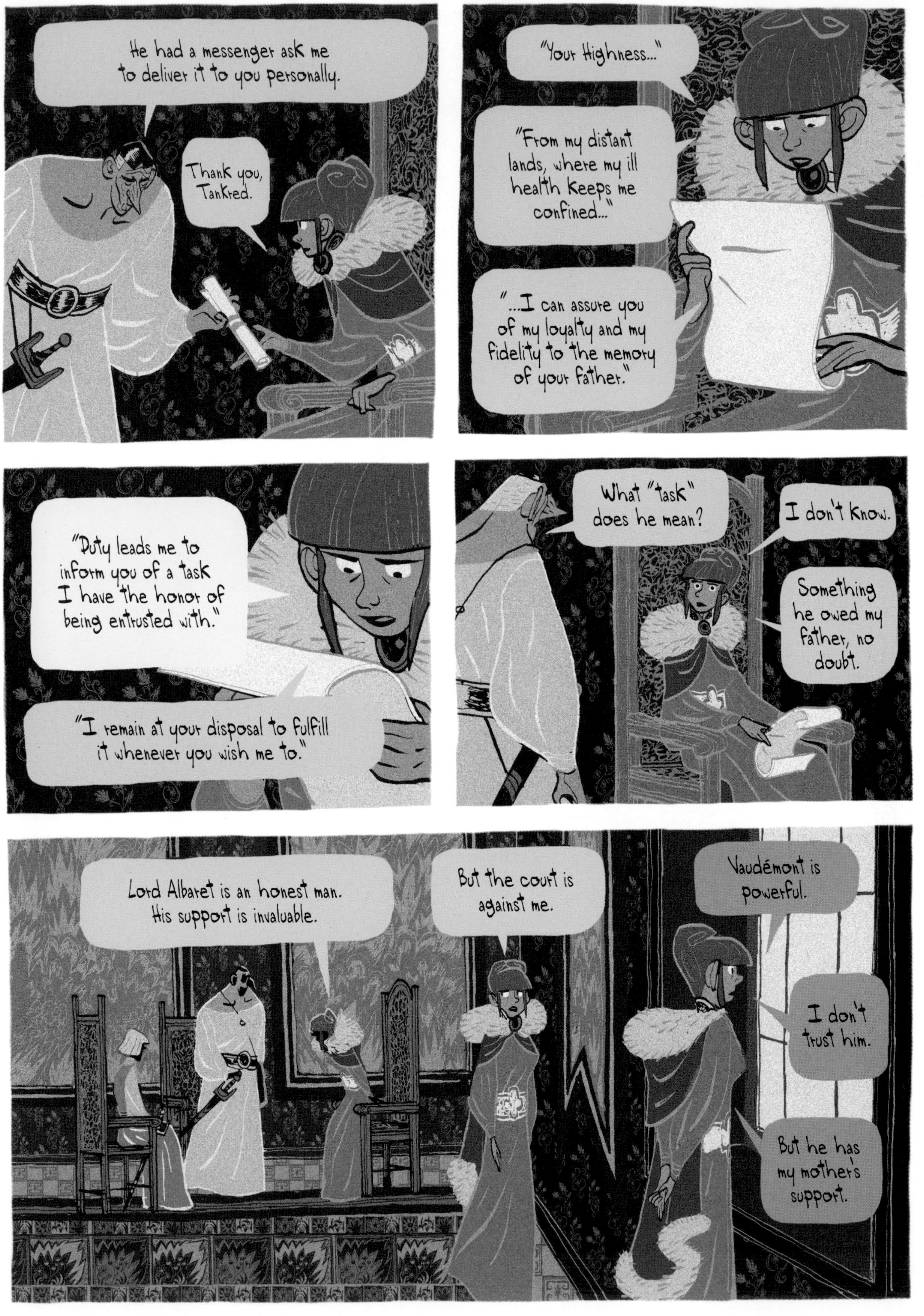
He had a messenger ask me to deliver it to you personally.
Thank you, Tankred.
"Your Highness..."
"From my distant lands, where my ill health keeps me confined..."
"...I can assure you of my loyalty and my fidelity to the memory of your father."
"Duty leads me to inform you of a task I have the honor of being entrusted with."
"I remain at your disposal to fulfill it whenever you wish me to."
What "task" does he mean?
I don't know.
Something he owed my father, no doubt.
Lord Albaret is an honest man. His support is invaluable.
But the court is against me.
Vaudémont is powerful.
I don't trust him.
But he has my mother's support.

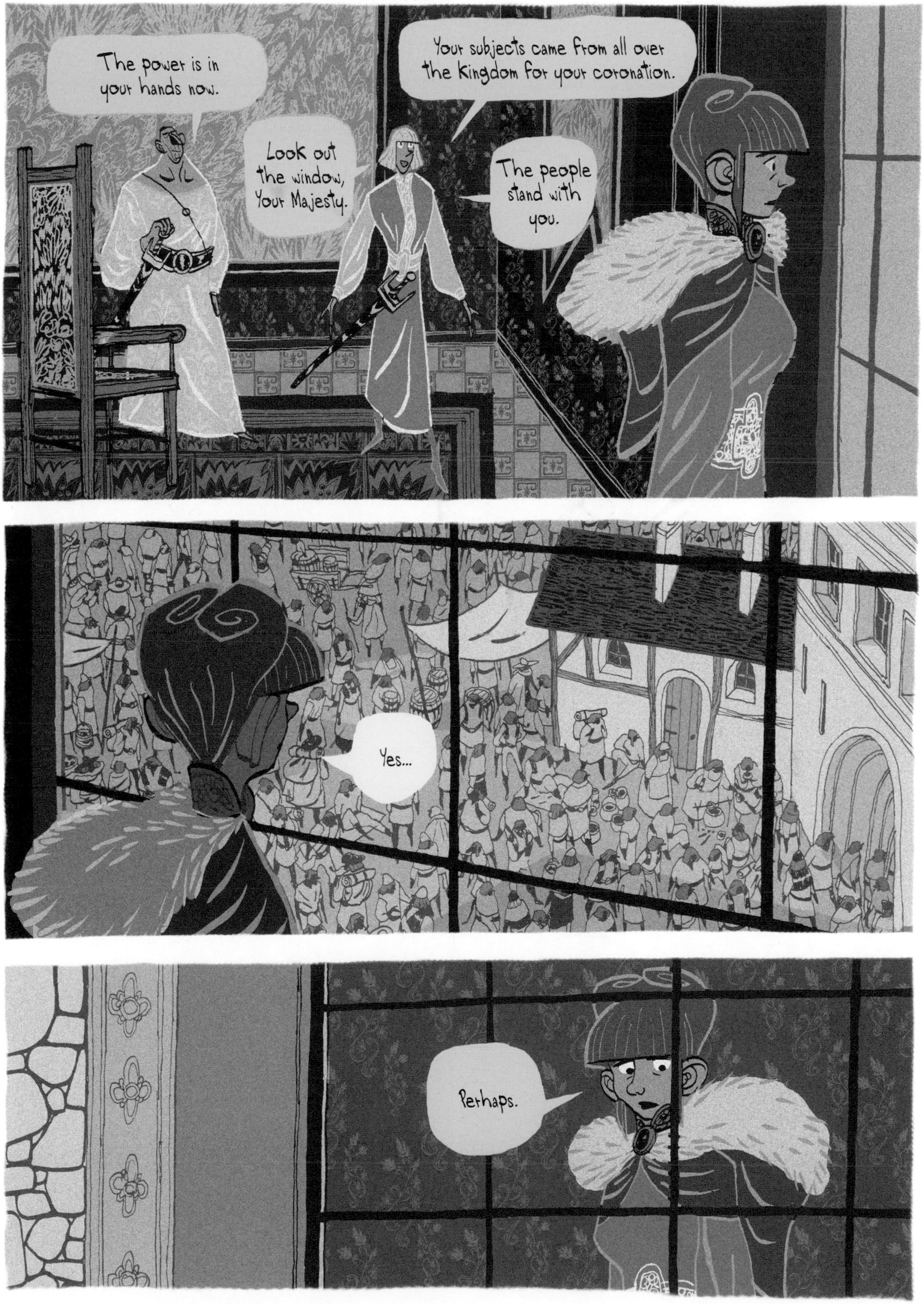
The power is in your hands now.
Look out the window, Your Majesty.
Your subjects came from all over the Kingdom for your coronation.
The people stand with you.
Yes...
Perhaps.

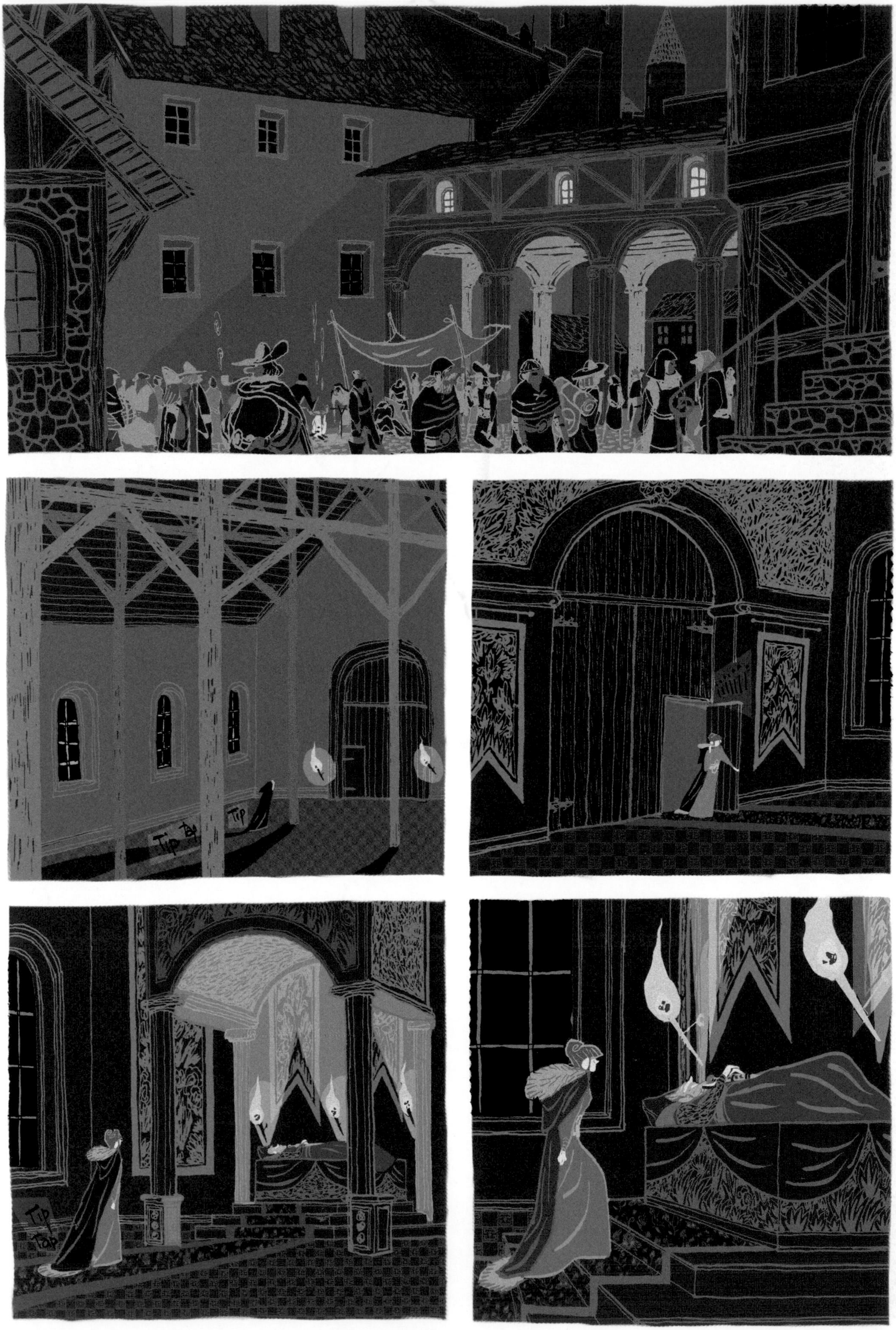
Tip Tap
Tip
Tip
Tap

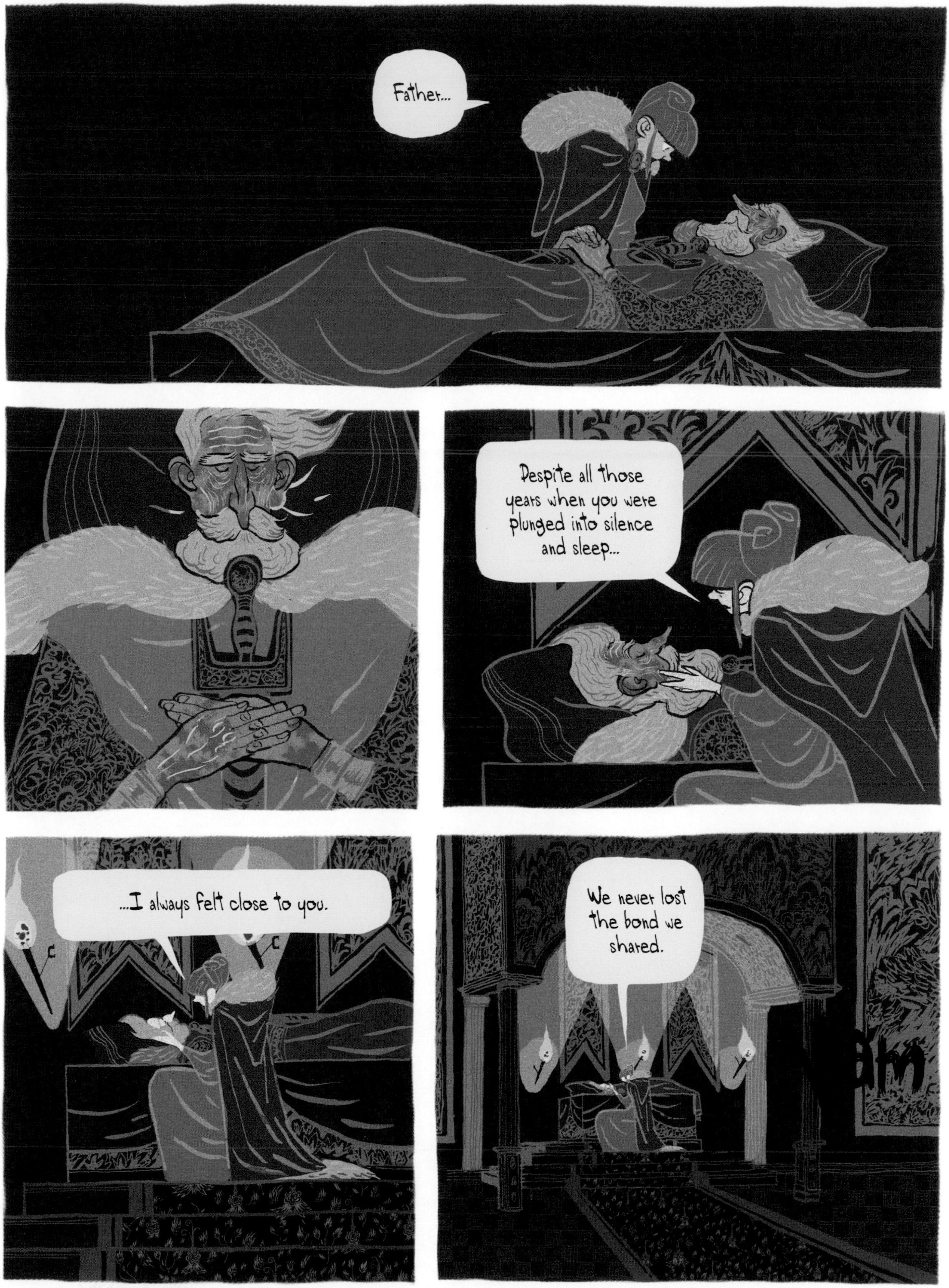
Father...
Despite all those years when you were plunged into silence and sleep...
...I always felt close to you.
We never lost the bond we shared.

Cling
Bing
Clang
Bing
Who are you?
By the Devil's horns...
Stand back!!
Calm down, Sister.

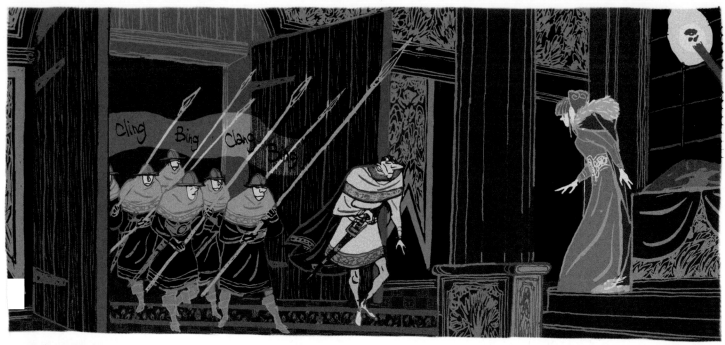

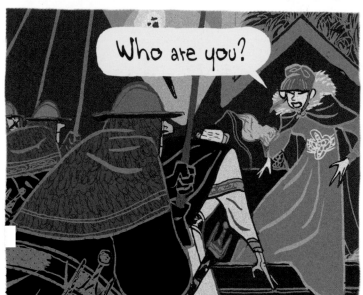

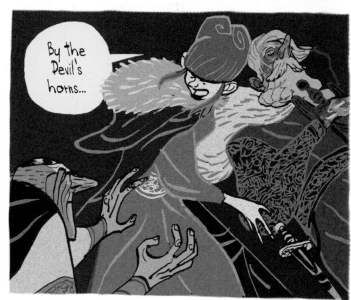

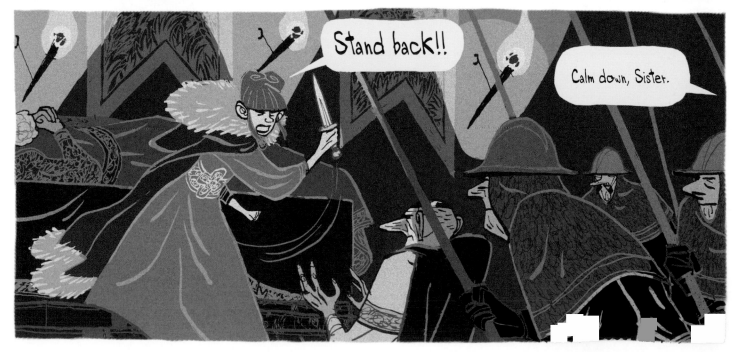

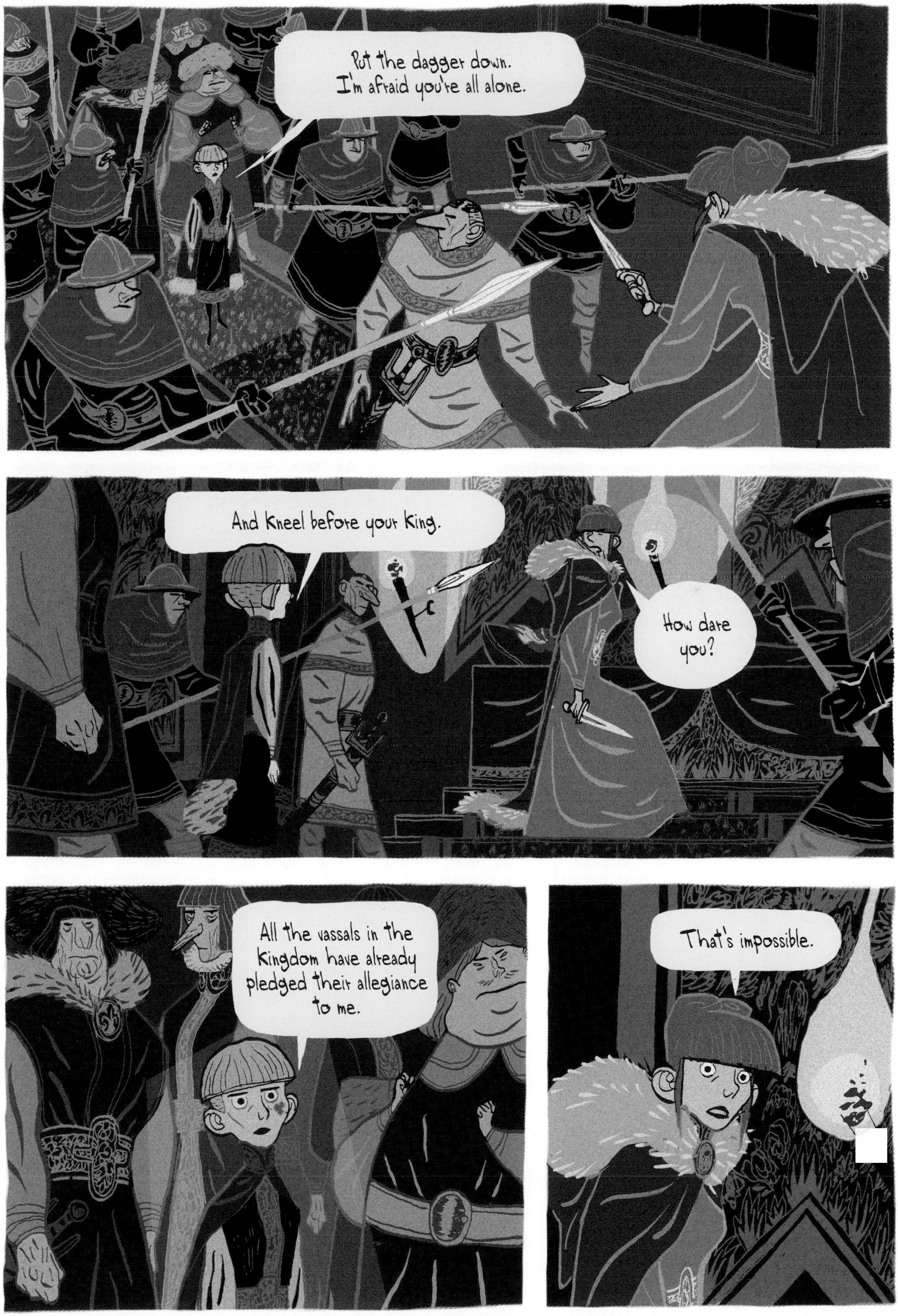
Put the dagger down.
I'm afraid you're all alone.
And kneel before your king.
How dare you?
All the vassals in the kingdom have already pledged their allegiance to me.
That's impossible.

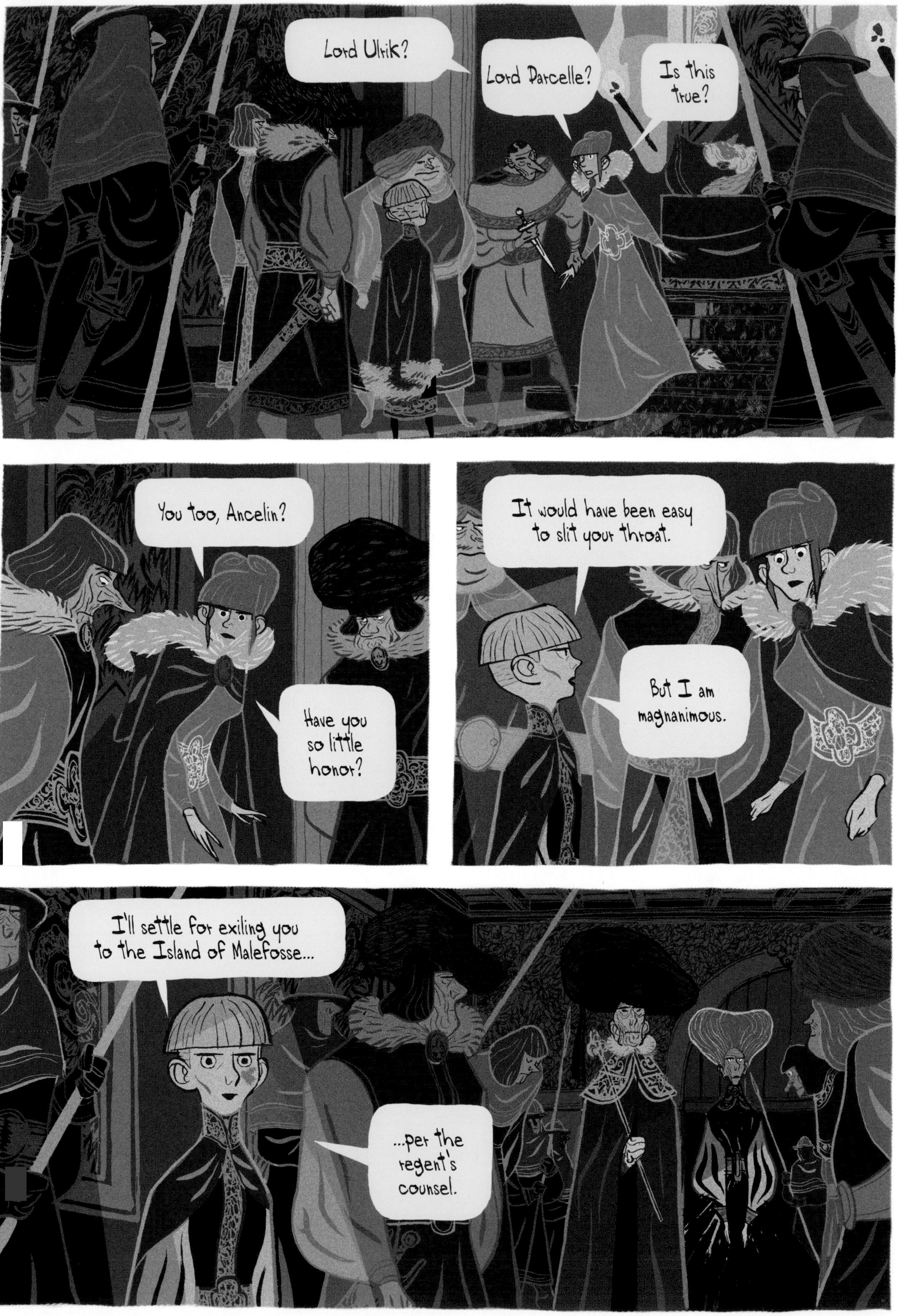
Lord Ulrik?
Lord Darcelle?
Is this true?
You too, Ancelin?
Have you so little honor?
It would have been easy to slit your throat.
But I am magnanimous.
I'll settle for exiling you to the Island of Malefosse...
...per the regent's counsel.

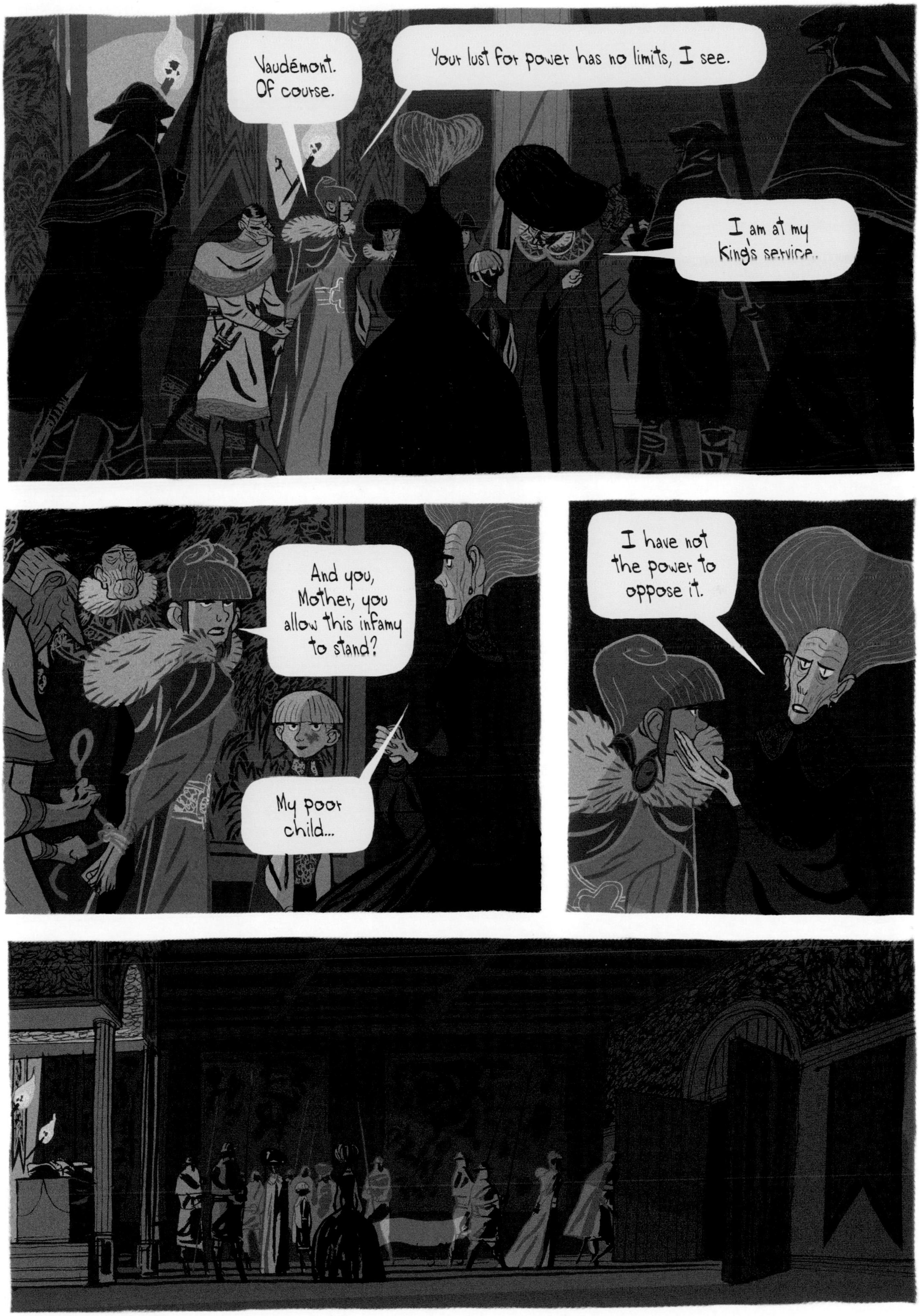
Vaudémont. Of course.
Your lust for power has no limits, I see.
I am at my King's service.
And you, Mother, you allow this infamy to stand?
My poor child...
I have not the power to oppose it.

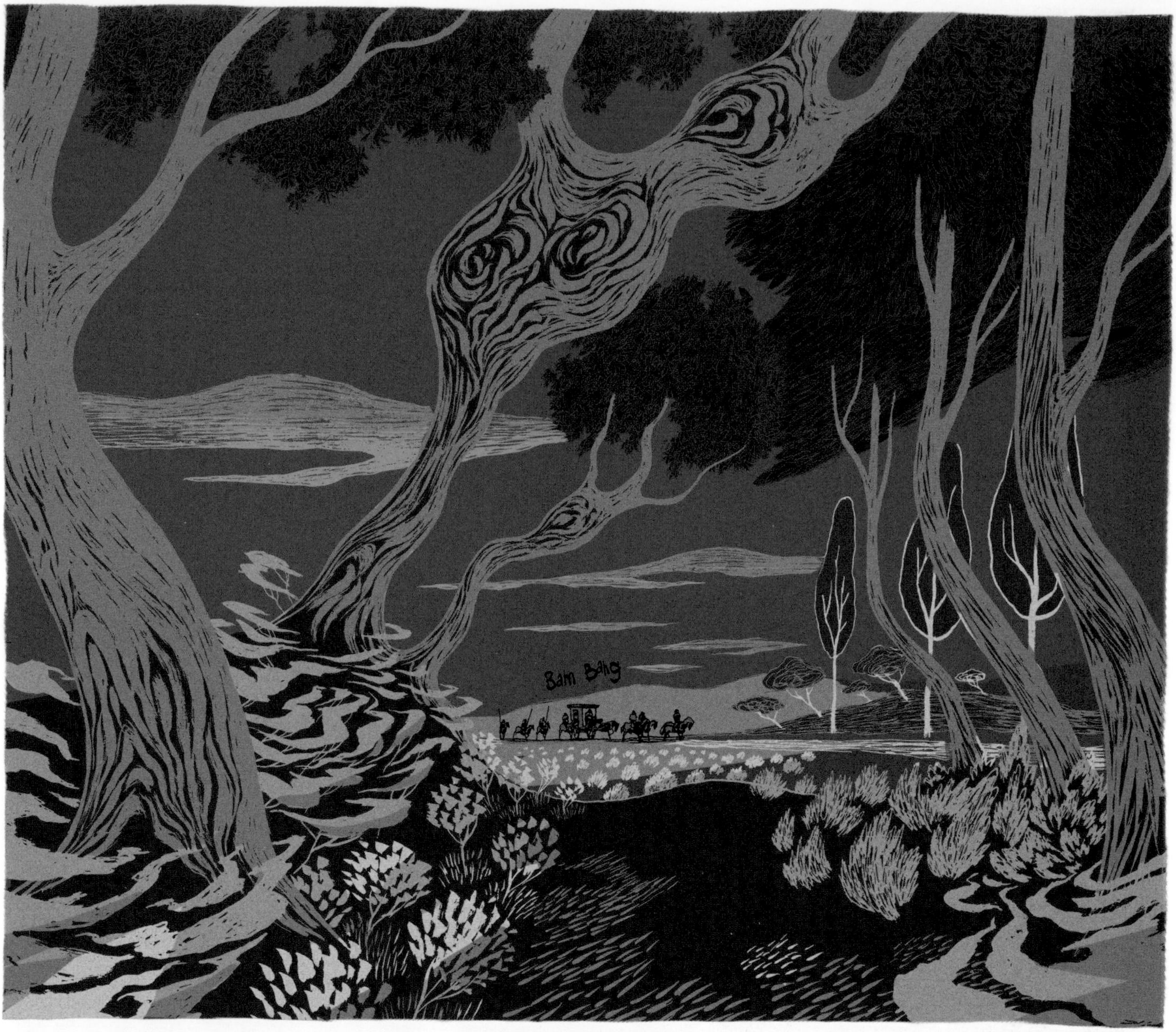
Bam Bang

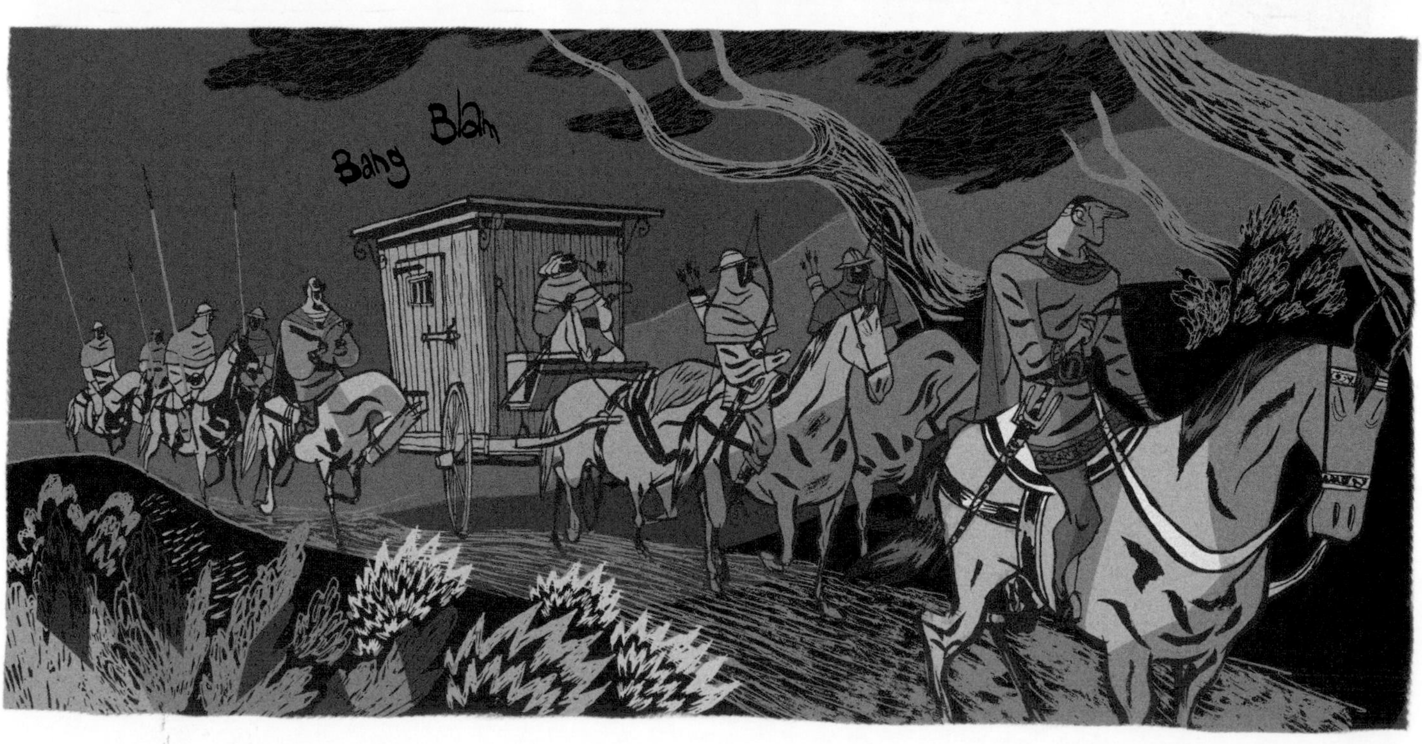
Bang
Blam

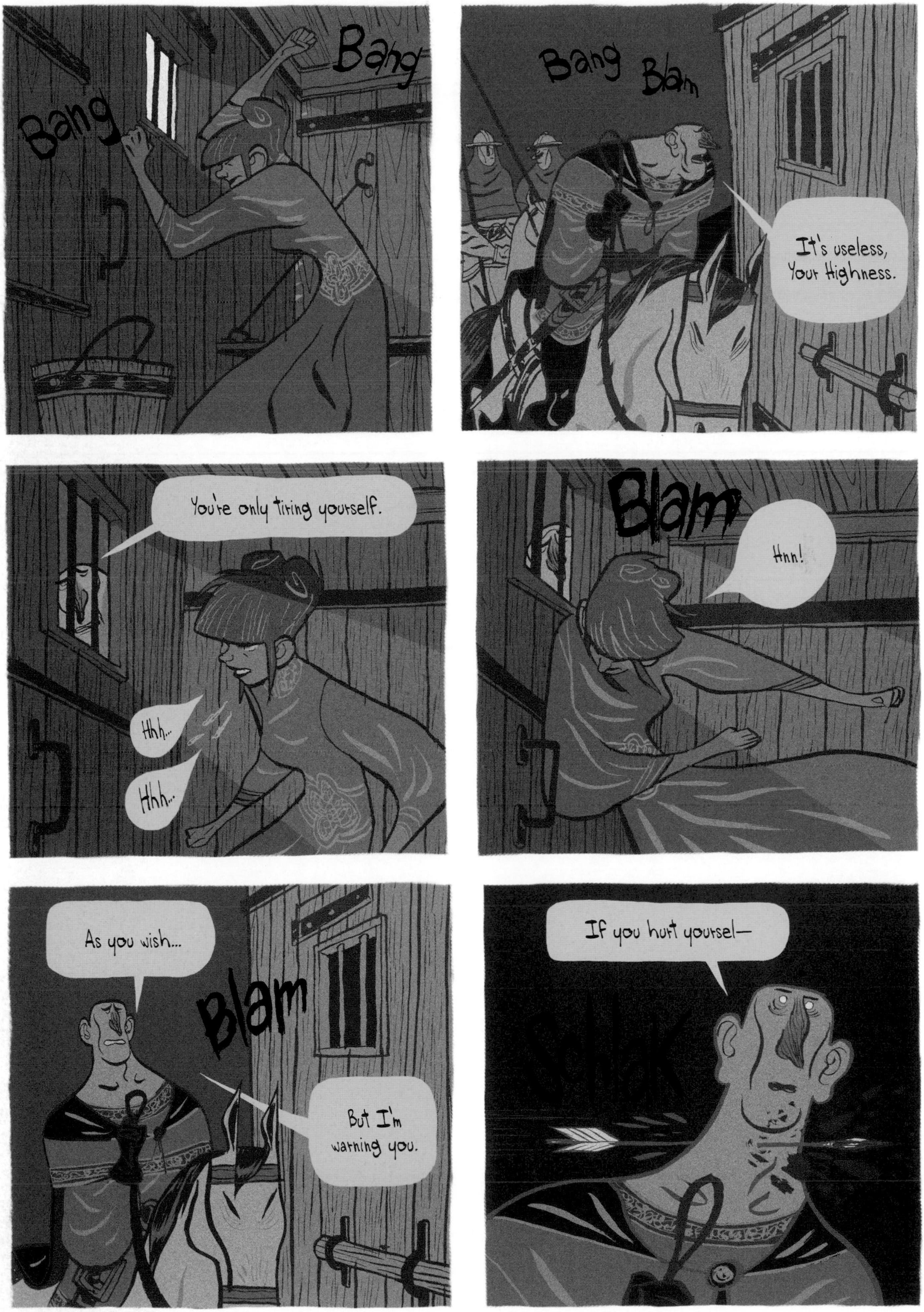
Bang
Bang
Bang Blam
It's useless, Your Highness.
You're only tiring yourself.
Hhh...
Hhh...
Blam
Hnn!
As you wish...
Blam
But I'm warning you.
If you hurt yoursel—

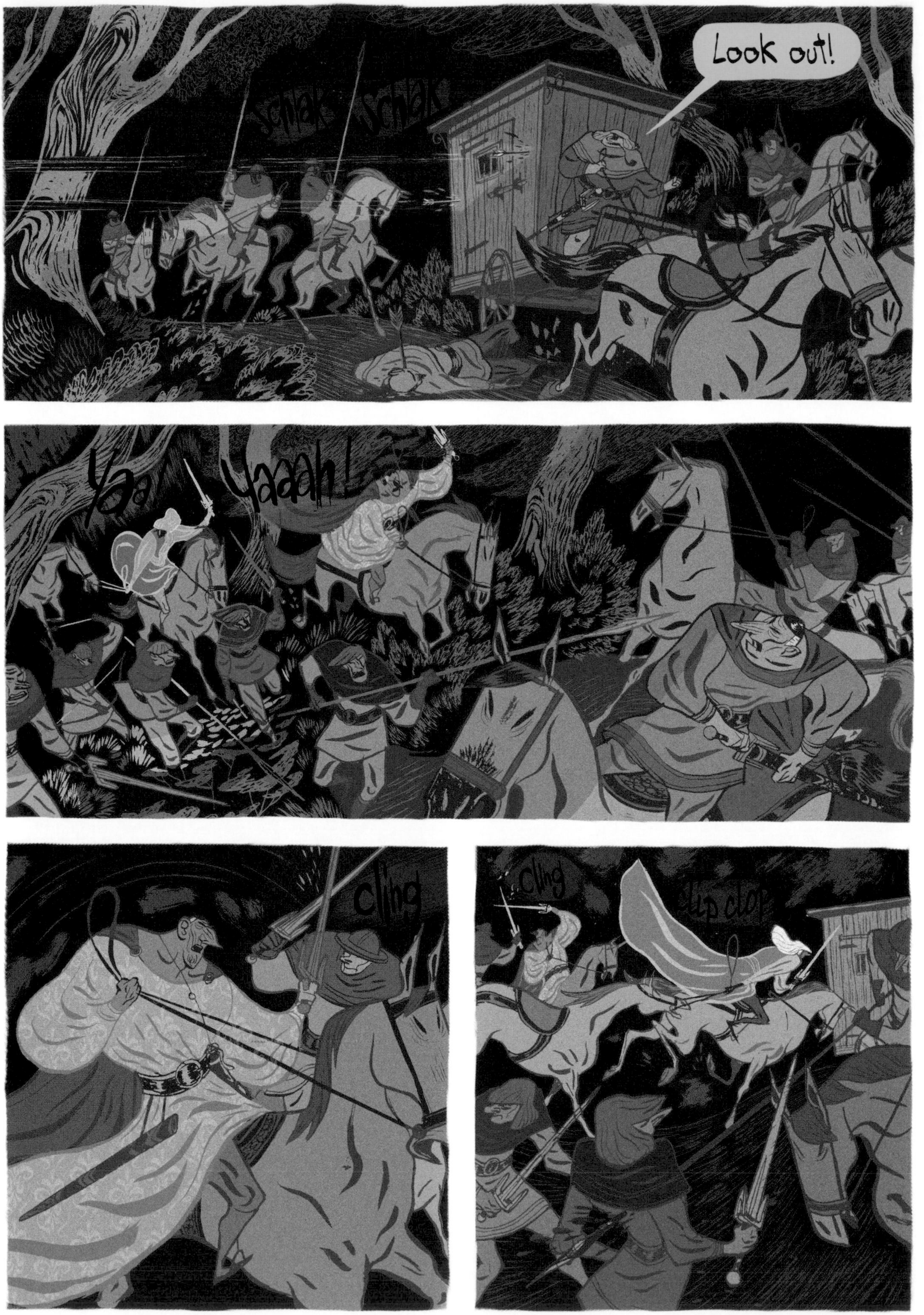
schlak schlak
Look out!
Ya Yaaah!
cling
cling
clip clop

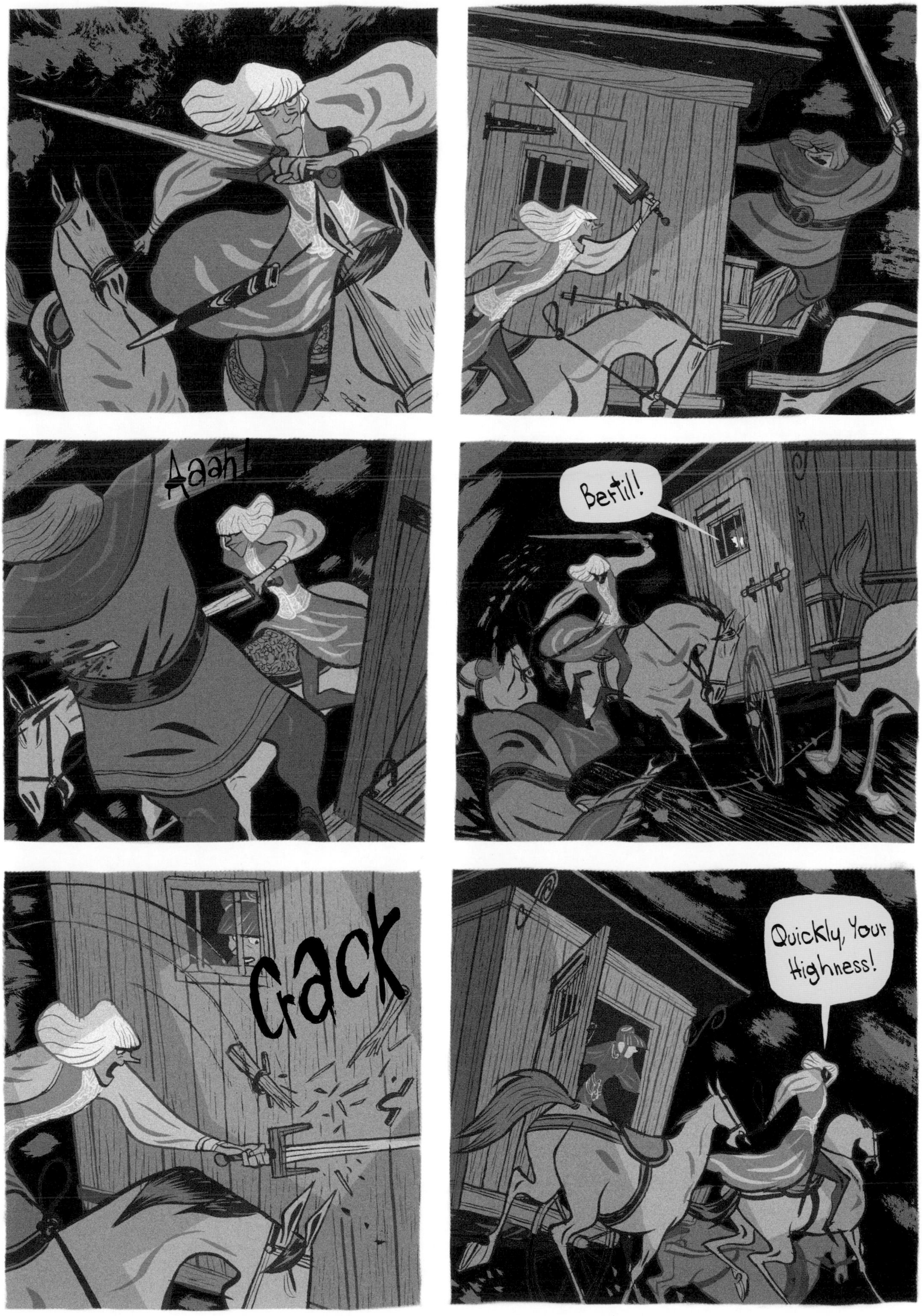
Aaah!
Bertil!
Crack
Quickly, Your Highness!

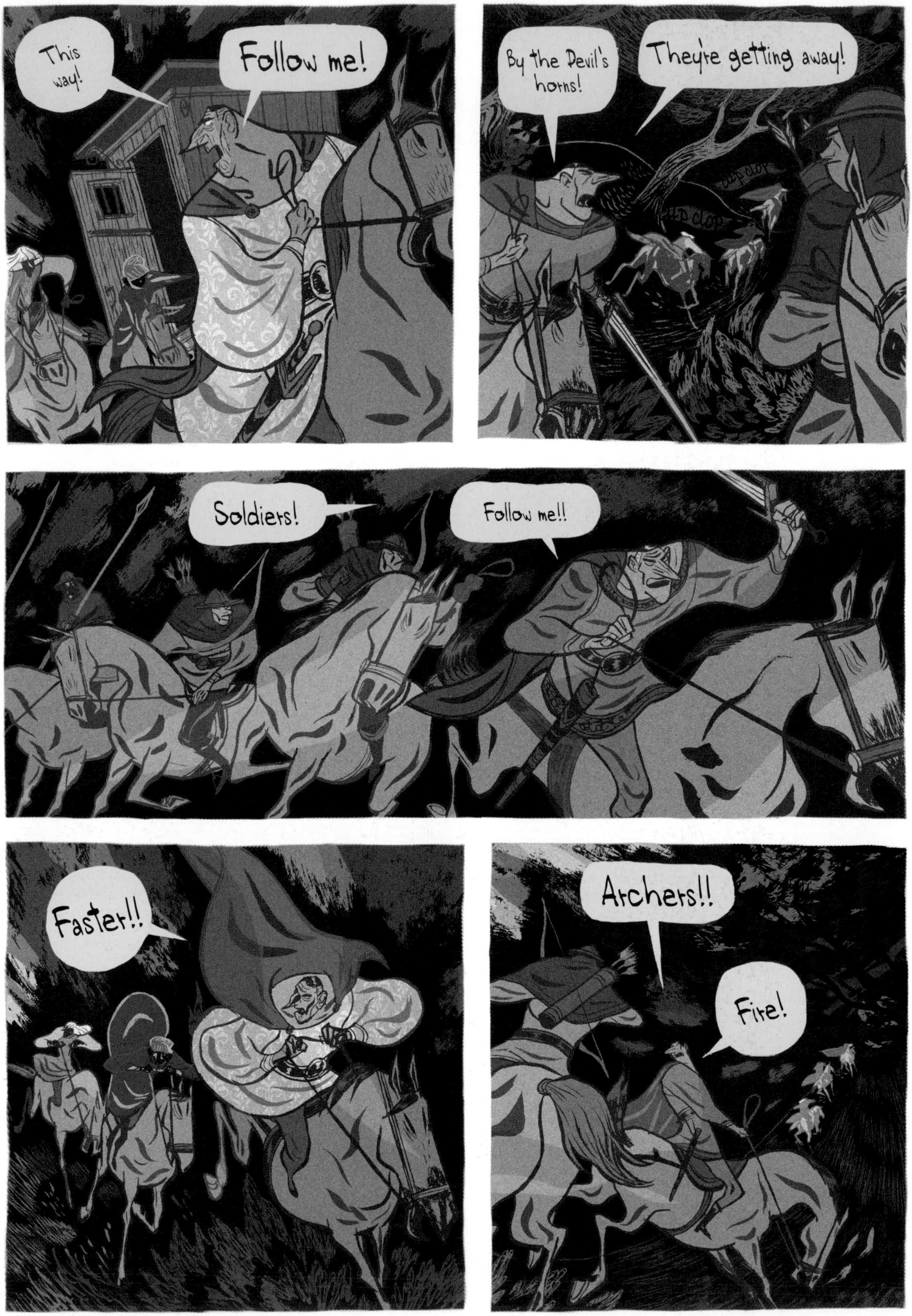
This way!
Follow me!
By the Devil's horns!
They're getting away!
Soldiers!
Follow me!!
Faster!!
Archers!!
Fire!

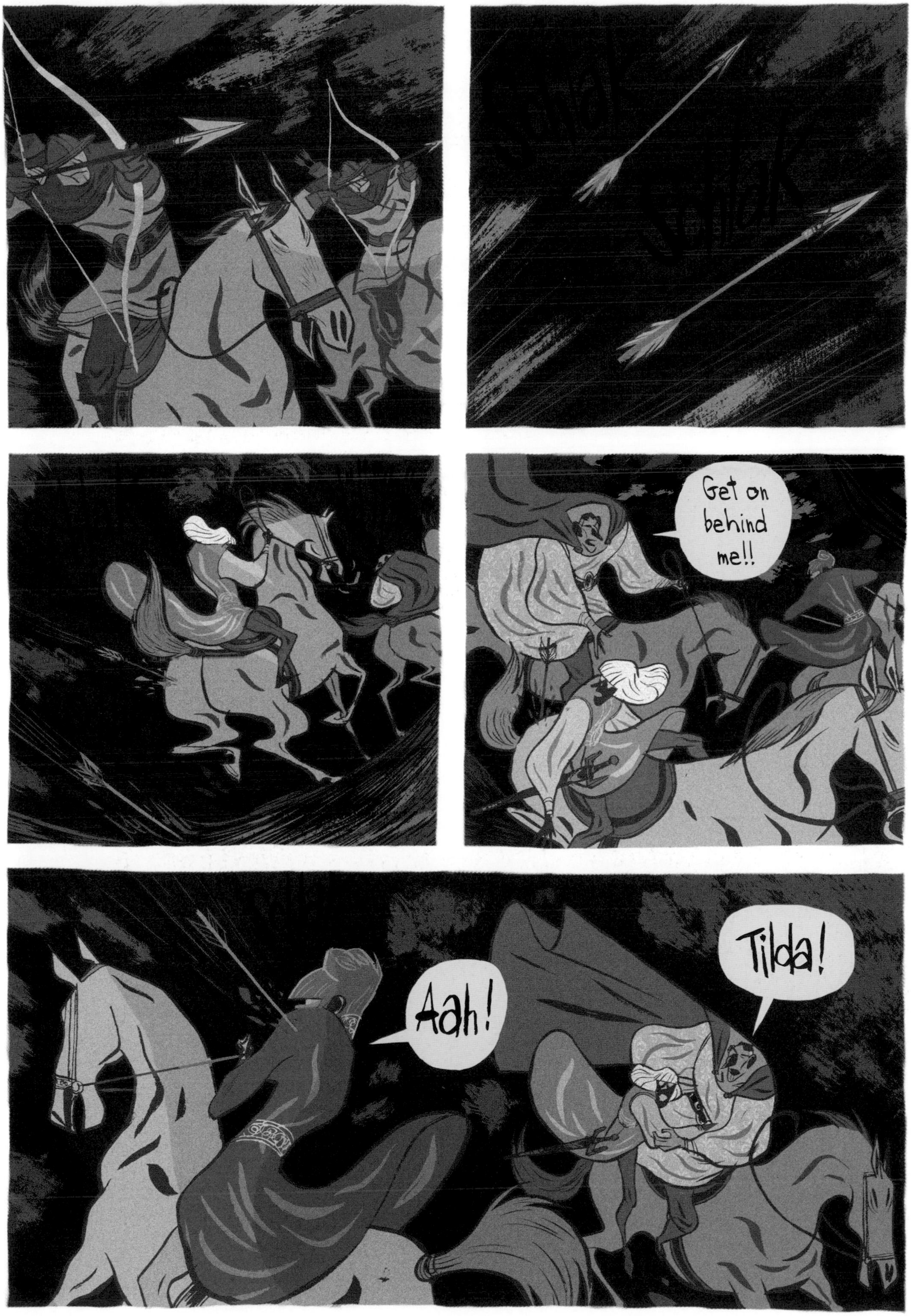
Get on behind me!!
Aah!
Tilda!

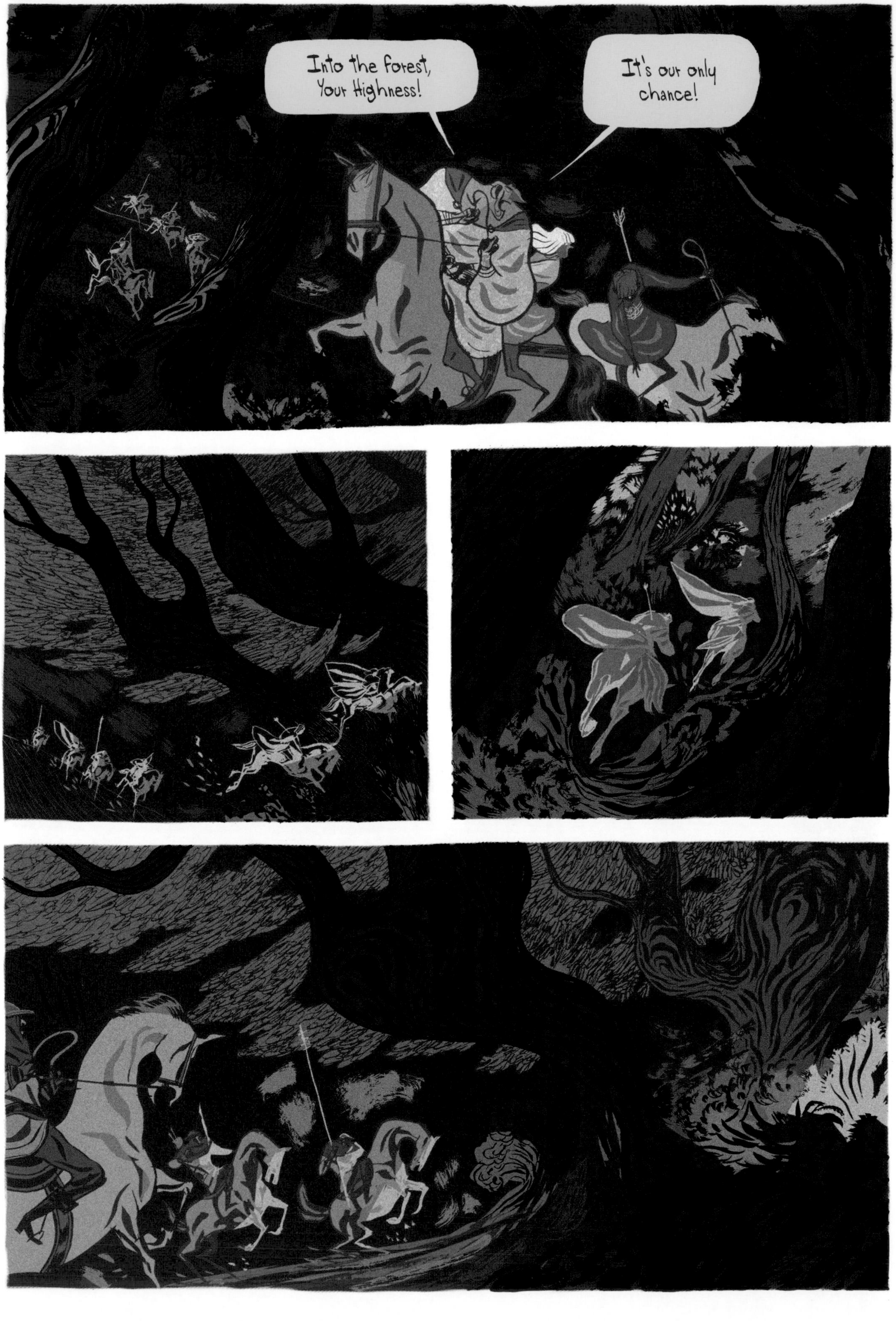
Into the forest, Your Highness!
It's our only chance!

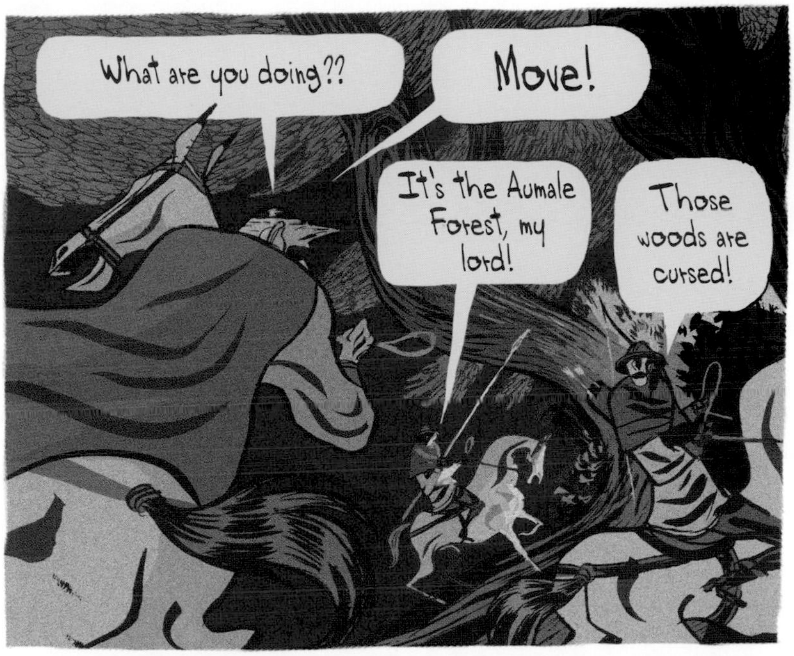
What are you doing??
Move!
It's the Aumale Forest, my lord!
Those woods are cursed!

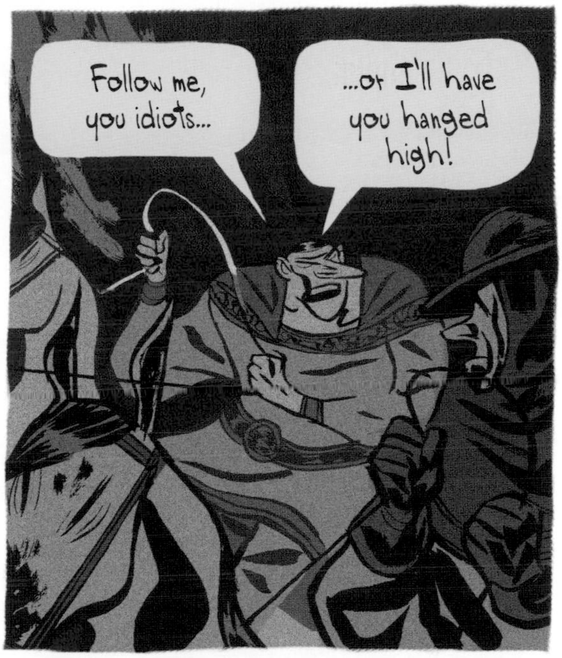
Follow me, you idiots...
...or I'll have you hanged high!

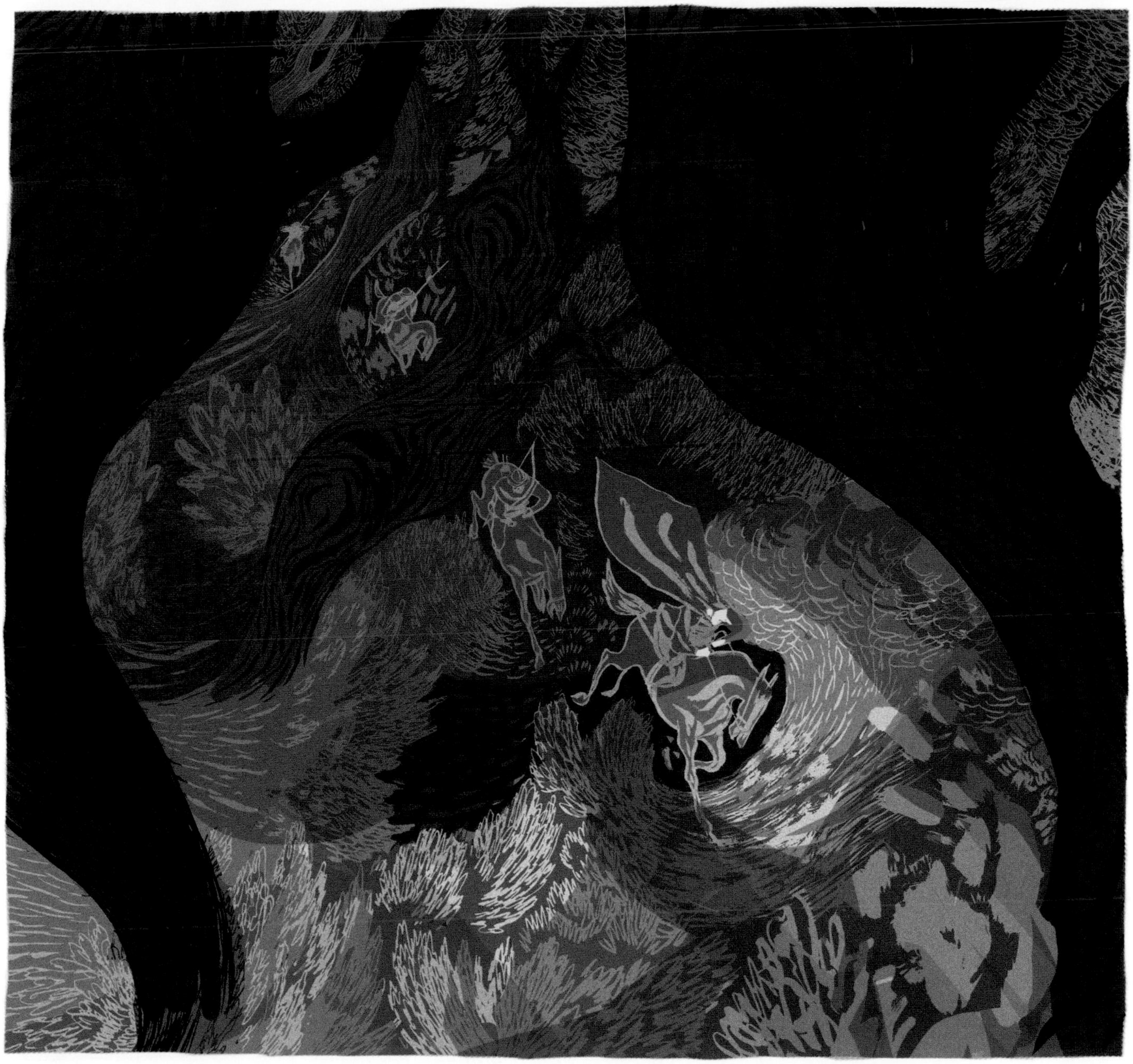

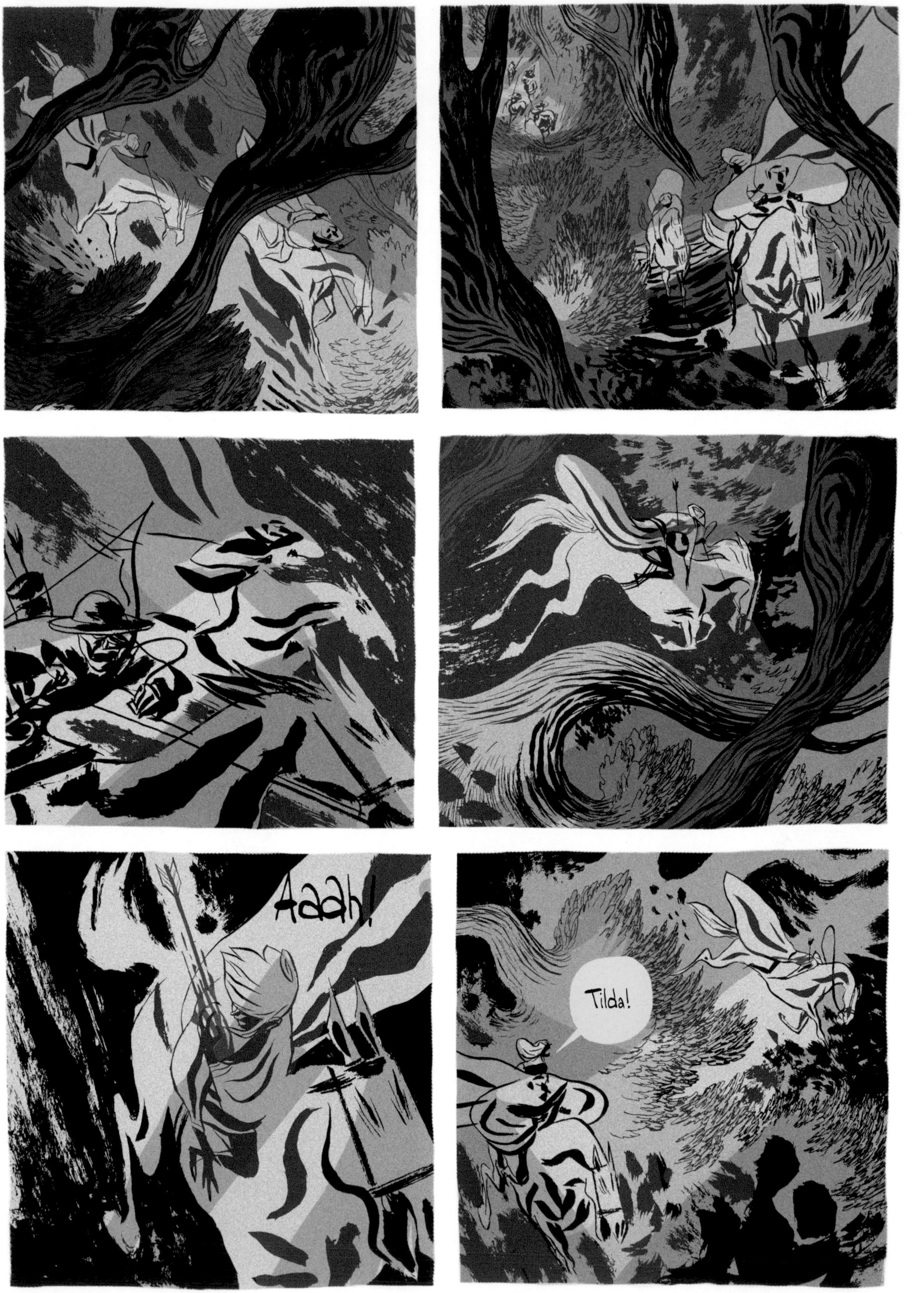
Aaah!
Tilda!

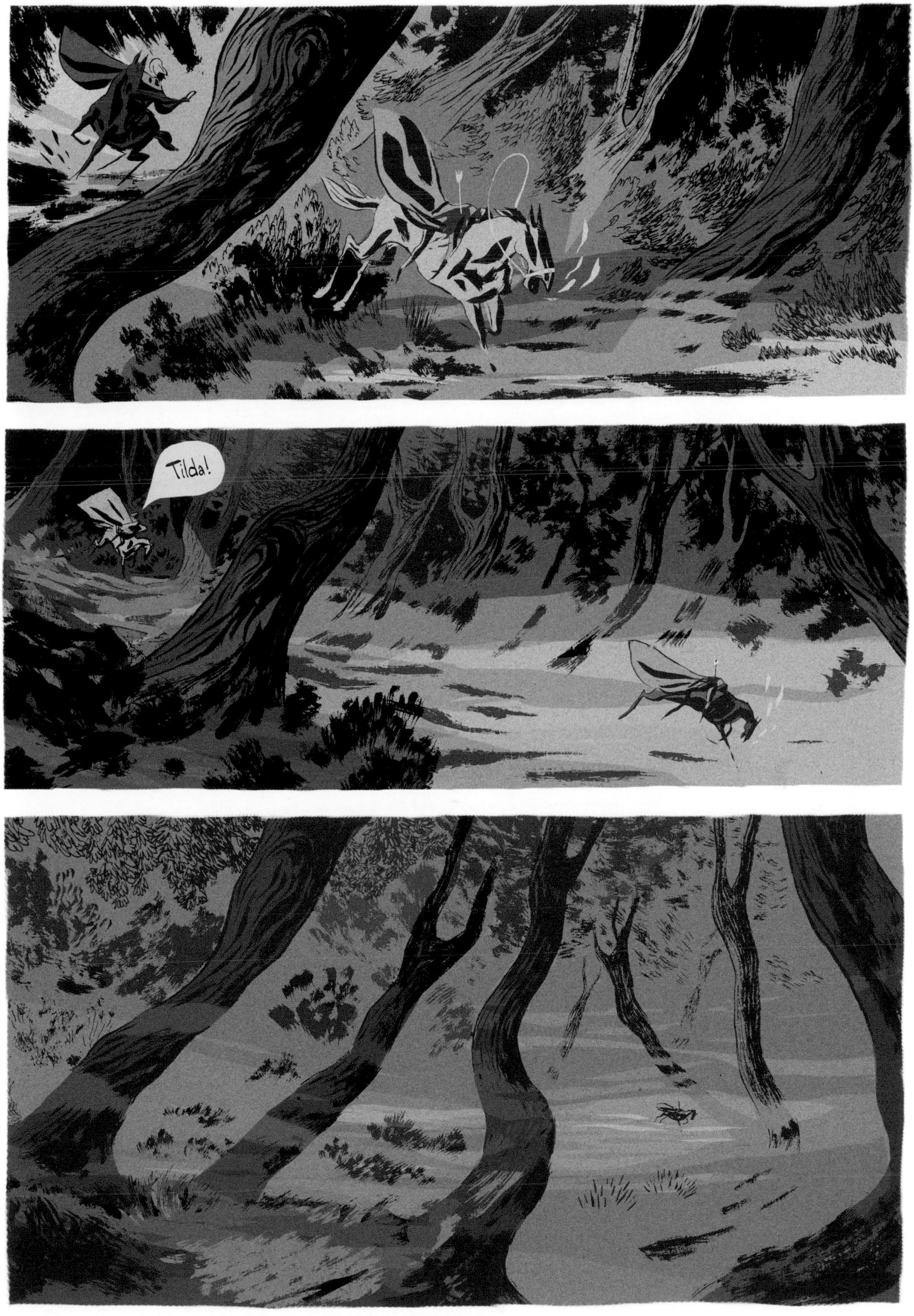
Tilda!

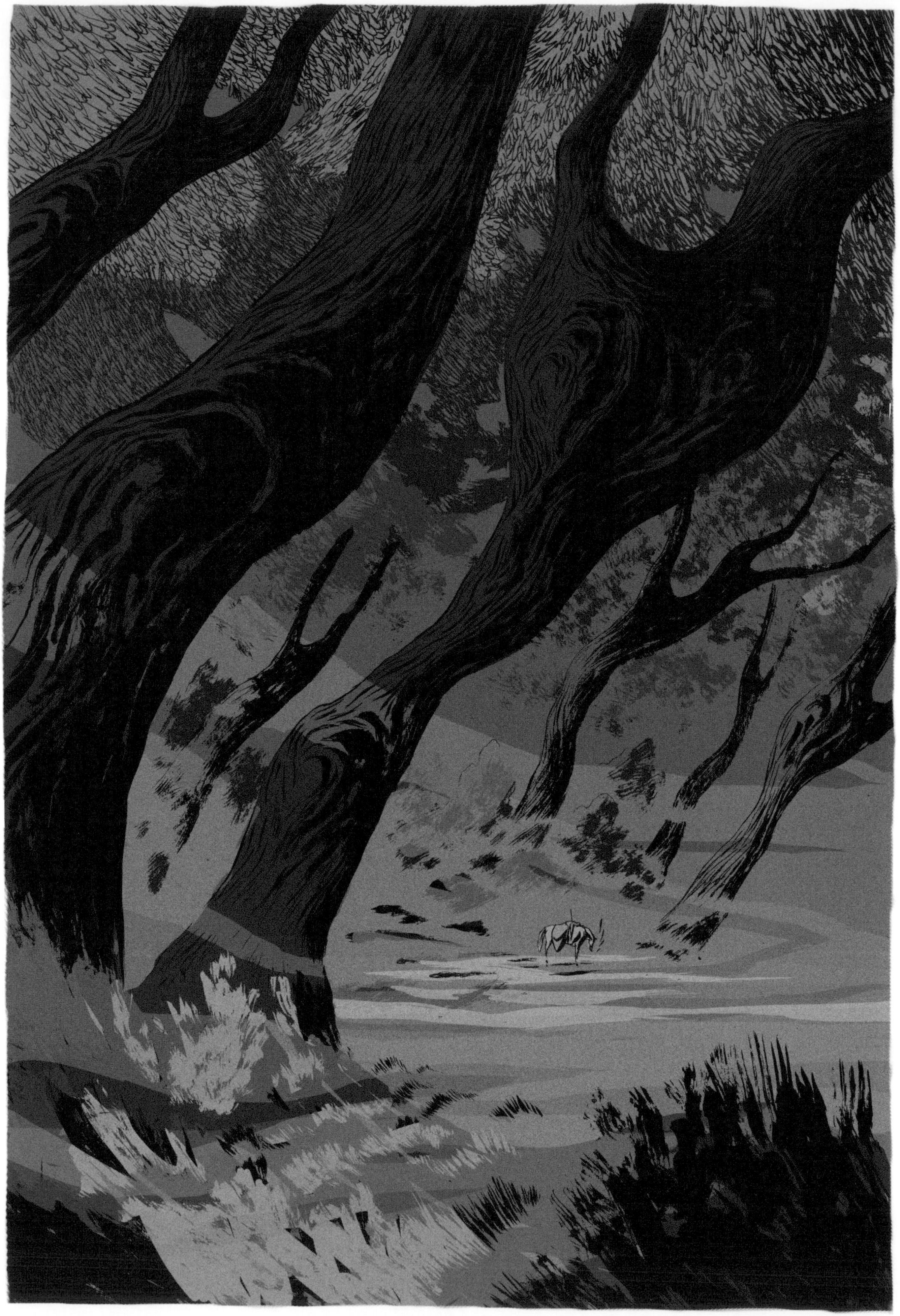

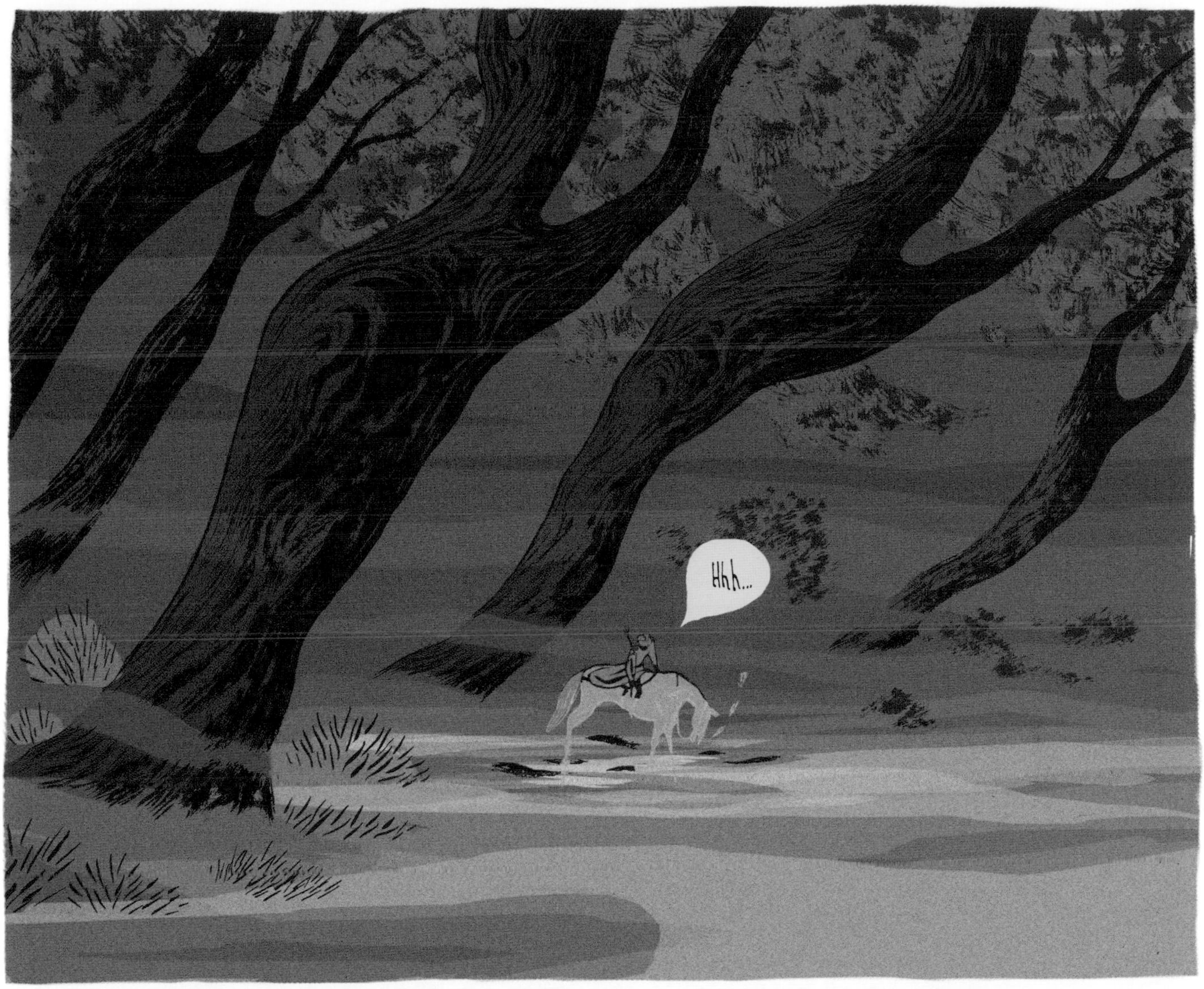
Hhh...

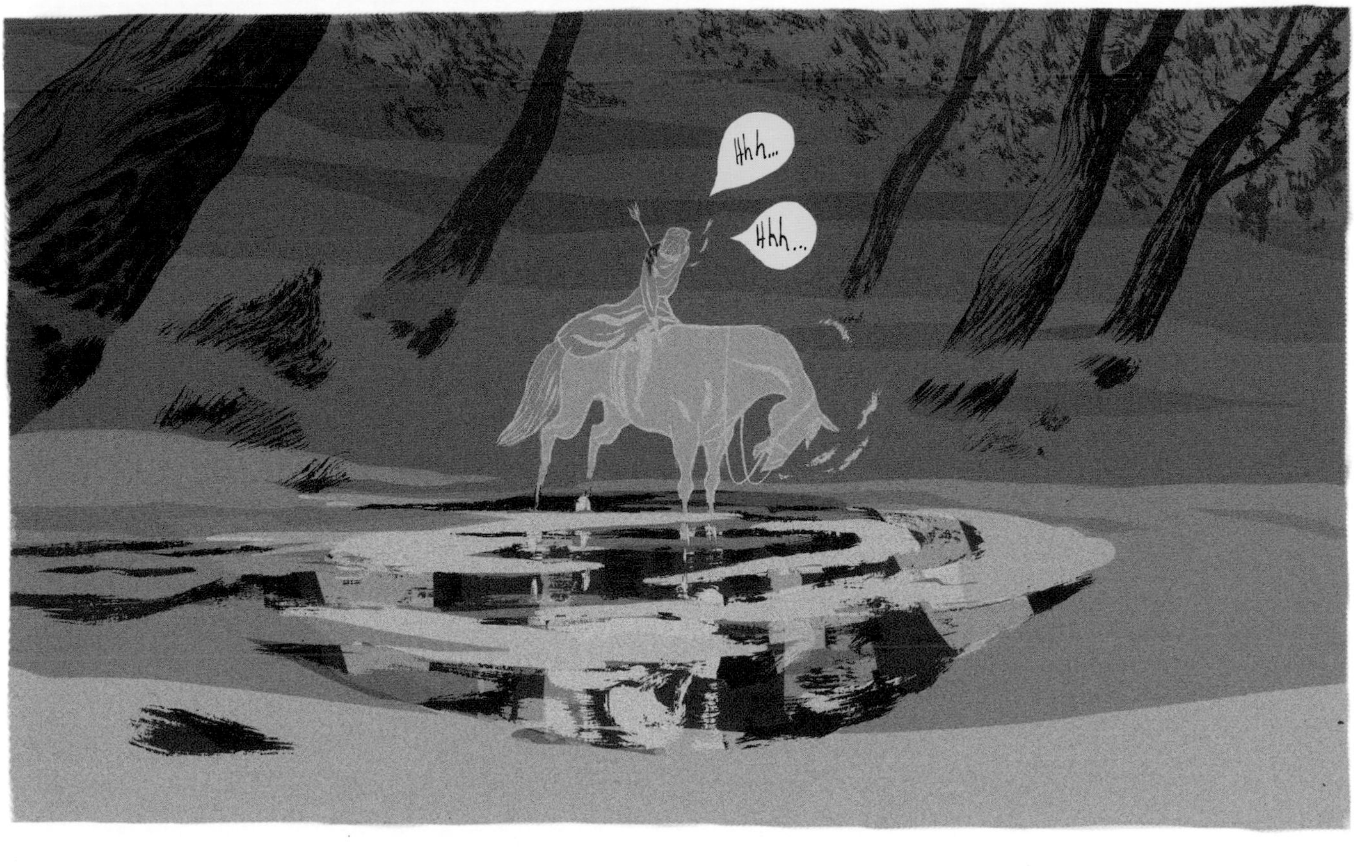
Hhh...
Hhh...

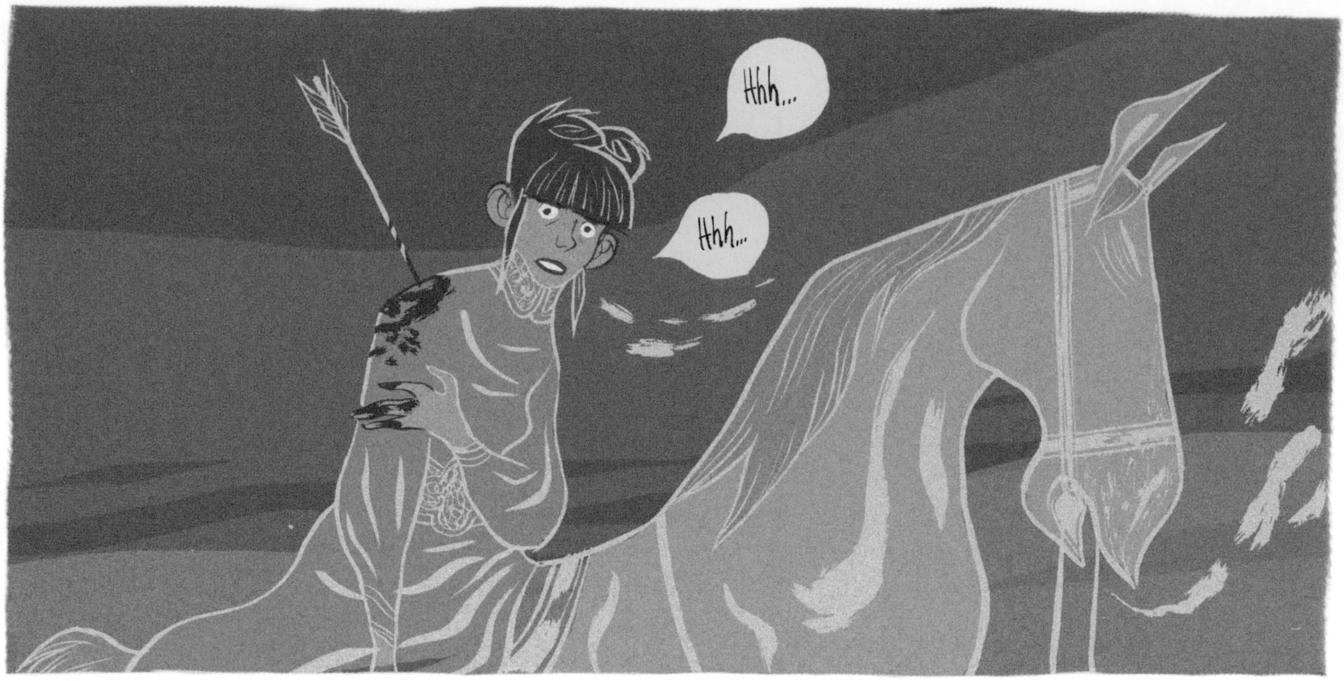
Hhh...
Hhh...

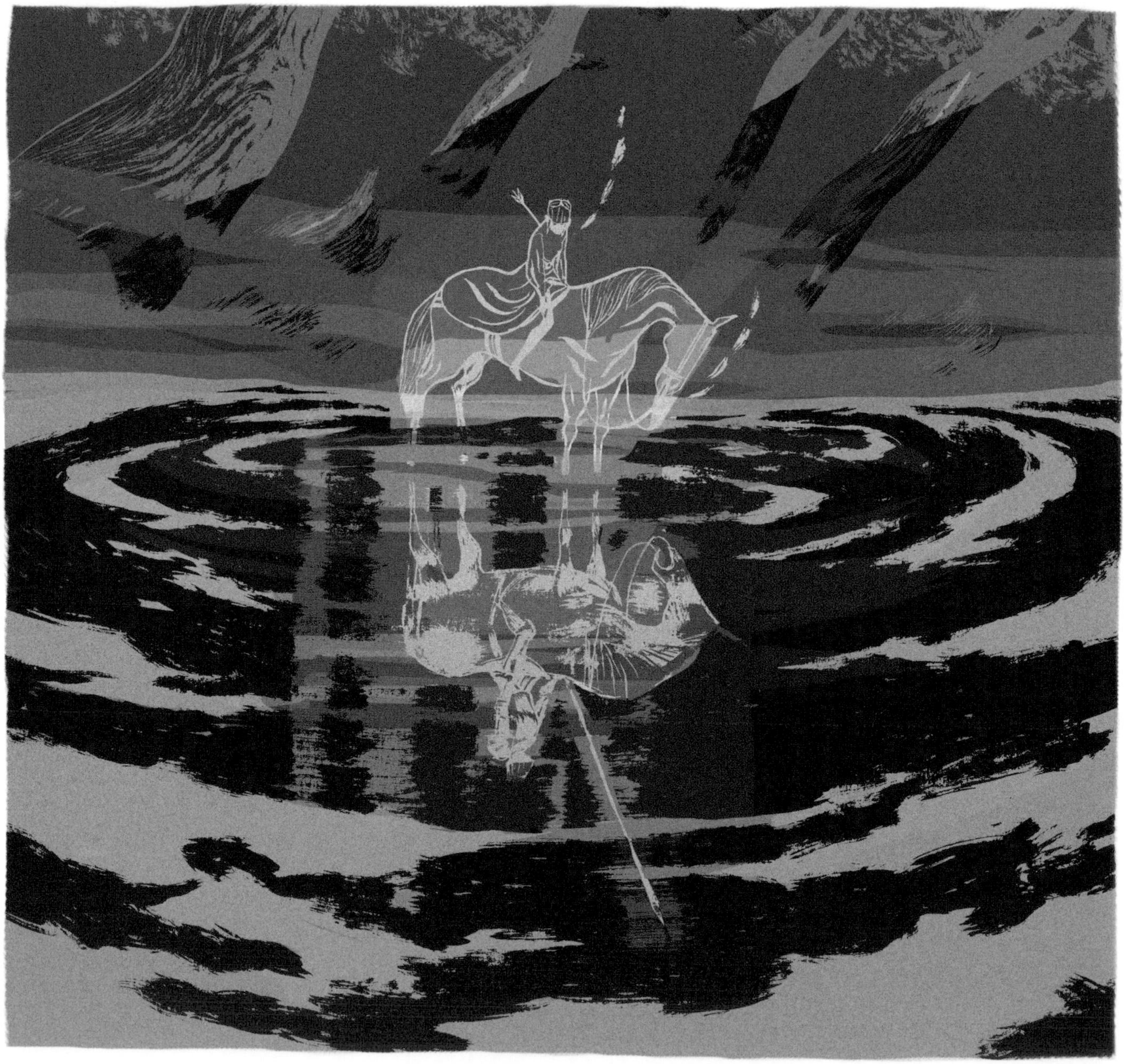

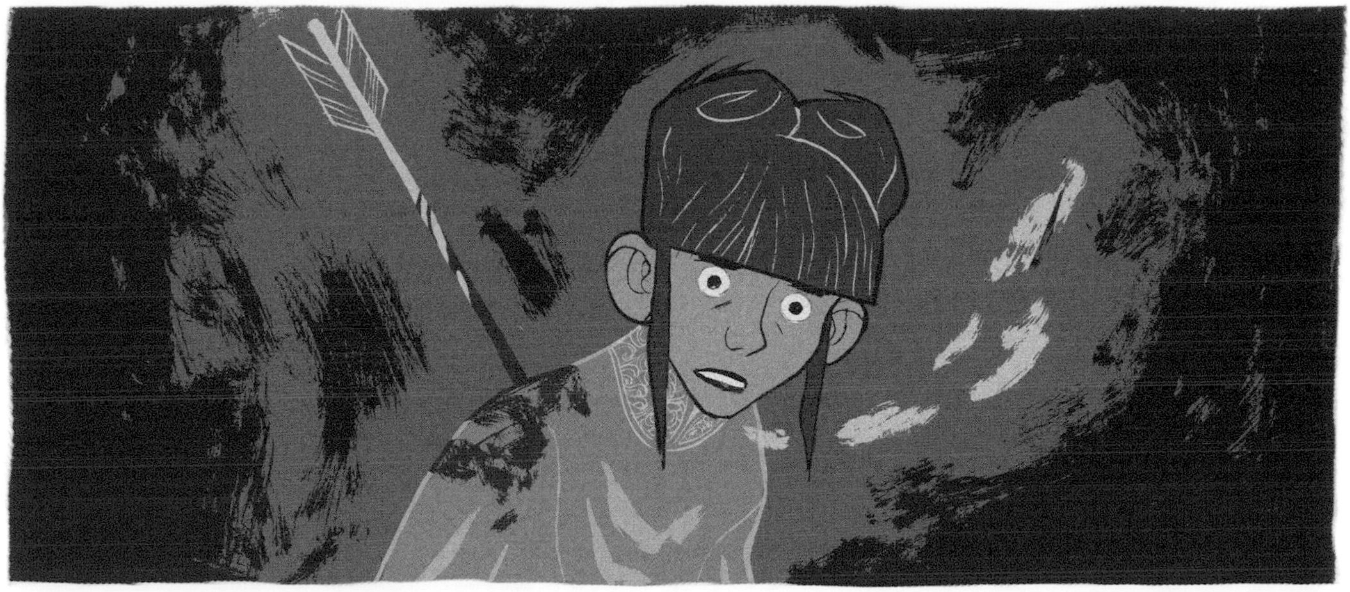

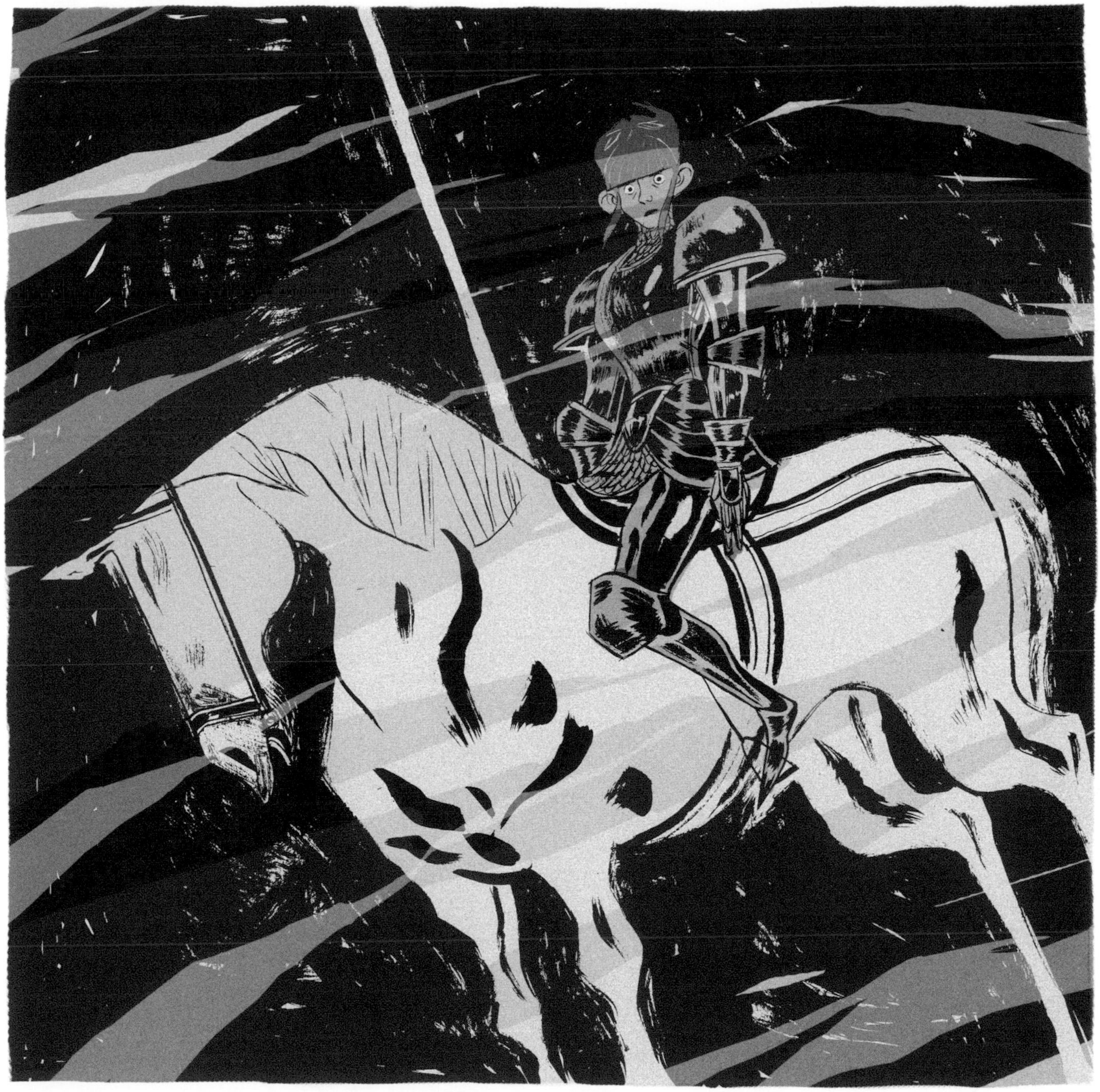

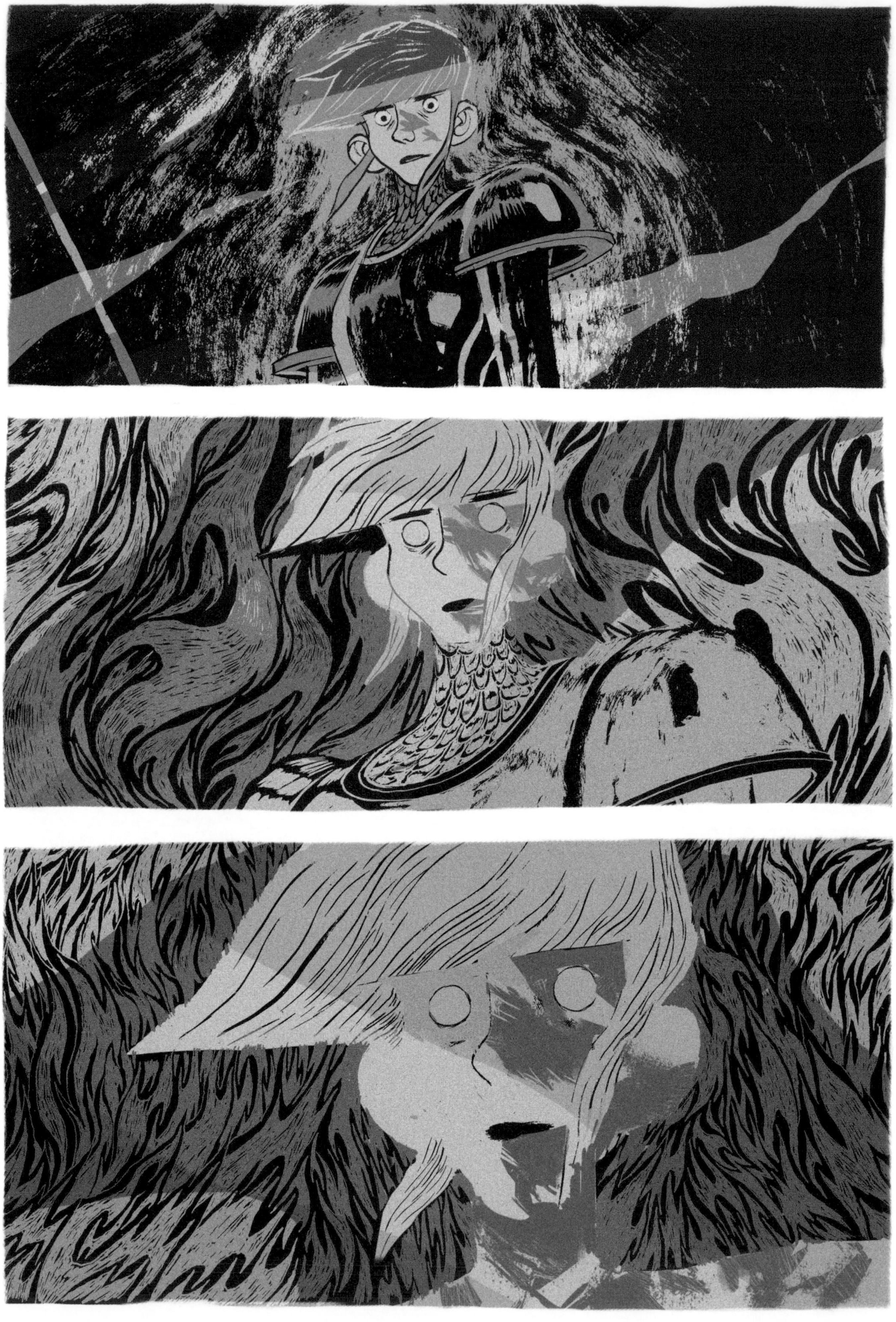

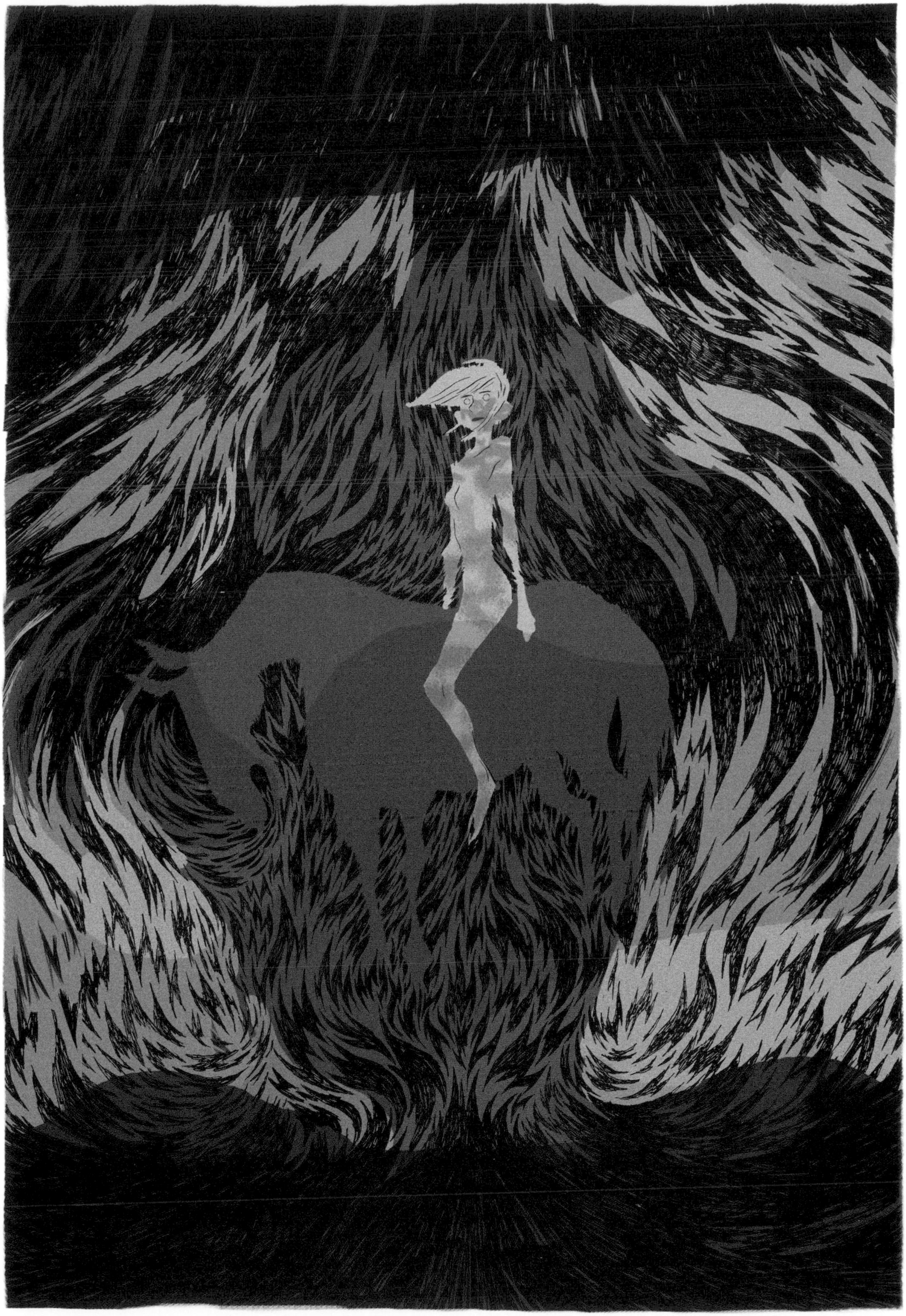

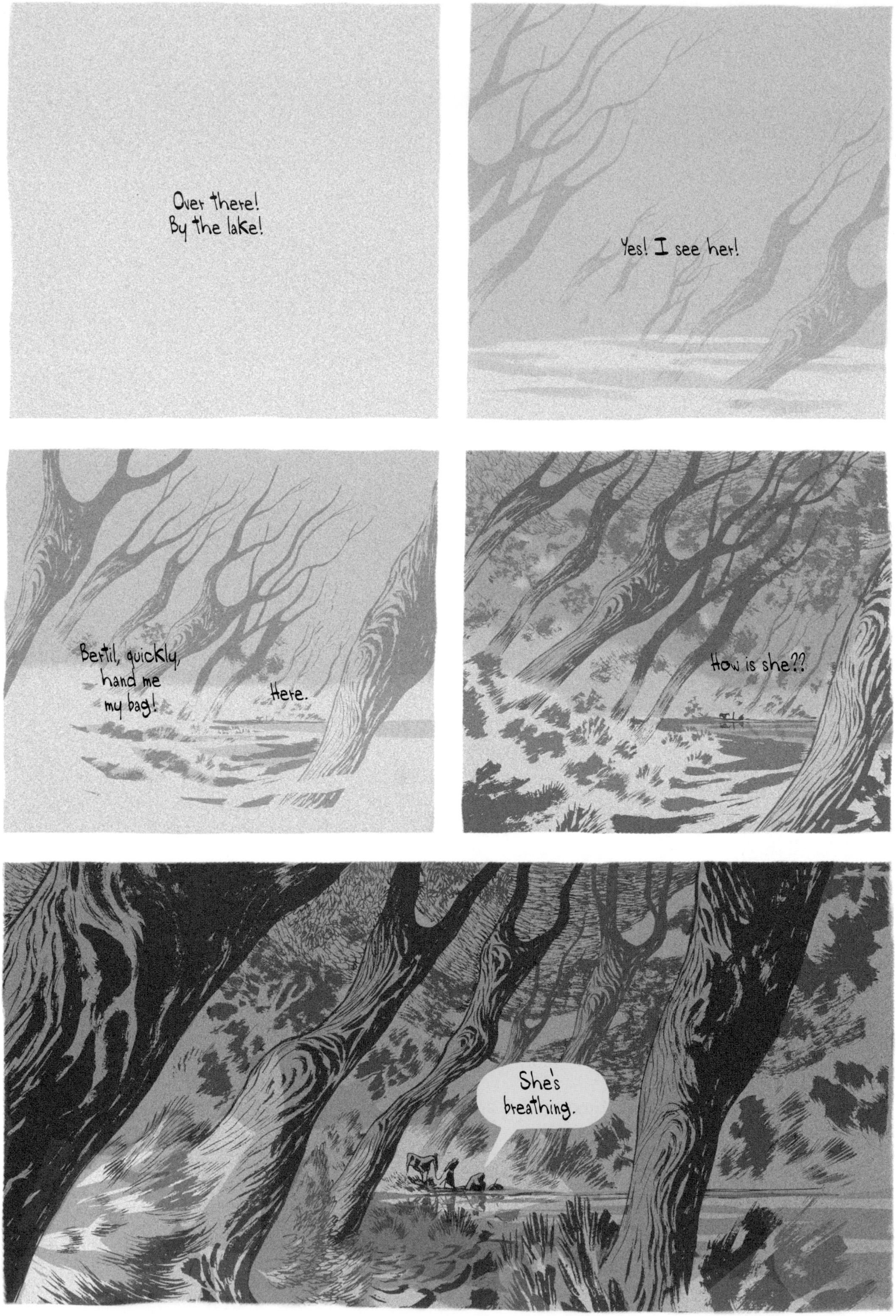
Over there!
By the lake!
Yes! I see her!
Bertil, quickly, hand me my bag!
Here.
How is she??
She's breathing.

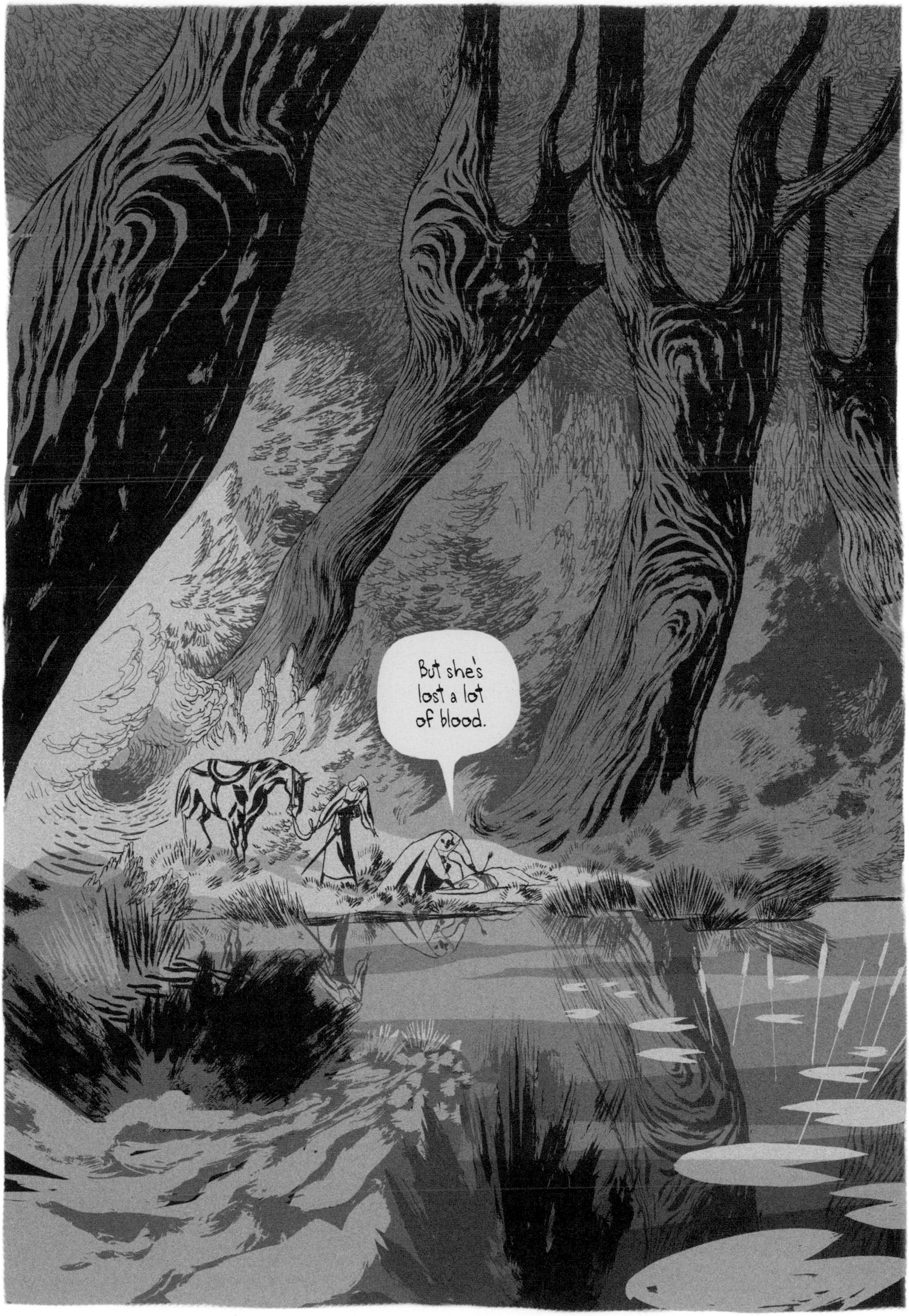
But she's lost a lot of blood.

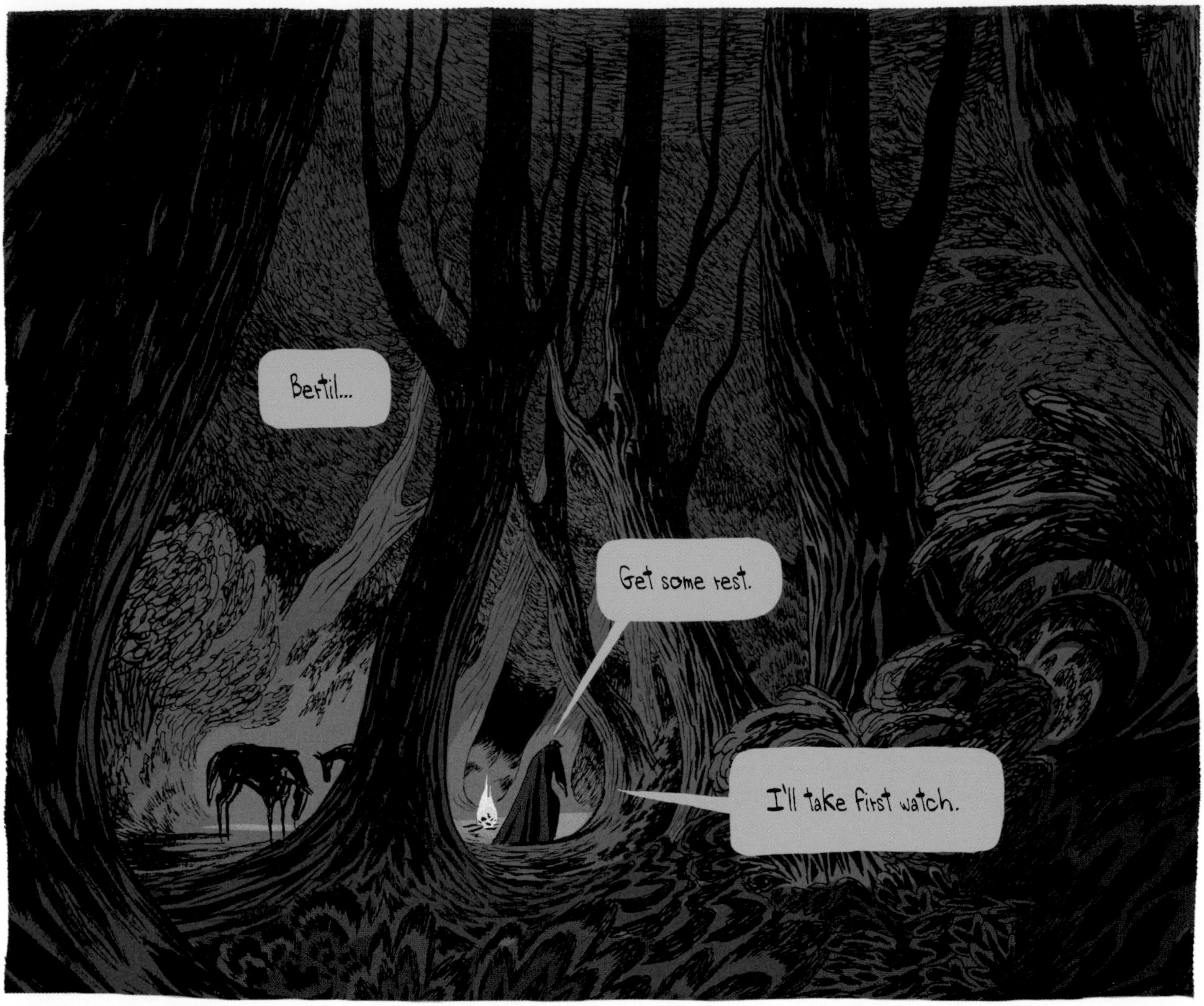
Bertil...
Get some rest.
I'll take first watch.

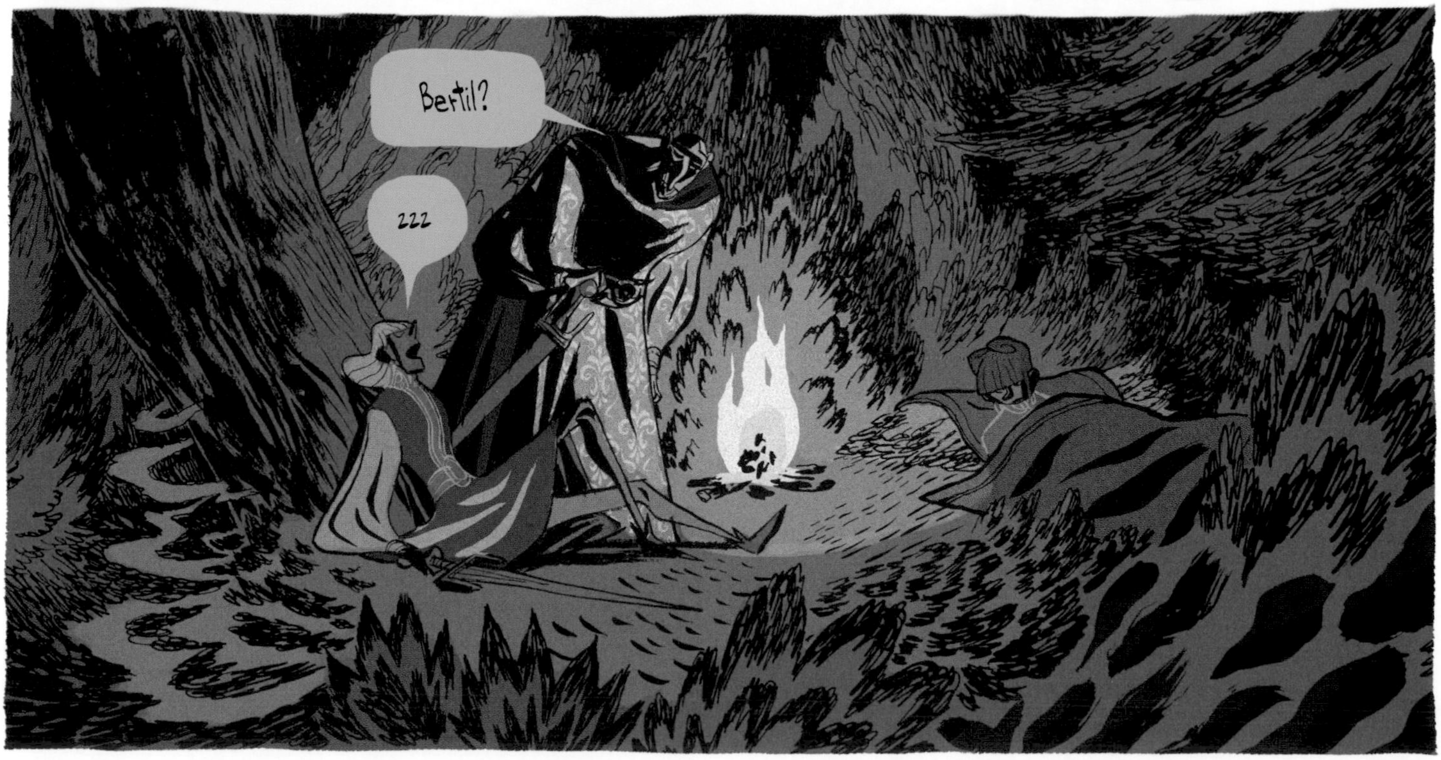
Bertil?
zzz

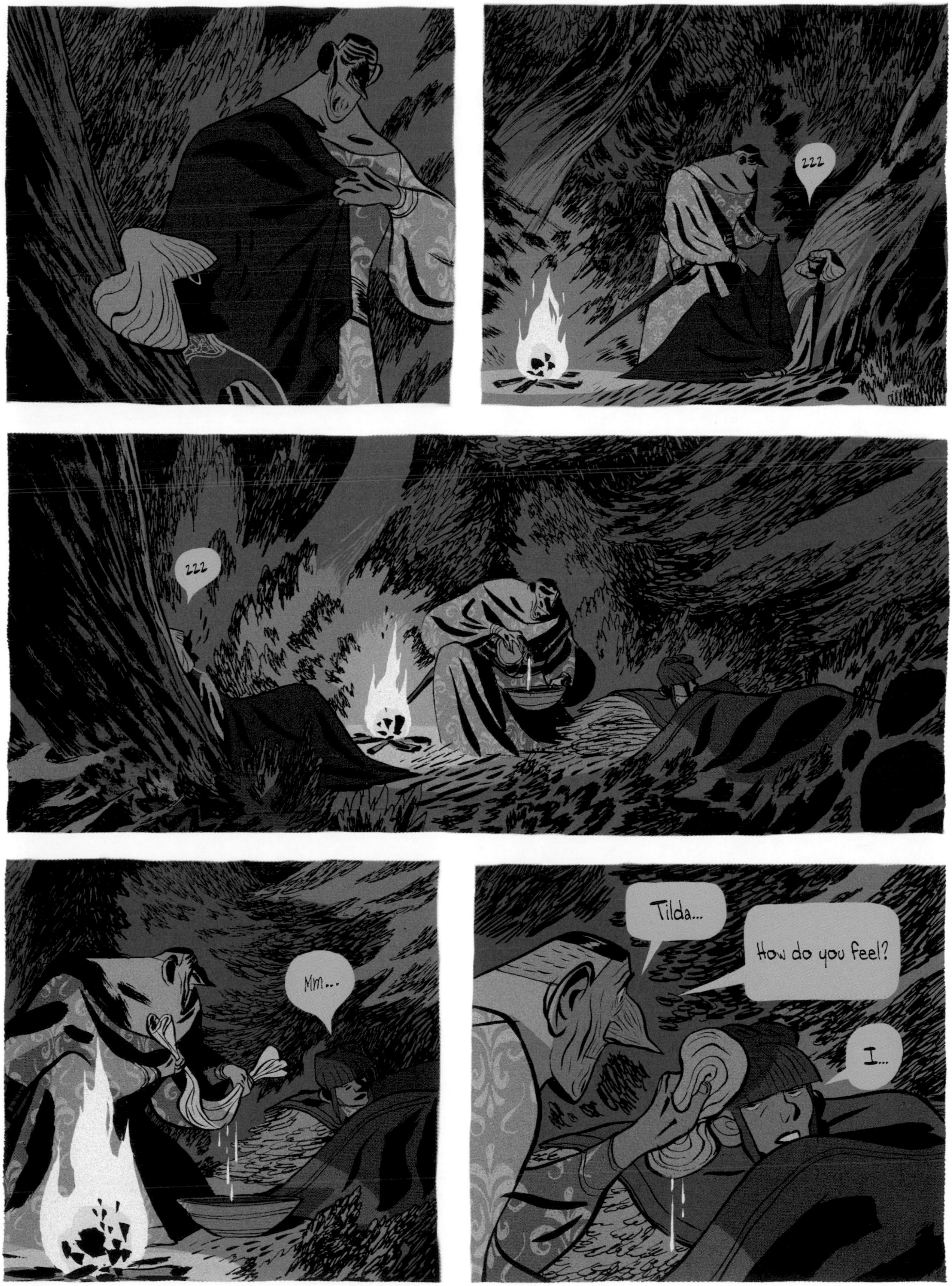
zzz
zzz
Mm...
Tilda...
How do you feel?
I...

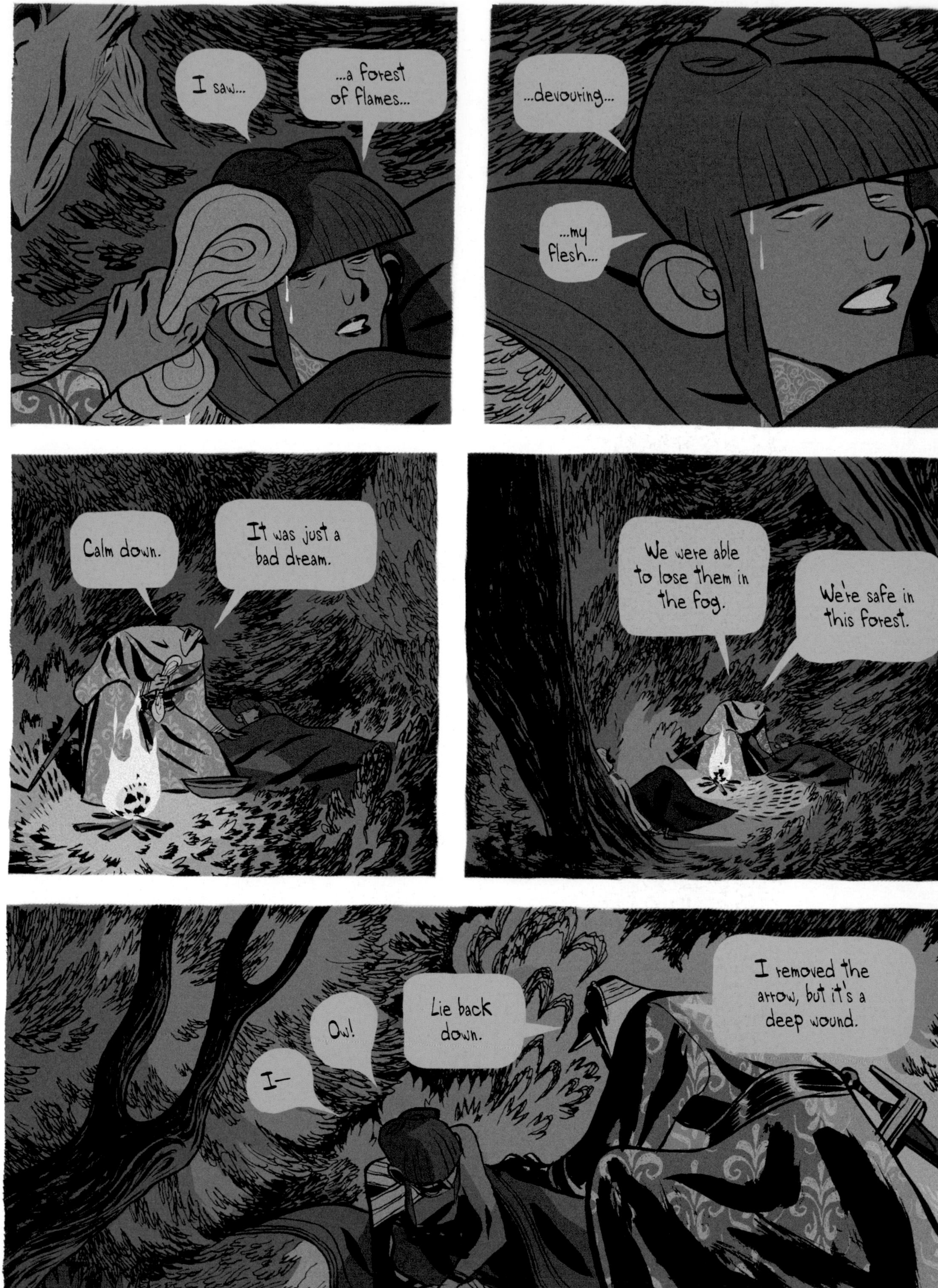
I saw...
...a forest of flames...
...devouring...
...my flesh...
Calm down.
It was just a bad dream.
We were able to lose them in the fog.
We're safe in this forest.
I—
Ow!
Lie back down.
I removed the arrow, but it's a deep wound.

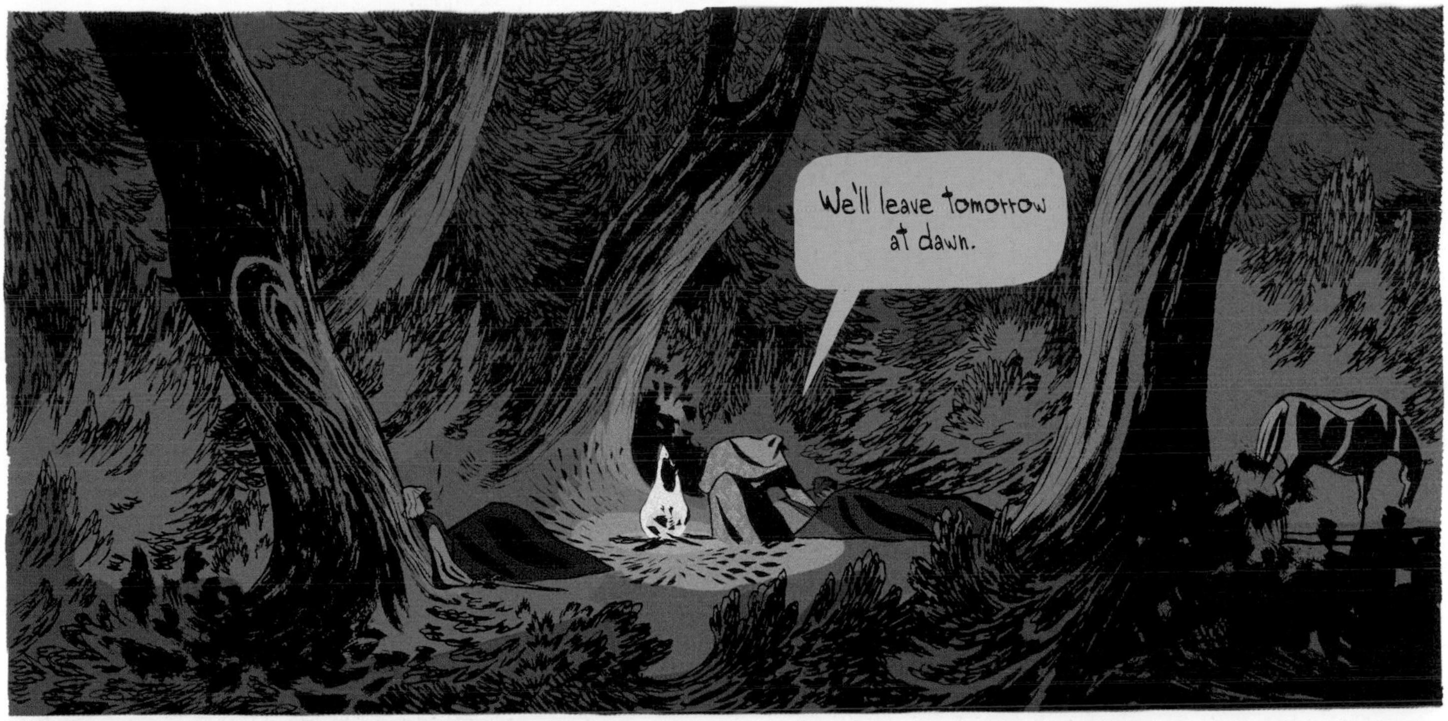
We'll leave tomorrow at dawn.

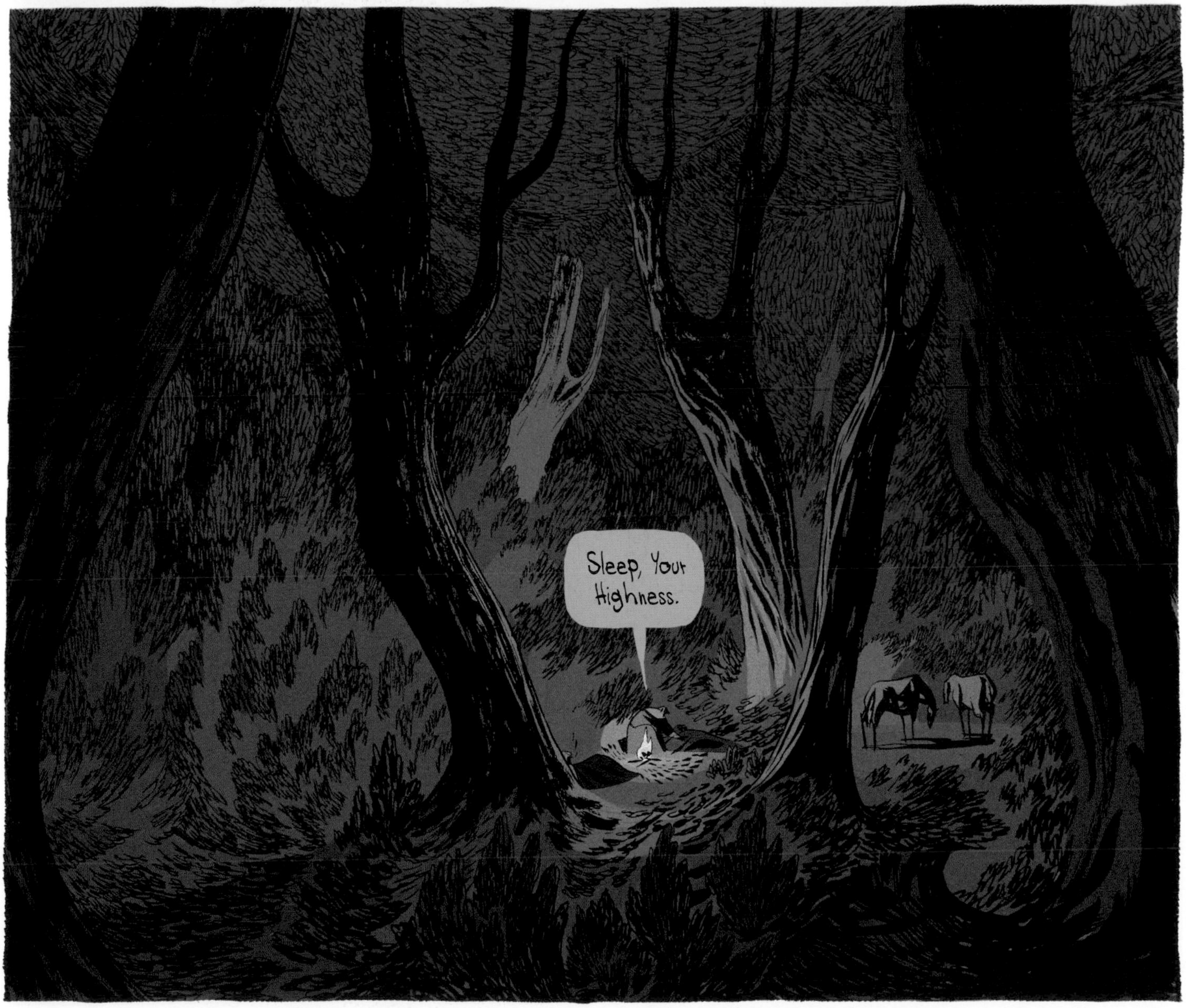
Sleep, Your Highness.

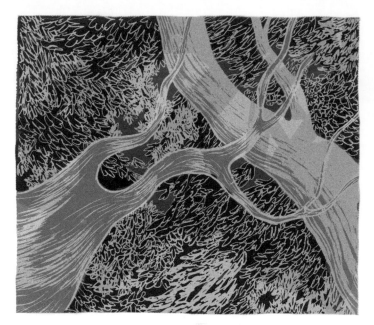

Your Highness...

Thanks, Bertil.

We need to look after your wound.

We'll make regular stops.

No need.

Ouch...

I will go on alone, Lord Tankred.

Turn around and return to your land.

There is still time.

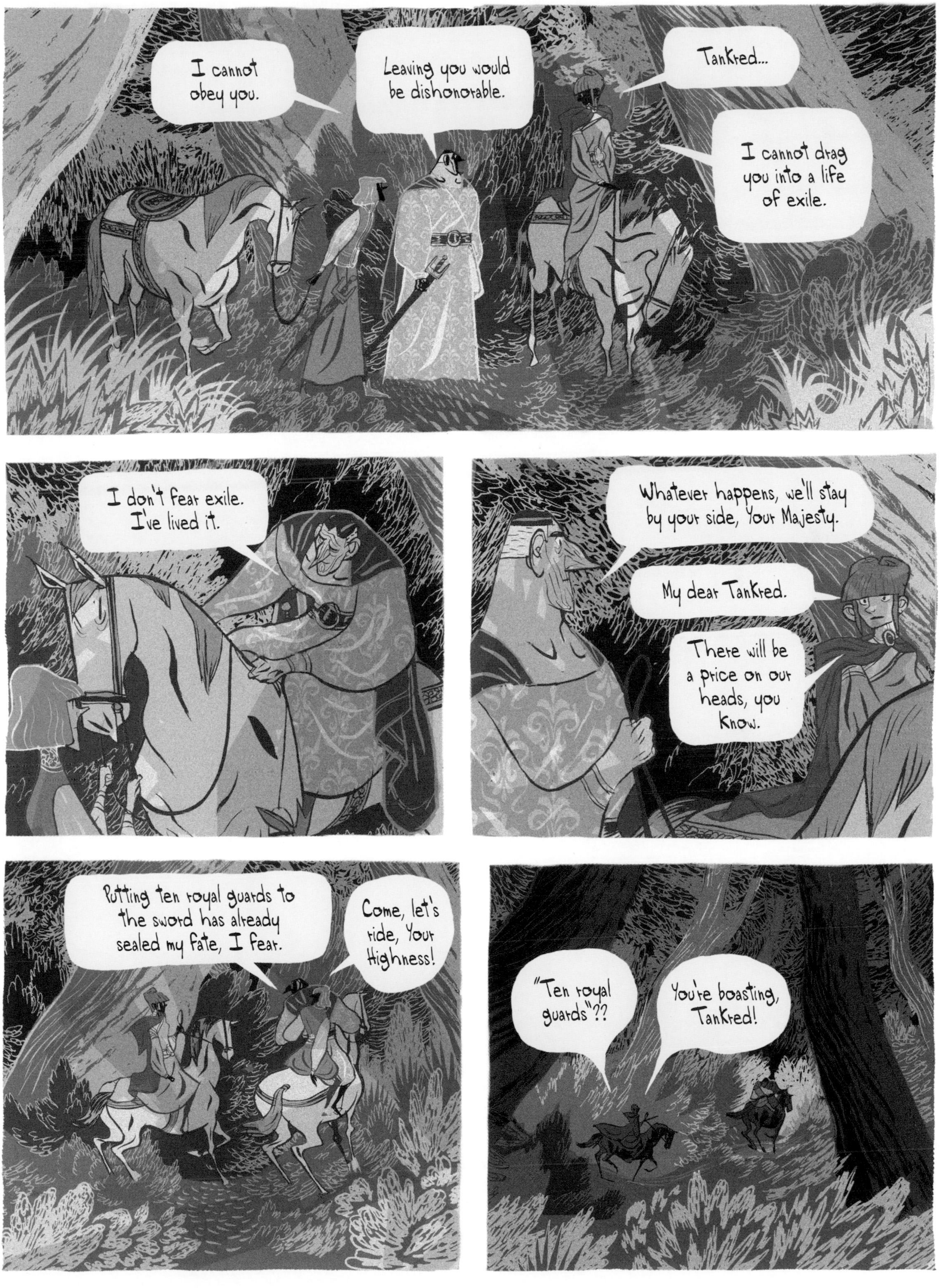
I cannot obey you.
Leaving you would be dishonorable.
Tankred...
I cannot drag you into a life of exile.
I don't fear exile. I've lived it.
Whatever happens, we'll stay by your side, Your Majesty.
My dear Tankred.
There will be a price on our heads, you know.
Putting ten royal guards to the sword has already sealed my fate, I fear.
Come, let's ride, Your Highness!
"Ten royal guards"??
You're boasting, Tankred!

Bertil... you seem troubled.
I don't like this forest, Your Highness.
Nobody ventures in here.
Fantastical creatures are said to dwell here.
The peasants speak of "evil warrior fairies"...
Good God, Bertil, don't be daft.
Don't mock the people, Tankred.
Peasants are like children. They love to frighten one another.
At least they didn't betray me.
You're right.
And we cannot stay in this forest forever.
We must go find support and protection in the provinces.
Anyone in particular?
Lord Albaret.
His letter proves his loyalty.
Can you ask him for sanctuary?

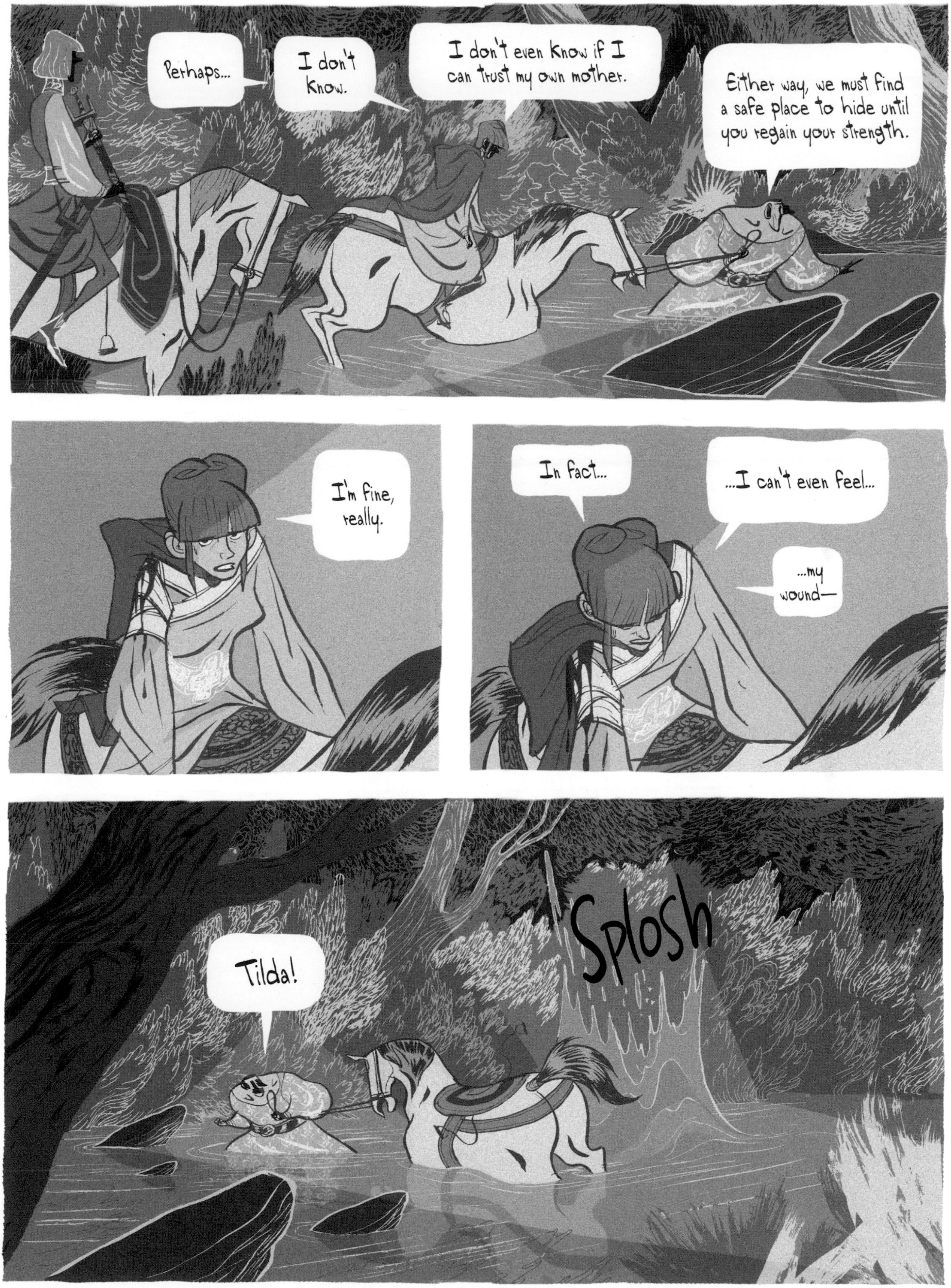
Perhaps...
I don't know.
I don't even know if I can trust my own mother.
Either way, we must find a safe place to hide until you regain your strength.
I'm fine, really.
In fact...
...I can't even feel...
...my wound—
Splosh
Tilda!

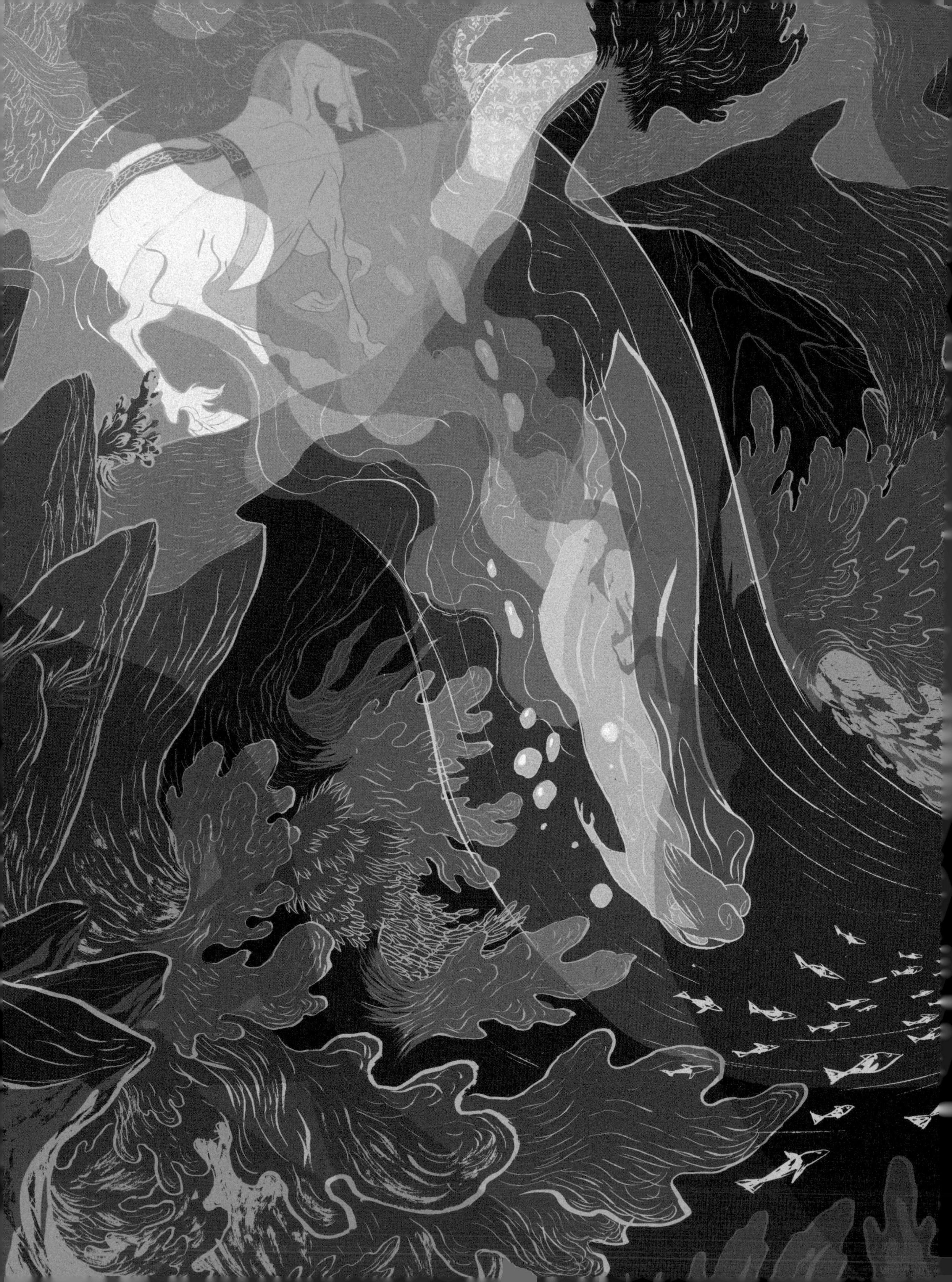

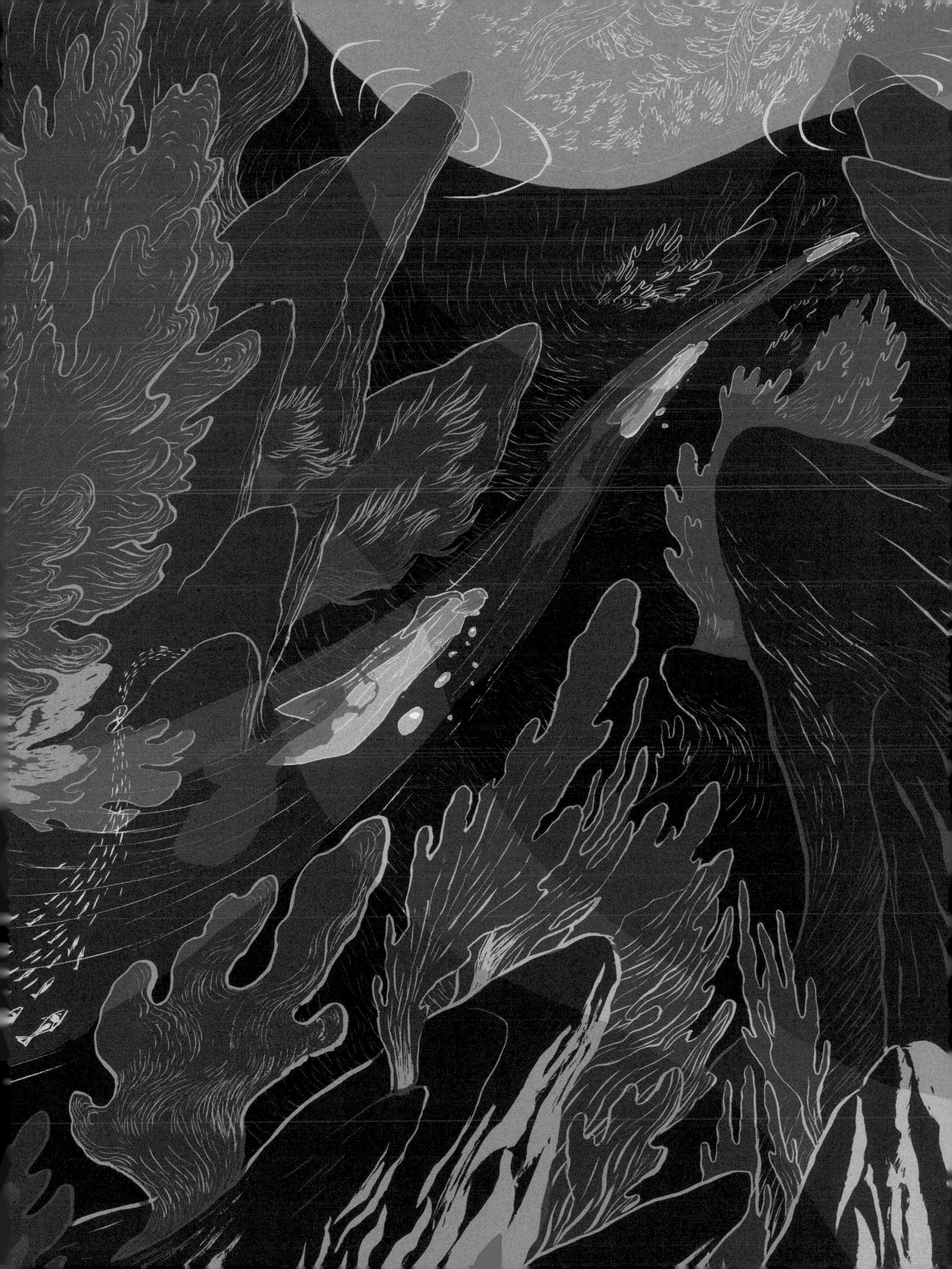

Plic
Plic

Frrr

Frrr

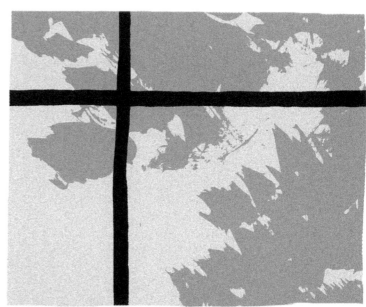

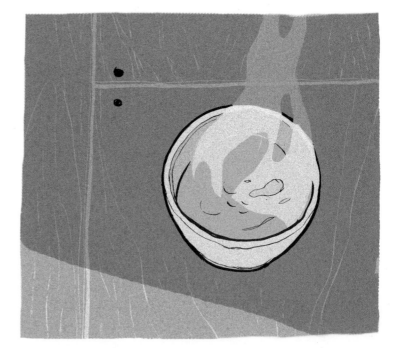

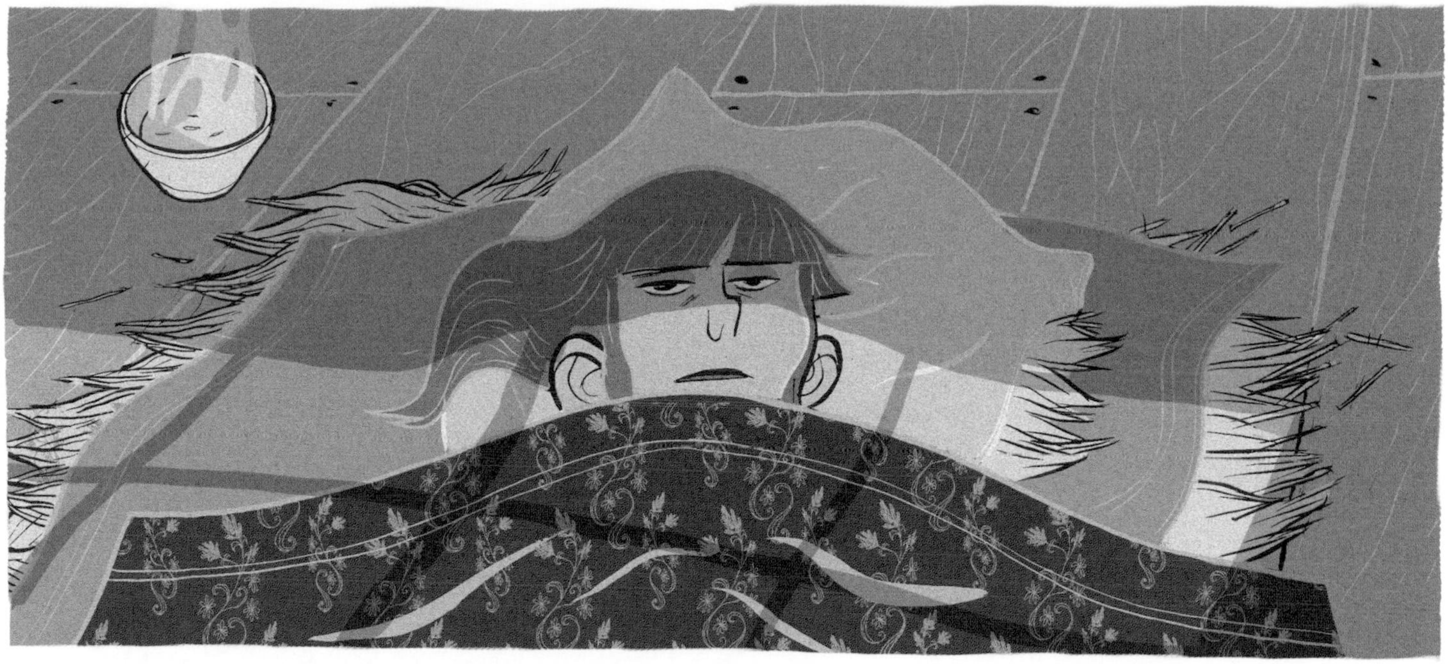

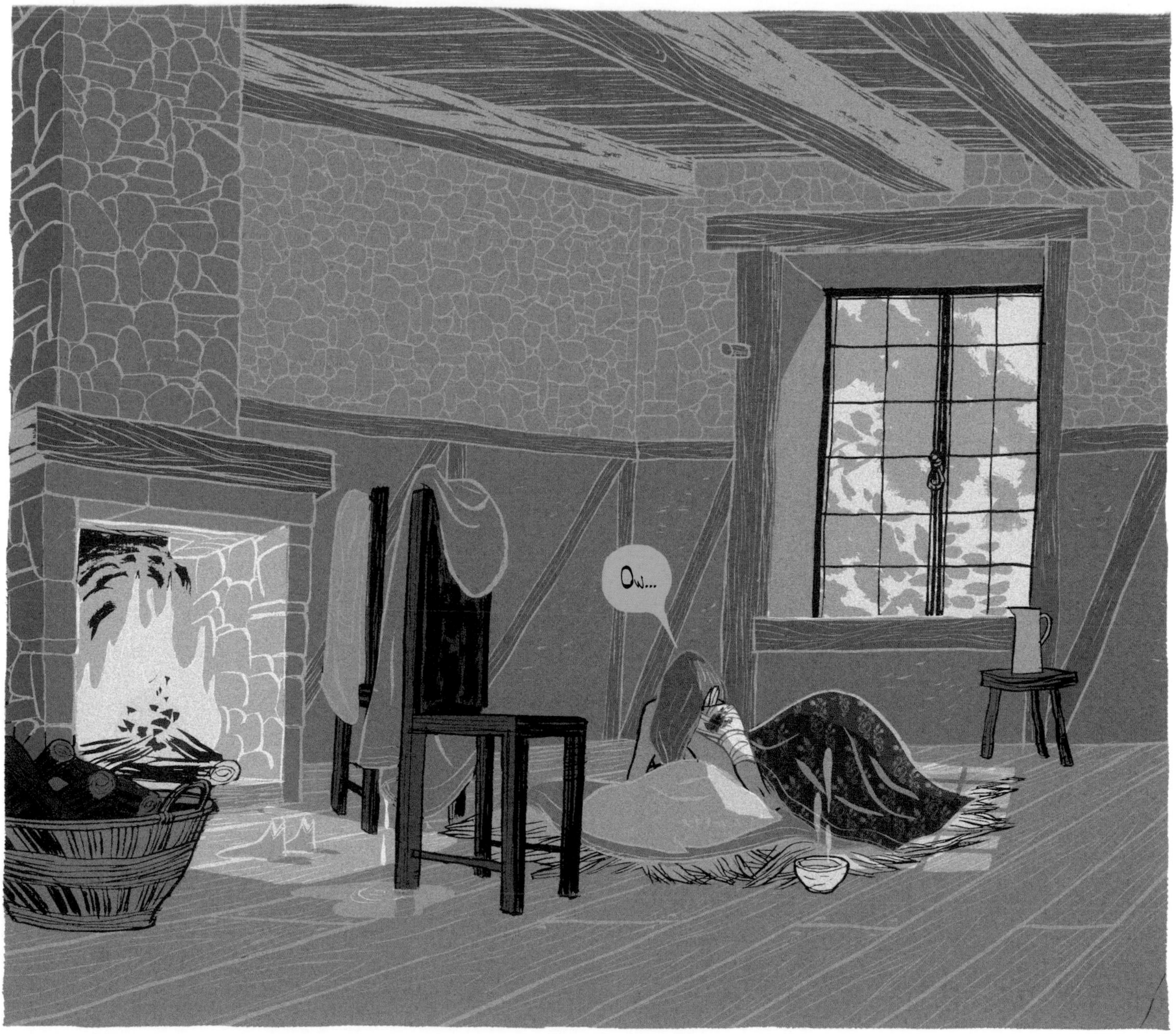
Ow...

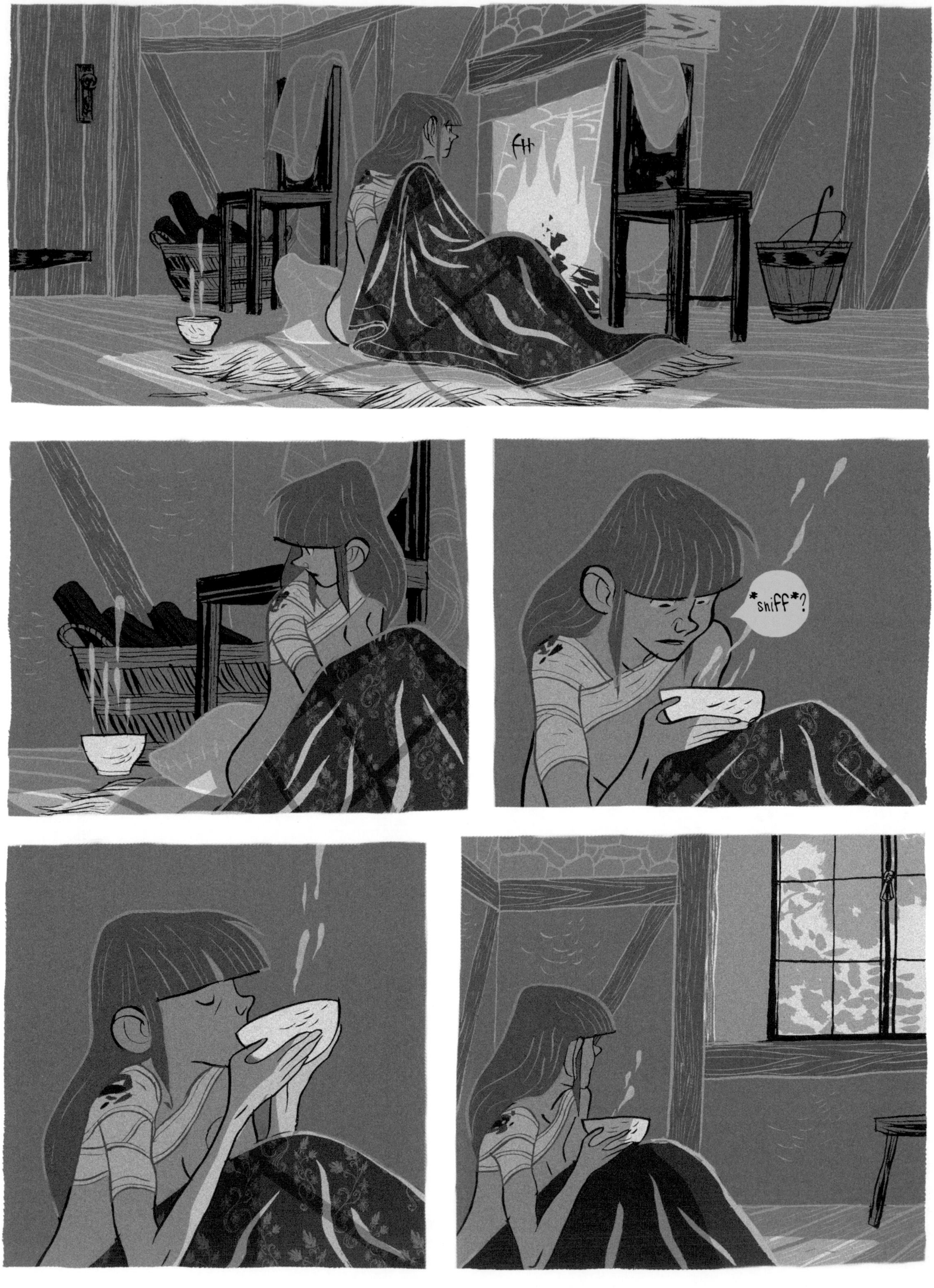
FH
sniff?

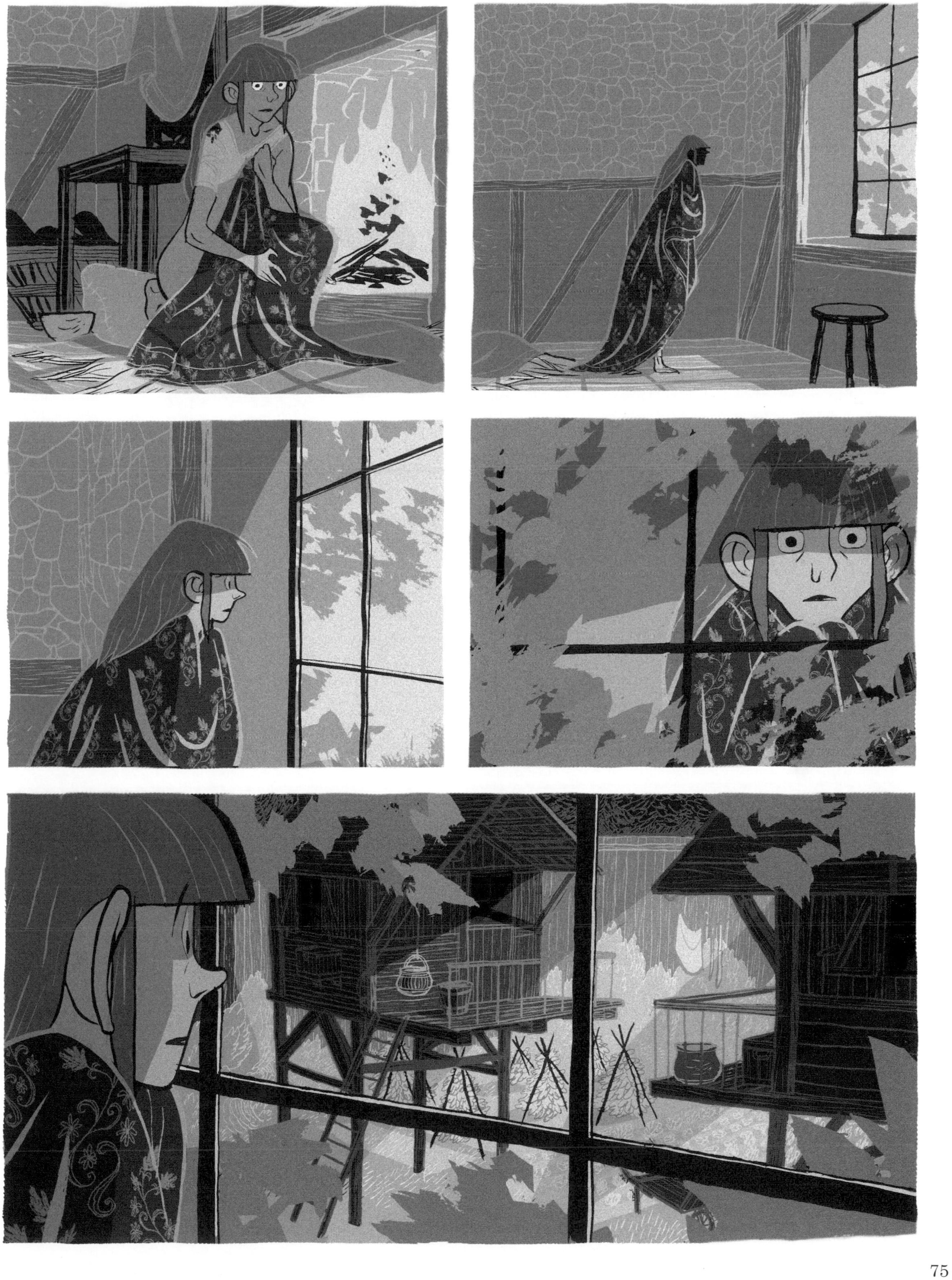

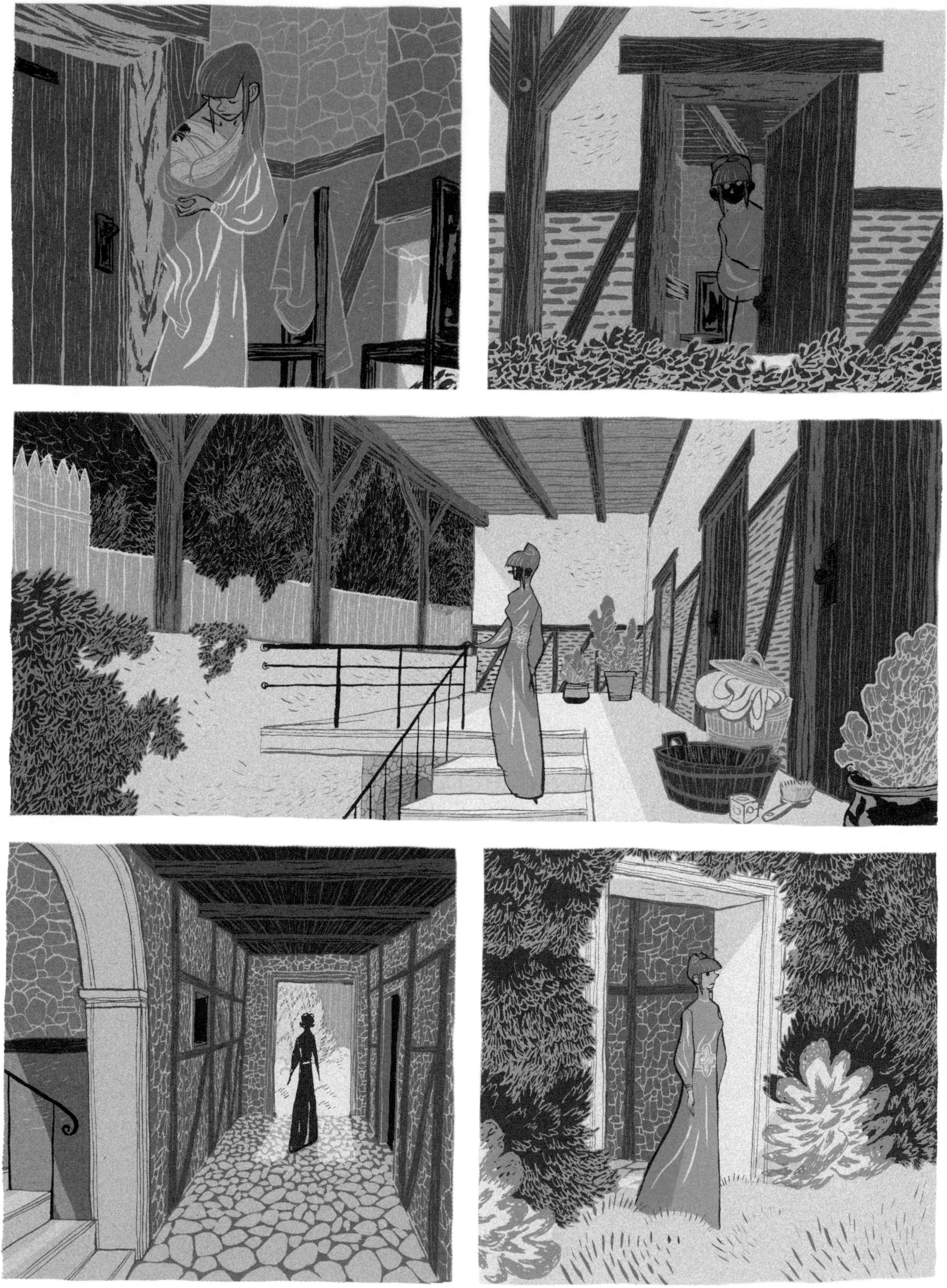

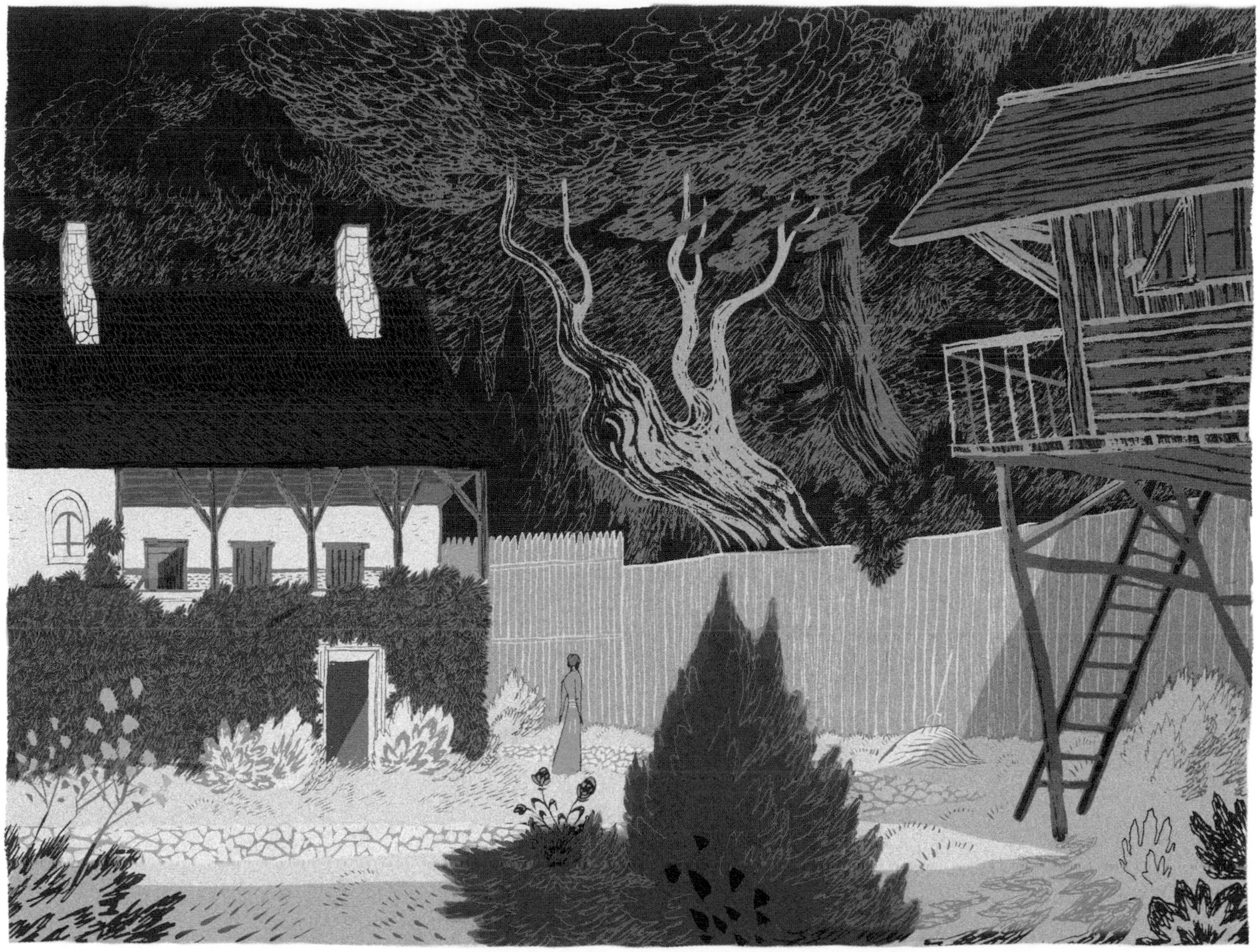

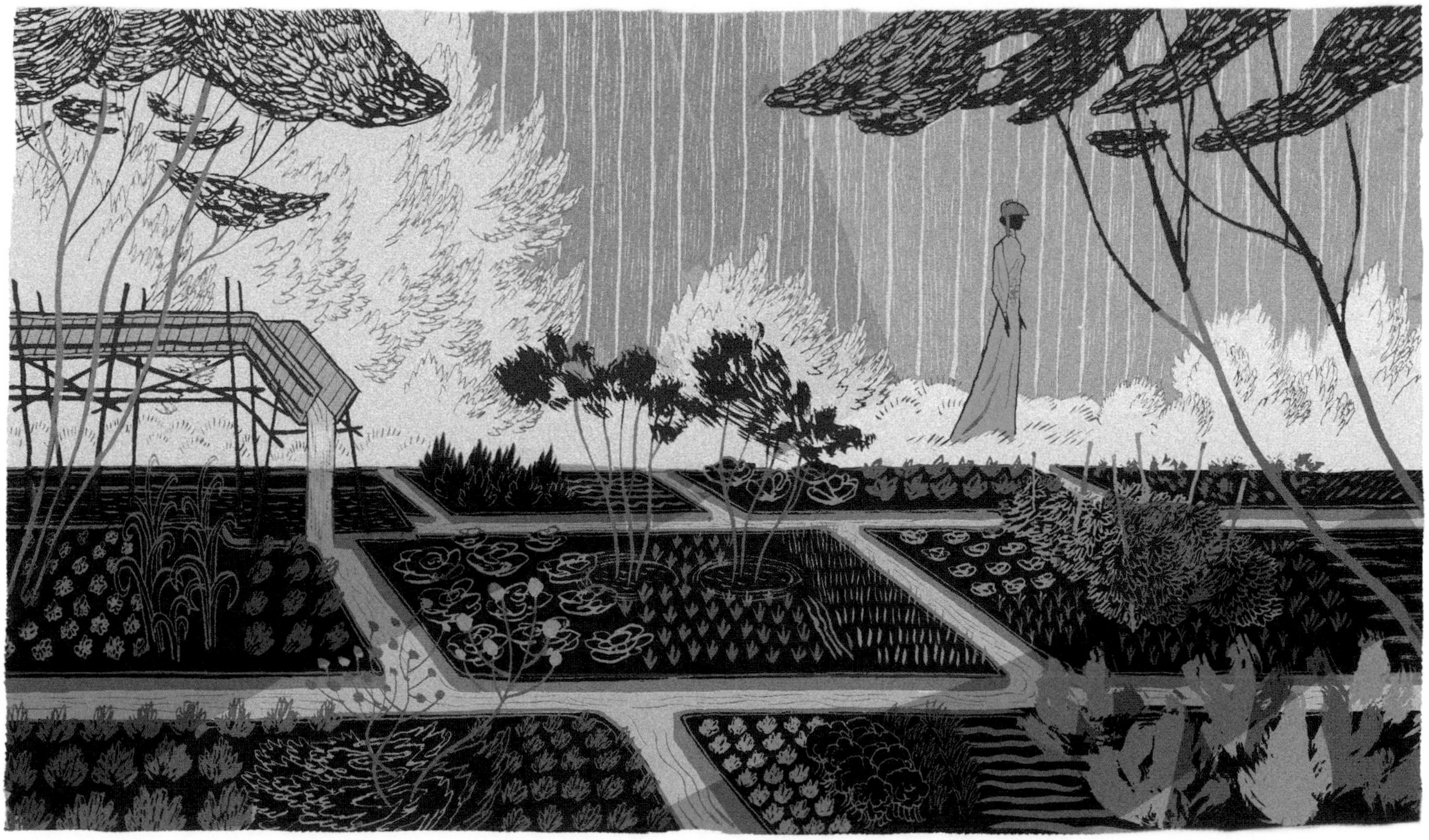

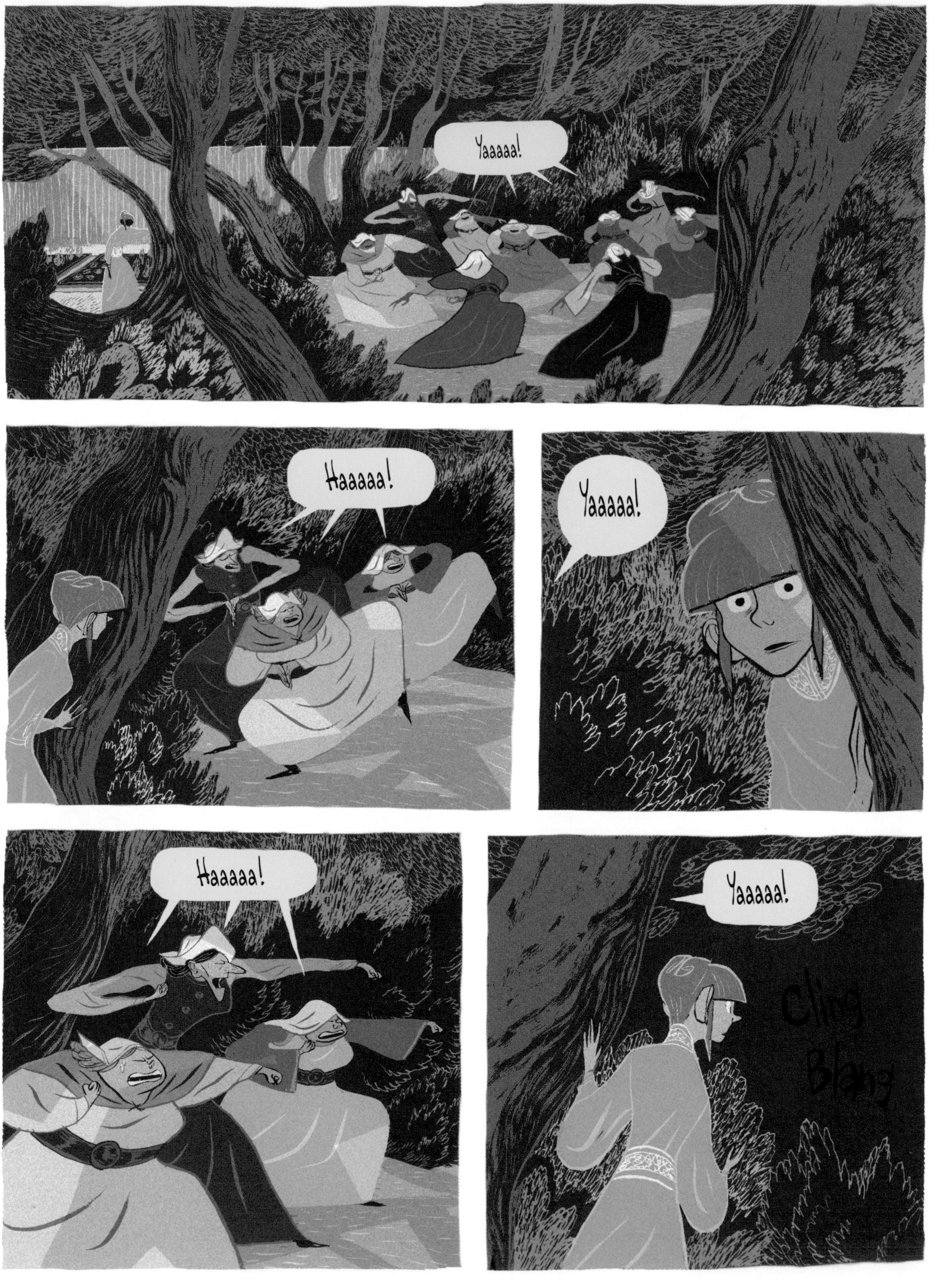
Yaaaaa!
Haaaaa!
Yaaaaa!
Haaaaa!
Yaaaaa!
Cling
Blang

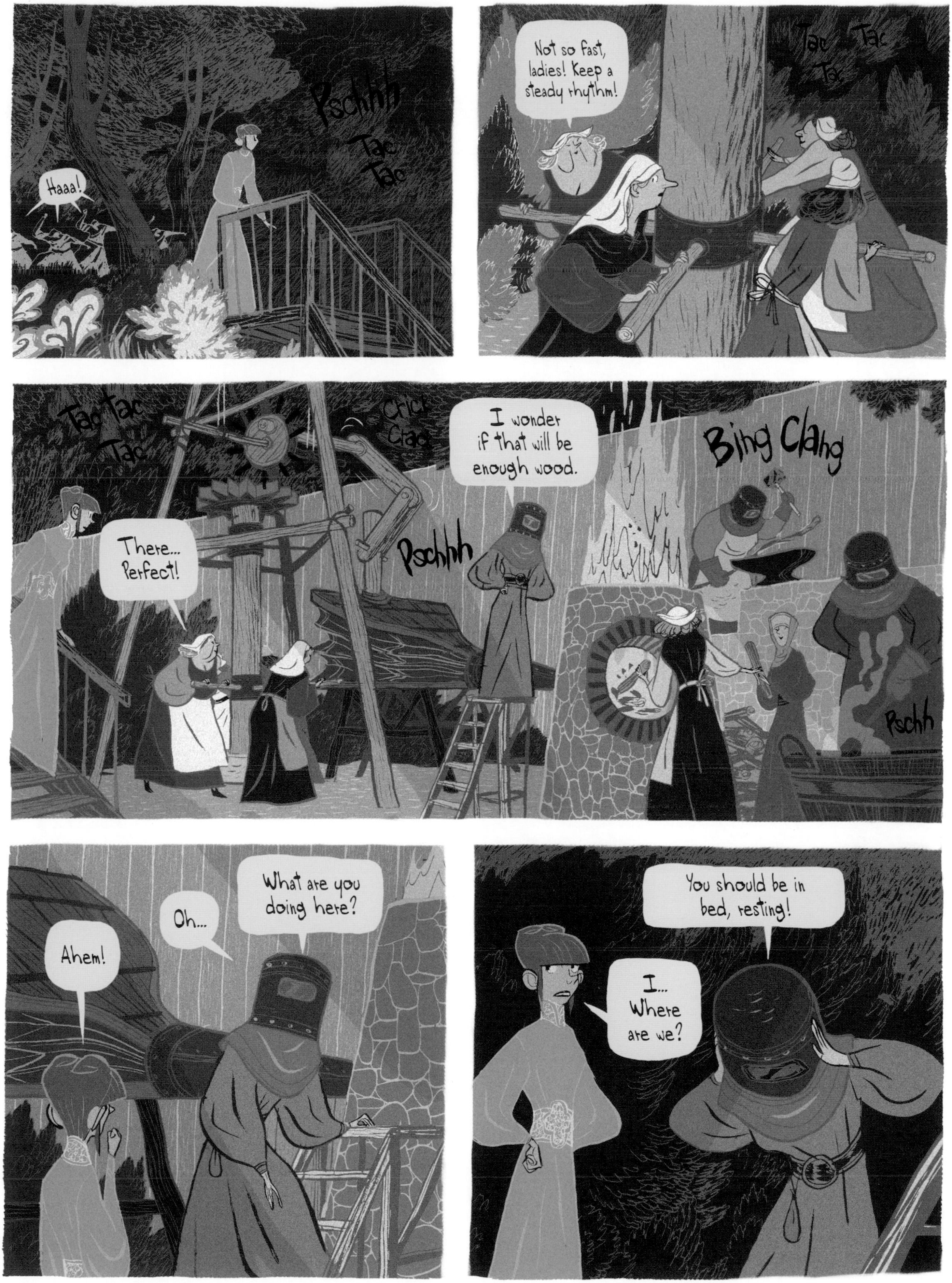
Haaa!
Pschhh
Tac Tac
Not so fast, ladies! Keep a steady rhythm!
Tac Tac Tac
Tac Tac Tac
Crick Crack
I wonder if that will be enough wood.
Bing Clang
There... Perfect!
Pschhh
Pschh
What are you doing here?
Oh...
Ahem!
You should be in bed, resting!
I... Where are we?

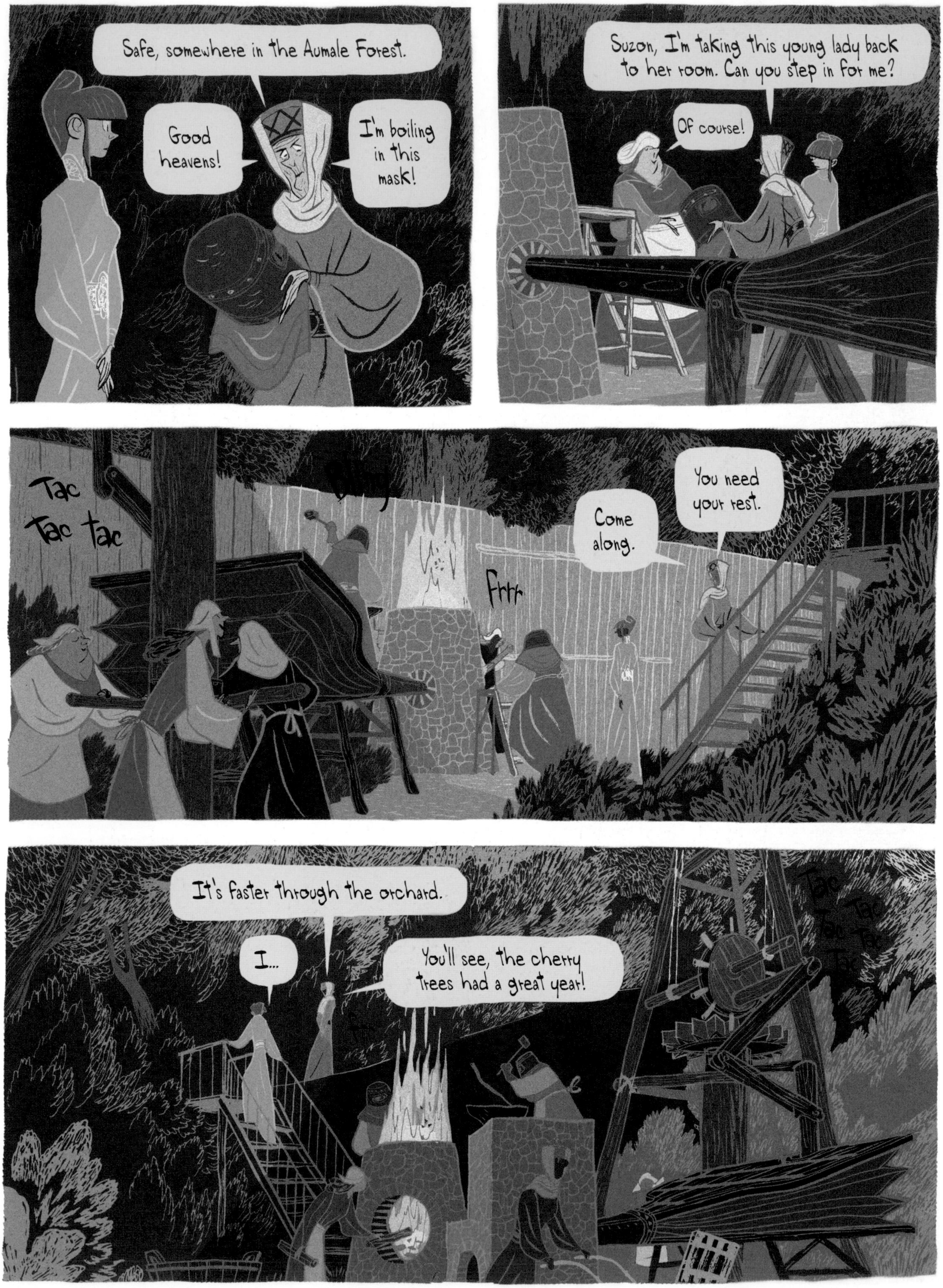

Safe, somewhere in the Aumale Forest.
Good heavens!
I'm boiling in this mask!
Suzon, I'm taking this young lady back to her room. Can you step in for me?
Of course!
Tac Tac tac
Frrr
Come along.
You need your rest.
It's faster through the orchard.
I...
You'll see, the cherry trees had a great year!

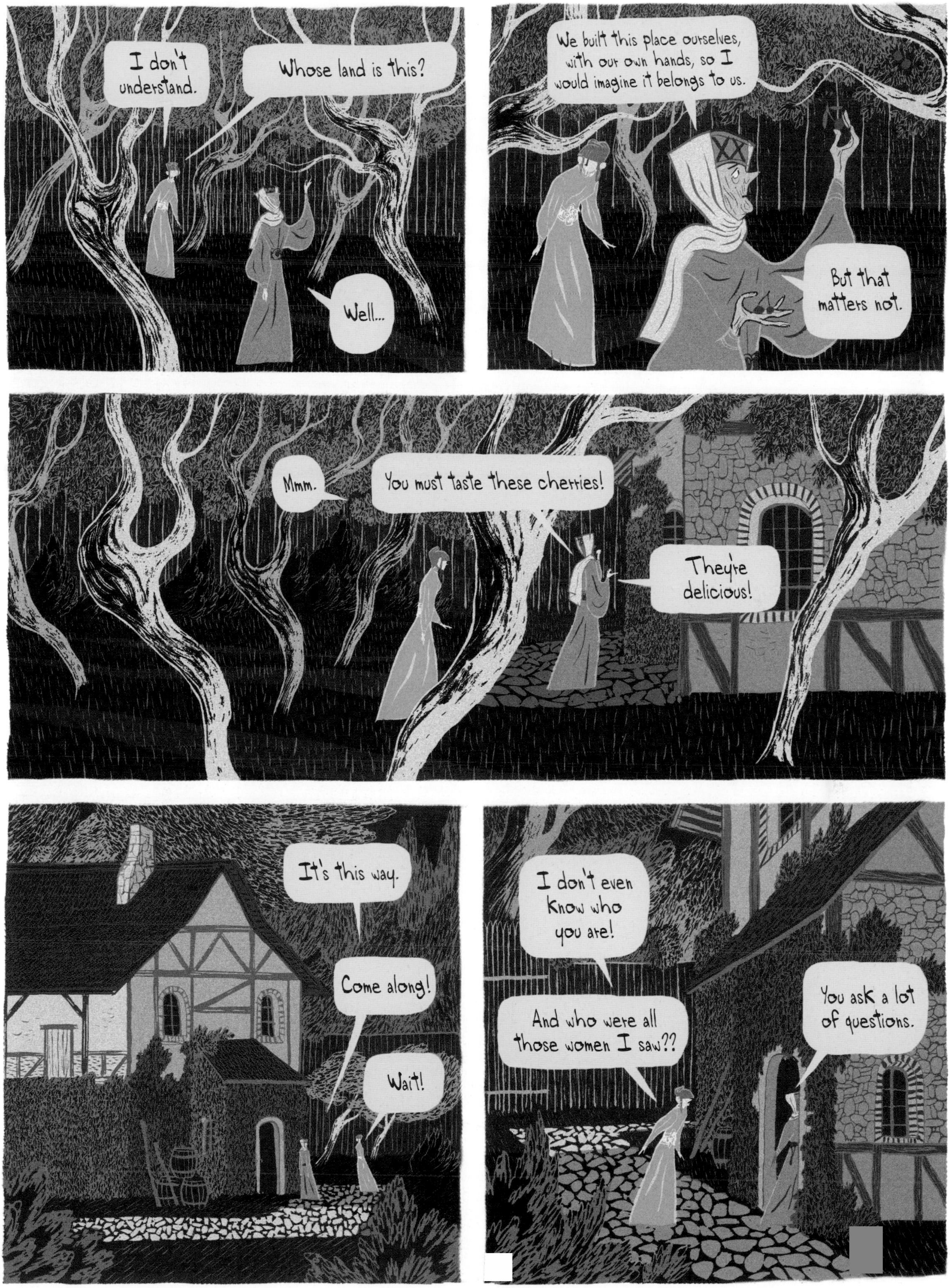
I don't understand.
Whose land is this?
Well...
We built this place ourselves, with our own hands, so I would imagine it belongs to us.
But that matters not.
Mmm.
You must taste these cherries!
They're delicious!
It's this way.
Come along!
Wait!
I don't even know who you are!
And who were all those women I saw??
You ask a lot of questions.

We found you unconscious on the riverbank.
Alone.
In the middle of the forest.
I, too, could ask you why.
Or what caused your injury.
I know nothing of those women. Their secrets are theirs to keep.
As for me...
...you may call me Abigail.

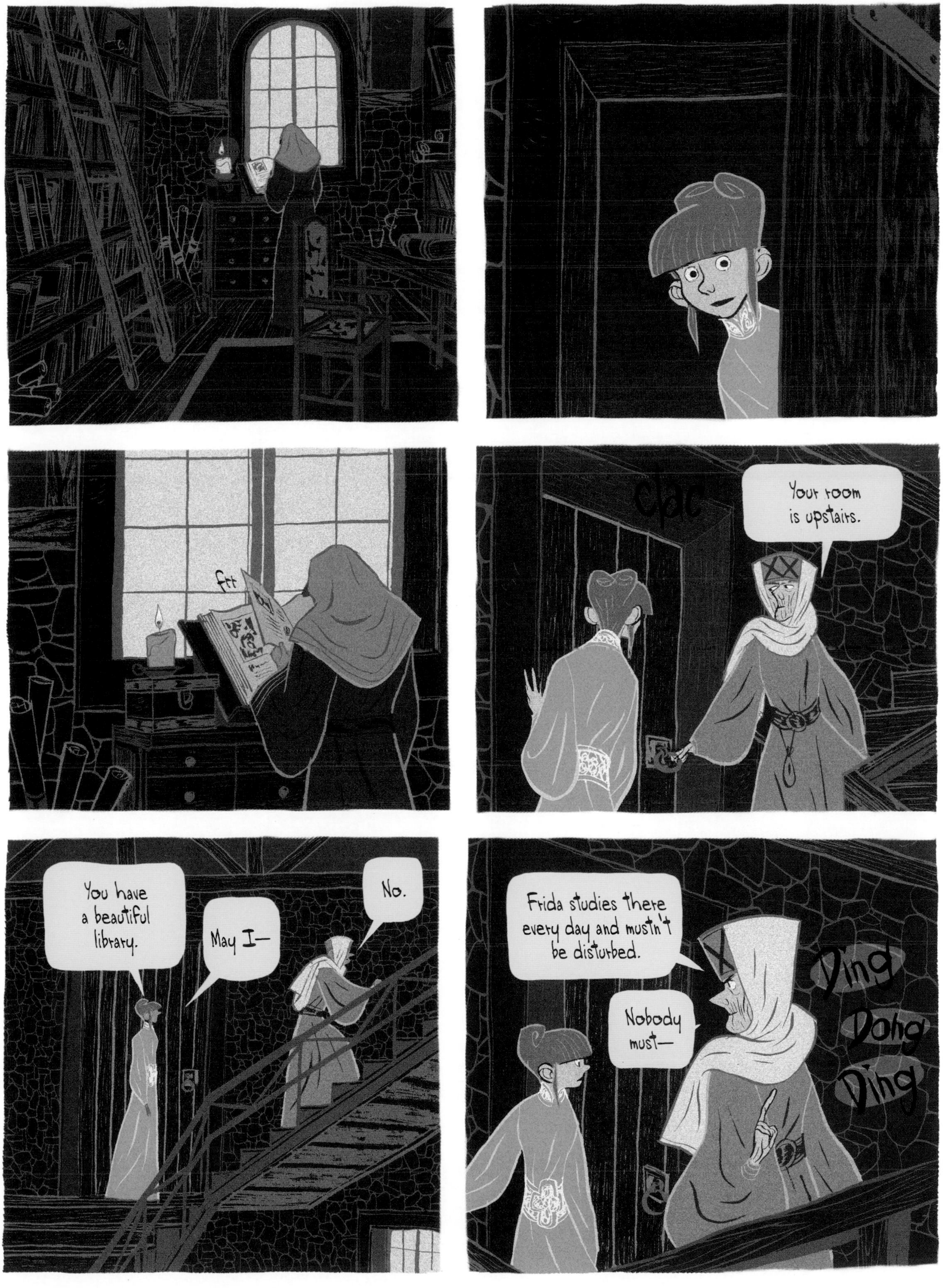

frr
clac
Your room is upstairs.
You have a beautiful library.
May I—
No.
Frida studies there every day and mustn't be disturbed.
Nobody must—
Ding Dong Ding

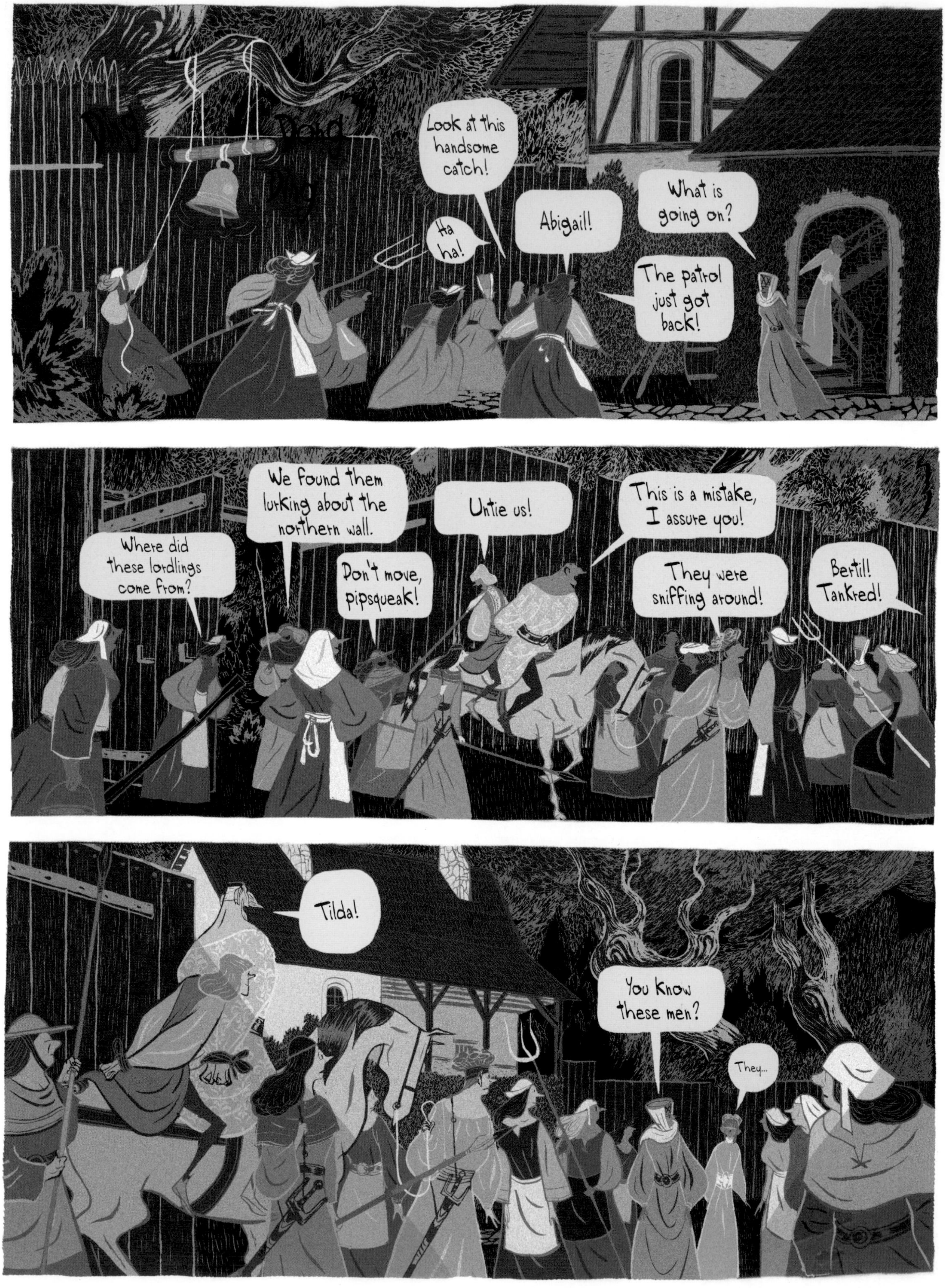
Ding
Dong
Ding
Look at this handsome catch!
Ha ha!
Abigail!
What is going on?
The patrol just got back!
Where did these lordlings come from?
We found them lurking about the northern wall.
Don't move, pipsqueak!
Untie us!
This is a mistake, I assure you!
They were sniffing around!
Bertil! Tankred!
Tilda!
You know these men?
They...

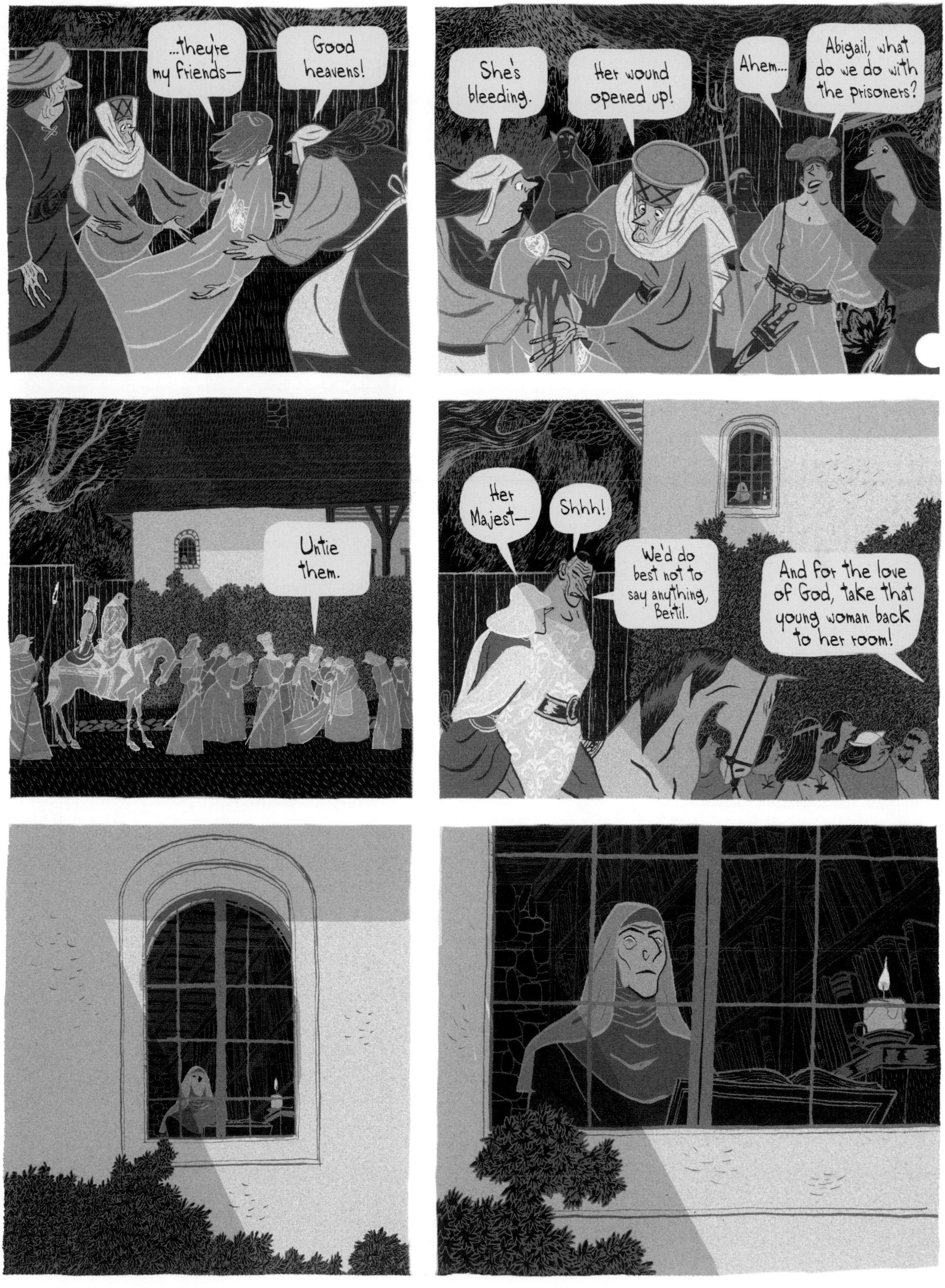
...they're my friends—
Good heavens!
She's bleeding.
Her wound opened up!
Ahem...
Abigail, what do we do with the prisoners?
Untie them.
Her Majest—
Shhh!
We'd do best not to say anything, Bertil.
And for the love of God, take that young woman back to her room!

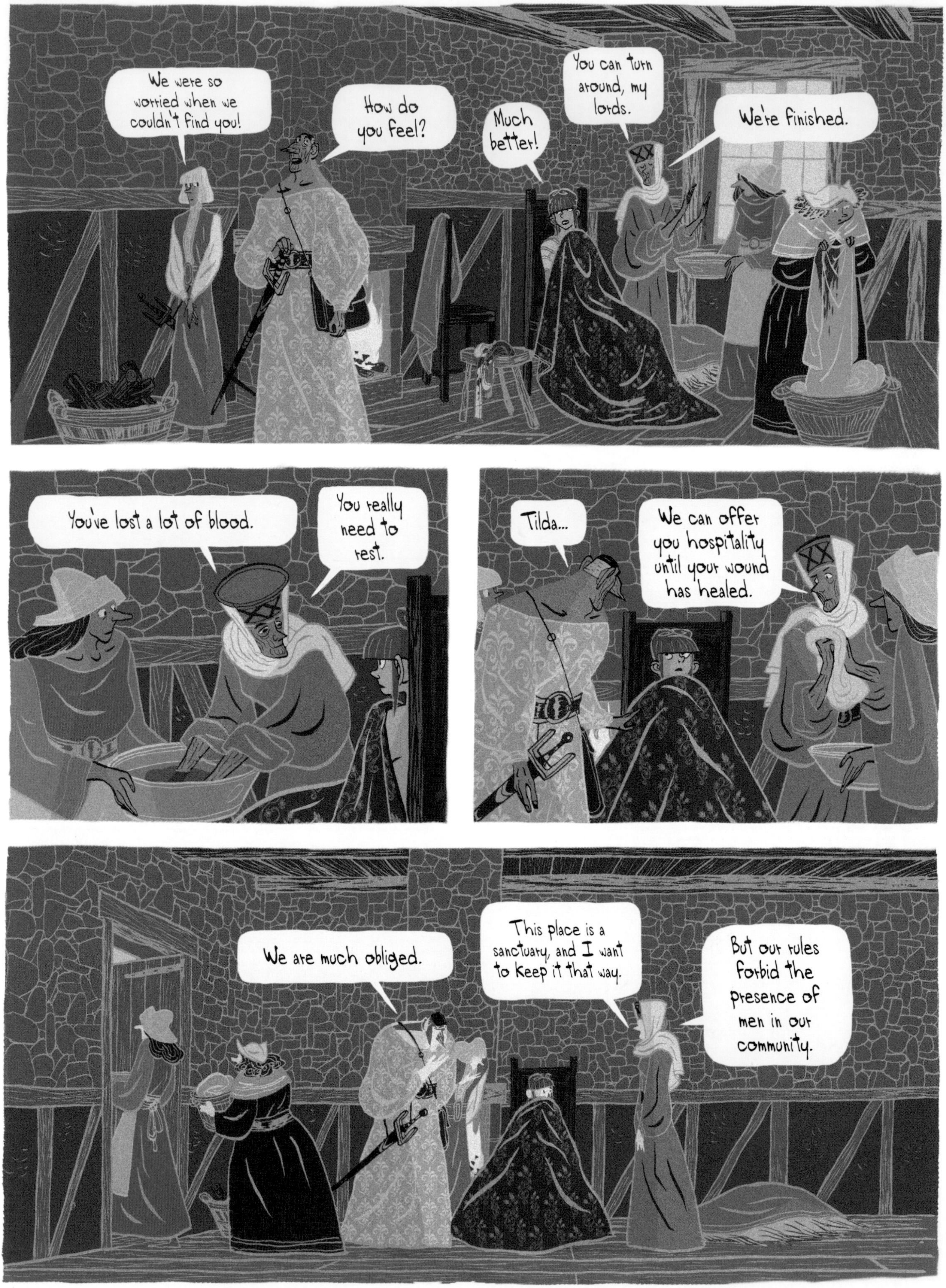
We were so worried when we couldn't find you!
How do you feel?
Much better!
You can turn around, my lords.
We're finished.
You've lost a lot of blood.
You really need to rest.
Tilda...
We can offer you hospitality until your wound has healed.
We are much obliged.
This place is a sanctuary, and I want to keep it that way.
But our rules forbid the presence of men in our community.

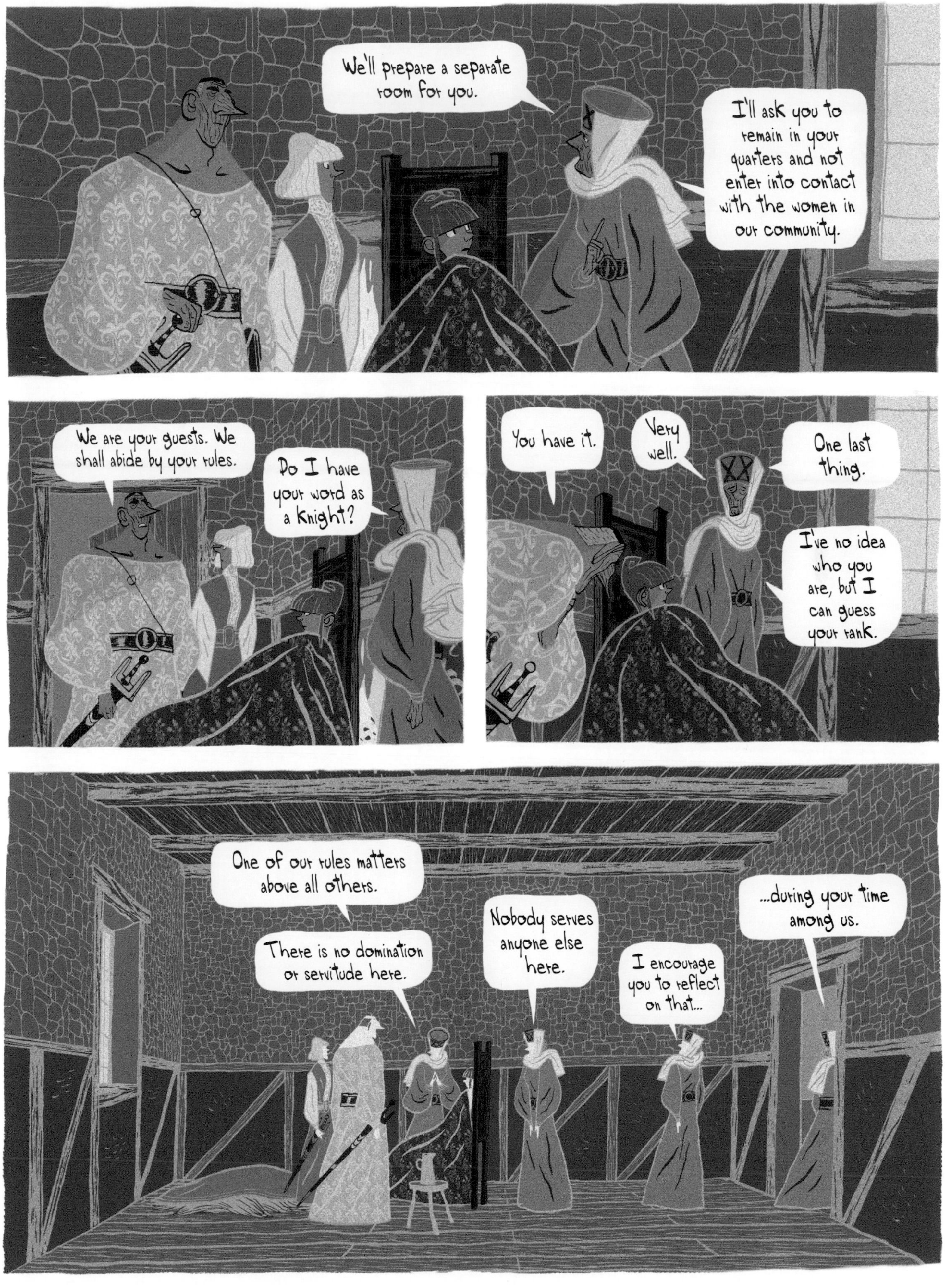

We'll prepare a separate room for you.
I'll ask you to remain in your quarters and not enter into contact with the women in our community.
We are your guests. We shall abide by your rules.
Do I have your word as a Knight?
You have it.
Very well.
One last thing.
I've no idea who you are, but I can guess your rank.
One of our rules matters above all others.
There is no domination or servitude here.
Nobody serves anyone else here.
I encourage you to reflect on that...
...during your time among us.

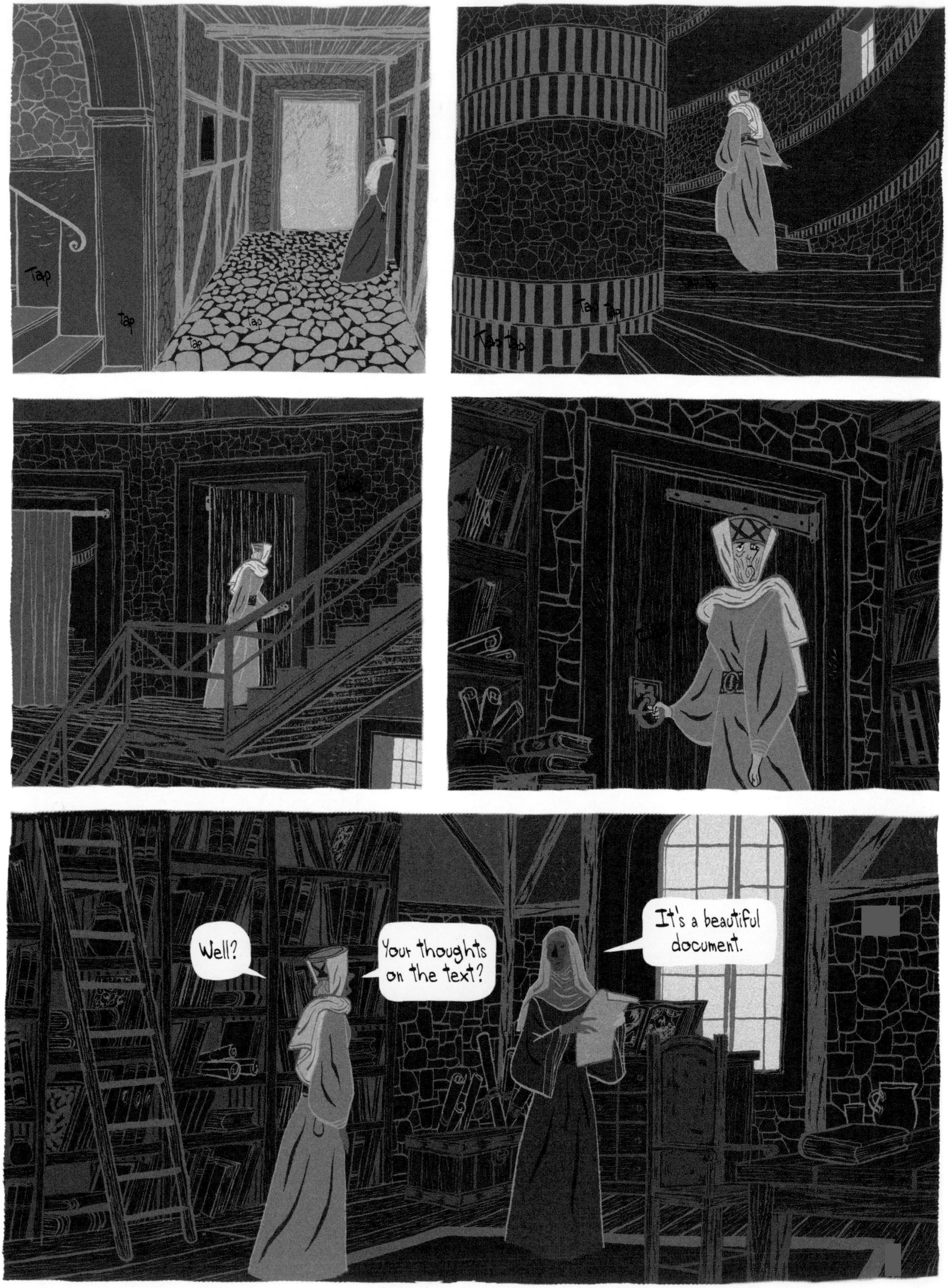
Tap
tap
tap
tap
Tap Tap
Tap Tap
Tap Tap
Well?
Your thoughts on the text?
It's a beautiful document.

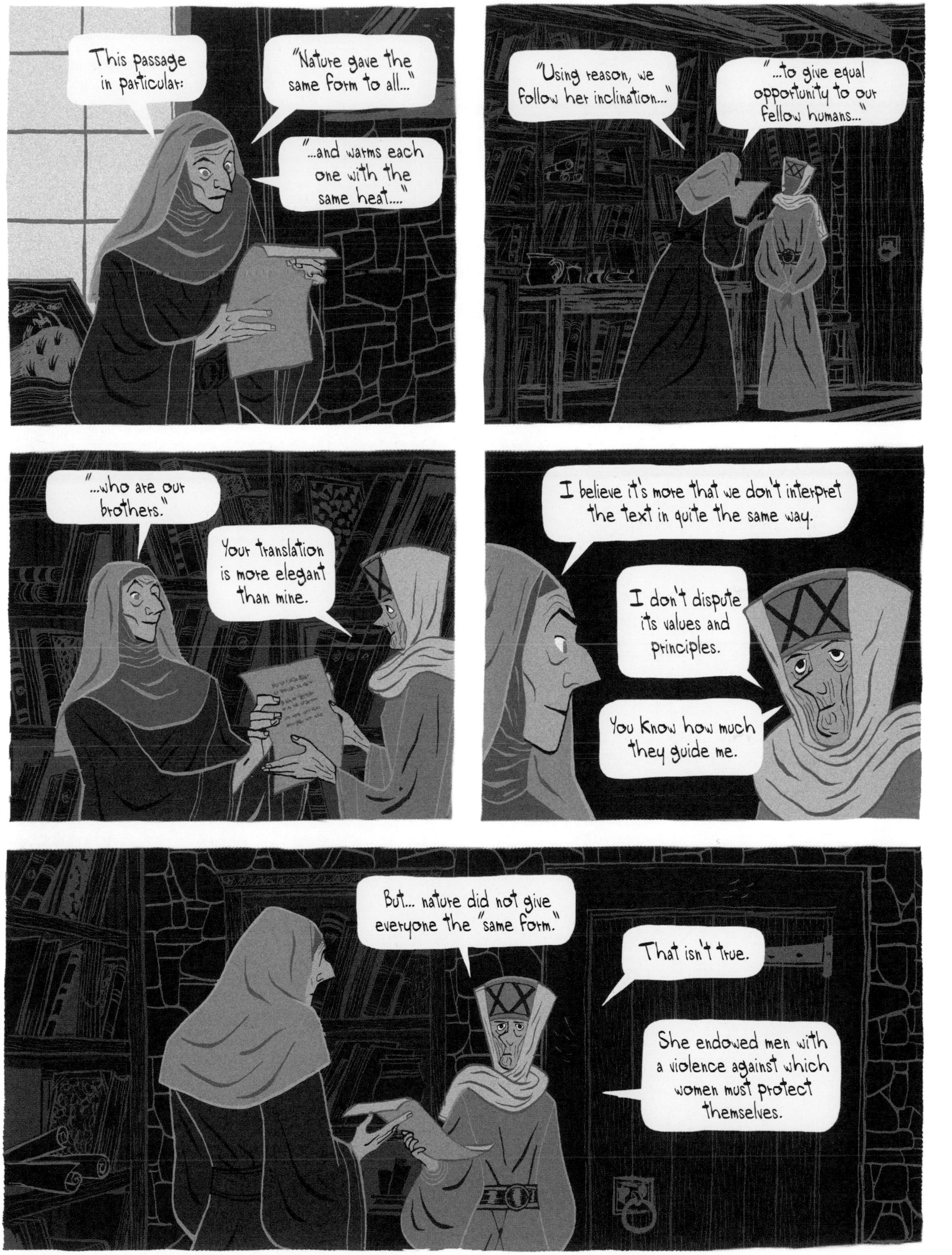
This passage in particular:
"Nature gave the same form to all..."
"...and warms each one with the same heat...."
"Using reason, we follow her inclination..."
"...to give equal opportunity to our fellow humans..."
"...who are our brothers."
Your translation is more elegant than mine.
I believe it's more that we don't interpret the text in quite the same way.
I don't dispute its values and principles.
You know how much they guide me.
But... nature did not give everyone the "same form."
That isn't true.
She endowed men with a violence against which women must protect themselves.

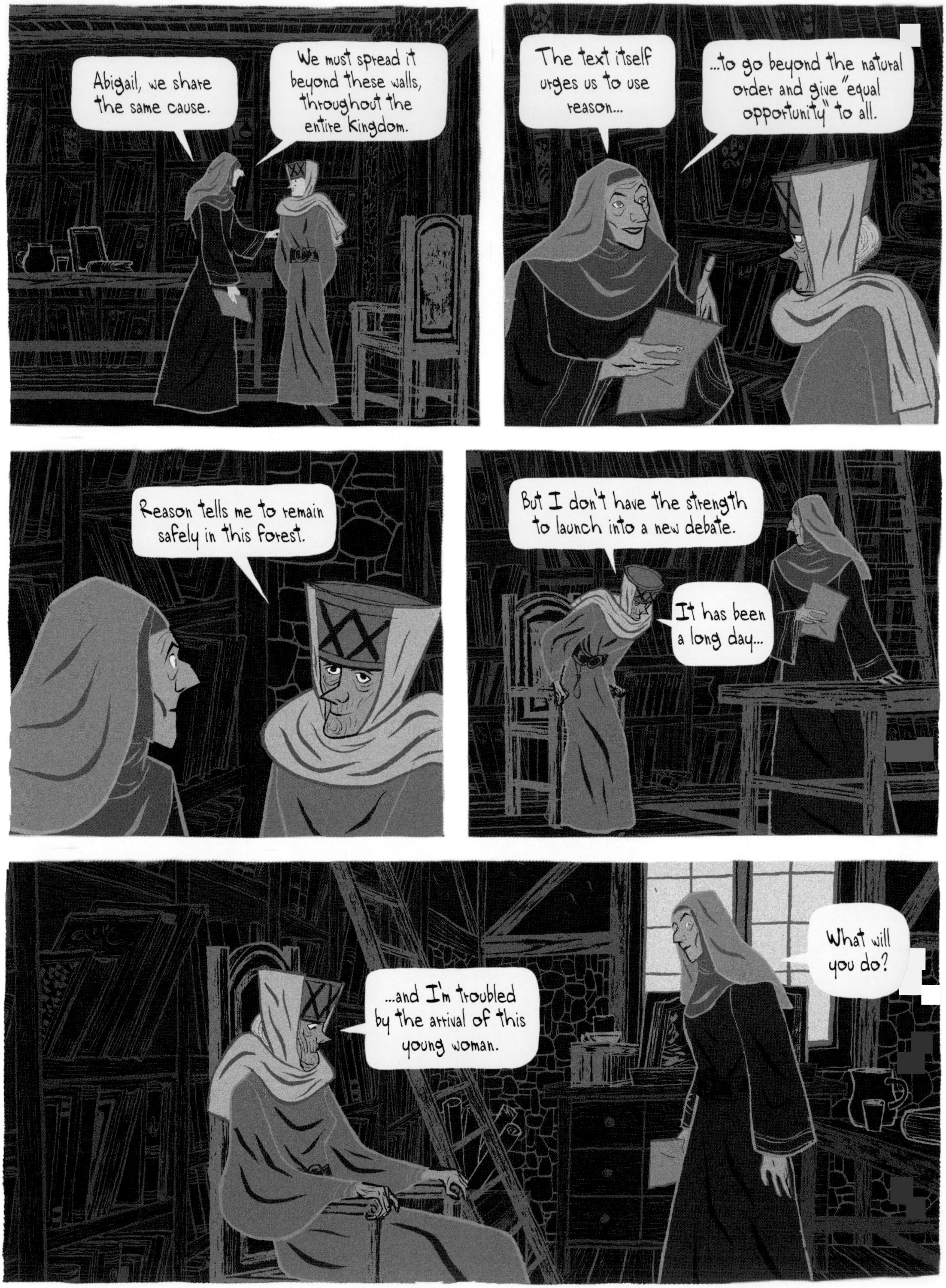
Abigail, we share the same cause.
We must spread it beyond these walls, throughout the entire Kingdom.
The text itself urges us to use reason...
...to go beyond the natural order and give "equal opportunity" to all.
Reason tells me to remain safely in this forest.
But I don't have the strength to launch into a new debate.
It has been a long day...
...and I'm troubled by the arrival of this young woman.
What will you do?

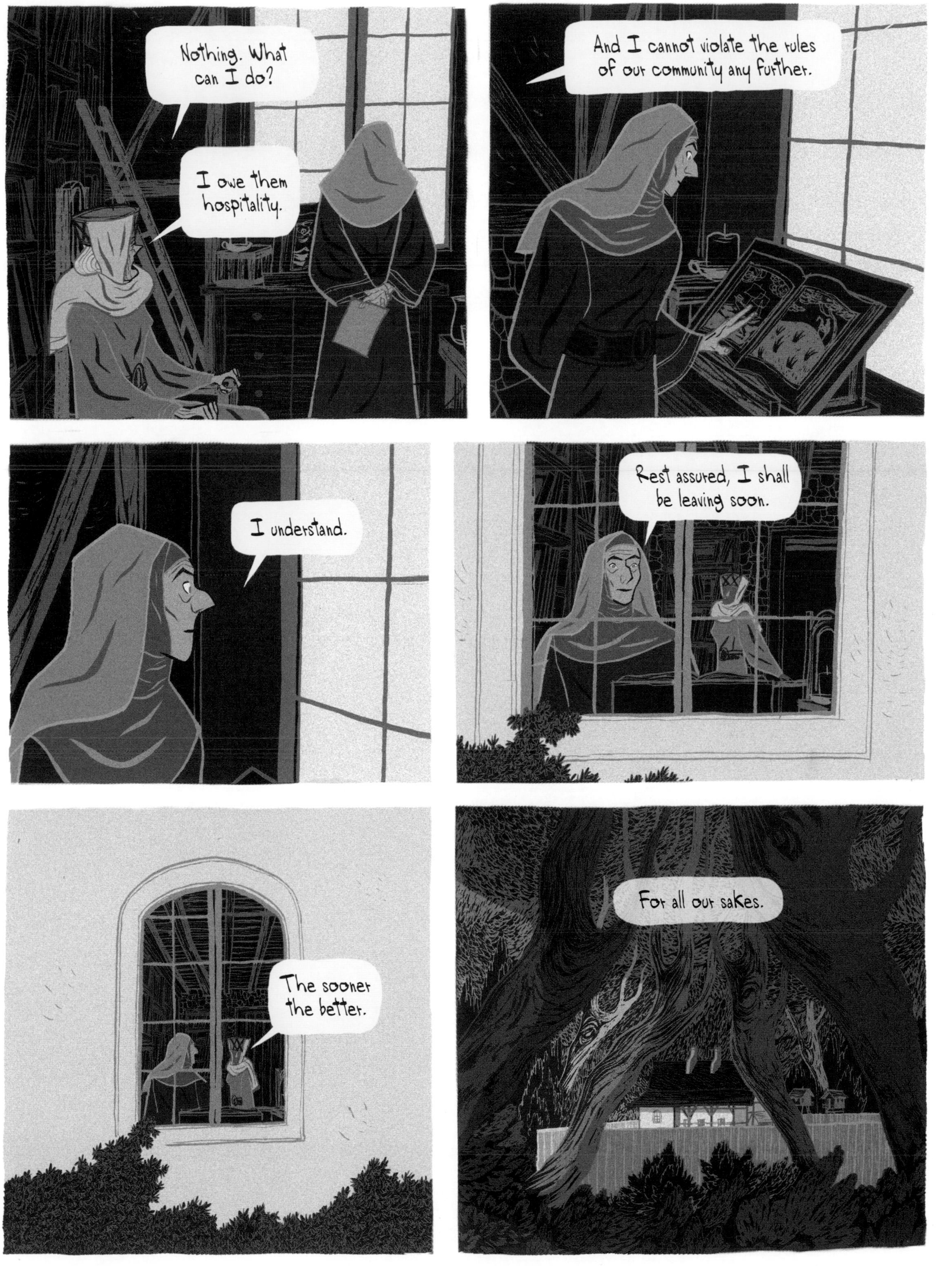
Nothing. What can I do?
I owe them hospitality.
And I cannot violate the rules of our community any further.
I understand.
Rest assured, I shall be leaving soon.
The sooner the better.
For all our sakes.

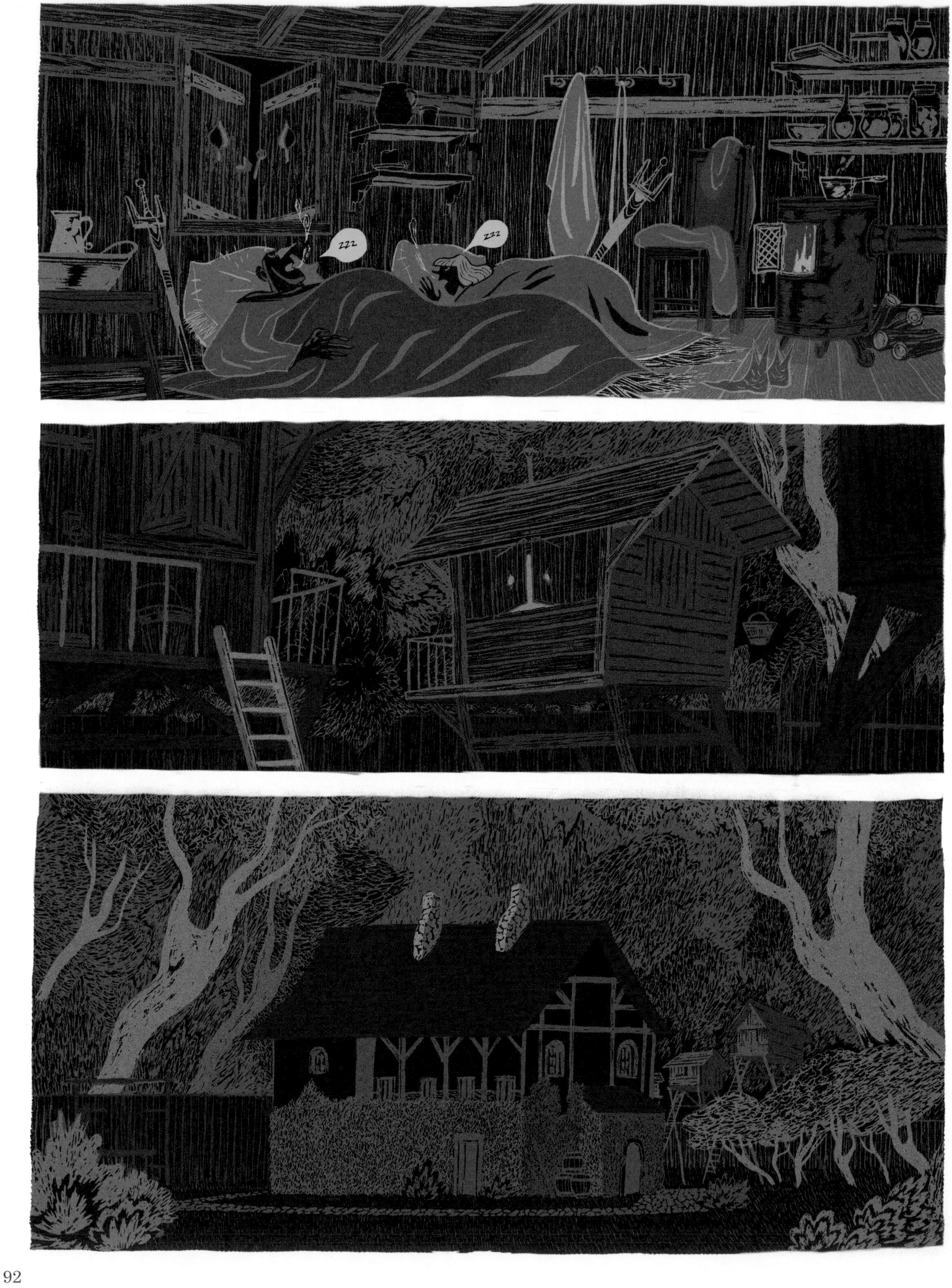
ZZZ
ZZZ

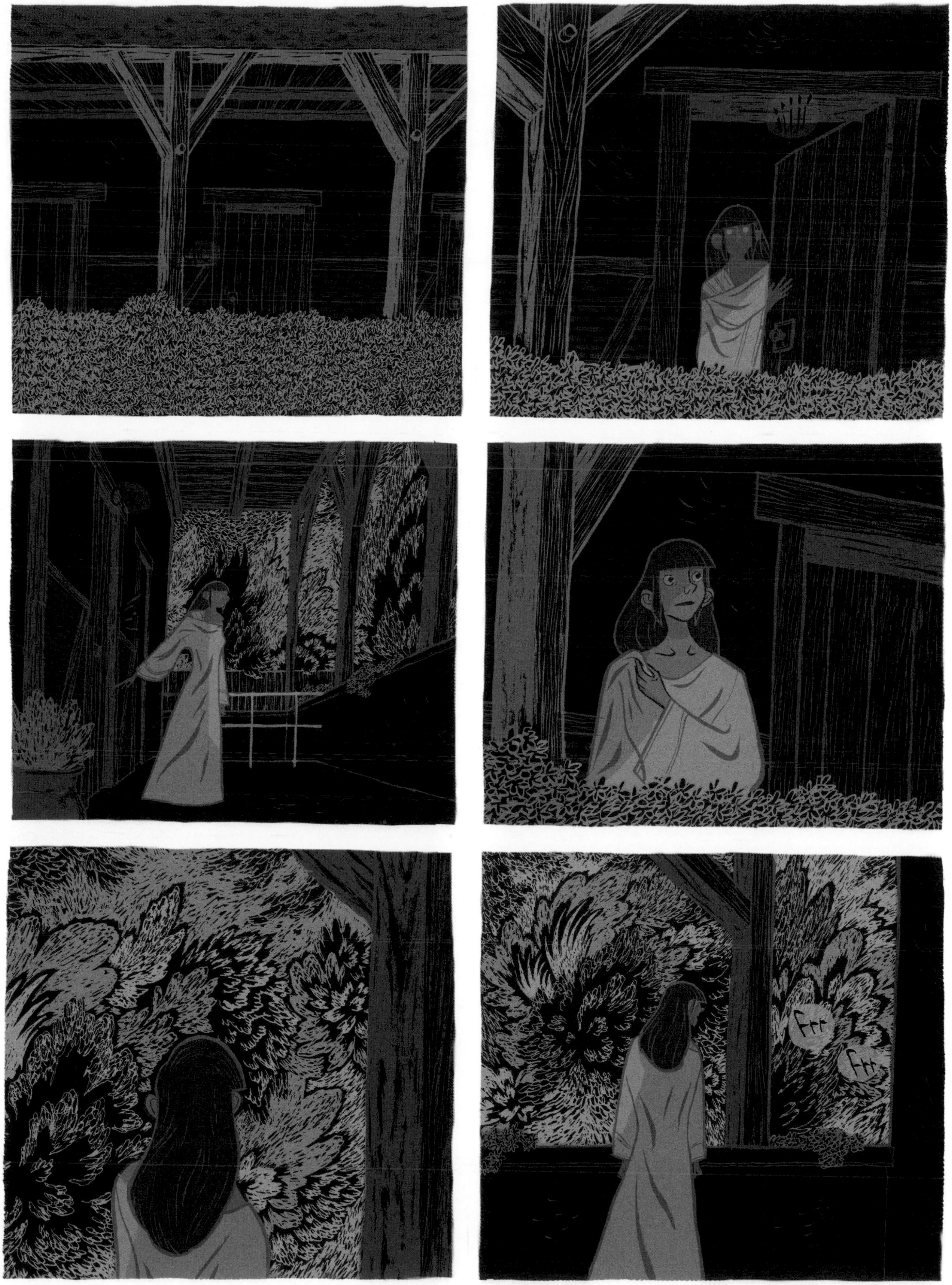
Fff
Fff

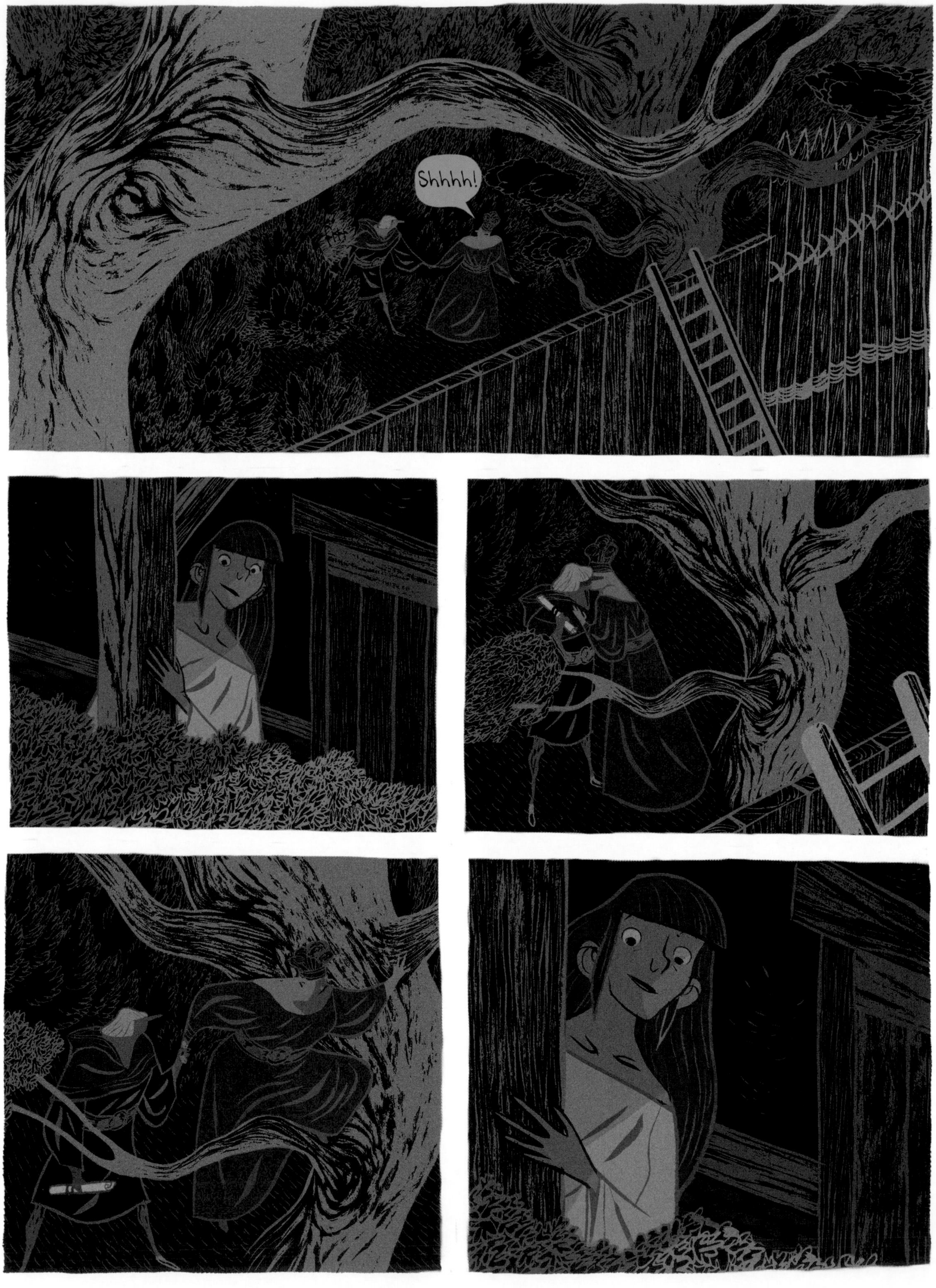
Shhhh!

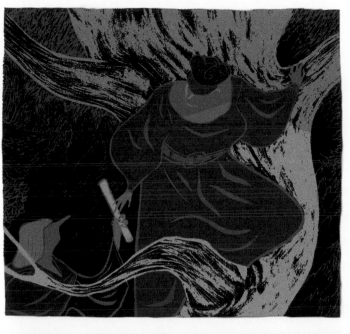

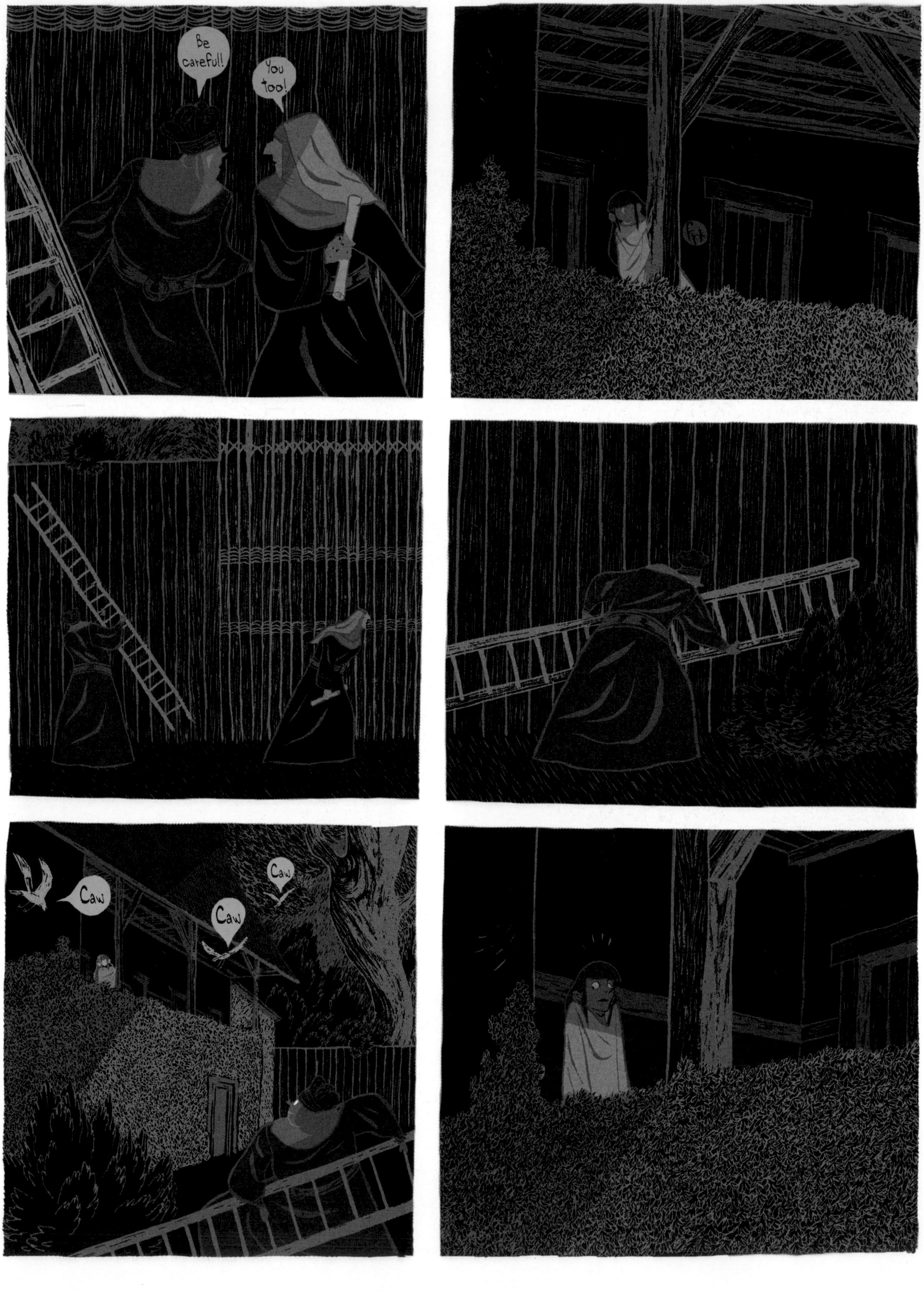
Be careful!
You too!
Caw
Caw
Caw

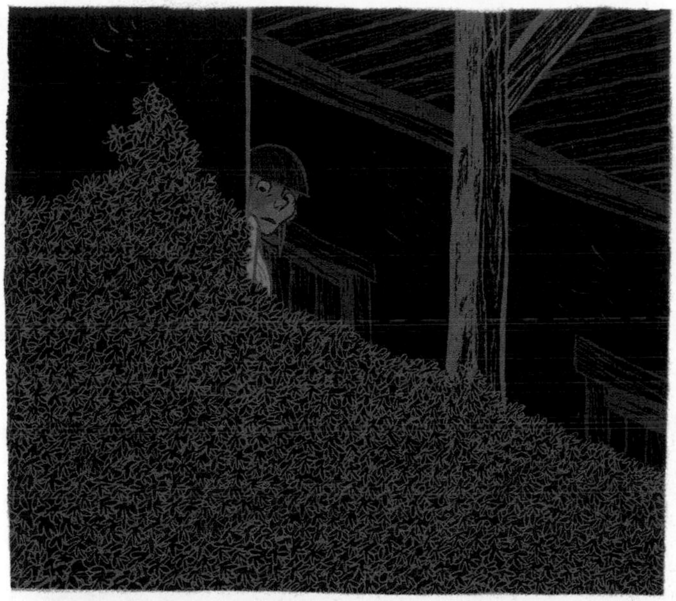

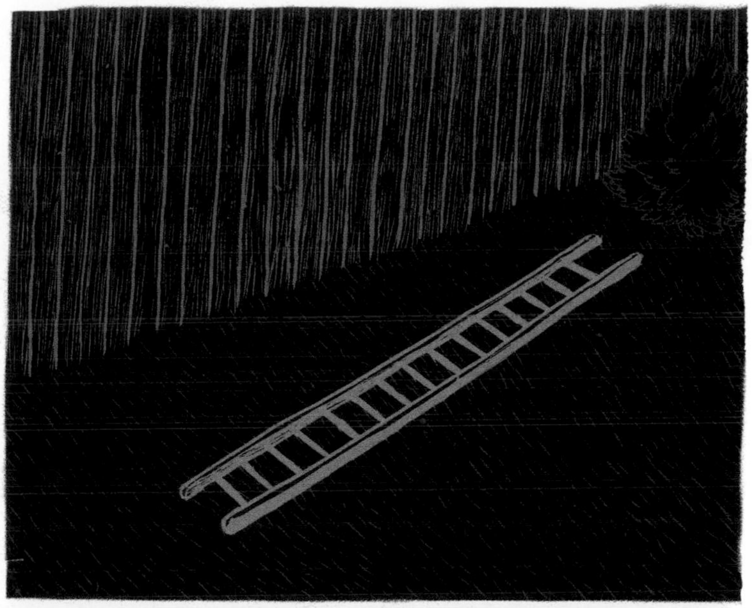

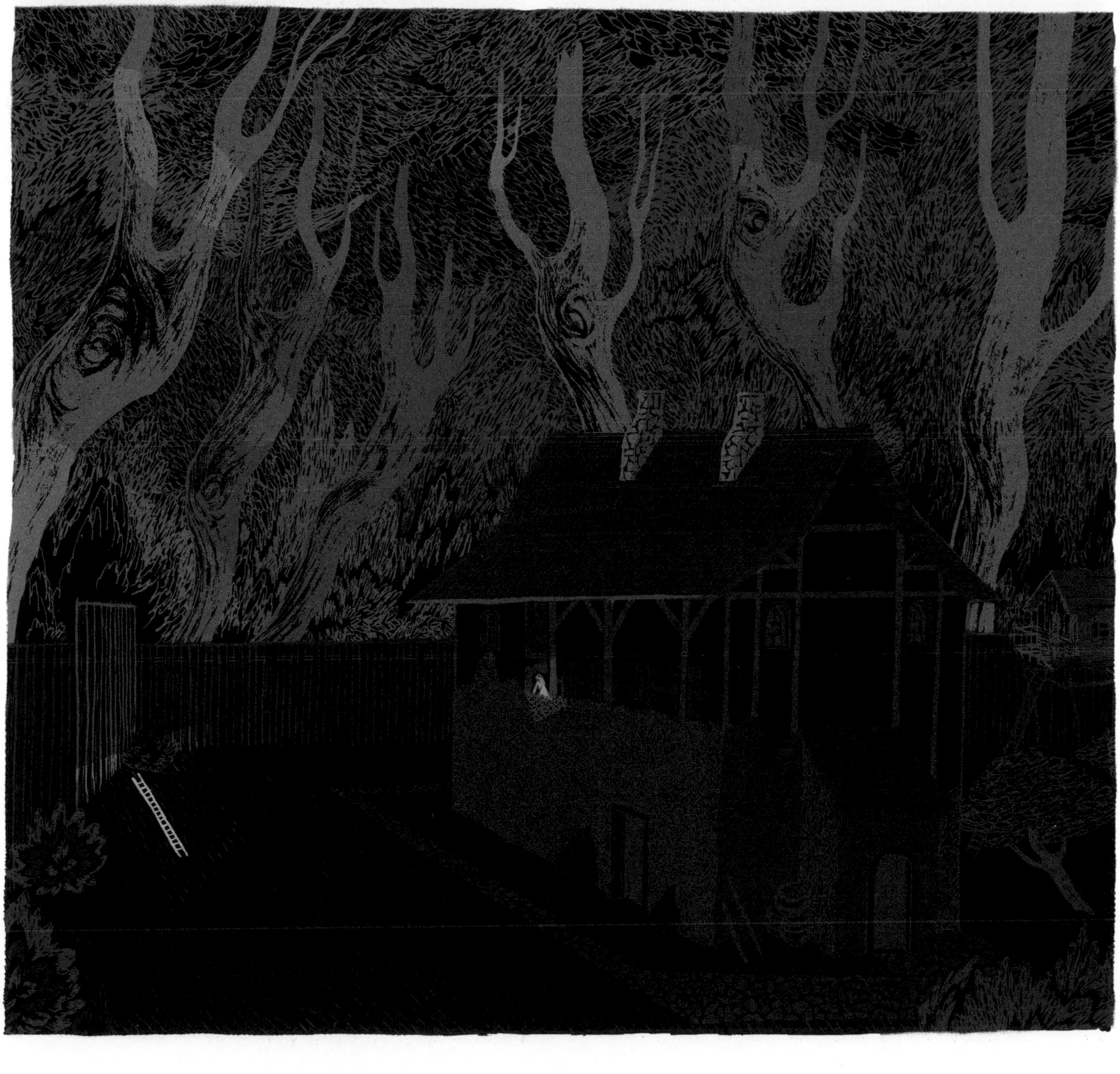

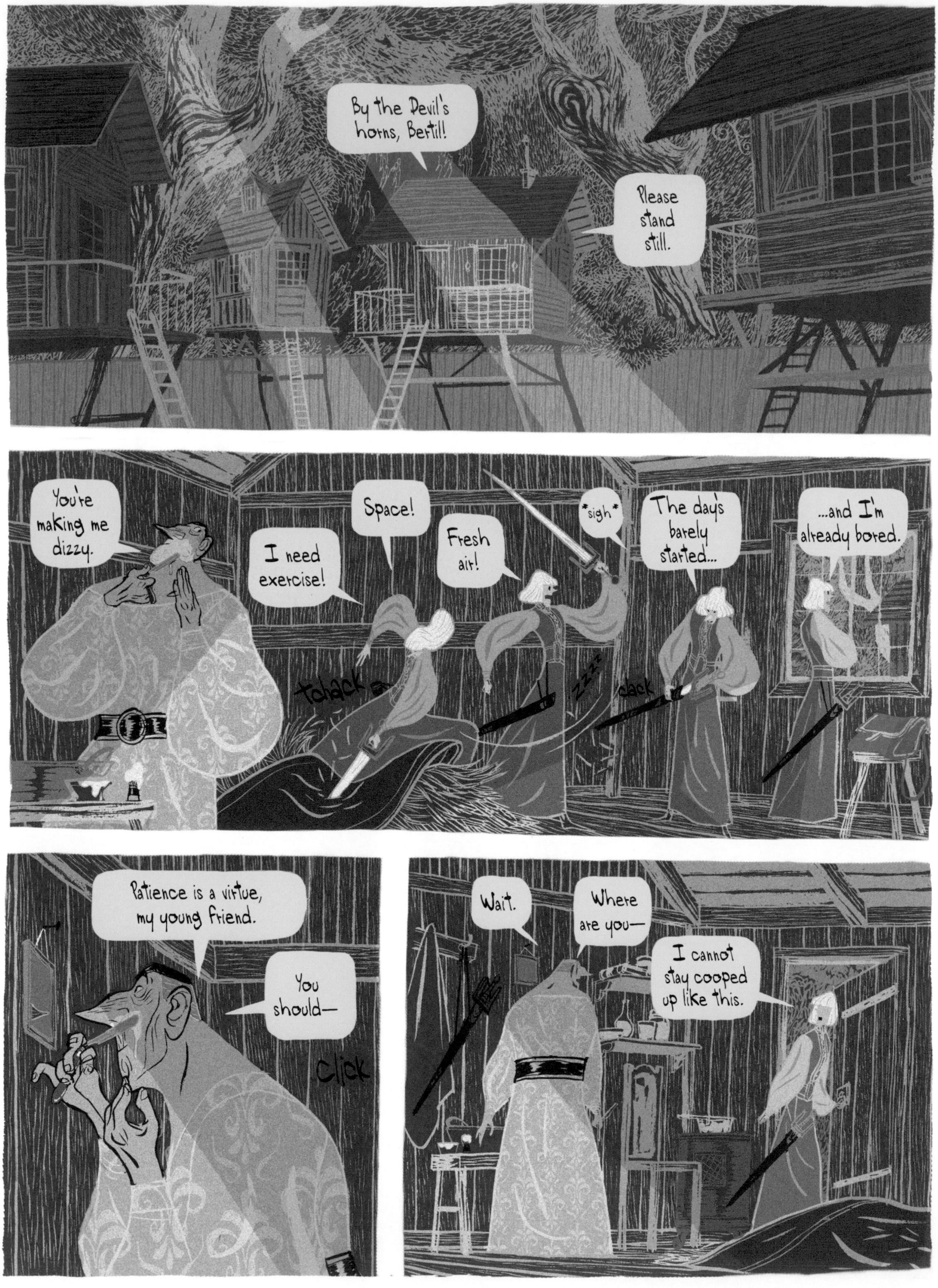
By the Devil's horns, Bertil!
Please stand still.
You're making me dizzy.
I need exercise!
Space!
Fresh air!
sigh
The day's barely started...
...and I'm already bored.
TCHACK
ZZZZ
CLACK
Patience is a virtue, my young friend.
You should—
CLICK
Wait.
Where are you—
I cannot stay cooped up like this.

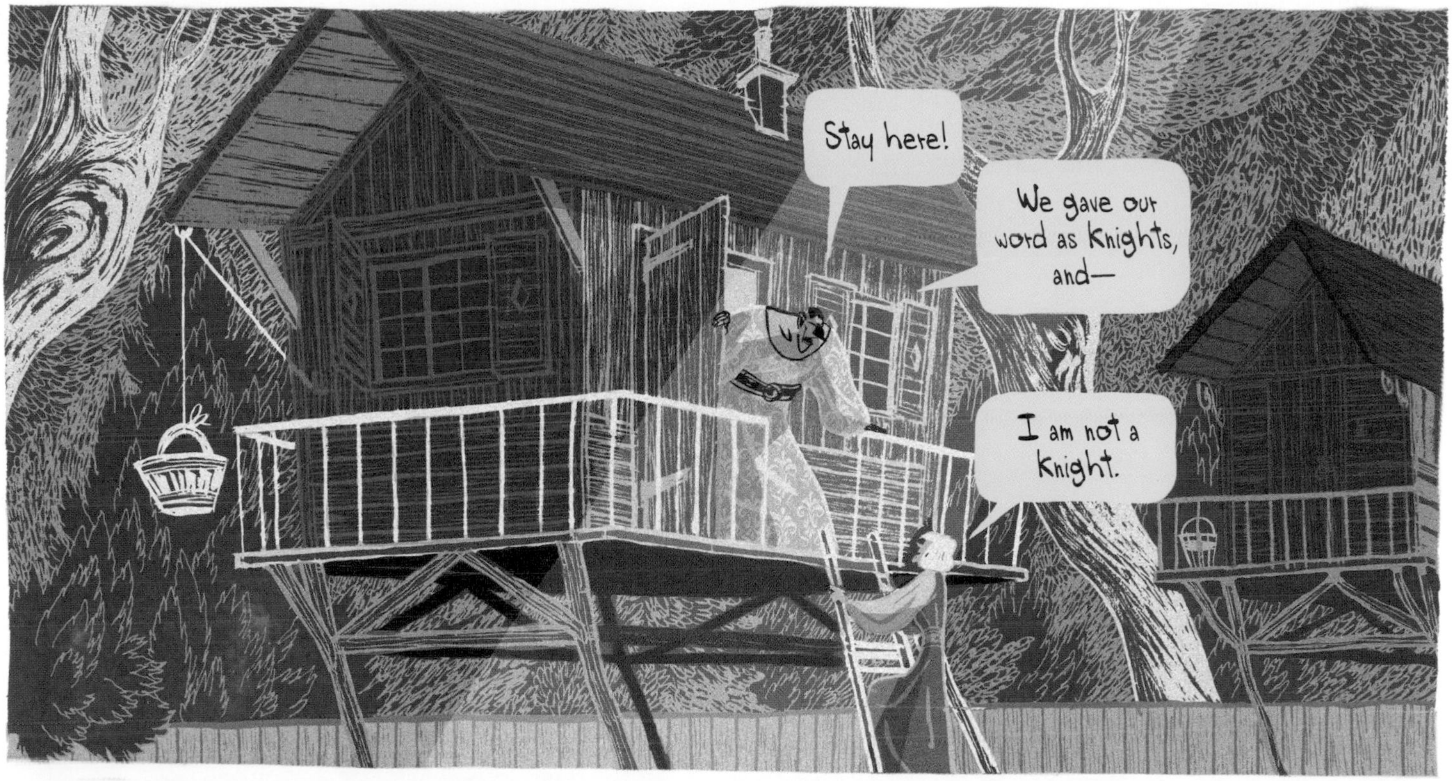
Stay here!
We gave our word as Knights, and—
I am not a Knight.

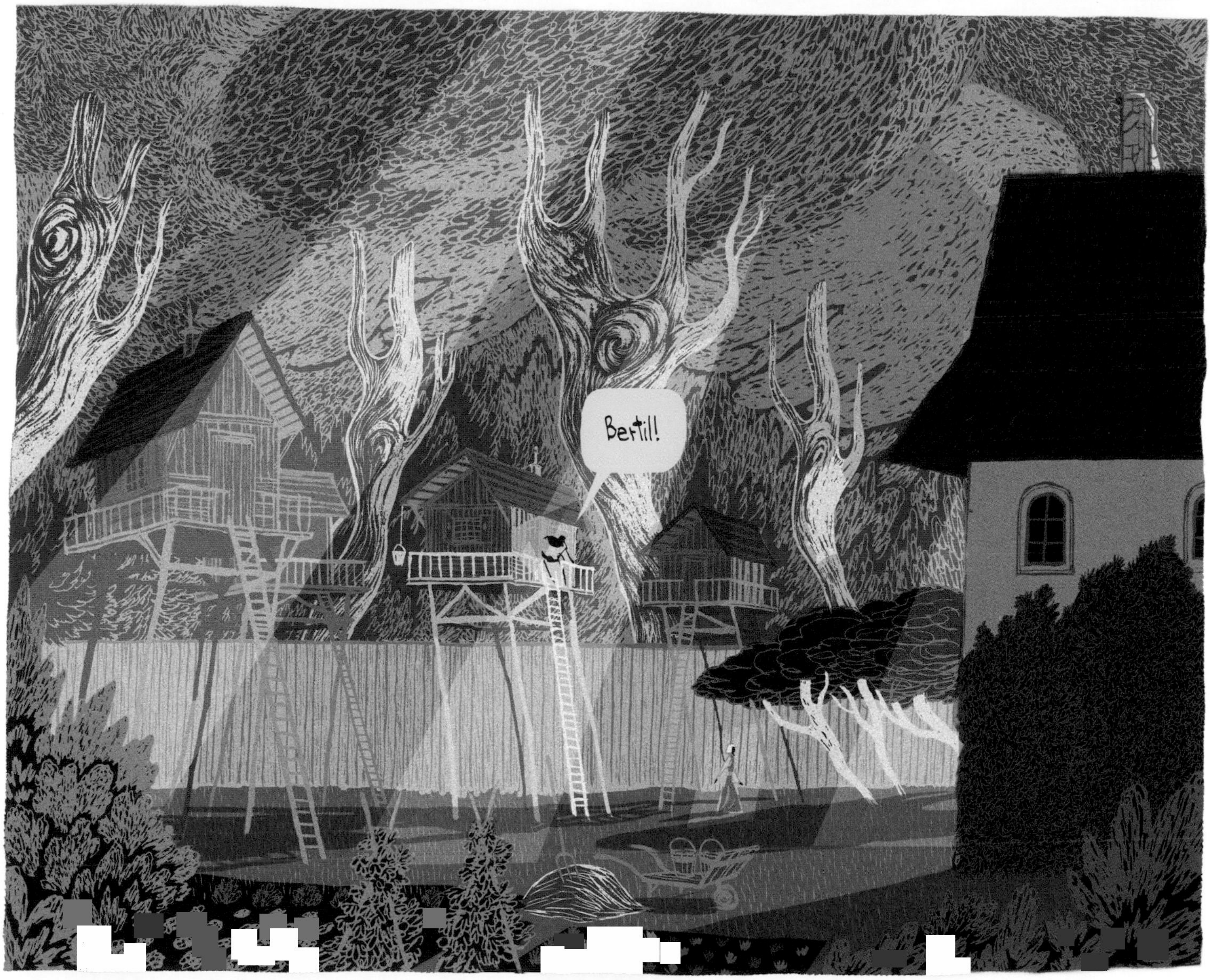
Bertil!

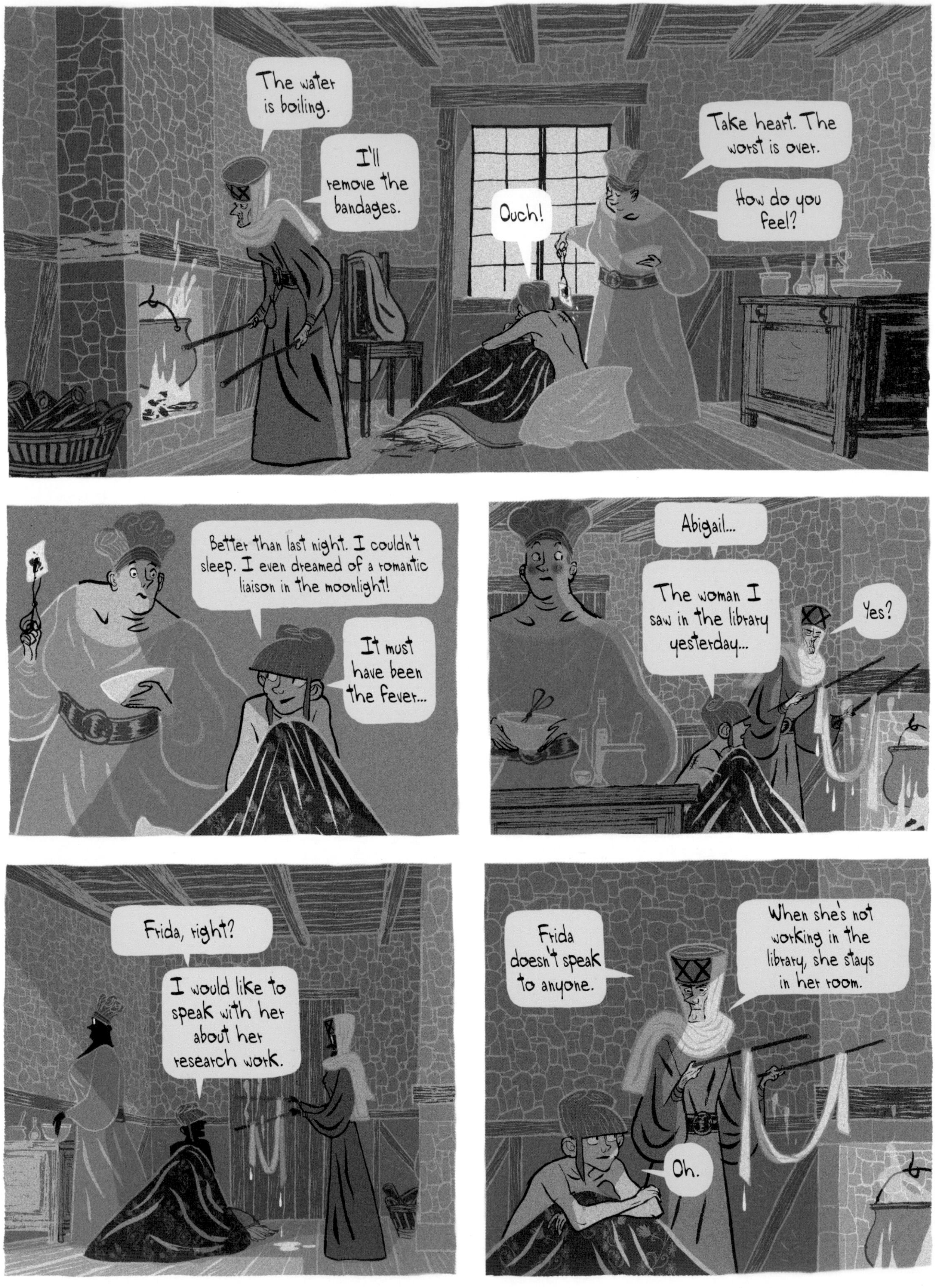

The water is boiling.
I'll remove the bandages.
Ouch!
Take heart. The worst is over.
How do you feel?
Better than last night. I couldn't sleep. I even dreamed of a romantic liaison in the moonlight!
It must have been the fever...
Abigail...
The woman I saw in the library yesterday...
Yes?
Frida, right?
I would like to speak with her about her research work.
Frida doesn't speak to anyone.
When she's not working in the library, she stays in her room.
Oh.

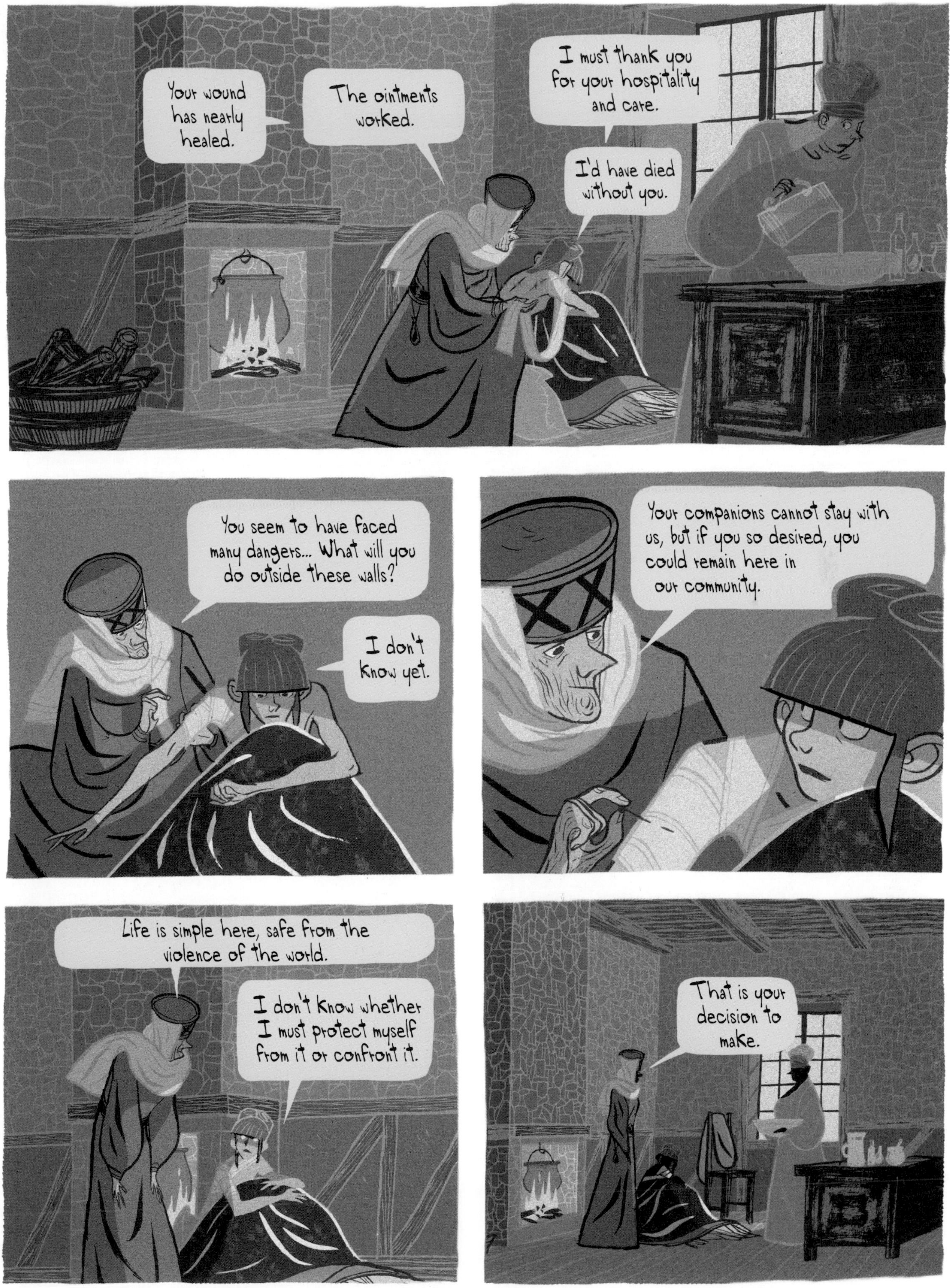

Your wound has nearly healed.
The ointments worked.
I must thank you for your hospitality and care.
I'd have died without you.
You seem to have faced many dangers... What will you do outside these walls?
I don't know yet.
Your companions cannot stay with us, but if you so desired, you could remain here in our community.
Life is simple here, safe from the violence of the world.
I don't know whether I must protect myself from it or confront it.
That is your decision to make.

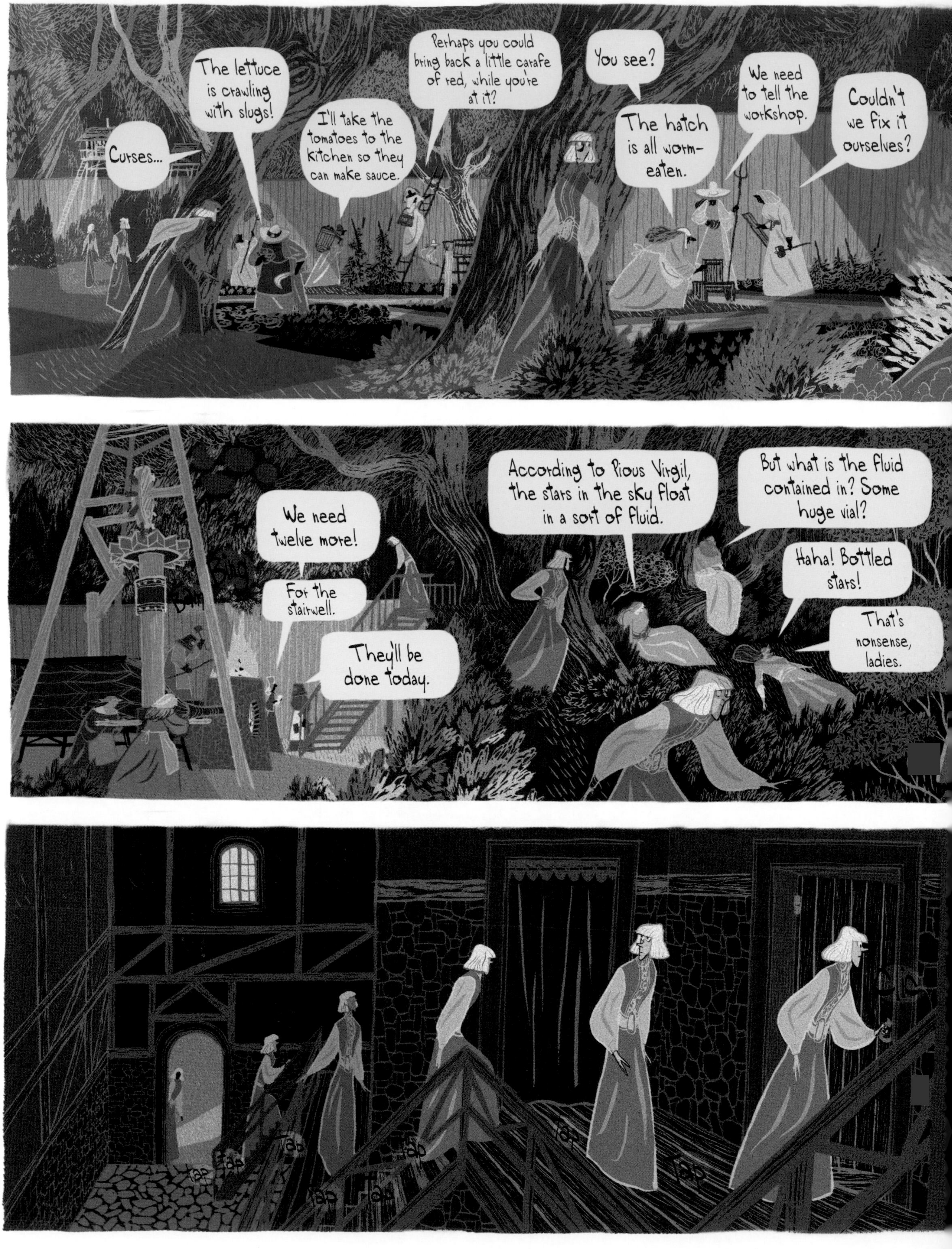

Curses...
The lettuce is crawling with slugs!
I'll take the tomatoes to the kitchen so they can make sauce.
Perhaps you could bring back a little carafe of red, while you're at it?
You see?
The hatch is all worm-eaten.
We need to tell the workshop.
Couldn't we fix it ourselves?
We need twelve more!
For the stairwell.
They'll be done today.
According to Pious Virgil, the stars in the sky float in a sort of fluid.
But what is the fluid contained in? Some huge vial?
Haha! Bottled stars!
That's nonsense, ladies.
tap tap tap tap tap tap tap tap

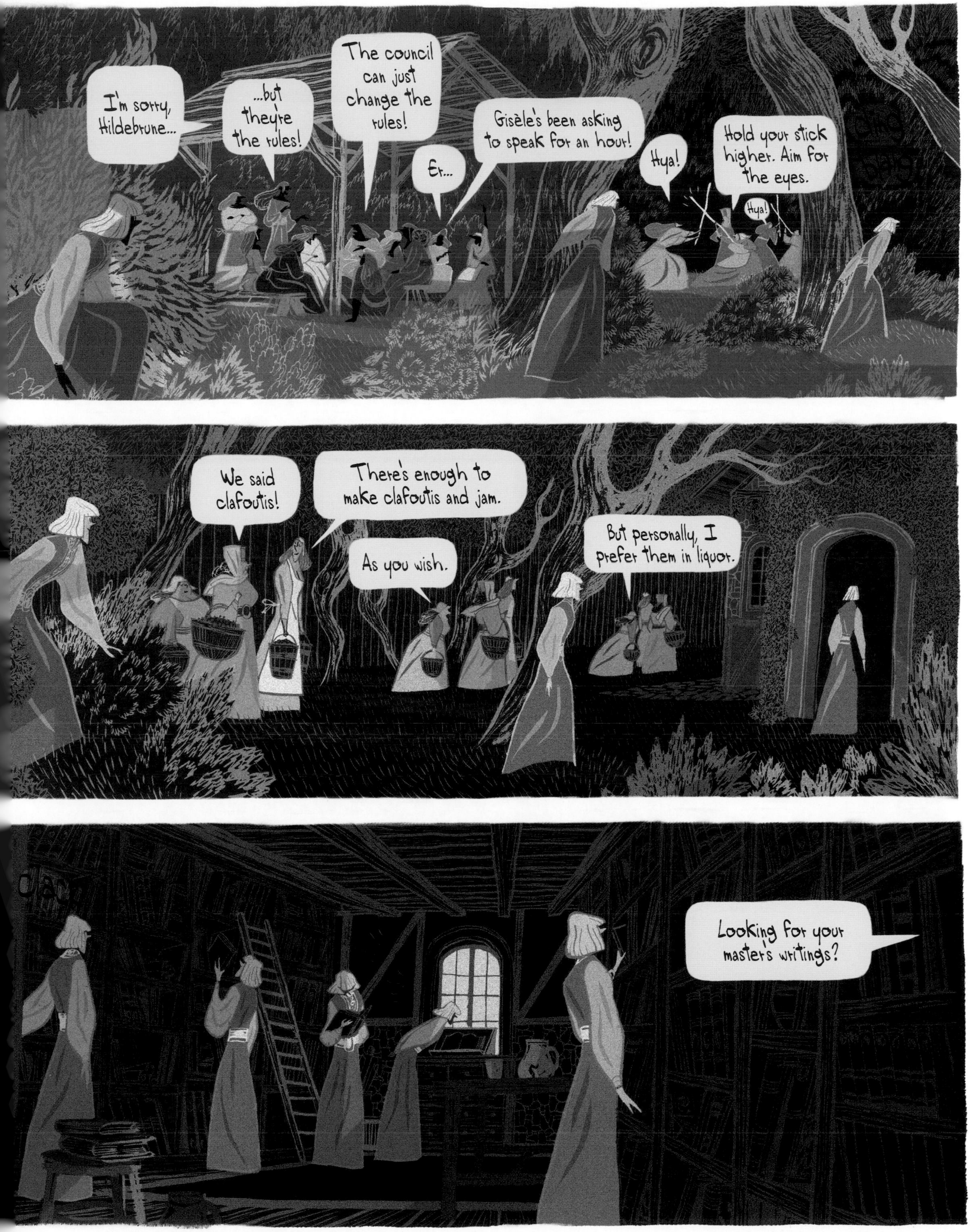
I'm sorry, Hildebrune...
...but they're the rules!
The council can just change the rules!
Er...
Gisèle's been asking to speak for an hour!
Hya!
Hold your stick higher. Aim for the eyes.
Hya!
We said clafoutis!
There's enough to make clafoutis and jam.
As you wish.
But personally, I prefer them in liquor.
Looking for your master's writings?

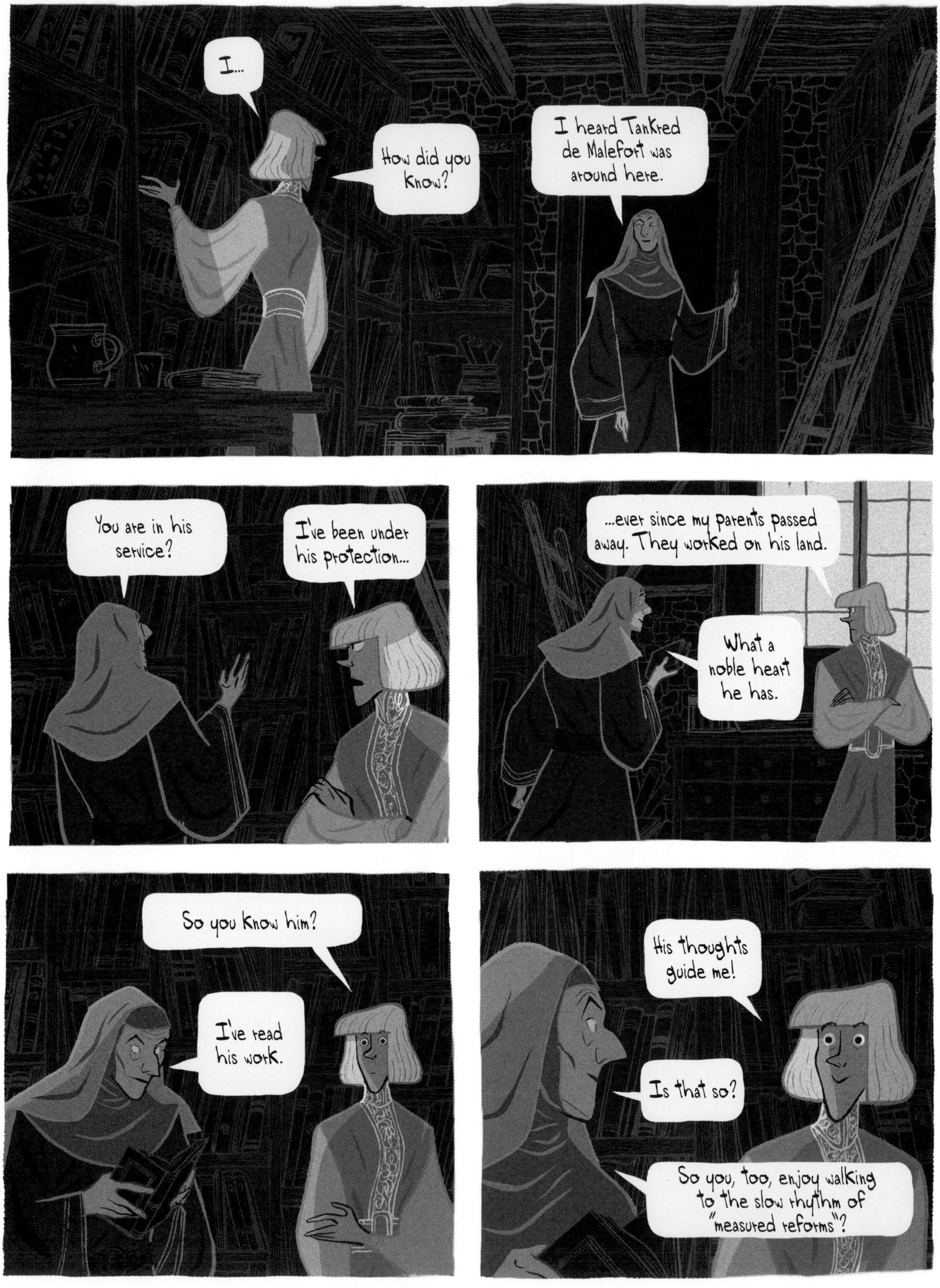

I...
How did you know?
I heard Tankred de Malefort was around here.
You are in his service?
I've been under his protection...
...ever since my parents passed away. They worked on his land.
What a noble heart he has.
So you know him?
I've read his work.
His thoughts guide me!
Is that so?
So you, too, enjoy walking to the slow rhythm of "measured reforms"?

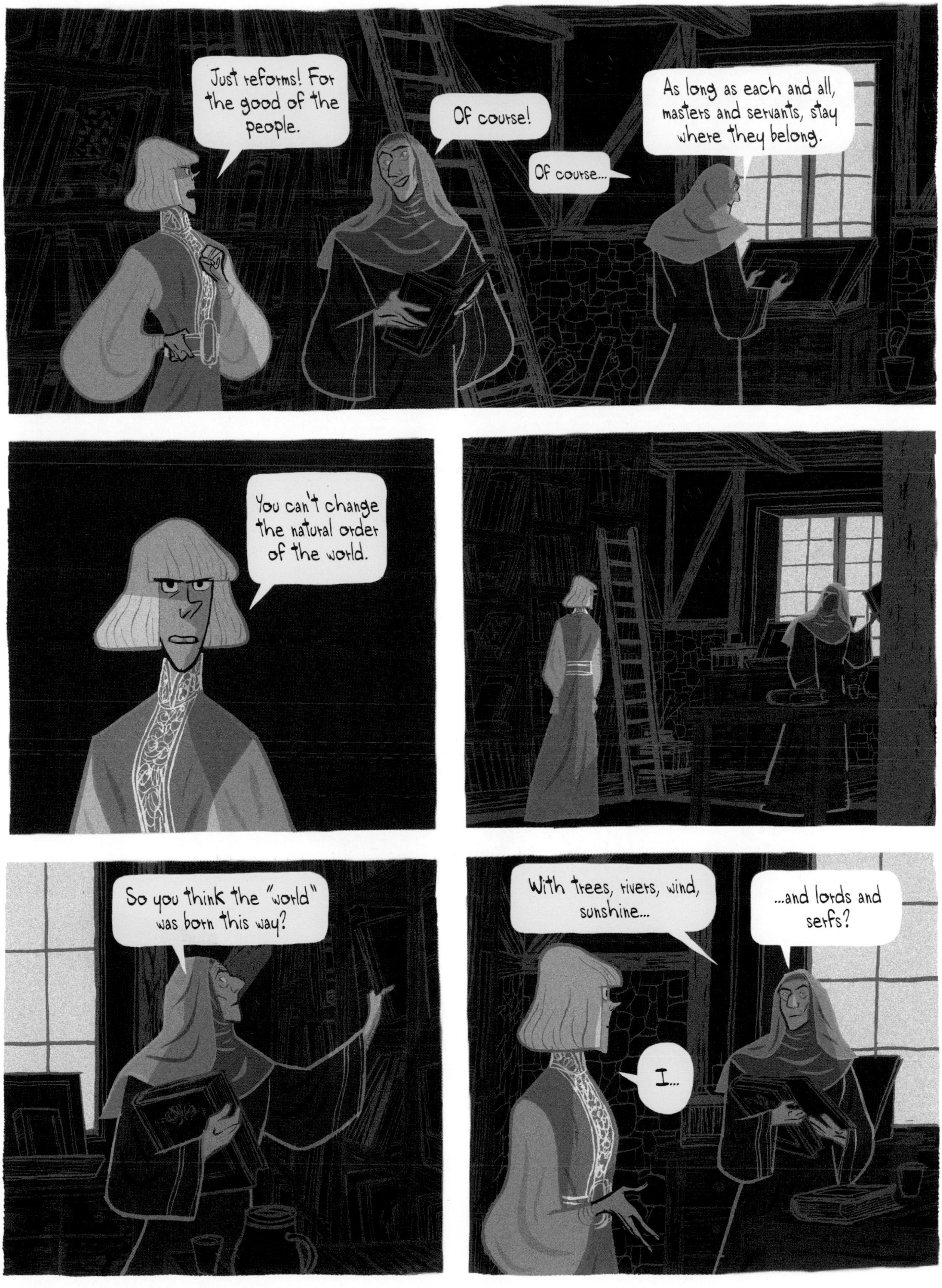
Just reforms! For the good of the people.
Of course!
Of course...
As long as each and all, masters and servants, stay where they belong.
You can't change the natural order of the world.
So you think the "world" was born this way?
With trees, rivers, wind, sunshine...
...and lords and serfs?
I...

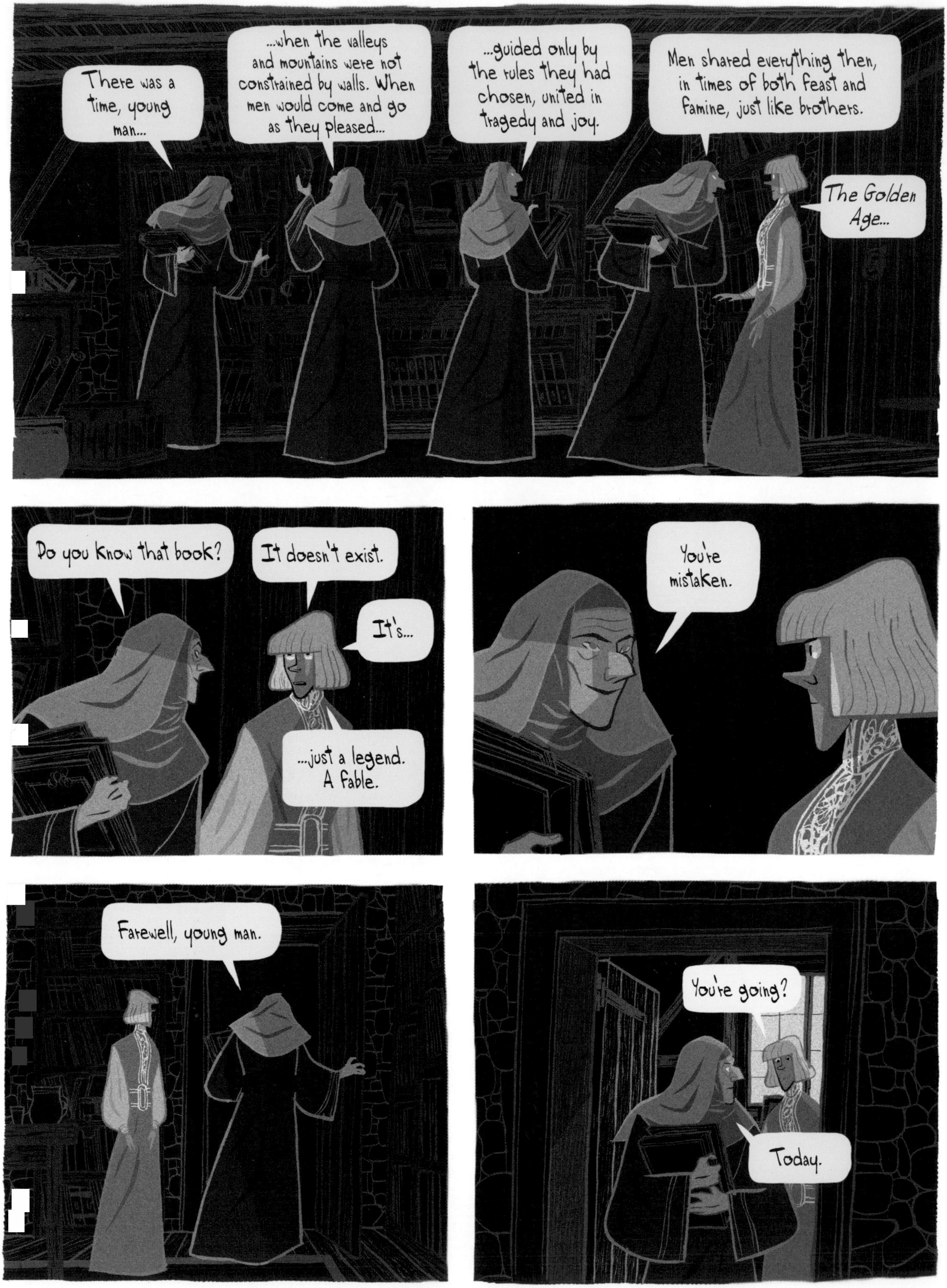
There was a time, young man...
...when the valleys and mountains were not constrained by walls. When men would come and go as they pleased...
...guided only by the rules they had chosen, united in tragedy and joy.
Men shared everything then, in times of both feast and famine, just like brothers.
The Golden Age...
Do you know that book?
It doesn't exist.
It's...
...just a legend. A fable.
You're mistaken.
Farewell, young man.
You're going?
Today.

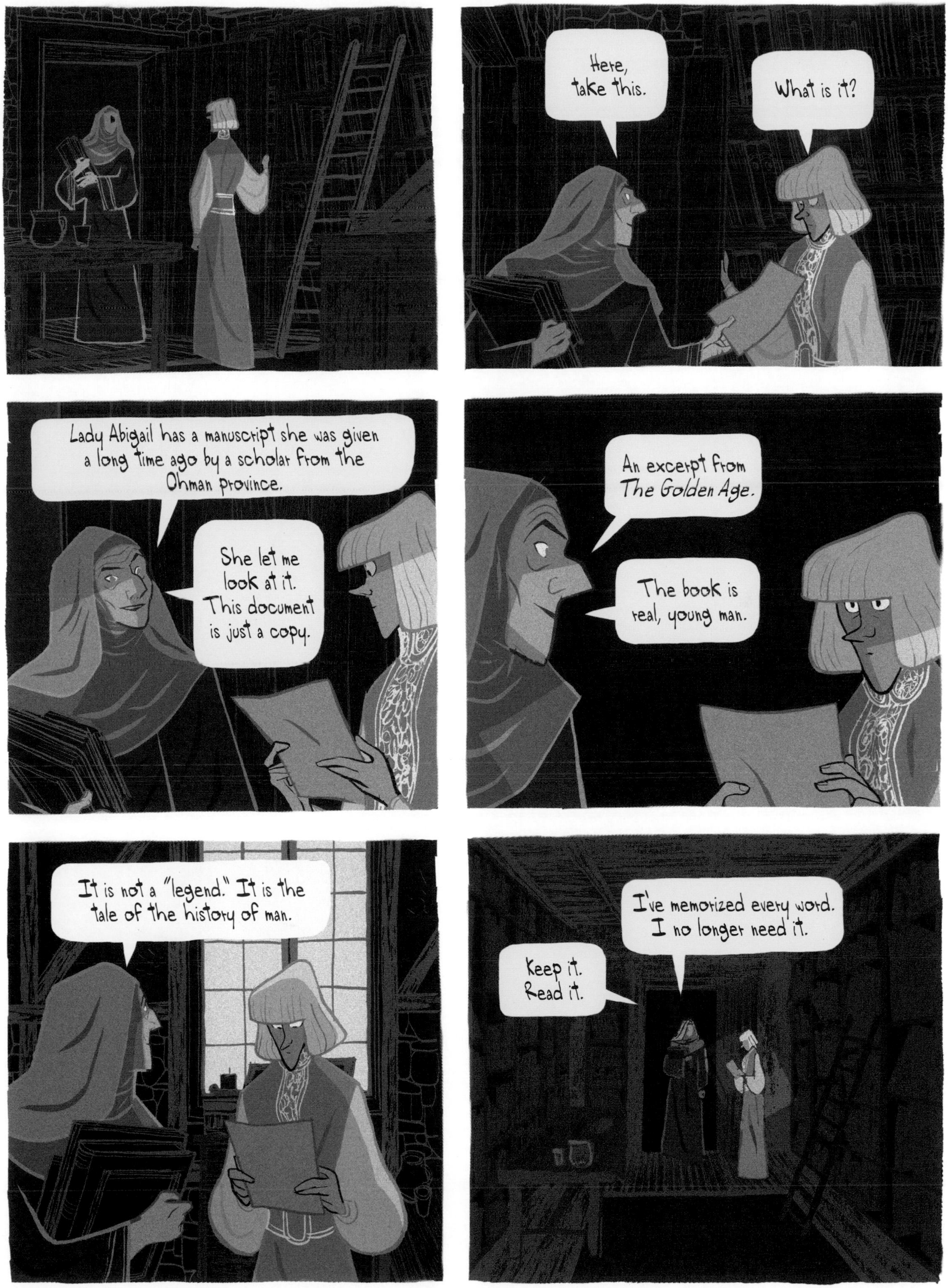
Here, take this.
What is it?
Lady Abigail has a manuscript she was given a long time ago by a scholar from the Ohman province.
She let me look at it. This document is just a copy.
An excerpt from The Golden Age.
The book is real, young man.
It is not a "legend." It is the tale of the history of man.
I've memorized every word. I no longer need it.
Keep it. Read it.

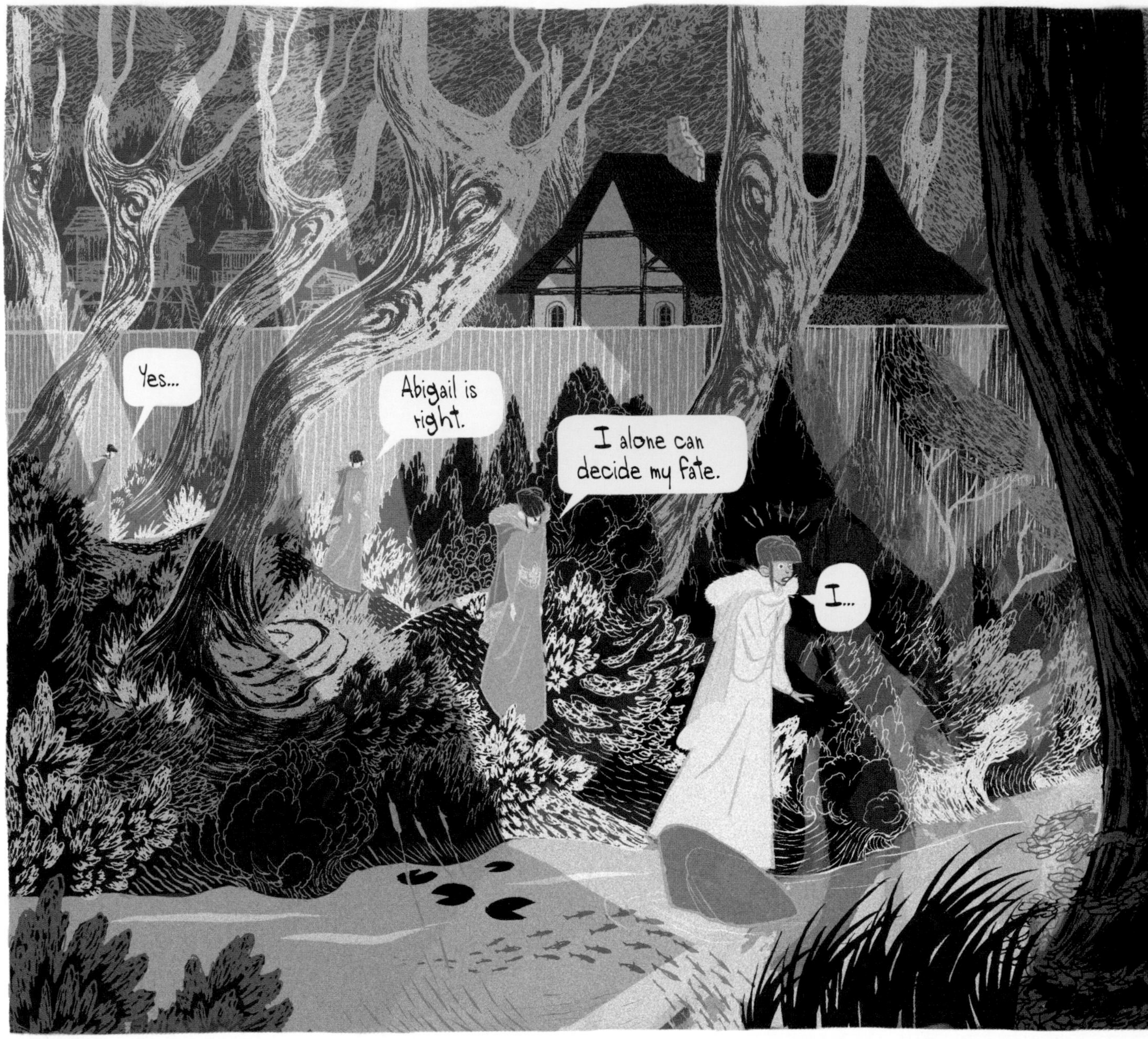
Yes...
Abigail is right.
I alone can decide my fate.
I...

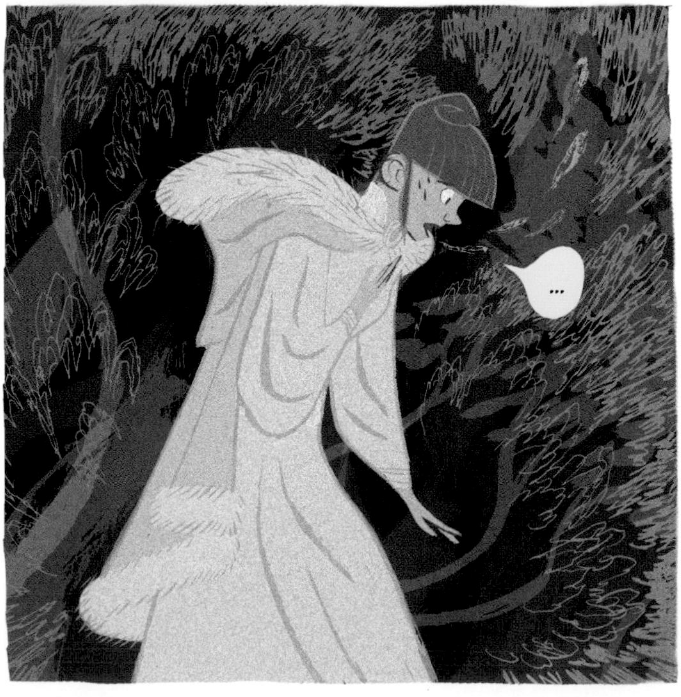
...

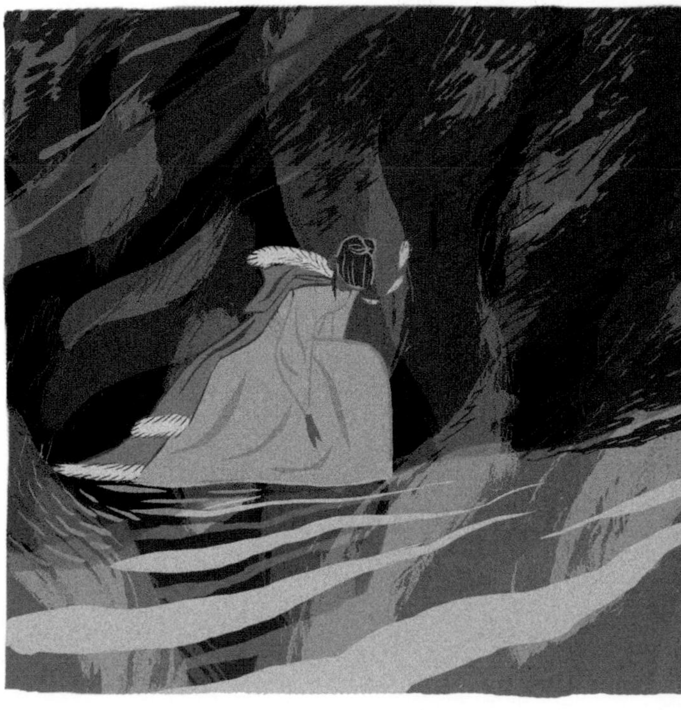

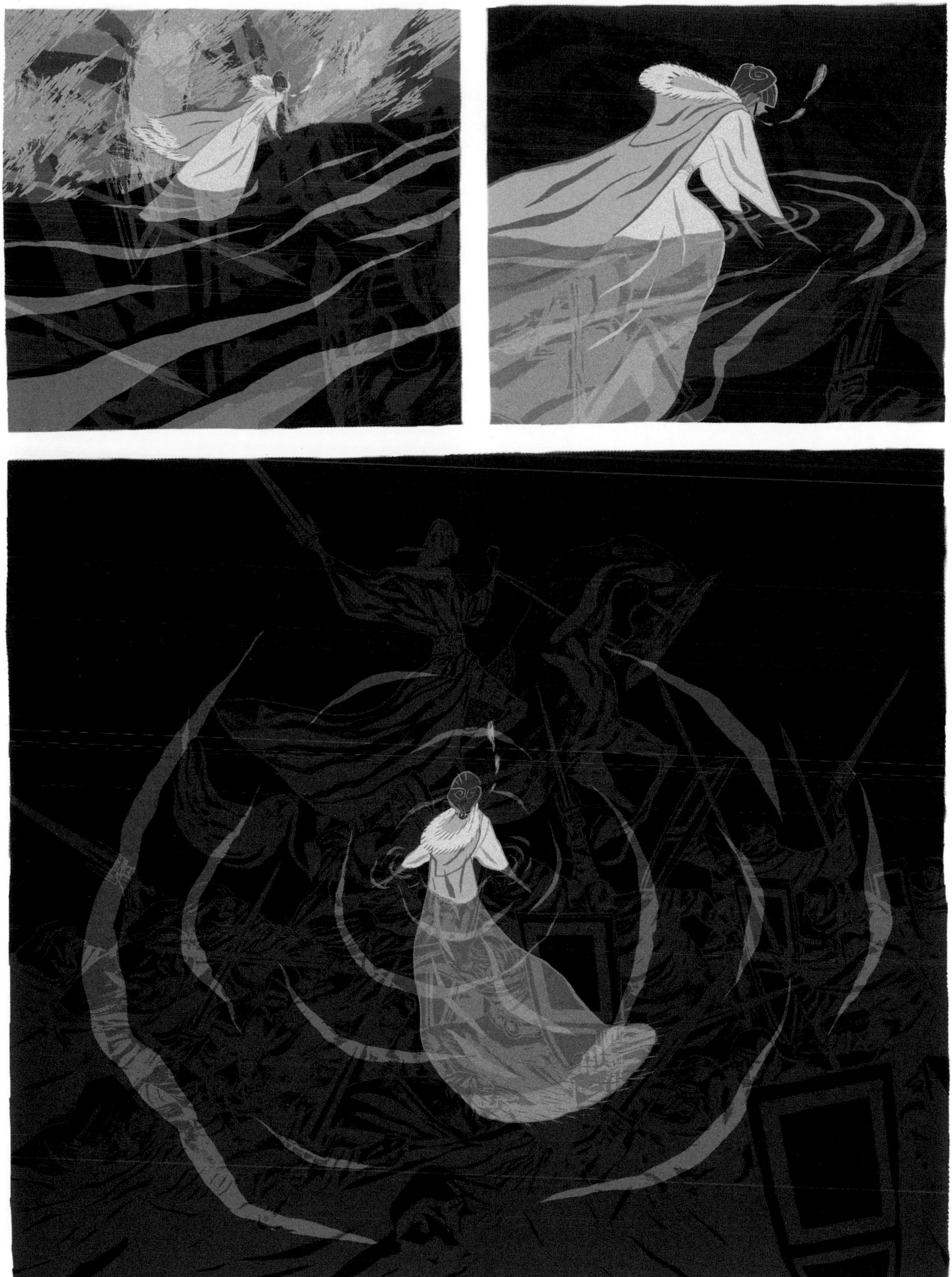

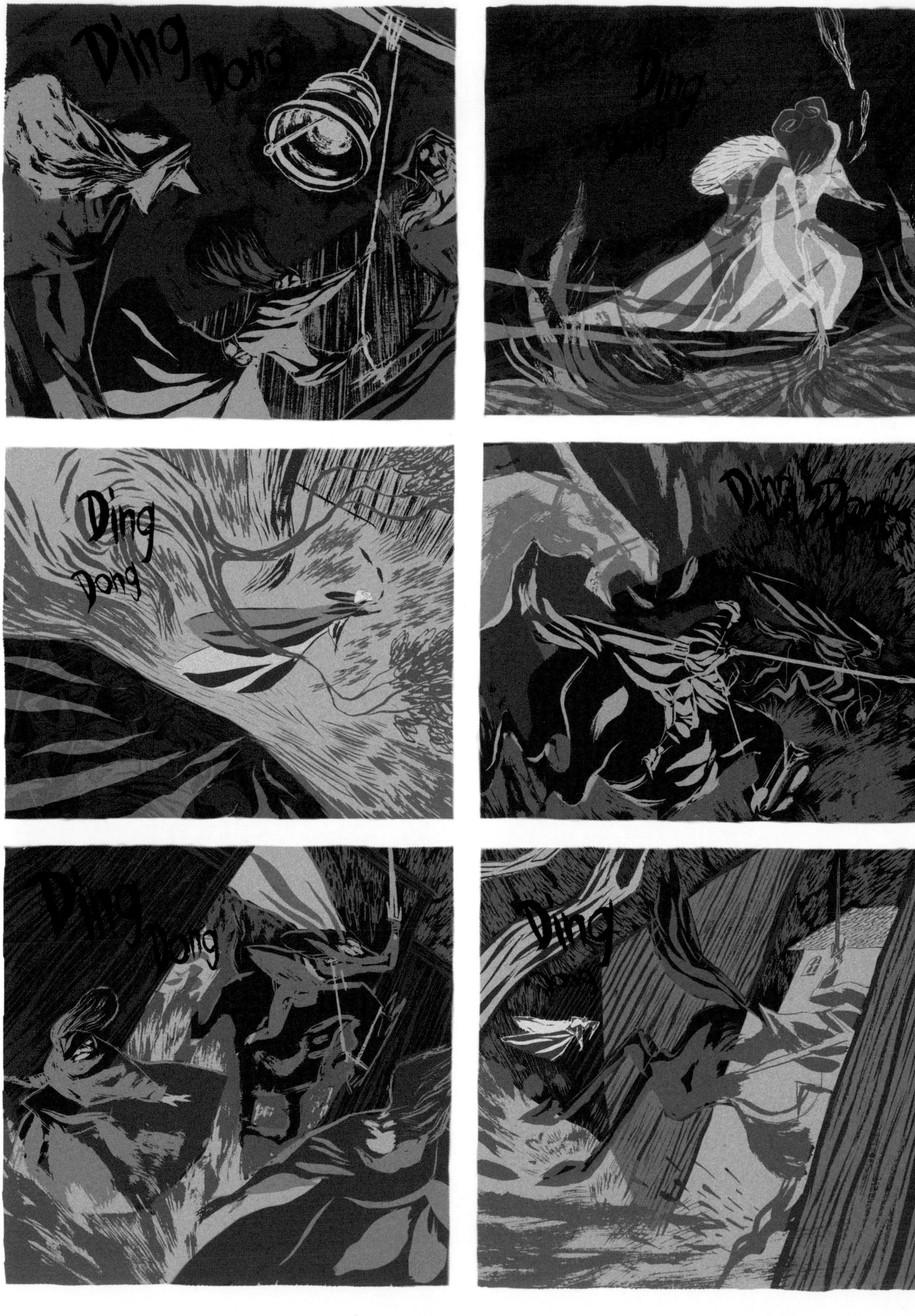
Ding Dong
Ding Dong
Ding Dong
Ding Dong
Ding Dong
Ding Dong

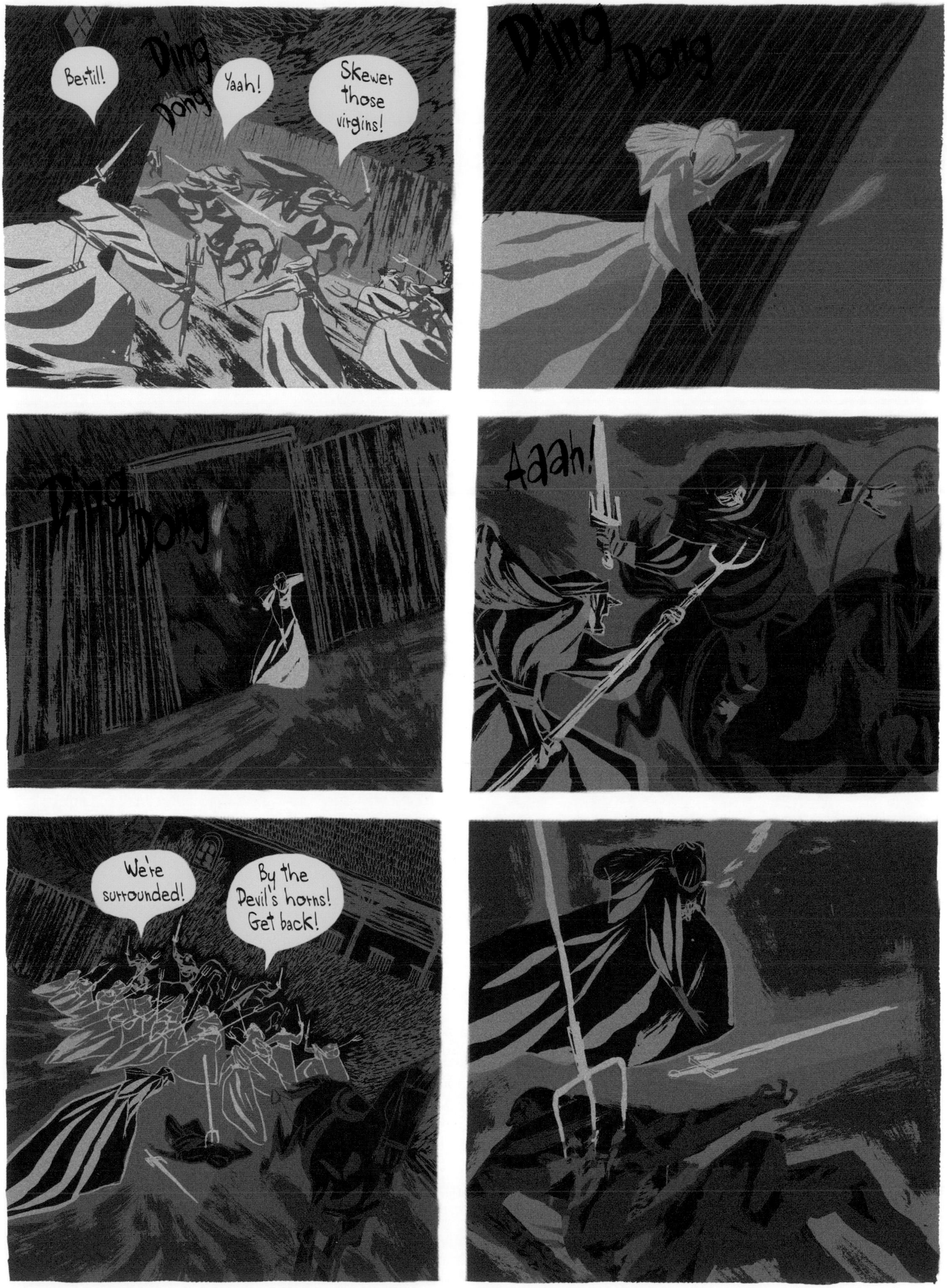
Bertil!
Ding Dong
Yaah!
Skewer those virgins!
Ding Dong
Ding Dong
Aaah!
We're surrounded!
By the Devil's horns! Get back!

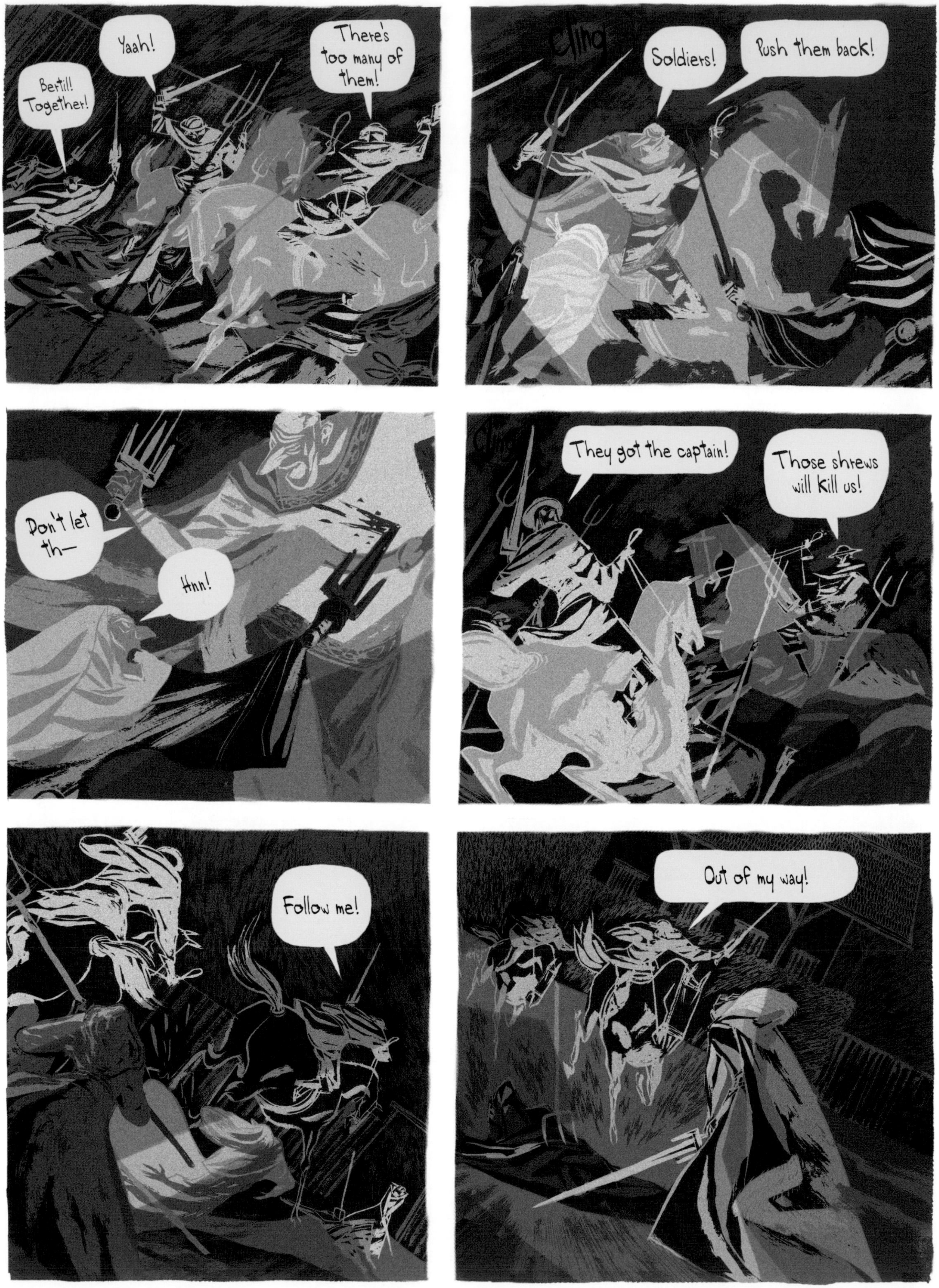
Bertil! Together!
Yaah!
There's too many of them!
Cling
Soldiers!
Push them back!
Don't let th—
Hnn!
Cling
They got the captain!
Those shrews will kill us!
Follow me!
Out of my way!

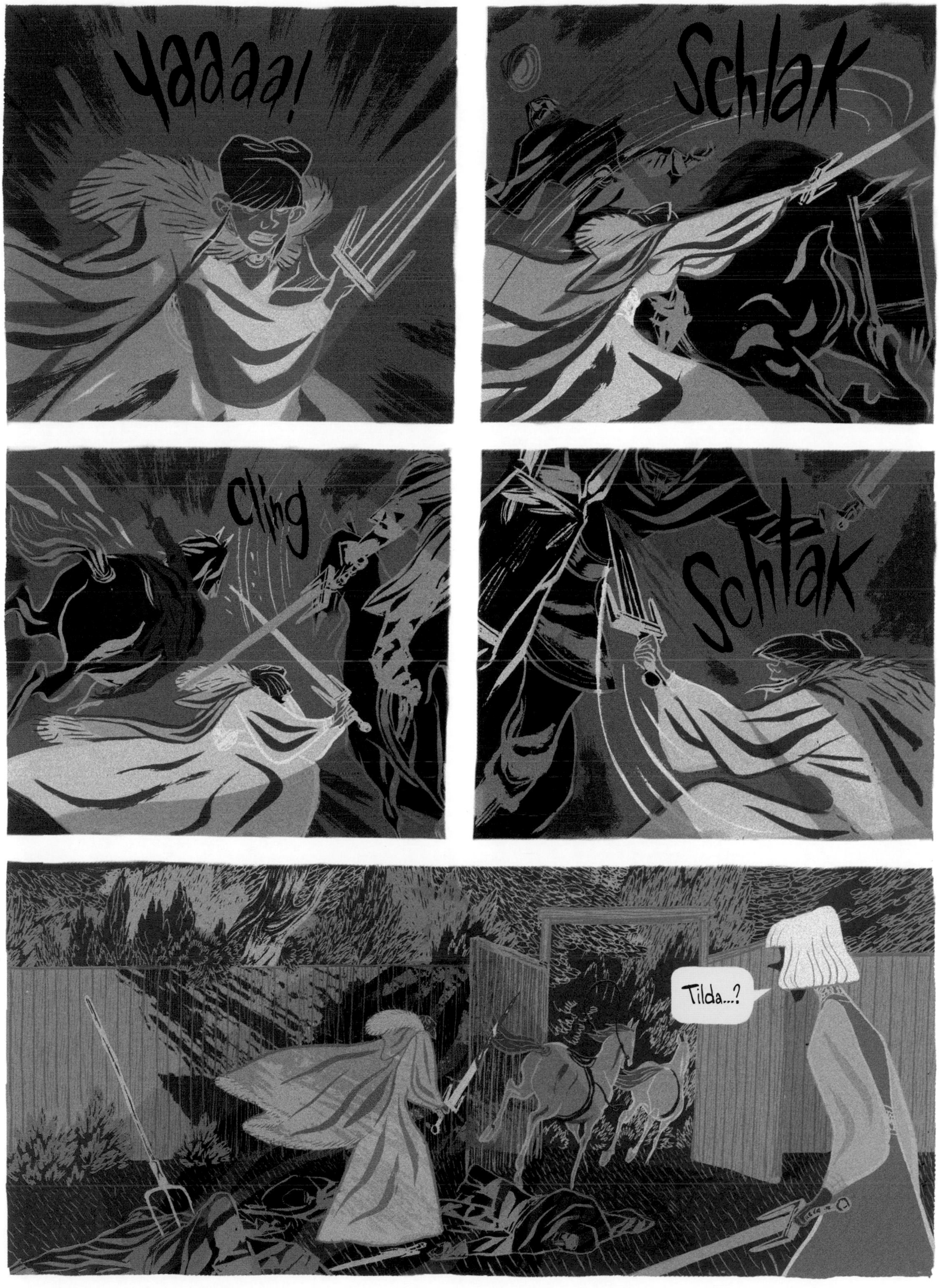
Yaaaaa!
Schlak
Cling
Schtak
Tilda...?

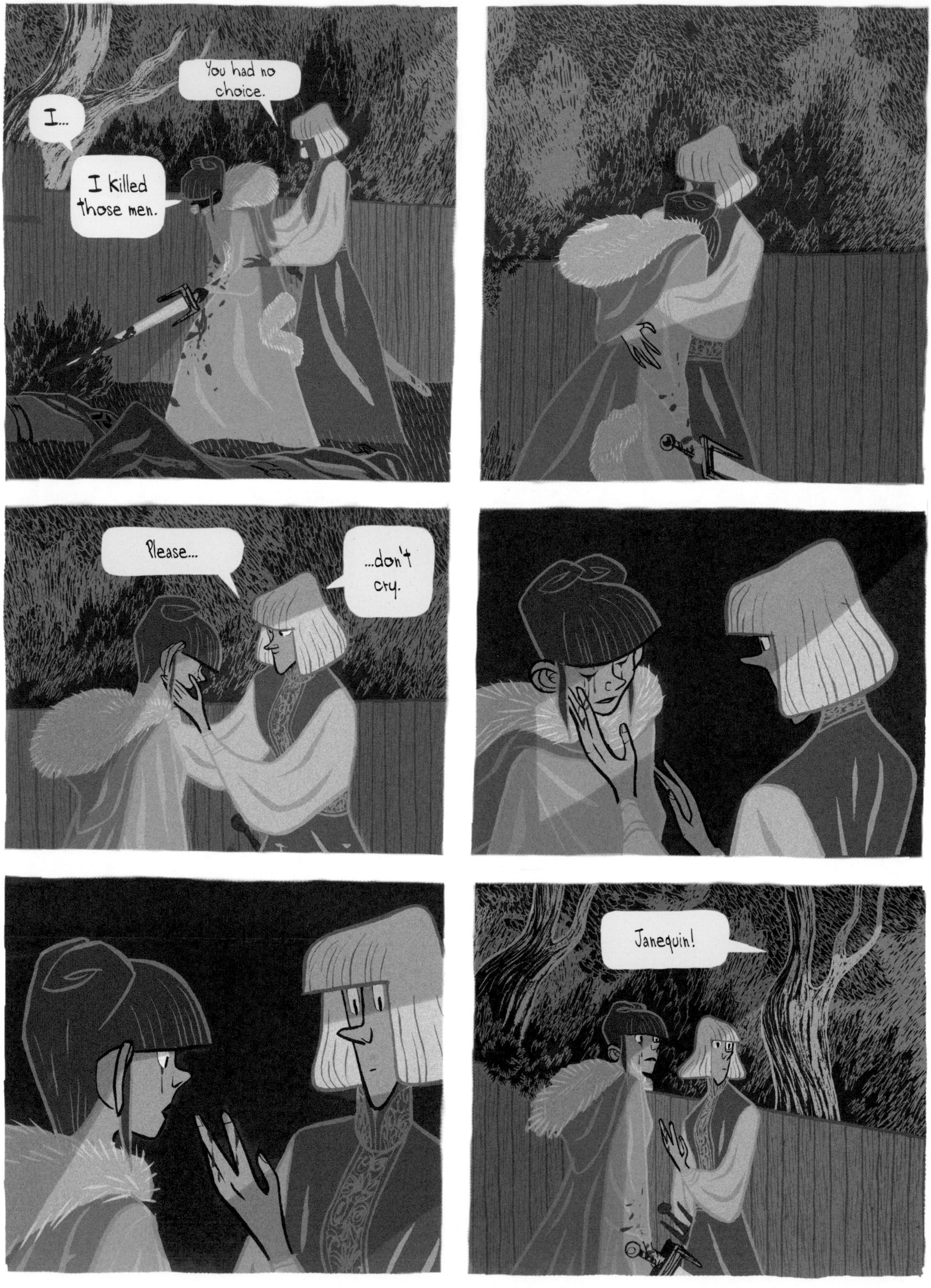

I...
You had no choice.
I killed those men.
Please...
...don't cry.
Janequin!

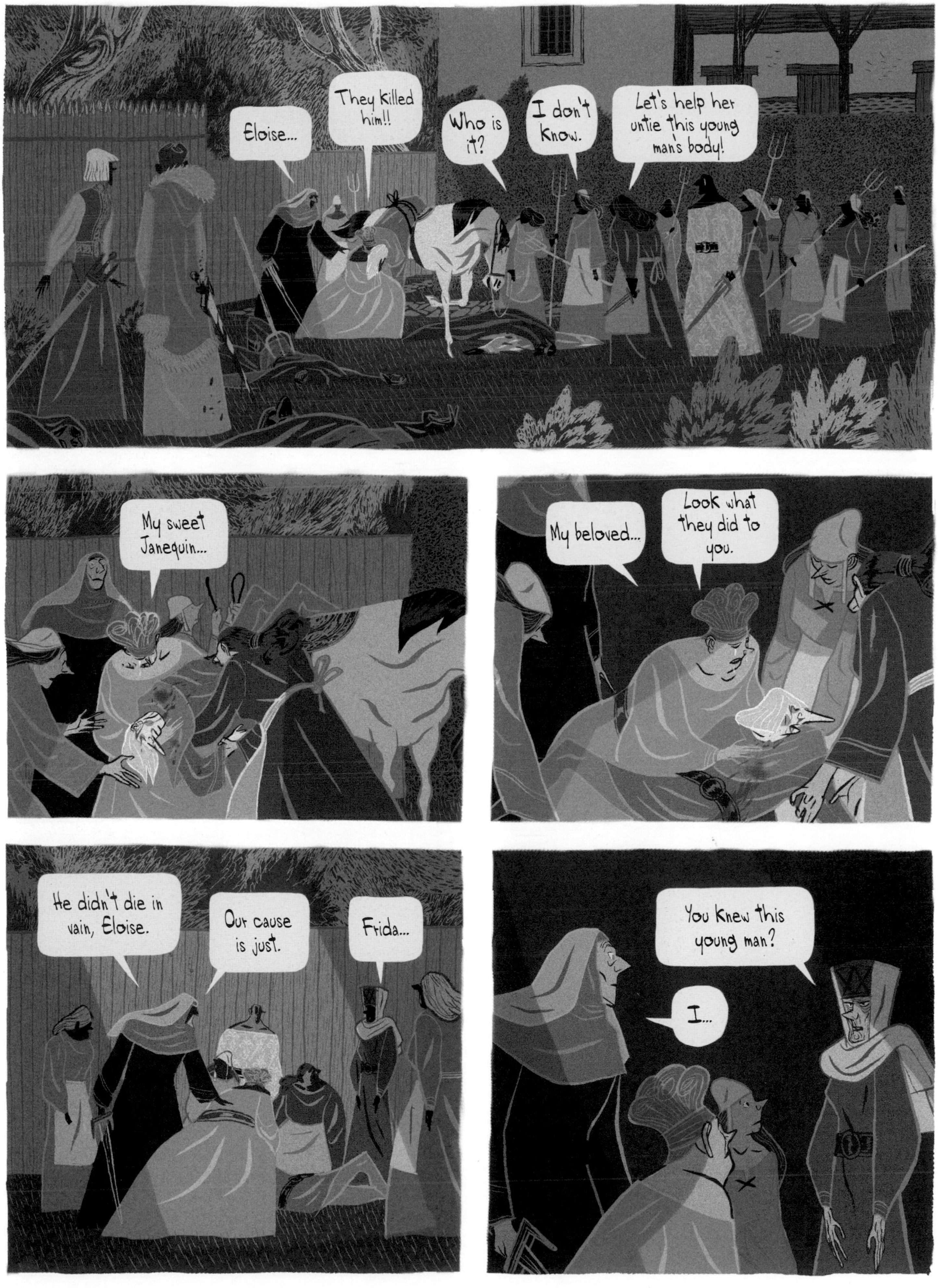
Eloise...
They killed him!!
Who is it?
I don't know.
Let's help her untie this young man's body!
My sweet Janequin...
My beloved...
Look what they did to you.
He didn't die in vain, Eloise.
Our cause is just.
Frida...
You knew this young man?
I...

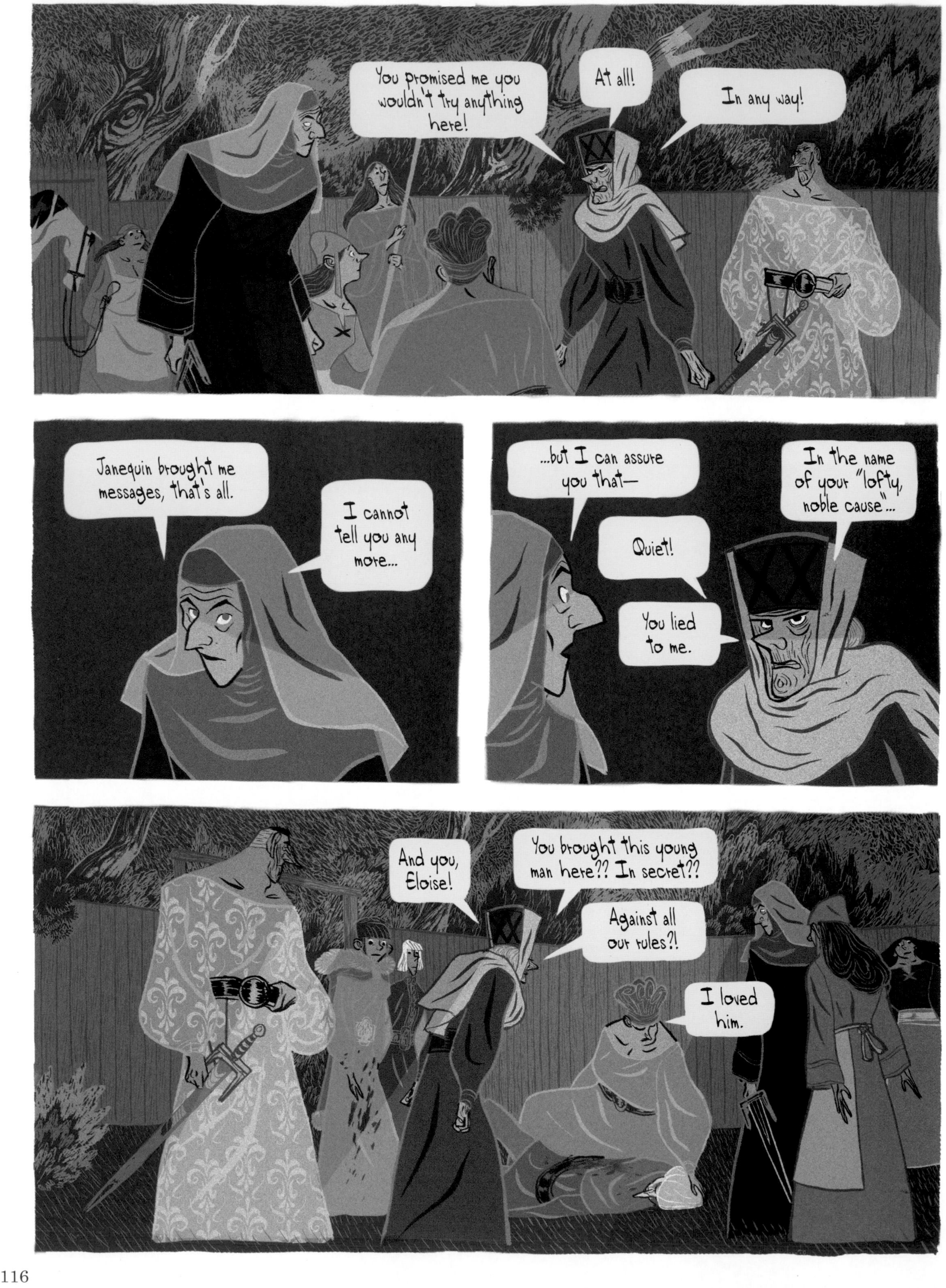
You promised me you wouldn't try anything here!
At all!
In any way!
Janequin brought me messages, that's all.
I cannot tell you any more...
...but I can assure you that—
Quiet!
You lied to me.
In the name of your "lofty, noble cause"...
And you, Eloise!
You brought this young man here?? In secret??
Against all our rules?!
I loved him.

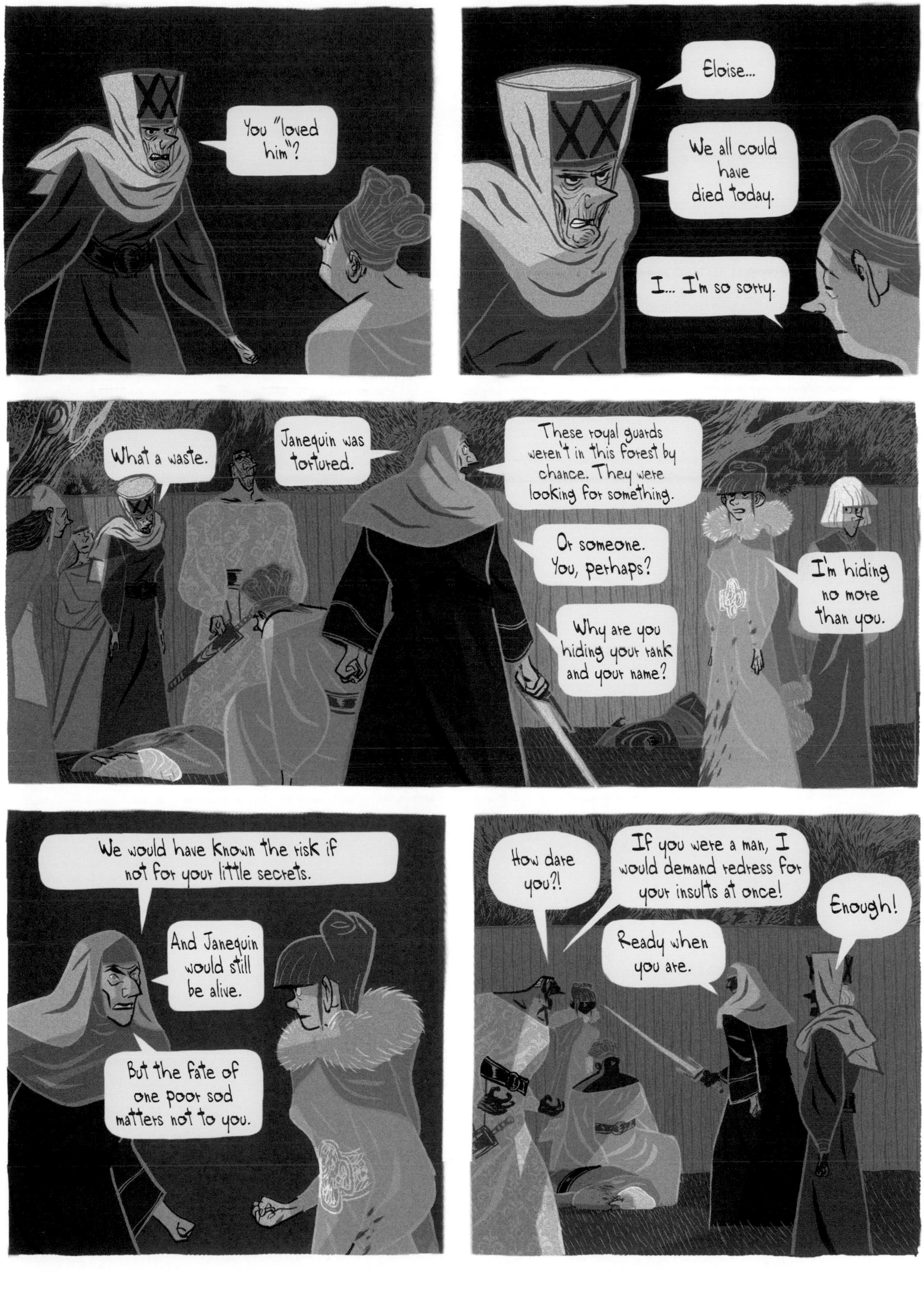

You "loved him"?
Eloise...
We all could have died today.
I... I'm so sorry.
What a waste.
Janequin was tortured.
These royal guards weren't in this forest by chance. They were looking for something.
Or someone. You, perhaps?
Why are you hiding your rank and your name?
I'm hiding no more than you.
We would have known the risk if not for your little secrets.
And Janequin would still be alive.
But the fate of one poor sod matters not to you.
How dare you?!
If you were a man, I would demand redress for your insults at once!
Ready when you are.
Enough!

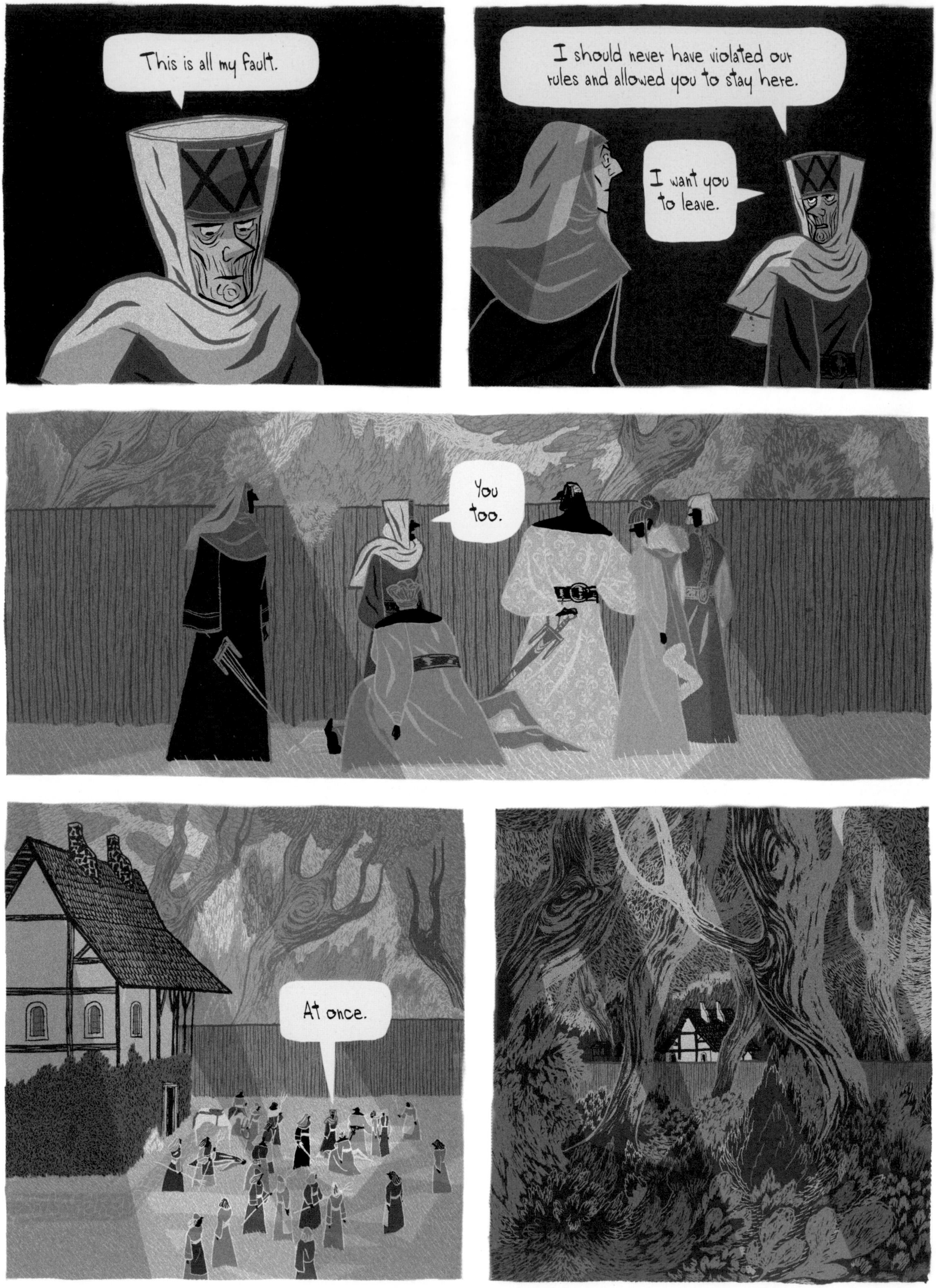
This is all my fault.
I should never have violated our rules and allowed you to stay here.
I want you to leave.
You too.
At once.

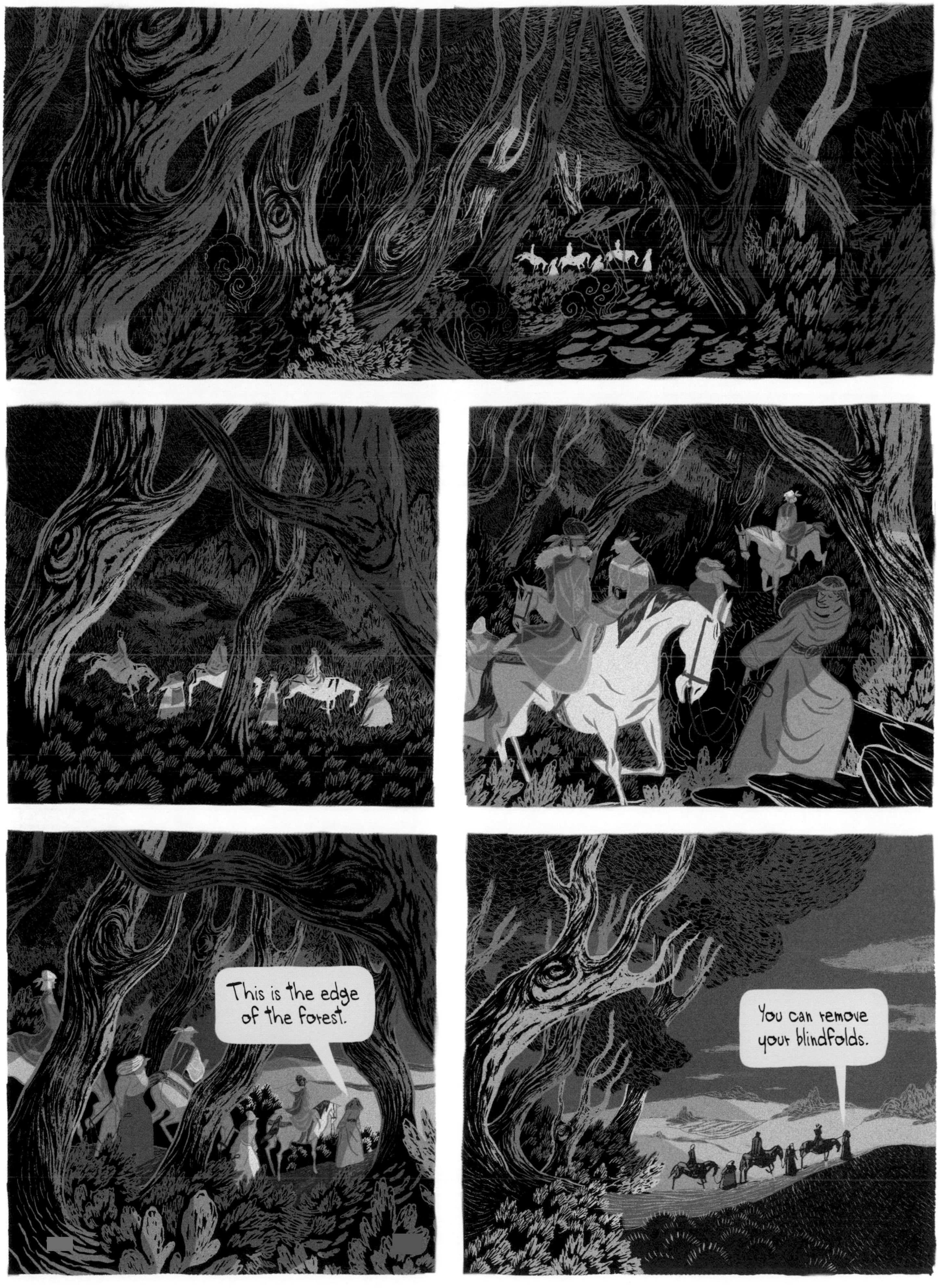
This is the edge of the forest.
You can remove your blindfolds.

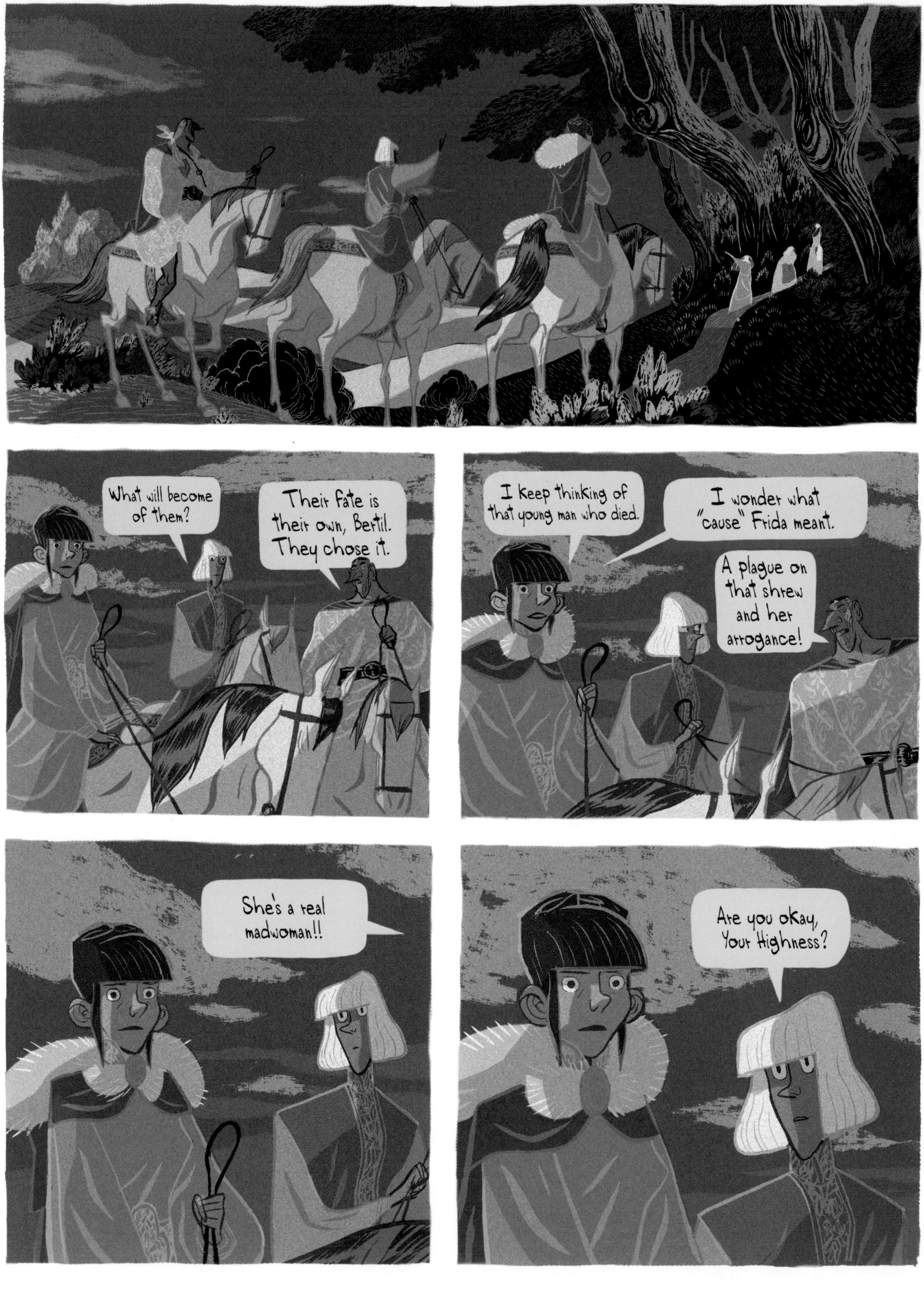

What will become of them?
Their fate is their own, Bertil. They chose it.
I keep thinking of that young man who died.
I wonder what "cause" Frida meant.
A plague on that shrew and her arrogance!
She's a real madwoman!!
Are you okay, Your Highness?

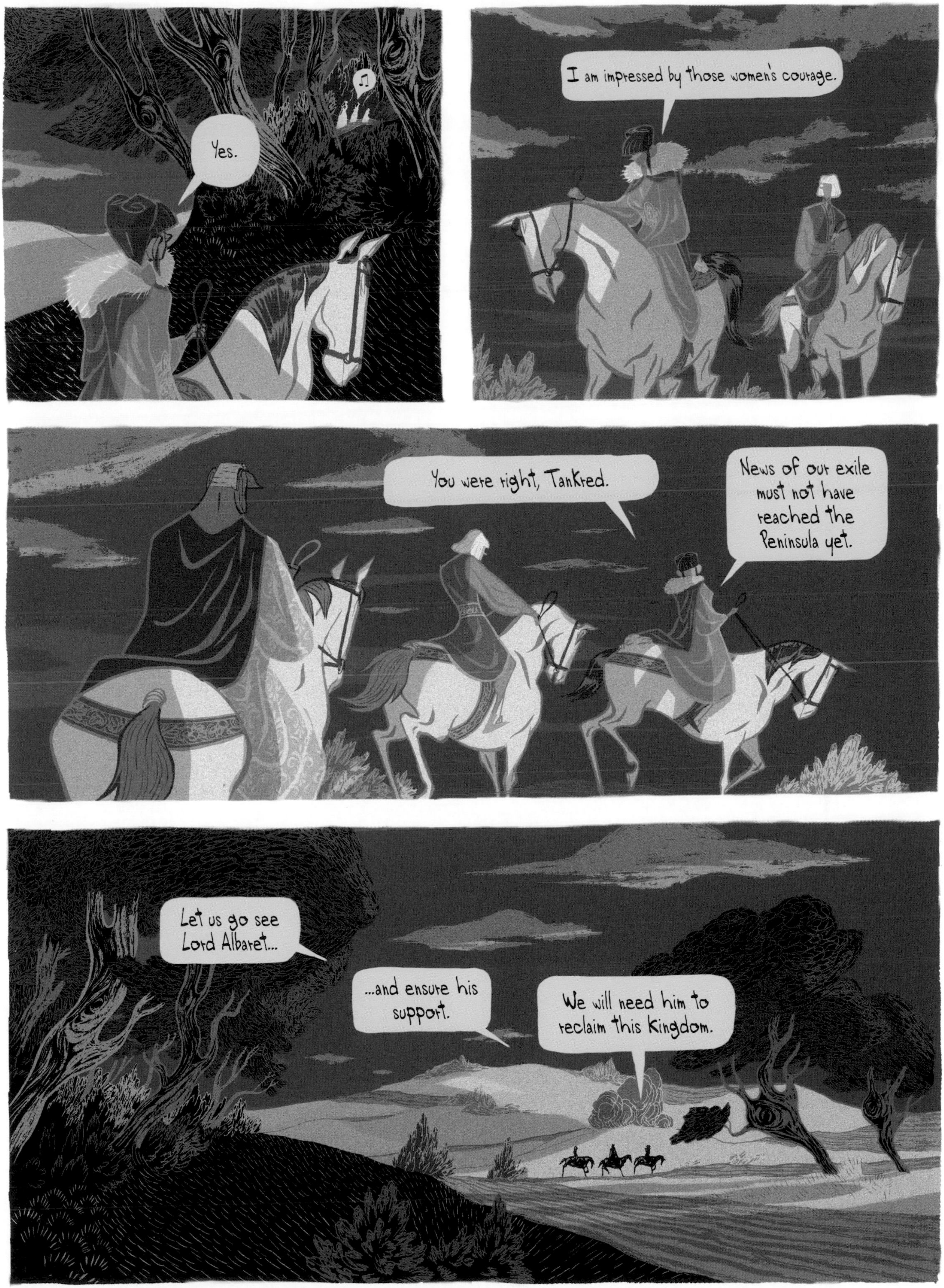
Yes.
I am impressed by those women's courage.
You were right, Tankred.
News of our exile must not have reached the Peninsula yet.
Let us go see Lord Albaret...
...and ensure his support.
We will need him to reclaim this Kingdom.

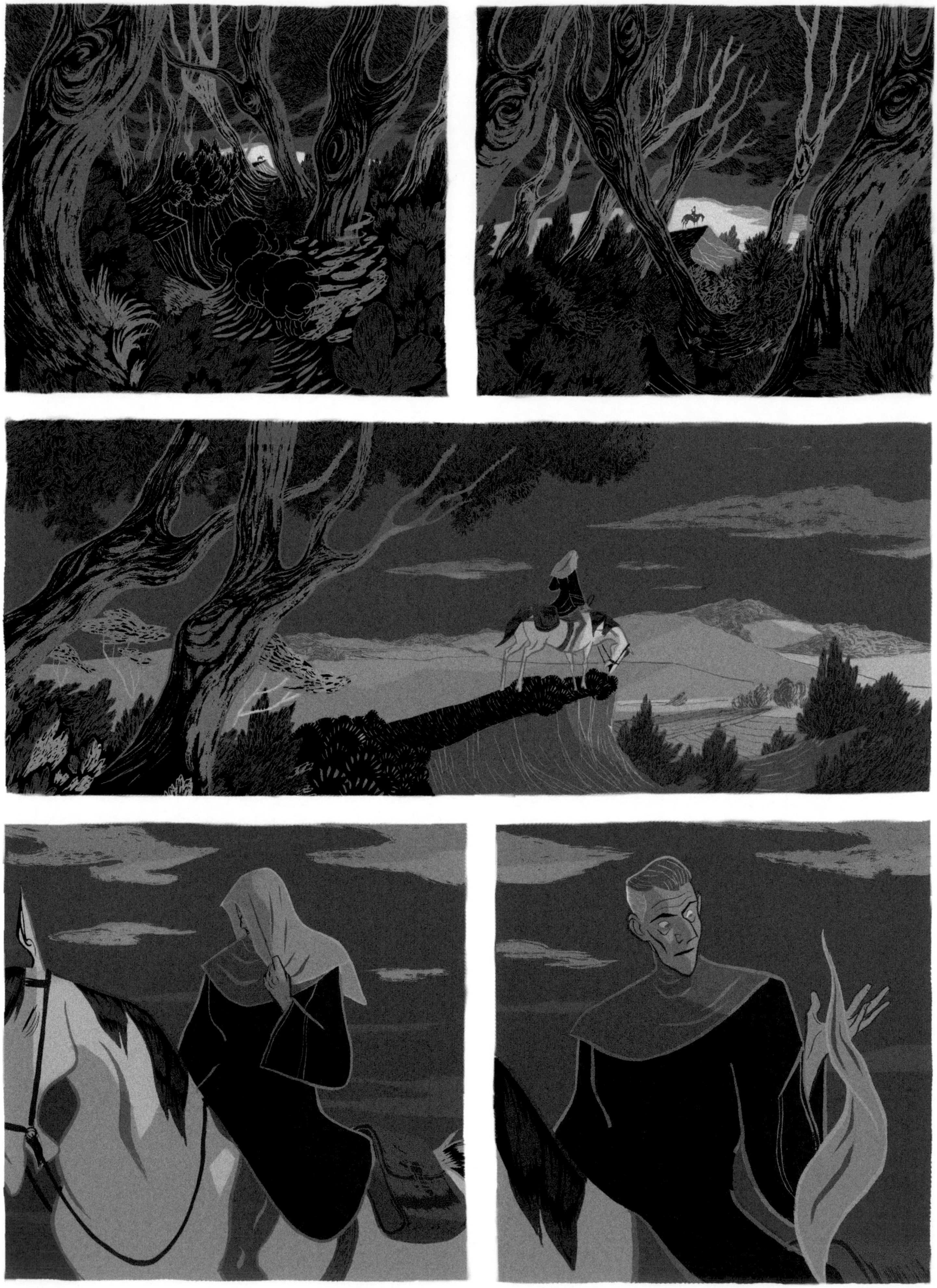

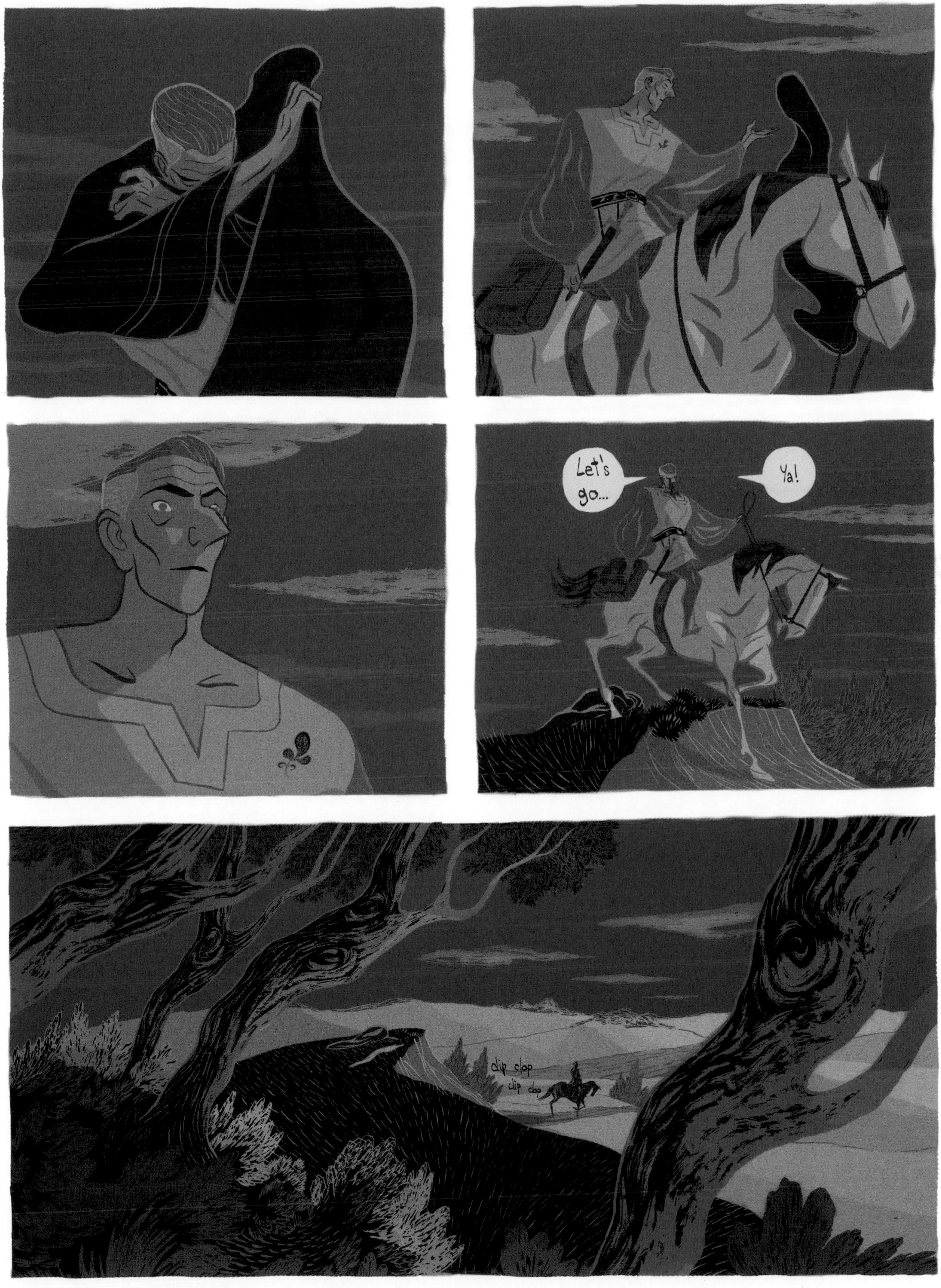
Let's go...
Ya!
clip clop
clip clop

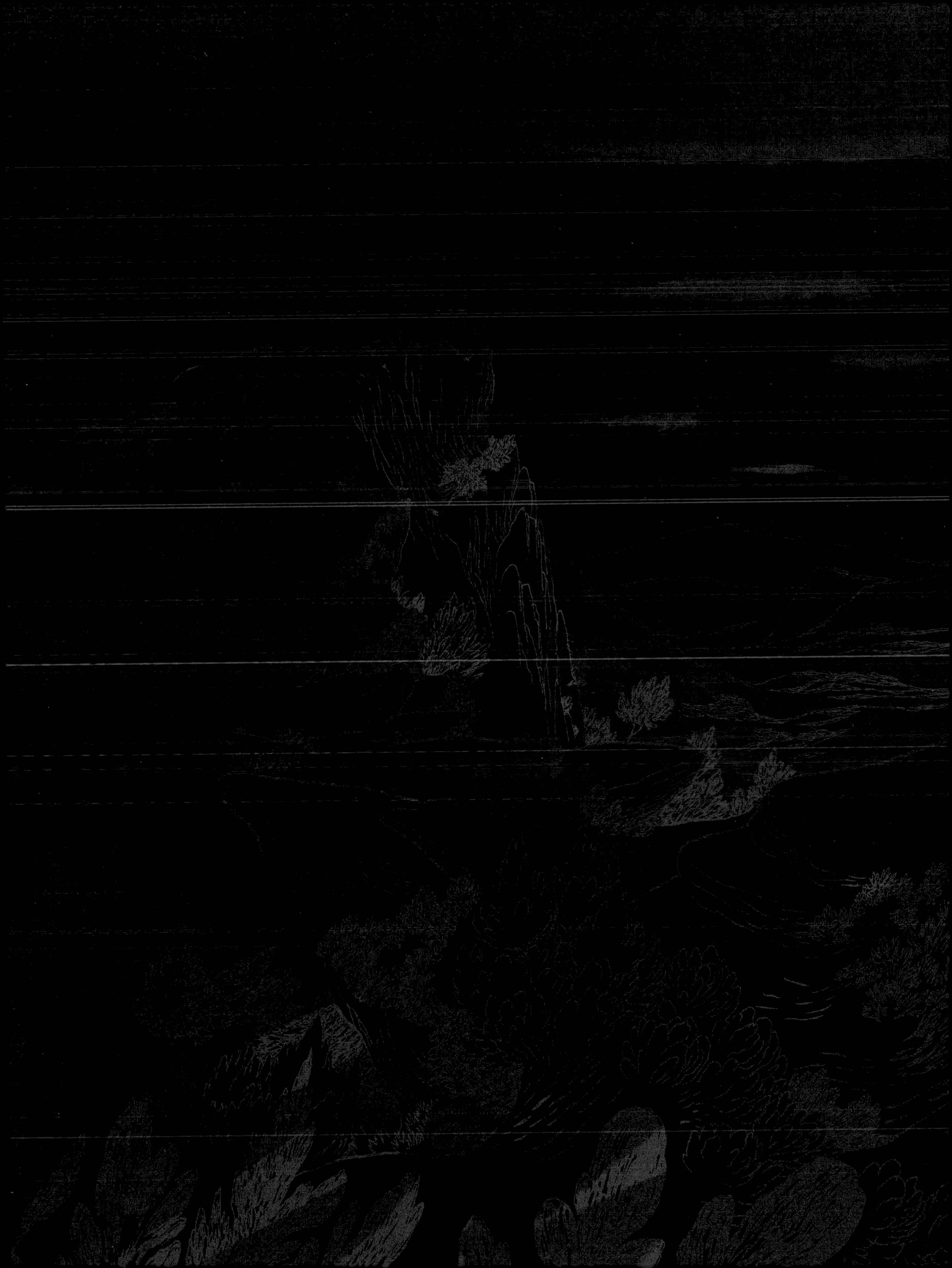

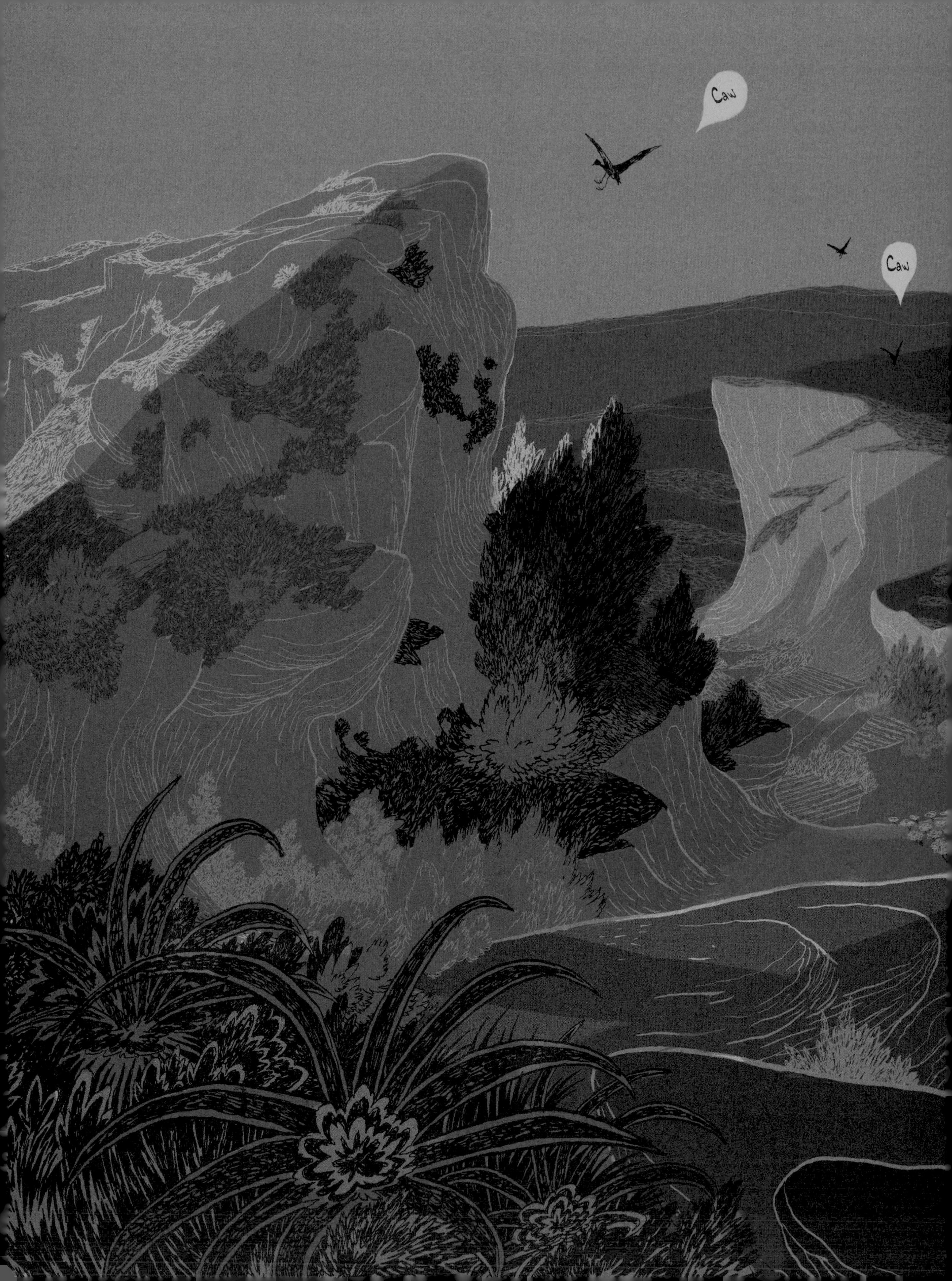
Caw
Caw

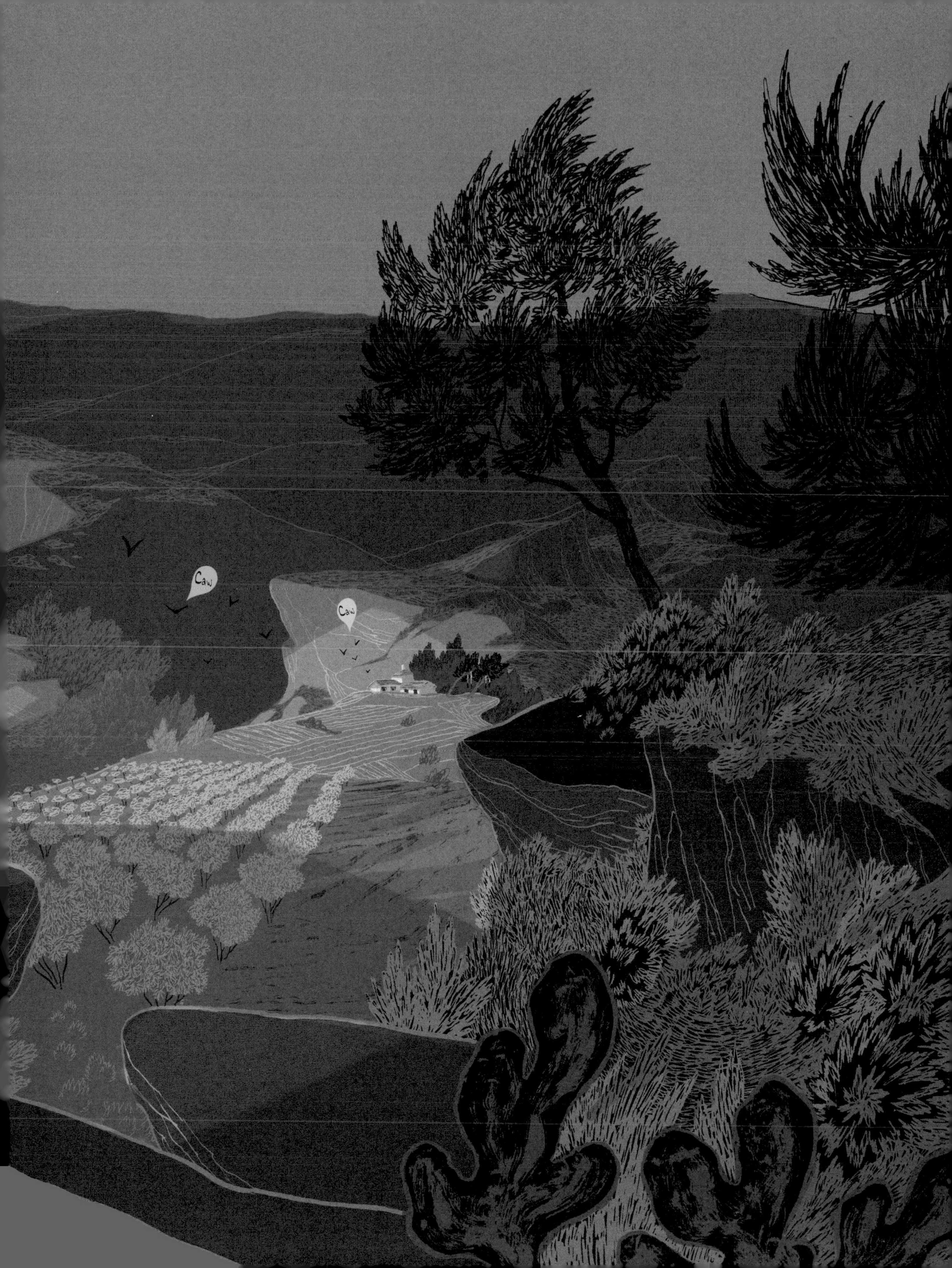
Caw
Caw

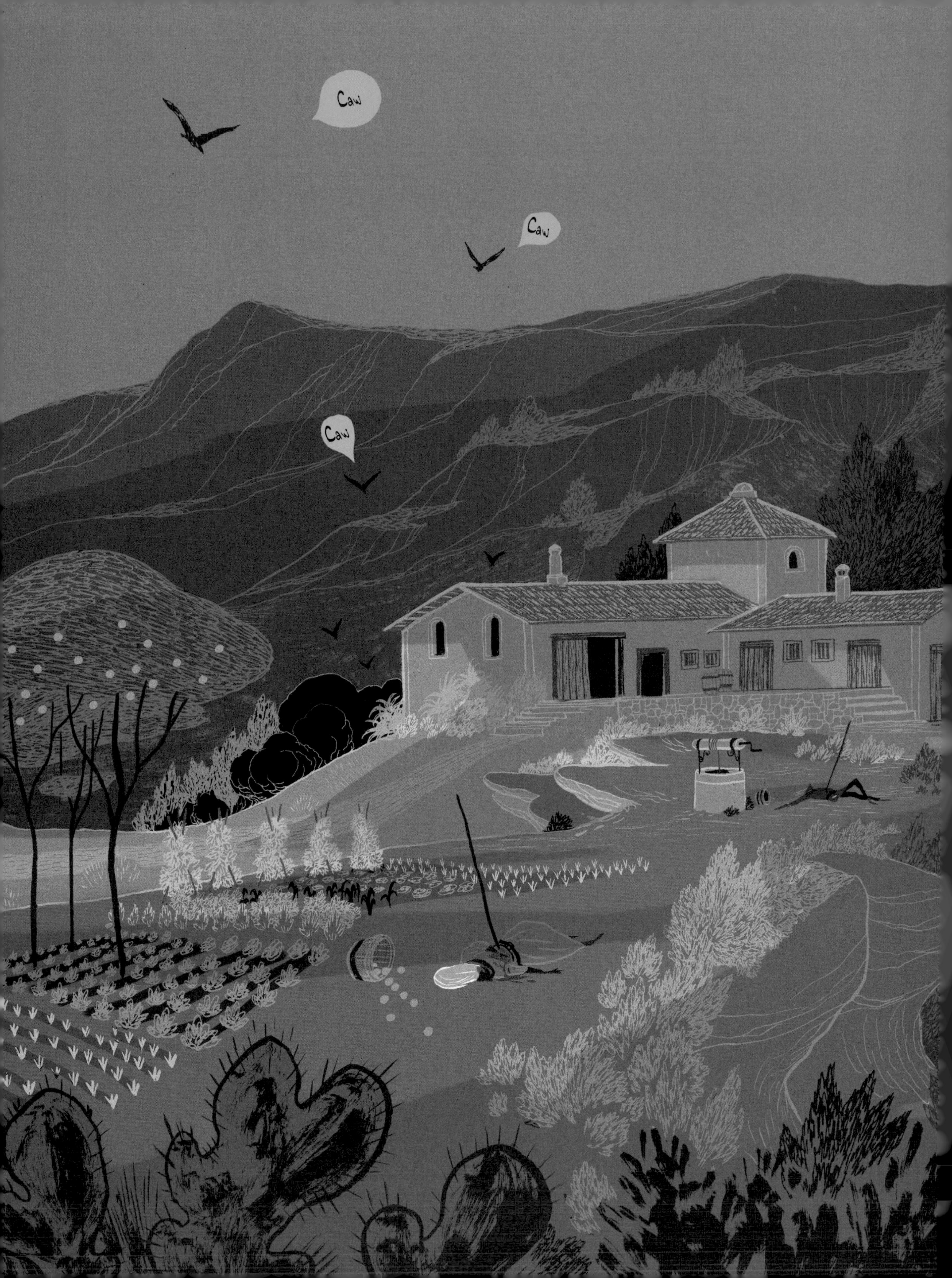
Caw
Caw
Caw

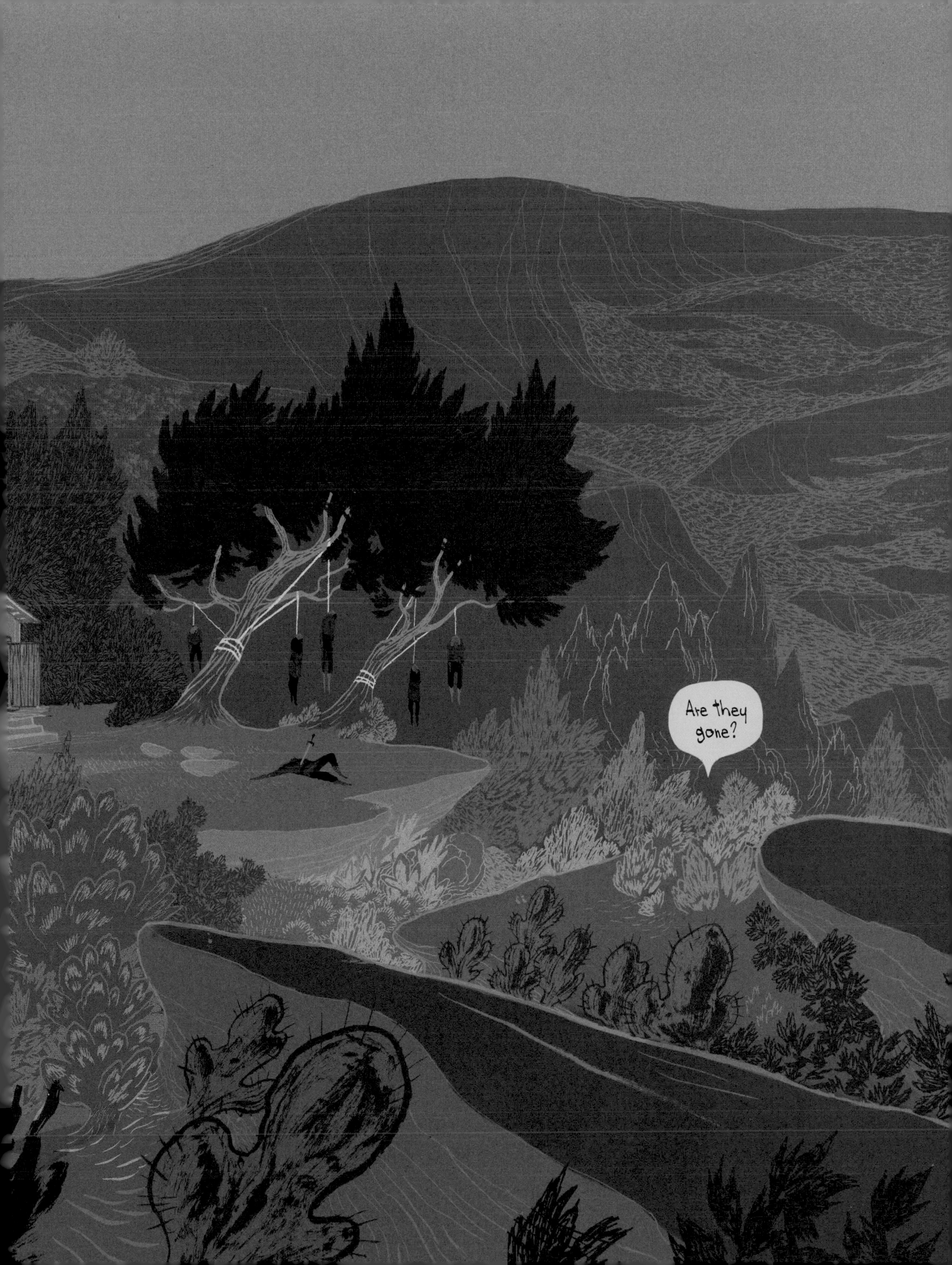
Are they gone?

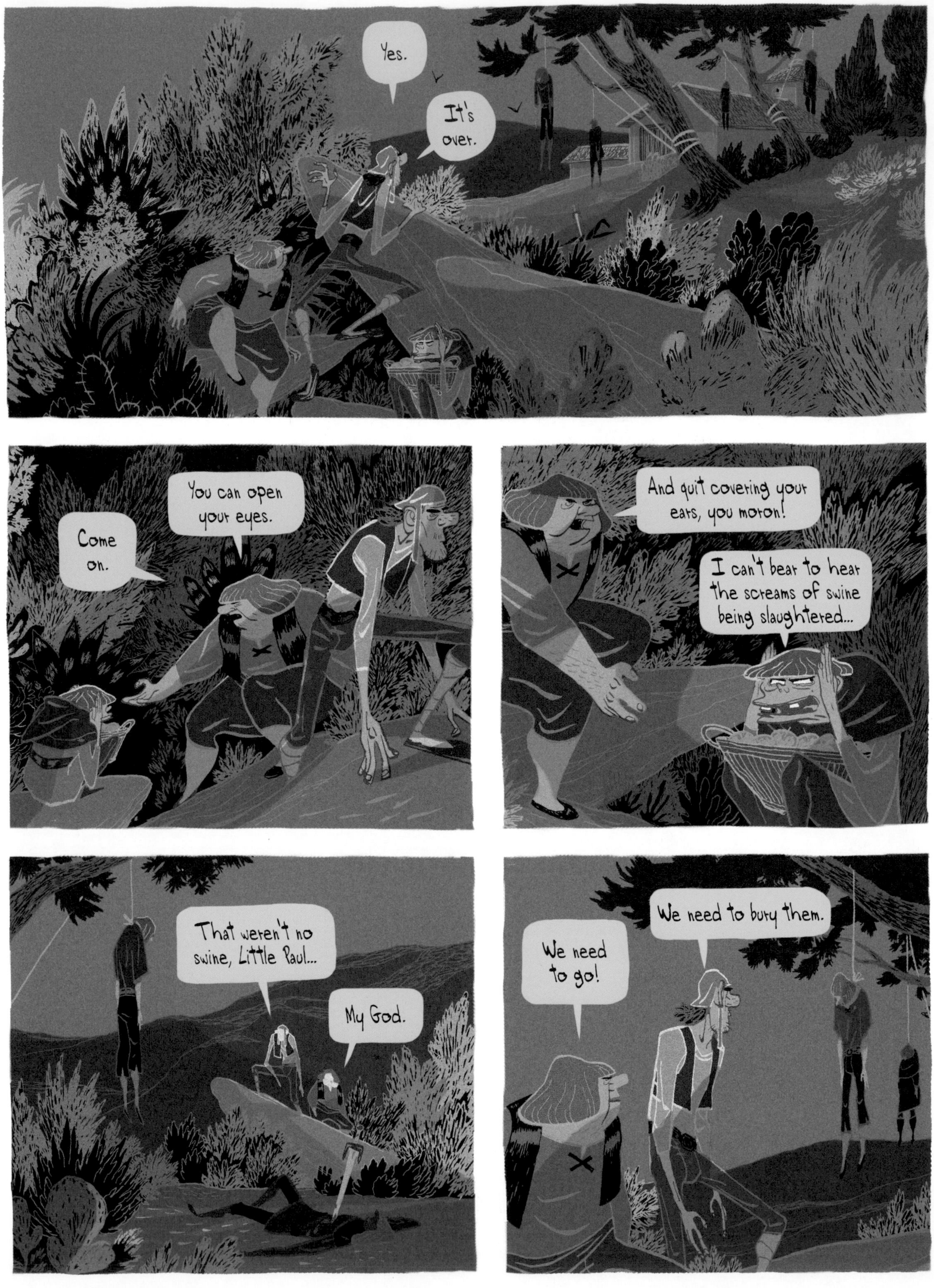
Yes.
It's over.
Come on.
You can open your eyes.
And quit covering your ears, you moron!
I can't bear to hear the screams of swine being slaughtered...
That weren't no swine, Little Paul...
My God.
We need to go!
We need to bury them.

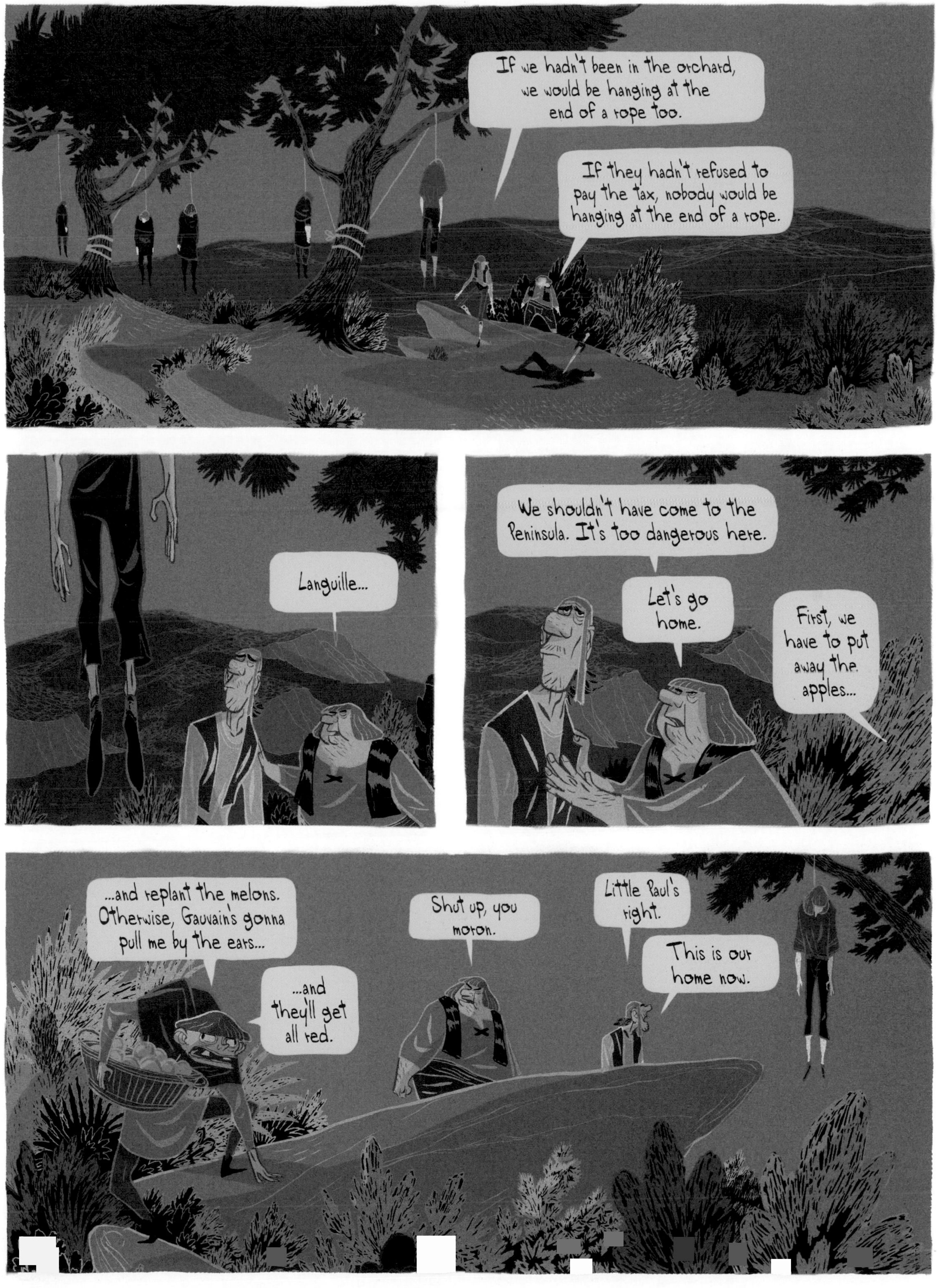
If we hadn't been in the orchard, we would be hanging at the end of a rope too.
If they hadn't refused to pay the tax, nobody would be hanging at the end of a rope.
Languille...
We shouldn't have come to the Peninsula. It's too dangerous here.
Let's go home.
First, we have to put away the apples...
...and replant the melons. Otherwise, Gauvain's gonna pull me by the ears...
...and they'll get all red.
Shut up, you moron.
Little Paul's right.
This is our home now.

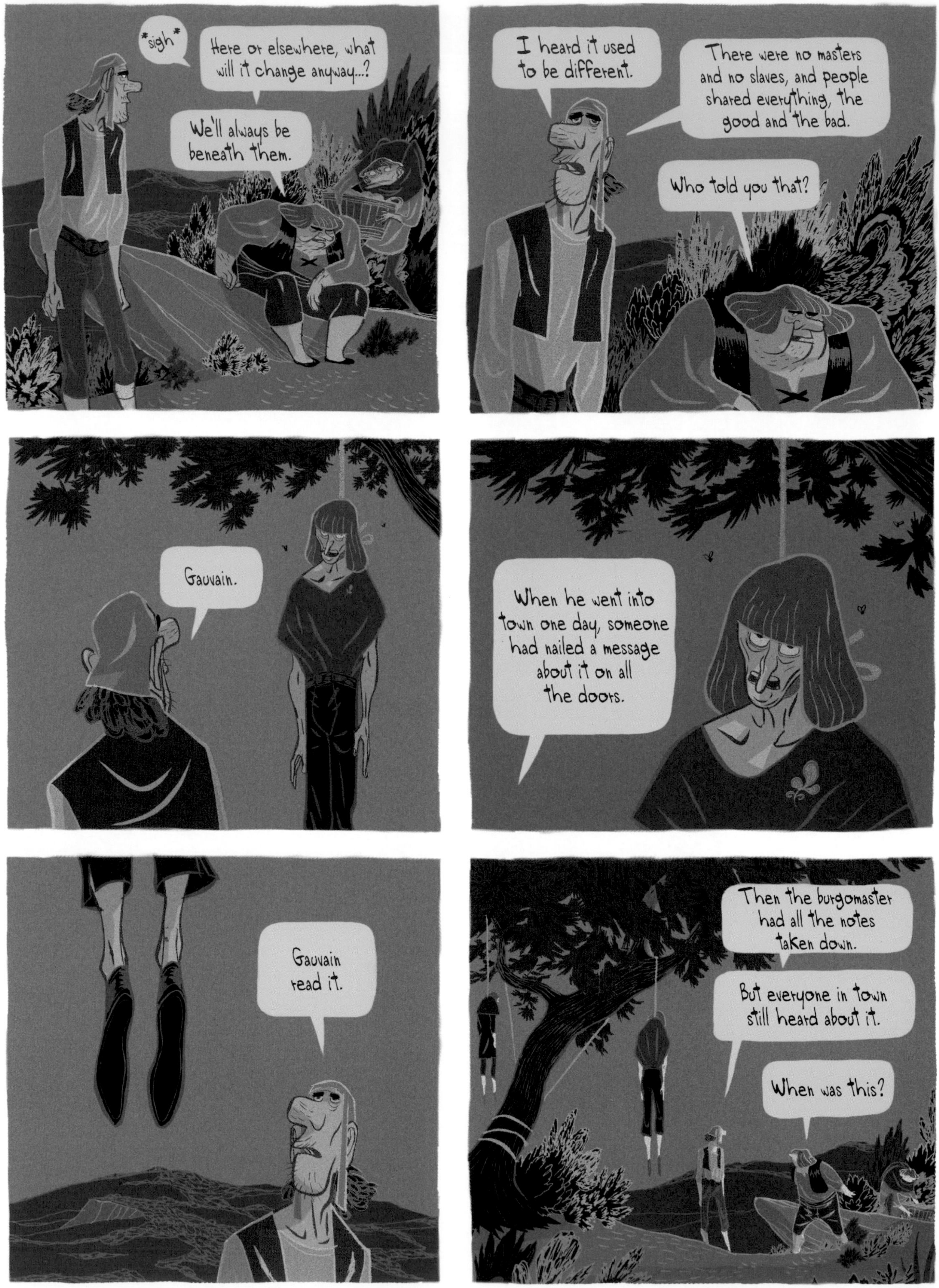
sigh
Here or elsewhere, what will it change anyway...?
We'll always be beneath them.
I heard it used to be different.
There were no masters and no slaves, and people shared everything, the good and the bad.
Who told you that?
Gauvain.
When he went into town one day, someone had nailed a message about it on all the doors.
Gauvain read it.
Then the burgomaster had all the notes taken down.
But everyone in town still heard about it.
When was this?

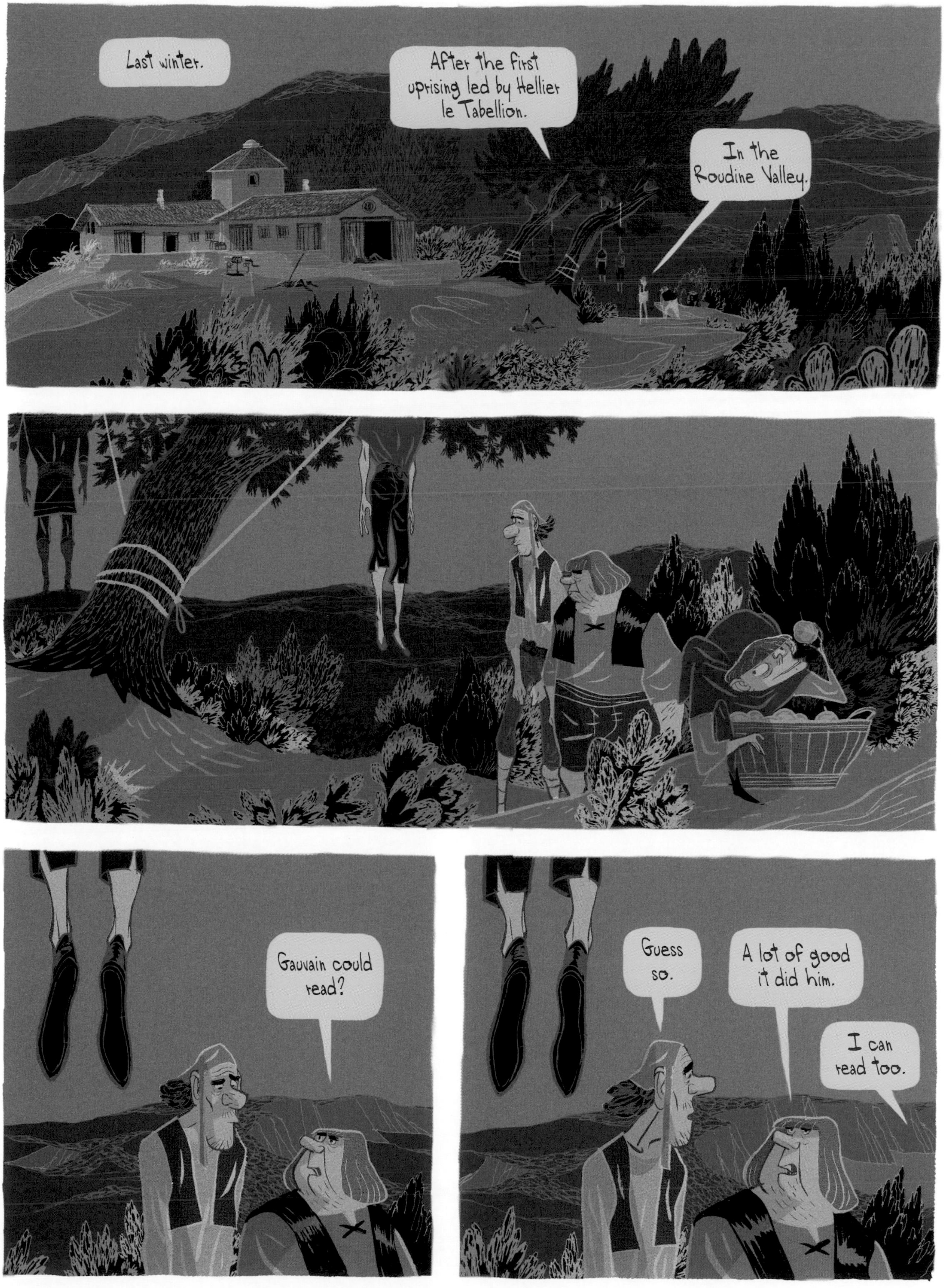
Last winter.
After the first uprising led by Hellier le Tabellion.
In the Roudine Valley.
Gauvain could read?
Guess so.
A lot of good it did him.
I can read too.

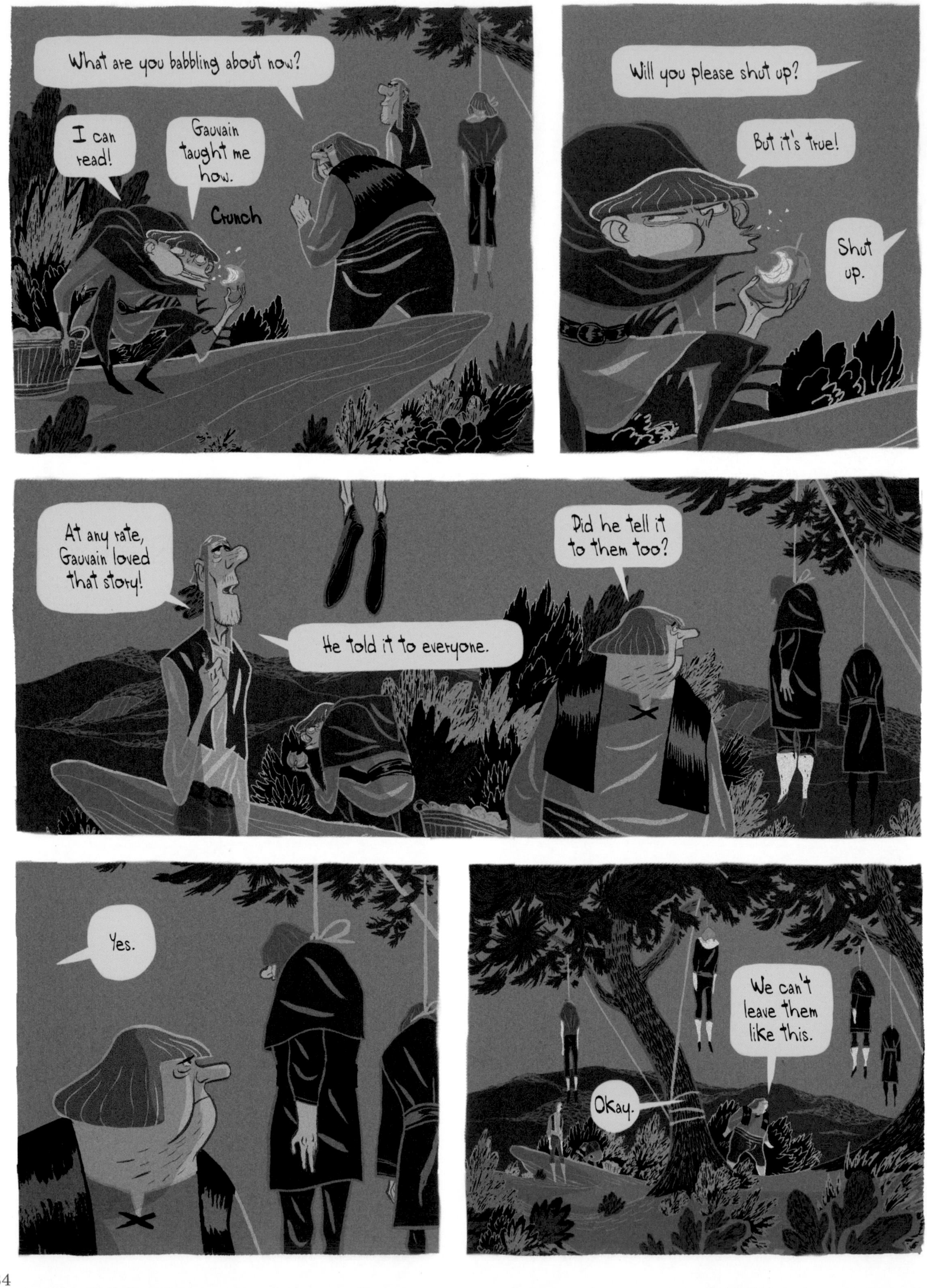

What are you babbling about now?
I can read!
Gauvain taught me how.
Crunch
Will you please shut up?
But it's true!
Shut up.
At any rate, Gauvain loved that story!
He told it to everyone.
Did he tell it to them too?
Yes.
We can't leave them like this.
Okay.

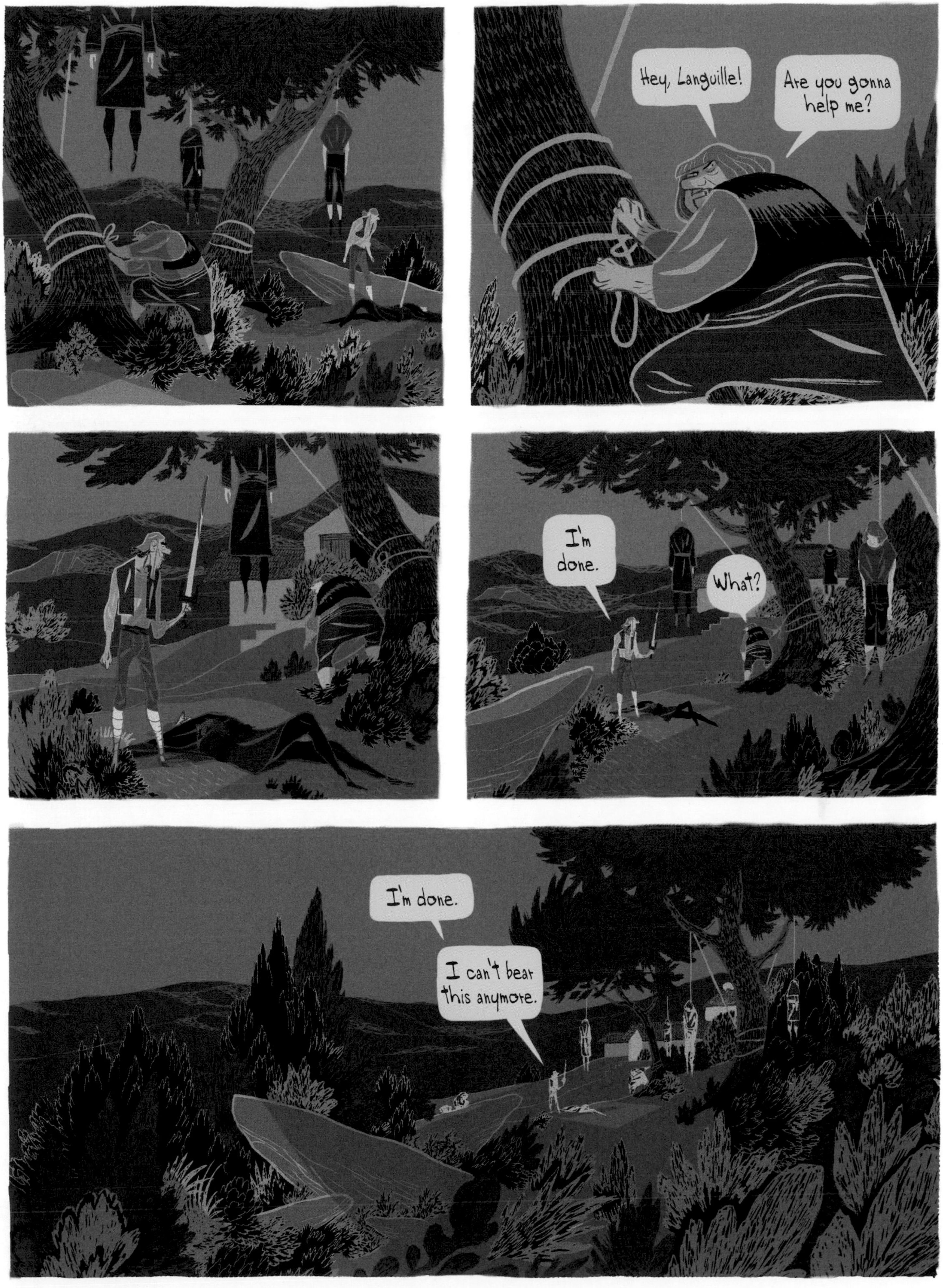
Hey, Languille!
Are you gonna help me?
I'm done.
What?
I'm done.
I can't bear this anymore.

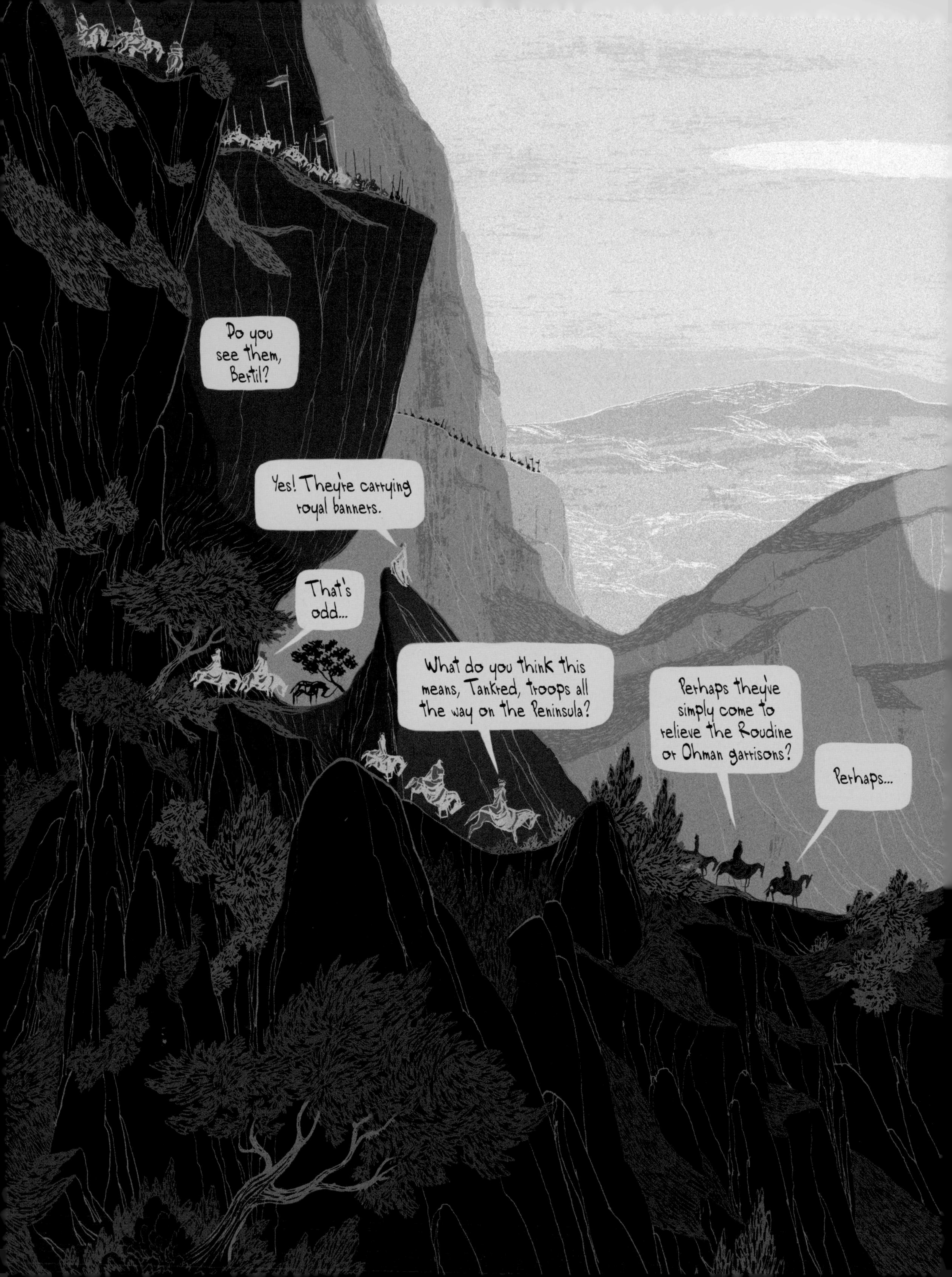
Do you see them, Bertil?
Yes! They're carrying royal banners.
That's odd...
What do you think this means, Tankred, troops all the way on the Peninsula?
Perhaps they've simply come to relieve the Roudine or Ohman garrisons?
Perhaps...

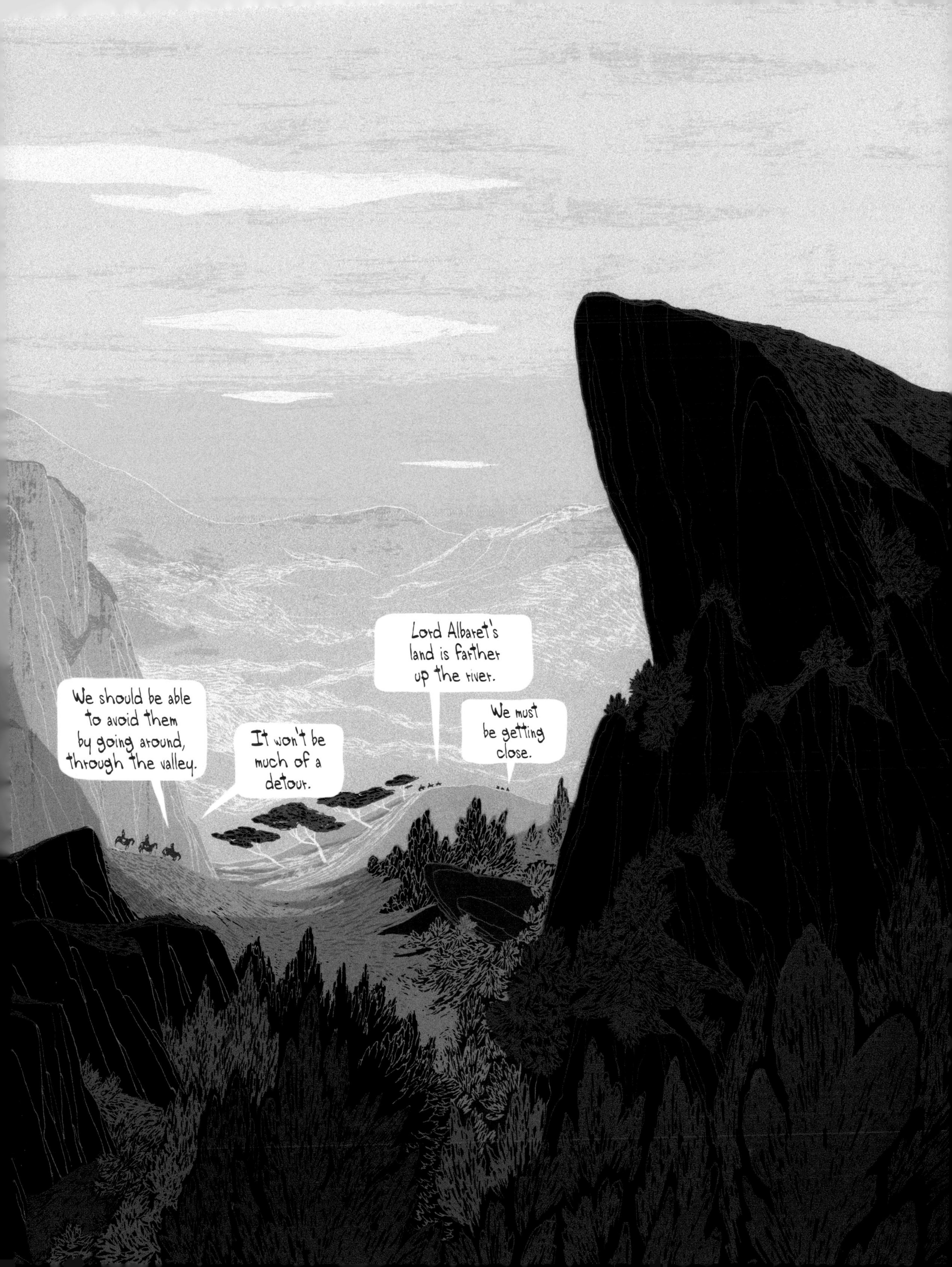
We should be able to avoid them by going around, through the valley.
It won't be much of a detour.
Lord Albaret's land is farther up the river.
We must be getting close.

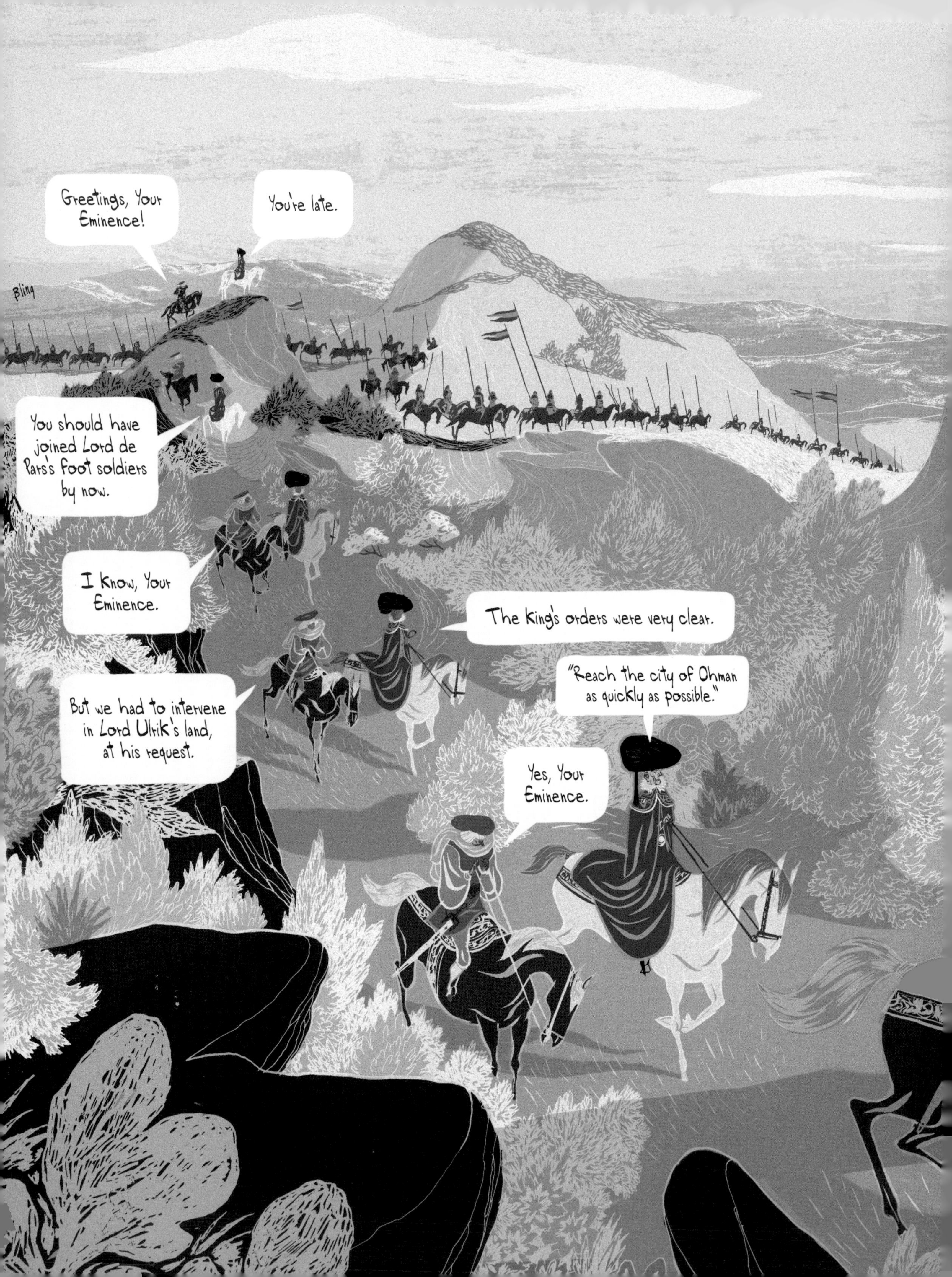
Greetings, Your Eminence!
You're late.
Bling
You should have joined Lord de Pars's foot soldiers by now.
I know, Your Eminence.
The King's orders were very clear.
But we had to intervene in Lord Ulrik's land, at his request.
"Reach the city of Ohman as quickly as possible."
Yes, Your Eminence.

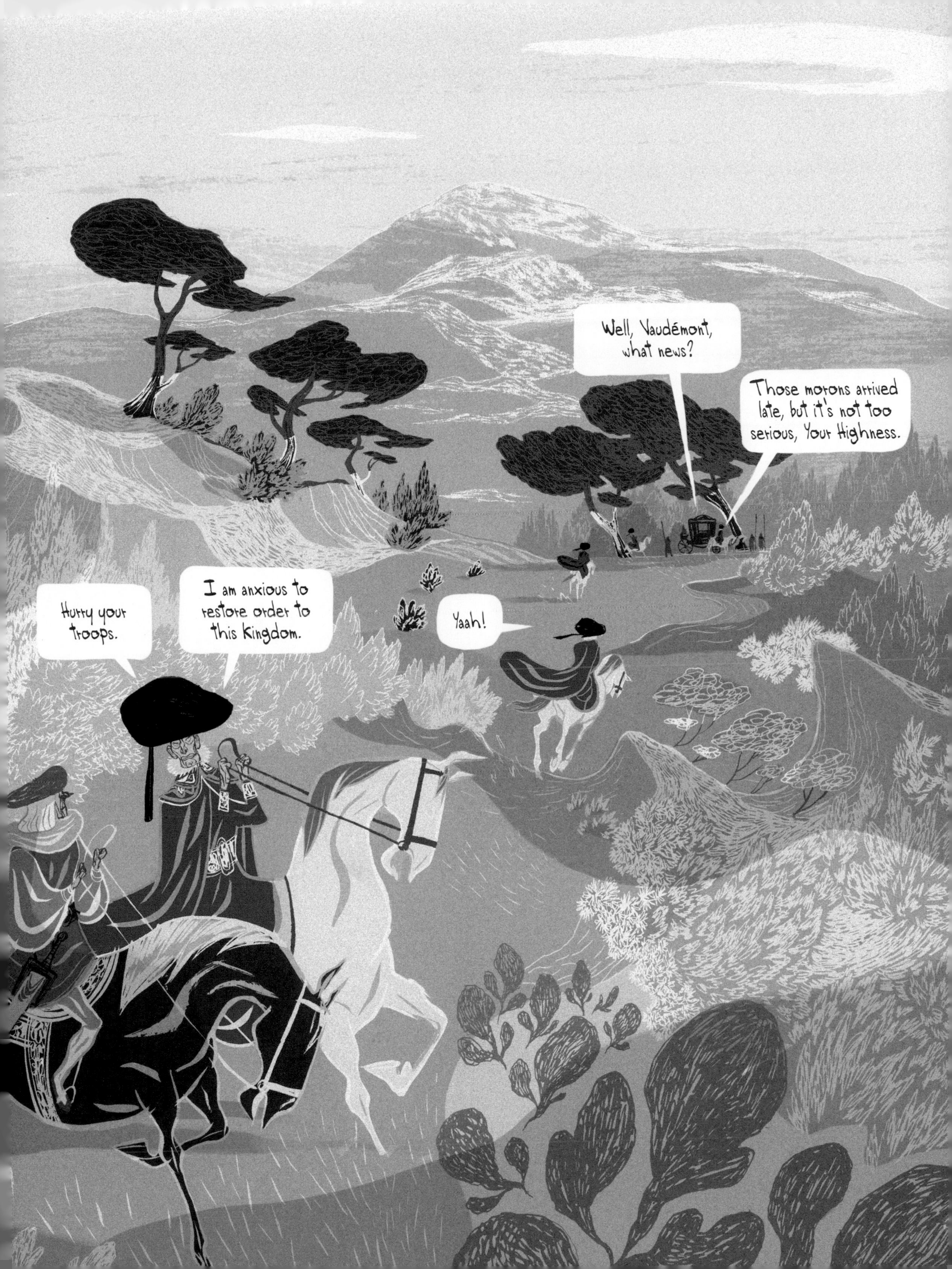
Well, Vaudémont, what news?
Those morons arrived late, but it's not too serious, Your Highness.
Hurry your troops.
I am anxious to restore order to this Kingdom.
Yaah!

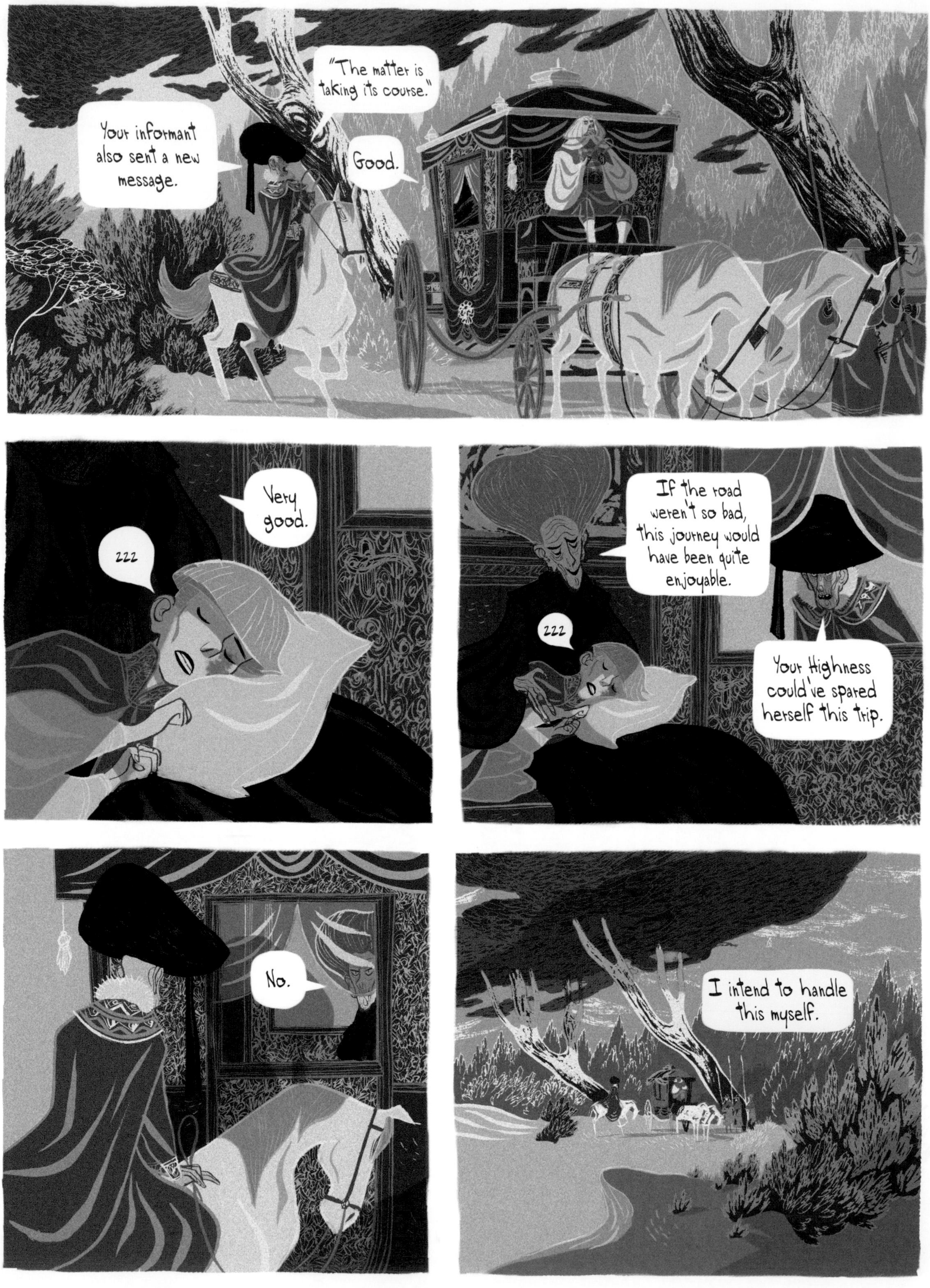
"The matter is taking its course."
Your informant also sent a new message.
Good.
Very good.
zzz
If the road weren't so bad, this journey would have been quite enjoyable.
zzz
Your Highness could've spared herself this trip.
No.
I intend to handle this myself.

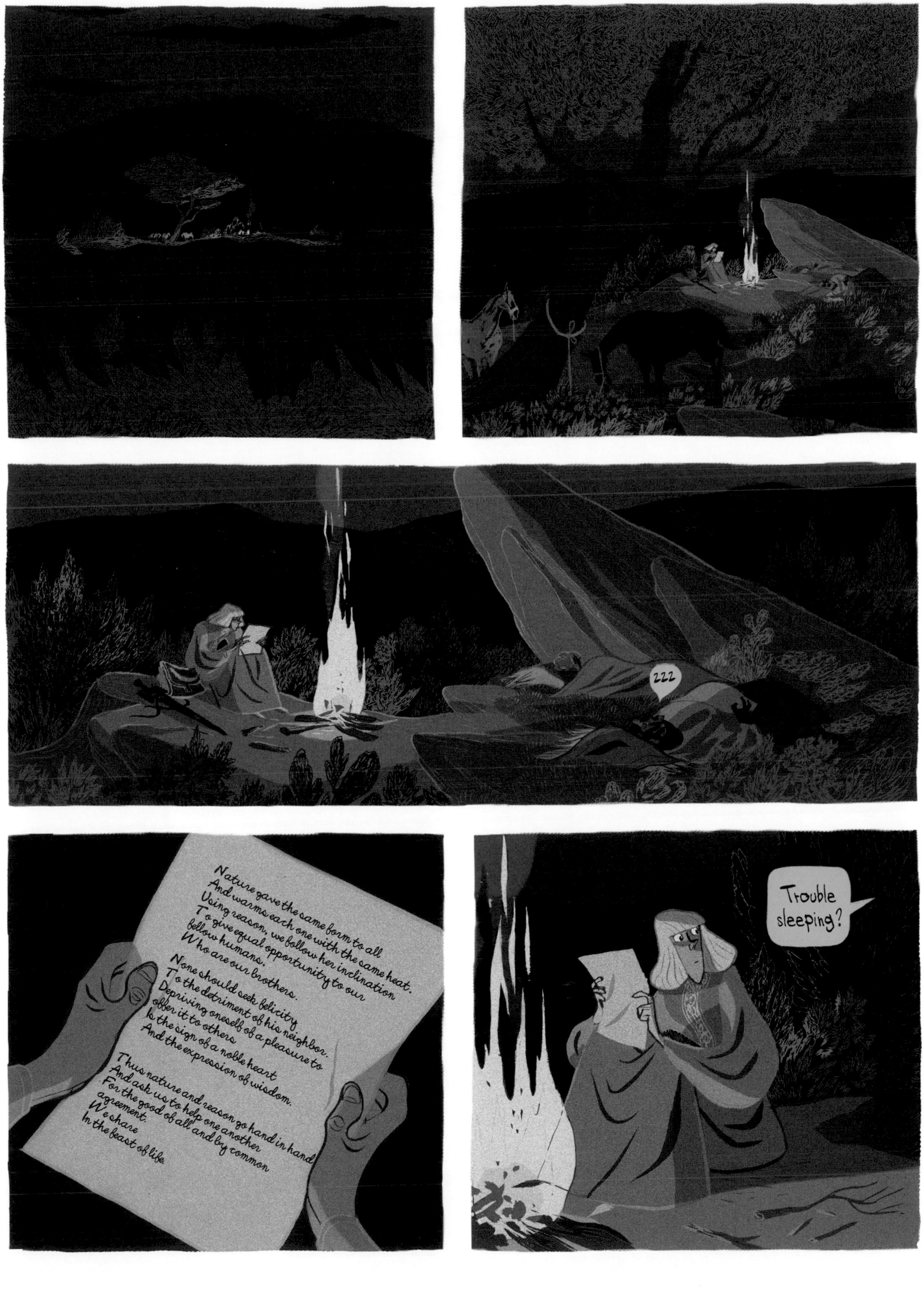

zzz
Nature gave the same form to all
And warms each one with the same heat.
Using reason, we follow her inclination
To give equal opportunity to our
fellow humans,
Who are our brothers.
None should seek felicity
To the detriment of his neighbor.
Depriving oneself of a pleasure to
offer it to others
Is the sign of a noble heart
And the expression of wisdom.
Thus nature and reason go hand in hand
And ask us to help one another
For the good of all and by common
agreement.
We share
In the feast of life.
Trouble sleeping?

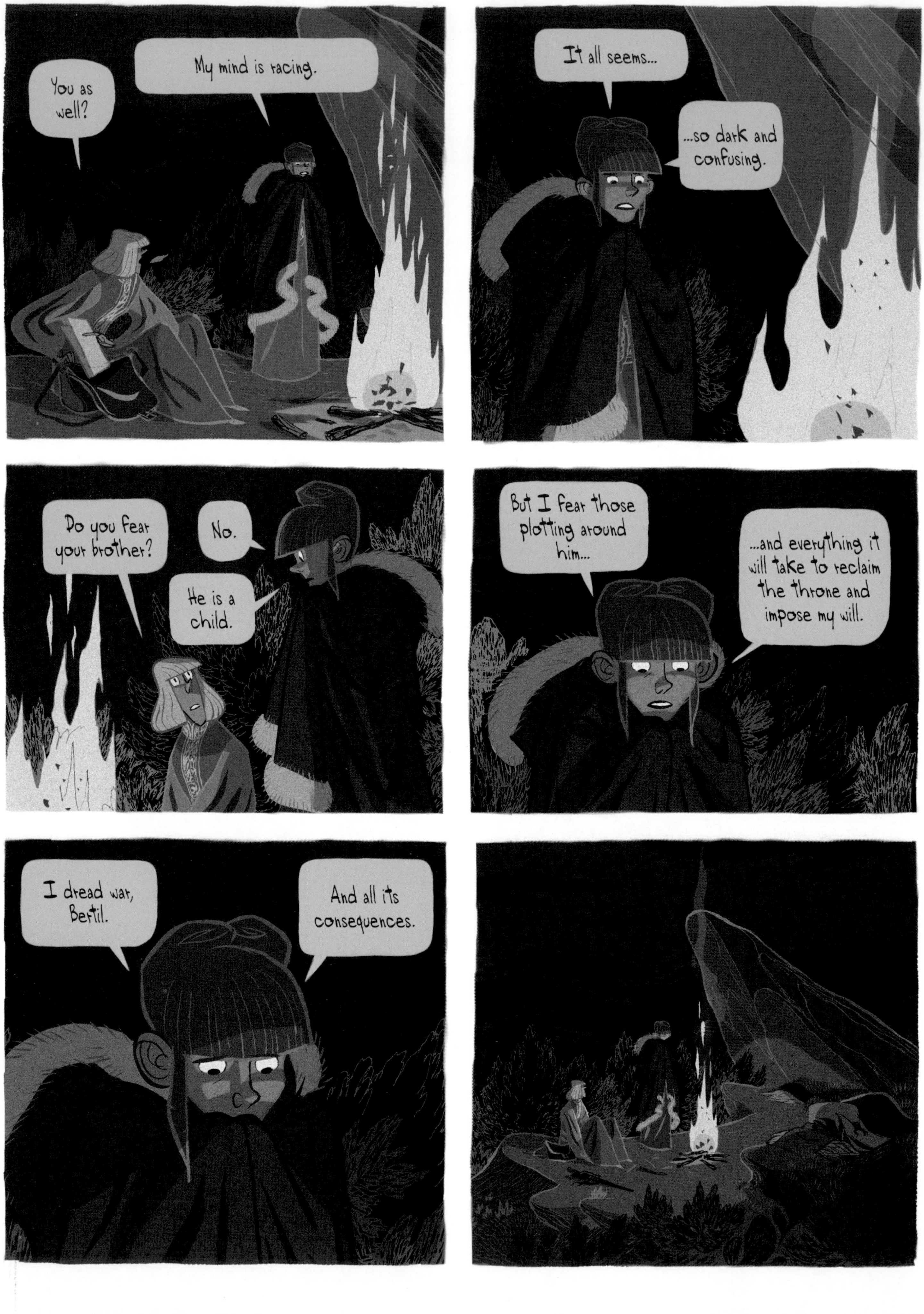
You as well?
My mind is racing.
It all seems...
...so dark and confusing.
Do you fear your brother?
No.
He is a child.
But I fear those plotting around him...
...and everything it will take to reclaim the throne and impose my will.
I dread war, Bertil.
And all its consequences.

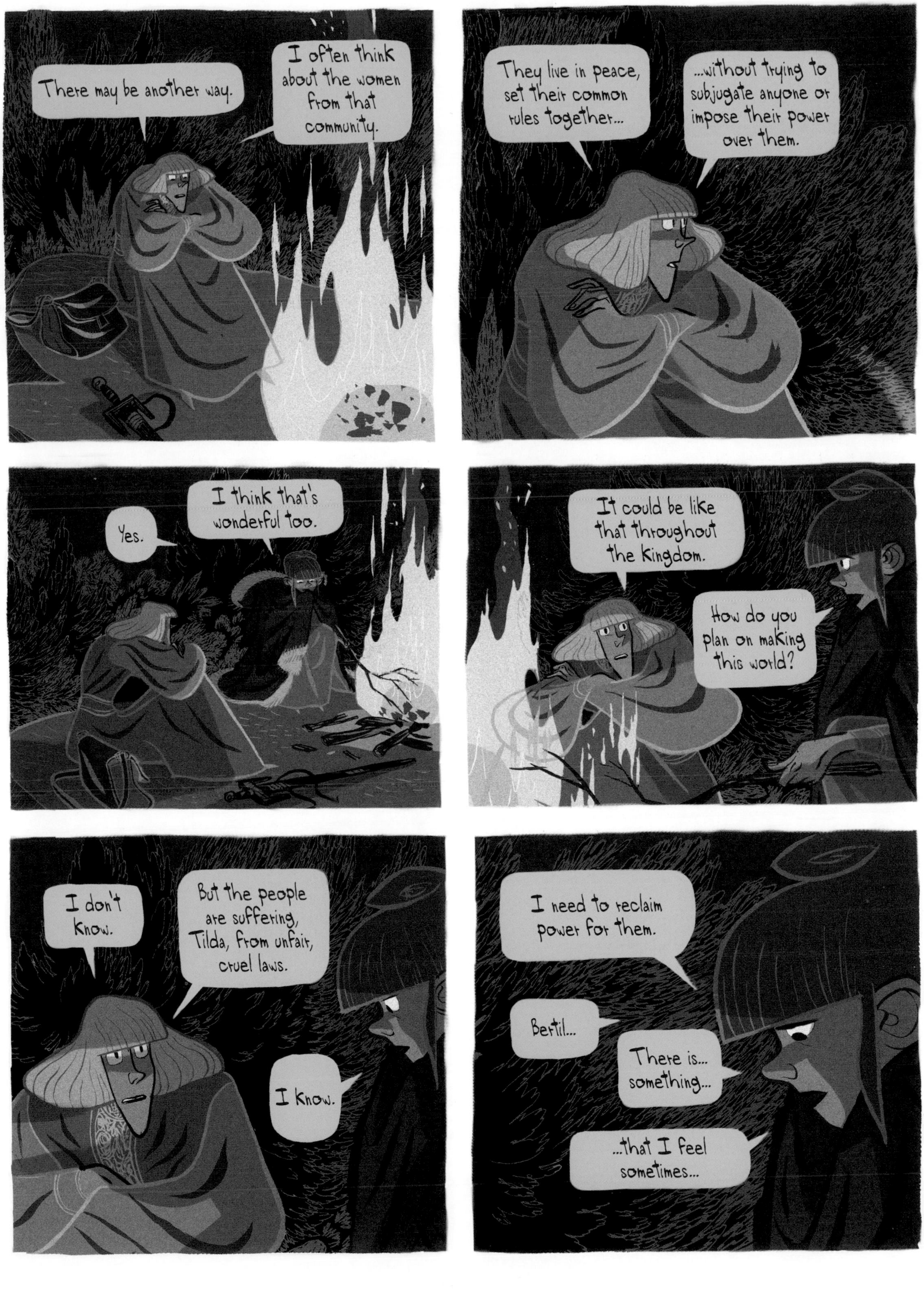
There may be another way.
I often think about the women from that community.
They live in peace, set their common rules together...
...without trying to subjugate anyone or impose their power over them.
Yes.
I think that's wonderful too.
It could be like that throughout the kingdom.
How do you plan on making this world?
I don't know.
But the people are suffering, Tilda, from unfair, cruel laws.
I know.
I need to reclaim power for them.
Bertil...
There is... something...
...that I feel sometimes...

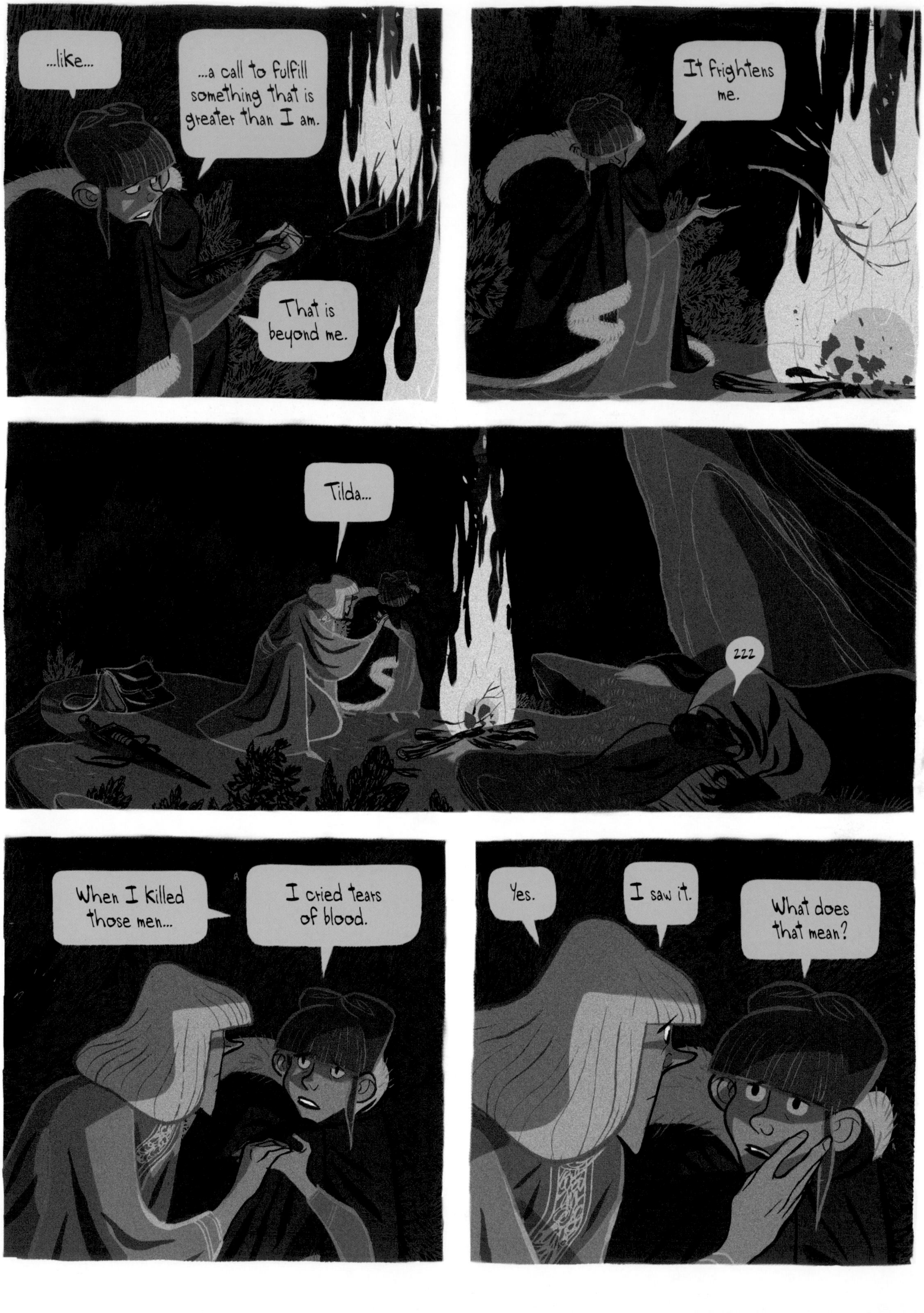
...like...
...a call to fulfill something that is greater than I am.
That is beyond me.
It frightens me.
Tilda...
zzz
When I killed those men...
I cried tears of blood.
Yes.
I saw it.
What does that mean?

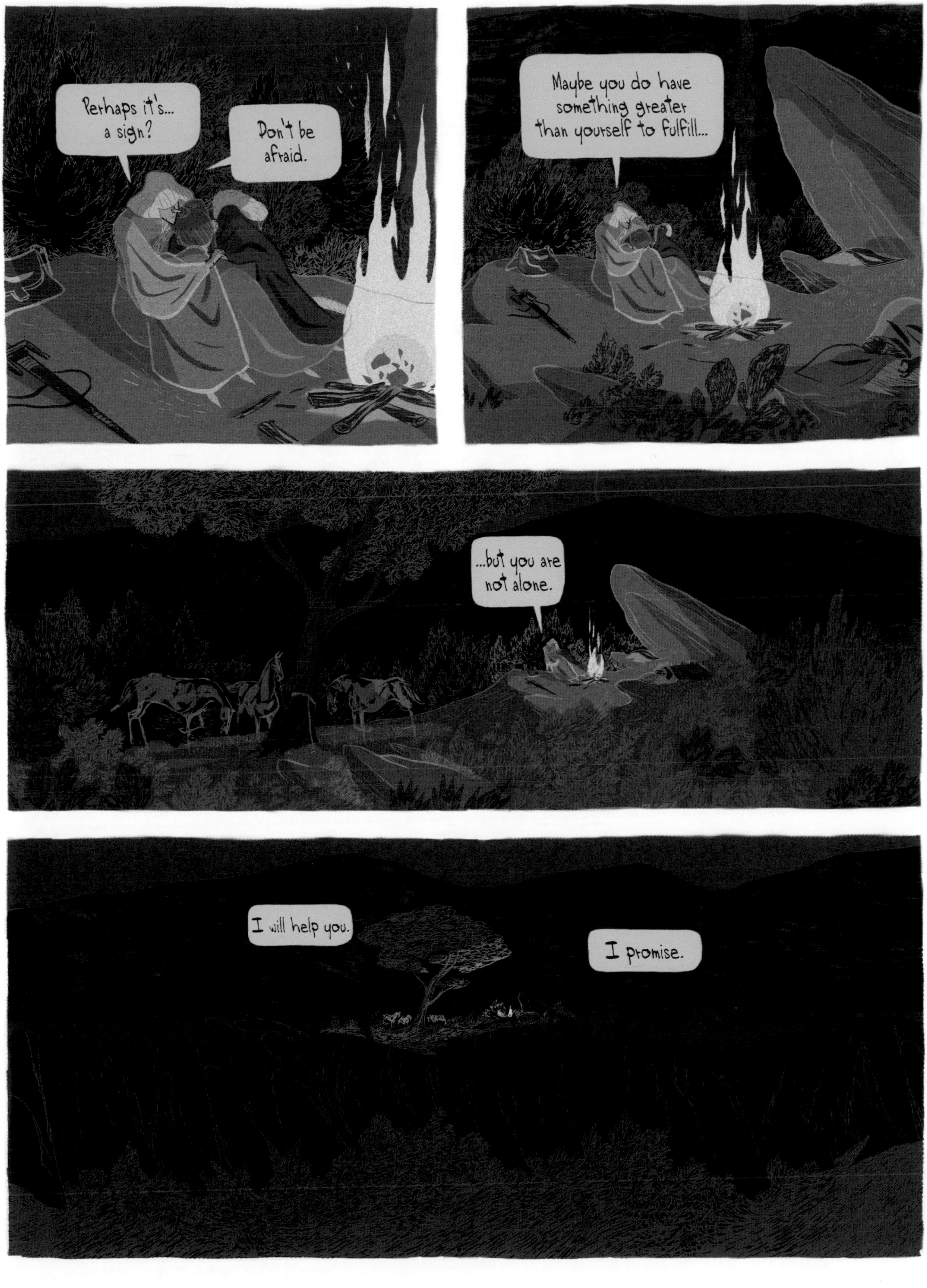
Perhaps it's... a sign?
Don't be afraid.
Maybe you do have something greater than yourself to fulfill...
...but you are not alone.
I will help you.
I promise.

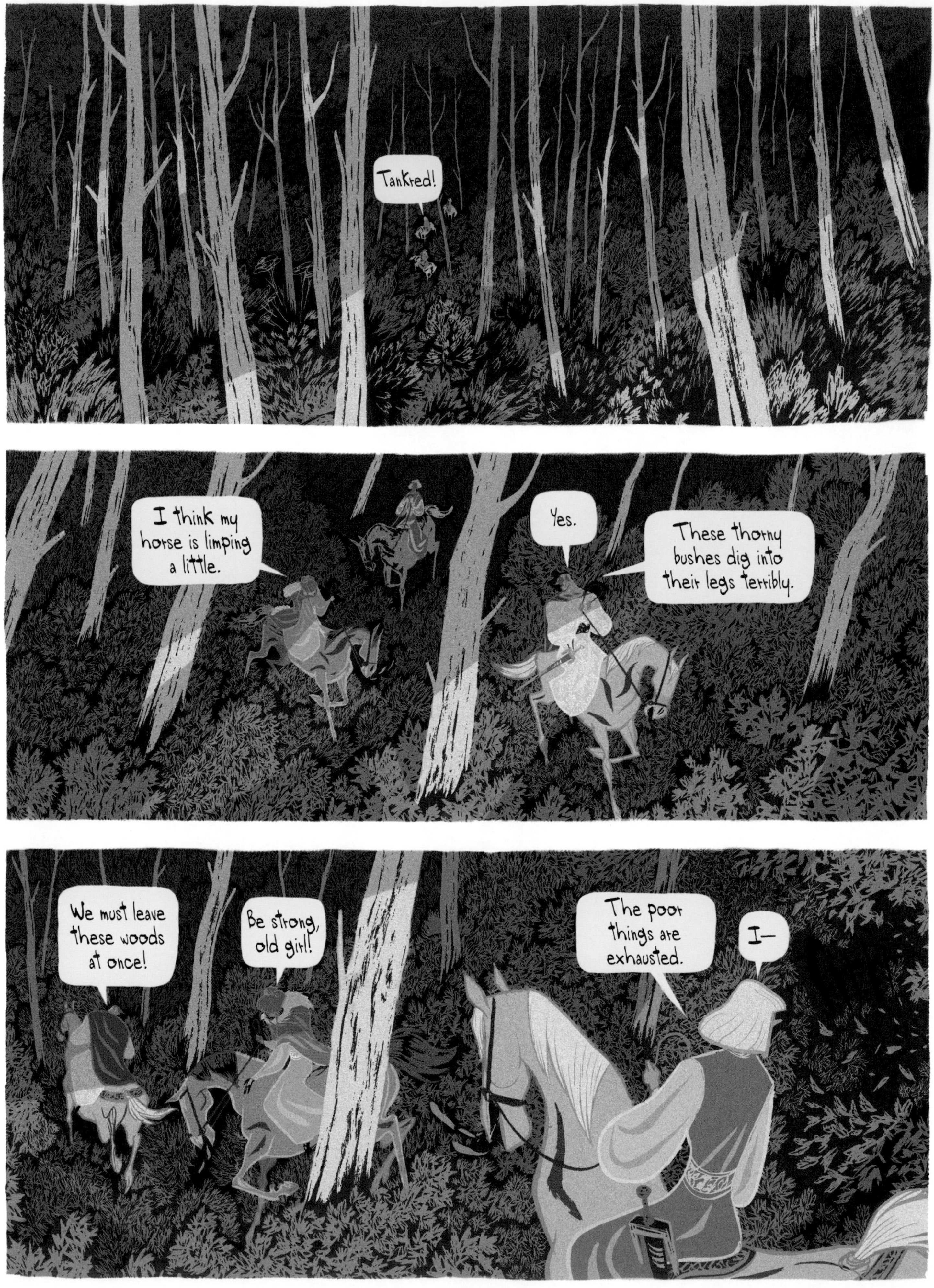
Tankred!
I think my horse is limping a little.
Yes.
These thorny bushes dig into their legs terribly.
We must leave these woods at once!
Be strong, old girl!
The poor things are exhausted.
I—

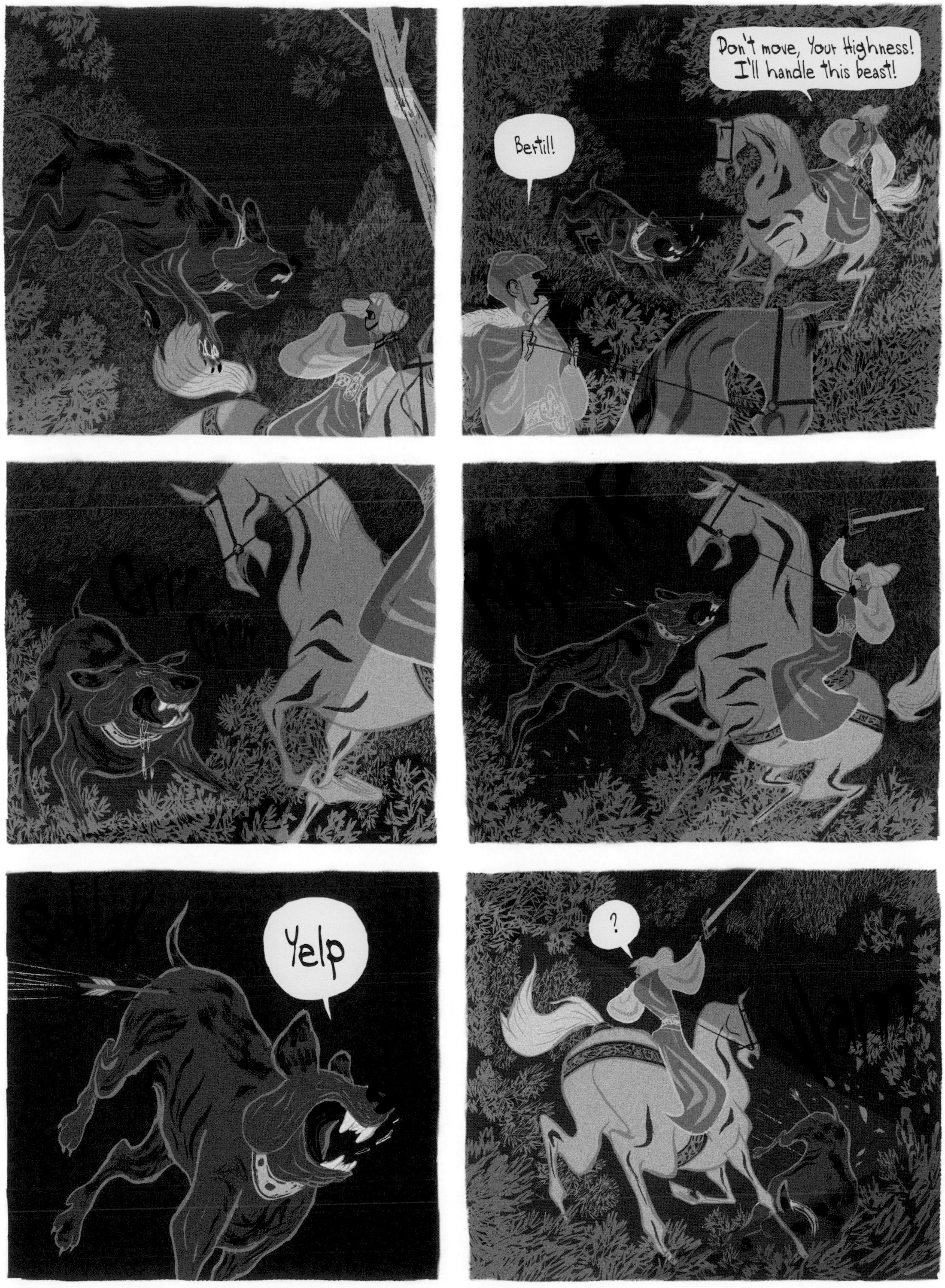

Don't move, Your Highness! I'll handle this beast!
Bertil!
Yelp
?

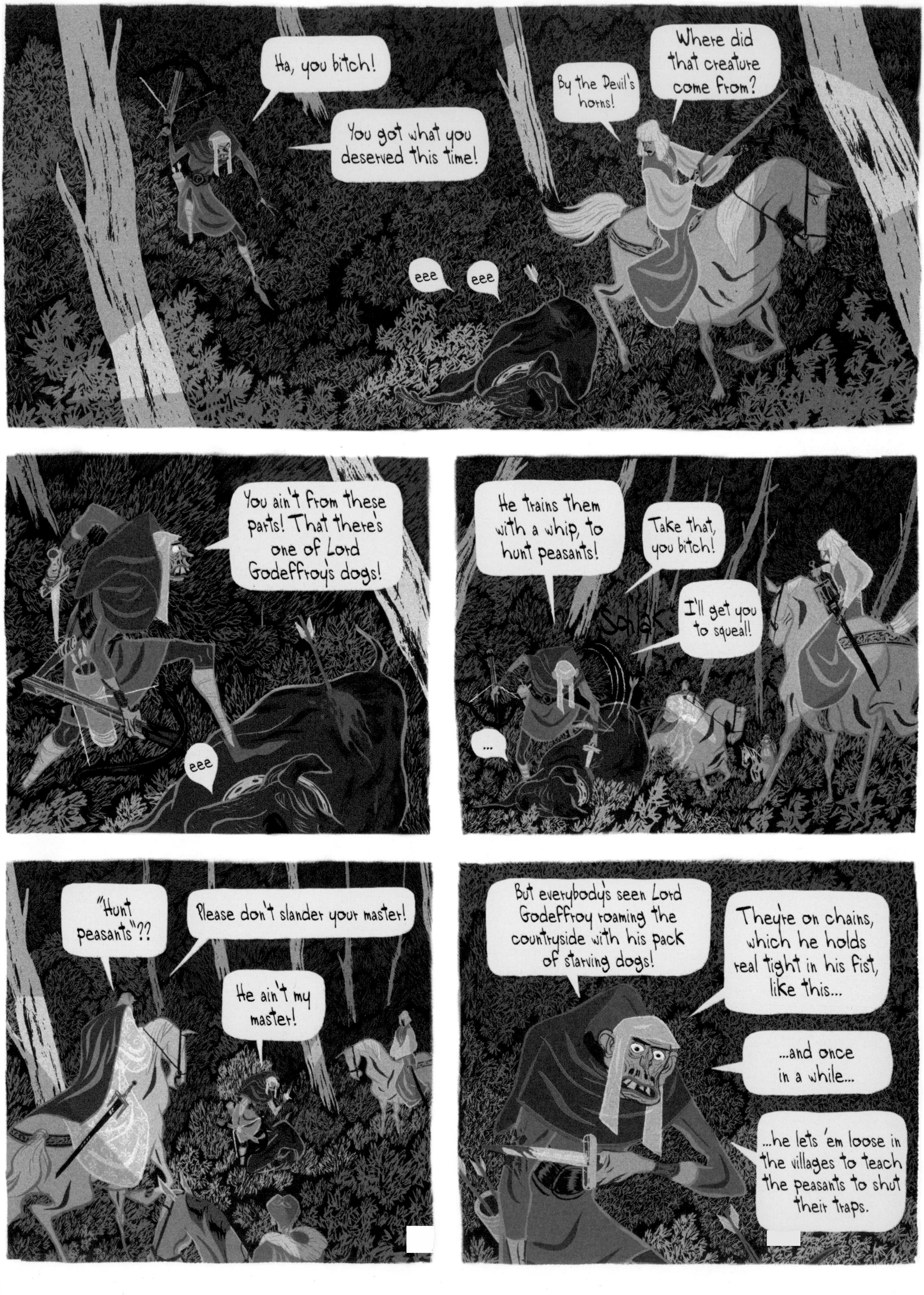
Ha, you bitch!
You got what you deserved this time!
By the Devil's horns!
Where did that creature come from?
eee
eee
You ain't from these parts! That there's one of Lord Godeffroy's dogs!
eee
He trains them with a whip, to hunt peasants!
Take that, you bitch!
I'll get you to squeal!
...
"Hunt peasants"??
Please don't slander your master!
He ain't my master!
But everybody's seen Lord Godeffroy roaming the countryside with his pack of starving dogs!
They're on chains, which he holds real tight in his fist, like this...
...and once in a while...
...he lets 'em loose in the villages to teach the peasants to shut their traps.

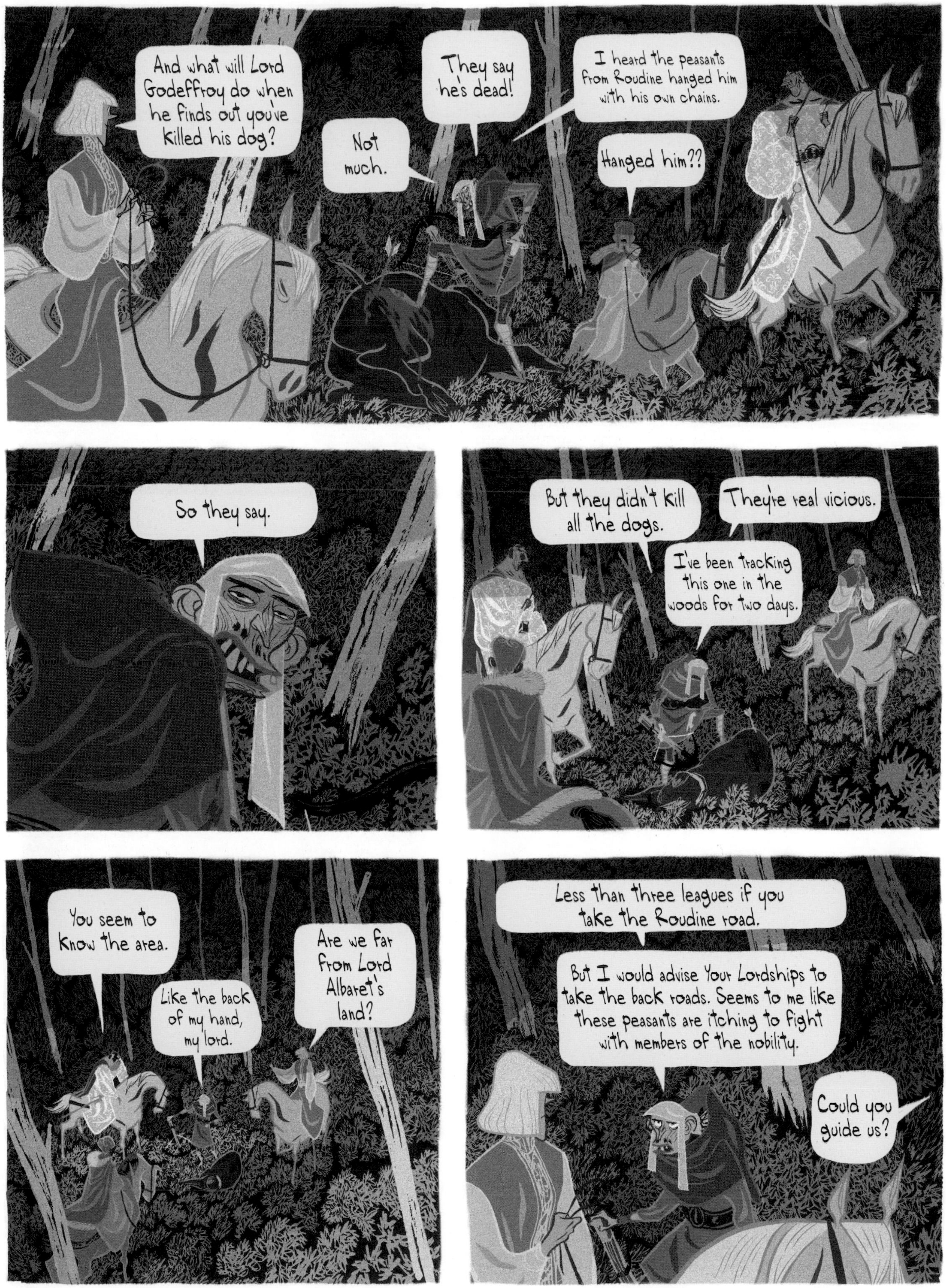

And what will Lord Godeffroy do when he finds out you've killed his dog?
Not much.
They say he's dead!
I heard the peasants from Roudine hanged him with his own chains.
Hanged him??
So they say.
But they didn't kill all the dogs.
They're real vicious.
I've been tracking this one in the woods for two days.
You seem to know the area.
Like the back of my hand, my lord.
Are we far from Lord Albaret's land?
Less than three leagues if you take the Roudine road.
But I would advise Your Lordships to take the back roads. Seems to me like these peasants are itching to fight with members of the nobility.
Could you guide us?

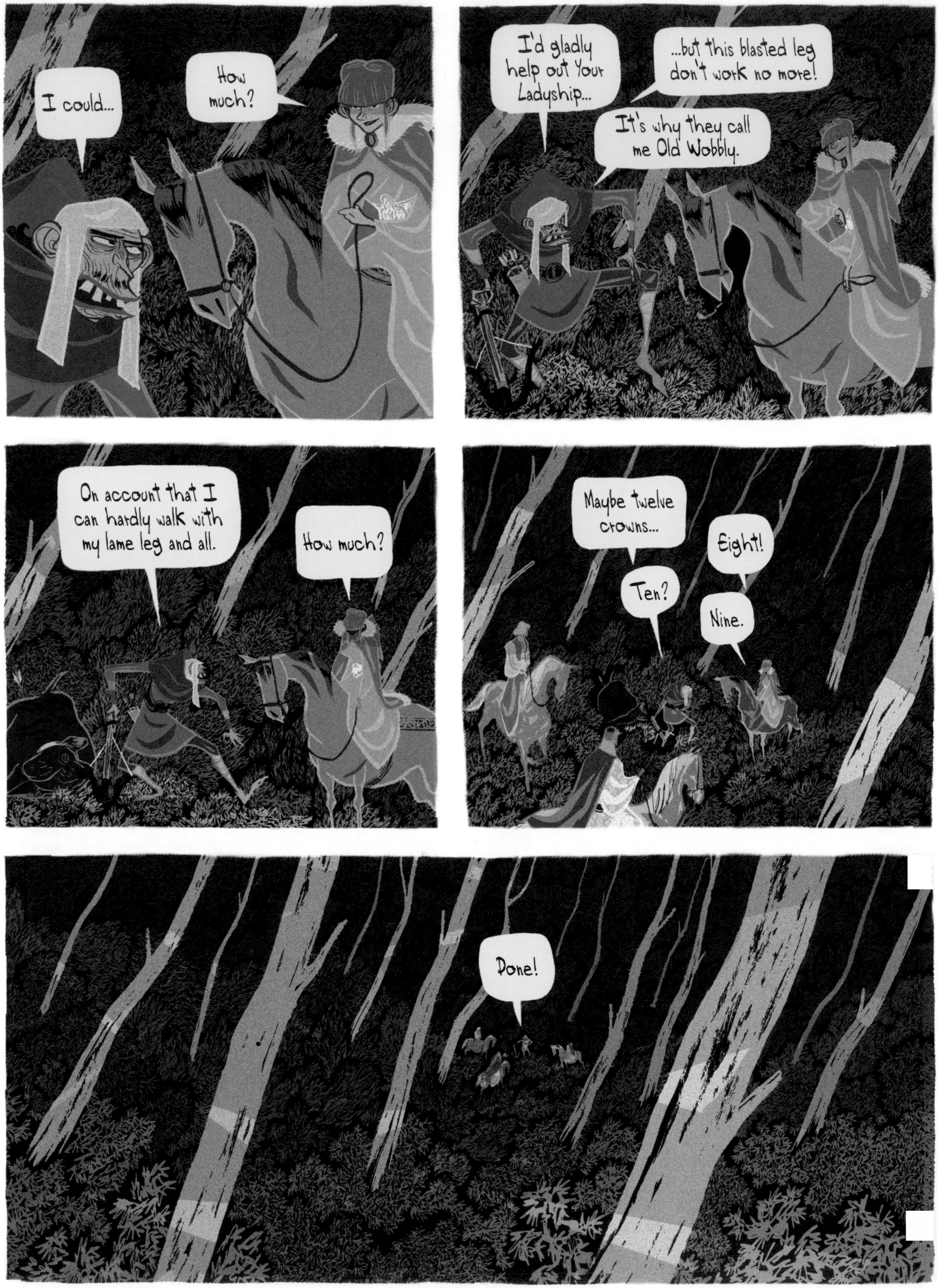
I could...
How much?
I'd gladly help out Your Ladyship...
...but this blasted leg don't work no more!
It's why they call me Old Wobbly.
On account that I can hardly walk with my lame leg and all.
How much?
Maybe twelve crowns...
Ten?
Eight!
Nine.
Done!

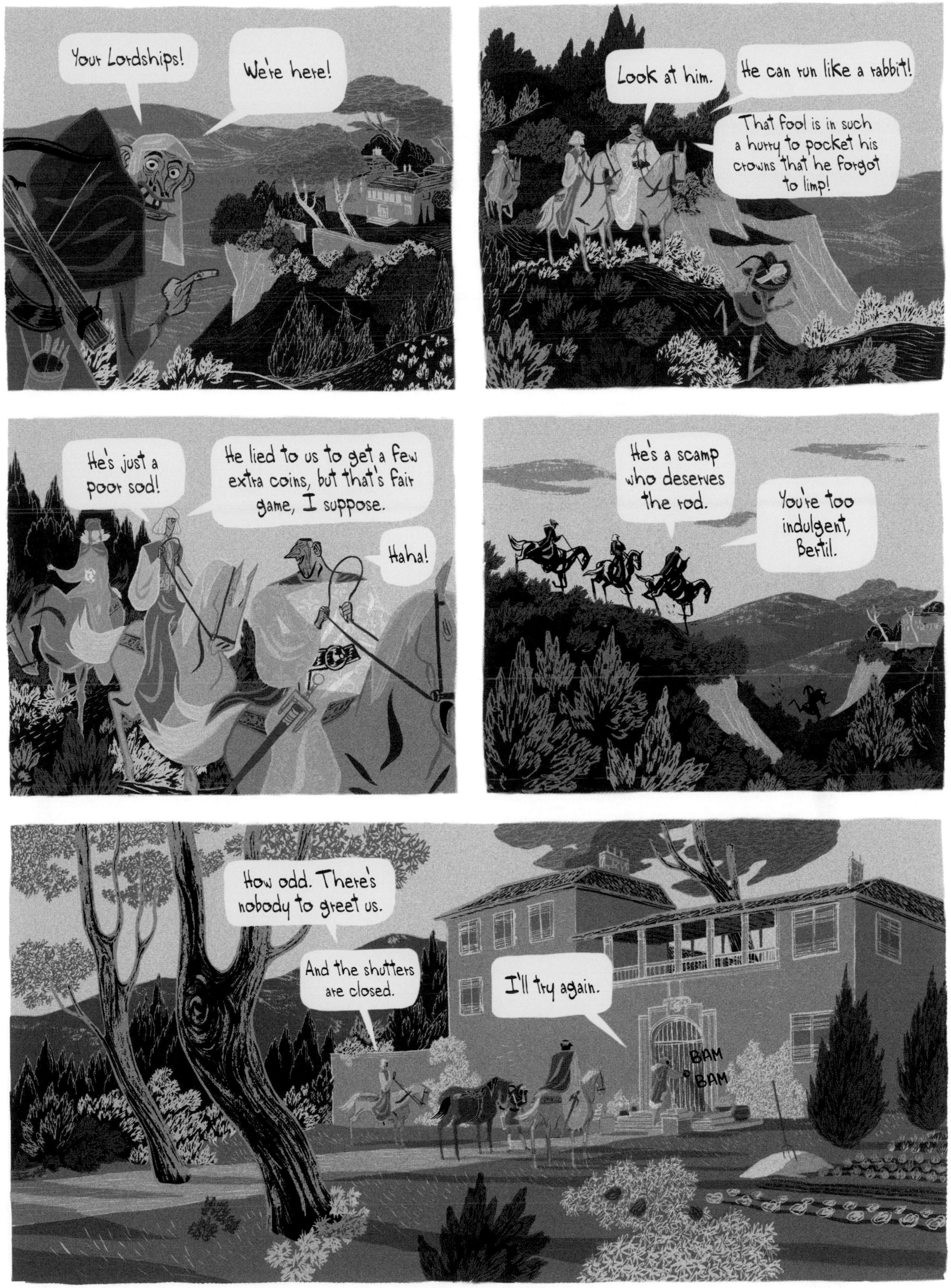
Your Lordships!
We're here!
Look at him.
He can run like a rabbit!
That fool is in such a hurry to pocket his crowns that he forgot to limp!
He's just a poor sod!
He lied to us to get a few extra coins, but that's fair game, I suppose.
Haha!
He's a scamp who deserves the rod.
You're too indulgent, Bertil.
How odd. There's nobody to greet us.
And the shutters are closed.
I'll try again.
BAM
BAM

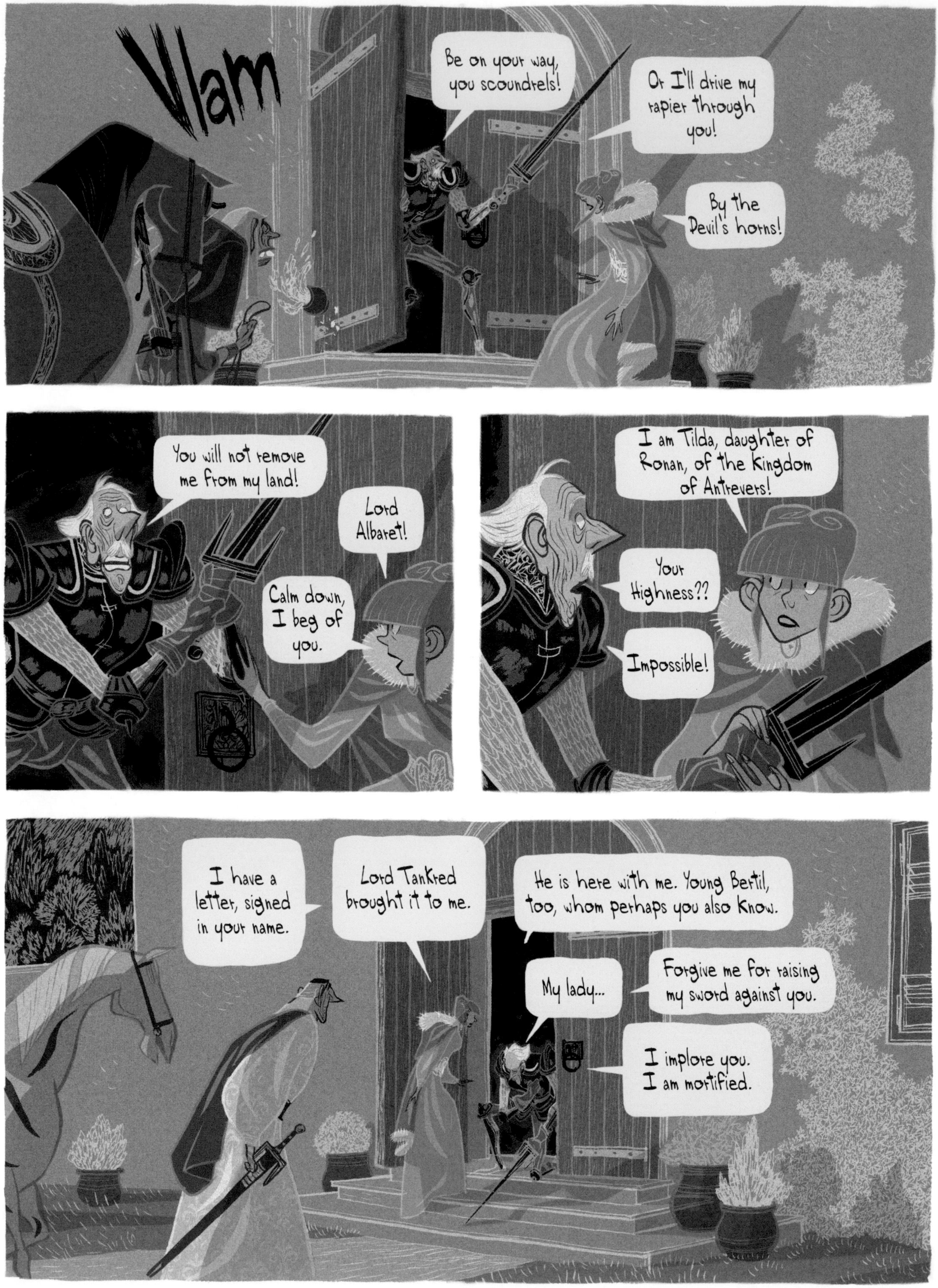

Vlam
Be on your way, you scoundrels!
Or I'll drive my rapier through you!
By the Devil's horns!
You will not remove me from my land!
Lord Albaret!
Calm down, I beg of you.
I am Tilda, daughter of Ronan, of the Kingdom of Antrevers!
Your Highness??
Impossible!
I have a letter, signed in your name.
Lord Tankred brought it to me.
He is here with me. Young Bertil, too, whom perhaps you also know.
My lady...
Forgive me for raising my sword against you.
I implore you. I am mortified.

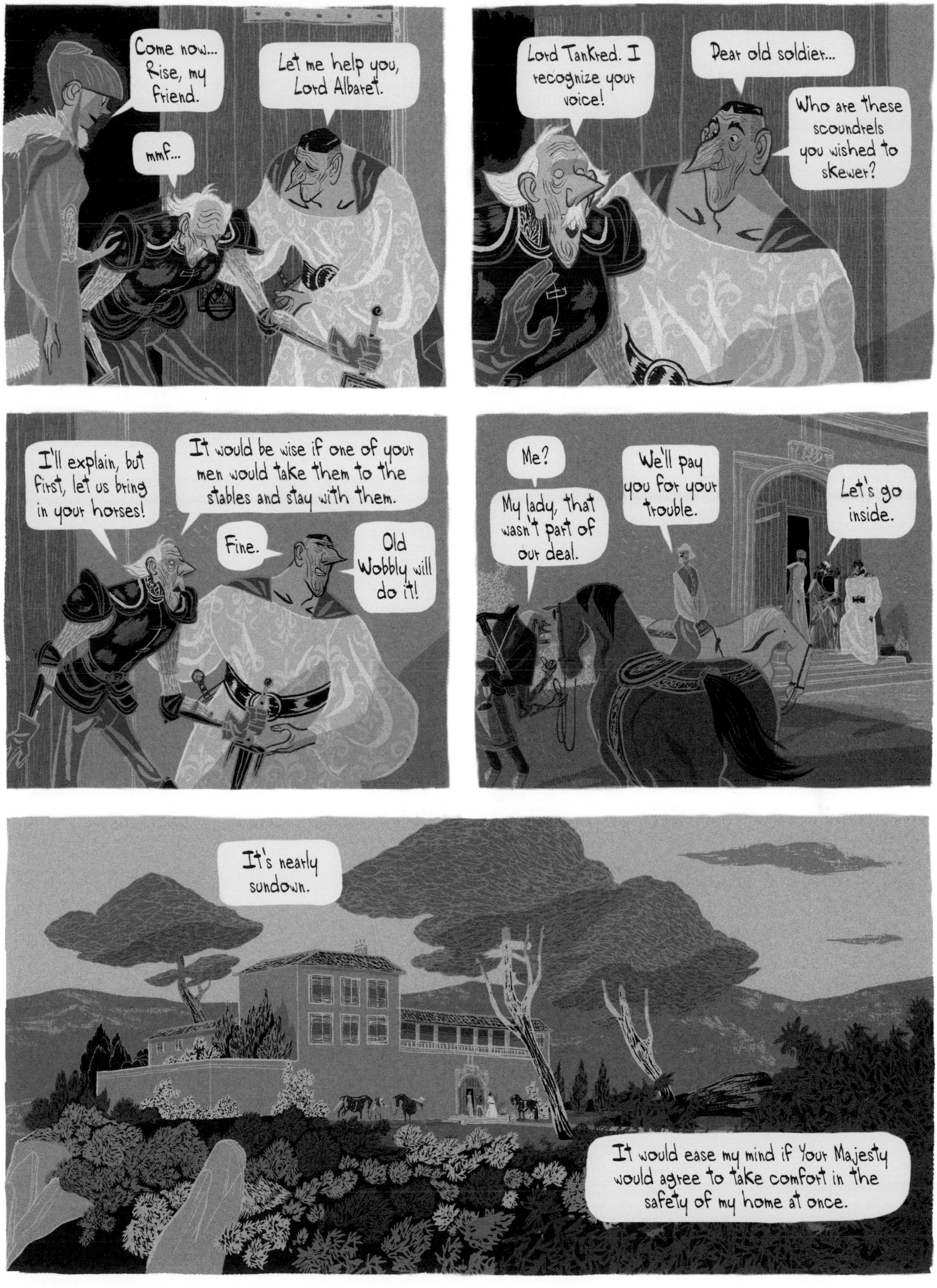
Come now... Rise, my friend.
mmf...
Let me help you, Lord Albaret.
Lord Tankred. I recognize your voice!
Dear old soldier...
Who are these scoundrels you wished to skewer?
I'll explain, but first, let us bring in your horses!
It would be wise if one of your men would take them to the stables and stay with them.
Fine.
Old Wobbly will do it!
Me?
My lady, that wasn't part of our deal.
We'll pay you for your trouble.
Let's go inside.
It's nearly sundown.
It would ease my mind if Your Majesty would agree to take comfort in the safety of my home at once.

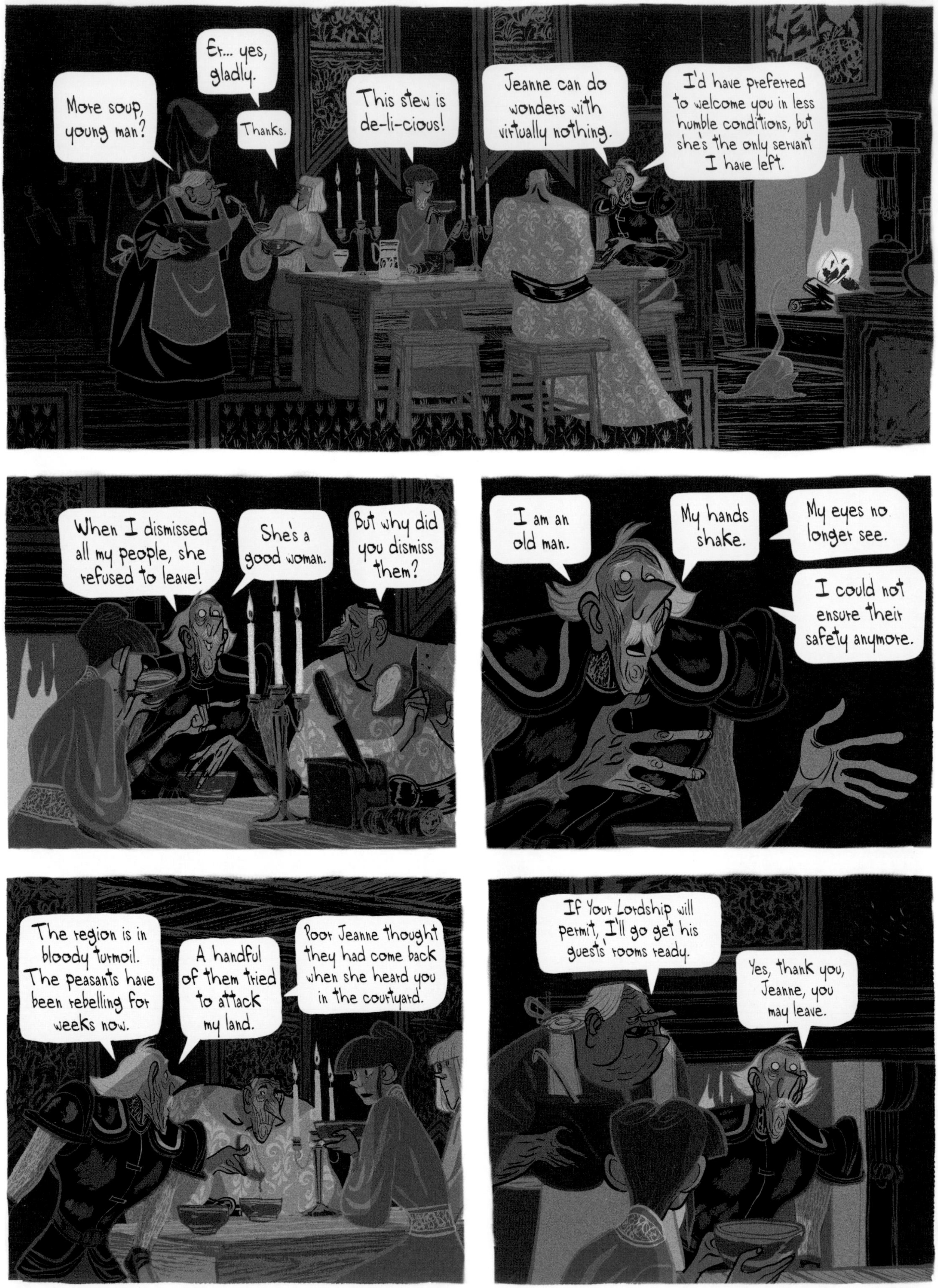
More soup, young man?
Er... yes, gladly.
Thanks.
This stew is de-li-cious!
Jeanne can do wonders with virtually nothing.
I'd have preferred to welcome you in less humble conditions, but she's the only servant I have left.
When I dismissed all my people, she refused to leave!
She's a good woman.
But why did you dismiss them?
I am an old man.
My hands shake.
My eyes no longer see.
I could not ensure their safety anymore.
The region is in bloody turmoil. The peasants have been rebelling for weeks now.
A handful of them tried to attack my land.
Poor Jeanne thought they had come back when she heard you in the courtyard.
If Your Lordship will permit, I'll go get his guests' rooms ready.
Yes, thank you, Jeanne, you may leave.

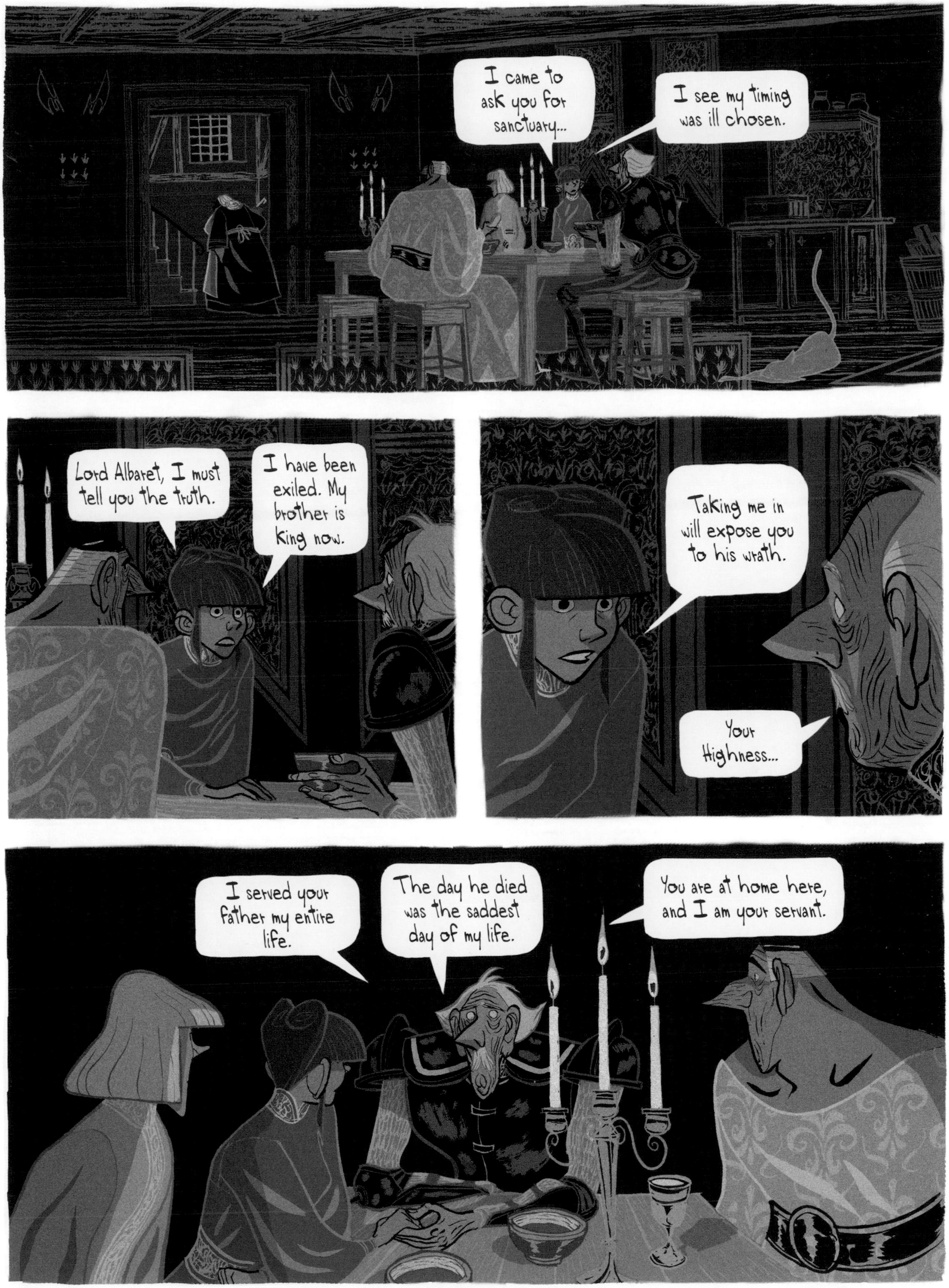
I came to ask you for sanctuary...
I see my timing was ill chosen.
Lord Albaret, I must tell you the truth.
I have been exiled. My brother is King now.
Taking me in will expose you to his wrath.
Your Highness...
I served your father my entire life.
The day he died was the saddest day of my life.
You are at home here, and I am your servant.

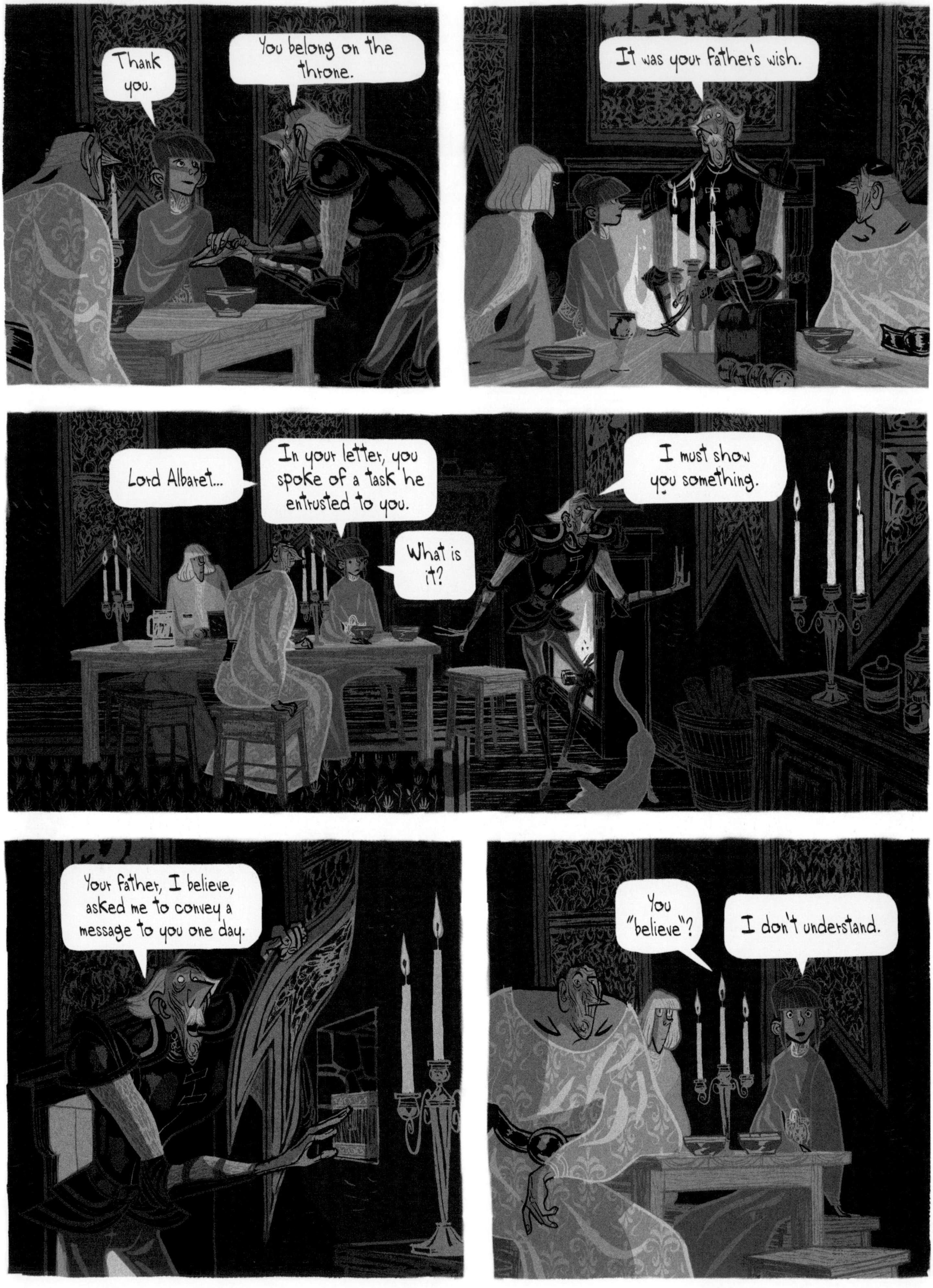
Thank you.
You belong on the throne.
It was your father's wish.
Lord Albaret...
In your letter, you spoke of a task he entrusted to you.
What is it?
I must show you something.
Your father, I believe, asked me to convey a message to you one day.
You "believe"?
I don't understand.

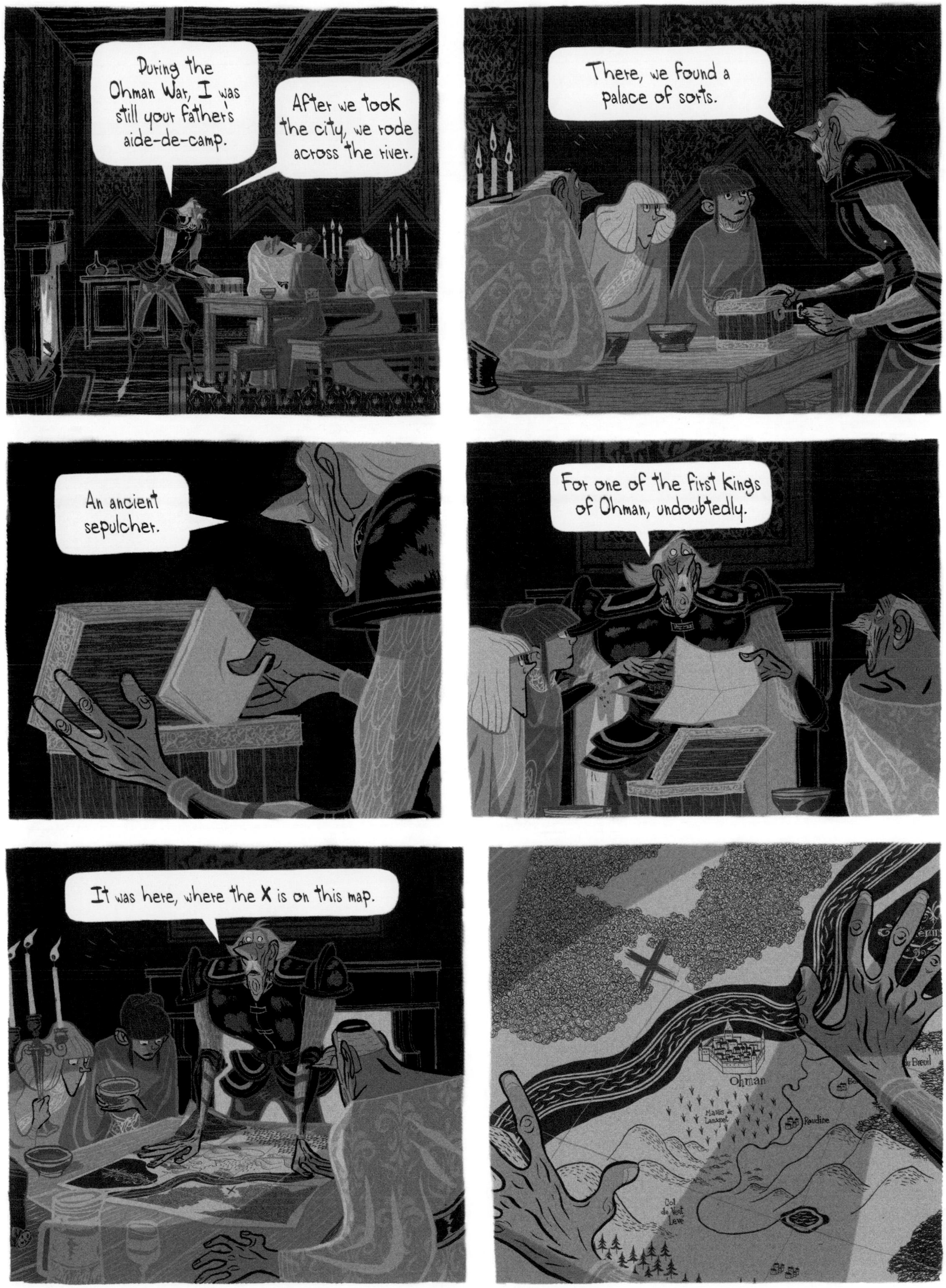
During the Ohman War, I was still your father's aide-de-camp.
After we took the city, we rode across the river.
There, we found a palace of sorts.
An ancient sepulcher.
For one of the first kings of Ohman, undoubtedly.
It was here, where the X is on this map.
Ohman
Marais de Lansquet
Raudine
du Breuil
Col de Vent Levé

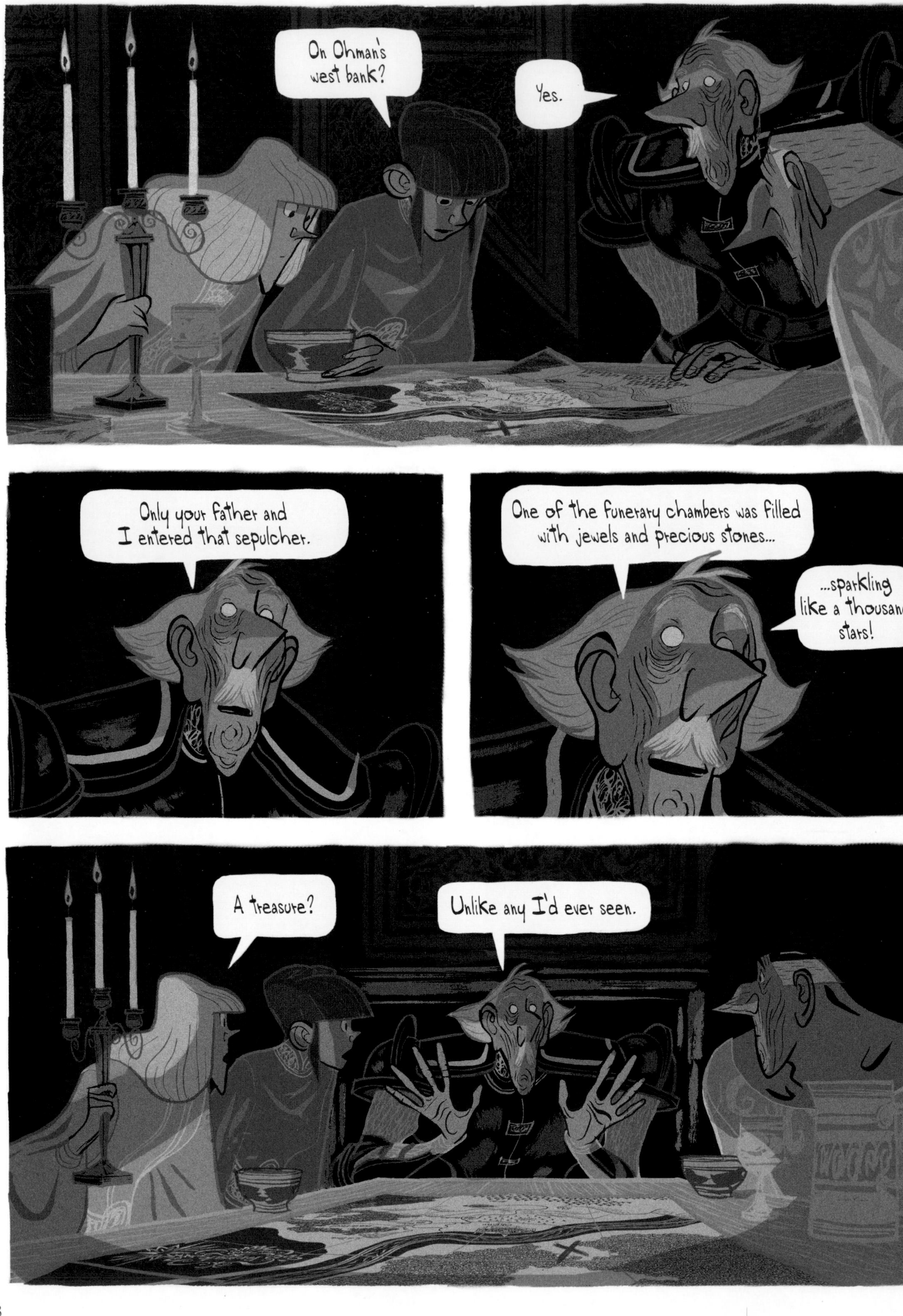
On Ohman's west bank?
Yes.
Only your father and I entered that sepulcher.
One of the funerary chambers was filled with jewels and precious stones...
...sparkling like a thousand stars!
A treasure?
Unlike any I'd ever seen.

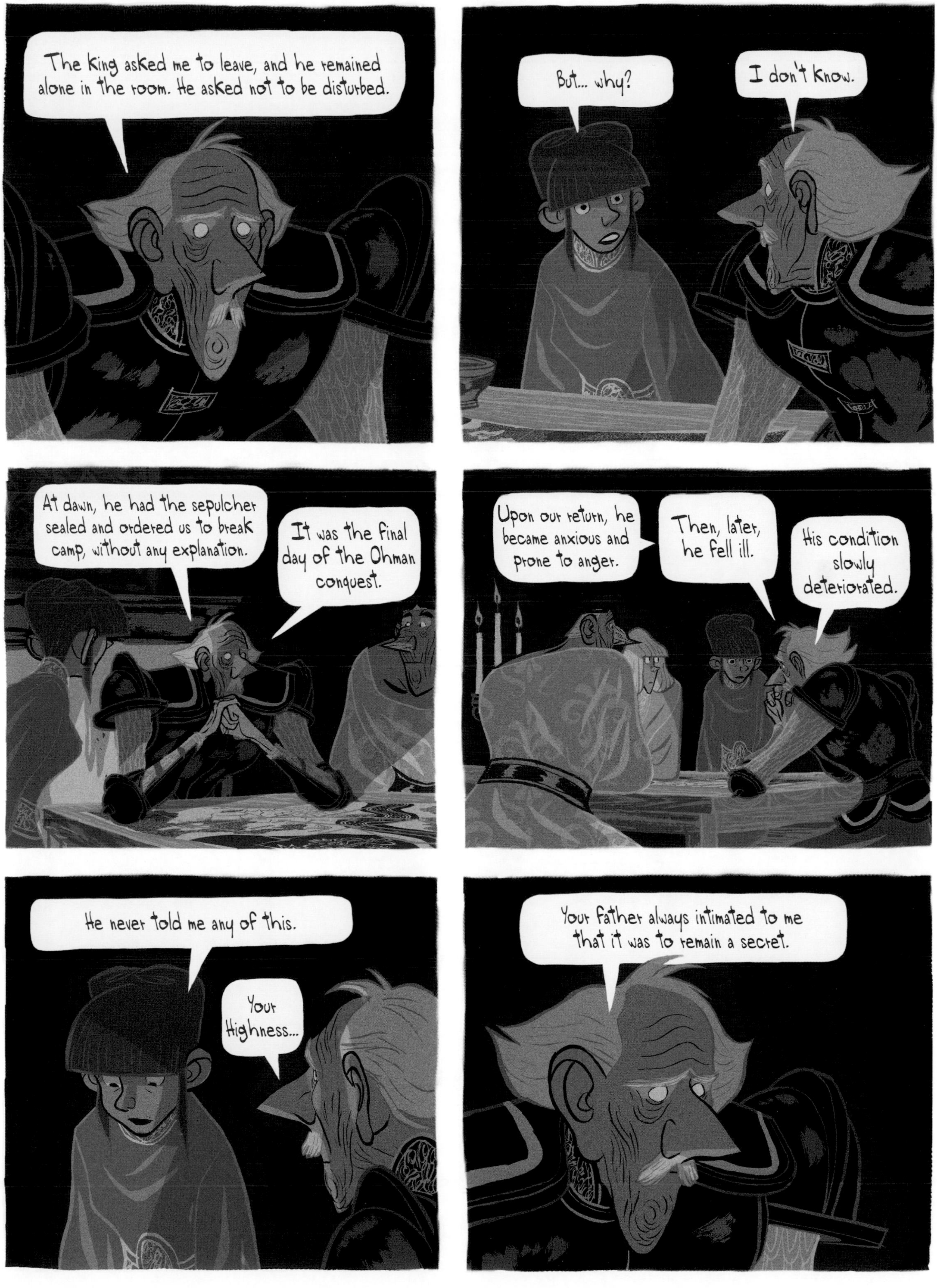
The King asked me to leave, and he remained alone in the room. He asked not to be disturbed.
But... why?
I don't know.
At dawn, he had the sepulcher sealed and ordered us to break camp, without any explanation.
It was the final day of the Ohman conquest.
Upon our return, he became anxious and prone to anger.
Then, later, he fell ill.
His condition slowly deteriorated.
He never told me any of this.
Your Highness...
Your father always intimated to me that it was to remain a secret.

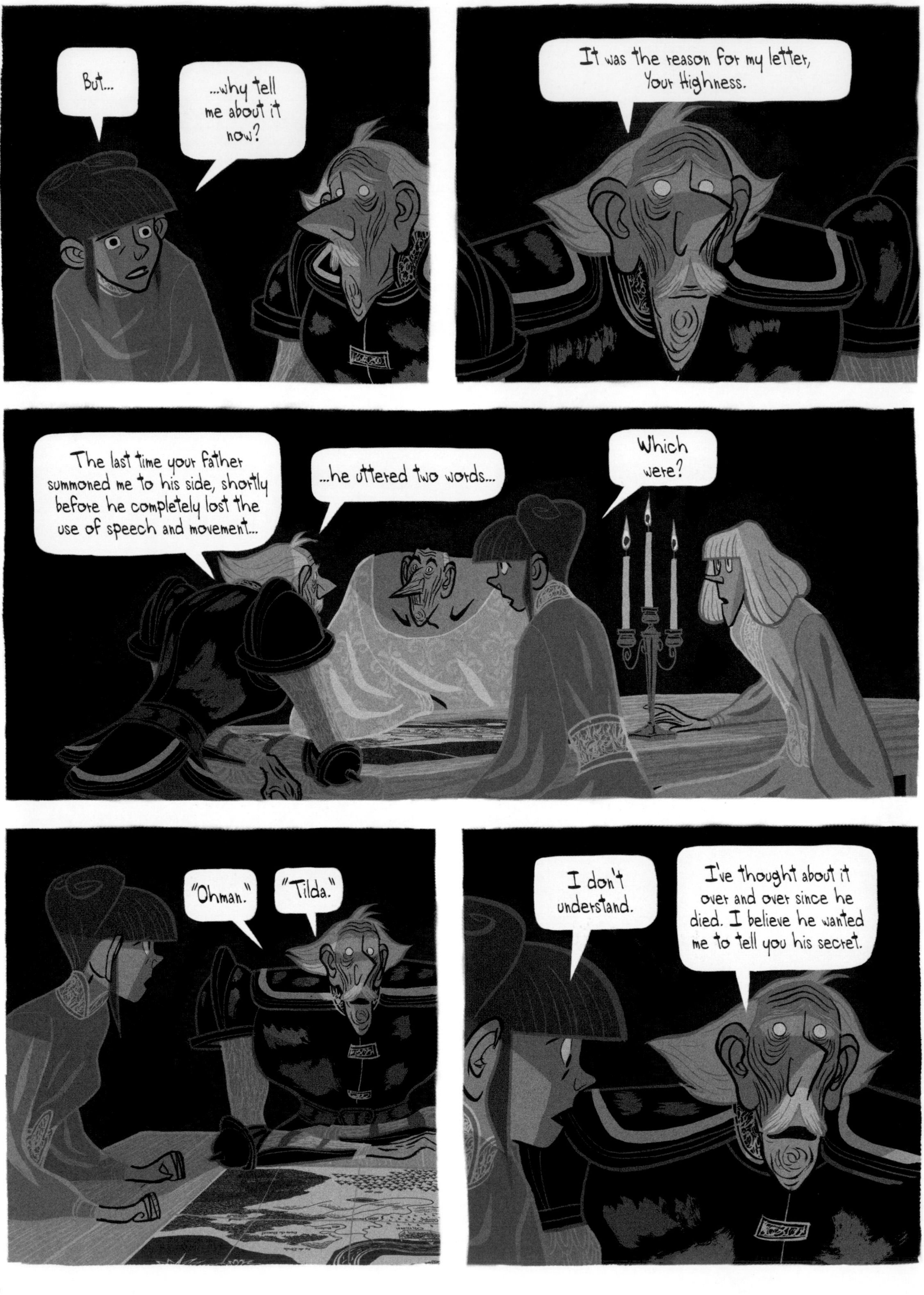
But...
...why tell me about it now?
It was the reason for my letter, Your Highness.
The last time your father summoned me to his side, shortly before he completely lost the use of speech and movement...
...he uttered two words...
Which were?
"Ohman."
"Tilda."
I don't understand.
I've thought about it over and over since he died. I believe he wanted me to tell you his secret.

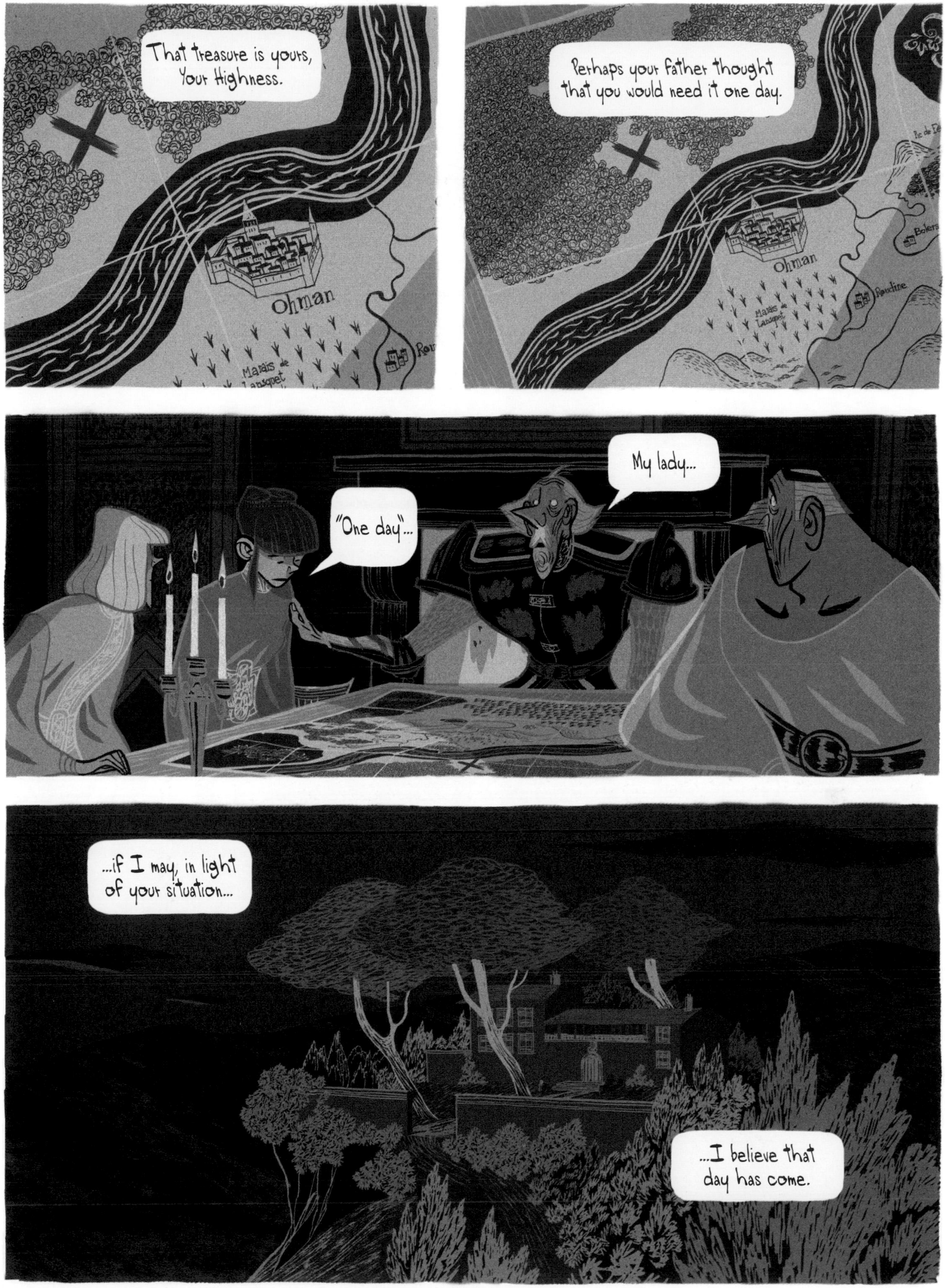
That treasure is yours, Your Highness.
Ohman
Marais de Lansquet
Perhaps your father thought that you would need it one day.
Ohman
"One day"...
My lady...
...if I may, in light of your situation...
...I believe that day has come.

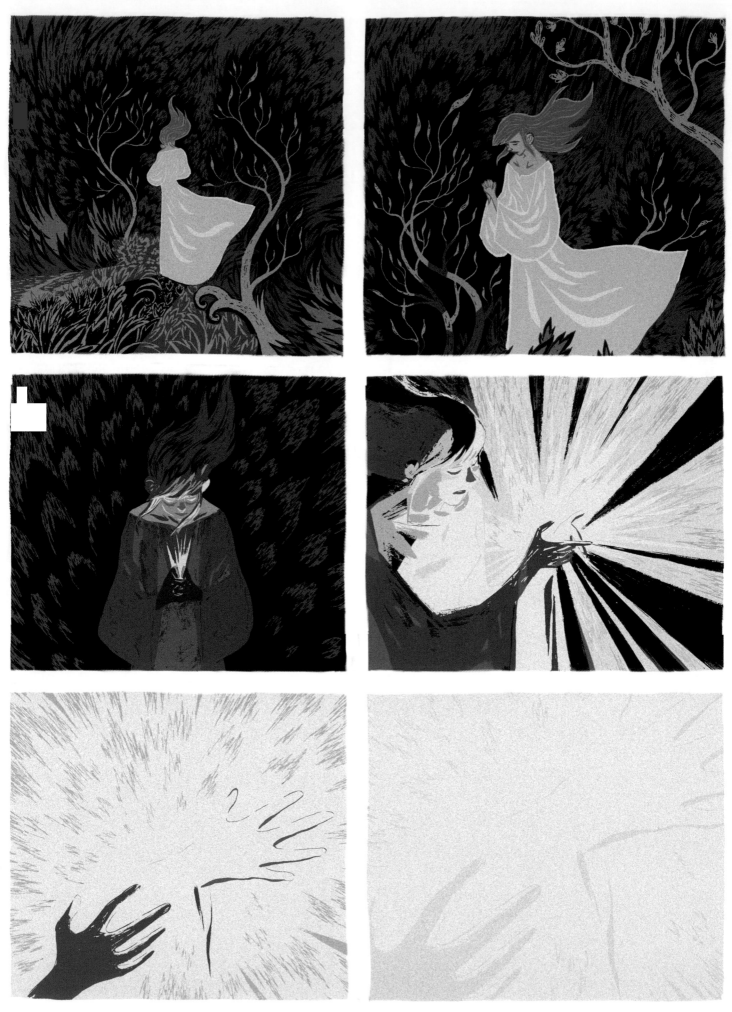

Your Highness?

Your Highness...

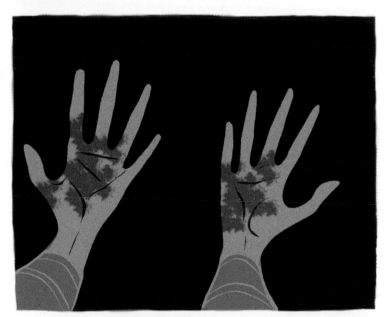

What's on your mind?

I....

163

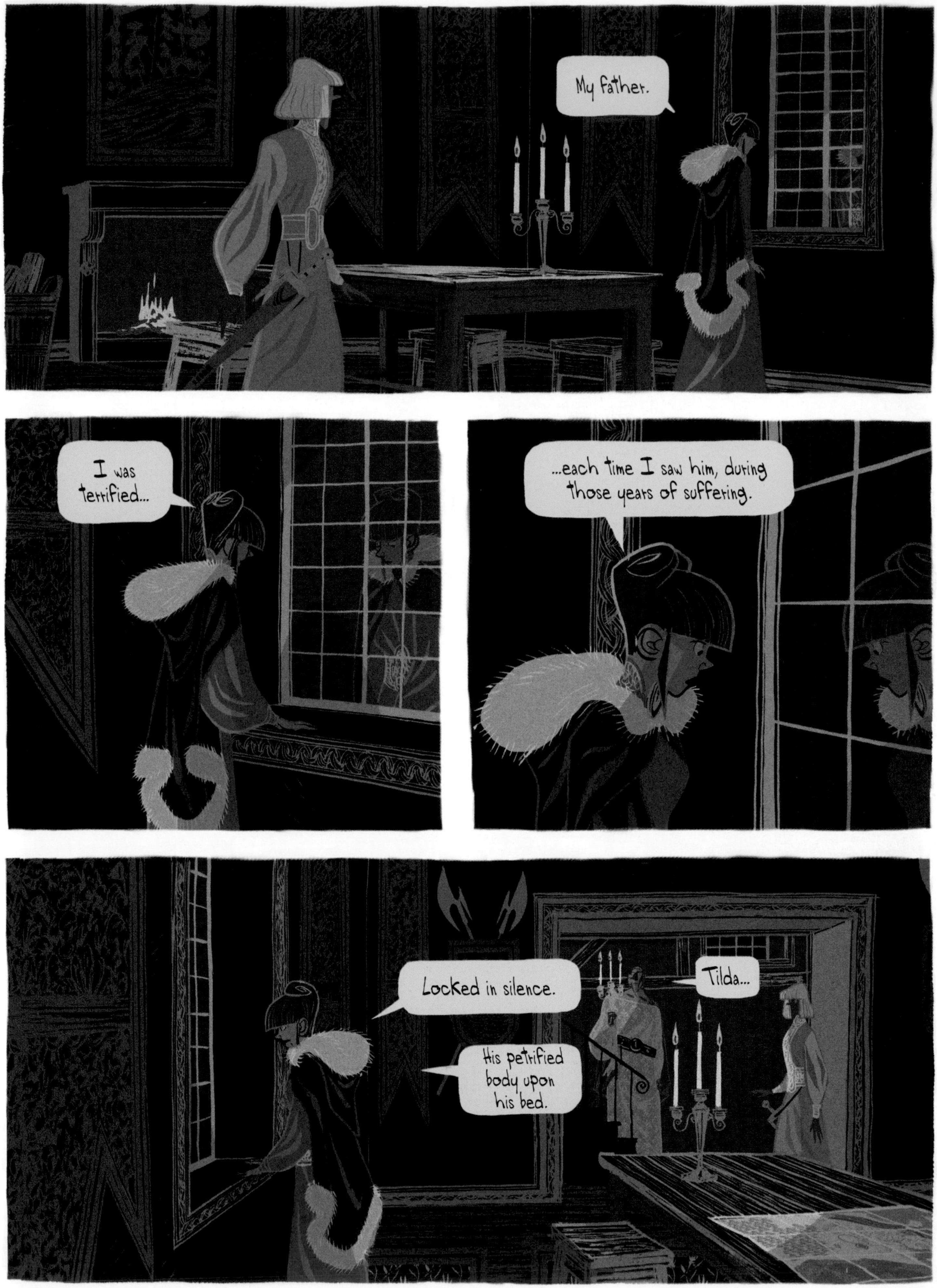
My father.
I was terrified...
...each time I saw him, during those years of suffering.
Locked in silence.
His petrified body upon his bed.
Tilda...

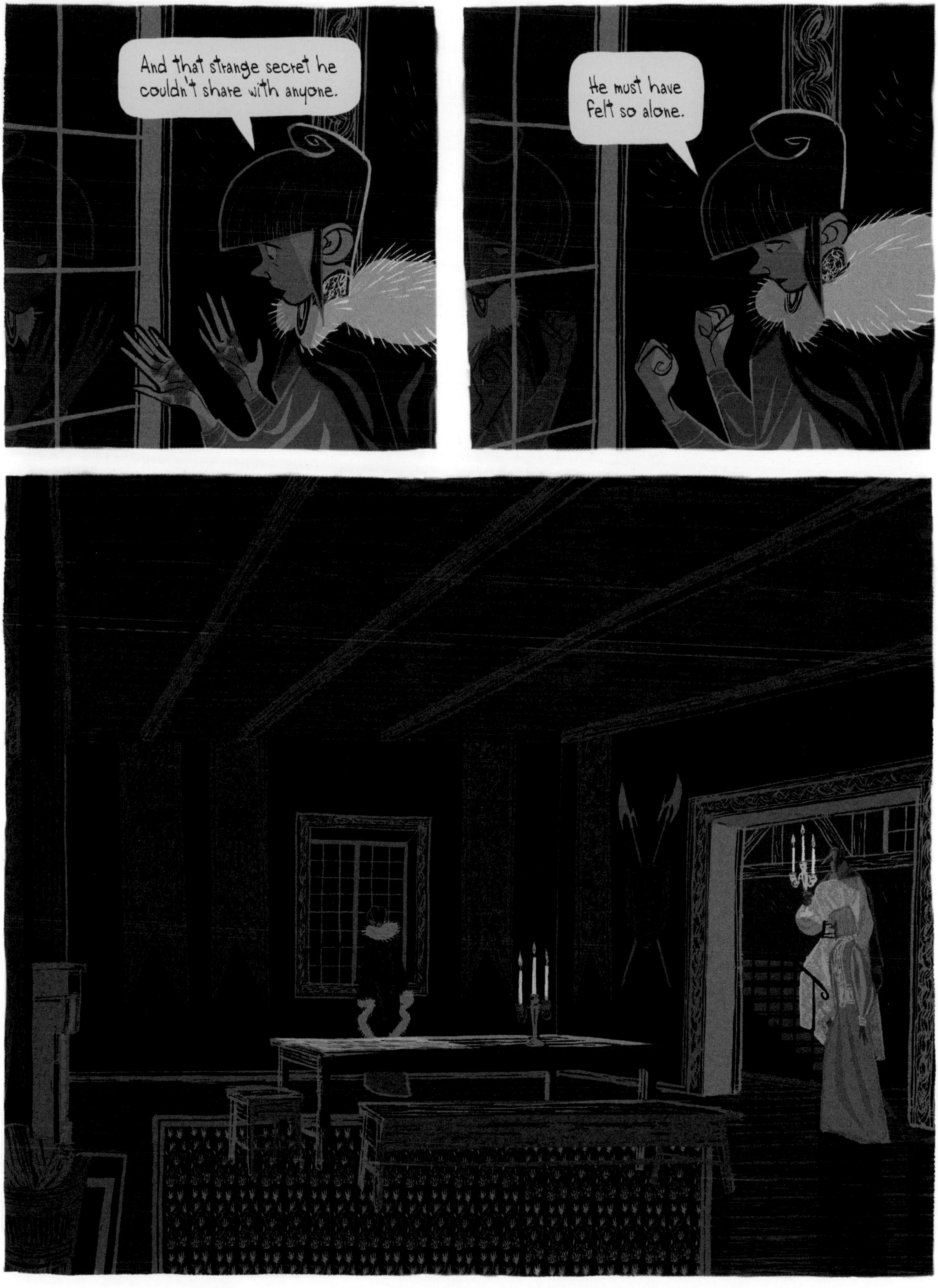
And that strange secret he couldn't share with anyone.
He must have felt so alone.

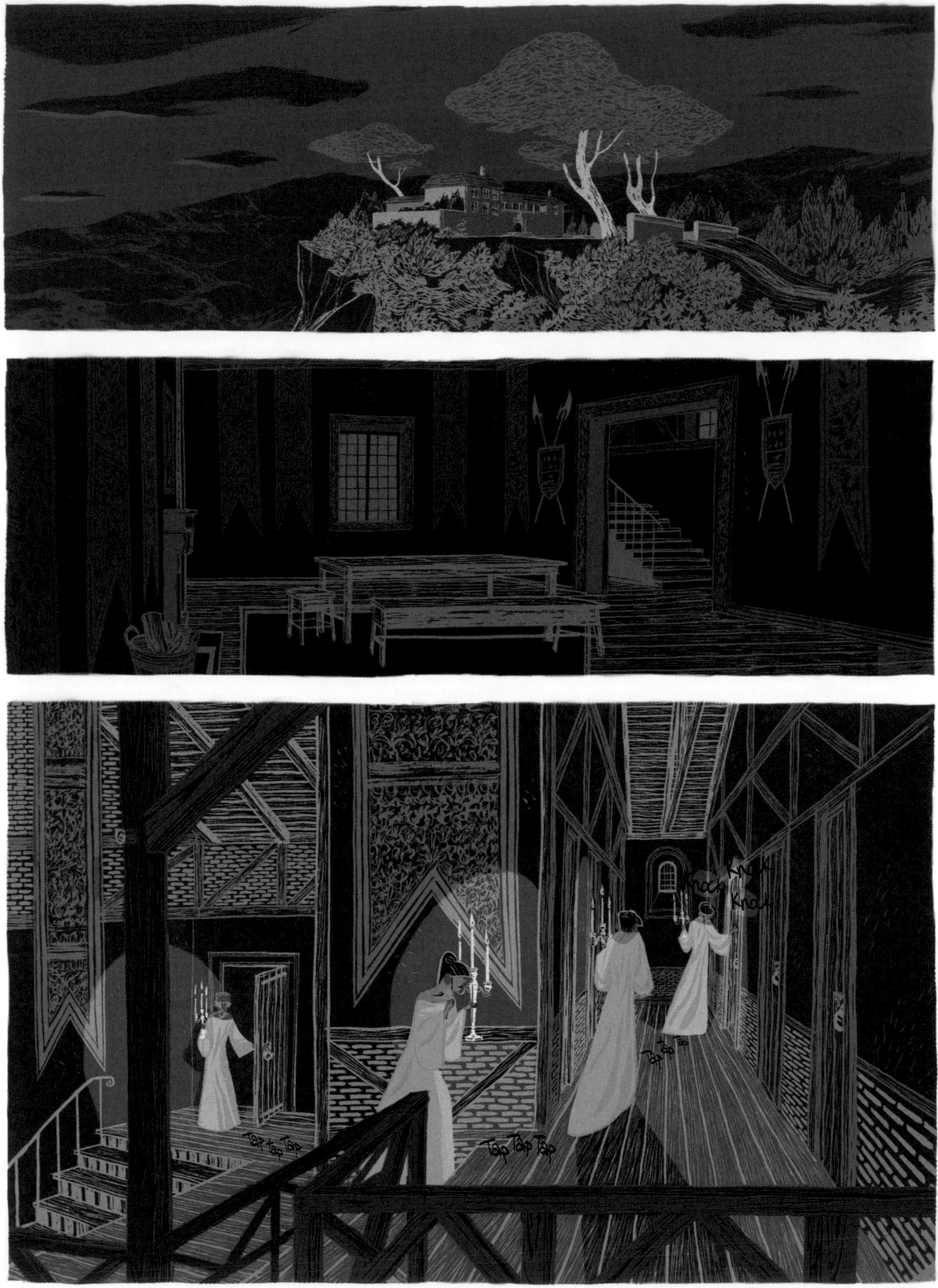
Tap tap tap
Tap Tap Tap
Tap Tap Tap
Knock
Knock
Knock

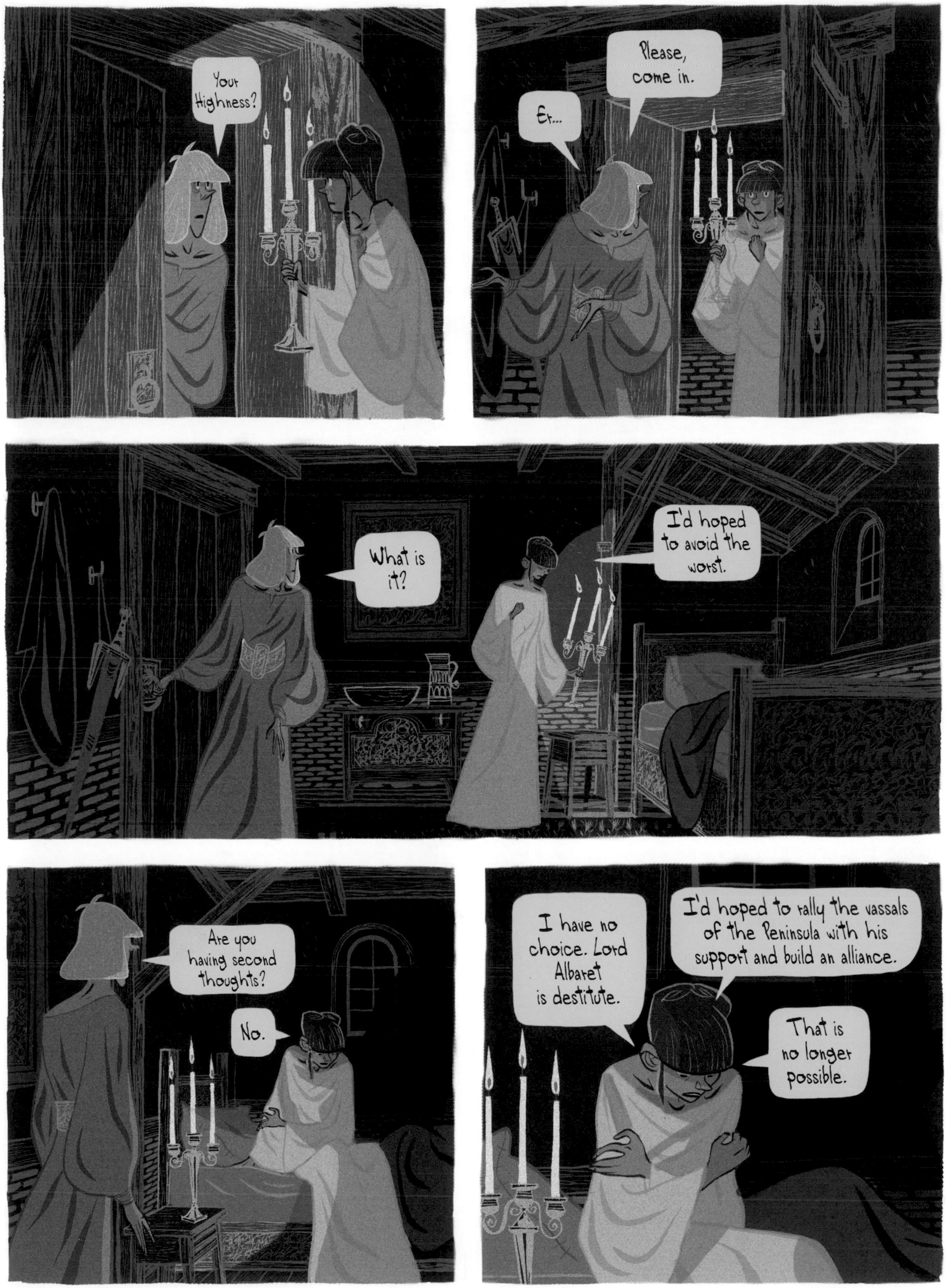
Your Highness?
Er...
Please, come in.
What is it?
I'd hoped to avoid the worst.
Are you having second thoughts?
No.
I have no choice. Lord Albaret is destitute.
I'd hoped to rally the vassals of the Peninsula with his support and build an alliance.
That is no longer possible.

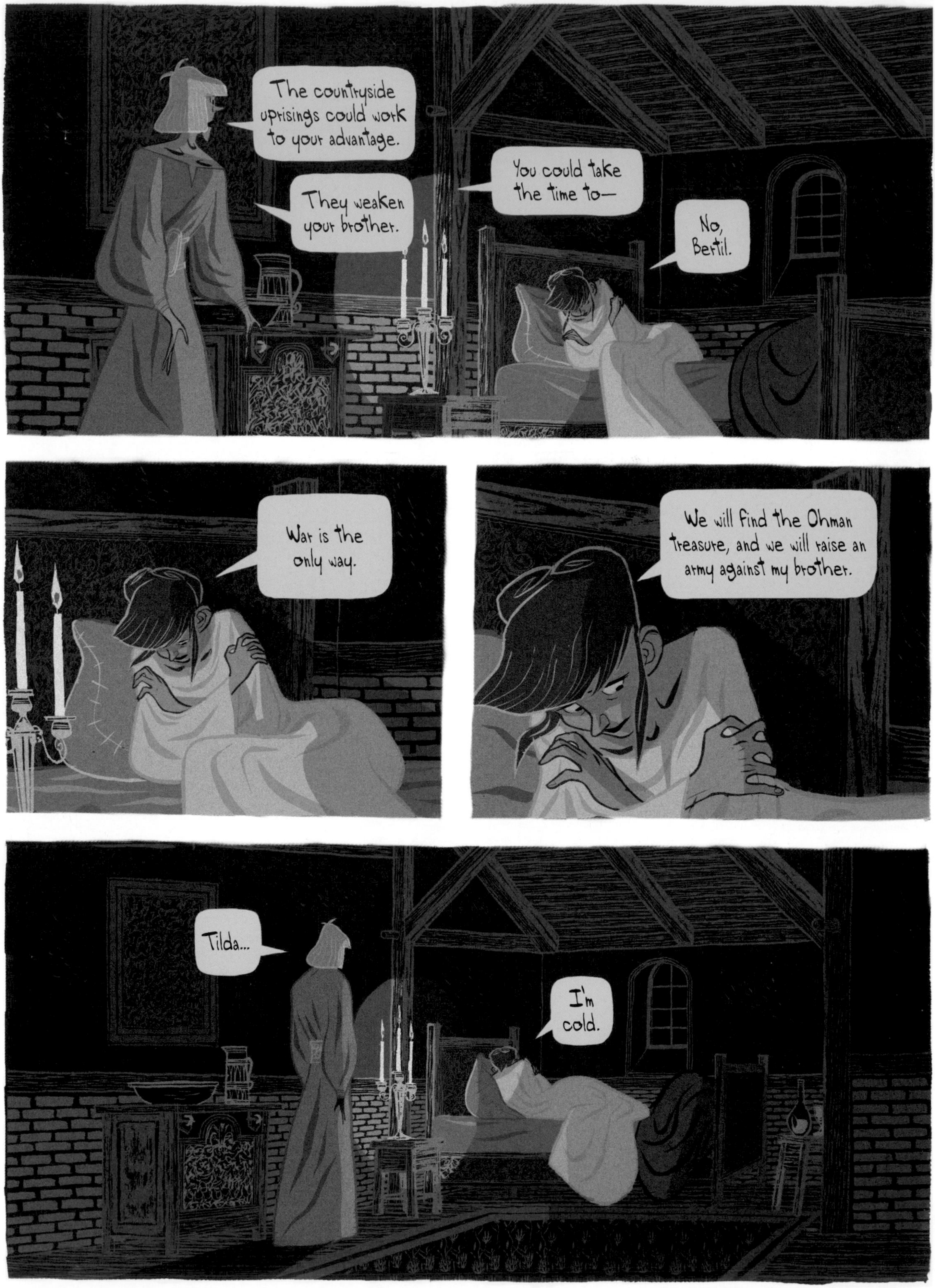
The countryside uprisings could work to your advantage.
They weaken your brother.
You could take the time to—
No, Bertil.
War is the only way.
We will find the Ohman treasure, and we will raise an army against my brother.
Tilda...
I'm cold.

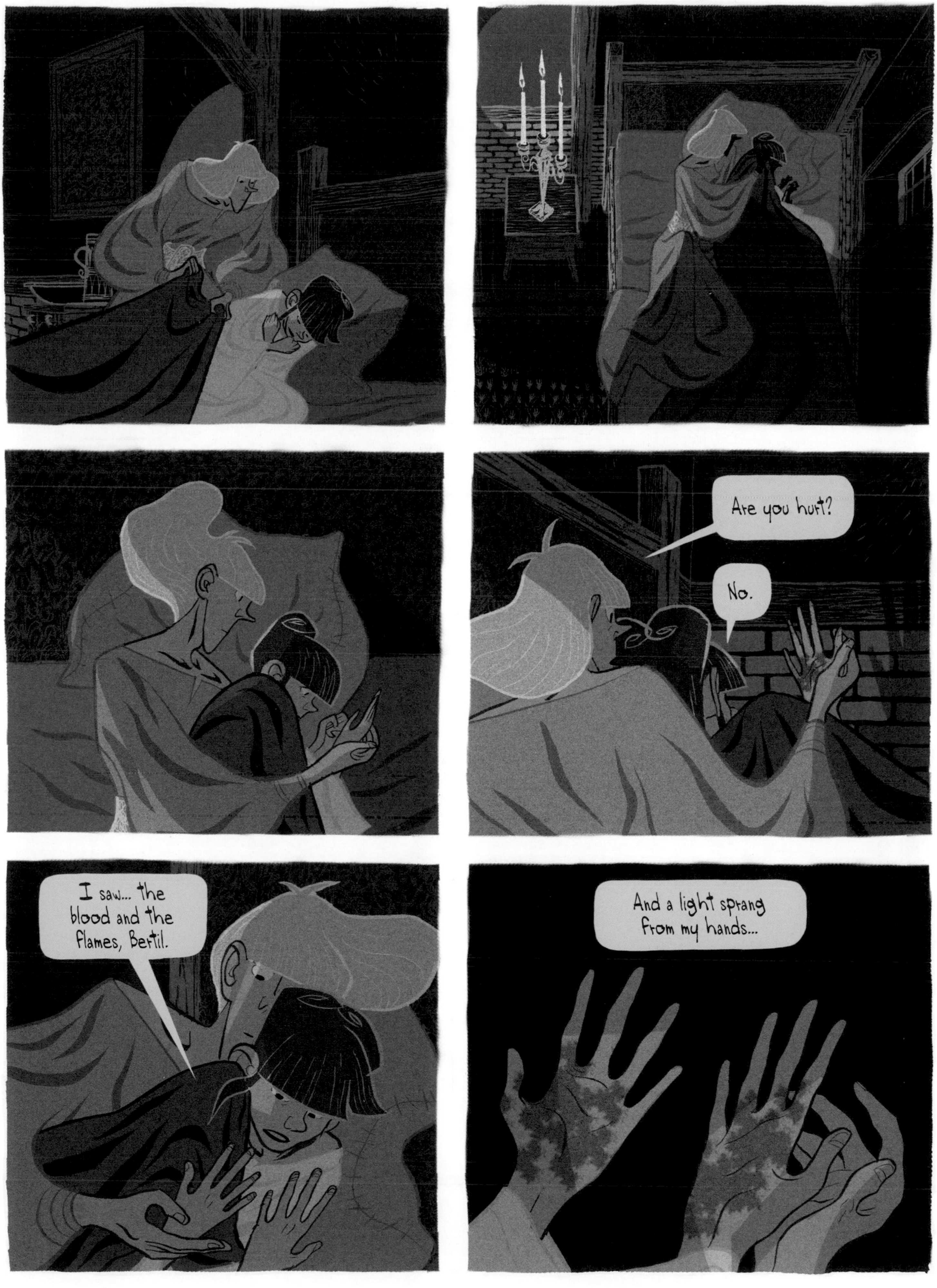
Are you hurt?
No.
I saw... the blood and the flames, Bertil.
And a light sprang from my hands...

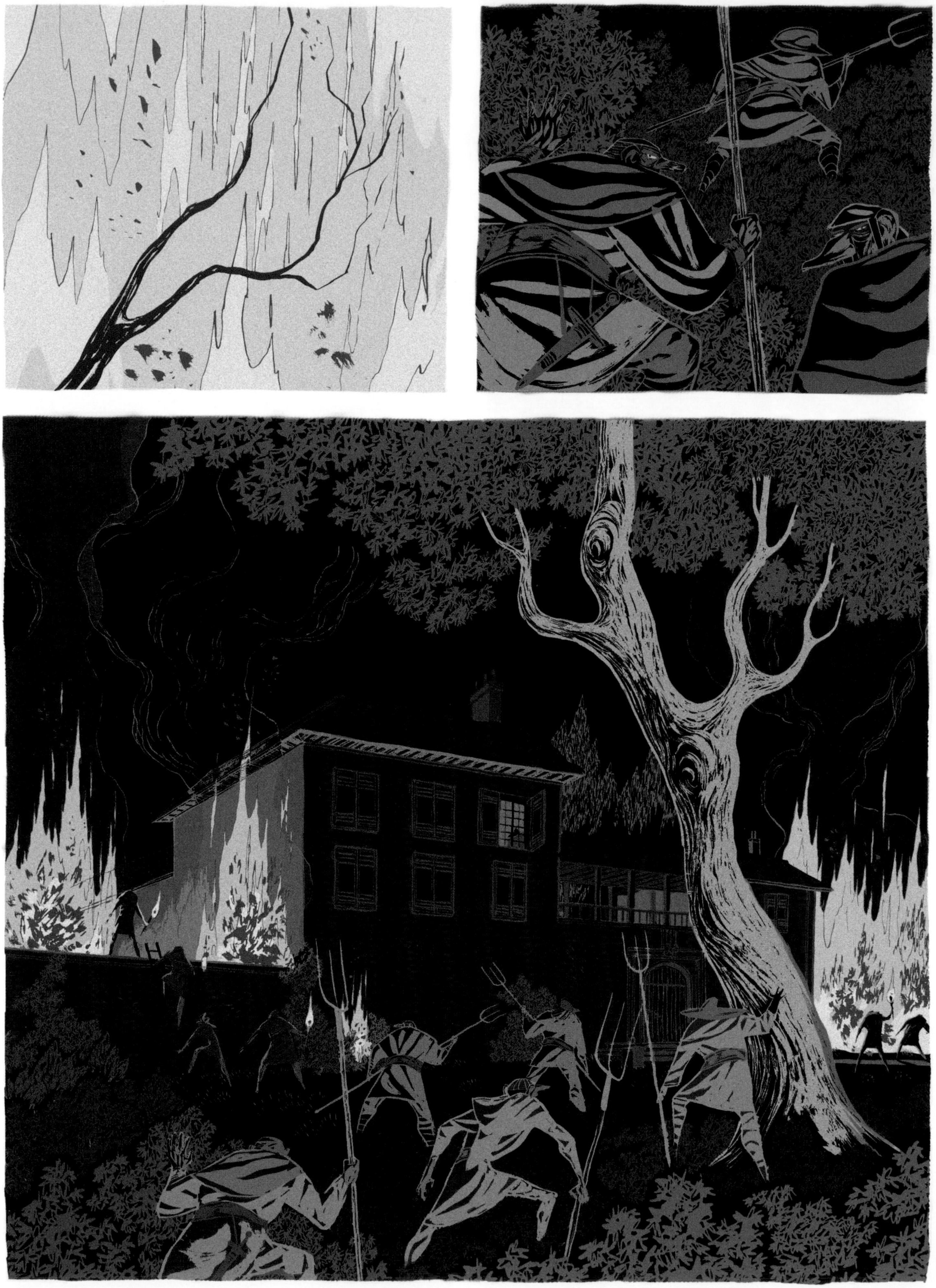

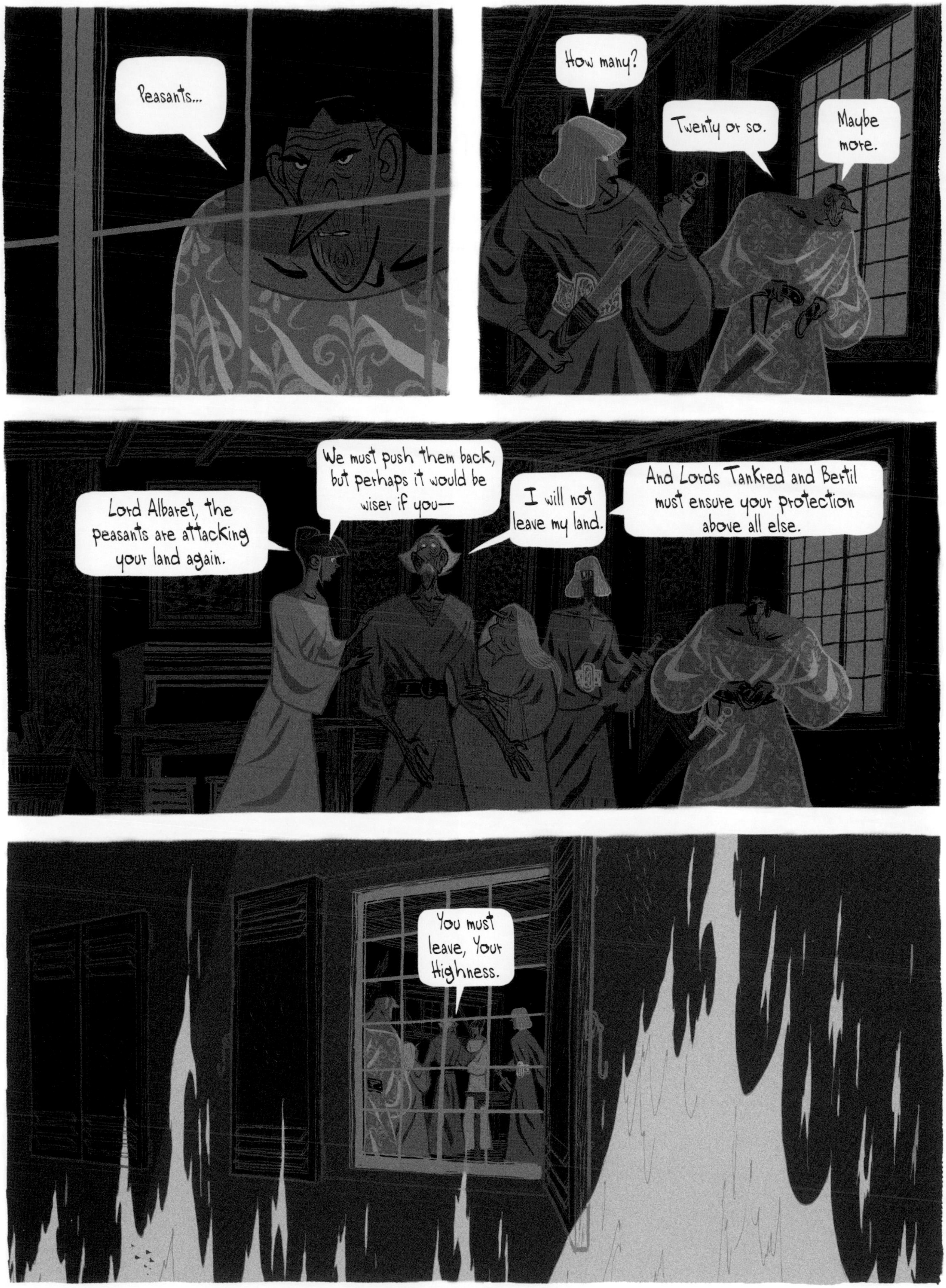
Peasants...
How many?
Twenty or so.
Maybe more.
Lord Albaret, the peasants are attacking your land again.
We must push them back, but perhaps it would be wiser if you—
I will not leave my land.
And Lords Tankred and Bertil must ensure your protection above all else.
You must leave, Your Highness.

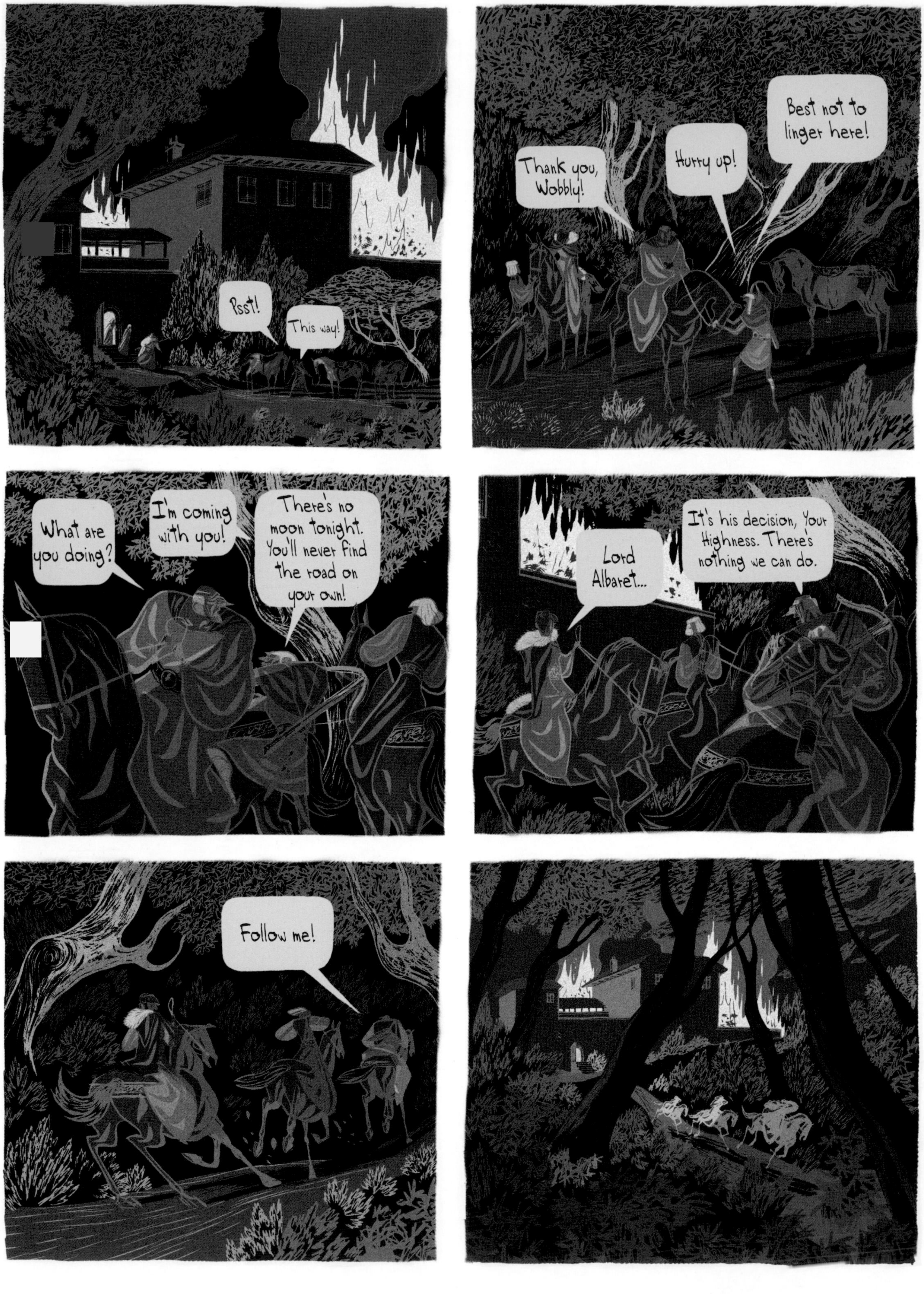

Psst!
This way!
Thank you, Wobbly!
Hurry up!
Best not to linger here!
What are you doing?
I'm coming with you!
There's no moon tonight. You'll never find the road on your own!
Lord Albaret...
It's his decision, Your Highness. There's nothing we can do.
Follow me!

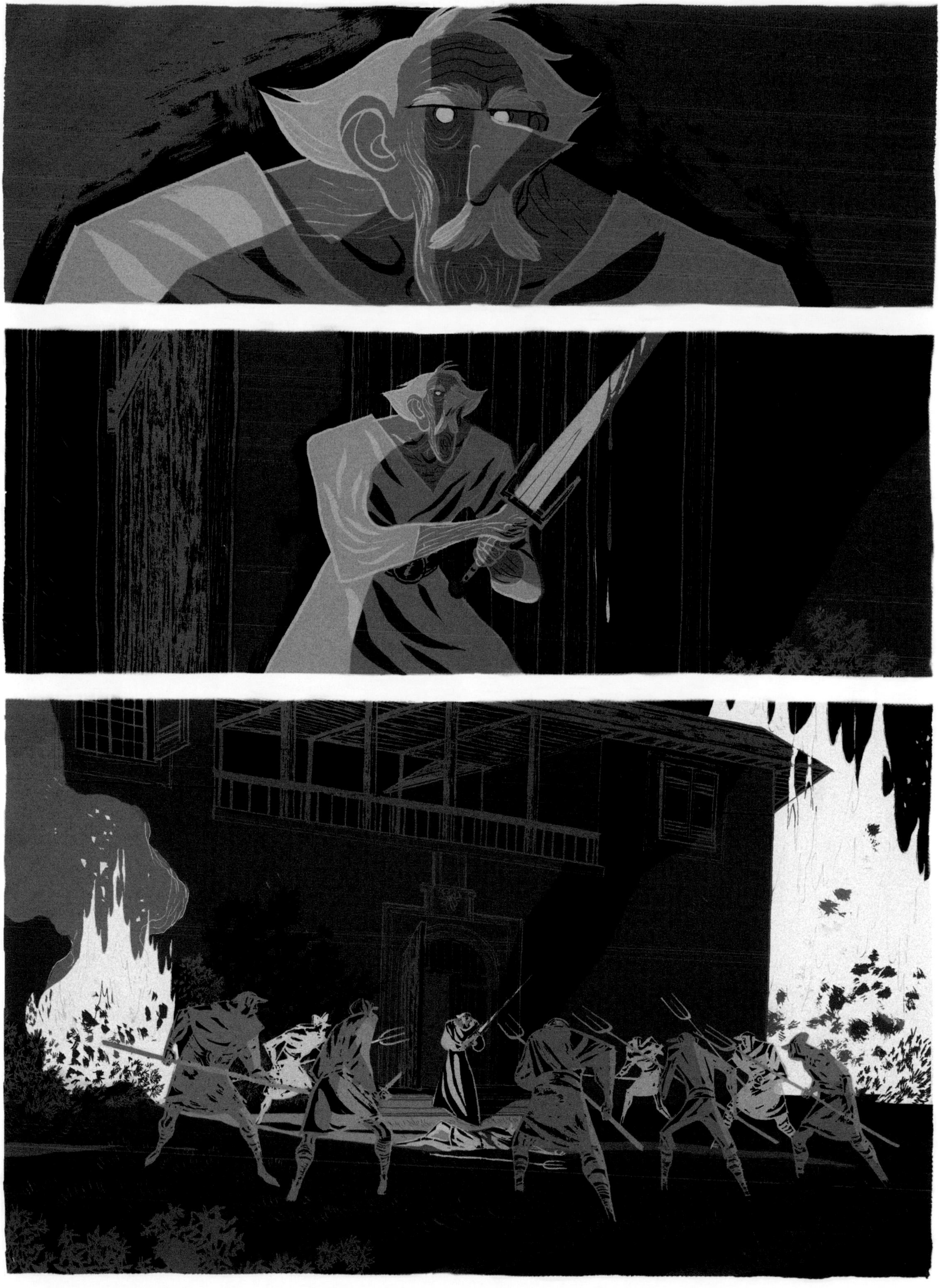

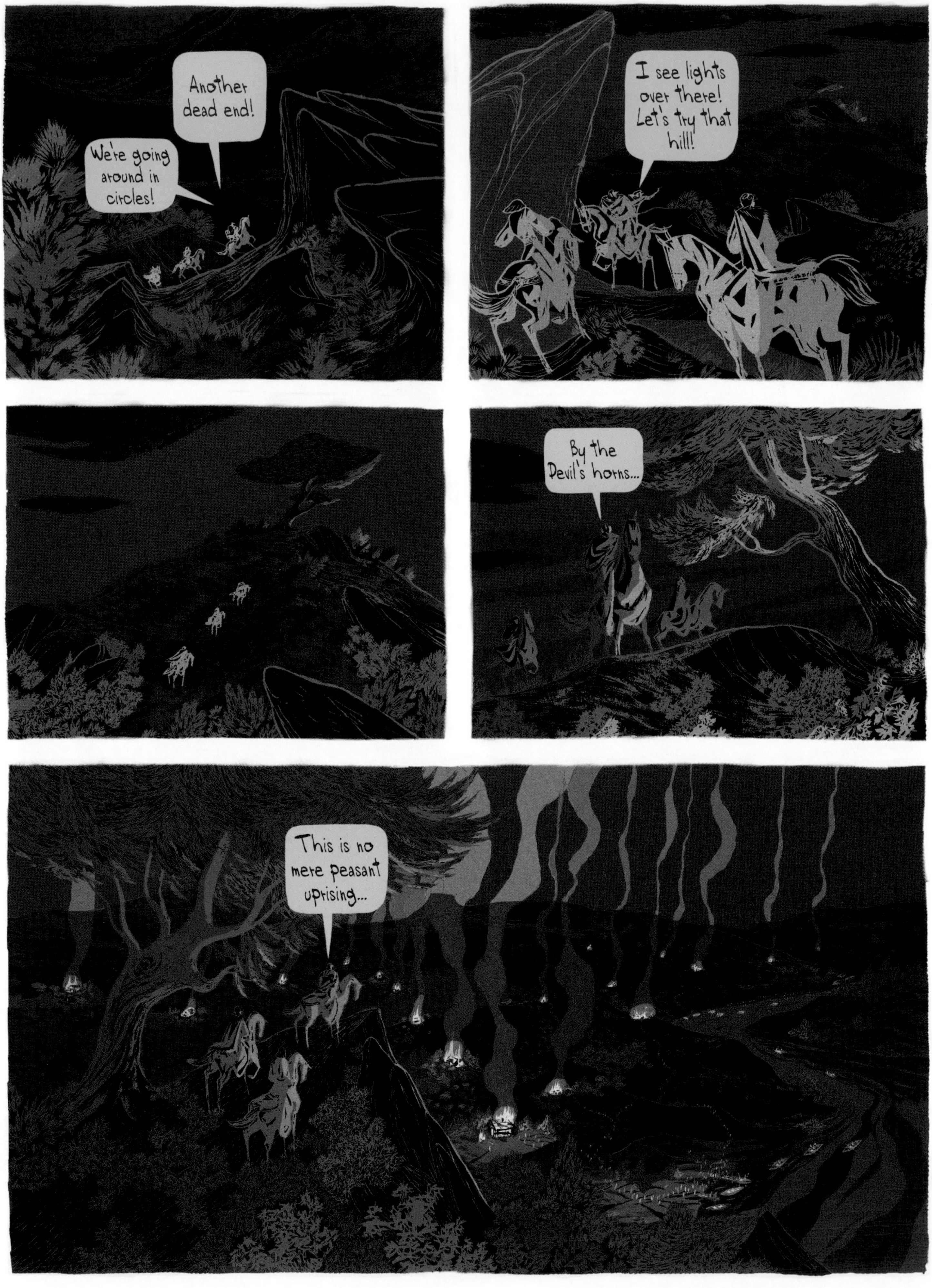
Another dead end!
We're going around in circles!
I see lights over there! Let's try that hill!
By the Devil's horns...
This is no mere peasant uprising...

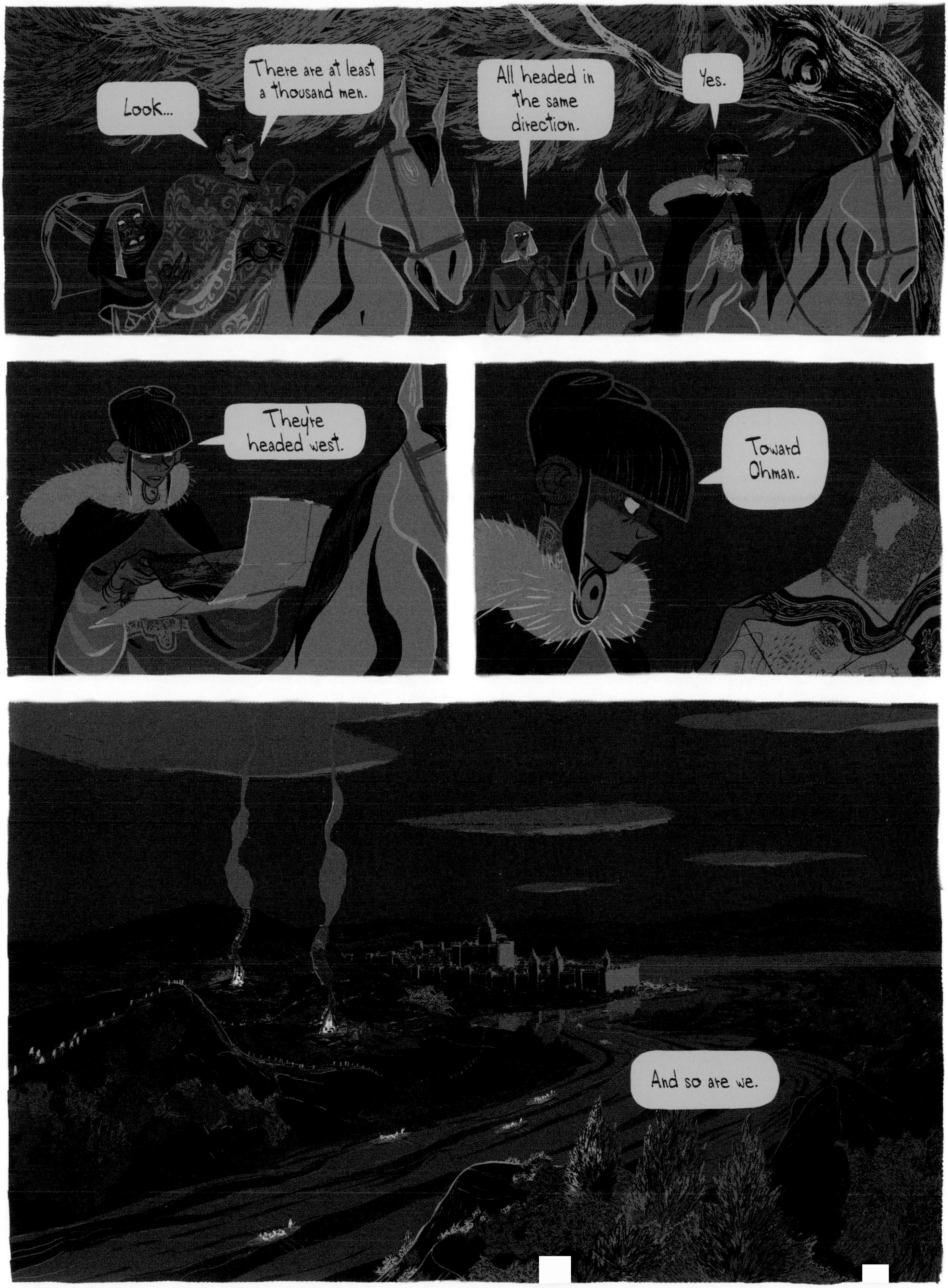

Look...
There are at least a thousand men.
All headed in the same direction.
Yes.
They're headed west.
Toward Ohman.
And so are we.

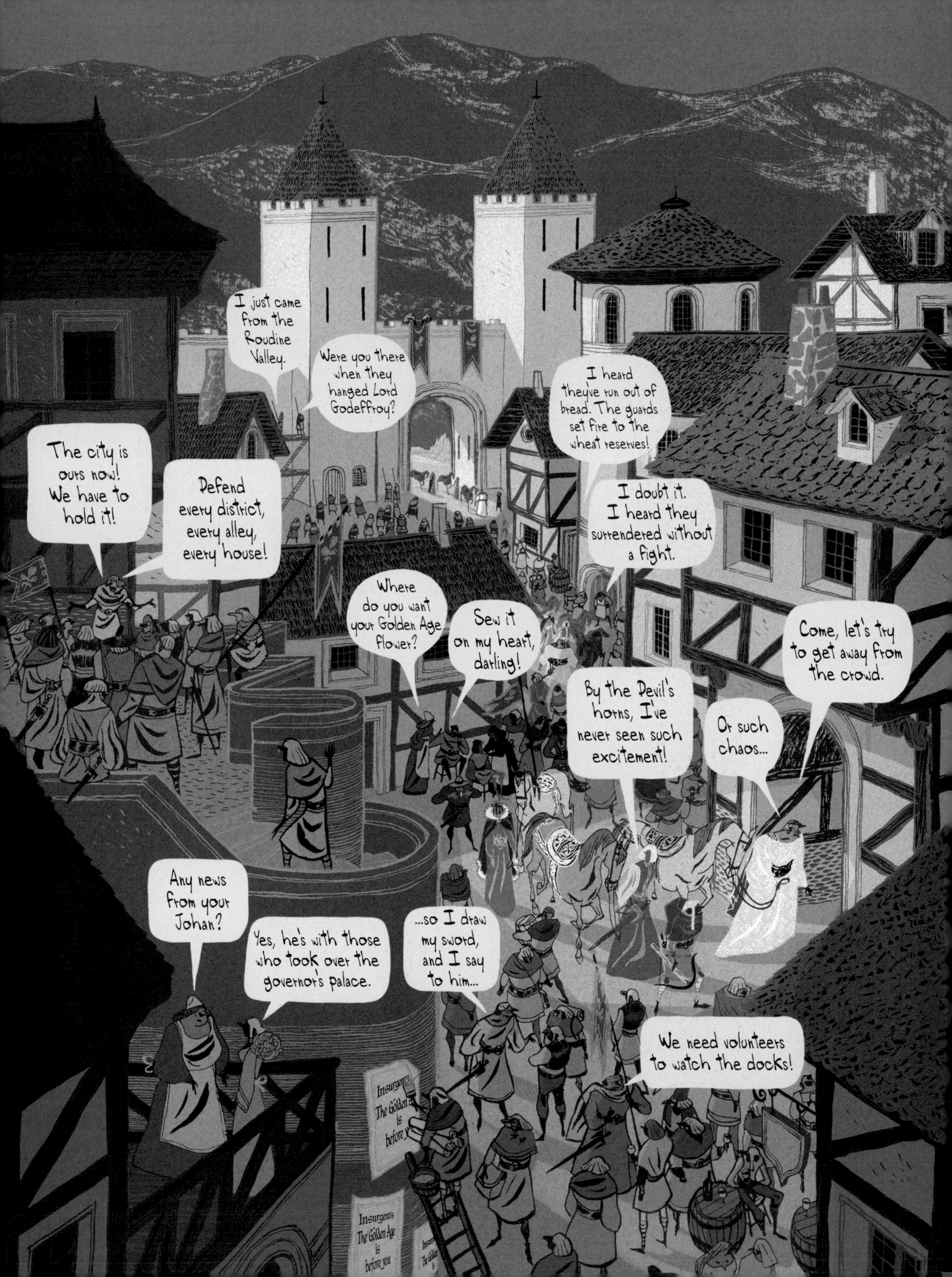
I just came from the Roudine Valley.
Were you there when they hanged Lord Godeffroy?
The city is ours now! We have to hold it!
Defend every district, every alley, every house!
I heard they've run out of bread. The guards set fire to the wheat reserves!
I doubt it. I heard they surrendered without a fight.
Where do you want your Golden Age flower?
Sew it on my heart, darling!
Come, let's try to get away from the crowd.
By the Devil's horns, I've never seen such excitement!
Or such chaos...
Any news from your Johan?
Yes, he's with those who took over the governor's palace.
...so I draw my sword, and I say to him...
We need volunteers to watch the docks!
Insurgents The Golden Age is before you

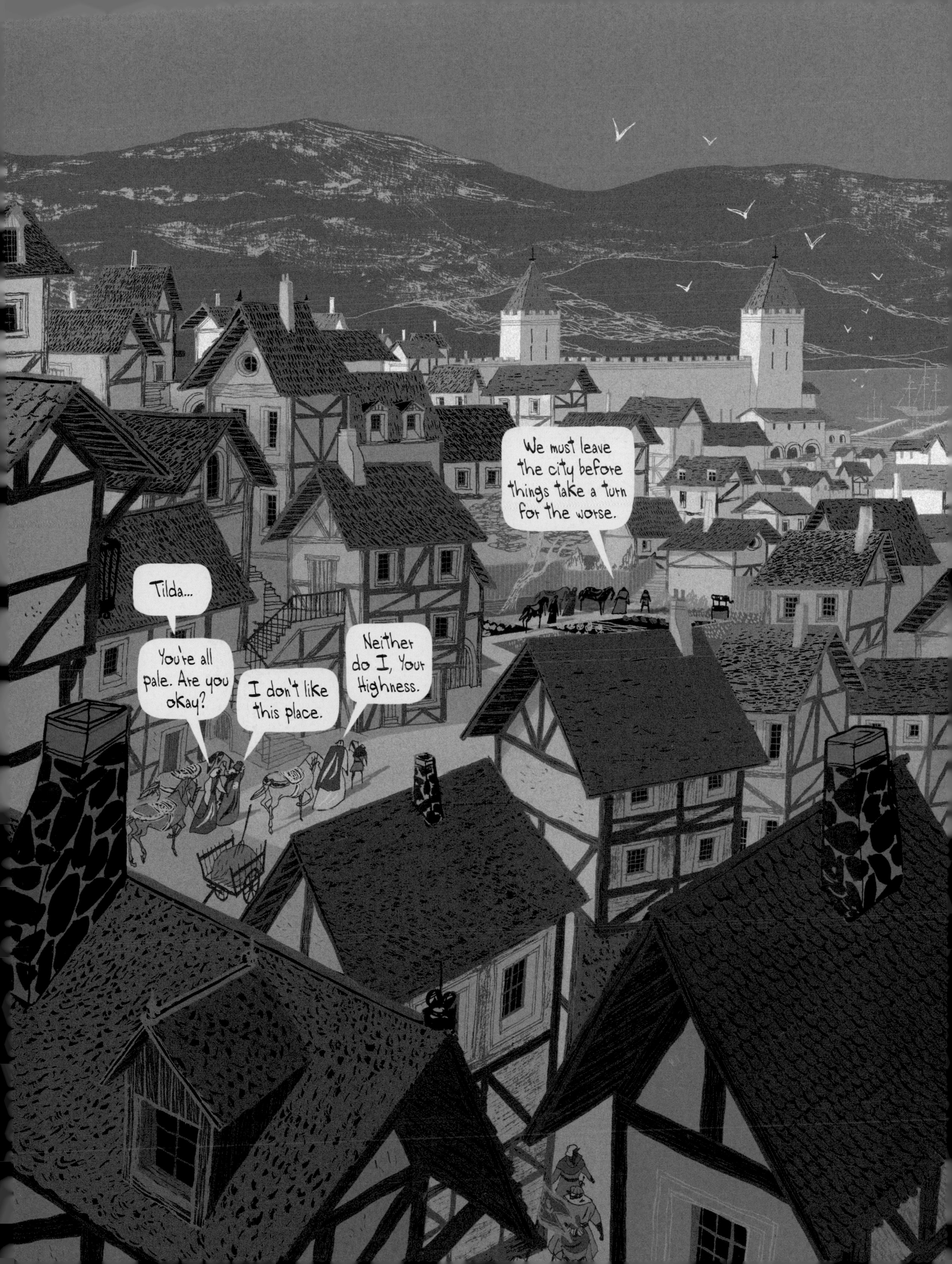
We must leave the city before things take a turn for the worse.
Tilda...
You're all pale. Are you okay?
I don't like this place.
Neither do I, Your Highness.

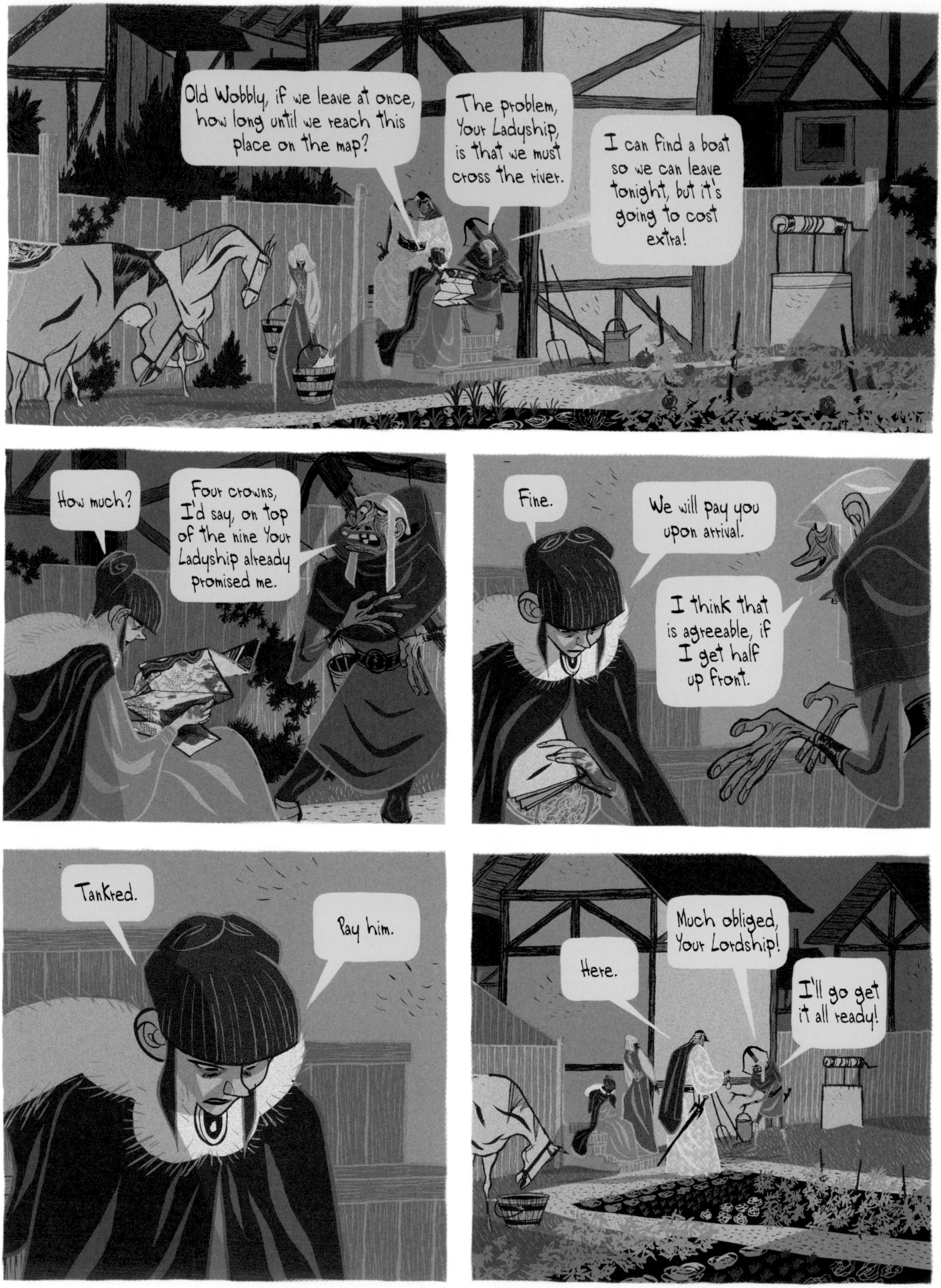
Old Wobbly, if we leave at once, how long until we reach this place on the map?
The problem, Your Ladyship, is that we must cross the river.
I can find a boat so we can leave tonight, but it's going to cost extra!
How much?
Four crowns, I'd say, on top of the nine Your Ladyship already promised me.
Fine.
We will pay you upon arrival.
I think that is agreeable, if I get half up front.
Tankred.
Pay him.
Here.
Much obliged, Your Lordship!
I'll go get it all ready!

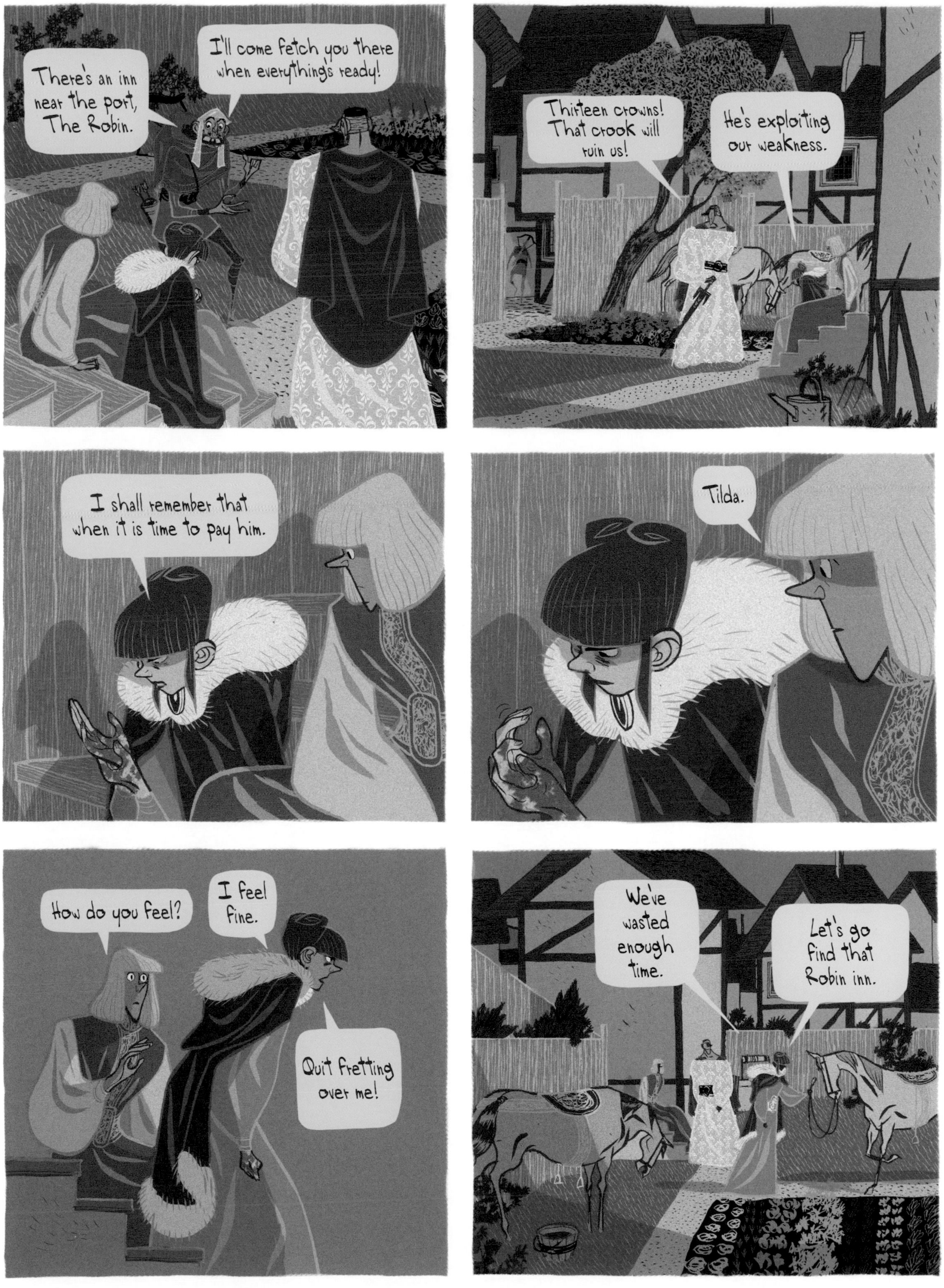
There's an inn near the port, The Robin.
I'll come fetch you there when everything's ready!
Thirteen crowns! That crook will ruin us!
He's exploiting our weakness.
I shall remember that when it is time to pay him.
Tilda.
How do you feel?
I feel fine.
Quit fretting over me!
We've wasted enough time.
Let's go find that Robin inn.

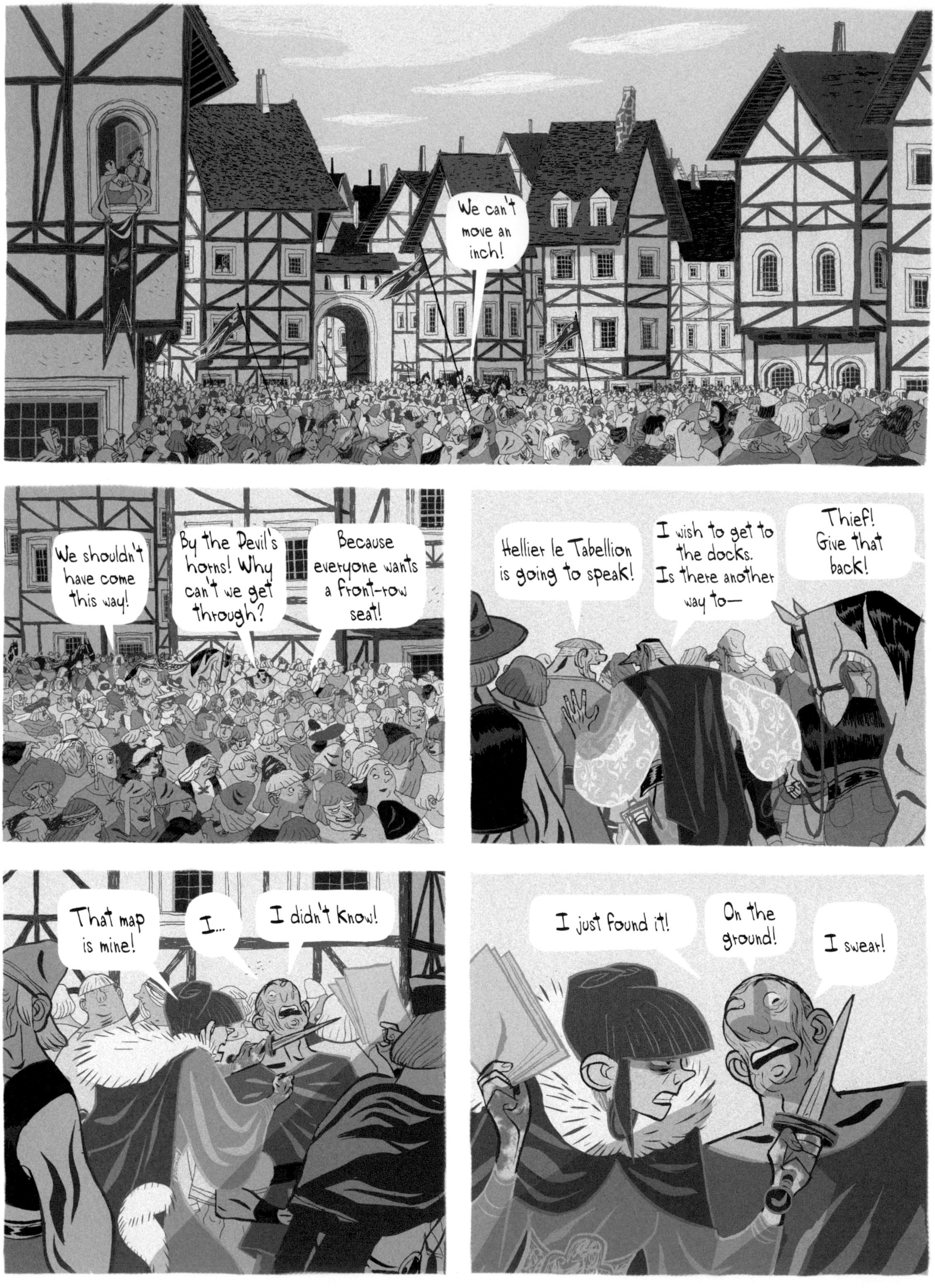
We can't move an inch!
We shouldn't have come this way!
By the Devil's horns! Why can't we get through?
Because everyone wants a front-row seat!
Hellier le Tabellion is going to speak!
I wish to get to the docks. Is there another way to—
Thief! Give that back!
That map is mine!
I...
I didn't know!
I just found it!
On the ground!
I swear!

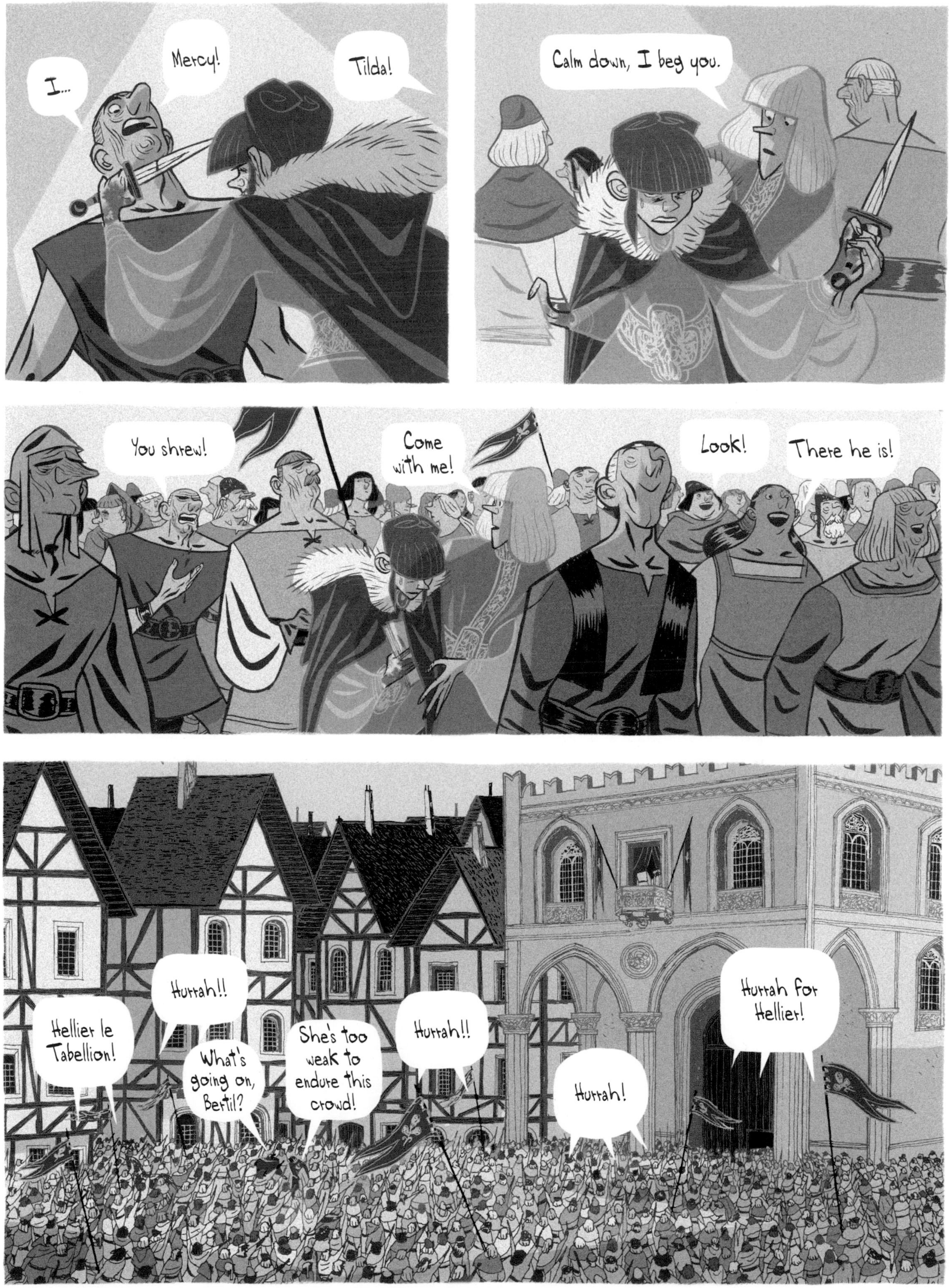
I...
Mercy!
Tilda!
Calm down, I beg you.
You shrew!
Come with me!
Look!
There he is!
Hellier le Tabellion!
Hurrah!!
What's going on, Bertil?
She's too weak to endure this crowd!
Hurrah!!
Hurrah!
Hurrah for Hellier!

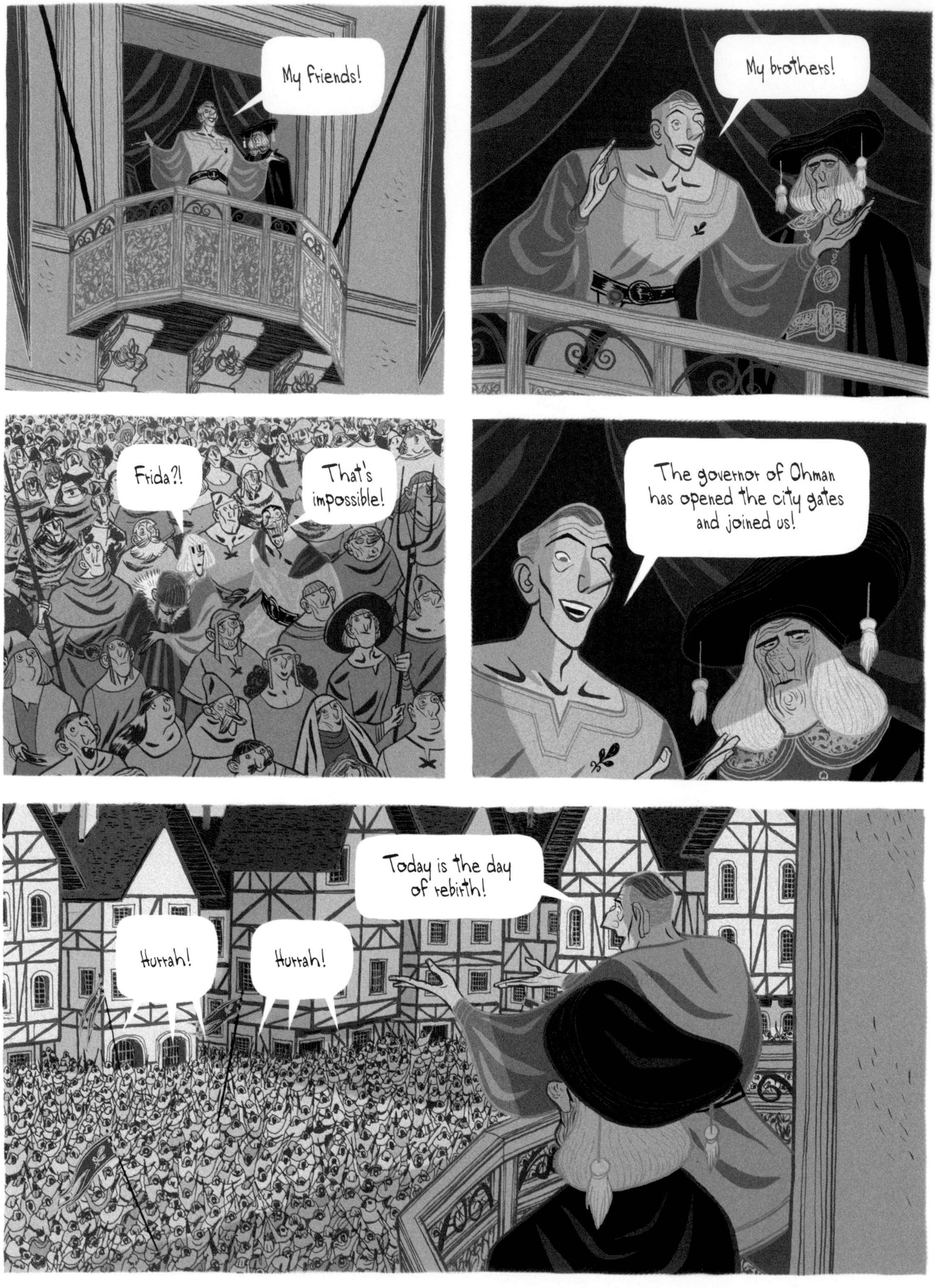
My friends!
My brothers!
Frida?!
That's impossible!
The governor of Ohman has opened the city gates and joined us!
Today is the day of rebirth!
Hurrah!
Hurrah!

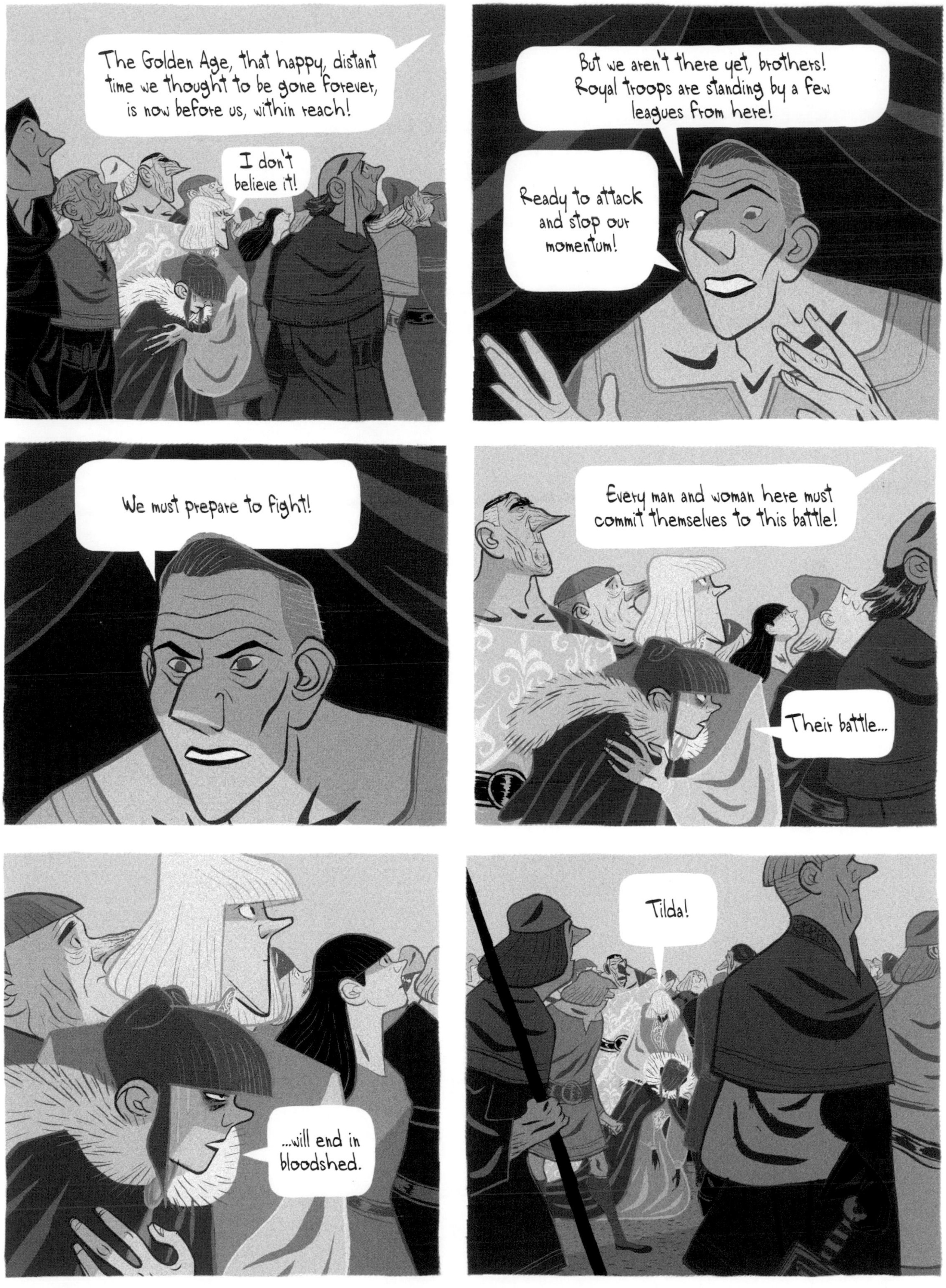
The Golden Age, that happy, distant time we thought to be gone forever, is now before us, within reach!
I don't believe it!
But we aren't there yet, brothers! Royal troops are standing by a few leagues from here!
Ready to attack and stop our momentum!
We must prepare to fight!
Every man and woman here must commit themselves to this battle!
Their battle...
...will end in bloodshed.
Tilda!

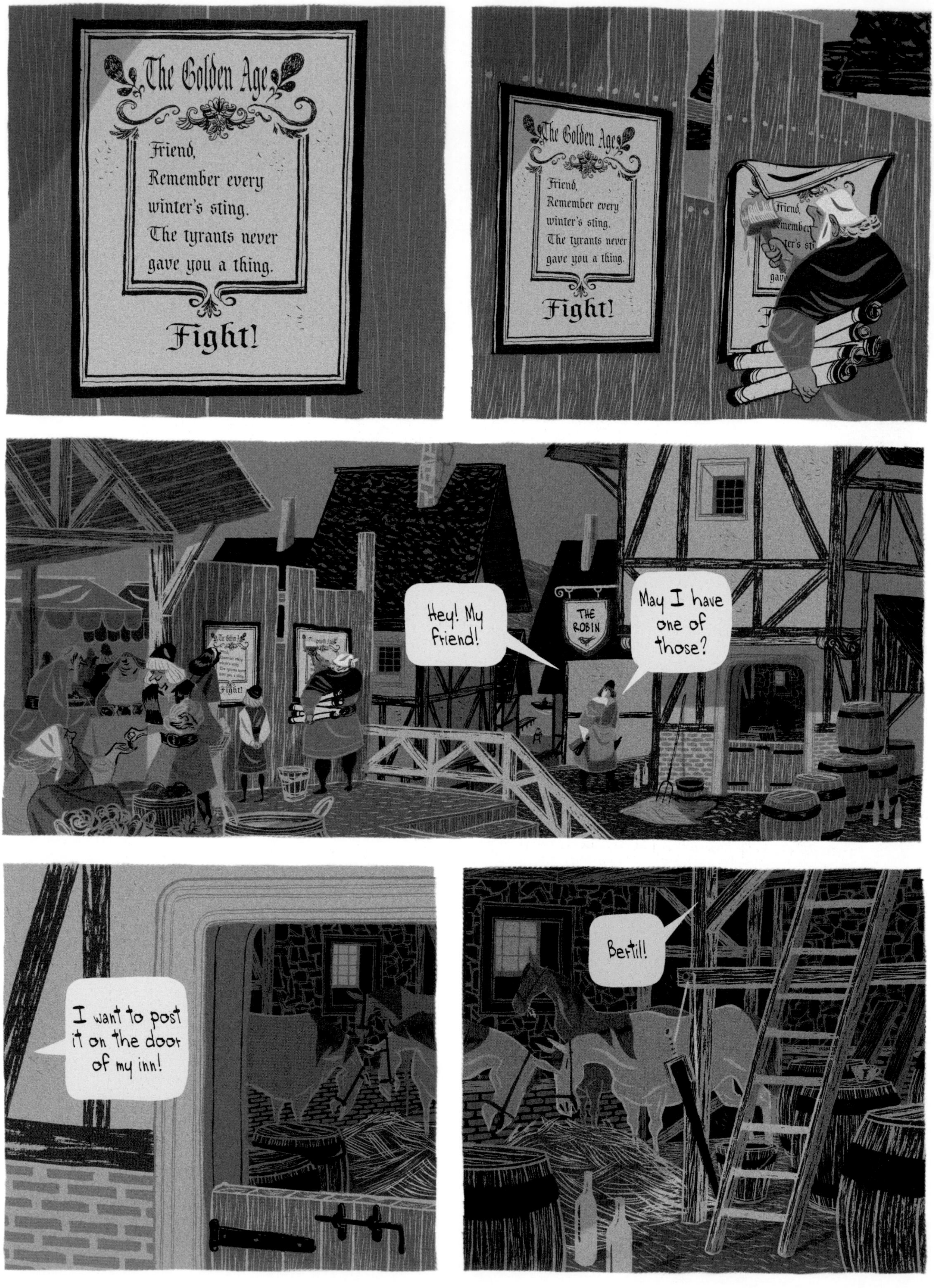
The Golden Age
Friend,
Remember every
winter's sting.
The tyrants never
gave you a thing.
Fight!
Hey! My friend!
THE ROBIN
May I have one of those?
I want to post it on the door of my inn!
Bertil!

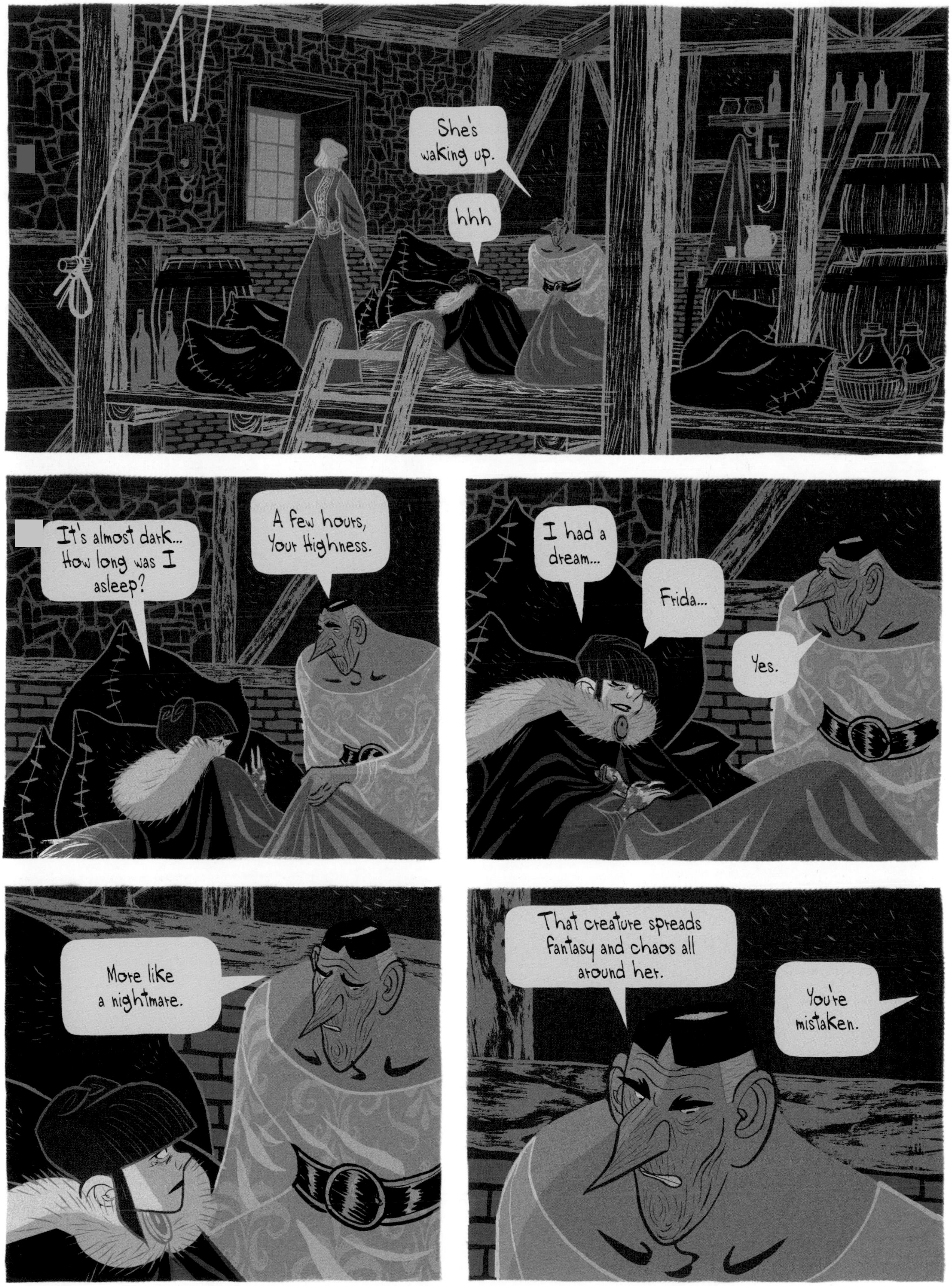
She's waking up.
hhh
It's almost dark... How long was I asleep?
A few hours, Your Highness.
I had a dream...
Frida...
Yes.
More like a nightmare.
That creature spreads fantasy and chaos all around her.
You're mistaken.

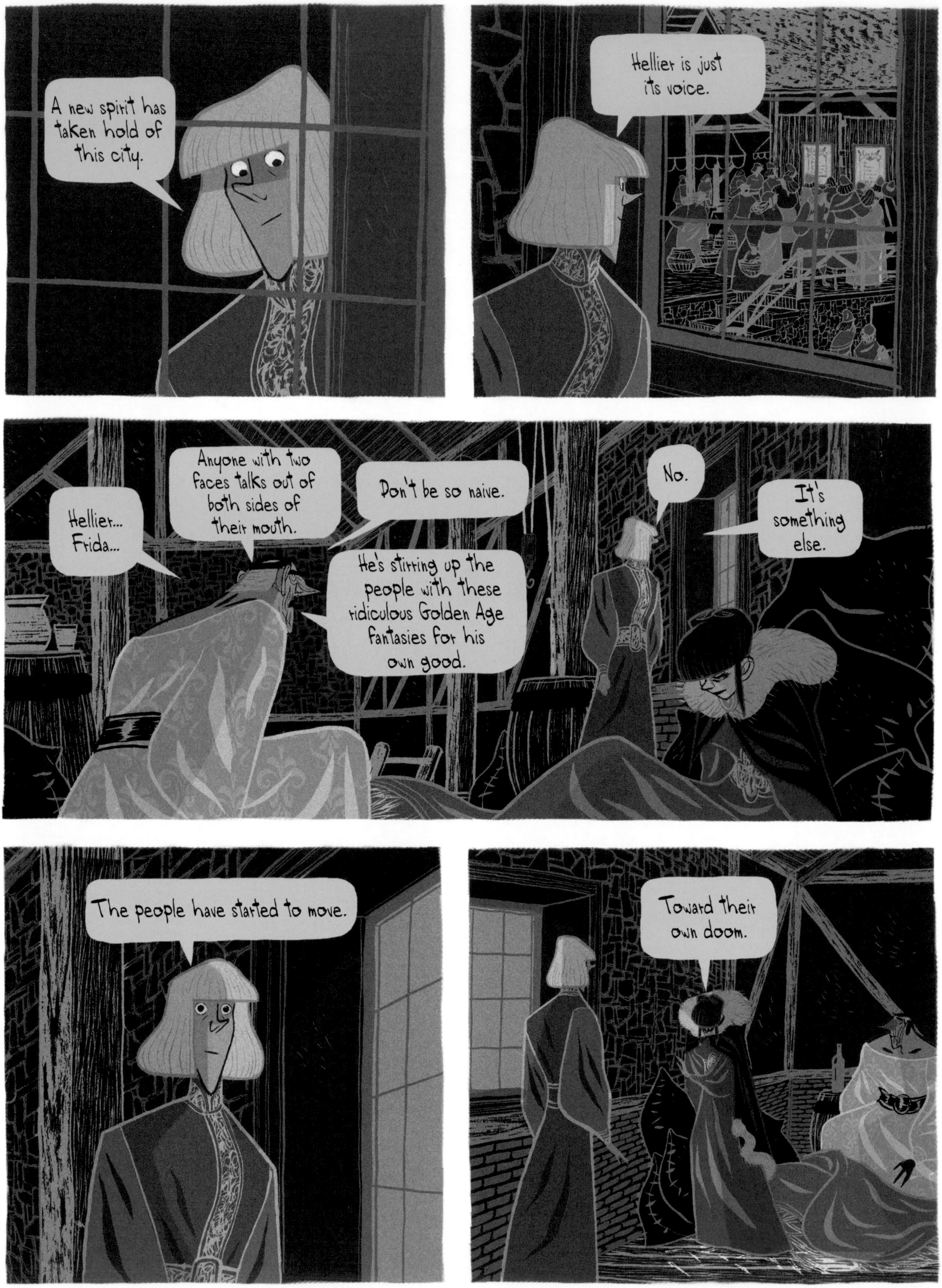
A new spirit has taken hold of this city.
Hellier is just its voice.
Hellier... Frida...
Anyone with two faces talks out of both sides of their mouth.
Don't be so naive.
He's stirring up the people with these ridiculous Golden Age fantasies for his own good.
No.
It's something else.
The people have started to move.
Toward their own doom.

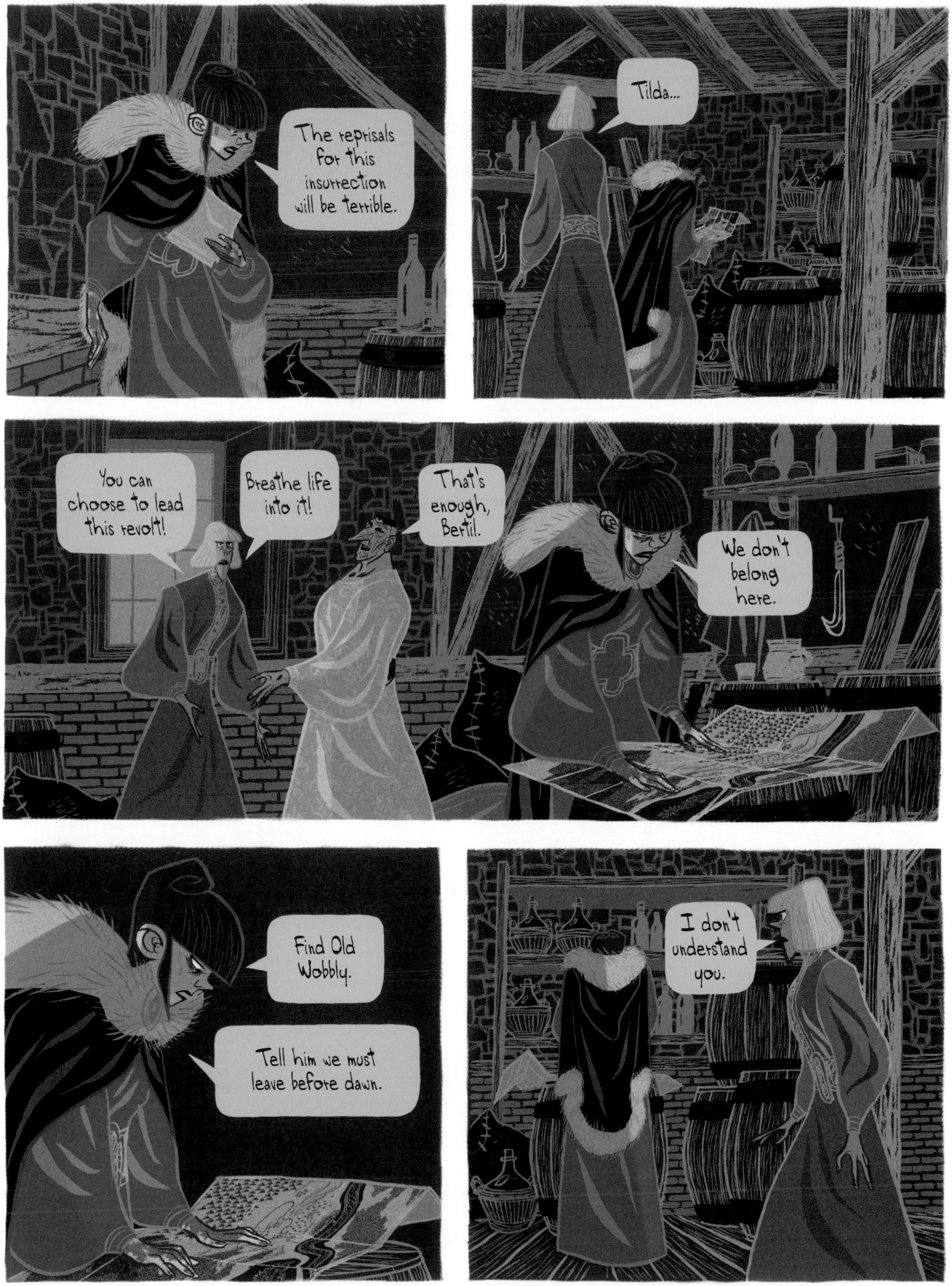
The reprisals for this insurrection will be terrible.
Tilda...
You can choose to lead this revolt!
Breathe life into it!
That's enough, Bertil.
We don't belong here.
Find Old Wobbly.
Tell him we must leave before dawn.
I don't understand you.

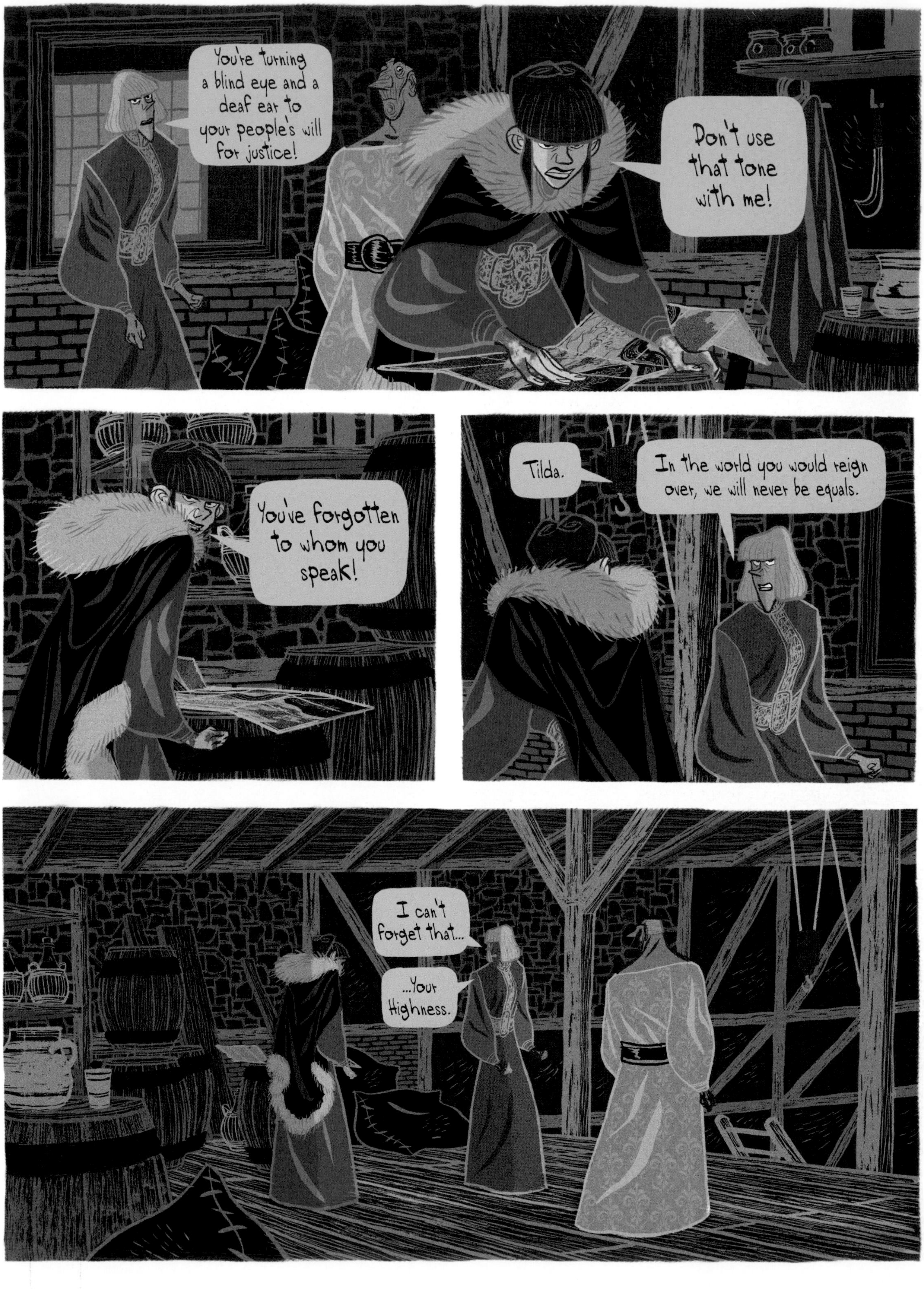
You're turning a blind eye and a deaf ear to your people's will for justice!
Don't use that tone with me!
You've forgotten to whom you speak!
Tilda.
In the world you would reign over, we will never be equals.
I can't forget that...
...Your Highness.

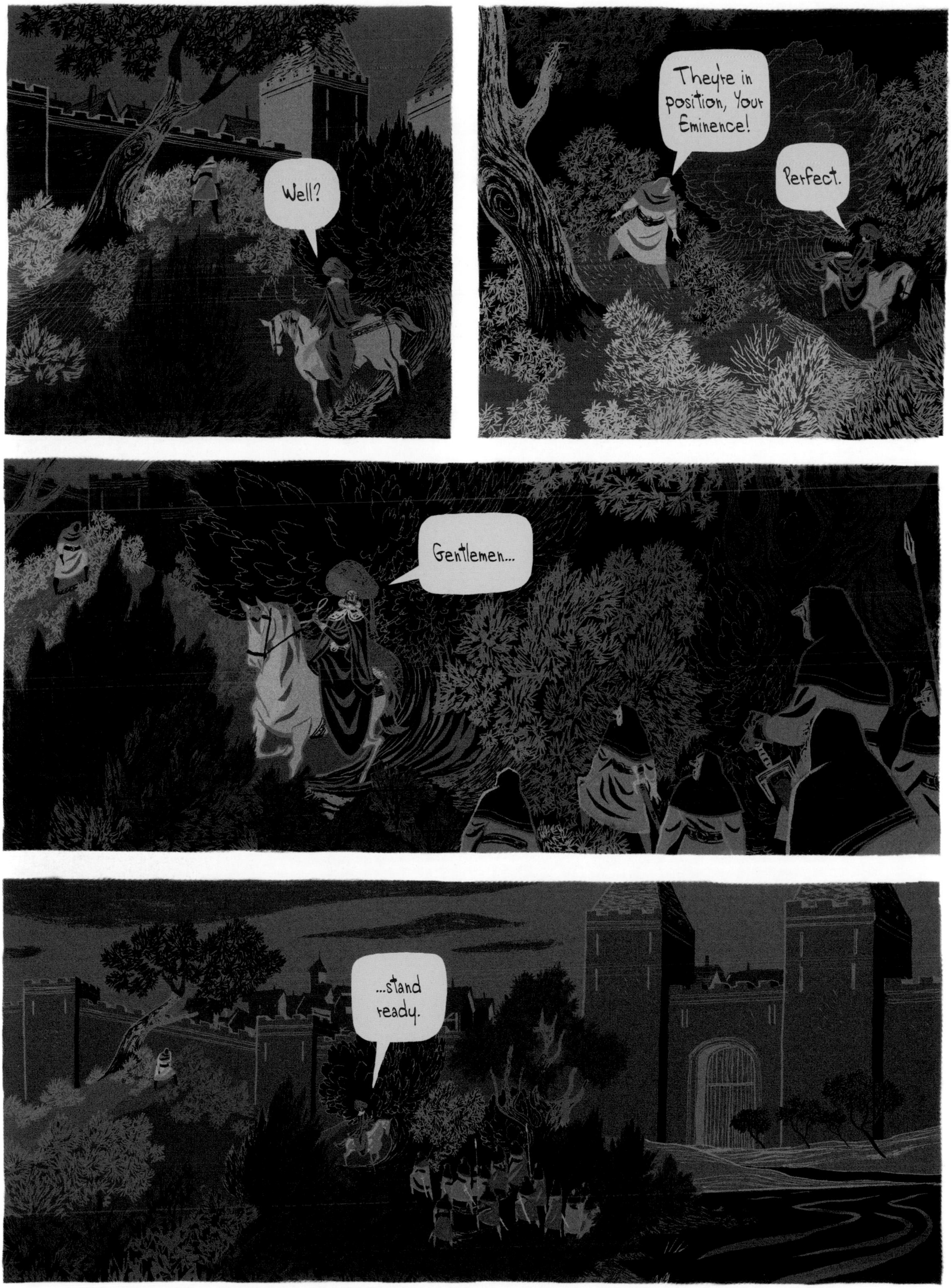
Well?
They're in position, Your Eminence!
Perfect.
Gentlemen...
...stand ready.

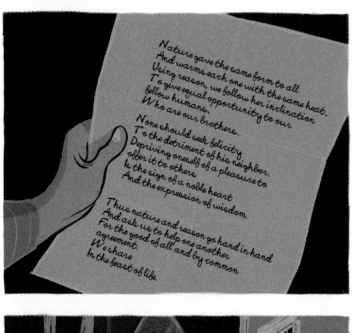

Nature gave the same form to all
And warms each one with the same heat.
Using reason, we follow her inclination
To give equal opportunity to our
fellow humans,
Who are our brothers.

None should seek felicity
To the detriment of his neighbor.
Depriving oneself of a pleasure to
offer it to others
Is the sign of a noble heart
And the expression of wisdom.

Thus nature and reason go hand in hand
And ask us to help one another
For the good of all and by common
agreement.
We share
In the feast of life.

How old are you, son?

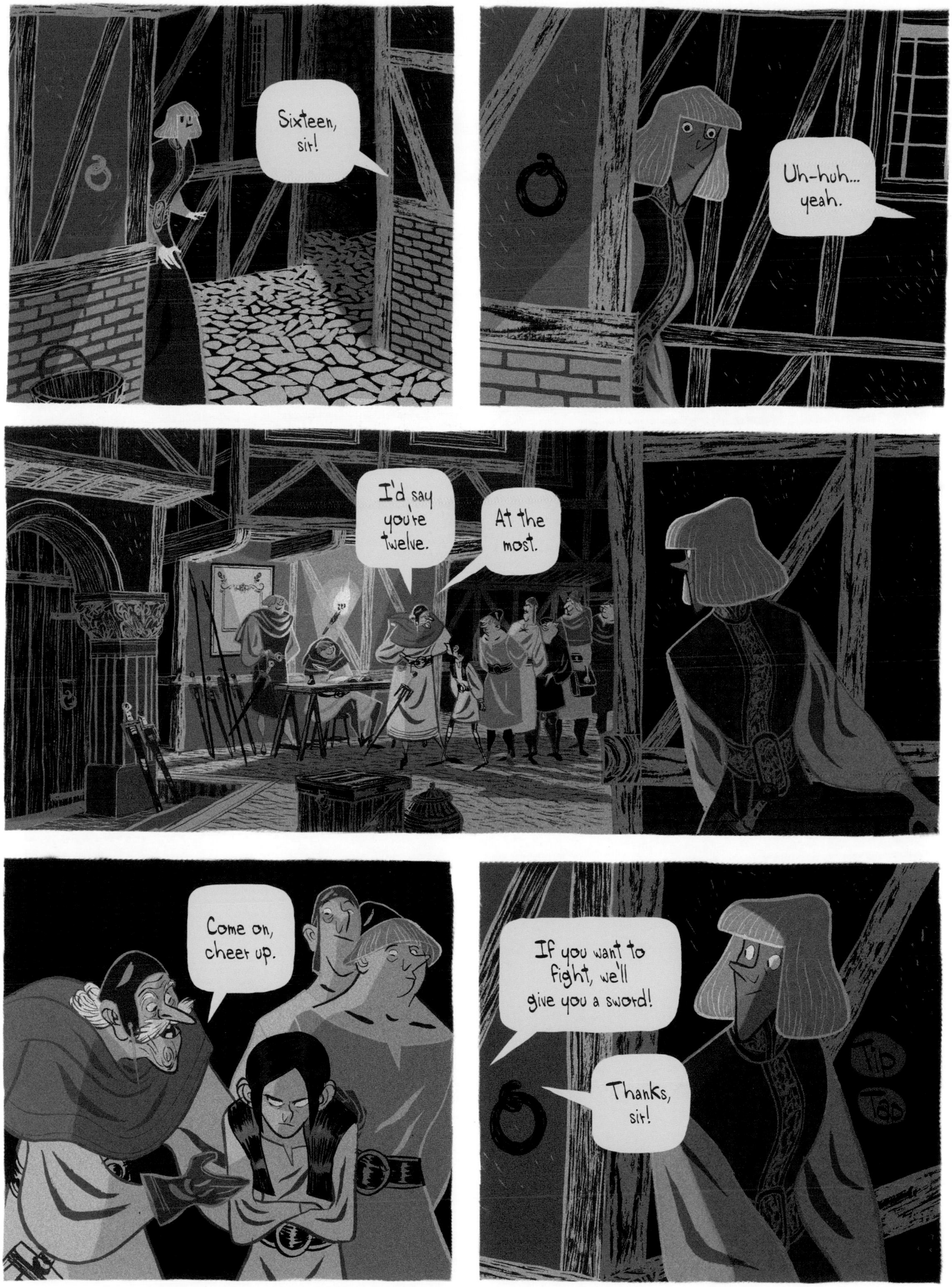
Sixteen, sir!
Uh-huh... yeah.
I'd say you're twelve.
At the most.
Come on, cheer up.
If you want to fight, we'll give you a sword!
Thanks, sir!
Tip
Tap

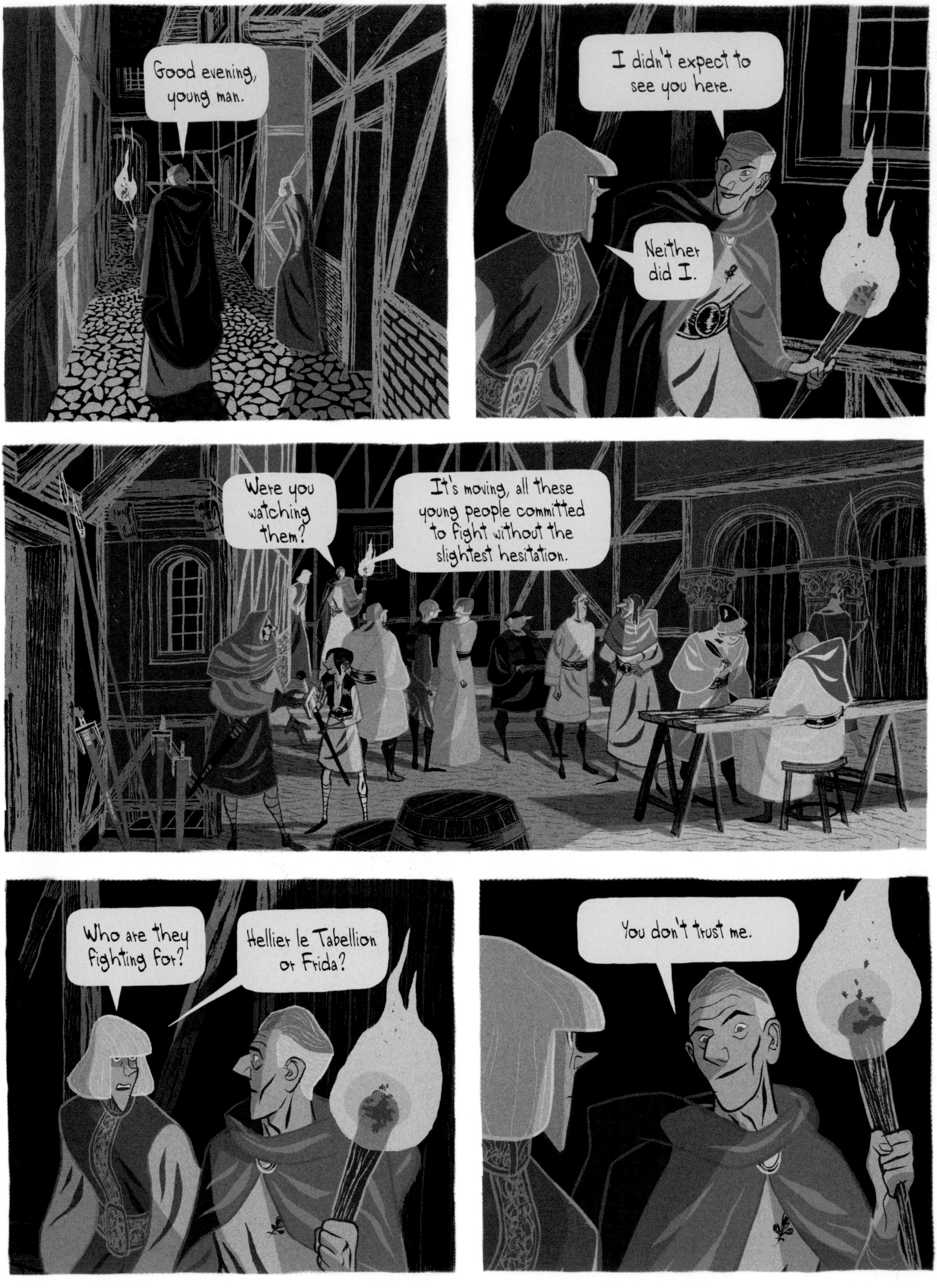

Good evening, young man.
I didn't expect to see you here.
Neither did I.
Were you watching them?
It's moving, all these young people committed to fight without the slightest hesitation.
Who are they fighting for?
Hellier le Tabellion or Frida?
You don't trust me.

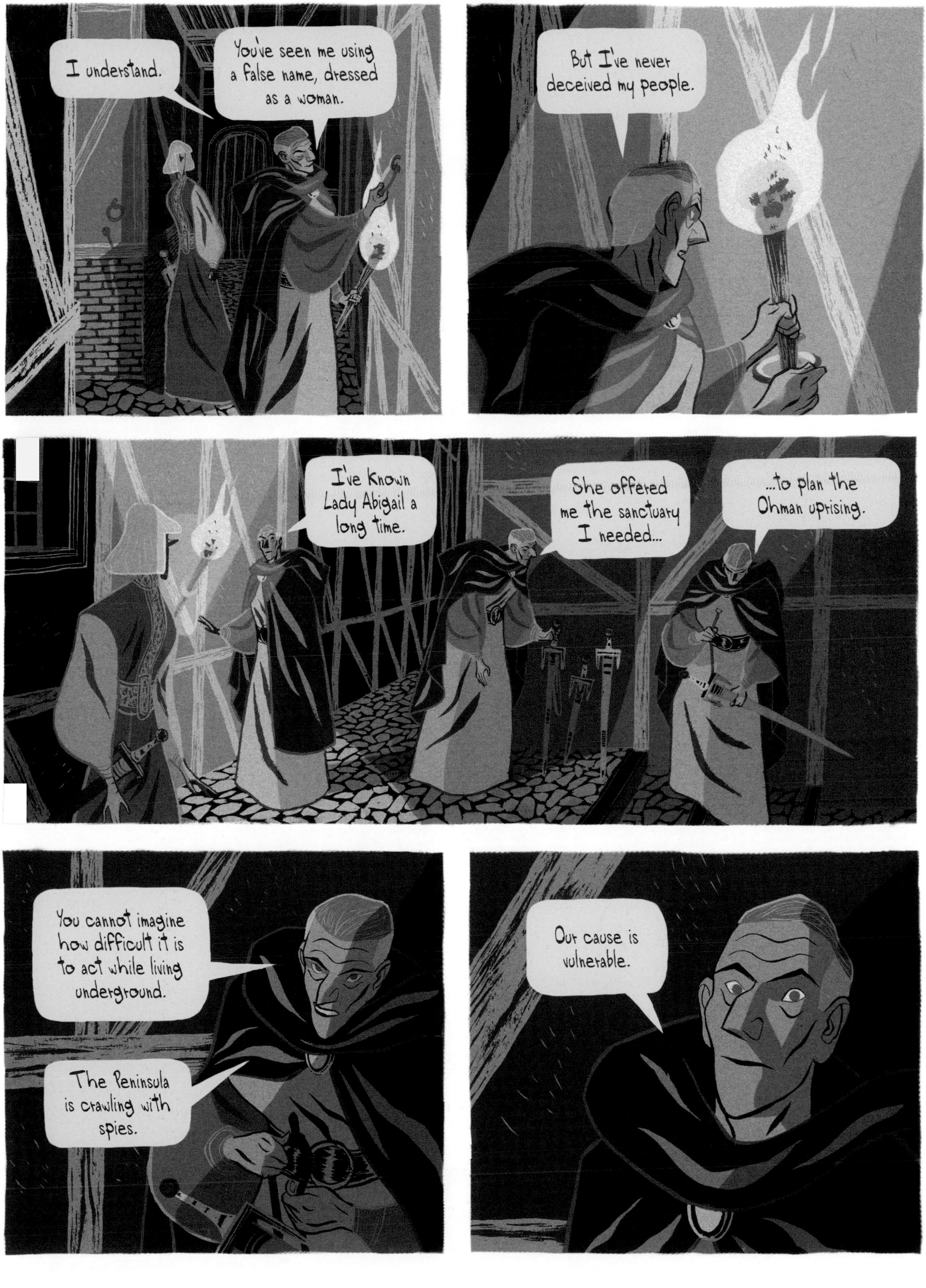
I understand.
You've seen me using a false name, dressed as a woman.
But I've never deceived my people.
I've known Lady Abigail a long time.
She offered me the sanctuary I needed...
...to plan the Ohman uprising.
You cannot imagine how difficult it is to act while living underground.
The Peninsula is crawling with spies.
Our cause is vulnerable.

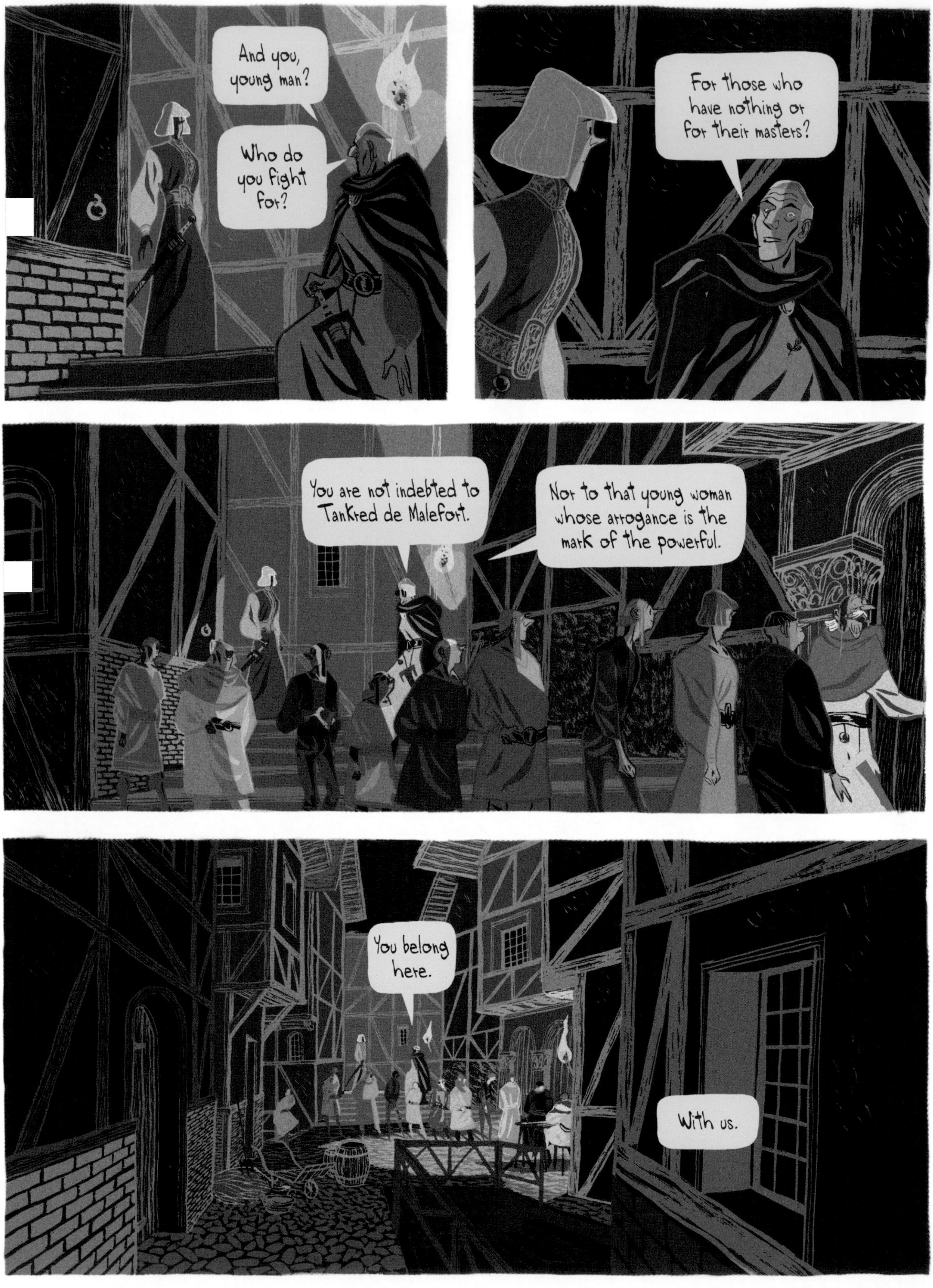
And you, young man?
Who do you fight for?
For those who have nothing or for their masters?
You are not indebted to Tankred de Malefort.
Nor to that young woman whose arrogance is the mark of the powerful.
You belong here.
With us.

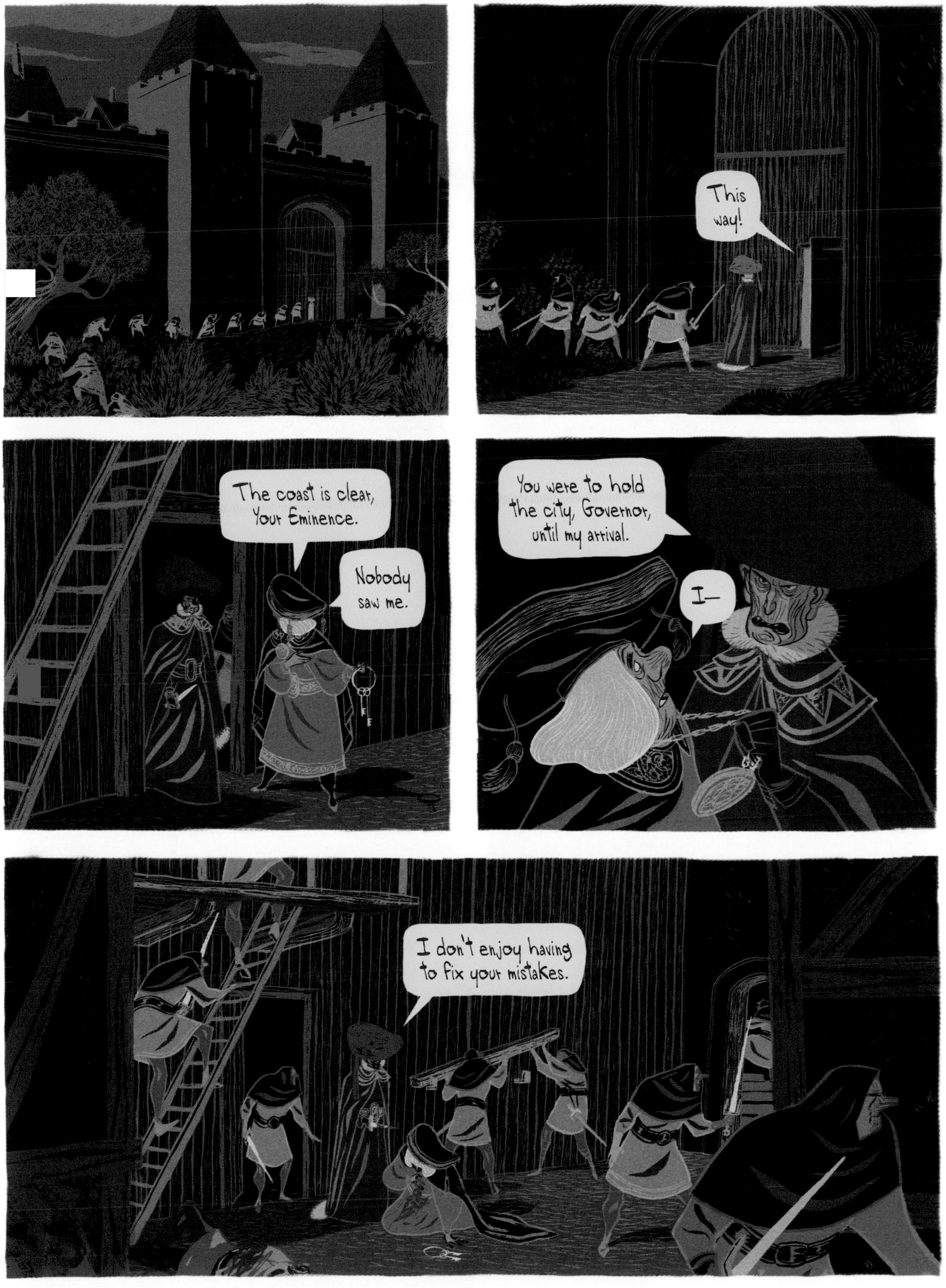
This way!
The coast is clear, Your Eminence.
Nobody saw me.
You were to hold the city, Governor, until my arrival.
I—
I don't enjoy having to fix your mistakes.

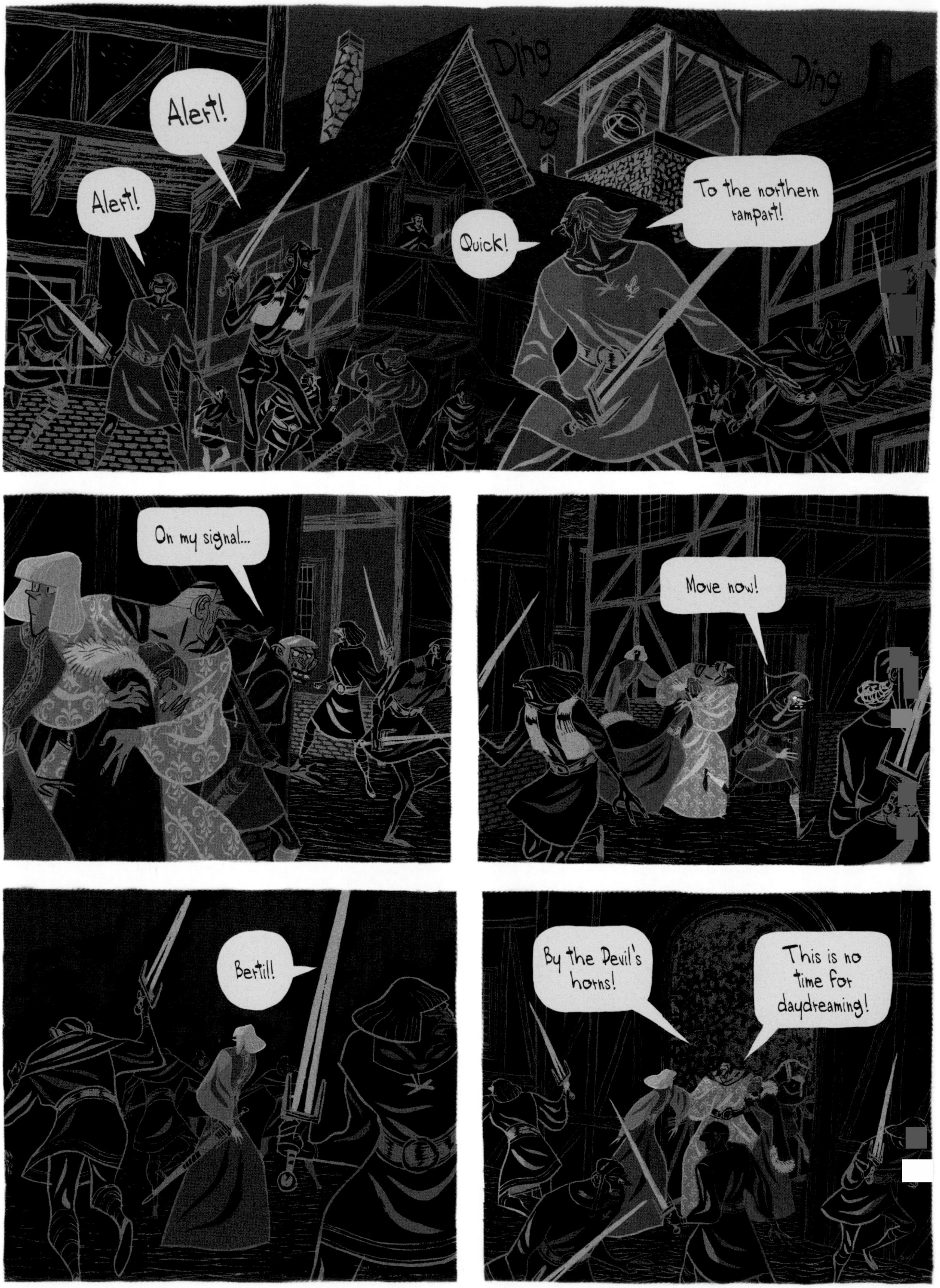
Ding
Dong
Ding
Alert!
Alert!
Quick!
To the northern rampart!
On my signal...
Move now!
Bertil!
By the Devil's horns!
This is no time for daydreaming!

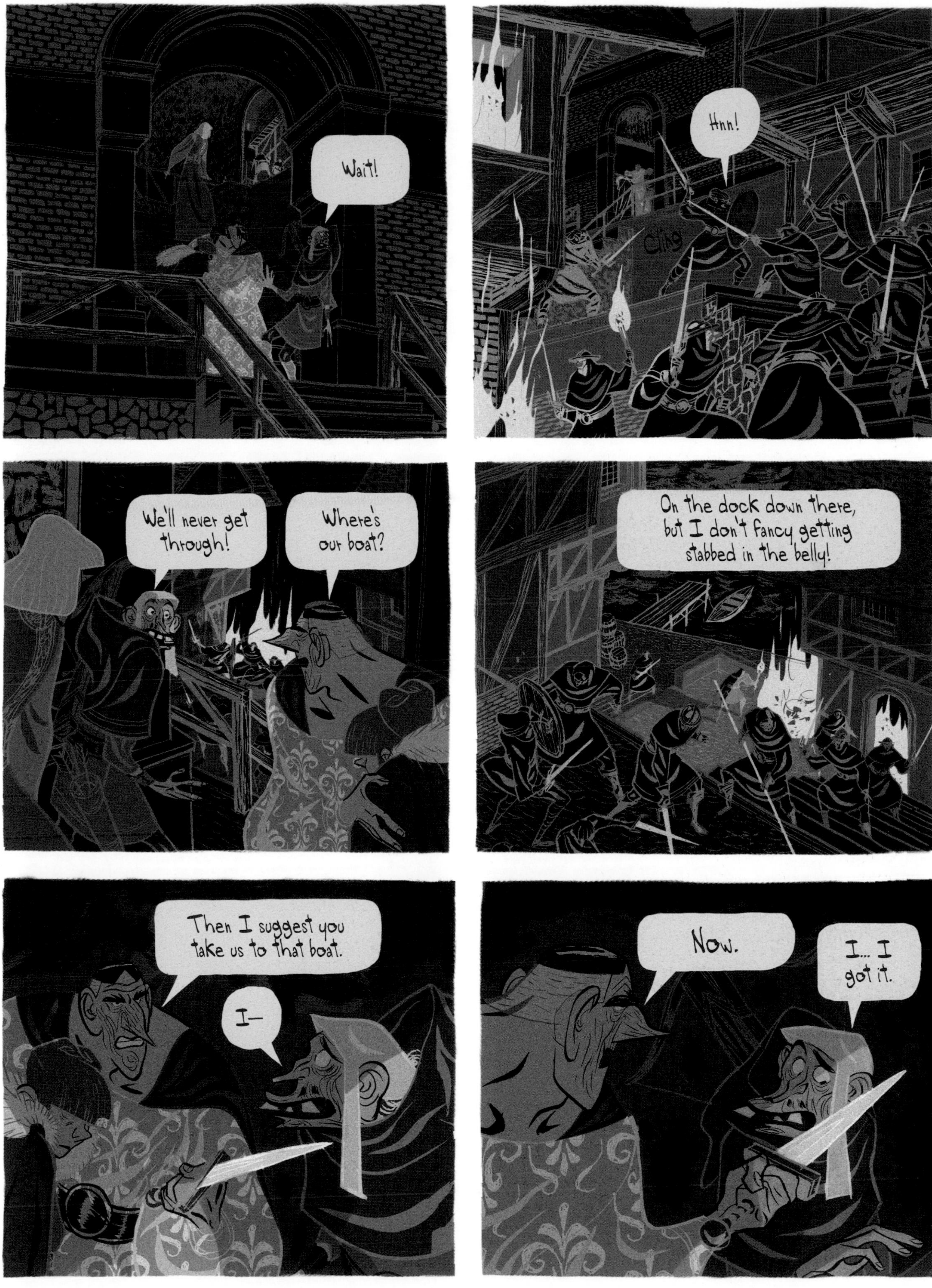
Wait!
Hnn!
Cling
We'll never get through!
Where's our boat?
On the dock down there, but I don't fancy getting stabbed in the belly!
Then I suggest you take us to that boat.
I—
Now.
I... I got it.

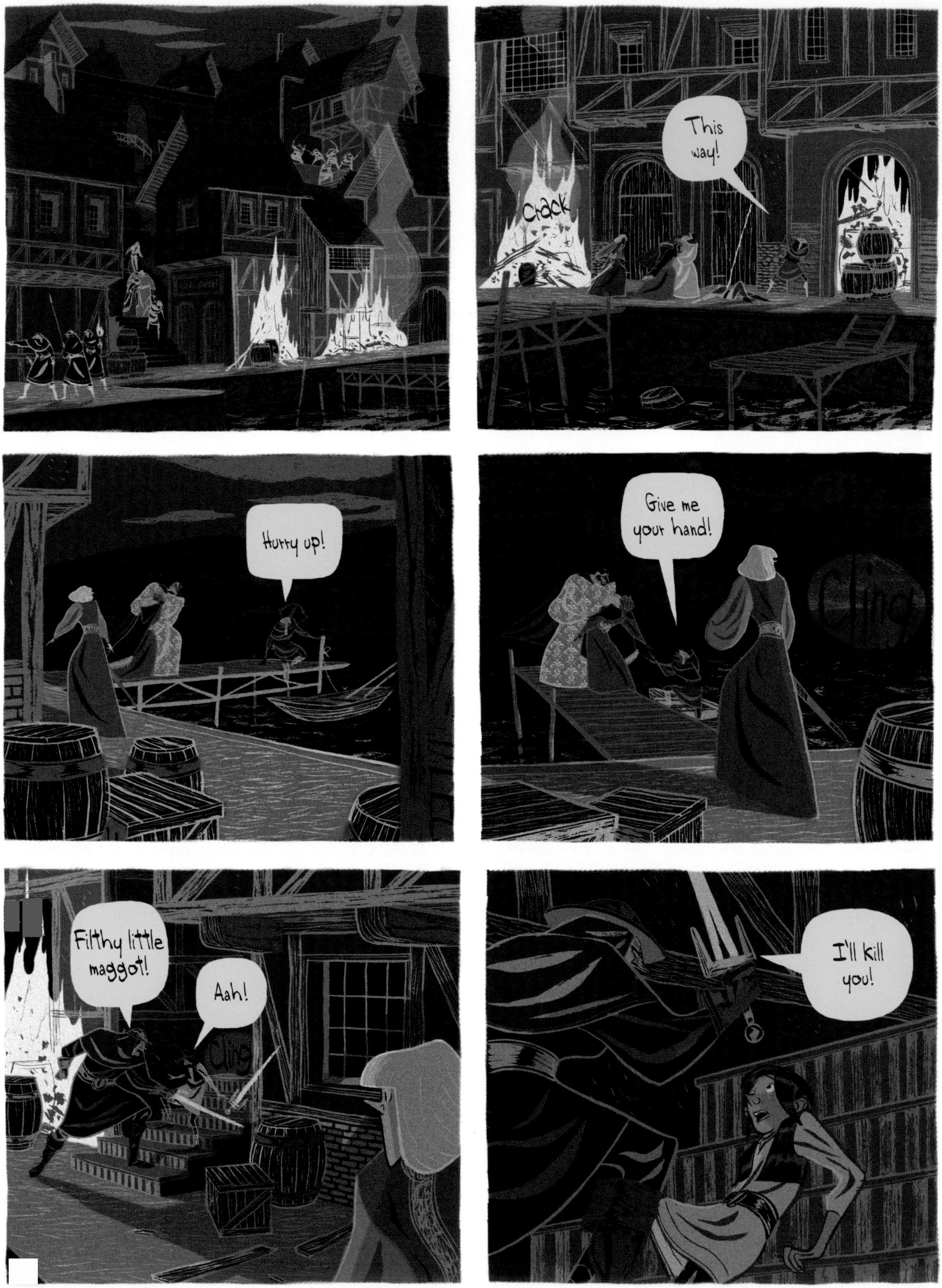
Crack
This way!
Hurry up!
Give me your hand!
Cling
Filthy little maggot!
Aah!
Cling
I'll kill you!

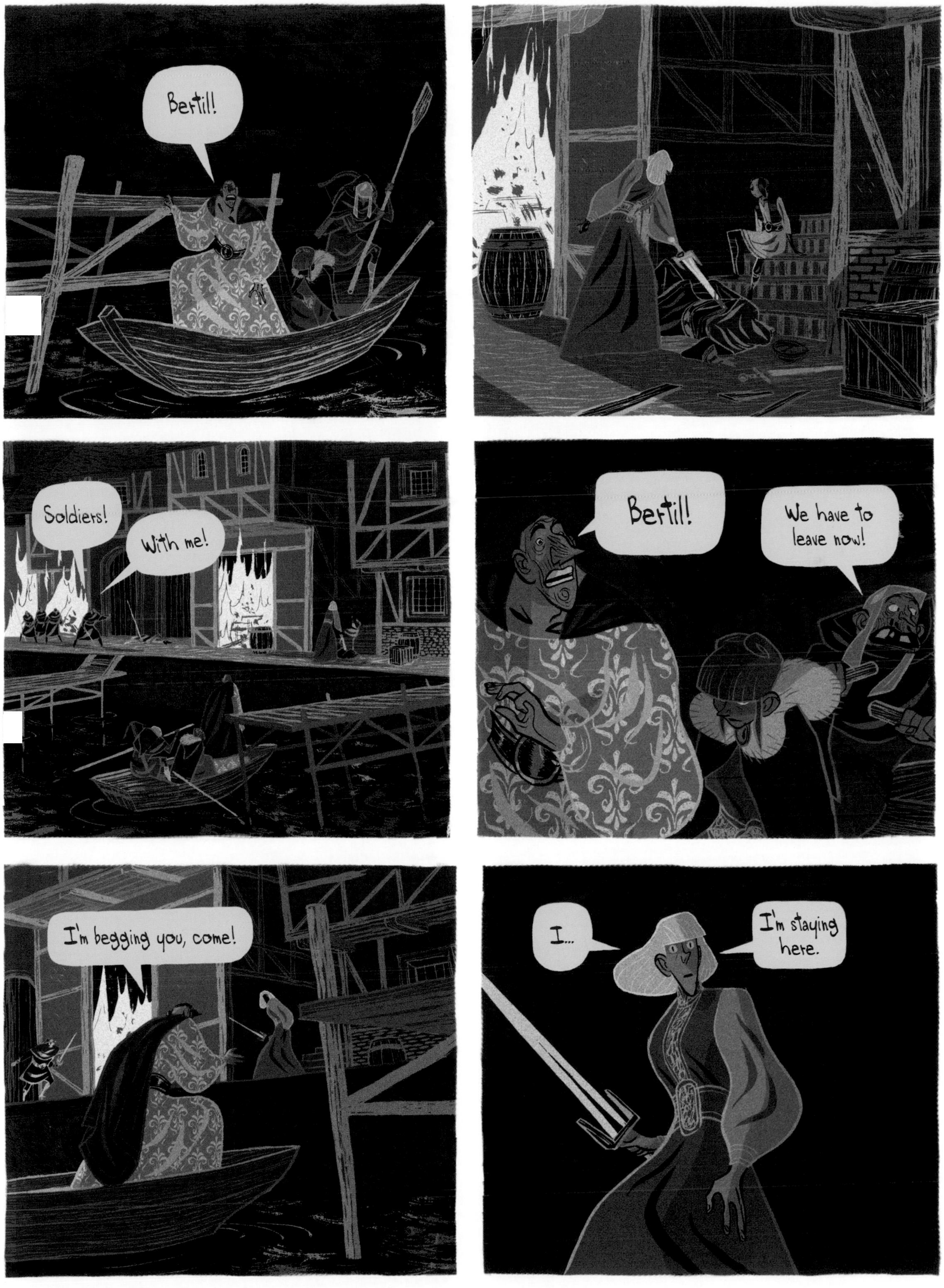
Bertil!
Soldiers!
With me!
Bertil!
We have to leave now!
I'm begging you, come!
I...
I'm staying here.

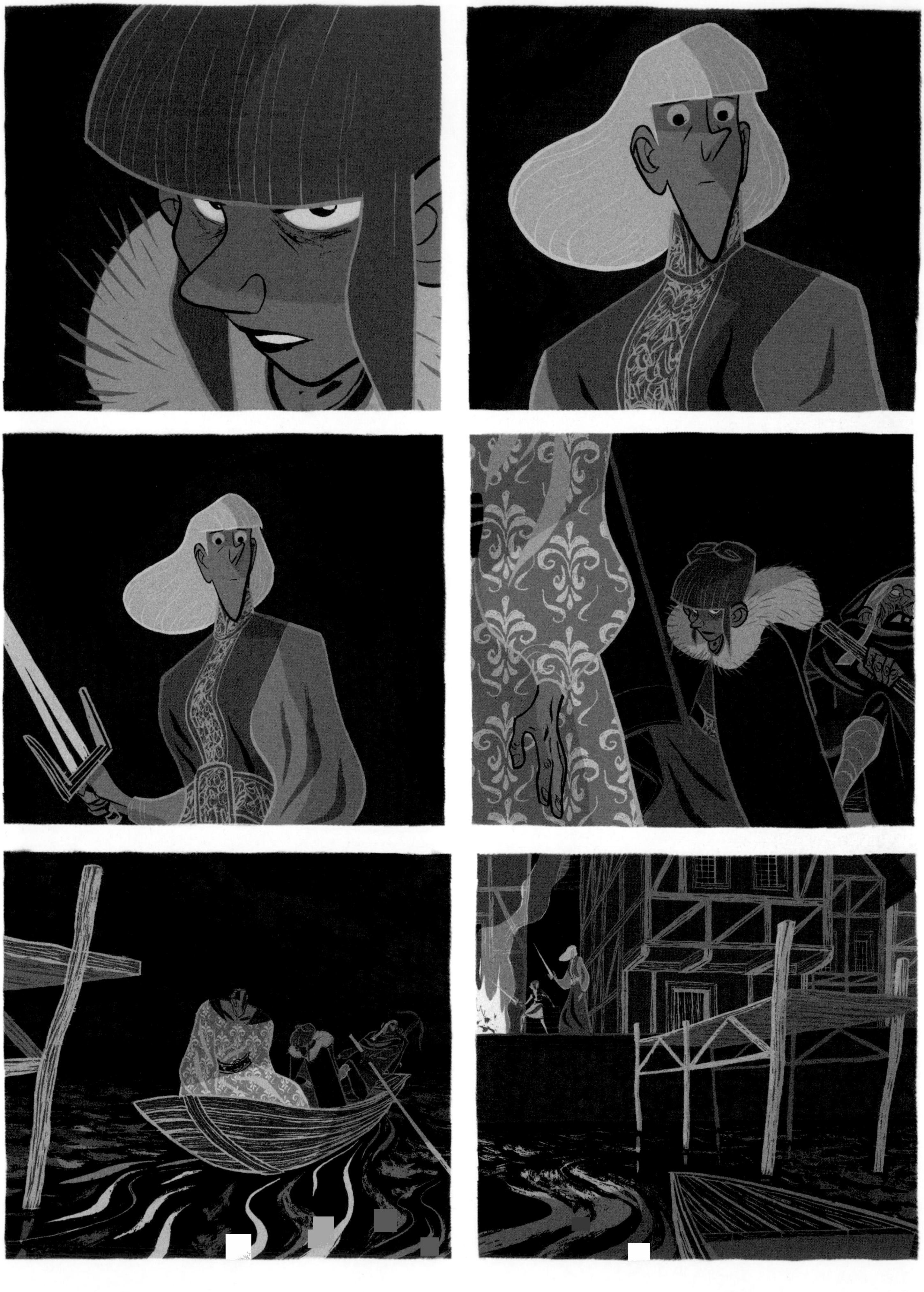

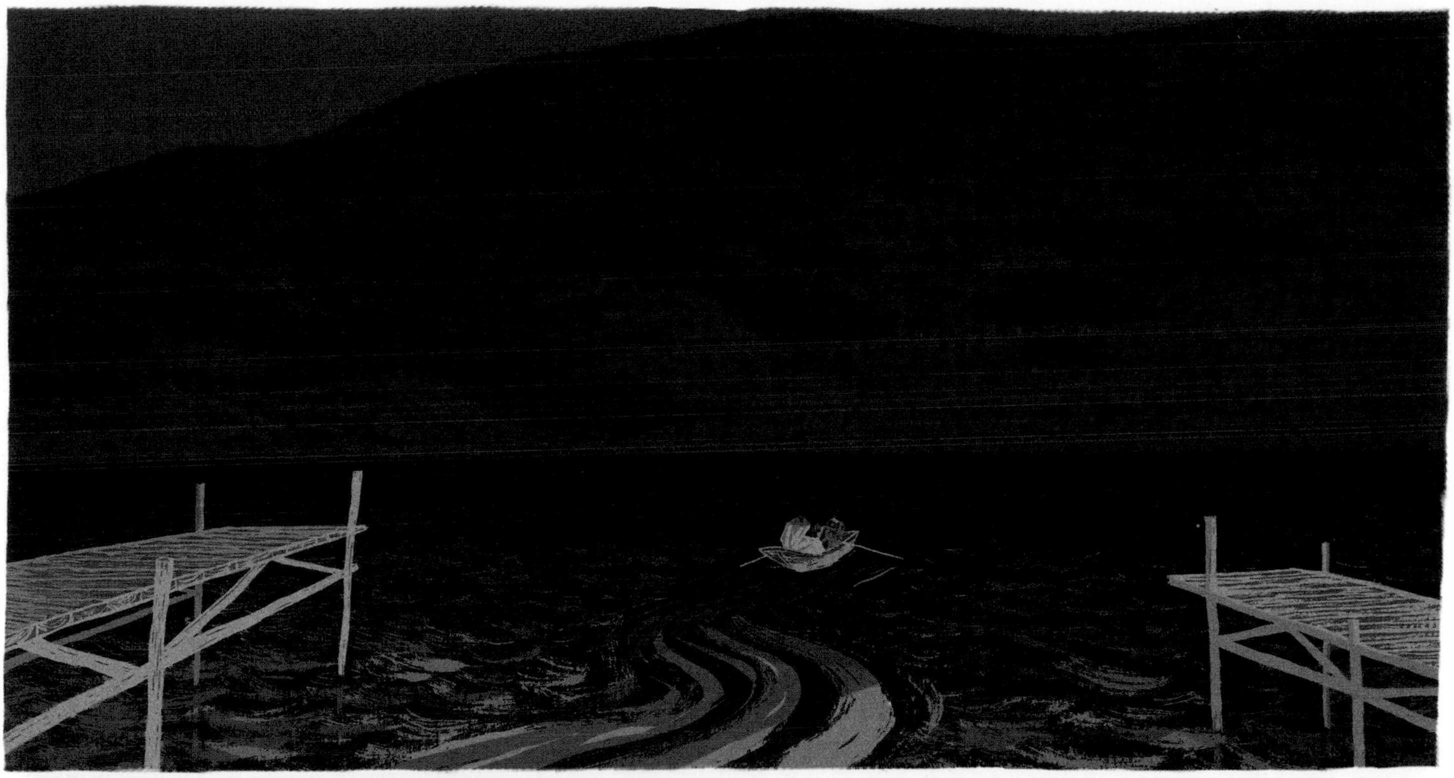

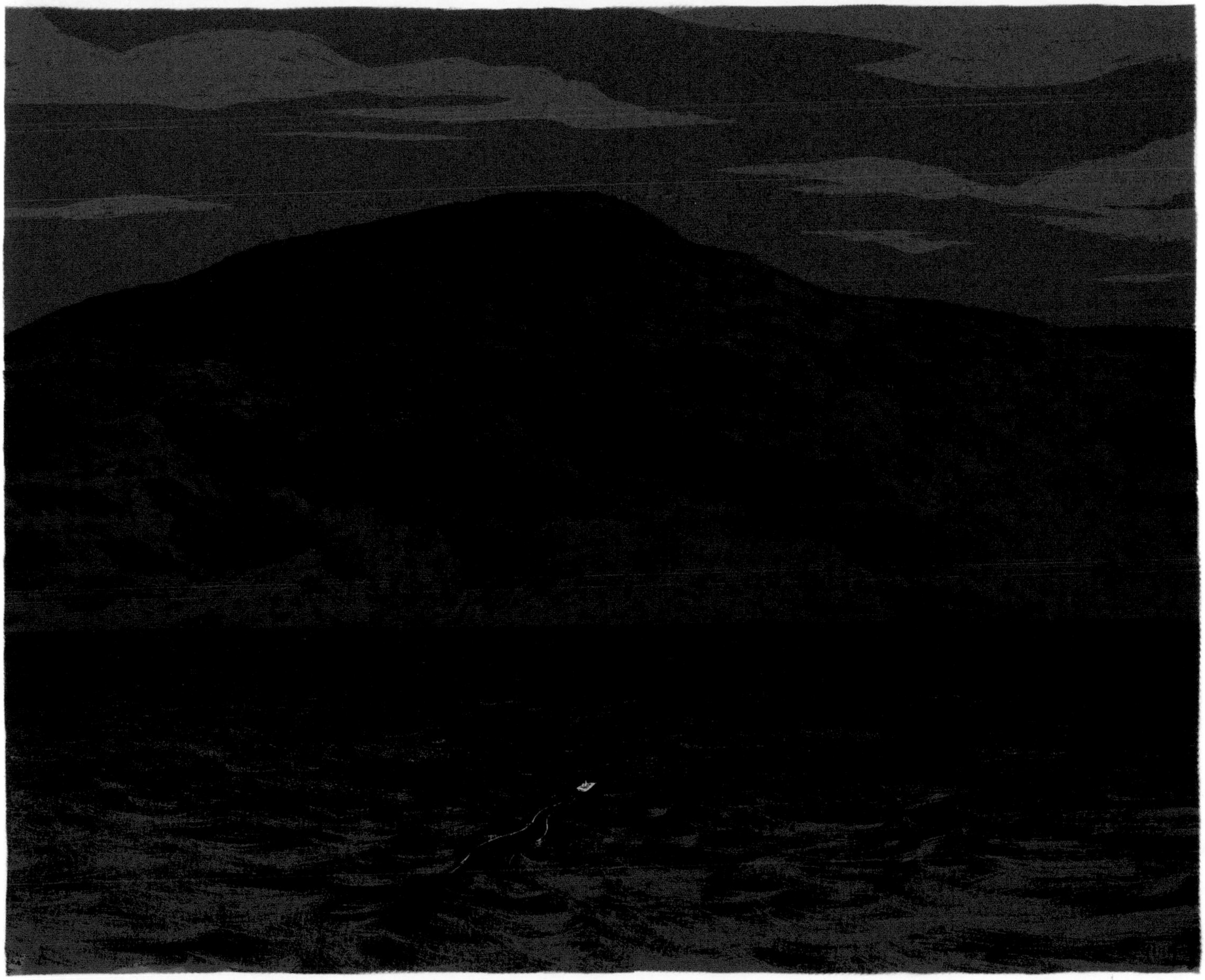

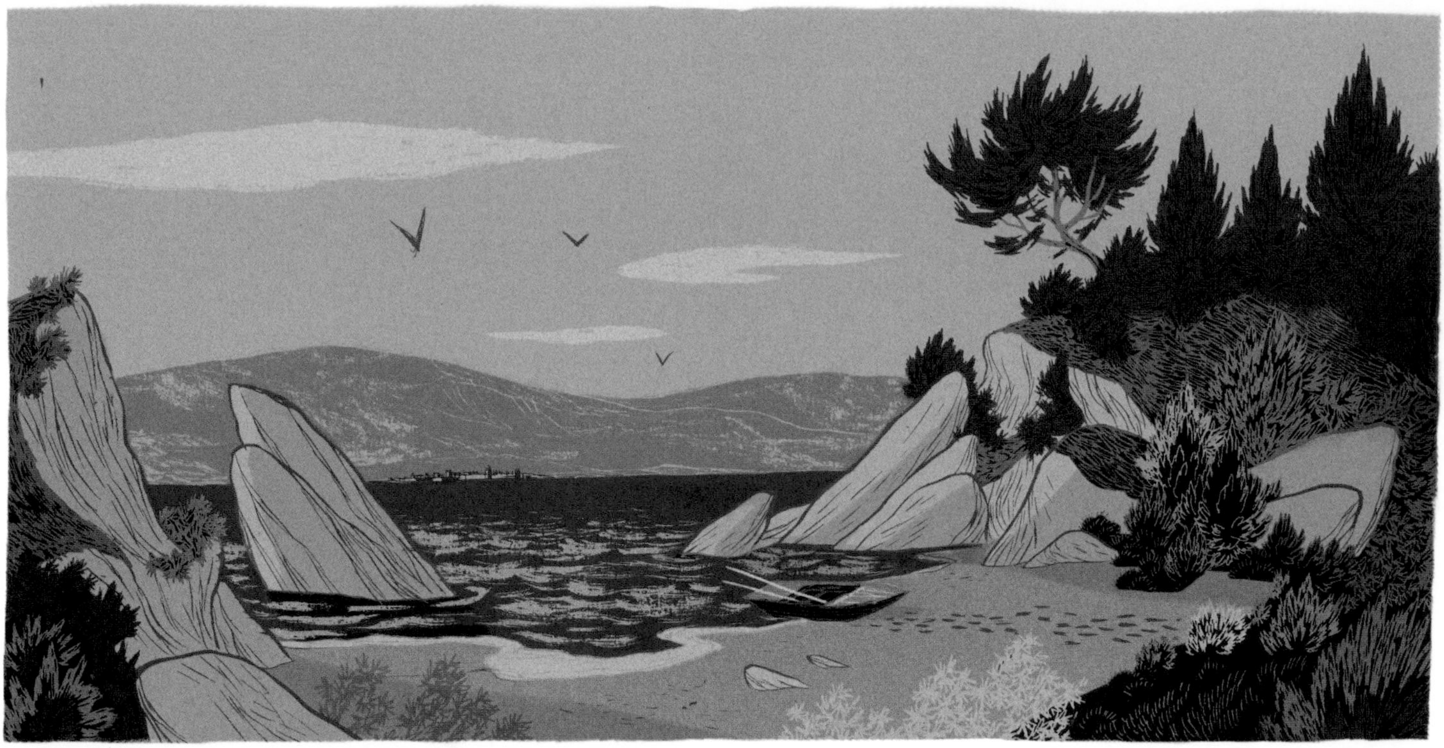

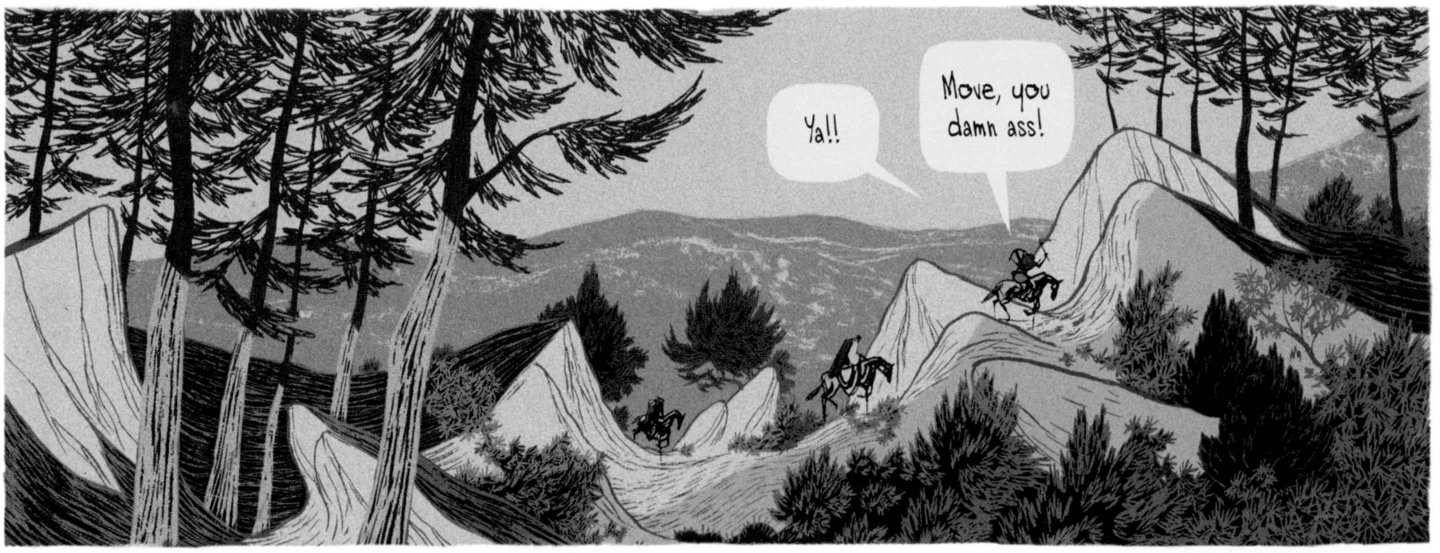
Ya!!
Move, you damn ass!

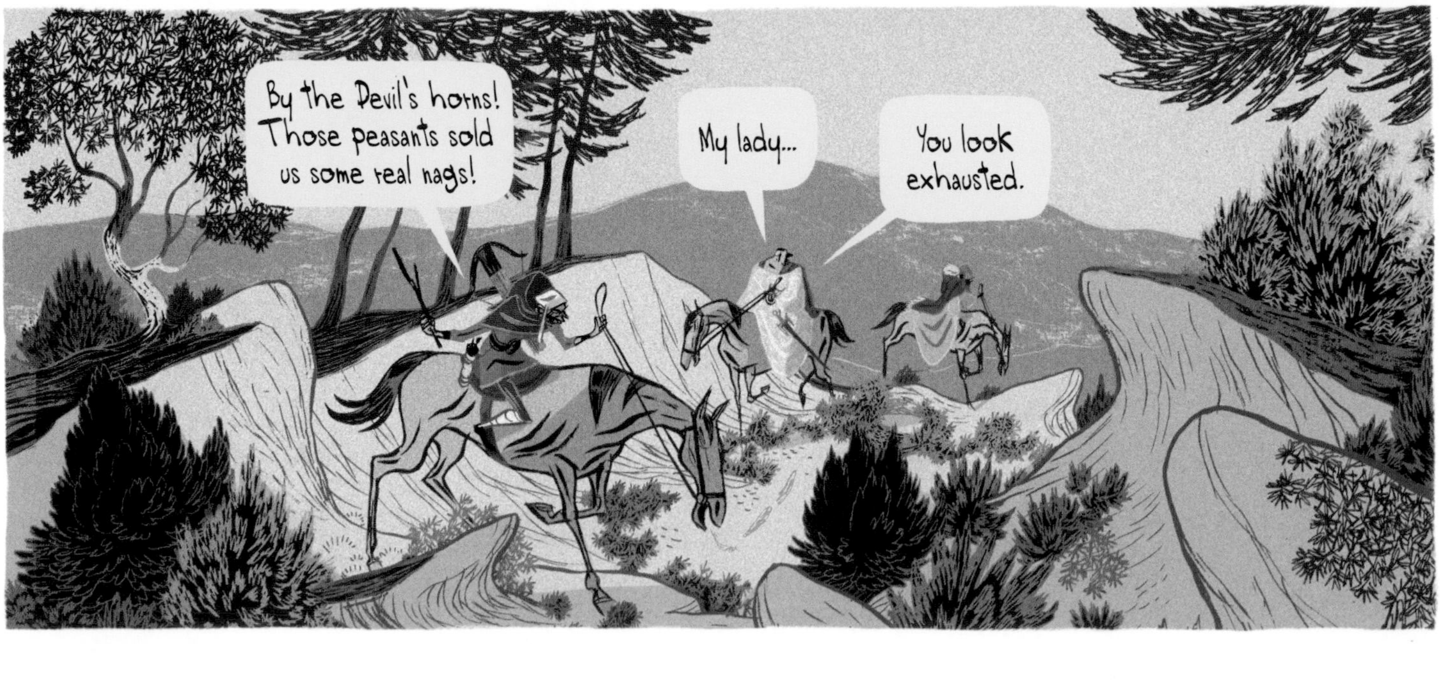
By the Devil's horns! Those peasants sold us some real nags!
My lady...
You look exhausted.

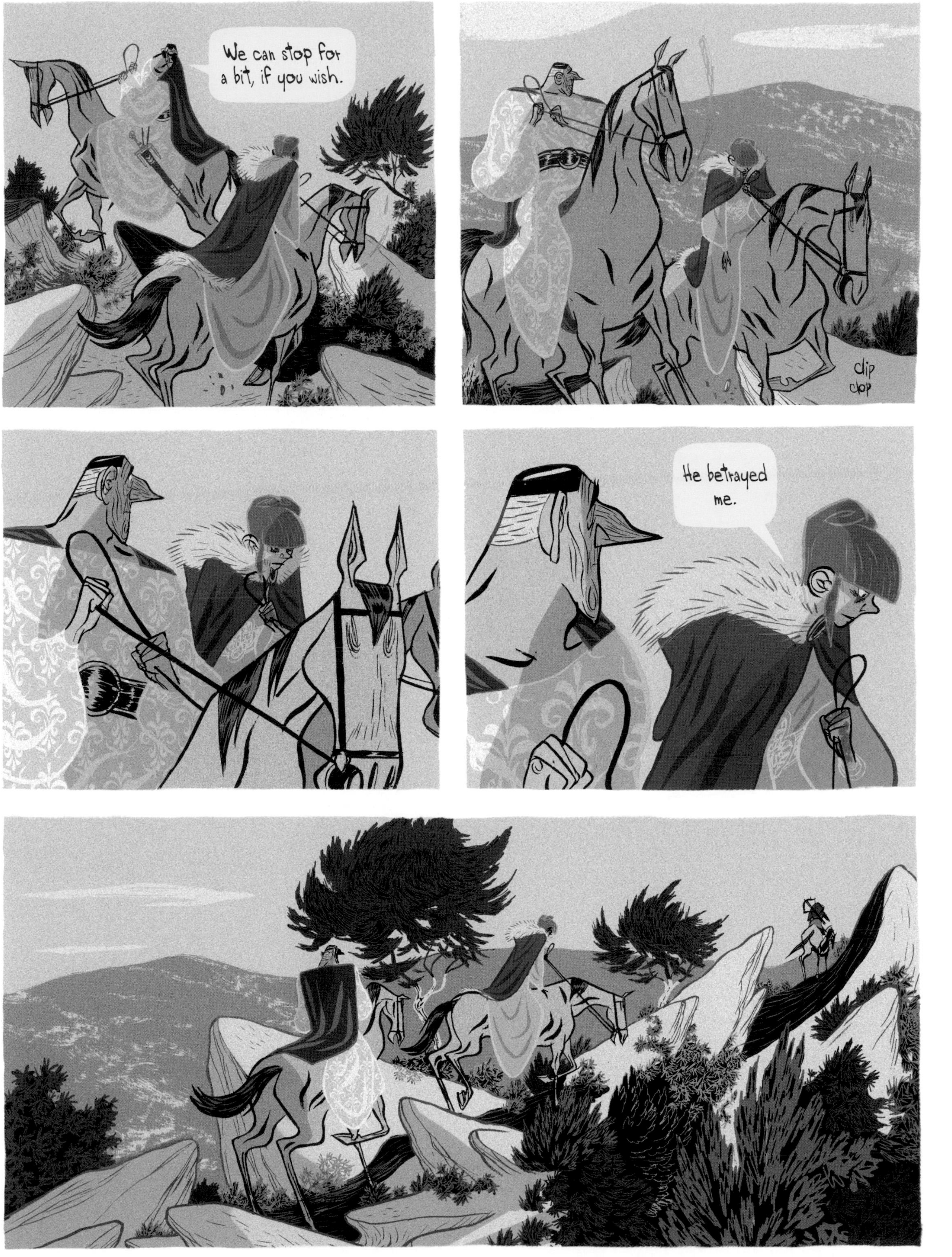
We can stop for a bit, if you wish.
clip clop
He betrayed me.

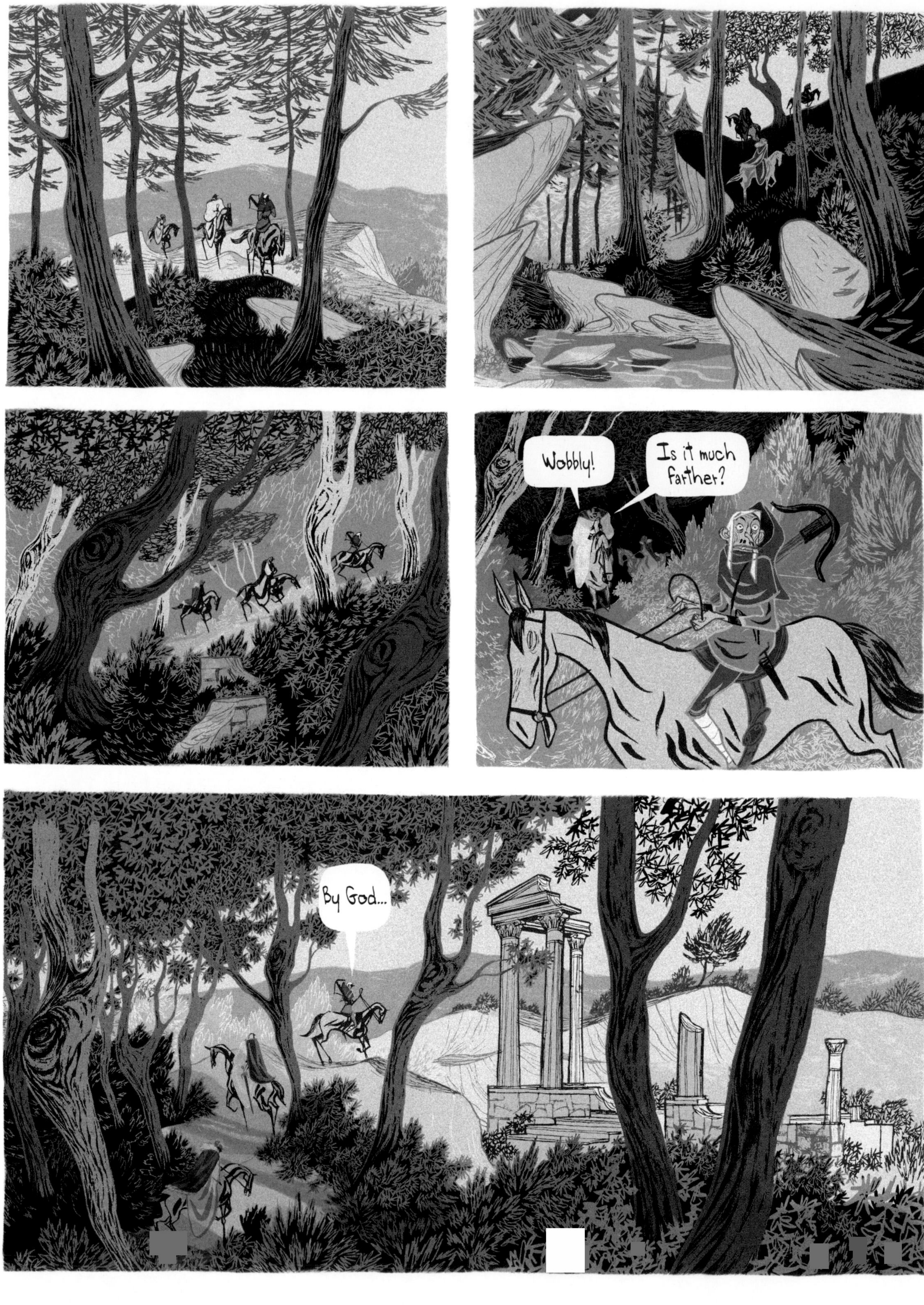
Wobbly!
Is it much farther?
By God...

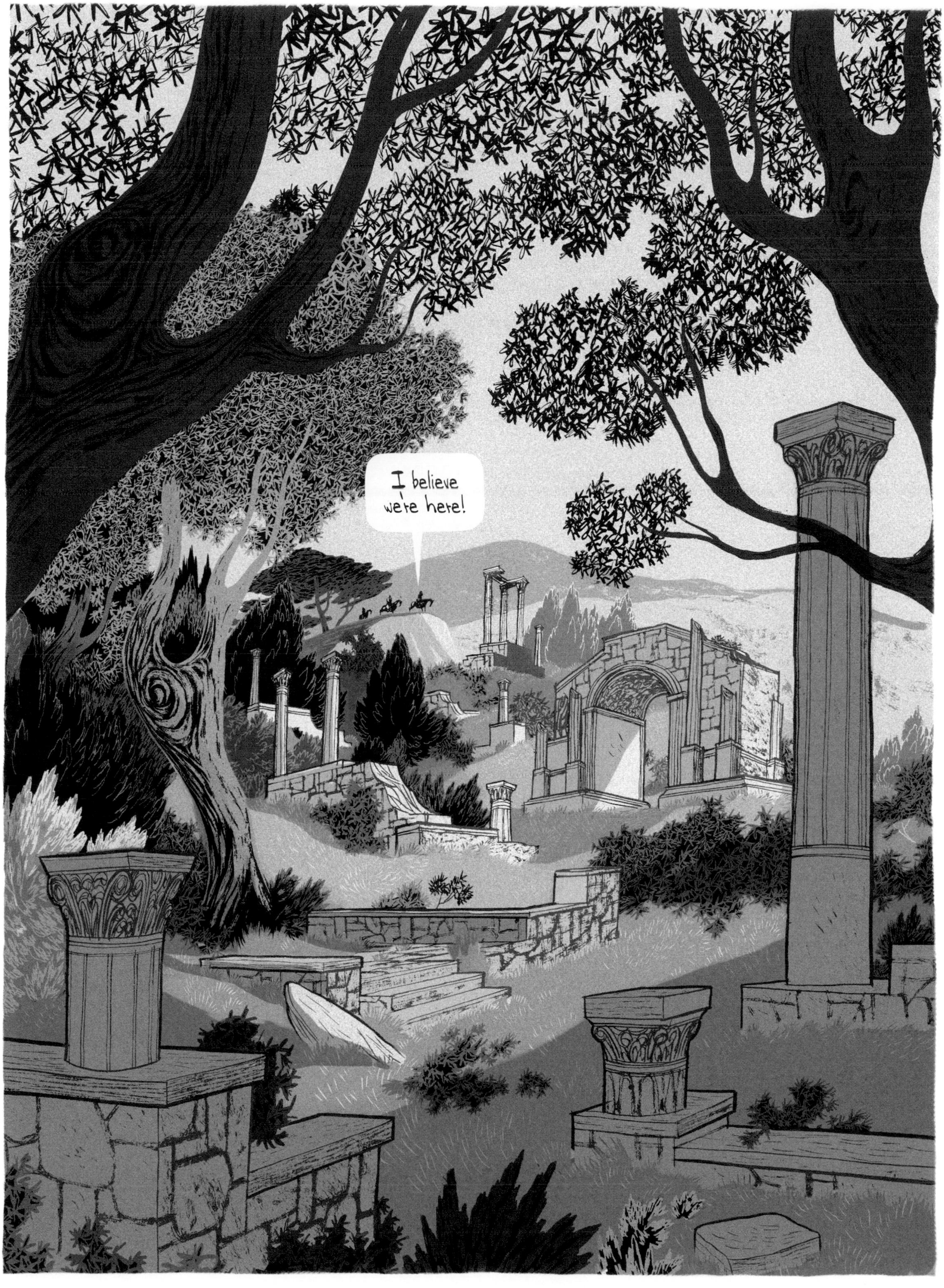
I believe we're here!

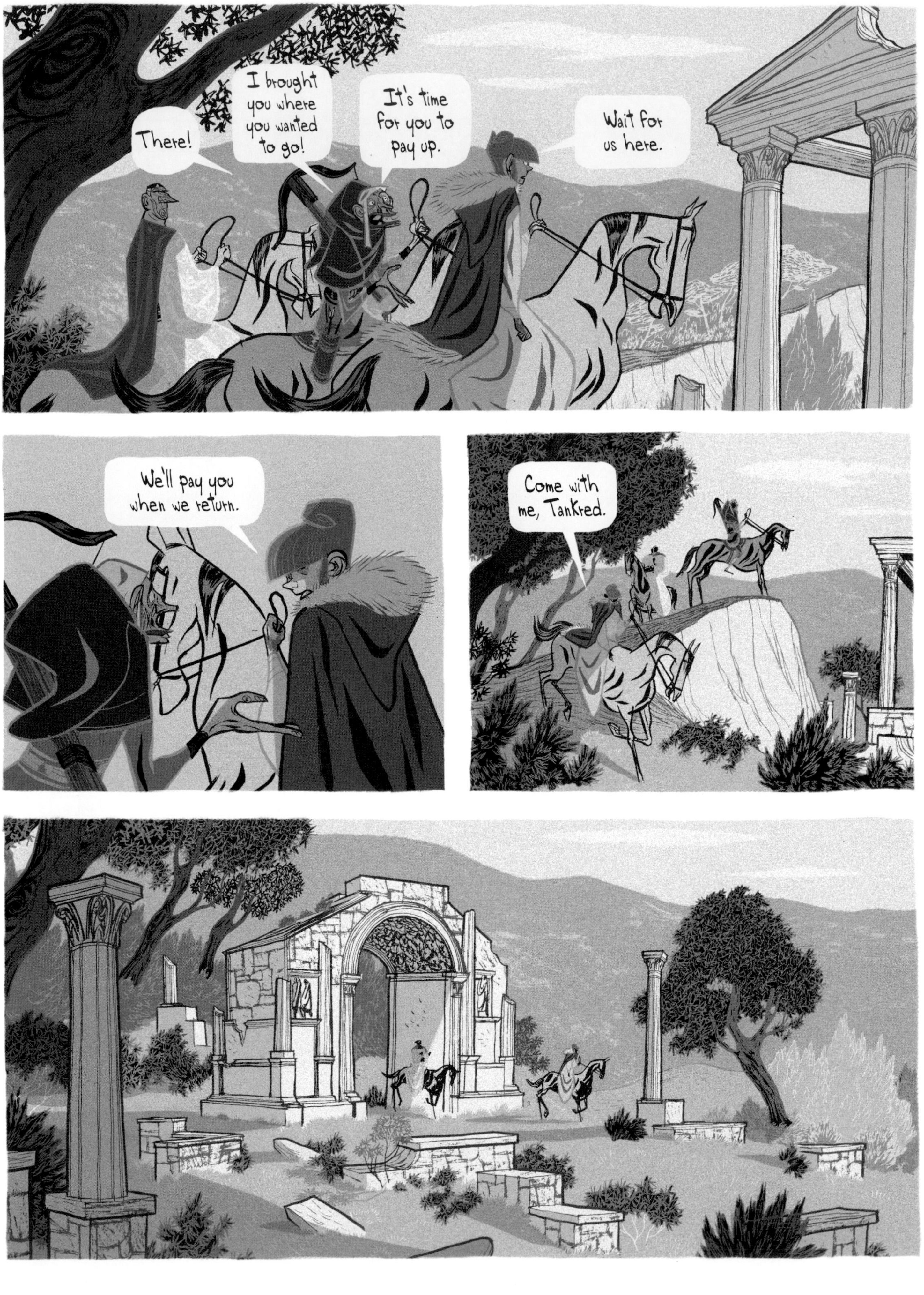
There!
I brought you where you wanted to go!
It's time for you to pay up.
Wait for us here.
We'll pay you when we return.
Come with me, Tankred.

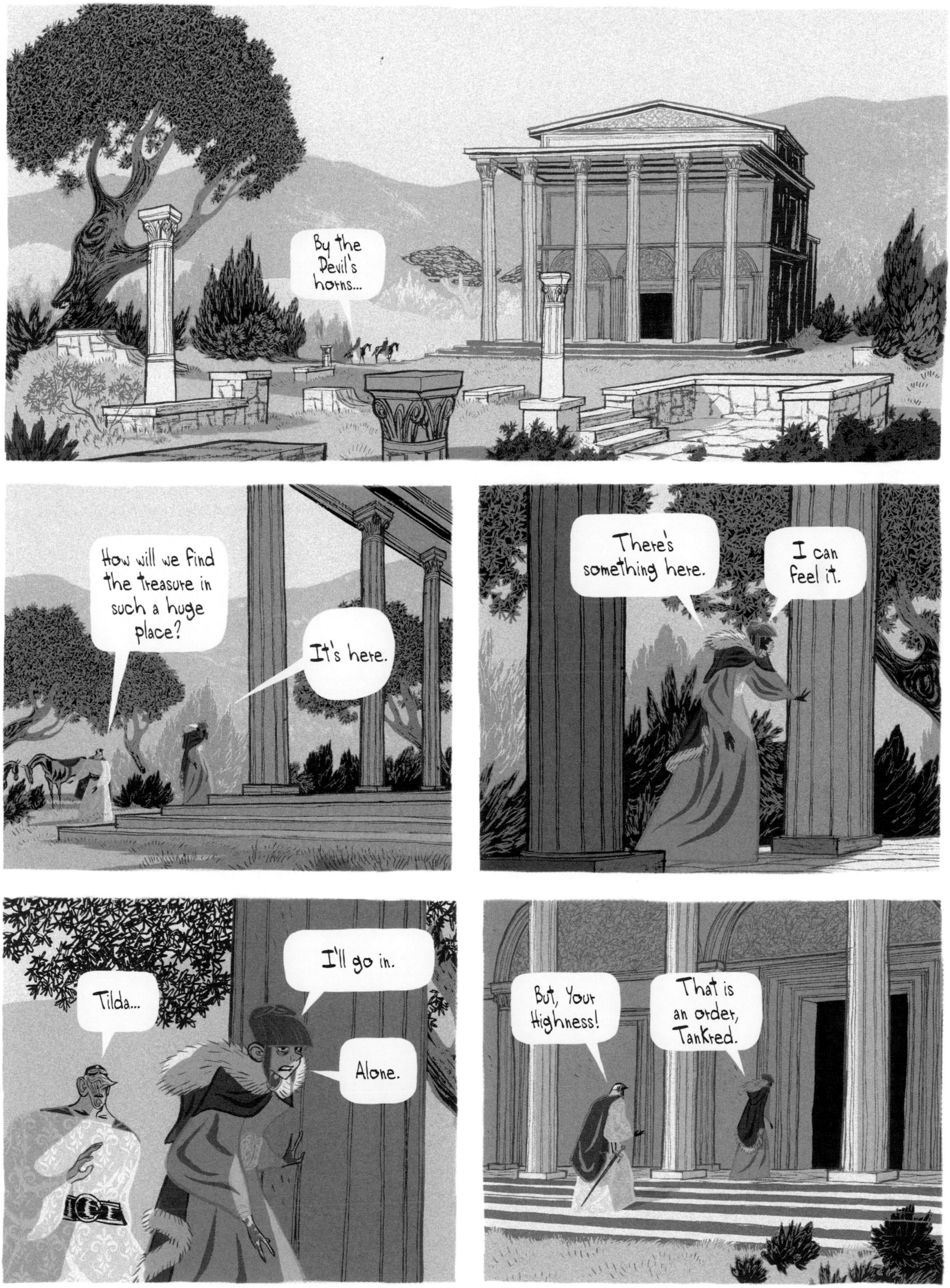
By the Devil's horns...
How will we find the treasure in such a huge place?
It's here.
There's something here.
I can feel it.
Tilda...
I'll go in.
Alone.
But, Your Highness!
That is an order, Tankred.

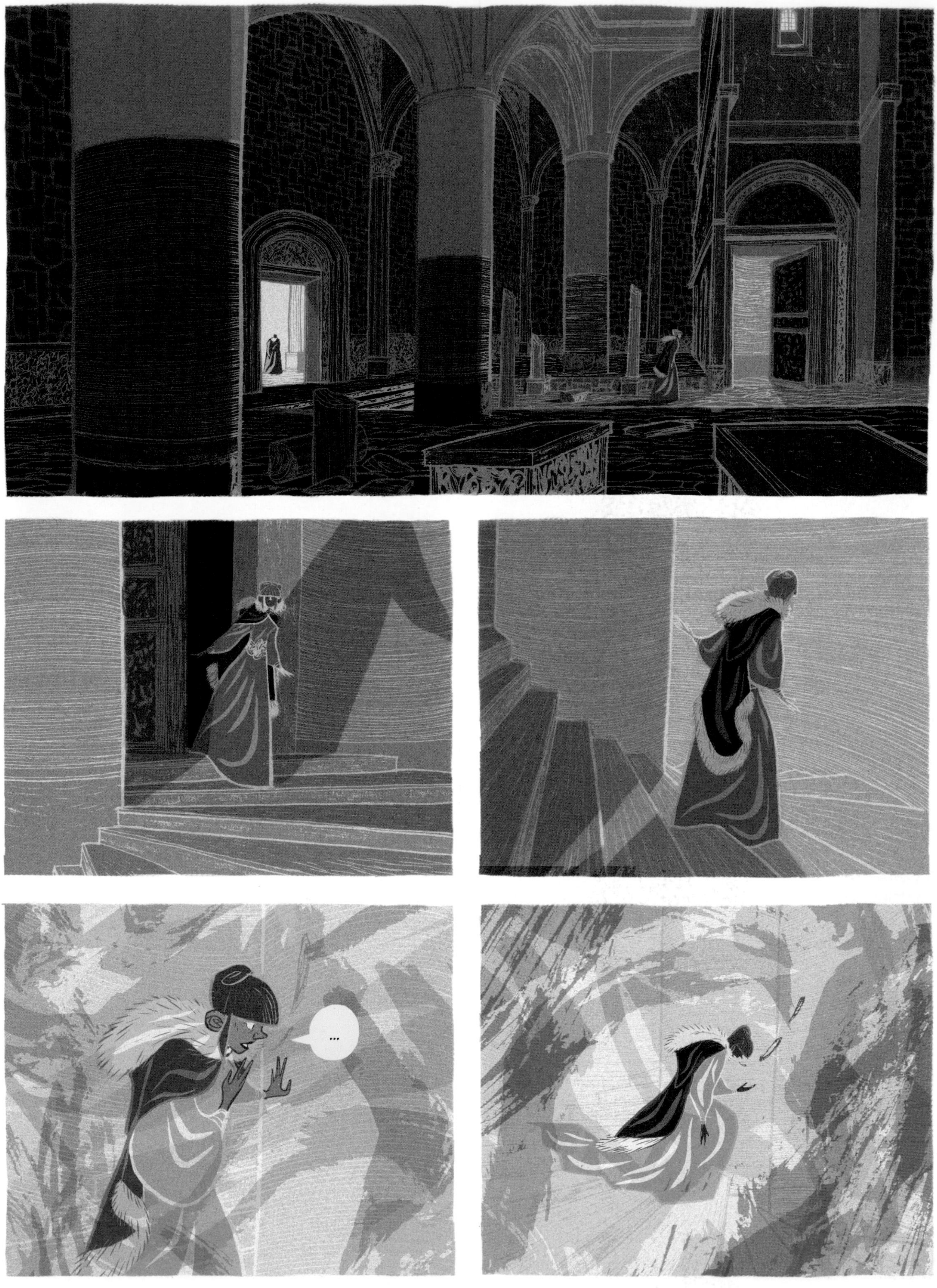
...

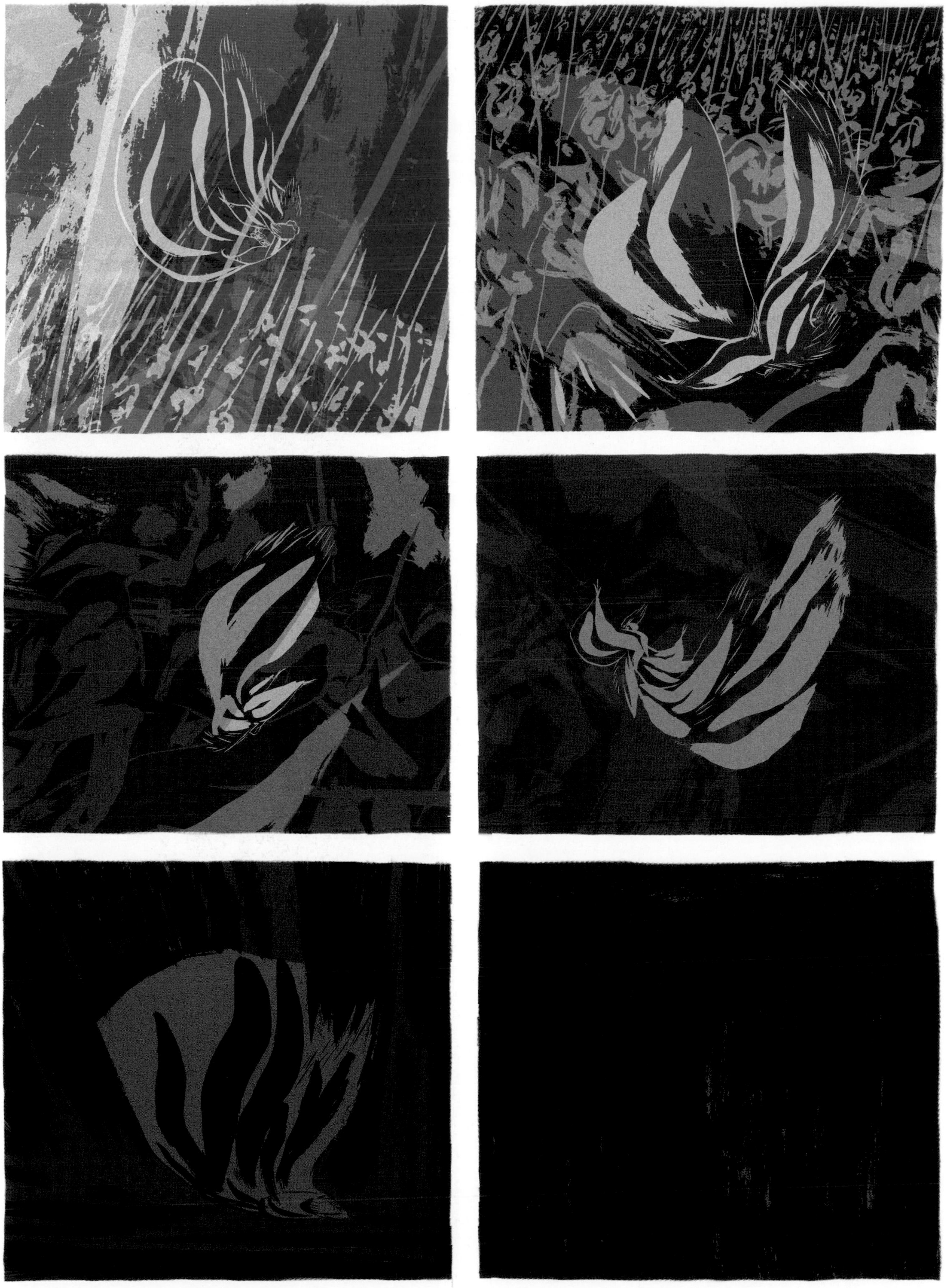

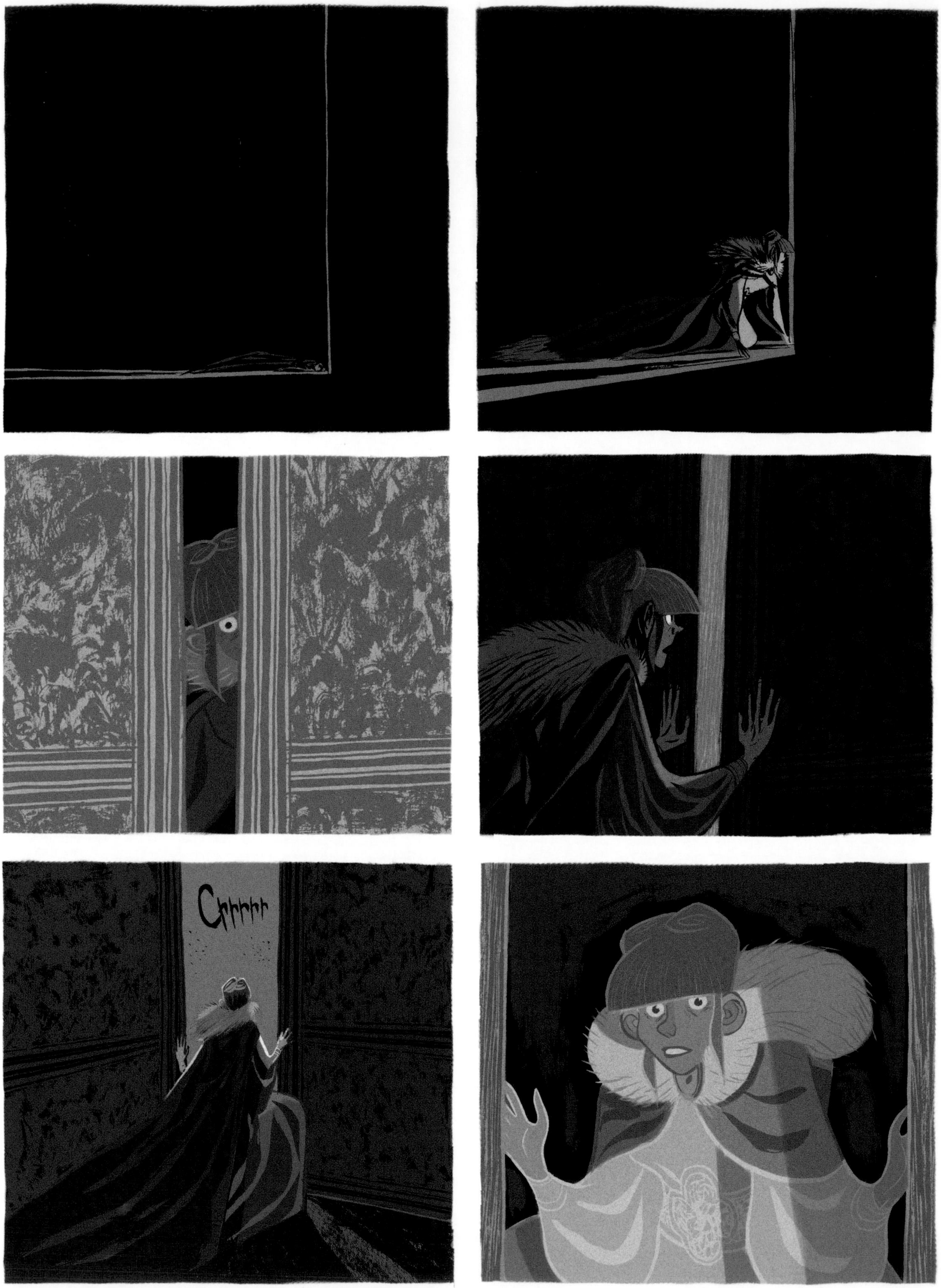
Crrrrr

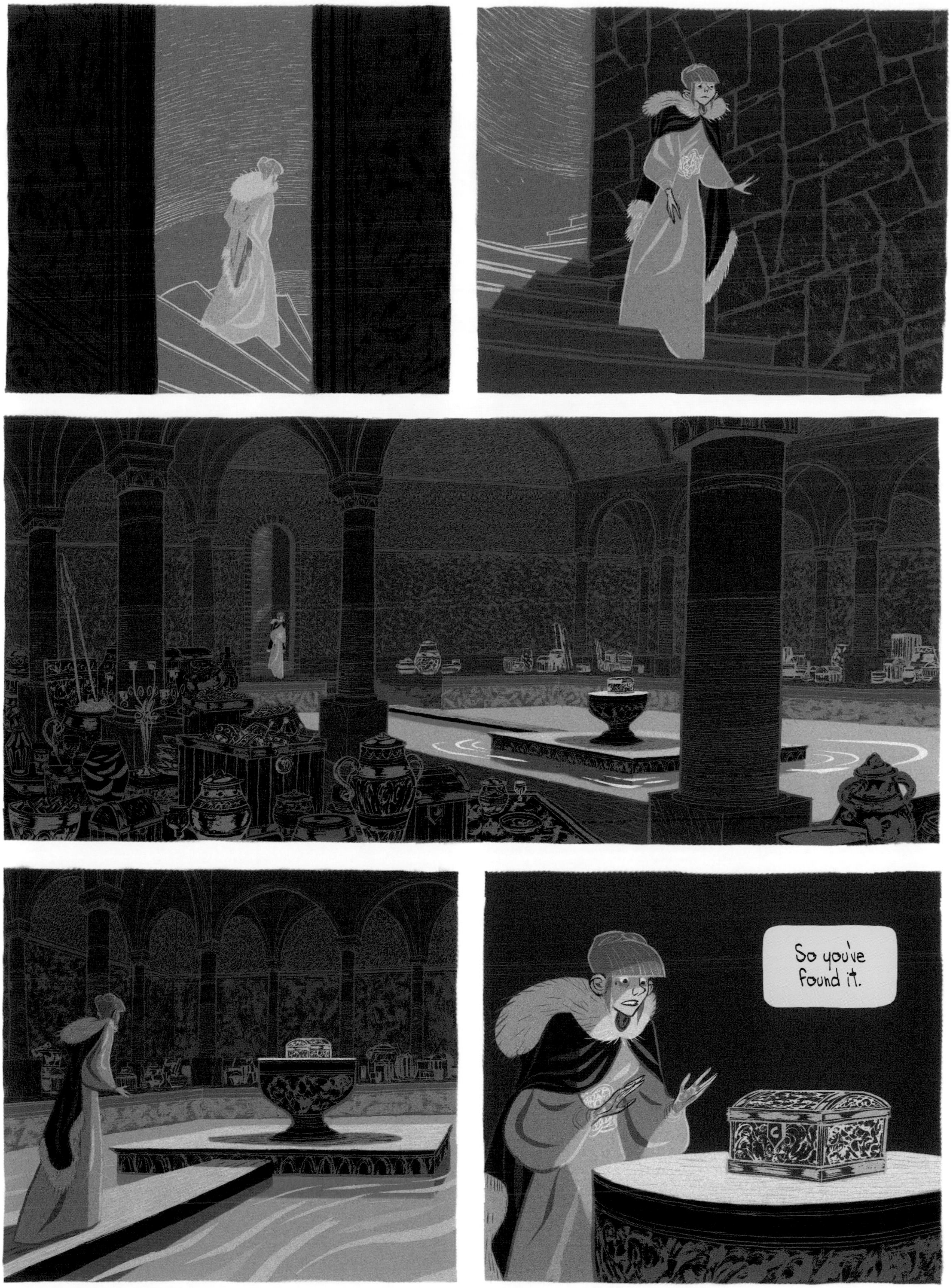
So you've found it.

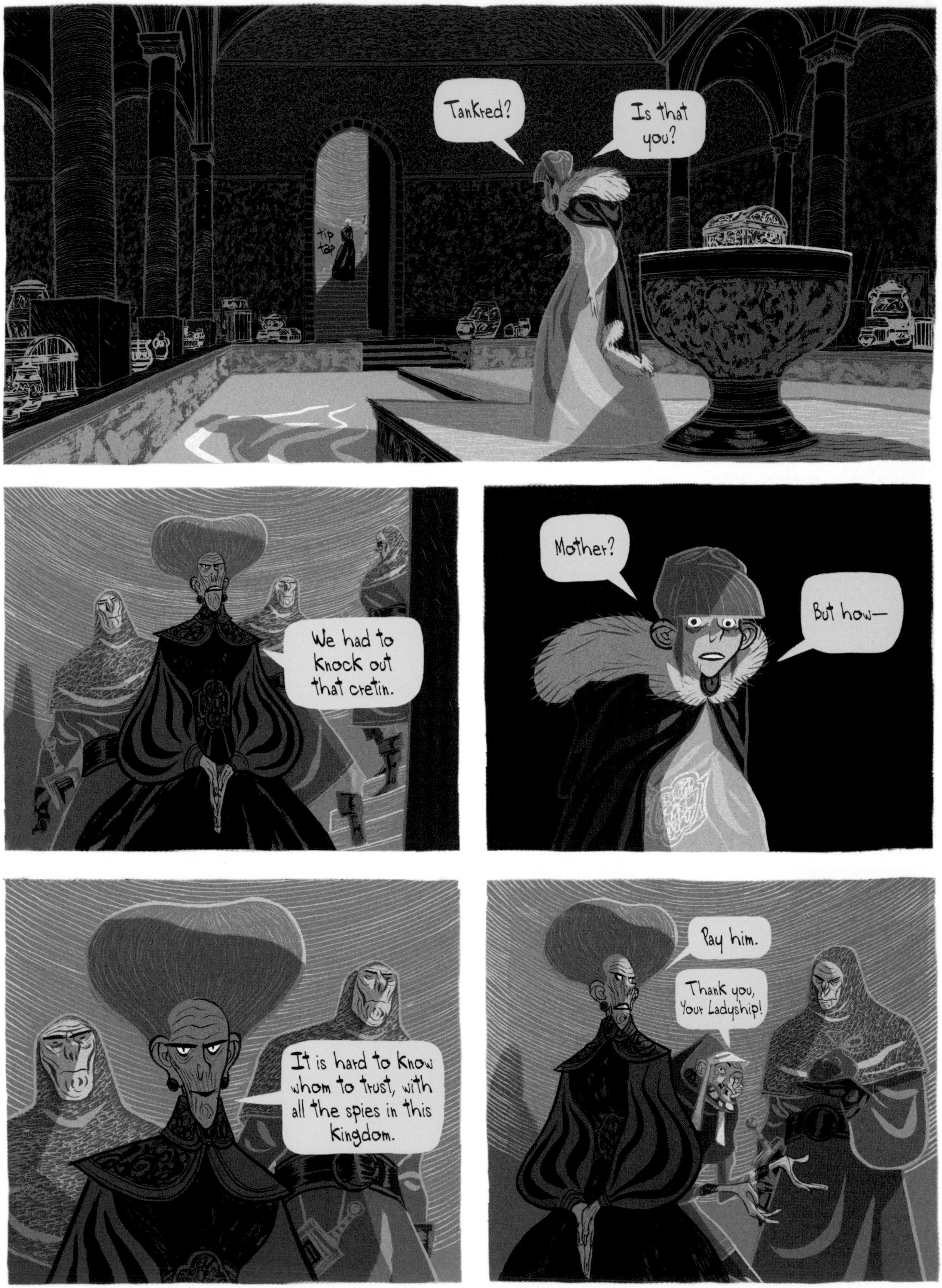

Tankred?
Is that you?
tip tap
We had to knock out that cretin.
Mother?
But how—
It is hard to know whom to trust, with all the spies in this kingdom.
Pay him.
Thank you, Your Ladyship!

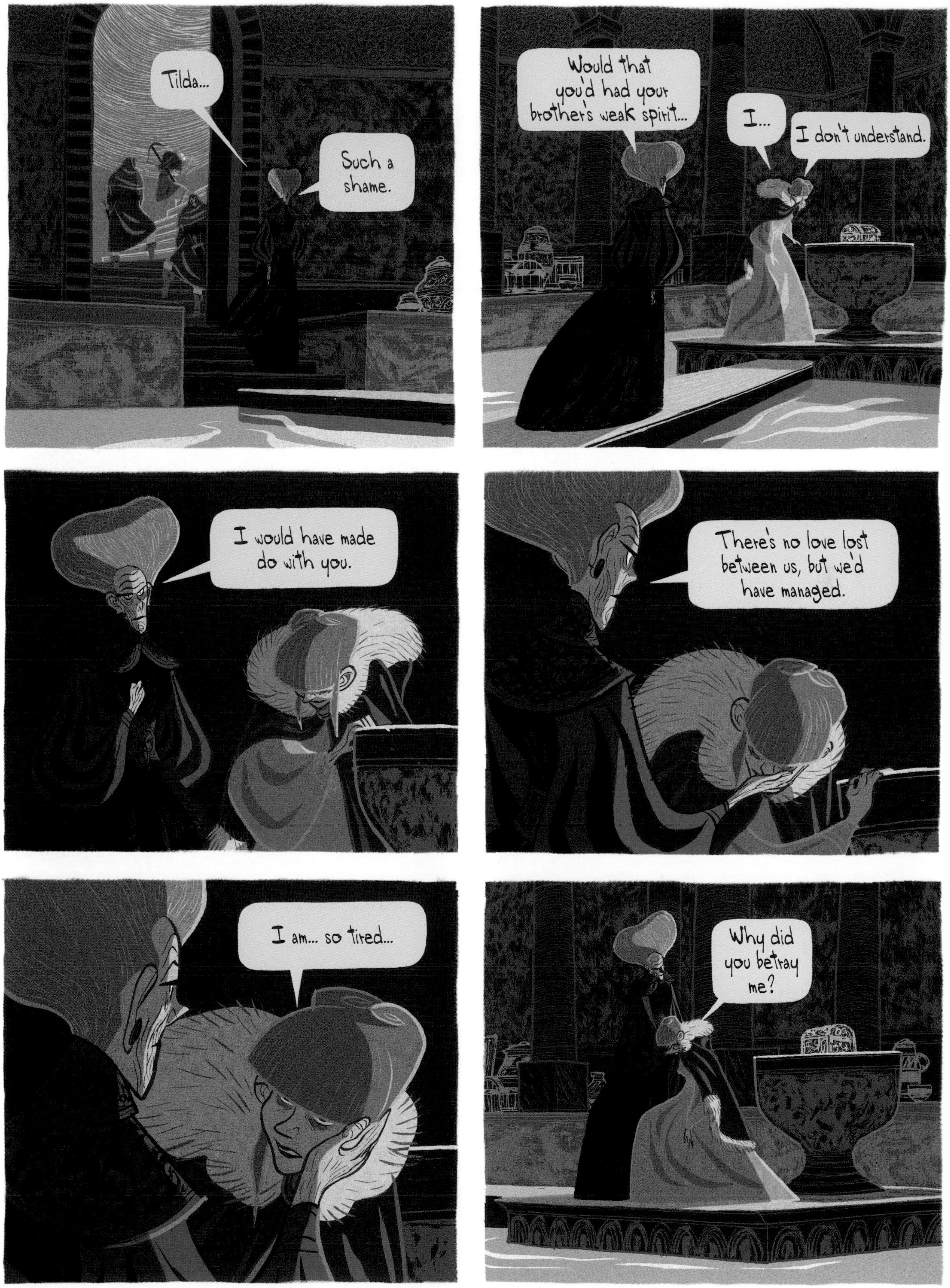
Tilda...
Such a shame.
Would that you'd had your brother's weak spirit...
I...
I don't understand.
I would have made do with you.
There's no love lost between us, but we'd have managed.
I am... so tired...
Why did you betray me?

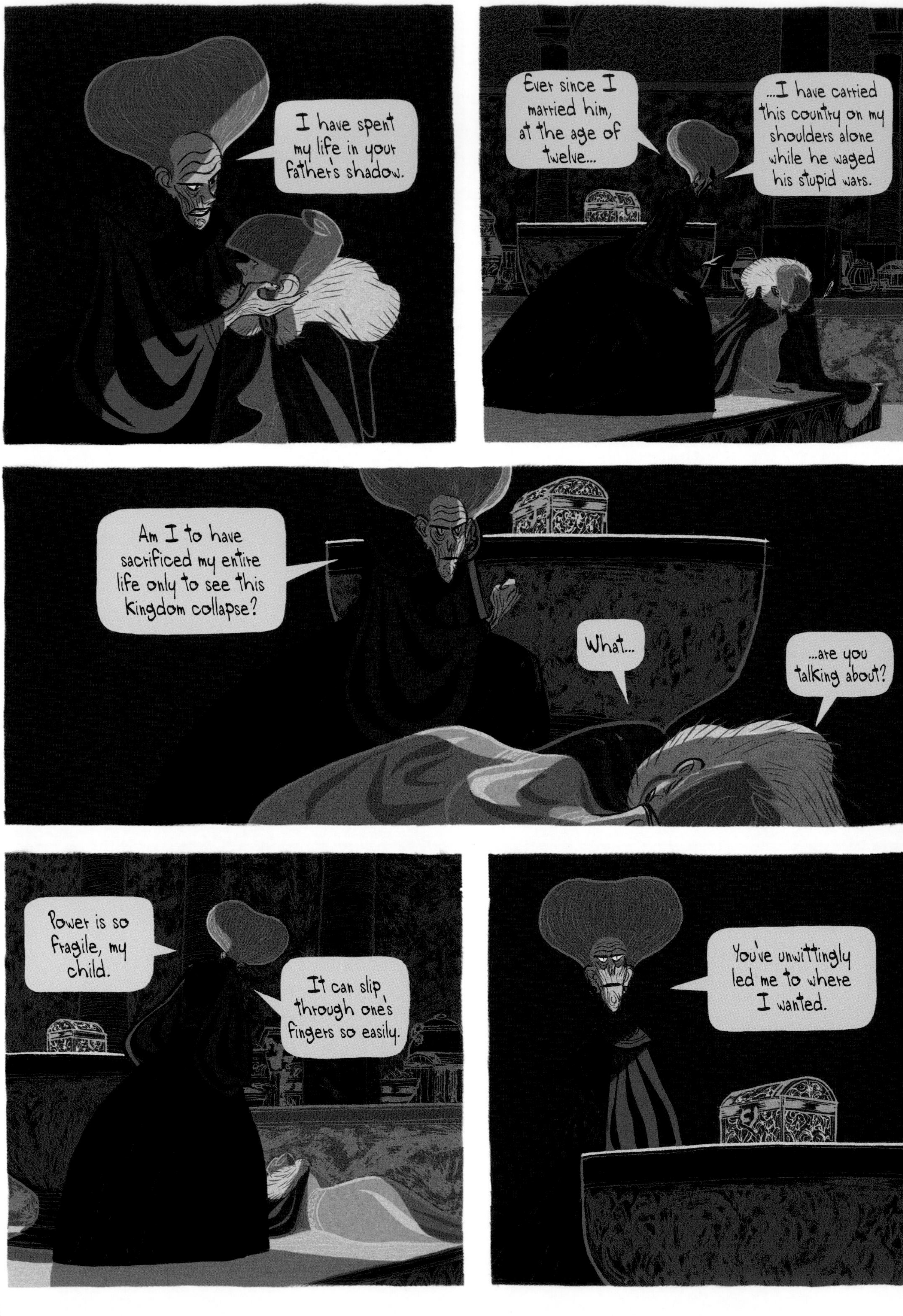
I have spent my life in your father's shadow.
Ever since I married him, at the age of twelve...
...I have carried this country on my shoulders alone while he waged his stupid wars.
Am I to have sacrificed my entire life only to see this kingdom collapse?
What...
...are you talking about?
Power is so fragile, my child.
It can slip through one's fingers so easily.
You've unwittingly led me to where I wanted.

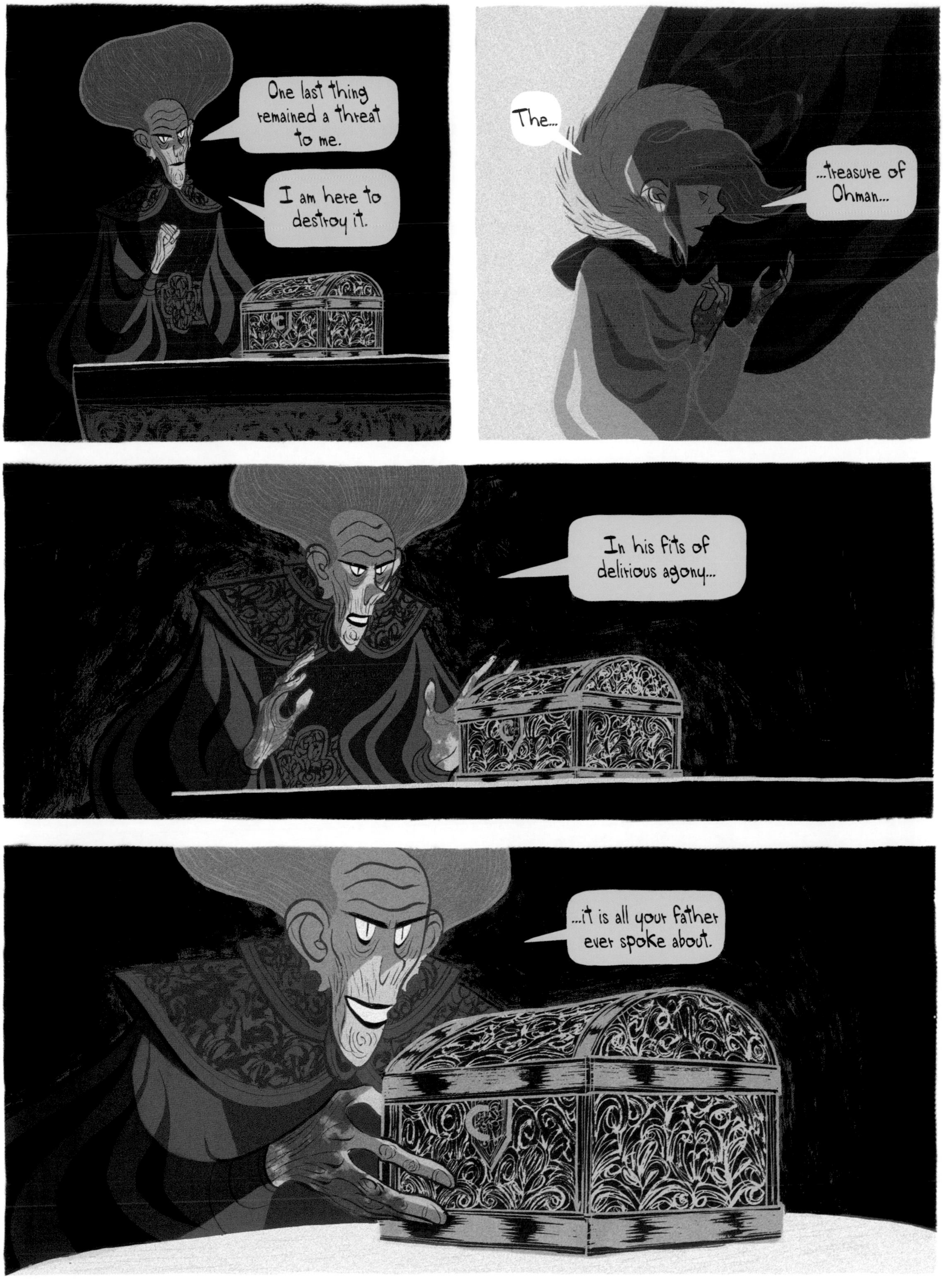
One last thing remained a threat to me.
I am here to destroy it.
The...
...treasure of Ohman...
In his fits of delirious agony...
...it is all your father ever spoke about.

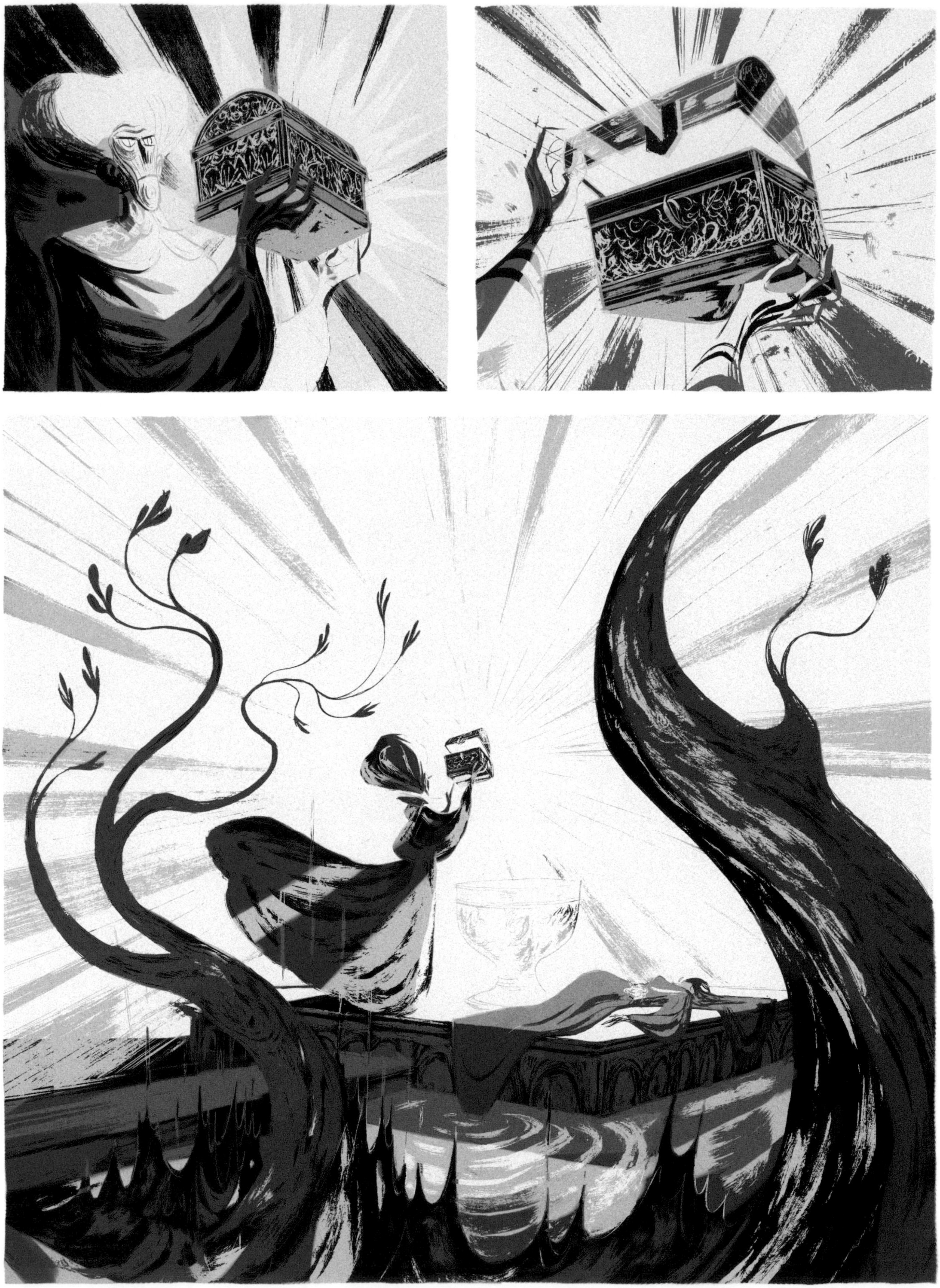

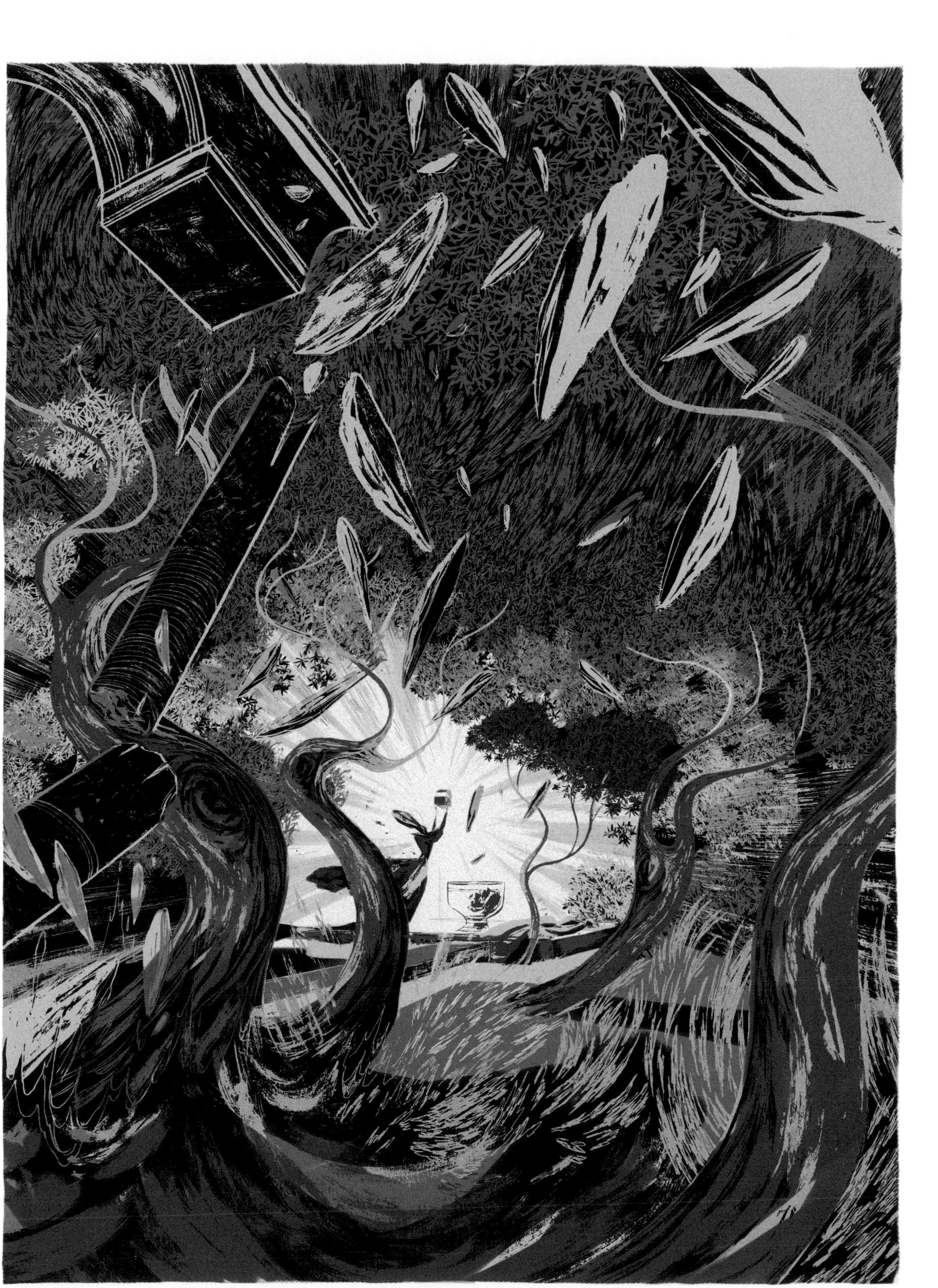

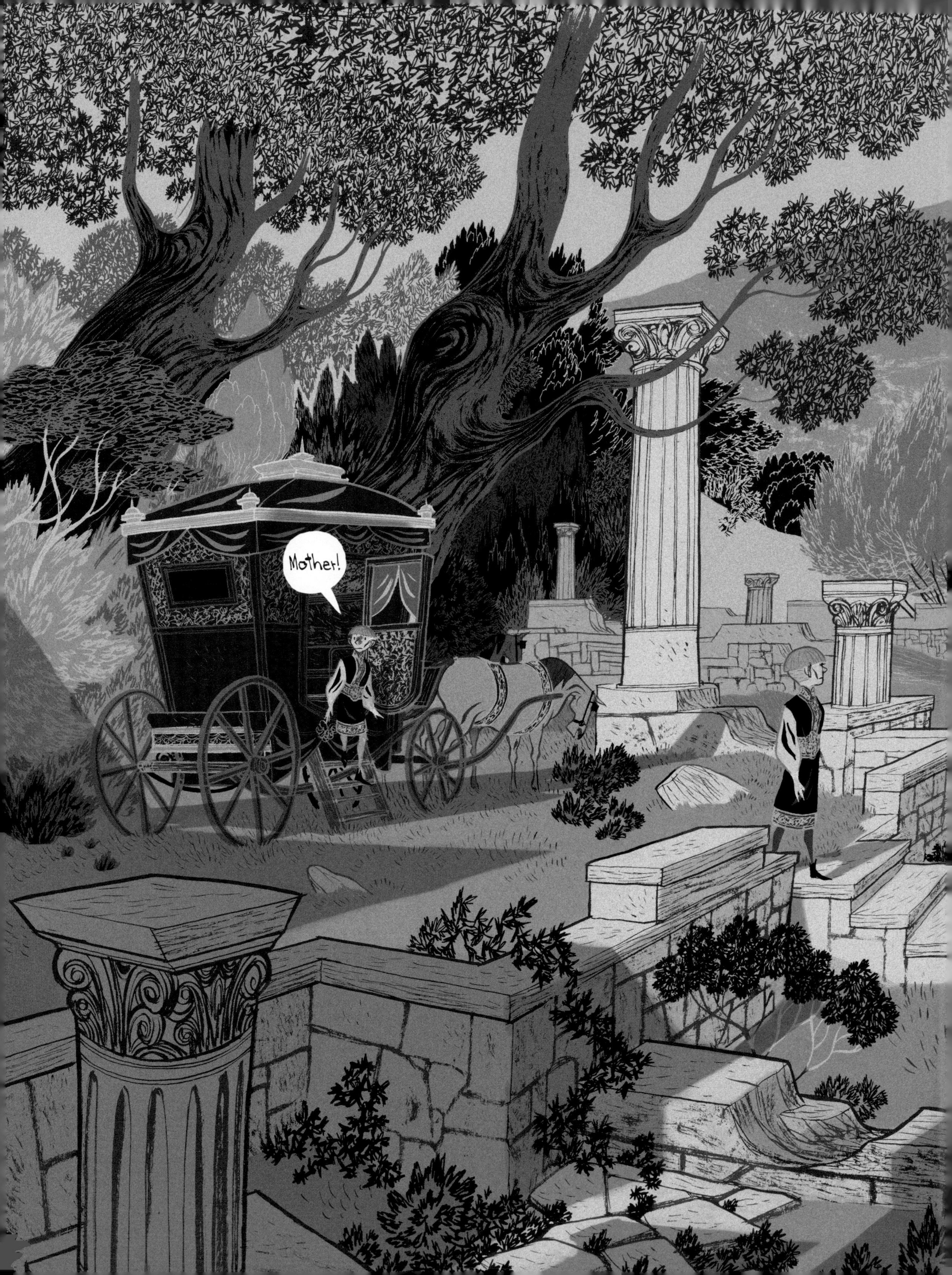
Mother!

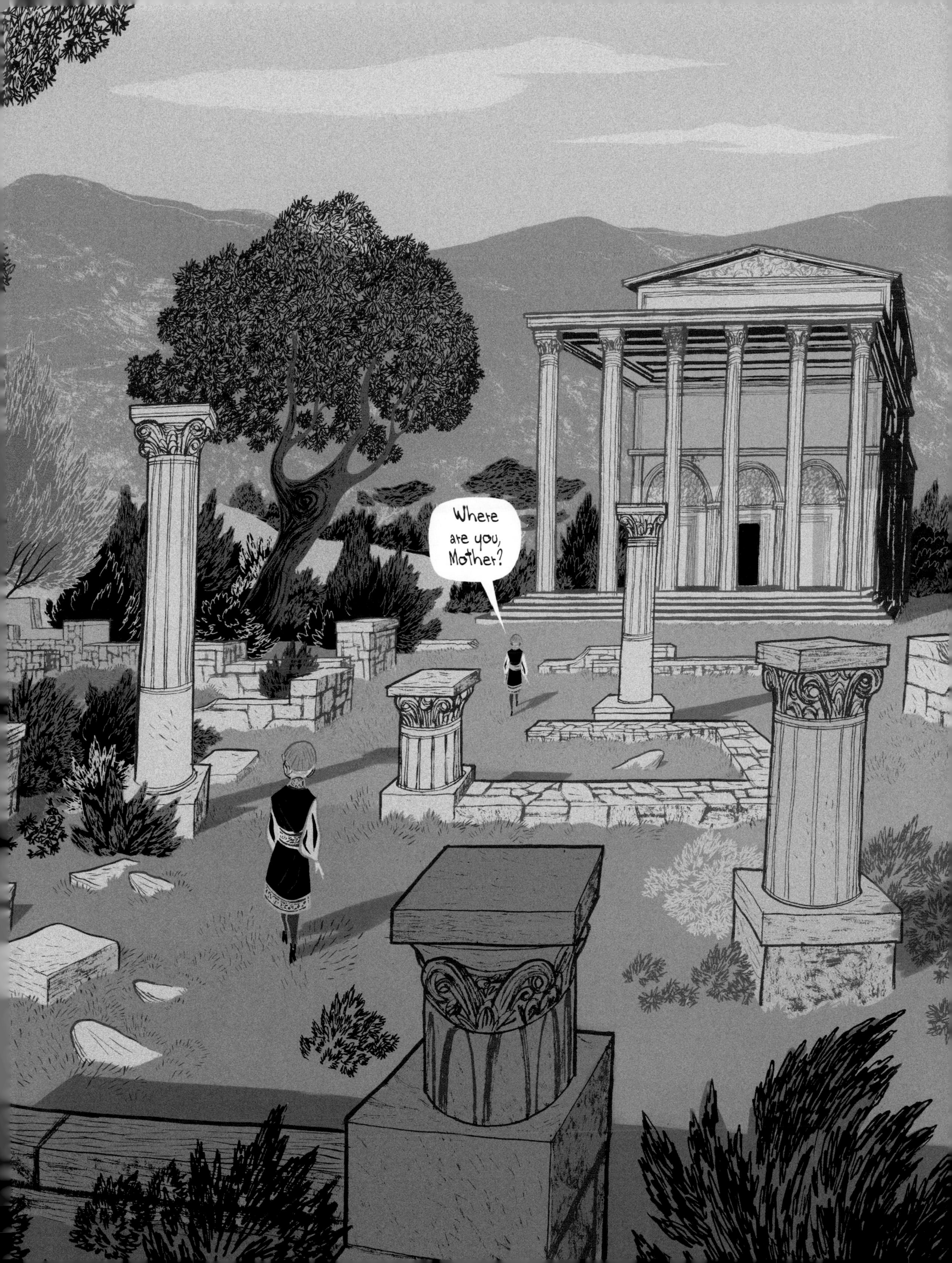
Where are you, Mother?

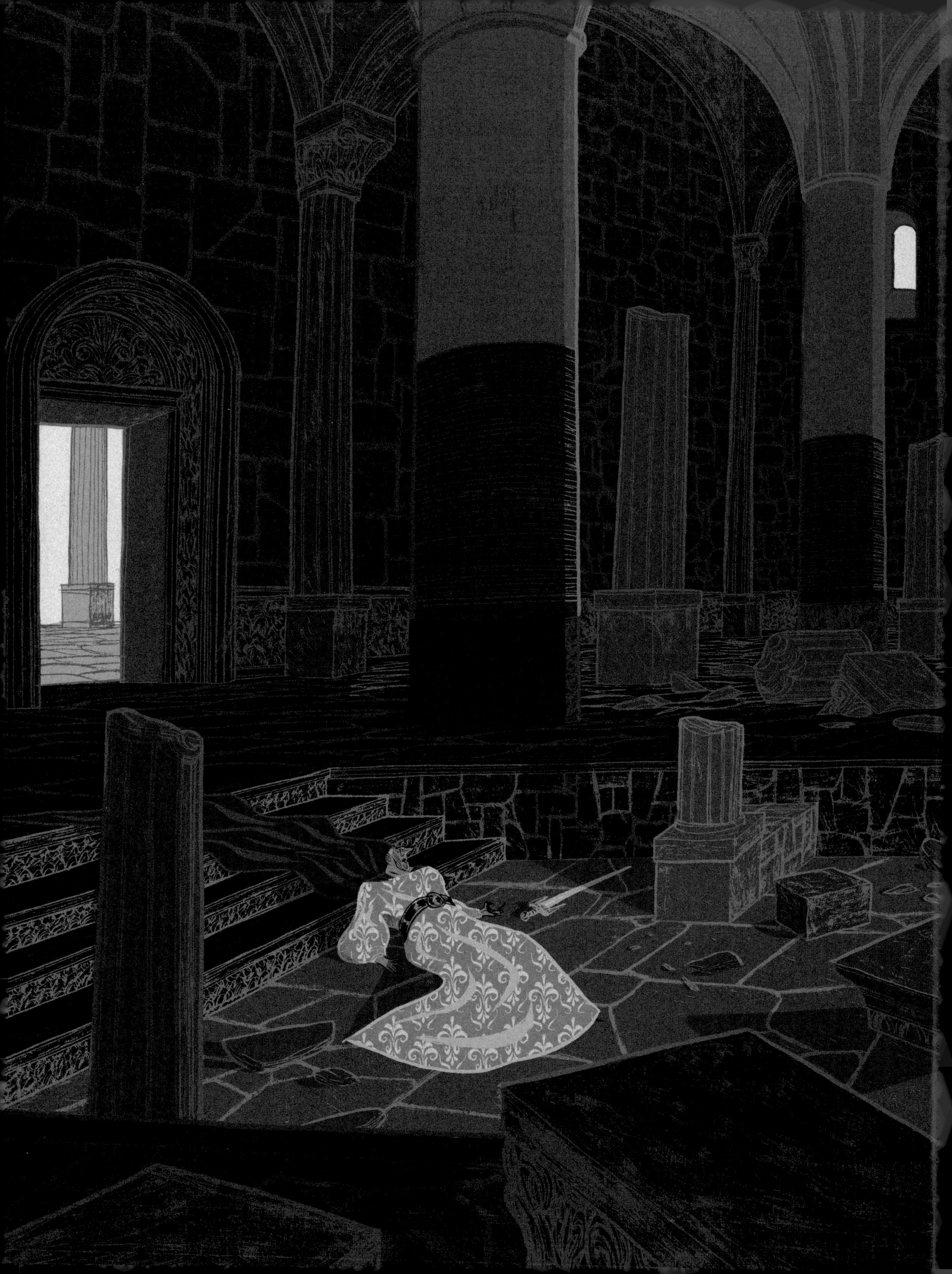

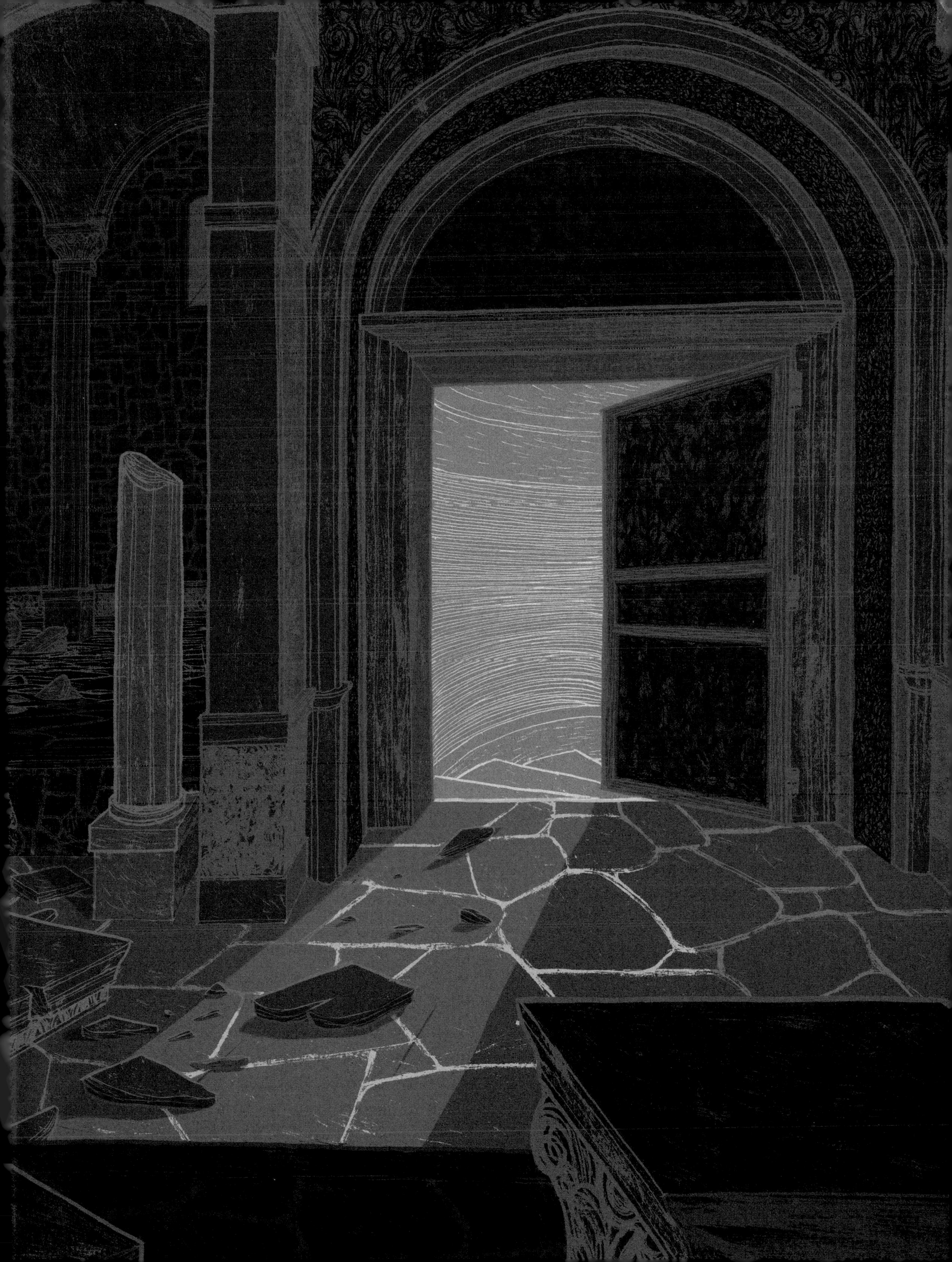

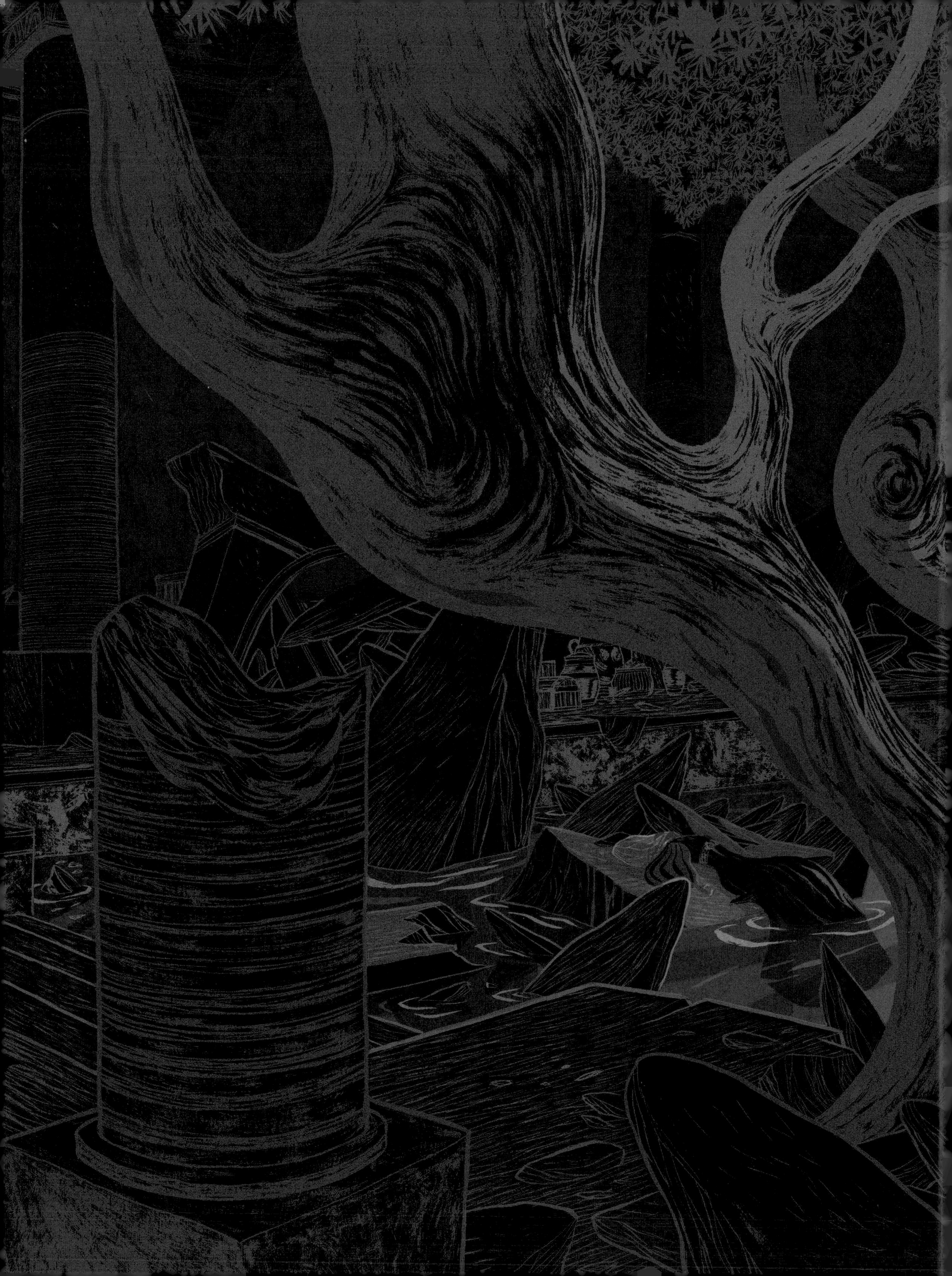

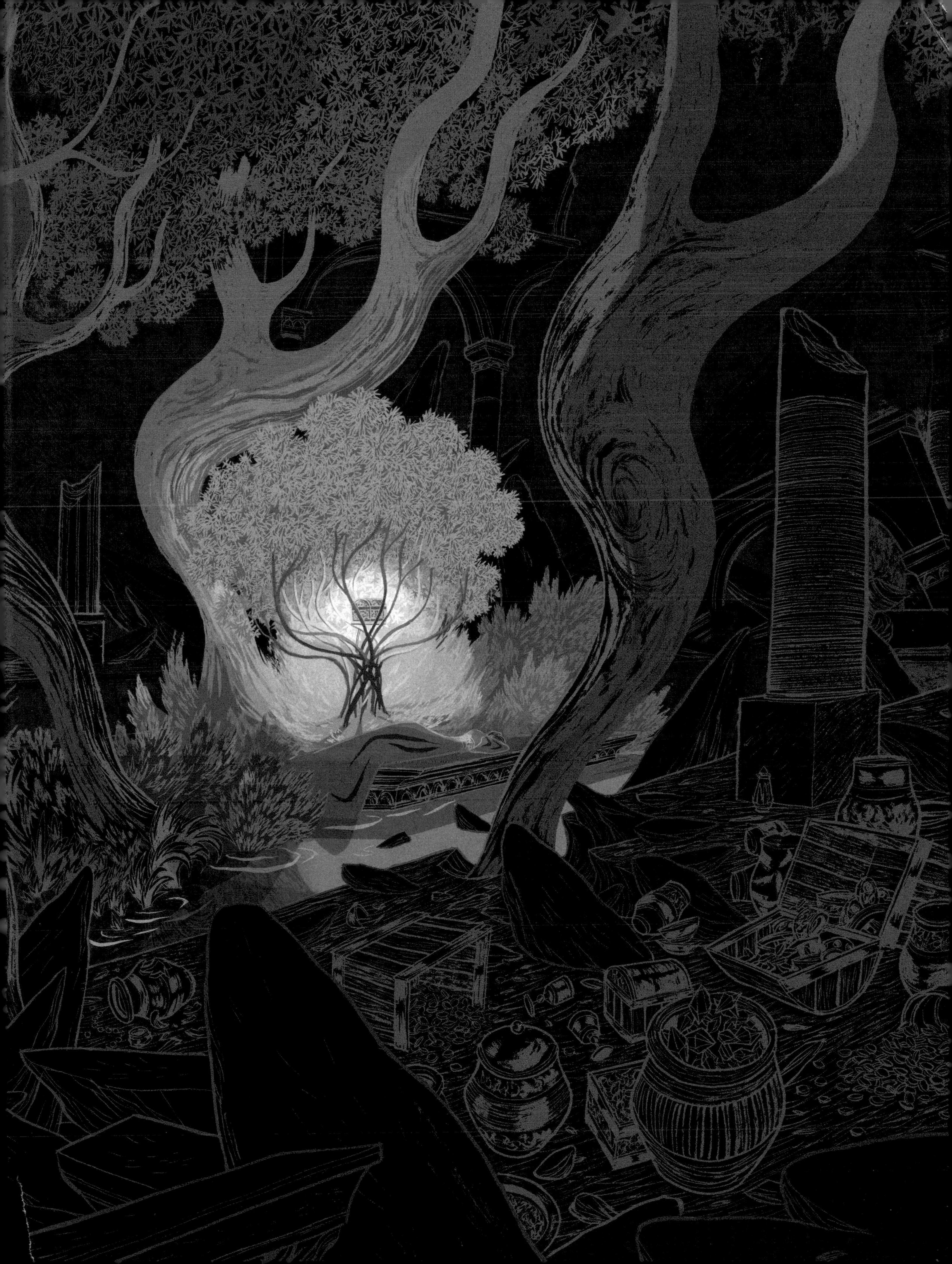

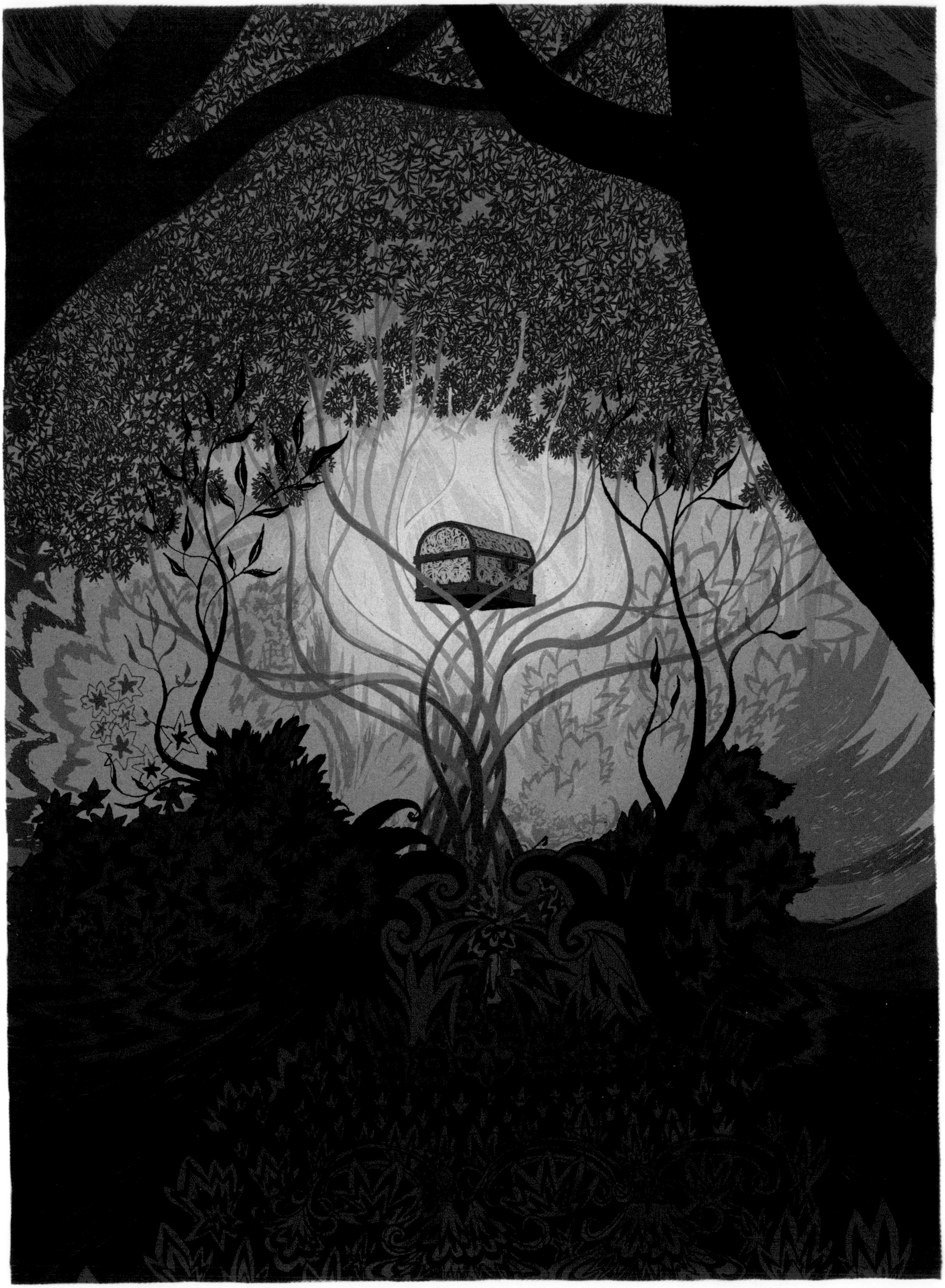

To be continued in

The Golden Age

Book 2